DATE DUE

F   Mahoney, Dan.
MAH
       Hyde

HAYNER PUBLIC LIBRARY DISTRICT
ALTON, ILLINOIS

OVERDUES .10 PER DAY. MAXIMUM FINE
COST OF BOOKS. LOST OR DAMAGED BOOKS
ADDITIONAL $5.00 SERVICE CHARGE.

HYDE

ALSO BY DAN MAHONEY

Edge of the City

Detective First Grade

BY DAN MAHONEY

◎

HYDE

◎

ST. MARTIN'S PRESS ✳ NEW YORK

Design by Pei Koay

Library of Congress Cataloging-in-Publication Data

Mahoney, Dan.
    Hyde / by Dan Mahoney.—1st ed.
      p.   cm.
    ISBN 0-312-15146-2
    I. Title.
    PS3563.A364H93   1997
    813'.54—dc20   96-43934
                                                        CIP

First Edition: January 1997

10   9   8   7   6   5   4   3   2   1

For

Detective First Grade Maureen Distasio, NYPD

and

Detective Second Grade Rita Kaplowitz, NYPD

Good cops, tried and true

It's been my pleasure

HYDE

Benny was a bully and was happiest when Kerri committed some transgression that permitted him to give her another disciplinary session. So Benny was very happy this day. Kerri had given him some sunshine in the middle of the coldest spell in New York memory. Once again she had broken his rules and now she had to be punished.

One look at her told Benny that she knew she had done wrong. Trouble was, she didn't look scared enough. Over the past year Benny had begun to suspect that Kerri might actually enjoy discipline, and that disturbed him. It took a lot of his fun away. But rules were rules, and whether she enjoyed it or not she still had to get hers.

He started with the blanket, her only source of comfort and her primary protection against the bitterly cold north wind blowing down Third Avenue. Kerri was sitting on their mattress spread on the ground, wrapped in her blanket, just staring at him with that mournful gaze while she shivered, waiting.

"Give me the blanket," he ordered. "Stupid people got to be cold."

Kerri didn't move except to gather the blanket closer around her shoulders.

Benny was surprised. He had come to expect immediate compliance to his orders. Good thing this happened, he thought. Bitch needs a tune-up. He took a step toward her and was gratified when he heard her whine.

"Benny, please. Not the blanket. I'm too cold already. I didn't mean nothin' by it."

Kerri's pleas were music to Benny's ears. He stood over her and savored the moment as she closed her eyes and cringed, waiting and braced for the blow.

This is one pitiful white woman I got me involved with, Benny thought. Sitting there with her eyes closed. I can do whatever I want. Stupid. Then he bent over and grabbed the two handles stitched into the sides of the mattress and pulled up with all his might. Kerri rolled over backwards and wound up on her back on the pavement, with her head resting just inside the doorway of the closed print shop. She was still clutching her blanket, her eyes still tightly closed, unmoving.

Benny looked at her contemptuously while he stood over her, holding the mattress by the handles. What to do next? He took a look around him. The street

1

was full of people, but everybody was walking fast, with someplace else to go and something else to do. Nobody cared what the homeless were doing.

Benny wasn't surprised. He had been through this before. He reached a decision. Time to throw a real scare into her. He placed the mattress on top of the hospital laundry cart that held all their worldly possessions and rolled the cart in front of Kerri so that she was invisible to anyone walking by. She lay in the stall he had created like a young calf waiting to be slaughtered. Placing his foot on her gut, he pressed hard, hard enough to force all the air from her lungs and stomach, but she kept her eyes screwed shut.

Ain't no fun like this, Benny thought, so he reached down, took hold of the blanket, and growled, "I'm leaving and I'm taking what's mine."

Kerri's eyes popped open. No more blank stare. Only terror. She let go of the blanket and Benny pulled it away. She watched him fold up the blanket and place it under the mattress in their laundry cart. Then he picked up the rest of their things and neatly placed them in the laundry cart, each in its accustomed place. Satisfied with his work, he turned back to Kerri. She was still staring at him, terror-stricken.

Benny liked the way she looked. But maybe I can make it better, he thought. Let's see. "I'm going over to the Citibank. Come get your shit later once I get unpacked."

It worked well. Kerri rolled onto her stomach and crawled over to him until she was lying at his feet like a dog. She put her hands over her head and dug her chin into the sidewalk. "Beat me, Benny. But don't leave me. I'll die out here without you. I can't do this by myself."

"Then why you always breakin' the rules?" Benny asked in a low, threatening voice. "Why can't you learn to live right out here?" His voice was rising. "Why can't you listen and show me some respect?"

Like a parent scolding a child, he waited for an answer but got none. Kerri's silence enraged him. "Why do I got to be stuck with the dumbest bitch on the planet?" he yelled as he gave her the first kick. It was short and sharp and caught her in the side of the ribs, but Kerri didn't seem to notice. She had known it was coming and she was ready for it. "Not now, Benny," she wailed. "You gonna have a crowd."

Her reasoning stopped him. She's right, he thought. No reason to do this now. Who needs a crowd? Later is better, when the streets are clear.

Benny brought his anger under control and looked around him. None of the people walking by showed any interest in him or her. Not used to the cold like he was, they were bundled into their gloves, overcoats, and scarves as they passed with heads down against the wind, paying no attention to the two souls who sometimes lived in front of the recessed print shop, partially protected from the elements by the ten-foot overhang of the apartment building over the shop.

But someone was watching, and had been watching them for days. The thin, bearded man was sitting at a table next to the window in the Japanese restaurant across the street, oblivious to the other customers. He picked at his second order of sushi and stared out at the street, apparently lost in thought. He didn't hear the waitress approach his table, which made her uncomfortable as she stood there, waiting to be acknowledged. She followed his gaze and saw nothing of interest outside as she wondered what had recently made this strange and silent man into such a regular customer.

She reached no conclusion. At one time or another during the past week he had tried everything on the menu and, although he ate slowly, it appeared to her he ate without pleasure.

At first she had thought that he was trying to gain weight. The clothes he wore looked like they belonged to someone a size larger than he was, and she speculated that maybe he was trying to fit into clothes someone else had given him. After all, she thought, they are nice clothes.

She waited as long as she politely could while he continued staring out the window, but he didn't notice her presence so she picked up his small bottle of sake from the table and shook it.

Her move startled him and he turned to her quickly.

"More sake?" she asked, smiling as she looked down to his empty cup.

"Yes, please. That would be fine."

She poured the remainder of the bottle and stood waiting for his next request.

"Check, please."

She smiled politely at him, then shuffled to the cash register and watched him while the cashier computed the bill. The customer picked up his last piece of sushi with his chopsticks and placed it in his mouth. He was staring out the window as he chewed, watching a bum push his laundry cart down East 30th Street. A sloppy woman was following abjectly, five steps behind. The waitress lost interest and looked away, but the customer didn't. He knew Benny and Kerri's routine well and knew where they were going.

He chewed slowly, pleasantly surprised that he could actually taste his food. He washed it down with the last of his sake, savoring every sip.

Once again, he had murder on his mind.

2

Wednesday, January 31   *Midtown Manhattan*

It was even colder the next morning when Detective First Grade Brian McKenna got out of the taxi in front of the 17th Precinct on East 51st Street, but the cold didn't bother him. Looking out of place with his deep tan, he was bundled in his overcoat, scarf, and gloves, ready for the weather. After a frustrating year of working in police headquarters, followed by a month on vacation, he was also ready for his new assignment in the 17th Detective Squad.

The headquarters people had thought he was out of his mind when he'd opted to give up his large office with a view and his fancy title of assistant commissioner in order to be a detective again, but for McKenna it was the only way. He had found that pretending to work was harder than actually working. He would be happy never to hear another word about management surveys, cost analysis studies, integrity review boards, supervisory ratio formulas, administrative rule reviews, and promotional screening standards. In the entire year he had stopped no crimes, solved no cases, and made no arrests; those tasks simply weren't done by an assistant commissioner, he had been told many times. It got so that sometimes he forgot his gun at home and his handcuffs were always on his desk holding down a pile of reports he somehow never found the time or the interest to read.

The worst part of it was that nobody in headquarters noticed what he did. They complimented him at every turn and thought he was performing splendidly, just like they were. They could have been, for all McKenna knew. He had no idea what they were supposed to be doing, but was sure it had nothing to do with police work. To keep his self-respect, McKenna knew he either had to quit or get his hands dirty being a cop again.

But not too dirty, at first. He knew he was rusty, so he had chosen the 17th Squad. He figured it would be a slow start because the 17th Precinct was a far cry from some of the war zones he had worked in over the years. It covered the East Side of Midtown Manhattan, encompassing some of the most expensive real estate on earth and most of the Fortune 500 companies, the United Nations, the best hotels, and the trendiest restaurants in the most expensive city in the United States.

As far as McKenna was concerned, there was only one minor drawback in starting out in the 17th Detective Squad: Everything that happened in the precinct was deemed important and invariably made the papers, so that a purse-snatch on Fifth Avenue in Midtown was a page-two event while a triple homicide on Fifth Avenue in Brooklyn would get a paragraph on page thirty-six, if it was covered at all. Press coverage aside, McKenna figured he would start with the mundane stuff like burglaries and car break-ins. There were enough stars in a squad like the 17th to handle anything heavy that came along, so he could take his time while he relearned the ropes.

Just then, another reason McKenna had chosen the 17th Squad got out of a cab in front of him, impervious to the cold with her overcoat over her arm. Detective First Grade Maureen Kaplowitz was primly dressed in a business suit, as always, was smiling, as always, and looked to be in good physical condition for a woman in her midforties, which was one of those matters of speculation in the detective bureau that had taken on a life of its own. Only McKenna and Police Commissioner Ray Brunette knew she was actually fifty-nine, though neither of them would ever admit to the knowledge. Maureen had been in the detective bureau for nineteen years, and she had learned all the tricks of the trade. A master at paperwork with an uncanny memory for names and faces, she was one of the few detectives who actually had accomplished that feat of police work they all lied and claimed they had accomplished: More than once she had arrested a bad guy on the street because she recognized his face from a wanted poster.

But Maureen's greatest asset in any investigation was that she always seemed to know what everyone around her was thinking, a skill that made her the perfect interrogator. Because she looked prim and proper and was so nice, suspects just had a hard time lying to her, and when they tried to pull it off, she always knew. In those cases she would put that hurt look on her face and say something like, "Young man, you don't really expect me to believe that. . . ." Then the suspect would realize how silly he was being and either yell for his lawyer or give it up. "It's like trying to lie to your kindergarten teacher. It can't be done," one prisoner

4

had complained after confessing to Maureen that he had killed his girlfriend.

Maureen made it to the station house door before she turned around and saw McKenna. At once, she bounded across the street like a schoolgirl and threw her arms around his neck, hugging him like he was her long-lost son. Then she held him at arm's length while he stood for inspection. "You look adorable with that tan," she said. "Florida?"

"Yep. A whole month."

"Good for you. Been working out, I see."

"Whenever I can," McKenna said, knowing what was coming next, but hoping she wouldn't.

She did, anyway, grabbing his chin with one hand and tousling his hair with the other. "Still got enough on top, but it's getting a little gray on the sides," she observed.

"Maureen, I don't care what color it is, as long as it's there."

"Nonsense. No need to look old when you don't have to. You should dye it."

"Dye it?"

"Everybody does here. This is Midtown," she explained to him as if he just got off the boat. She let him go and said, "Now do me, and be honest."

McKenna made a show of looking her up and down before his verdict. "Perfect. Getting younger every day."

And she heard that every day. "Okay, don't be honest," she said as she grabbed his hand. "Come on. Thomas must be waiting for you."

"Thomas?"

She looked pityingly at him, then remembered that the slow children needed special attention. "You know. Lieutenant Ward. He's a nervous wreck. Got everything spick-and-span yesterday."

McKenna made the attempt to pull himself out of remedial kindergarten, remembering that there was no rank in Maureen's life. The squad commander was *Thomas* just like the police commissioner was *Ray*. They were her boys, and she had helped to put many of them into the best positions. "Why's he nervous?" he asked.

"Because you're an assistant commissioner. He's very impressed with titles."

"*Was* an assistant commissioner. Now I'm just another detective working for him."

"You'll know he believes that when he sends you out to get him a sandwich," she said, pulling him across the street and into the station house.

A young cop was sitting at the reception desk, reading the paper. He glanced up at Maureen and McKenna before returning to his sports. Then he looked up again and did a double take as his eyes went wide. He popped up straight and yelled "Attention!" so loud that McKenna came to attention himself. Everything stopped in the large room, with every cop standing straight with eyes front. Everybody, that is, but the two astonished prisoners being booked at the desk. But eventually even they got into the act and began earning their time off for good behavior, snapping to attention in their own way.

Good God! was all McKenna could think. He felt warm and knew he was blushing when Maureen started giggling. He didn't know what to say, but she did. "Everybody, this is Brian. He's a friend of mine and he's going to be working here," she announced.

The desk lieutenant was the first one to relax and the others quickly followed his lead. McKenna read the room. A friend of Maureen's? So he's not a problem?

The lieutenant hurried from around the desk and offered his hand. "Sorry, Commissioner. Nobody told us you were coming."

McKenna self-consciously shook his hand. "It's just detective now, Lieutenant. We don't all have to go through this every time I come in or go out."

"Detective?"

"Yeah. Detective. I'm coming back to work," McKenna explained, but saw he wasn't getting through.

"Why?" the lieutenant asked.

"It's a long story," seemed to be the best explanation for the moment.

"But what do I call you?"

"Brian if you like me, McKenna if you don't."

"Oh! Okay, Commissioner. I'll be right here if you need anything. Name's Lieutenant Leavey, but you can call me Jay."

This is gonna be harder than I thought, McKenna told himself, glad that Maureen was dragging him toward the stairs. Still, he felt the need to say something. "Okay, Jay. I'll be upstairs if you need me for anything."

"Welcome aboard, Commissioner," he heard as the stairwell door closed.

In the squad office on the second floor things were different, but not much better. They obviously knew he was coming, which led McKenna to conclude that detectives aren't necessarily smarter than their uniformed brethren, just better informed. Three detectives were pecking away at the typewriters on their neatly arranged desks in their immaculate office, each one pretending he was so busy that he didn't notice the new arrival. All their shirts were whitest white, all top buttons buttoned, and all ties snug at the neck.

McKenna had never seen anything like it, especially at ten to eight in the morning. All hands present and accounted for, busy as beavers ten minutes before their tour of duty officially began. Although he had memorized the roster, he couldn't fit the faces with the names.

"Don't mind them. They think this is a trick," Maureen said to him, then shouted, "Everybody, let's not forget our manners! This is my friend Brian McKenna."

McKenna smiled like the new kid in class and looked from one to another, but nobody said a word. He focused on the detective he perceived to be the senior man and searched his mind for a name. It came to him: oldest one here, has to be Detective Second Grade Billy Mercurio, twenty-one years on the job, a real star. McKenna walked over and held out his hand. "Billy Mercurio, right?"

Mercurio responded with suspicion as he shook. "Brian, right?"

"All the time."

"What's this all about?"

"Simple. Ever notice how every time you go to headquarters, you get a feeling like you have to pee?"

"Yeah?"

"Well, I just spent a year there and I'm all pissed out. I've had enough of the clown show."

Apparently that made sense to everyone. The ice was broken and the introductions commenced. "Steve Birnstill," a well-built and well-dressed detective said. "I don't know how you stood it for so long with them slimeballs."

"Kenny Bender." This one looked like he jumped into the office straight from the front panel of a box of Wheaties. "Welcome aboard, but I have to tell you, you must've been out of your mind to spend a year with them low-life, do-as-I-say-not-as-I-do, hypocritical, back-stabbing, make-work phony fucks."

McKenna was glad to hear that the relationship between headquarters and the field was still intact and exactly as he remembered it. It was apparent to him that detectives were still expected to be profanity proficient, and he had grown a little rusty hobnobbing with all those whatever-they-call-them types in headquarters.

"The lieutenant's been waiting for you," Mercurio said. "He asked me to tell you to go in whenever you're ready."

"Then I guess I'm ready." McKenna went to the squad commander's office and knocked on the door, feeling very much like a kid caught smoking in the boys' room summoned to see the principal.

"Come in, please," Ward's voice immediately sounded from the other side.

Ward was one of those tall, thin men who always managed to look meticulously correct while having more fun than anyone else. His posture was formal, his jacket was buttoned, his tie up, and both of his hands rested in front of him on his desk as McKenna entered.

It was to be a real job interview, McKenna surmised, and he knew if Ward didn't want him, then he wouldn't be staying. "Been a long time, Brian," Ward said, pointing to the chair opposite his desk.

McKenna took it. "Yeah, Lieutenant, a long time, and I guess you've got some questions."

"Lots of them. I assume you sent yourself here?"

"Yeah, my last act as a big shot."

"Had enough of the headquarters crowd?"

"I got really comfortable there until one day it occurred to me that I couldn't stand the place."

"I figured that would happen to you sooner or later, but you're not making a real common move. It's a big cut in pay, isn't it?"

"More pay, more taxes. As a first-grader, I'm doing okay. Lieutenant's pay without the headaches. Besides, I wasn't earning what they were giving me."

Then came the big question. "You and the commissioner still tight?" Ward asked.

"Best of friends, but that doesn't mean anything here. I'm no spy and Ray wouldn't ask me a thing about what was going on around here. He put you in that chair, so he'd ask you."

McKenna could see that his answer sat well with Ward, but he wasn't in yet. "Why'd you choose a precinct squad?" he asked. "Why not something more glamorous like the Major Case Squad?"

"Their office is in headquarters and I wanted out."

"Why not a homicide squad?"

"I'm sick of bodies."

"Robbery Squad?"

"I'll leave that to the young breed. I've had enough shooting in my life for a while."

"You've toned down a bit, I see. Good. Makes me happy to know I'm not gonna be spending half my time documenting McKenna adventures."

"Not for a while, I promise you that. Not till I'm sure I know what I'm doing again."

Ward took it in stride. "Fair enough," he said. "Last question. Why this particular squad?"

"You and Maureen, mainly. Besides, it's Midtown, it's close to home, and it's a good place to ease back in."

"So you're here to stay a while?"

"If you want me," McKenna said.

Ward liked McKenna's answer. He loosened his tie and extended his hand across his desk. "Welcome aboard, Brian," he said. "It's good to have you."

"Thanks," McKenna said, shaking Ward's hand before he loosened his own tie.

"You know, when I heard you were coming it made me a little nervous," Ward admitted, waving his hand at that foolish concern when McKenna gave him his best hurt look. Then the phone on Ward's desk rang. "Calls before eight o'clock are never good news," he observed as he picked up the receiver.

It was a short call, with Ward mostly listening while leaning back in his chair. McKenna surmised from the conversation that it was the precinct commander calling with a problem. "I've got just the man for the job, Captain," Ward said before he hung up, and McKenna knew he was in trouble.

"You still one of the press's glamour boys?" Ward asked with a sardonic smile.

"I guess so. I haven't stepped on their toes recently and a few of them owe me dinners."

"Good, because I'm gonna put you right to work. The precinct CO's pulling his hair out and dodging the press. Another one of our homeless citizens froze to death last night at Thirty-first and Second."

"Another one?"

"Second one for him this week, so the captain's in real trouble since Plan B is in effect. He's not a bad guy, so take Maureen with you and do what you can for him."

3 No one knows for sure how many there really are, but the estimates of the number of homeless people living on the streets of the City of New York range from 10,000 to 100,000. Whatever figure one chooses to believe, a walk around Midtown will convince anyone that the problem is enormous. There are panhandlers everywhere, and at night the homeless sleep on the street in the cardboard beds they fashion for themselves. There are so many of them that it would be easy to draw the conclusion that nothing is being done to help the downtrodden.

That would be a mistake. Available to each homeless adult is a monthly stipend of $382.00 from the Department of Social Services, in addition to food stamps and free medical care provided at the city hospitals. The problem is that $382.00 buys little in the way of housing in New York City. So, at great expense, the taxpayers of the most generous city in the world are paying for a network of shelters to house and feed the homeless street people and protect them from the elements.

The problem is that the shelters are not really a place to live, just a place to spend the night. Most provide beds in a warehouse-type setting and evict their guests at eight every morning. Still, it's a warm, dry place to spend the night, which would indicate to the uninitiated that the homeless shouldn't be sleeping on the streets.

Most of them wouldn't, if it weren't for the crime. Ludicrous as it seems, the shelters are infested with criminals, also homeless. Since the homeless have all their worldly possessions with them in one place while they sleep as guests of the city, they are frequently preyed upon by their fellow indigents and awake to find themselves owning even less than they started with before their stay. So the weak and the infirm, those people the system was designed to protect from the ravages of nature, avoid staying in the city shelters whenever possible. Some refuse to go no matter what the weather outside. But not all of them; the worse the weather, the more crowded the shelters become.

The city administration is aware of the problem, of course, and has hired a number of private security agencies to provide guard services at the shelters, and they do something to improve the situation. But the city hires these guard agencies on a lowest-bid contract format, so the guards working the shelters are low paid, poorly trained, and they haven't gained a reputation for fairness or efficiency. When the weather gets cold and the shelters get crowded, they are overwhelmed by the job.

But homeless people freezing to death on the streets of the most generous city in the country makes for very bad publicity, so the mayor placed the problem in the hands of the police department. Cold Weather Emergency Plan B is the response developed by police administrators.

According to the plan, whenever the wind-chill factor falls below ten degrees Fahrenheit, the police are charged with searching for the homeless and directing them to the shelters, and even bringing them and their belongings there, if requested to do so.

On paper, the plan works when the patrol officer finds a homeless person who agrees to go to one of the shelters. The problem arises when the subject doesn't want to go because in the United States, if a person hasn't committed a crime, then the police have no constitutional authority to force that person to stay anywhere against his or her will. So police administrators in New York City have devised a line of reasoning under the Mental Health Law that disregards the conditions in the shelters. To convince those reluctant to check into the shelters, the police tell themselves that if someone won't come in from the cold, then he or she must be crazy. They then cart this person to one of the city hospitals to consult a psychiatrist who will, presumably, concur with the street opinion rendered by the officer and order that the homeless person be locked in a warm place for the night. Sometimes Plan B works as intended and a few lives are saved.

But not always. The problem is that homeless people might be cold and might be crazy, but frequently they aren't stupid. As the temperature drops, the more streetwise among them have learned to avoid the police. If one fails and finds himself talking to a cop, he will say something like, "Good to see you, Officer, and thanks for stopping by. Unfortunately, I can't stay to chat because I'm on my way to the shelter.'' He then makes a show of pushing his belongings in the direction of the nearest shelter until the satisfied officer leaves.

But he's not really going to the shelter and, in spite of Plan B, a number of homeless people freeze to death every year. When that happens, unfavorable publicity for the city is generated, heads must roll, and the chiefs know exactly what to do.

According to departmental reasoning and tradition, anything that goes wrong in a precinct is ultimately the fault of the precinct commanding officer, so the chiefs vent their wrath on this unfortunate, reacting as if they found the body in the captain's freezer at home. They mark him as unworthy for further advancement and end his career by banishing him to the large police prison the department calls Patrol Borough Brooklyn North.

The two luxury high-rise apartment buildings comprising the Kips Bay Towers apartment complex seemed almost out of place in Manhattan, very pleasant and more suburban than urban in character. Separated by a large private park, one building looked onto East 33rd Street between First and Second Avenues and the other faced East 30th Street. On the Second Avenue side of the complex was a row of small stores, a supermarket, a movie theater, and a Citibank branch, all set back from the street behind a row of trees and bushes. This commercial strip was elevated four feet above street level, so that shoppers from outside the Kips Bay Towers complex must climb a short staircase to get to the stores.

Two radio cars, an ambulance, and a press van were already parked at the curb on Second Avenue at East 31st Street when McKenna and Maureen arrived. McKenna parked behind them and they got out of their car, McKenna marveling at Maureen's total disregard of the cold wind whipping down Second Avenue. He hunched his shoulders inside his overcoat while she took a minute to remove a few imaginary specks of dust from her skirt. Looking around, the two detectives saw no sign of the uniformed cops.

''They'll be over here,'' Maureen said, and McKenna followed her up the stairs leading to the row of stores set back from the street.

Maureen was right. The uniformed sergeant, two young cops, and the ambulance crew were gathered around a body on the ground outside the Citibank branch. As McKenna and Maureen approached, one of the cops removed a blanket from a laundry cart parked next to the bank entrance and spread it over the body. A small group of well-dressed people stood to the side watching while the news crew filmed Heidi Lane, a pretty, blond Fox Five News TV reporter in her late twenties. She was talking into a microphone, with the laundry cart, the body, and the cops in the background.

Heidi saw McKenna and she pointed at him. The cameraman switched his focus to him as Maureen left her partner's side and walked to the group of cops. The camera stayed on McKenna as he stopped next to Heidi.

''Standing with me is Assistant Commissioner McKenna,'' Heidi said into her microphone before turning and placing it in front of McKenna's face. ''Would you care to make a statement on this tragedy, Commissioner?''

McKenna didn't. He turned his back to the camera and stood between Heidi and her news crew. "I just got here, Heidi, and it's Detective McKenna now," he said, trying to keep his annoyance out of his voice. "If you turn your equipment off and give me a chance to look around, maybe I'll be able to give you a statement later."

McKenna's attitude caught Heidi by surprise. She glared back at him for a moment before giving him a contrite smile. "Sorry, Brian. I get carried away sometimes," she said, lowering her microphone. She waved to her cameraman, who lowered his camera from his shoulder and shut it off. "Satisfied?" she asked.

"Yeah, thanks. You know, I just came over to say hello, not to make a fool of myself on the evening news."

"Then hello it is," she said, giving McKenna her hand. "I heard about this detective stuff, but didn't know if it was true."

McKenna gave her hand a businesslike shake, surprised at how warm Heidi could look with such a frozen hand. Over Heidi's shoulder, he saw Maureen giving him an amused smile. "It's true," he said, feeling a little self-conscious as he let go. "I'm back in the trenches."

"Why? Did you have some problem in headquarters?"

"No, I just like this job better."

It took Heidi a moment to digest the information. "Might be a good human-interest angle in there somewhere," she speculated. "You gonna give me a story on it?"

"No. Let's just stick to this one. How are you playing it?"

"You know. Tragedy, poor unfortunate homeless person, large uncaring city. We'll do some background on him once you tell us who he is, but I'd like to wrap it up quick. There's some crews from the other stations on the way."

"Then let's make a deal. You're here first, so just give me a little time and I'll give you the statement."

Heidi smiled. "An exclusive?"

"Not exactly, but you're the only one I'll go on camera for."

"That's a deal. We'll wait in our van 'til you're ready. See you later."

Heidi turned and walked down the stairs, followed by her news crew. Maureen was talking to the uniformed sergeant, an old-timer in his fifties, when McKenna joined them. The two cops and the ambulance attendants were chatting quietly, trying not to notice McKenna as the sergeant gave him a crisp salute.

The salute surprised McKenna and left him no choice but to return it. "I'm just a detective, Sarge," he said. "I'm supposed to salute you, not the other way around."

"Got it," the sergeant said, entirely unconvinced. "You want to take a look at him?" he asked.

McKenna nodded. The sergeant bent down and grabbed the blanket, pulling it off so McKenna could inspect the body on the ground.

The dead man was black and in his forties. He looked content and perfectly at ease with death, stretched out on a large piece of cardboard spread on the sidewalk in front of the door to the bank, with his arms extended and his eyes closed. He had been dressed for the cold, wearing a hooded polyester jacket with a scarf wrapped around his face and gloves on his hands. All of his clothes were old and dirty.

"Got the call at 7:35," the sergeant said. "Anonymous male caller to 911 stated there was a body on the sidewalk here. Sector Charlie responded and found him here. Pronounced dead at 7:45 by Ambulance Attendant Chavez."

"Any ID on him?" McKenna asked.

"We were waiting for you before we did the search."

"His name's Benny Foster," Maureen said, surprising everyone. "Date of birth September 9th, 1947. Been living on the streets as long as I can remember. He's a mean, rotten snake. His body's frozen, but his soul is burning in Hell."

"How do you know all this?" McKenna asked.

"Because I locked him up last year for beating up that poor little thing," Maureen said, pointing inside the bank.

Then McKenna and everyone else saw Kerri for the first time. She was in the bank in the front section where the ATM machines were located. She was easy to miss because she huddled under the counter where the deposit slips were, sitting on a blanket on the floor and hiding behind two plastic trash cans she had placed in front of her.

McKenna guessed that Kerri was around thirty. She had a red round face, stringy blond hair, and a potbelly that looked out of place on her thin body. But it was her eyes that got McKenna. Scared and doleful, her face was bruised and she peered at him through eyes that were almost swollen shut. He could see that she was shaking. "Looks like he threw her another beating last night," he observed.

"I'm not surprised," Maureen said, turning back to Benny's body. "She'll keep in there until we're done out here. Let's hurry and get this piece of garbage off the street."

Mildly surprised by the vehemence in Maureen's voice, McKenna turned and looked back toward the sidewalk. He could just make out the roof of his car through the bushes and knew that the entrance to the bank was not visible from the street. Any cops driving by the night before couldn't have seen Benny and Kerri, leading McKenna to conclude that Benny's location was the main reason he was dead. He turned back to the sergeant. "Let's get the search done."

"Time for the search," the sergeant loudly ordered over his shoulder to the two cops. They abruptly ended their conversation with the ambulance attendants and hurried over. Although young, both were experienced and knew what they were doing. From their tags McKenna saw that their names were Smith and MacGregor.

MacGregor pulled a pair of latex surgical gloves from his pocket, put them on, and bent over the body while Smith took out his memo book, pen poised and ready to write. MacGregor started with Benny's jacket pockets and found another pair of gloves and three handkerchiefs. He gave them to his partner, then zipped open the jacket. Benny was wearing two sweaters and a flannel shirt. The sweater and shirt pockets were empty. Then MacGregor searched the pants pockets and found more than fourteen dollars in change. "Panhandling profits," he speculated as he gave the change to Smith before resuming the search.

Benny was wearing another pair of pants under his outer pair and those pockets produced the stash—$189.00 in cash, two welfare checks, and a wallet containing Benny's Department of Social Services ID card. MacGregor gave it all to Smith, who logged it into his memo book before handing the checks to McKenna.

Both checks were for $382.00. One was made out to Benny Foster and the other to Kerri Brannigan. McKenna returned the checks to Smith, examined the ID card, and saw that Maureen had been correct right up to Benny's date of birth. He gave it back to Smith, then watched as MacGregor tried to turn Benny over. The body was frozen solid and Smith had to help because Benny's arms were stretched straight out. They struggled to lift the body three feet off the ground before they were able to turn it over and place it back on the sidewalk.

The only thing MacGregor found in Benny's back pockets was a squashed half-roll of toilet paper. Finished, he stood up and looked to McKenna.

McKenna bent over the body, looking for a wound or mark, but found nothing. Lifting up Benny's sweater, McKenna saw no postmortem lividity, leading him to conclude that Benny's blood was frozen solid. He knocked on Benny's back and found it was like knocking on a hollow log. Benny's skin was frozen rock-hard, and the knock echoed in Benny's chest.

There was nothing to indicate a time of death to McKenna. With MacGregor's help, he turned over the body again and repeated the process, looking for wounds. Finding none, he placed his face close to Benny's and smelled a strong odor of alcohol. McKenna tried to pry Benny's mouth open, but couldn't. It was frozen shut.

Finished, McKenna stood and the sergeant gave a signal to the ambulance attendants. They lifted the frozen body onto a stretcher, covered it with a blanket, and carried it to the ambulance. McKenna followed them halfway down and saw that Heidi and her cameraman were filming. Another news van had arrived and the camera crew was setting up.

Having nothing to say yet, McKenna turned and rejoined Maureen at the bank. "Ready to talk to Kerri?" he asked.

"Sure." Maureen took a Citibank card from her purse and opened the bank door while Kerri watched them, cowering behind her garbage cans in her hideout. Once they were inside, Maureen asked, "Do you remember me, Kerri?"

Kerri didn't answer, so Maureen got down on her knees in front of the counter. "I'm going to move these cans so I can see you," she said, but Kerri still didn't answer. When Maureen pulled the cans out of the way, Kerri pushed herself closer to the wall. She was shaking, looking at Maureen, then up at McKenna.

"Kerri, do you remember me now?" Maureen asked again, softly.

Kerri stared at Maureen blankly through her half-closed eyes. Then McKenna saw a flicker of recognition cross her face. "Detective Kaplowitz?" Kerri asked.

It was the voice of a child, soft and afraid.

"That's right. Maureen Kaplowitz. Remember I took you to court last year when Benny beat you up?"

"I remember now. That was a long time ago. You bought me some food in the restaurant," Kerri said, thinking hard. From her accent, McKenna knew she was from someplace down South.

"That's right. Are you hungry now, Kerri?"

Kerri nodded, then focused on McKenna.

"This is my friend Brian, Kerri. He's a nice man," Maureen said. "If you'd say hello to him, we'll go get some breakfast. Okay?"

"Okay. Hello, Brian."

That was easy enough, McKenna thought. He got down on his knees so he could look Kerri in the eye, but she avoided his gaze. "Hello, Kerri," he said, trying to sound as nonthreatening as possible. "I'm pleased to meet you."

"Me too," Kerri murmured.

"Kerri, did Benny beat you up again?" McKenna asked.

When Kerri didn't answer, McKenna tried another tack. "Can we talk about it while we eat?" he asked.

Kerri nodded, but McKenna saw it wasn't going to be easy. "What about Benny?" she asked.

"Benny had to go to the hospital."

"He's mad at me, you know. He doesn't want me to talk to anyone."

"Don't worry about him now, Kerri," Maureen said. "He can't hurt you anymore."

Kerri didn't look convinced. "He will, you know," she said after a minute. "He'll do it when nobody's looking."

"He won't do it anymore, Kerri," Maureen said. "Benny's dead. He can't hurt you anymore."

McKenna watched as this information registered with Kerri. He saw first sadness on her face, then joy followed by confusion. "What's going to happen to me?" Kerri asked.

"That's one of the things we're going to have to talk about," McKenna said. "Can I help you up?"

"Okay, Brian," Kerri said, holding up her arms like a baby wanting to be picked up. McKenna grabbed her arms and helped her to stand, surprised that she seemed smaller and even more pitiful when she stood than when she was hiding under the counter. Then Kerri remembered her blanket. She reached under the counter and smiled as she folded it.

"Ready?" McKenna asked.

Kerri nodded and followed the two detectives outside, stopping for a moment to place her blanket in the laundry cart. Then confusion overtook her again. "What about all our stuff?" she asked Maureen.

"It's all yours now, Kerri," Maureen answered.

"All mine? Really?" Kerri was ecstatic at her good fortune.

"Yes, all yours. The police are going to bring it to the station house to see what you have, but I'll make sure they bring everything back to you, okay?"

Kerri was very happy with the arrangement until McKenna said, "We'll even give you a list of everything you have." Then her face showed pure bewilderment.

"Kerri doesn't want a list," Maureen said. "She doesn't like to read."

You mean she can't read, McKenna thought. This poor lost soul can't read and has no place to go, but it should be better for her today than it was yesterday. Probably the worst thing that ever happened in her life is dead.

McKenna asked the sergeant to have the laundry cart brought to the station house, then stopped at Heidi's van and found her shivering in the front seat. She rolled down her window and he said, "I'll give you a statement in front of the station house in an hour or two."

"Why not now?" Heidi asked.

"Got a few things to think over before I tell you anything. That's how long it'll take me."

"The guy did freeze to death, right?"

"I don't know. We'll have to wait for the autopsy," McKenna said.

Heidi's displeasure showed on her face. "That's going to take more than two hours, isn't it?"

"Much more. The body has to thaw out."

"This puts me in a spot, you know. If this guy didn't freeze to death, then there's really no news story here."

"Then I'd wait a bit on this one if I were you," he suggested. "If you must, you can say it looks like he froze to death, but you should add that you might be wrong."

Heidi didn't like that idea, either. Then a thought struck her. "It isn't a murder, is it?" she asked in a sly tone, catching McKenna by surprise.

"No, I think he just died of natural causes."

"Then I'll see you later. As soon as you hear from the medical examiner, you'll talk to me before you talk to any other reporters, right?"

"We have a deal, don't we?"

"Glad to hear you remember. Who's the girl?" Heidi asked, pointing to Kerri.

"Let's leave her out of this for now. She's pretty fragile and she's going to be taking a little trip to the hospital after breakfast."

Heidi took a good look at Kerri and obviously agreed with McKenna's assessment. She just shrugged her shoulders and rolled her window back up.

4 With Kerri between McKenna and Maureen, the three walked across Second Avenue to a diner. The waitress didn't look happy with having Kerri for a customer, but she took their breakfast order anyway. As soon as the waitress left, McKenna got down to business.

"Can you tell us why Benny beat you?"

Kerri looked to Maureen before answering. Maureen smiled encouragement and placed her hand on top of Kerri's. "Because I talked to a man," Kerri whispered. "He don't want me talking to no one."

"Who was the man?" McKenna asked.

"I don't know. We was working the copy store and the man talked to me."

"Working? What kind of work?"

"You know. Just working."

"Panhandling?" Maureen asked.

"Yeah, I guess so."

"Where's the copy store?" McKenna asked.

Kerri pointed west, toward the back of the restaurant. "One block that way and one block down."

"Second Avenue and East Thirtieth Street?"

"I don't know."

"That's it," Maureen volunteered. "Tower Copy. It's recessed into the building, so there's an overhang out front. The homeless are always there because it's out of the wind and rain. Soon as the place closes, they set up camp."

"Okay. Tell me about the man," McKenna said.

Kerri squinted her eyes as she tried to remember. "He was just a man. He asked me if I wanted someplace to stay and I told him I stayed with Benny. Then Benny came back and . . ."

"Where was Benny?"

"He went around the corner to pee."

"Okay. Benny came back. What then?"

"The man told Benny he should get me off the street. Benny got mad and told him to shut up, but the man didn't. He said that Benny was a worthless bum. Then he put ten dollars in my cup and told me I should leave Benny."

"So Benny beat you up over that?"

"Yeah. He kicked me a little there, then told me he was going to Citibank. But we didn't go there, yet. We walked around a while. He hit me a lot and made me cry."

"What time did you and Benny get to the Citibank?" McKenna asked.

"I don't know. Late. We always get there late, when there's not too many people."

"How did you get into the bank?"

"I'm smart," Kerri answered proudly. "Someone always lets me in with one of those cards. I just tell them I'm real cold and I'm just going to stay for a little while. Sometimes they give me money from the machine, too."

"And then you let Benny in, after they leave, right?"

"Right."

"But not last night. Kerri, how come Benny was sleeping outside when you were in the bank?" McKenna asked.

Kerri's smile vanished and she looked to Maureen. "It's all right, Kerri. You can tell him," Maureen said.

"Because he was being mean to me," Kerri said. "I made believe I was asleep when he tried to come in."

"But you weren't asleep?"

"No. I was fooling him." Suddenly, Kerri was enjoying the little joke she had played on Benny.

For a moment, McKenna thought it strange that Maureen also found it funny, and then he figured it out. If Benny hadn't beaten Kerri, she wouldn't have locked him out of the bank and he'd still be alive. Maureen caught McKenna staring at her, made an effort to take the smile off her face, and nodded at him to continue.

"What time was it when you were pretending to sleep?" he asked Kerri.

"I don't know."

"Did you see Benny lie down outside?"

"No. He was talking to another man when I really fell asleep. They were drinking together outside."

"Do you know this other man?"

"No, but Benny must. He don't drink with just anybody."

"What were they drinking?"

"I don't know. Some kind of alcohol. The man had a bottle and he gave Benny some in his cup."

"What happened to the man?"

"I don't know." Kerri was getting bored with the questioning and was having a hard time concentrating.

"Would you know him if you saw him again?"

"I don't know. Maybe, maybe not."

McKenna wanted to pursue that line of questioning, but the waitress came with their breakfast orders and Kerri was no longer in the mood for talking. McKenna and Maureen just picked at their food, while Kerri attacked hers with enthusiasm but very little in the way of table manners as she devoured her order. Maureen gave Kerri her half-finished plate, and Kerri polished that one off too.

"You want more?" McKenna asked.

"Not now. I'm full," Kerri stated.

"Kerri, did Benny always use his own cup?" Maureen asked. It was her first question and gave McKenna an indication that his partner had something on her mind.

"Sure, always," Kerri answered. "He didn't want to get nobody else's germs. He was real careful about germs."

"Where's his cup now?" McKenna asked.

"I don't know. I guess he put it away. He's real neat, you know."

"What does his cup look like?"

"It's white with some kind of writing on it."

"What kind of writing?" he asked.

Kerri's face went blank. She showed her displeasure at the question by ignoring it and turning to Maureen.

"Kerri. This might be important," Maureen said softly. "What kind of writing did Benny's cup have?"

Kerri's brows furrowed as she concentrated. "I don't know, but it was red-colored. Maybe it said his name."

"That's probably it," McKenna agreed, which caused Kerri to smile. "Thanks, Kerri. You've been a big help. Is it okay if we talk about you now?" he asked.

"I guess," Kerri said, noncommittally.

"How come you stayed with Benny?"

Kerri looked surprised. "Because he's my man. He takes care of me most of the time."

"But he beats you."

"Everybody beats me. He ain't no different."

"Where are you from, Kerri?"

"Down South."

"What state?"

It was a hard question for Kerri. "Is Mississippi a state, or is it just a river?"

"It's both," McKenna said.

"That's where I'm from."

"How long have you been in New York?"

"I don't know. A long time."

"How long have you been with Benny?"

"A long time."

"How did you get here?"

"I hitchhiked."

"Do you have any family in Mississippi?"

"My mother, I think. I know she moved, but maybe she's still in Mississippi."

"Did you go to school in Mississippi?"

"When I was little, but it was too hard for me."

I'll bet it was, McKenna thought as he watched Kerri grimace while she remembered. Then she said, "I don't like to talk about school."

"Okay," McKenna said. "Let's talk about something different. How old are you, Kerri?"

"Old. I was born in 1968."

Yeah, that's real old, McKenna thought. Twenty-eight long and miserable years old. "You're a big girl now. I want to thank you for answering our questions," he said.

Kerri preened at the compliment, but had more important things on her mind. "I have to go to the bathroom."

Maureen pointed out the rest rooms in the rear of the restaurant. "Well, what do you think?" she asked McKenna as soon as Kerri left.

"I think your pal Benny deserved to freeze, but I'm not sure that's what happened to him. He looked too relaxed lying out there, not all huddled up the way a person lies when they're cold. Maybe he just drank till he passed out, then froze, but he sounds too sharp for that."

"He was," Maureen agreed. "Benny drank, but he was on the street a long time and he was very careful. He would never drink enough to pass out and take a chance on getting robbed. Not when he had all that money on him."

"Then my bet is he died of natural causes. Maybe a heart attack."

"Hope you're right," Maureen said. "It'll get the cops off the hook."

"What's your feeling on it?"

"I've got a feeling he was murdered," Maureen said.

It was a leap of faith that surprised McKenna, but only for a moment. He had found no marks on Benny's body, but it was common knowledge in the detective bureau that Maureen's feelings were never to be disregarded. Of the 2,400 NYPD detectives, she was one of the ninety-nine who had been recognized and promoted to detective first grade, a promotion that never came easy and took more than dedication and hard work to achieve. It required the indefinable insight on their cases that intangible crime writers call a hunch. McKenna knew that Maureen's brain generated a prodigious number of hunches, a fair share of which turned out to be correct. "Poison?" he asked, trying not to sound skeptical.

"I don't know. Maybe," she answered, deep in thought.

"Why would anyone poison a bum?"

"I don't know that either, yet," Maureen answered, staring McKenna straight in the eye. "What I do know is that Benny was always a pretty healthy guy."

It didn't make sense to McKenna, but if Maureen said it, then the possibility had to be explored. "If Benny was poisoned, then the murderer was probably the guy he was drinking with."

"Unless he had a real unhealthy snack while Kerri was sleeping," Maureen said. "We'll know more when we send Benny's cup to the lab, if it's still there. There might be some residue of his last drink left in it."

"And if the cup's not there?" McKenna asked, knowing the answer.

"Then that's good and bad," Maureen answered. "If the cup's gone, then we'll know between ourselves that we've got a murder, but we'll have to rely on the medical examiner and the autopsy to make us look smart."

Somehow I don't feel so smart around this woman, McKenna thought. But she's right. If someone went to the trouble to poison Benny, then he might have been smart enough to take his cup. "Then Benny's cup is our first order of business," he said, stating the obvious.

"Your case and your first order of business," Maureen answered. "My first order of business is Kerri."

"Kerri? That's it?"

"Sure. If it is a murder, she's going to have to be warm, safe, and available to tell you everything she knows about Benny."

She's right again, McKenna thought. I'm gonna need some idea on the motive if it was murder, and Kerri might be the only person who can give it to me. Without her, I've got no idea how to start tracing the life of a street person to find out who disliked him enough to kill him. Where would I even start? "What happened when you locked Benny up?" he asked.

"Nothing. I had to talk Kerri into pressing charges, but she was terrified of him. She just refused to go to court after the arraignment, so the charges were dropped."

"What are you going to do with Kerri now?"

"After I have a doctor look at her face, I'll make sure she gets the cash Benny had on him and I'll get her set up for a couple of days, just in case you need her."

She makes it sound so easy, McKenna thought. Violate all the rules by giving Kerri the decedent's money and, on top of that, keep her off the street and available. Even for Maureen, that's a lot to accomplish. "How are you gonna do all that?" he asked.

"Take my advice and don't worry about anything," Maureen answered, dismissing his question. "I've been working this precinct long enough to earn some favors."

Great, McKenna thought. So for my first case, I might be looking at a very-hard-to-solve murder. How am I gonna handle this one?

McKenna silently pondered his situation for a few minutes while Maureen watched him, smiling wryly. In the end, he decided to take her advice. He didn't worry about it.

5 Maureen dropped McKenna off at the station house, then left to drive Kerri to Bellevue Hospital for treatment before finding her a place to stay for a while.

Behind the desk, Lieutenant Leavey was writing in the blotter, but he stopped as soon as he saw McKenna. "How can I help you, Brian?" he asked, causing McKenna to wonder if that was the first time a desk lieutenant had ever asked a detective that question.

"I'd like to take a look at the stuff they brought in from Thirty-first Street."

"Sure. It's in the property room."

"Has it been inventoried yet?"

"Not yet. You want me to have someone do it now?"

Second time history's being made, McKenna thought. When did a desk officer ever care what a detective wanted? "Naw, it's not important. Just show me where it is."

"Sure." Leavey gave McKenna a key and brought him to the property room behind the desk. "Just give a holler if you need anything else."

Benny's cart was in the middle of the room. McKenna didn't relish going through all the dead man's possessions, but found it easy once he got started. Benny had been meticulously neat and organized in his packing.

Under the mattress, Benny's and Kerri's clothes were packed in cardboard boxes along with a radio, a Coleman lantern, two sleeping bags, and a blanket. McKenna went through the clothes first and found nothing of interest, but a small suitcase at the bottom of the cart contained some things that told McKenna quite a bit about Benny.

There was his birth certificate registering his arrival in Fulton County, Georgia, on September 9, 1947. He came into the world as Benjamin Harrison Foster at seven pounds, one ounce, and was Clara Foster's third child. The space for the father's name was blank.

Then there was a report card from the fifth grade indicating that Benny had never been a rising star, although he had earned a B in penmanship. Absent nineteen times and late thirteen, the rest of his grades were D's and F's. Rounding out his performance were U's in conduct and effort.

Benny's DD-214 form documented that his conduct and effort hadn't improved. He had served for nine months before the army ended his military career with a bad-conduct discharge on December 24, 1969.

Wrapped with a rubber band was a stack of business cards from seven different lawyers, all Legal Aid, with dates written on the back ranging from 1974 to 1996. McKenna surmised that Benny had been arrested at least seven times and his attorneys had each given him a business card after writing the date of Benny's next court appearance on it.

A small photo album at the bottom of the suitcase held McKenna's attention for a few minutes, although it only contained four old black-and-white snapshots. One was of Benny in his army uniform, two were of teenage girls, and the last was a group photo showing a middle-aged black woman posing with seven kids in front of a ramshackle home. He guessed Benny was the precocious-looking boy in front, sitting on the ground with legs crossed and his mother's arms on his shoulders. Benny looked like he wanted to be someplace else.

McKenna closed the album and tried to put his mind in order as he repacked the cart. What Benny had left told the story of a sad and wasted life. He had grown up poor and stayed that way, succeeding in nothing.

Something his mother had always said to him as a child popped into McKenna's mind. Time and again she had told him that if he didn't do well in school, he would grow up to be a bum. Benny's life was proof she had been right. But there was more to it than that, he realized. Benny's childhood and his were a world apart, causing McKenna to wonder how his own life would have turned out if he had started out in life black, poor, and fatherless in the rural South of the fifties.

He couldn't find an answer, and gave up trying. What disturbed him more was that Benny's cup hadn't been in the cart, buttressing Maureen's suspicion that

Benny had neither frozen to death nor died of natural causes. Although it made no sense to McKenna, he could stretch to imagine that a meticulous planner had poisoned Benny and taken the cup with him. But why would anyone go to the trouble of poisoning him? McKenna wondered again. Finding the motive—if there was a motive, if Benny had really been murdered—would be the key, but there were other things to be done before he could even think about that.

McKenna locked the door and returned the key to Leavey, then decided to see how much weight he carried with the lieutenant. "Are the guy's money and checks in the safe?" he asked.

"Sure."

"That and everything in the cart is all community property shared by Benny Foster and a Kerri Brannigan, so don't bother to inventory it. I'd like you to turn it over to Maureen when she asks for it."

McKenna expected Leavey to voice some objections. According to procedure, it should all go through the Office of the Public Administrator. McKenna knew Kerri was not equipped to deal with the bureaucracy that process would entail.

But there were no objections coming from Leavey. "Whatever you say, Brian. Anything else?"

Lots of weight, McKenna thought. What else? "When Maureen asks for the stuff, could you have someone help her deliver it to Brannigan?"

"No problem."

Mercurio was the only one left in the squad office when McKenna got there. "The lieutenant's been asking for you," he said casually, but it gave McKenna a jolt.

First mistake, he thought. It's never good when a squad commander has to look for one of his detectives. I should have given Ward a call.

He was right. Ward was seated at his desk looking unhappy. "Get lost out there?" the lieutenant asked as soon as McKenna entered.

"Sorry, I should have called," McKenna offered.

"Yeah, you should have. The captain, the chief, and the press have all been calling me and I'm left up here looking stupid and holding my johnson. What's happening?"

"We think it might have been a murder."

Ward had no reaction except, "We? Maureen too?"

"She came up with the idea, but I agree with her."

Still no reaction from Ward, which left McKenna feeling uneasy while watching the boss think over the implications. Finally Ward said, "Let me get this straight. I send you out to give the captain some support, and you wind up telling me I've got a homicide?"

What am I supposed to say to that? McKenna wondered. Apologize to him because somebody killed one of his citizens? Okay. "Sorry."

That wasn't it. "Know what my homicide clearance rate was last year?" Ward asked.

McKenna did know. "One hundred percent."

"That's right. One hundred percent, meaning that for every murder committed in this precinct last year, those guys outside brought me the guy who did it. Made me look better than any other squad commander in the city and I like how that feels. You see where I'm leading?"

This isn't the time to be humble or subtle, McKenna thought. "Sure, it's simple. If it's a homicide, I bring you the killer."

It was all Ward wanted to hear. "Good. Pull up a chair and tell me about it."

In the end, Ward agreed, although McKenna got the feeling the lieutenant was agreeing more with Maureen than with him. McKenna pointed out that they were going out on a limb calling it a homicide before the autopsy, but that didn't bother Ward. Once he was on board, he wasn't the kind of guy to hedge his bets; he was prepared to sink or swim with his decision. He listened while McKenna outlined his plan of action, and had nothing to add. In the end, it was resolved that Ward would call the chief and try to get the heat off the precinct captain for a while. He assigned McKenna the task of handling the press as best he could.

As soon as he left Ward's office, McKenna called Fox Five News and left a message for Heidi Lane to call him. Then he made himself a cup of coffee and hadn't sat down before the phone rang. Mercurio picked it up and announced, "Heidi Lane for you on line two."

McKenna sat down at a vacant desk and took a moment to think out strategy. He decided on the sweet approach. "McKenna here. Sorry I took so long getting back to you, Heidi."

"You sure did. How's my story?"

"Might not be a story. I still think there's a good chance Benny Foster didn't freeze to death."

"Still going with that?" Heidi asked skeptically. "What was it, a heart attack?"

"There's a chance he was poisoned, but like I told you before, we won't know until the autopsy. You'll have to wait for a statement."

"How long?"

"Tomorrow, I'd say."

McKenna had expected Heidi to object at once, but she didn't. She was silent while she thought over this turn of events. "You know, while I've been waiting for you, just like you asked, all the other stations are running the story at noon that he froze to death," she said at last.

"Then it looks like you're the smart one."

"And I'm gonna use the opportunity to scoop them all."

"Good thinking," McKenna offered. "You'll look pretty good tomorrow if I'm right."

"You've got that wrong," she countered. "Things that happen tomorrow aren't called news, they're called forecasts. That's not my department. I'm a newswoman, so I'll need a statement today that it's possible the guy they're all saying froze to death was really murdered."

Oh-oh, McKenna thought. If I do that, I could wind up looking like the prime-time news-at-five dope if the ME tells us I'm wrong. Got to get out of this. "Bad idea, Heidi. If he wasn't murdered, we'd both look pretty silly," he tried.

"Not *we*. Just *you*, but that would still be news."

It sure would be, McKenna realized, picturing the lead: *You remember yesterday when that dope McKenna told us all the guy was murdered? Well, Viewers, turns out that poor homeless man just froze to death after all. See what you've got running our police department?* McKenna had the feeling that would be a better story as far as Heidi was concerned. "I think tomorrow would be better."

"That's not our deal. I thought you were the kind of guy who made a deal and kept it."

Our deal? McKenna thought. What exactly did I tell her I'd do?

But Heidi wasn't going to give him time to think about it. "You do keep your promises don't you?" she asked.

"Well, yeah. Of course I do."

"Good. I'll take that exclusive statement today then, if you don't mind."

"No, I don't mind," McKenna said. But maybe first you'll have to catch me, he thought. I plan to be real busy real soon and we just might miss each other. "When will you get here?"

"I'm right outside. We're set up and waiting for you."

Damn!

6 McKenna tried to keep it brief and vague with Heidi, but he didn't get away with it. On camera in front of the station house she started with an introduction that made him blush, giving an outline of his famous cases as if his history were common knowledge. She appeared to be his biggest fan, but with a number of pointed questions she still got him to say it. What it boiled down to was that no matter how cold the weather, no matter how it looked, and no matter what the silly folks on those other stations said, that poor man on East 31st Street didn't freeze to death. Ace Sleuth McKenna thought he had been murdered. Poisoned, no less.

Just wonderful! McKenna thought as Heidi wrapped it up. Tune in tomorrow for continuing developments and future pronouncements from our hero. He really knows how to handle the press.

But Heidi had still another surprise for him. As soon as her cameraman turned off his camera, she grabbed him and gave him a kiss on the cheek, then whispered in his ear, "Thanks, Brian. Was it good for you?"

One or two responses immediately came to mind, but he brought himself under control in time. "Just swell," he answered, a rigid smile on his face. "How can I ever repay you for your kindness?"

"Easy. No matter what, think nice thoughts about me."

That was far from easy for McKenna, but he managed to keep his smile on until Heidi got into her van. Then he walked to Third Avenue and hailed a taxi. "Thirty-first and Second," he told the driver.

McKenna had called the morgue before his interview with Heidi, hoping for something to support his theory, but they hadn't started on Benny yet. He was still being defrosted.

The pressure was building, and McKenna thought the best way to use the time before the autopsy was to go over the crime scene. He knew that, in many cases, it was difficult for a pathologist to determine categorically whether a person was poisoned without an idea of the reagent used. The cup would fit the bill. If there was anything left in it, the forensic technicians could use the lab's trace spectrometer to determine the chemical composition.

He wasn't out of the taxi long before he realized how slim his chances were of finding that cup. He thought the murderer might not have discarded it in the first place, but rather kept it as some kind of trophy. Then he found that the Department of Sanitation had already picked up the garbage from the apartment buildings at seven that morning, before McKenna knew about Benny. That left only the corner refuse baskets, so he spent a cold hour at the unpleasant task of searching every refuse basket in the neighborhood around East Thirty-first Street and Second Avenue. His fingers were numb by the time he was satisfied that Benny's cup was not in any of them.

His next stop was the Citibank branch, although he thought he was grasping at straws questioning the bank workers about the homeless people who spent the nights in their lobby. But he found something there that he hadn't noticed that morning, something that gave him a glimmer of hope. Just inside the lobby were two cameras mounted in a corner of the ceiling. One focused on the lobby ATM machines and the other was pointed at the front door. As he opened the bank door, he saw the red light on the front of the camera flash. It was a lot to ask, but he had always been considered a lucky detective; just maybe Benny's companion had been captured on film.

The cold was keeping people home, so McKenna was next in line to see the branch manager. Considering that a lucky sign, he took a seat and waited. Then he noticed the manager's nameplate on her desk and welcomed it as another lucky sign. Charity Bucks was the most unlikely name for a bank manager, but there she was, a black woman, thirty-something, slim, and smartly dressed in a gray pin-striped business suit that said: Don't mess with me, I'm the boss around here. However, the attempt was in vain because the intended effect of the suit stopped short at her neck. She had a kind face, the perfect background for a friendly smile.

Trying to decide if she was beautiful or just plain pretty, McKenna was so intent on her smile that he didn't notice it was for him until she asked, "You're here to see me, aren't you?"

"Sorry, I was daydreaming," he said, feeling foolish.

"Detective McKenna, isn't it?" she inquired, keeping the smile on as she pointed to the chair next to her desk.

Now how did she know that? McKenna wondered. "Yes, Brian McKenna," he said, sitting down. "I'm investigating the death of the man who died outside last night."

"And you want the film from our lobby cameras, right?"

McKenna was stunned and realized his mouth hung open as he stared. Ms. Bucks was smiling and looking like she was really enjoying herself at his expense.

Wait a minute, he thought as he recovered. Nobody can be this sharp. But how can she know I'd want the film when I just thought of it myself? Then it came to him and he realized he was wrong. There *was* somebody that sharp. "I guess you're a friend of Maureen's, aren't you?"

Charity's smile faded just a little. McKenna could see she was sorry the joke

24

was over, almost. "Very good, Brian," she said, looking at her watch. "She said you'd be around asking about the film sometime this morning."

McKenna couldn't help himself. He had to check his own watch and saw that it was five minutes to twelve. Just made it, he thought, but it didn't give him much satisfaction knowing he was only five minutes away from being a dope, as far as Maureen was concerned. Maybe as far as Charity was concerned, too.

"I was beginning to get worried about you," she said.

"I would have been here sooner, but I had a lot to do this morning. When was Maureen here?"

"She wasn't. She called me about cashing some checks for Kerri and getting her some help."

"You know Kerri too?"

"Of course. I've been at this branch for six years and I've lived in this neighborhood for ten. Lots of people around here know her. She's a nice girl, in her own crazy way."

"How about Benny? Did you know him, too?"

"Well enough to avoid him, whenever I could. He didn't like me at all."

That lowered McKenna's opinion of Benny even further. He figured anyone who didn't like Charity had to be no good. "Why didn't he like you?"

"Because we tried to get Kerri away from him."

"We? You mean you and Maureen?"

"I mean the Kips Bay Rotary Club. Maureen and I are both members and we got the club to put her up a few times. Even got her an apartment, but she always left and went back to Benny."

She said it like it almost made sense, which indicated to McKenna that she was the kind of person who gave her time and money without demanding results. "Maybe this time it'll be different," she added.

"You're getting her another place?"

"Not me. Maureen took her to Ben Rosen. He's a good friend of hers."

McKenna knew that Maureen had friends everywhere, but Ben Rosen was a surprise. Rosen, a wealthy and influential retired lawyer, ran an advocacy group called the Grand Central Coalition for the Homeless. He always managed to get publicity for his cause and had become something of a gadfly to the police department, critical of its sporadic efforts to remove to city shelters the homeless people living in Grand Central Station and the connecting subway stations and adamant in his conviction that panhandling was a guaranteed constitutional right under the First Amendment.

What especially bothered the chiefs was that Rosen always seemed to have advance notice of any police sweep and could get an injunction barring the operation quicker than any lawyer in the city. Knowing that he had to lose at the hearing, he would then manage to postpone it many times, in the process generating unfavorable publicity for the department at each court appearance. He was tireless and financially unsparing in his efforts, but McKenna found him personally obnoxious and suspected Rosen was in it mainly because he liked being in front of the cameras.

But Rosen's personality was just one thing that surprised McKenna about Maureen's friendship with him. The other also worried him, and it had to do with politics. Being known as a friend of Rosen's would have to be detrimental to a detective's career, even a detective like Maureen Kaplowitz. After all, Rosen always seemed to know.

McKenna was certain that Maureen would never divulge official business to Rosen, but the chiefs can be a paranoid and vengeful lot when their plans are thwarted, especially when they wind up with bad publicity in the process. McKenna didn't expect Charity to know that. "This may sound silly, Charity, but I wouldn't mention Maureen's and Rosen's name in the same sentence," he cautioned her.

At first, Charity appeared startled by McKenna's advice. Then she smiled at him, reprovingly. "I know that, but you're a friend of hers, aren't you?"

Once again, Charity had made him feel foolish. He realized it wasn't his advice that had startled her; it was that he had felt a need to offer it. Like him, she knew Maureen was special. Friendship with a person like her was a privilege that carried certain responsibilities. Loyalty was chief among them.

"Yes, I'm a friend of hers, and proud of it." Enough said in that department, he thought. Let's get back to business. "Do you know any of Benny's friends?"

That was a tough one for Charity. She had to think a while before answering, "He knew a lot of people, but I don't think he had any friends."

A man without a single friend? What an epitaph, McKenna thought. He noticed that Charity must have thought the same thing and was kind enough to be bothered by the prospect. She kept thinking, then smiled. "Father Hays, maybe."

"The priest from Saint Francis of Assisi?"

"Yes. Do you know him?"

"Not personally, but I heard about him. He's an honorary police chaplain."

"He also runs a soup kitchen at the church and works with Operation Intercession, trying to keep the homeless people in touch with their families. You might want to talk to him."

"Thanks, I will."

"Anything else I can help you out with?"

"The film?"

"Oh, you've kept me so busy talking that I forgot to tell you. We don't have the keys to the cameras here. That's handled by bank security. I called them and they told me they'd have somebody here before closing time to get the film out."

"They're single-frame stills, aren't they?"

"I guess so. All I know is that one camera goes on every time the front door opens and the other one snaps a picture five seconds after somebody takes out cash from the ATMs. It's a new system, so I've never seen any of the pictures."

Then I sure hope they're working like they're supposed to, McKenna thought. Someone must have walked in and used the machine while Benny was outside drinking with his pal. Just maybe he gave Benny a swig somewhere near the front door. Now here comes the hard part. "I'll need just one more favor, but it's a big one."

"Whatever I can do."

"I'll need the names, addresses, and phone numbers of all the people who used the ATMs last night, along with the times they used the machines. I'm hoping that at least one of them will be able to describe the guy Benny was drinking with."

McKenna could see by Charity's reaction to his request that it was indeed a big one. He thought she was mulling over bank rules and regulations, but that wasn't it at all. "It seems such a shame to bother all those people over someone like Benny," she said.

From what he had learned about Benny so far, McKenna found himself in agreement with her. Benny's death was what detectives in the Homicide Squad call a "Public Service Murder," and he thought it unfortunate that he had a personal stake in solving this one. "I'm sorry, but I need the information," he said.

"I understand," Charity said. "I can give you everything on the people who used a Citibank card. For the people who used cards from another bank, all I'll be able to get is the name of their bank and their account number."

"That's fine. If I need to, I'll get it from the other banks. Can I pick up the information and the pictures at three o'clock?"

"Sure. If you want, I can have the security people deliver it to you if it's ready before then."

"No, that's all right," McKenna said. "I'll be here to pick it up at three. I'm gonna be at the Bellevue Morgue until then and I don't think they'll want to go there."

Charity shuddered at the mention of the morgue. "You're probably right. I feel sorry for you, going to that place."

McKenna was busy repressing his own shudder. I feel sorry for me, too, he thought.

Although he had spent three years in the Manhattan North Homicide Squad and had seen more than his share of gore, McKenna had never gotten used to the morgue and hated going there. Having been present at many autopsies, he was almost past the point where the sight of the scalpel slicing through dead flesh put his stomach in knots, although it still made his skin crawl. But those were just physical reactions, things he could get past. What bothered him about the morgue was that it was the place where death was treated impersonally. At the morgue a body just represented another case, a collection of bone and tissue to be cut and probed in order to find out how it arrived there. Finish one and on to the next was the attitude; at the Bellevue Morgue, the supply of bodies requiring autopsy was endless.

That attitude troubled McKenna. Unlike most cops, he could never bring himself to regard a dead human body as something commonplace, as part of the Job. When he saw a body at the morgue, he grieved, no matter who they had been.

Naturally, he grieved for the victims, those whose lives had been ended by accidents or by an act of violence prompted by avarice on the part of others. However, they weren't all victims. He knew that many of those occupying the freezers were not innocents, and the lifestyles they had led had much to do with their cold position. Violence begets violence, and criminals rarely die in bed on social security. Those who live as drug dealers, robbers, burglars, and murderers frequently wind up as an ME case, on the slab before their thirtieth birthdays.

McKenna grieved even when he saw those bodies, but his grief wasn't for them. He had seen good people crying over the bodies of criminals whom, common sense dictated, no one should miss. He reasoned that they all had a mother, and rare is the person who goes through life without touching someone; character is not a prerequisite for love.

As he left the Citibank and walked to the Bellevue Morgue, two blocks away at East 30th Street and First Avenue, McKenna's only consoling thought was that Benny Foster might have been that rare person no one would miss.

The Chief Medical Examiner's secretary looked like she had just escaped from one of the freezers downstairs. Dour and pale, she was transferring entries from a logbook to a piece of paper when McKenna entered. While he stood waiting in front of her desk, trying to decide if she was forty years old or sixty and if her hair was light blond or gray, she pointedly ignored him. According to the nameplate on her desk, she was Ms. S. Lacey.

"Brian McKenna to see Dr. Andino," he announced after a full minute.

She didn't look up. "Do you have an appointment?"

"No, but he'll see me if he's in. We're old friends."

McKenna's pronouncement earned him a small, derisive chuckle from Ms. Lacey. "Really?" she asked, still writing. "I've been here for fifteen years and I know all his old friends."

Oh-oh, McKenna thought. Dr. Andino's placed an F-14 class fighter-interceptor in my path. He's a nice enough guy, but I guess he doesn't welcome unannounced intrusions while he's working. What to do now?

The truth was all he could come up with. "Well, I'm really more of a good acquaintance. I used to be an assistant commissioner in the police department and we met at a few cocktail parties."

Ms. Lacey wasn't impressed. "Take a seat while I check," she said, but continued writing for another minute before she picked up the phone.

Dr. Andino was in, and he would see McKenna. Ms. Lacey escorted him into what looked to be Dr. Frankenstein's office. There was a standing skeleton in one corner and a floor-to-ceiling bookcase that ran the length of one wall. On a long table against another wall were a large microscope and an assortment of other gadgets, none of which McKenna could divine a use for. The decor was completed by an assortment of photos hanging on the walls, all of them pre-autopsy shots of bodies exhibiting the most gruesome wounds imaginable.

John Andino was seated at his desk while reading one of the autopsy reports from the stack in front of him. He was one of the most average-looking of people: middle-aged, slightly balding, and of average height and weight.

But then Andino did the thing that made him special. He looked up from his report and smiled, showing the twinkle in his eye that proved his intelligence and the grin that let one know that here was the life of the party. Despite being one of the premier pathologists and medical administrators in the world, and despite the surroundings he had chosen for himself, John Andino was one of the funniest and most popular guys around.

"Good to see you, Brian," he said, standing up and offering his hand. "Pull up a chair."

McKenna shook Andino's hand and sat down, but Ms. Lacey remained standing in front of the desk.

"That's all for now, Sunshine," Andino told her.

Ms. Lacey spun around and left without a word, closing the door behind her.

"Sunshine? Is that what the *S* stands for?" McKenna asked as soon as she was gone.

"Ironic, isn't it? She's a hardworking girl, but as you can see, not much on personality."

"Is she the best you can get?"

"Absolutely, unless you know of some gorgeous, highly efficient gal who wants to spend the next twenty years working in the morgue," Andino answered. "Do you?"

"No."

"Well, I'm just as happy. I don't think Sunshine likes people much, but she's good at keeping my guest list small. I don't get many interruptions."

"Interruptions like me, I guess."

"You're not interrupting, I've been expecting you."

How come everyone knows where I'm going to be today before I do myself? McKenna wondered. "What made you think I'd be here today?" he asked.

"Simple. Reporters don't operate in a vacuum, and none of them want to be scooped by Heidi Lane. All the TV stations have been calling me for the last hour, wanting the details on the demise of Mr. Foster. Seems your little chat with Heidi's put some pressure on both of us."

"More on me than on you," McKenna said.

"Maybe, if I can prove you wrong about the poison. If not, you still have a problem, but I've got a bigger one."

To McKenna, Andino suddenly looked like he had the weight of the world on his shoulders. The smile was gone and his brow was furrowed, a look McKenna had never seen on the happy-go-lucky chief medical examiner before.

What could cause Andino to worry so? McKenna wondered. Secure in his job and at the top of his profession, my dilemma should evoke nothing more than a good-natured chuckle from him, along with a joke or two to cheer me up. There's more to this than I'm seeing right now, because this guy is scared. Now what is it? "Could your bigger problem have anything to do with the first one?" he asked.

McKenna knew he'd hit it because Andino looked even more unhappy. The doctor leaned back in his chair and gazed at the ceiling, shaking his head. "Yeah. Rodney Bailey, the guy I said froze to death last week. I might've been wrong."

McKenna was surprised by Andino's reaction. He knew that self-pity and self-doubt weren't normally in Andino's repertoire. He felt better when Andino straightened up in his chair and stared at him, looking like a toreador about to take the bull by the horns. "If Foster was poisoned, I'm gonna have to take another good look at Bailey," Andino said. "If I was wrong, I'll take the lumps I deserve."

"Did you do the autopsy on him?"

"No, but one of my people did. Dr. O'Malley. He's good, but I was just reading the autopsy report and there's some things in it I'd like to go over with him."

"You mean that maybe he screwed it up?" McKenna asked.

"No. He reached the logical conclusion. You see, death resulting from hypothermia is very difficult to define in a pathological sense because there's no damage to the internal organs. A person who freezes just slows down and stops, one organ at a time."

"So how is it determined that someone froze to death?"

"By the process of elimination. When we get a frozen body in, we look for all the other things that might have caused death. If there's no serious wounds and if the internal organs are intact and healthy, then the logical conclusion is that hypothermia was the cause of death."

"But what about a poison?"

"Naturally, a routine toxicology workup is done for alcohol and drugs, the same as in any other case."

"Routine? What does that mean?"

"It means tests to determine if narcotics, alcohol, barbiturates, corrosives, or the drugs commonly used in suicides were in the body."

"If Bailey had been poisoned, would it show up in a routine toxicology workup?"

"Some poisons would, but Bailey had a pretty good load in his system. In his case, finding anything but the common poisons would require a lot of time and work."

"A good load?" McKenna asked. "What does that mean?"

"It means he'd ingested most of the things that the majority of the folks in the freezers downstairs did whenever they had the chance. You want a breakdown?"

"Sure."

Andino picked up the autopsy report he had been reading and turned back a few pages. "Here we go. He had a blood-alcohol reading of point-one-two, which meant he was legally intoxicated, but not smashed. There was the usual load of THC, indicating heavy marijuana use. Rounding out the drugs, there was methadone and codeine."

"But none of those killed him?"

"Nope. Either alone or in combination, there wasn't enough of any of those drugs in his system to kill him, although I'm sure they slowed him down. Except for the codeine, he was on the usual high-octane diet and about as street-ready as most of our clients."

"Any idea why he was taking codeine?"

"For pain. He had AIDS, and it was manifesting itself with lymphatic cancer under his arms. But that didn't kill him, either, although Dr. O'Malley estimated that, in any event, he only had between three and six months left."

"Did he look like he was in poor health?"

"You tell me. Here's his picture," Andino said, passing McKenna a photo from the autopsy report.

It was a full-length shot of Rodney Bailey, taken before the autopsy. He was naked and lying on one of the tables downstairs. Black, emaciated, and unshaven, Bailey appeared to be in his forties. His body was a mass of scars, with oid surgical incisions under both armpits and down the front of his chest. He looked pitiful, causing McKenna to wonder why anyone would go to the trouble to poison someone so obviously close to death anyway. It seemed illogical to him, so he concluded that no one would.

"I wouldn't worry too much about this one," McKenna said, handing the photo back to Andino. "My bet is that he froze to death, just like you said."

McKenna's pronouncement did nothing to alleviate Andino's concern. The doctor just sat back and smiled, more to himself than to McKenna, like he was telling himself a joke he had never heard before.

McKenna watched Andino a moment before he asked, "What else should I know, John?"

McKenna expected Andino to hedge, but that wasn't the doctor's style. "You should know that this place has become unusually busy in the last month, processing cases that nobody really cares about."

"You've had an increase in homeless people dying?" McKenna guessed.

"We've got more cases, but I don't know yet exactly who they were."

"How big an increase?"

"January of last year we processed two hundred and ten cases. This is the thirty-first and already we have two hundred and twelve. Roughly a one percent increase."

"One percent? That doesn't sound like much," McKenna said. "After all, everyone knows that AIDS-related deaths have been increasing all year."

"Yeah, but those aren't usually ME cases. They die at home or in a hospital and the body doesn't wind up here for autopsy. Ordinarily, I wouldn't be too worried about the numbers, except the homicide rate has been down eleven percent since last year. Those are my cases, and there aren't as many of them. I should have less cases this year, not more."

"Maybe it's just a statistical anomaly."

"I like to think of myself as a scientist," Andino said, shaking his head. "That leaves me no room to blame statistical anomalies if there's something going on here."

"The weather this winter must have something to do with it," McKenna offered. "After all, without the two who might have frozen to death, you'd be just even with last year."

"Even isn't good enough," Andino said. "I should be down, but I was hoping that maybe the cold could explain it until I did some checking. For once, it's been colder here than in Chicago, but not by much. I called the Chicago medical examiner and he told me their caseload is down four percent this month over January last year."

"And their murder rate?"

"Down six percent."

"They have anybody freeze to death?"

"Not one. Worse, if Bailey and Foster did freeze to death, they're the second and third ones this year."

"Seems strange that two out of three were in one precinct," McKenna said. "Where was the other one?"

"In the Bronx, New Year's Day. What's stranger is that we've never had three people freeze to death in one year."

"But we've never had this many homeless on the streets, and this winter has been colder than usual."

"That also sounded good until I did some checking," Andino said. "It doesn't wash. I called the medical examiner in Moscow."

Moscow? Boy, you really did some checking, McKenna thought. But it makes sense. It's got three million fewer people than New York, but they're in bad shape. Their homeless population is up, everybody drinks a lot, and it's sure cold enough. "And what did they tell you?" he asked.

"That three people freezing to death is a lot for New York, considering that they think we're living in the Sun Belt. It's been ten degrees colder there all month, and they've only had two people freeze."

"Maybe they're just used to it. You know, thinner blood."

"Might have a little to do with it, but consider that they don't have the social safety valves we have, like shelters, food stamps, and public assistance, and you have to come to the conclusion that we have at least two more bodies than we should. Maybe a lot more."

Andino had just about said it, so McKenna didn't feel foolish stating the obvious conclusion. "You believe that some madman out there is poisoning our bums?" he asked.

"I don't jump to conclusions like that. I'm just saying it deserves a good look. Like I told you, I don't even know yet if our homeless population accounts for the increase."

"When will you know?"

"Soon," Andino answered, giving McKenna a smile he found strange.

"I've got those figures you asked for, Doctor," Ms. Lacey announced loudly from behind him. McKenna hadn't heard her come in and she startled him so that he jumped in his chair.

"Are you okay, Brian?" Andino asked, enjoying himself. "You seem a little jumpy."

"Just a nervous tic," McKenna answered. "I'm fine."

"Good. Let's have it, Sunshine."

"Twenty-nine of our clients last January were listed as homeless," Lacey said, reading from the book she had been writing in earlier.

"And this year?" Andino asked, bracing himself.

"Forty so far this month."

Andino made a face like he was going to cry, but then he smiled, which surprised McKenna until he figured it out. Andino had just received bad news with career-threatening implications from Lacey, but if it bothered him, he wasn't showing it. Instead, he was pleased that he had found a problem to solve. "Thanks a lot, Sunshine. Go take a nice lunch at Pasta Presto and charge it to my account."

McKenna expected to hear a thank-you from Ms. Lacey, but didn't. He waited a moment, then turned in his chair. She was gone, vanished without a sound.

"Isn't she wonderful?" Andino asked.

"How does she do it? She doesn't make a sound."

"I watch her do it and I still don't know," Andino answered, still smiling. "She's just about scared the life out of me more than once. I never get used to it."

"So what now?" McKenna asked.

"That depends. You're the one who said Foster was poisoned. Got any ideas on his particular brand?"

"Sorry. Not yet."

"Well, then it's gonna cost the taxpayers a bundle. Fortunately, this place is well equipped, but running down poisons is a very tedious, time-consuming, and expensive business. I'm gonna be using all my toys."

"When?" McKenna asked, worried that Andino appeared to be getting happier by the minute.

"Starting right now. I'm going to personally take Mr. Foster apart, and then I'm going to do the most exhaustive toxicology workup I can on his body fluids and organs. If you're right and Foster was poisoned, I'm gonna know it."

"And if he was?"

"Then Rodney Bailey gets the treatment. Fortunately, no one ever claims the homeless bodies and he's still downstairs."

"And if *he* was?" McKenna asked, shuddering as he anticipated the answer.

"Then you're going to get many, many court orders to exhume a whole bunch of bodies. We'll grab some shovels and head up to Potter's Field in a very large truck."

Just wonderful, McKenna thought. This is better than being retired in the Florida sunshine, waterskiing, fishing, and hitting golf balls all day long? Now I hope I was wrong about Foster and I don't care what they say about me. "How long do you think it will take to finish with Foster and Bailey?" he asked.

"Depends. Maybe today, tomorrow if the poison is rare, and three or four days if the stuff is real exotic."

Andino looked excited at the prospect and absolutely content. McKenna didn't understand it at all. "John, mind if I ask you a personal question?"

"Shoot."

"Aren't you going to be in some trouble if it turns out that a good number of people were poisoned and your autopsies didn't catch it till now?"

"Sure, I'll get some heat over it. I'm responsible, even if I wasn't here. But I've been around a while and it'll be pretty difficult to knock me out of the box."

"You weren't here?"

"No. I was at an international conference in Italy, and then I took three weeks' vacation over there. I just got back last Friday."

"Who was in charge while you were gone?"

Andino laughed. "Assistant Supervising Medical Examiner Dr. James Wright, that's who."

"Then I guess he might be in some trouble," McKenna speculated. "Do you like him?"

"You tell me," Andino said, standing up. "Do you like duplicitous, back-stabbing, pompous, overly ambitious, lying scumbags who are always looking over your shoulder while they're after your job?"

"No."

"Neither do I. Isn't it wonderful?" Andino looked at McKenna like he expected an answer.

"I guess so," McKenna said. This is sure one crazy place, he thought. I shouldn't hang around here too long.

Foster was thawed and ready. First he was measured, weighed, and photographed. Then he was undressed by two attendants and his clothes were examined by McKenna and Andino before they were tagged, bagged, and saved for a more detailed microscopic examination. A close survey of Foster's body revealed no marks, bruises, or wounds. The entire body was X-rayed and no fractures were found. McKenna fingerprinted him, thinking Foster looked like he was asleep, stretched out on the autopsy table. With his eyes closed, the deceased looked healthy, as if he shouldn't be where he was for at least another twenty years.

While they were working, McKenna did his best to ignore the other tasks being performed in the large room. There were four autopsy tables, and all were occupied and in use. Foster was on the end table, so McKenna was able to keep his back to the other procedures. But he couldn't ignore the high-pitched whine of the circular saws the pathologists working behind him used to cut through skull and bone.

Then Andino turned up the heat, pressing the point of his scalpel into the skin at Foster's right armpit. Halfway expecting Foster to sit up and scream, McKenna watched Andino cut the standard Y-shaped incision on the torso of the body.

McKenna desperately wanted to be somewhere else, and then he remembered. He was *supposed* to be somewhere else. "I gotta go, John," he said. "Got another appointment at three o'clock."

Andino placed his scalpel on Foster's chest and checked his watch. "Better hurry. It's ten after three. You coming back?"

"No, not today," McKenna was happy to say.

Maureen was waiting for McKenna outside, double-parked in front of the morgue. As soon as he got into the car she handed him a large, bulky manila envelope.

"The bank film?" he asked.

"From both cameras, along with the list of customers from last night. Charity told me you were here, so I figured you were pressed for time," Maureen answered.

"Thanks. I am." He opened the envelope and dumped two black cassettes on his lap.

"It has to be developed," Maureen said. "Should we head for the Photo Unit first?"

"Where else?"

"Charity told me you want to speak to Father Hays, so I set up an appointment for four-thirty. We'll have to hurry if we go downtown first."

"Let's try."

Maureen headed downtown on Second Avenue, weaving in and out of traffic like a cabbie. Once he realized she was an excellent driver, McKenna relaxed a bit, then took out his cellular phone and called Ward. By the time he finished reporting to the lieutenant, they were in the garage at police headquarters.

McKenna left Maureen in the car and brought the cassettes to the Photo Unit.

The clerk recognized him, but still handed him a photo request form before he would accept the cassettes. Once he filled it out, McKenna was told it would take at least a day to process the pictures.

"No good," McKenna said, putting all the authority he could muster into his voice. "I need it done now. I'll wait." He was gratified to see the clerk's face contort into that old reluctant-disruption-of-routine frown.

"We can't do that, Commissioner. We'd have to stop everything else," the clerk protested.

"That's fine. Do it," McKenna said, happy that the folks working in the basement seemed to be late in getting the gossip and news. "I'll take responsibility."

"Okay, if you say so."

"I say so. Thanks."

While he waited, McKenna found his thoughts wandering to Maureen. He had learned for himself what others said, that Maureen did always seem to know what people around her were thinking, or at least what he himself should be thinking. It was one thing to hear that about a person and quite another to experience it. She was always a half-step ahead of him, something that hadn't happened to him before.

He found this disconcerting, so he went through the list of customers who had used the Citibank ATM machine the night before. There were six pages of Citibank customers, listed chronologically. Next to each of the names were the times they visited the ATM, their account numbers, and their addresses. The list was computer generated, but Charity had taken the time to look up most of the phone numbers and write them in.

McKenna began counting the names, but quickly became discouraged. He stopped counting at a hundred and turned to the list of customers who used credit cards or cards from other banks at the ATMs. That list contained only two pages of names with the names of their banks and their account numbers, but he figured there were just as many customers.

It took forty-five minutes before the pictures were ready. When the clerk handed McKenna the tall stack of photos, he saw why. "How many are there?" McKenna asked.

"Seven hundred and thirty-two."

"You guys did quite a job on short notice. Thanks."

The clerk didn't appear to appreciate the compliment, but McKenna didn't care. Balancing his stack, he walked back to the garage. Maureen was out of the car and waiting for him, holding open the passenger door.

During the drive back uptown, McKenna shuffled through the stack of photos and saw that the shots taken by the camera focused on the bank door were on top. They were grainy black-and-white five-by-sevens. Each photo showed a customer entering or leaving the bank and had a date/time stamp at the bottom. They were in chronological order.

McKenna quickly went through a couple of hundred photos before he finally found something of interest. It was a shot taken at 11:21 P.M. and showed an elderly white man holding the door open for Kerri. She had already been worked over by Benny. The next shot showed the same man leaving, putting his wallet in his back pocket as he opened the door. Kerri wasn't captured in that one, or the next thirty. They showed only customers entering and leaving, bundled against the cold. McKenna concluded that Kerri was already under the counter, either asleep or feigning sleep.

There was no sign of Benny until 12:15 A.M., but the only evidence of his presence in that photo was his laundry cart parked near the door and the worried look on the female customer's face as she glanced to her left and opened the door. The next photo showed the same customer leaving five minutes later, this time looking to her right at the place where McKenna figured Benny was standing, waiting for business to drop off so Kerri could let him in.

Benny had timed his arrival just about perfectly. Business at the bank had died down considerably, with only six customers entering and leaving during the next hour. All had been men and none gave any sign of Benny's presence outside the bank, although his cart was still there.

McKenna could imagine Benny's frustration, standing outside in the cold while Kerri pretended to be asleep. The worst part for Benny must have been knowing there wasn't much he could do about it. He had been on the street a long time and must have known that the police had become very responsive to any report of suspicious activity in the vicinity of an ATM; make a racket, make someone suspicious, or even offend someone by following them in, and he ran the risk of the police showing up.

To Benny in that weather, the police meant the shelter or the hospital, the last places he wanted to go. So he played it cool and raged in silence, figuring he'd get a chance to straighten Kerri out later.

Benny's plans for Kerri's future had started going awry at 1:21 A.M., the first time he actually appeared in the photos. A male customer in his twenties and wearing work clothes was entering the bank. Over the customer's right shoulder McKenna could see Benny in profile, twenty feet from the bank entrance, talking to someone standing in front of him. Except for an extended hand, the customer's body blocked the camera's view of Benny's friend.

Frustrated, McKenna lowered the photo and stared at it from a different angle, as if by doing so he could look over the customer's shoulder and see who had been with Benny. Then he realized what he was doing and laughed at himself before he placed the photo on the dashboard and examined the next one from the stack.

That one turned out to be even more frustrating, showing the same customer leaving the bank three minutes later, his back to the camera as he looked straight ahead at Benny and his companion. Benny was once again in profile, this time holding a cup in his hand as his companion poured him a drink from a wine bottle; once again the customer was blocking his view so that little was visible of Benny's gracious visitor.

McKenna held the photo closer and stared at it. No matter how hard he looked, all he could see was an extended arm tilting the bottle over Benny's cup and the top of a knit hat showing above the customer's bare head.

There wasn't much, but there was enough to permit McKenna to make a few deductions: The man with Benny was about five foot nine and he wasn't dark-skinned. The top of the man's head and the top of Benny's head lined up in the photo, and Benny was five foot nine. The hand holding the bottle looked white, so he was white, Hispanic, Asian, or a light-skinned black.

McKenna tried to content himself with the thought that he had just eliminated at least 95 percent of the people in New York as suspects, but failed when he did some quick arithmetic and figured that still left him with 400,000 possibles.

The only other thing he learned from the photo was that Kerri had been right about the cup. It was a light-colored ceramic cup with something written on the front, but the photo was too grainy and the distance too great for McKenna to make out the inscription.

McKenna also placed that photo on the dashboard and examined the next one. This time it was a black man in his sixties, entering the bank a half hour later, at 1:55 A.M. Benny and his companion weren't visible, but the laundry cart still was. Four minutes later the customer was out, looking down and to his right as he left the bank.

Is he looking at Benny lying on the ground, dead or dying? McKenna wondered. He shuffled through another twenty photos, bringing him to 4 A.M. Ten customers had entered the bank during that time and most of them seemed to be looking at the spot in front of the bank where Benny had been found dead. Some had looked when they entered, some had looked when they left, and three had done both.

He wanted to finish going through the photos, but they were almost at their next appointment. Maureen turned into West 31st Street and stopped in front of the St. Francis of Assisi Church. The block was crowded with double-parked trucks, but Maureen still managed to find a small parking spot. As she backed up and maneuvered in, McKenna picked up the two photos from the dashboard and studied them one more time.

What kind of luck is this? he thought. Here we have two good shots of Benny and none of the guy standing right next to him the whole time. Is it possible that he's aware of the camera?

Maureen finished her parking job and turned to McKenna. "Can I see those before we go in?" she asked.

He gave her the two photos and watched her closely while she studied them.

It didn't take Maureen long. "Looks like he knows about the camera," she said a minute later as she handed them back to McKenna.

9

McKenna's Catholic school education and at least a dozen Hollywood movies had given him a preconceived notion of what a priest's office should look like. He wasn't disappointed in that regard; the place where Father Hays worked was exactly what McKenna had expected, straight from *The Bells of St. Mary's*. There was the mahogany decor, the crucifixes, the pictures of Christ, and the statue of Mary, complete with a row of candles in front.

On the other hand, nothing in his experience prepared him for Father Hays. The first surprise was the priest's choice of clothes. It wasn't the black traditional garb nor the hipster jeans and flannel shirt activist priests seemed to favor; Father Hays was wearing khaki slacks and a white shirt, both with sharp, military creases. Tall, well built, in his late thirties, and sporting a full head of light brown curly locks, he looked like a cross between Harrison Ford and Robert Redford, the kind of man some women swoon over.

It didn't add up to McKenna that a man who looked like Father Hays had chosen a celibate lifestyle, so he looked for an angle, but didn't find one. Father Hays turned out to be his kind of guy.

It started when Hays just about bounded from his desk to give Maureen a kiss and a hug as soon as they entered. He then took her in, head to toe, before he told her how wonderful she looked. Him Maureen believed, because right before McKenna's eyes she blushed like a schoolgirl.

Then it was McKenna's turn. Hays took his hand in a strong grip and said, "So good to finally meet you, Detective McKenna. I've been following your remarkable career for years."

"Thank you very much, Father," McKenna said, wondering if he was blushing himself. "Why don't you just call me Brian?"

"Okay, Brian. Let's relax while we chat," Hays said. He took two chairs from along the wall and placed them in front of his desk, then took his own seat behind his desk. Maureen and McKenna sat down and got comfortable.

"Maureen tells me you think my low-life pal Benny was poisoned," Hays said, and waited for McKenna to begin.

For a moment, McKenna didn't know what to say. He had expected to meet a man of God who would tell him that Benny Foster had been a poor, misguided, and misunderstood individual who had been sent to his untimely final reward after a life of unjustifiable suffering. "You find any redeeming qualities at all in Benny?" McKenna asked.

"No, and believe me, I looked," Hays said.

"Was he bad enough for someone to want to murder him?"

"Tough question." Hays had to think about that for a moment before arriving at a conclusion. "No, he wasn't that bad, although most everyone who knew him wouldn't mind smacking him around a bit. Felt like doing it myself most of the time."

"What do you know about him?"

"A lot. At one time, he was one of the people I had some hope for, and there aren't too many of the homeless we can say that about."

"You mean hope in a spiritual sense?" McKenna asked.

"No, I never had any spiritual hope for Benny. If there's a Hell, then that's where he is. What I meant was, he didn't have the physical, mental, or dependency problems many of them have that make them hard-core unemployable."

"You mean he didn't have to be homeless?"

"That's what I'm saying. I think he was smart enough to have made some kind of life for himself."

Maureen disagreed. "I'd say he was crafty, not smart," she said. "Crafty enough to get everything he could without doing a lick of work."

"Maybe I was being too kind," Hays said. "Crafty might be a better word, but he was still no dope."

"So what was he?" McKenna asked. "Just lazy?"

"No, not lazy. Benny was the best panhandler in the city and he worked at it. He had more scams than anybody out there. Did the wounded-Vietnam-vet thing, the working-guy-who-ran-out-of-gas-and-just-needed-a-dollar-to-get-going thing, the I've-got-AIDS-and-I'm-not-on-welfare thing, the my-house-burned-down thing, you name it." Hays shook his head and smiled. "Whichever one he used, he made more than anybody else at it."

Having walked around the streets of New York for the past year, McKenna had already seen all the ploys Hays had mentioned, and quite a few more. "Looks like you admire his creativity," he commented.

"Yeah, not that it means that much. In panhandling, the difference between the best and mediocre can't be more than a hundred a week. Not enough to have a life or get a place to live."

"Not even with the help he was getting from the city?" McKenna asked.

"Three hundred and eighty-two dollars a month? Maybe in Nebraska, but not here."

"But there were two of them. Kerri gets a check, too. Between the food stamps and the panhandling, that should have been enough to set them up."

"Unfortunately, that's not the way the system works. Once they share an apartment, the Department of Social Services treats them as a family unit. Just one check, maybe four and a quarter. And you're not figuring in furniture, utilities, or security deposits, even if you could find a landlord willing to rent to them. Besides—"

"I know," McKenna interrupted. "Benny liked living on the streets."

"I don't know if I'd say *liked*. Preferred, maybe. He knew how to cope and, on the street, Benny was respected by his peers."

"But not liked?"

"Not at all. He treated them all as inferiors and was always conning even them out of money, one way or another."

"Can you think of any enemies in particular? You know, badasses?"

"No. There are some retired badasses among our clients, but Benny was smart enough to leave them alone."

"How about the rest?"

"For a suspect? On paper, maybe. If you checked their criminal records you'd find that many of them had been to jail for one thing or another when they were younger. But being homeless has a way of sapping your self-respect, even criminal self-respect if you ever had any. They might have done bigger things once, but now a little shoplifting would be the extent of it, and most of them wouldn't even do that."

"So there's nothing violent about them?"

"Generally, no. Sometimes a psychotic or neurotic forgets to take his medication and acts up, but that has nothing to do with this case. Regarding Benny, a few might cut him in a fit of rage, but you suspect that this is a poisoning case, right?"

"Yeah, something requiring planning."

"Then I'd say you have to look somewhere else for a suspect. I don't think any of my clients pulled it off."

"Any suggestions?"

Hays shrugged. "Maybe someone from his past."

I'm not getting much help here, McKenna thought. "Mind if I ask a personal question?"

"No, go ahead."

"You've been described to me as the only friend he had," McKenna said. "Do you think that's accurate?"

"As far as I know."

"But you didn't like him, right?"

"No, I didn't like him. He burned me a few times," Hays admitted.

"Burned you? How?" McKenna asked.

Hays started running the ways off on his fingers. "He used the church's name to collect funds for himself. He set himself up as a supervisor in our soup kitchen and collected food stamps from our slower clients for their meals here. He sold to bodegas right on the church block the cheese the government gives us to distribute. He . . ."

"He stole cheese from you?" McKenna asked.

"No, he bartered for it from our other clients after we gave it to them."

"What did he use to barter with?" McKenna asked. "Food stamps?"

"Worse than that," Hays answered, looking to Maureen.

"He used Kerri," she said. "He used that poor simpleminded girl in the vilest ways just to get cheese. He rented her out."

"So he rented his girlfriend for cheese," McKenna said, looking to Hays. "Why didn't you cut him off, throw him out and keep him out? Maybe even have him arrested for some of his stunts?"

"I'd like to say that it's because I believe that each of us is created in God's image and therefore we all have the capacity to be good. Even the worst of us," Hays sighed, leaning back in his chair.

"But that's not it?"

"No, that's not it. Unfortunately, I'm not that fine a person. The truth is, Benny found a loophole, a way to keep scamming me over and over. I knew it, but there was nothing I could do about it."

Hays smiled, but McKenna saw sadness in it. Now how could Benny keep scamming this guy, a sharp guy who's been around enough to recognize Benny for what he was? McKenna asked himself. Figuring it must have something to do with religion, he ventured a guess. "Confession?"

"You got it," Hays said. "Confession. Benny became a Catholic and had me feeling good about it until I finally realized it was a scam. Every time I caught him doing some shenanigans, he pulled the confession angle on me."

McKenna understood, but was gratified to see that for once Maureen didn't.

Hays caught it, too. "As a priest, I'm required to hear confessions from any Catholic whenever he or she feels the urge," he explained to her. "So Benny would confess his sins to me and ask God's forgiveness. Acting in God's name, I'm required to give it. So who am I not to forgive him if God does? he always had me asking myself. I knew better, but he still managed to pull all my strings."

"I see how he put you on the spot with that one," Maureen said. "He was despicable."

Hays nodded, then turned his attention back to McKenna. "Now, mind if I ask you a question, Brian?"

"Shoot."

"You don't have to answer this, but aren't you investigating more than just Benny's murder?"

McKenna was stunned by the question and cast a sidelong glance at Maureen.

She gave him an unconcerned, innocent smile, although he figured she had broken one of the cardinal rules of protocol and had divulged details of his investigation without his permission. Even though Hays was a police chaplain, it still wasn't done.

When and how? he wondered. He reached the conclusion that she had been listening while he reported to Ward during their trip to headquarters and that she had then called Hays while he was waiting for the photos. He felt anger rising within him, but Hays's question still had to be answered. "Yes, it's possible that more than one person has been murdered," he admitted.

"More than one homeless person?"

"Yes. Maybe a lot more."

"I thought so," Hays said to McKenna, but he was smiling at Maureen. It appeared to McKenna that they were both sharing a little joke on him. Then Hays turned back to McKenna. "If it's possible there's a good number murdered, then why are we going so deeply into Benny's background? Wouldn't it seem to be random killings of homeless people?"

McKenna thought it was a good question, and it was one he had even asked himself after he had talked to Andino. He gave Hays his conclusion. "Maybe, if there is more than one. I can't even say for certain yet that Benny was poisoned, but all the bases still have to be covered and investigative procedures still have to be followed. Now I need a favor from you."

"You mean keep all this to myself?"

"Exactly," McKenna said, trying to smile pleasantly while struggling to keep his anger under control. If Father Hays knows that, why doesn't Maureen? he wondered.

10 There was another one. As soon as they got in the car after leaving Father Hays, McKenna called Ward to report and was told that the body of a homeless man had been discovered in the playground at Second Avenue and East 29th Street. Although the location was in the 13th Precinct, one block south of the 17th Precinct dividing line, Ward figured McKenna ought to look into it. He offered no further details, as the body had been found at 4:00 P.M., just an hour before.

In a perverse sort of way, the assignment fit McKenna's mood. He needed something to occupy his mind and didn't feel like talking to Maureen. Since he liked and respected Maureen, he had already given her the benefit of the doubt, assuming she had her own good reasons for talking over details of his case with Hays without so much as a nod in his direction.

But her reasons weren't his reasons. Although nothing written in any of the manuals barred her from discussing his case with Hays, and even though Hays wasn't about to go running to the press, she had still violated the protocol that stated it was *his* case and *his* responsibility, win or lose, so that he was the one who should call the shots on who gets told what, and when.

McKenna silently went back to the bank photos while Maureen drove. If she detected anything wrong with his mood, she didn't show it. By the time they got to Second Avenue, McKenna had finished scanning the rest of the photos without finding another sign of Benny, Kerri, or the man in the knit cap. He had hoped for more.

As soon as Maureen turned the corner, McKenna saw that his poisoning theory had hit home in the upper echelons of the department. Whoever the deceased had been, he was receiving more attention for his demise than he probably ever had throughout his life. Sitting along the curb in front of the playground were a row of radio cars, both marked and unmarked, an ambulance, and the morgue wagon. Double-parked next to them were the Crime Scene Unit's station wagon and a very shiny unmarked car with enough antennae on the rear to monitor communications from the space shuttle, indicating to McKenna the presence of a chief.

The press vans were across the street, roof antennae raised and prepared to broadcast. The park had a steel fence around it and had been closed by the police, with yellow crime-scene tape strung across the entrance. Despite the cold, the curious had gathered along the fence and were mingling with the reporters. The guest of honor lay in the rear of the playground next to the rear fence by the handball courts, his body surrounded by uniformed cops, detectives, and ambulance attendants.

Maureen pulled up behind the chief's car. As soon as she shut off the ignition she began her dusting process again, removing invisible specks of dirt from her suit while McKenna watched. Then she turned to him for approval. "How do I look?" she asked.

"Marvelous."

"No, really. How do I look?"

McKenna had been through this same routine with his wife a million times before and knew there was only one answer. "Marvelous. Really, you look just marvelous."

Just like Angelita, she never believed him but always had to ask. "I hate this," she said, regarding him as if she had just caught him in a lie. "The cameras show every wrinkle and make you look so fat," she complained, looking like she really loved it.

As soon as they left the car, the press was on them at a trot, advancing with microphones held forward. Leading the pack, still a little sharper and a little faster, was Heidi Lane. She skidded to a stop in front of McKenna, blocking his path.

"Not now, Heidi," McKenna said as he tried to move around her.

Heidi had moves and speed that, despite her size, could have placed her on the defensive line of any professional football team. No matter which way McKenna tried to maneuver, Heidi was in front of him with her microphone held to his mouth. "Commissioner McKenna, does your presence here indicate—"

"What time was this morning's interview first shown?" he asked, cutting her off and throwing her off balance.

"Five-twenty."

"What time you got now?"

Heidi took a moment to look at her watch and McKenna was by her, running through the newspeople toward the two cops guarding the entrance to the park. They were ready for him and held up the crime-scene tape for him, saluting as he ducked under. He got to the center of the park before he looked back and discovered he was no longer the focus of attention.

Maureen was. Heidi and she were slowly strolling toward the park entrance, Heidi's microphone held in front of Maureen's face while her cameraman backed up to keep them in focus as they walked. It seemed to McKenna that Maureen had a lot to say before she reached the park entrance. There she stopped and talked a little more on camera before she ducked under the tape and joined McKenna with that innocent smile on her face.

The many questions he had for Maureen he kept to himself. Detective Cisco Sanchez from the 13th Squad had detached himself from the crowd around the body and was approaching them. Sanchez and McKenna had worked together before and respected each other's talents. McKenna thought Cisco was a good detective, but a little too cocky; Cisco thought that, next to himself, McKenna might be the best detective on the job. Sanchez was the picture of the Midtown detective: well dressed, well groomed, and carrying himself proudly like the man in charge.

"How's it going, Cisco?" McKenna asked.

"Okay, until you invited all these people to my playground," Sanchez said, nodding in the direction of the body. "Some bum croaks and you got me putting up with the press and the brass."

"Doing a good job with it?"

"Sure. I figured you were gonna make a big thing out of this, so I took care of a few things while awaiting your arrival. Although she denies it, we have the woman who called 911. I listened to the tape and the voice matches."

"Why's she denying it?" McKenna asked.

"Who knows? Anyway, she's knocking a tennis ball against the wall with her new yuppie racket when her ball lands next to the dearly departed. It's still there, which is why I first figured she was the caller."

"She was practicing in this weather?"

"What can I tell you?" Sanchez answered, shrugging his shoulders. "She's real hard-core."

"And he was just lying there while she was improving her game?" McKenna asked.

"Sure. In this place the bums are part of the landscape. The Bellevue Shelter's two blocks away and they like to hang out here and refresh themselves until nap time. Nothing unusual."

"She knew he was dead just by looking at him?"

"Wait'll you see him. You get close enough to him, this guy looks like he should've been dead six months ago. Heavy-duty AIDS, sarcomas all over his hands."

"Was she the only one in the park?"

"There was another bum hanging around when I got here, passing the time and doing a little drinking."

"Does he know the dead guy?"

"Yeah, knows him as Juan Bosco. Says he doesn't like hanging out with him on account of the AIDS."

"Where is he now?"

"I set up a temporary headquarters in the Madison Boys Club across the street. I've got him over there being force-fed some coffee."

"And the tennis nut?"

"Yeah, she's over there, too, squawking about how she don't know nothing and breaking the cops' balls."

"Why's she so upset?" McKenna asked.

"Because it's her nature and she doesn't like cops. I had to have her dragged over there."

Sanchez was smiling, but McKenna could see he was worried. "Is she gonna be a problem?" he asked.

"Let me put it this way, Brian. You better have a homicide here or she's gonna be after my pension."

McKenna understood Sanchez's concern. By taking the witness someplace against her will, Sanchez had, in effect, unlawfully arrested her, even though he would never say so. Although it's not written down anywhere, as a matter of practice judges recognize that a homicide represents a special case and they allow the police more latitude than is permitted by the Constitution. Consequently, judges generally turn a deaf ear to lawsuits instituted by reluctant witnesses who were detained by the police immediately after a murder, but there has to have been an actual homicide, not just a suspicious body, or chances are the plaintiff will collect.

"You know, I've never seen this park so clean," Maureen observed cheerfully, making her first comment and ending McKenna and Sanchez's ruminations. "Usually it's a disgrace with bottles and cans everywhere," she added, looking around.

The worried look left Sanchez's face. Forgetting for a moment that he was angry with her, McKenna had to conclude that Maureen was a genius. She had found a way to cheer up Sanchez by giving him a chance to shine.

"That's because all the trash that was in the park is now in the Boys Club," Sanchez said proudly.

Both McKenna and Maureen put on their best awestruck expressions, prepared to marvel at Sanchez's expertise as soon as he explained to them how real crime-fighters do things. *Take the trash? Now why would you do that, O Magnificent One?*

Sanchez savored the moment before he climbed on his soapbox. "You see, I heard that if this is a homicide, then it's probably a poisoning case. Now, as I'm sure you know, poisoning cases are difficult if you don't have an idea of the poison. So I figured that if yonder gentleman had been poisoned in this park, there's a chance that the Holy Grail was left here someplace. So I had the Crime Scene Unit pick up every can and bottle that was littering this park when I got here, along with all the stuff in the trash cans. Later on the lab can see if any of them contain the mystery poison."

"That's gonna be very expensive," Maureen commented.

"Hey, it's a McKenna case, isn't it?" Sanchez asked, smiling. "The taxpayers should be used to financing his adventures by now."

The lighthearted remark worried McKenna. If this guy wasn't poisoned, he thought, I'm going to look ridiculous. Even though I didn't choreograph this particular act of the show, the Job has reacted like they believe in me, spending time, manpower, and money, as only the largest police department can in its plodding and methodical fashion.

Once again, Maureen read his mind. "Don't worry, Brian. If this one wasn't poisoned, there will be other victims. Until you get the killer, all this is going to have to be done every time one of our homeless dies in the street. The man you're looking for isn't going to stop.''

McKenna thought Maureen was wrong. If this one was a murder, it had occurred before Heidi's interview with him had aired. However, he considered it likely that the killer would stop when he learned that the police were on to the murders. Thinking he was one up on Maureen made McKenna feel magnanimous. ''You did a great job here, Cisco,'' he said. ''I'm glad it was you who got the call.''

Sanchez took the praise in stride as something to be expected every time he showed up at a crime scene and did his thing. ''Thanks,'' he said perfunctorily.

''Who's the chief handling this?'' Maureen asked.

''Steve Tavlin.''

McKenna realized at once that all the praise shouldn't go to Sanchez, but he kept that to himself. Tavlin had recently been promoted to Chief of Detective Borough Manhattan and was one of the ablest police commanders McKenna knew. His presence at the scene explained a lot to McKenna. ''Where is he now?'' he asked.

''The Boys Club, waiting for you to finish the search here. He didn't want anyone touching the body until you got here.''

''And nobody did?''

''Just the ambulance attendants. They tried some useless first-aid stuff on him, but he's just the way we found him, except colder and stiffer.''

''Let's finish up here before we all freeze,'' McKenna said, walking to the group clustered at the far end of the playground. Maureen and Sanchez followed.

All eyes were on McKenna, making him feel self-conscious. Standing around the body were a uniformed sergeant, two cops, and the ambulance crew. They split up to let McKenna examine the deceased.

Bosco was a dark-skinned Caucasian, shabbily dressed in sneakers, old polyester pants, and a cheap hooded snorkel coat. Despite the cold, there were no gloves or scarf and the hood of his jacket was down. A green tennis ball lay inches from his right hand, as if he had just died and dropped it.

McKenna's first impression was that Sanchez had been right in every way. It was obvious the dead man had been suffering long before his last day; lying on his back two feet from the park fence, his eyes were closed but his face still showed the pain. AIDS could drastically change a person's appearance: Bosco was emaciated, jaundiced, clumps of his hair had fallen out, and he had black sarcomas on his hands and neck. McKenna could only guess an age range between thirty and fifty and thought Bosco looked Hispanic.

Again McKenna asked himself: Why would anyone subject himself to risk and waste his time by poisoning a person so obviously close to death anyway? He concluded that the man at his feet must have died of natural causes. For a moment he felt foolish, thinking he was wasting the department's money and time as well as his own reputation.

Then, behind him, he heard Maureen put her two cents in.

''It sure is a crazy world, isn't it?'' she observed to no one in particular.

Yes it is, McKenna thought, full of crazy people who do things for bizarre reasons that make sense only to themselves. Rodney Bailey had been in the same shape as Bosco, yet an authority like John Andino had conceded that Bailey might have been poisoned.

Straighten out and stay with it, McKenna told himself. He bent over the body and put his face close to the victim's. The odor of alcohol was unmistakable.

"Who was first on the scene?" he asked as he stood up.

The two uniformed cops stepped forward and saluted at attention. "We were, sir," one of them reported. "Sector Thirteen Boy." The name tag below the young cop's shield said he was Wilenski. The row of medals over his shield told McKenna that Wilenski knew his job and worked hard at it.

"Let's relax a bit," McKenna suggested. "I'm not a *Sir* and I don't get saluted. I'm a detective, not a boss."

Wilenski wasn't buying it. "Yes sir."

"Tell me about the job."

"Got a radio run at 3:50 of a man down in the park. When we got here, he was dead, just like you see him now."

"Anybody around him?"

"No."

"How many people in the park?"

"Just another bum sitting on a bench over there," Wilenski answered, pointing at a row of benches near the playground entrance.

"How about the person who called in the job?"

"We didn't see her," Wilenski admitted. "Detective Sanchez scooped her up after he got here. She was standing by the phone booths over there," he said, pointing at a bank of pay phones across the street at the corner of East 29th Street and Second Avenue.

If she can help, it was an impressive piece of police work on Sanchez's part, McKenna conceded. To see the tennis ball and connect it to the owner standing a half a block away was sharp. To check the 911 voice-tape and bring her in against her will was even sharper.

McKenna turned to the ambulance crew. They were two young white men who seemed uncomfortable as they huddled in their coats, trying to stay warm. "What did you guys do?"

The two attendants looked at each other for a moment before one of them stepped forward. "We arrived here at 3:56. Inserted an endotracheal tube, aerated with an ambu bag, and tried CPR. No response. Tried to insert an IV, but couldn't get a line. I suspect collapsed peripheal circulation due to hypothermia. He was dead and cold, body temp around eighty-nine degrees. Pronounced dead at four o'clock."

McKenna was impressed by the amount of emergency care they had given Bosco in four minutes before arriving at the inescapable conclusion that he was dead and gone. "You said something about hypothermia. You saying the cold killed him?" he asked.

"No. All I said was that the body was cold. It's about five degrees out here, so figure he was dead a half an hour when we got here."

Good information, but McKenna needed more than that. "So maybe he didn't freeze to death or die of natural causes?" he speculated, hoping for some sign of agreement from the ambulance attendant.

He wasn't getting it. "Can't say," the attendant answered, looking down at

Bosco's pitiful body. "From the shape of him, this guy could have died of ten things I could think of off the top of my head."

"If you had to pick one, what would it be that killed him?"

"Life."

So much for that. "Thanks. You guys can go now," McKenna said. The two attendants picked up their gear and were gone without another word.

It was time for the search of the body. Following protocol, McKenna turned to the patrol sergeant. "Can we get the search done now, Sarge?" he asked.

The sergeant, an unhappy-looking old-timer, had been around long enough to anticipate the request. "Certainly," he said, giving the barest nod to Wilenski and his partner.

It was all they needed, and they began the practiced procedure. Wilenski pulled a pair of latex gloves from his jacket pocket and put them on as his partner took out his memo book, poised to record the results.

The first place Wilenski searched was Bosco's jacket pocket. He took out a folded pink piece of paper and handed it to his partner. McKenna recognized the paper as a C-type summons, the kind that nobody but tourists, out-of-towners, or really legitimate people in New York ever worry about or bother to answer. The pink summonses were given by the police for nuisance things like dirty sidewalks, littering, jaywalking, and drinking in a park.

Hoping to get lucky, McKenna's heart raced as Wilenski's partner recorded in his memo book the information from the summons. Then he handed it to Mc-Kenna.

The summons stated that at 3:20 P.M. on January 31 Police Officer Chris Saffran of the 13th Precinct had personally observed one Juan Bosco drinking an alcoholic beverage in the playground at East 29th Street and Second Avenue in violation of Section 10-125 subdivision b of the New York City Administrative Code. Bosco's address on the summons was given as 421 East 30th Street and his date of birth was listed as August 18, 1965.

Realizing that he had evidence in his hand that a cop had seen Bosco drinking in the last hour of his life at the very place where he died, McKenna tried to contain his excitement while he watched the rest of the search. As he passed the summons to Maureen, his mind was focused on this Police Officer Chris Saffran. Whoever he was, Saffran was McKenna's new very favorite person on the planet. He wanted to buy Saffran dinner, meet his family, throw him a party, and be godfather to his children.

As it turned out, the rest of the search turned up very little of importance that McKenna didn't already know. In his pockets Bosco had $7.00 in bills, $4.46 in change, a Department of Social Services ID card, an expired learner's permit, two business cards from Legal Aid Society attorneys, and a half-smoked joint.

"Anything else?" the sergeant asked McKenna.

"A few things. What's at 421 East 30th Street?"

The sergeant looked at McKenna like he had just failed basic geography. "That's the Bellevue Shelter," he said, like everyone should know this.

"Who's Police Officer Saffran?"

McKenna got the same look again, as if only recently arrived tourists from Albania wouldn't know who Chris Saffran was. "A good cop, but a little strange. Works day tours on foot posts in this sector," the sergeant explained patiently.

"I need to talk to him."

"He got off at three-thirty. He should be in tomorrow morning at seven."

The sergeant's attitude was wearing on McKenna, but he understood it. Any detective making a fuss and drawing chiefs to the scene of a routine job like a dead homeless person who had obviously died of natural causes would be considered a stupid annoyance by any patrol sergeant.

How to handle this guy? McKenna wondered briefly before coming up with the answer. After all, this is civil service, so it's okay to be stupid and annoying as long as you're in charge. Time to see if I still have any weight to throw around.

"Sarge, I said I need to talk to him today. Wherever he is, find him and get him in. When you do, have him report to Chief Tavlin at the Madison Boys Club."

"Yes sir."

The indoor basketball courts of the Madison Boys Club had been transformed by the Crime Scene Unit into a scale version of the 29th Street playground: All cans and bottles were inside, each tagged and placed in the position on the courts corresponding to the place in the park where it had been found. The three park trash cans were also there, with a row of cans, bottles, and coffee containers lined up in front of each one. Signs taped on the floor denoted the positions of the monkey bars, the swings, the slide, and the handball court. Two Crime Scene Unit detectives were doing something chemical to wine bottles at a table set up by the entrance to the gym.

"See what you started?" Maureen asked McKenna as they surveyed the scene before them.

"Seems to me you started all this," he answered.

"Nope. I just gave you my opinion and you ran with it, but it's your case. I'm just here to help you, any way I can."

"Thanks. You've been a big help, Maureen," he said sarcastically, but Maureen took it as a compliment and gave him an appreciative smile.

Is it possible she doesn't get it? McKenna wondered. She knows it's my case, but she's sticking me at every turn. Most detectives I know would be ranting and raving at her by now if they were in my place, first for blabbing to Father Hays and then for talking to the press about my case. But here she is, constantly smiling like she's done nothing wrong. Why? She's certainly been around long enough to know the rules.

"Brian, you want to talk to me, right?" Maureen asked out of the blue, startling McKenna once again.

How does she do that? he wondered for the umpteenth time. "Yeah, we have to have a chat."

"Then why don't we?"

"Later. Once we're done in here we'll make some time."

"Okay, but I think it should be soon. You're wrong, you know." The smile was gone and Maureen looked hurt.

"I am?"

"Of course. But don't worry, I forgive you."

Forgive me for what? McKenna asked himself. What did I do?

Then Maureen's smile returned. "Let's get back to work," she said. "Steve must be wondering where we are. But no more snotty faces, okay?"

Good God, snotty faces? And Chief Tavlin is another one of her boys? "Okay."

McKenna asked one of the Crime Scene detectives for Tavlin's location and was directed to the administrator's office on the second floor. They found Tavlin there, sitting alone with his feet up on the desk reading Vernon Geberth's *Practical Homicide Investigation*.

McKenna wasn't surprised. Tavlin possessed that rare combination of investigative and administrative skill, which he constantly honed by reading what the other experts had to say. People who worked for him soon acknowledged that he wasn't the boss because he had passed some civil-service tests and went to the right parties; Tavlin was the boss because he *should* be the boss. The flip side was that if they were working for him, they'd better be good or they would soon find themselves working for someone else in a less desirable setting.

Looking and dressing more like a successful Wall Street executive than a chief, Tavlin had always run his outfits like a corporation. He was results oriented, a traditionalist fan of procedure and usually lacking in the sentimentality department. For that reason, McKenna was a little surprised at the reception they received from him.

As soon as they entered the office, Tavlin put down his book and bounded from his desk. McKenna was ignored for a full minute while Tavlin and Maureen went through the old-pal, kissy-huggy, How-have-you-been? routine. Tavlin's first words to McKenna were, "Brian, I hope you're treating this treasure like she deserves."

Good God! "We get along," McKenna answered. This lady is driving me nuts, he thought but didn't mention.

"Good. Now what do we do to catch this guy?" Tavlin was back to his desk and back to business.

There were a few things McKenna liked in Tavlin's simple question. First was the *we* part. Conforming to Tavlin's usual approach, this was to be a corporate team effort. What Tavlin hadn't said was, *"What makes you think there is a guy doing all this?"* or even the more usual *"How do we get out of this looking good?"* That wasn't Tavlin's way. McKenna surmised that Tavlin had already talked to Ward and heard about Dr. Andino's concerns. Even though a conclusive autopsy and toxicology finding of poisoning wasn't in yet, Tavlin believed and had firmly committed himself to the case. McKenna was also sure that, if he was wrong and there were no murders, Tavlin was prepared to fall on his sword and accept the consequences.

"First of all, I have to apologize," McKenna said. "I sort of used your name in vain to get something done."

"That's a switch. Just two months ago I was throwing your name around to get things done. Consider yourself operating with my full faith and authority. Next?"

McKenna took twenty bank photos and Charity's customer lists from his pocket and passed them to Tavlin. "I need the people in those photos interviewed," he said. "Just match up the time on the bottom of the photo with the time on the list to find out who they are."

Tavlin went through the photos and took out McKenna's two favorites. "This Benny Foster behind the customer?" he asked.

"Yep."

"And the guy pouring the wine is the killer?"

"I think so."

"I see that one customer got a good look at him," Tavlin said, then went through the bank list. "Here he is. Richard Cama of 621 Parker Place in Levittown, Long Island, is our one 1:21 A.M. customer. He was about thirty miles from home last night."

"Looks like he was working," McKenna said.

"We'll find out. What about the rest of these customers? They all appear to be looking at something on the ground. Is that where the body was found?"

"Yep. They all saw Benny Foster on the ground, either dead or dying. If he was still alive for a while after he lay down, maybe some of them can give us an idea of his symptoms to help Dr. Andino find the poison."

If there is a poison, McKenna expected Tavlin to add, but he didn't. All Tavlin said was, "Done. What next?"

Done? That's it? McKenna thought. Interviewing twenty people, some of whom don't live or work close by, is a time-consuming task requiring lots of manpower. Yet Tavlin's treating it as a minor chore. "How?" he asked out loud.

"Don't worry about the details," Tavlin said. "I put the day tour from the Seventeenth Squad on overtime and I've got the Homicide Squad on the way here. Your job is to keep thinking and tell me what you need."

"So they're all gonna be personally interviewed. You're not going to just call them up?"

Tavlin looked insulted by the question. "Of course not. Each of them will be getting a visit. Richard Cama and any of the others who have anything useful to add will be brought to you. I've been told to give this case the highest priority, and you know what that means."

McKenna did, and a few things happening around him suddenly became clear. It meant that his pal, the almost-all-seeing, almost-all-knowing, almost-all-powerful Police Commissioner Ray Brunette had found out about his case and had taken a personal interest in it. Money, manpower, and department resources weren't going to be much of a problem here. "Yeah, I know what that means," he answered.

"Good. Me too. What else?"

"Have the people from the park been interviewed yet?"

"No. I was waiting for you to interview the woman, but you better take a Bromo first. She's a real nasty one. Won't even give her name."

"And the other one? The bum?"

"Complacent and compliant, but I don't know how much help he's gonna be. He's on the Thunderbird Express and a little confused by all this."

"Let's do the woman first," Maureen suggested.

"Good idea," Tavlin commented. "I'll be back in an hour or two. Let me know how you do."

Sitting in the administrator's office, McKenna and Maureen had ample notice of the pending arrival of their very unhappy witness. They could hear her shouting in the hall, threatening to sue the mayor, the police commissioner, Cisco, and especially the unfortunate who was escorting her. McKenna and Maureen braced themselves as the threats reached the office door. Then there was silence for a moment. McKenna figured she was gathering her strength, looking forward to devouring them.

Maureen figured different. "Bad case of PMS," she whispered. "She'll probably be a sweetie in a day or two."

The office door opened and she was in, escorted by a uniformed cop who looked very glad to be rid of her. The witness was middle-aged, bleached-blond, and heavyset, wearing a black short-sleeved pullover shirt and a pair of spandex pants at least two sizes too small. She had a Yankees jacket and a tennis racket tucked under one arm. Her other arm was used exclusively to smoke her cigarette. She took drag after drag as she coldly eyed McKenna and Maureen, stopping only for a second to blow smoke in the uniformed cop's face.

Well, nobody told me any lies about this one, McKenna thought. She's tough as nails if she was out hitting her ball wearing only those clothes in this weather. He nodded to her escort and he left, closing the door behind him. "Please come in and have a seat," McKenna said as pleasantly as possible.

She dropped her cigarette on the floor and squished it out with her foot, then shuffled to the empty chair facing McKenna and Maureen. She dusted it off with her hand before she sat down and resumed glaring at them.

"I'm Detective McKenna and—"

"I know who you are, McKenna," she spat out in a distinctive, gravel-filled voice before turning to Maureen. "And I know who you are, too. Kaplowitz, right?"

So she was downstairs watching the news interviews on TV while she was waiting for us, McKenna realized. Very good. She's as smart as she is nasty. He caught a wink from Maureen and he was happy to defer to her.

"Do you mind if I call you Ms. Nasty?" Maureen asked.

"I certainly do."

"Good. Ms. Nasty, we are certainly having a bad day, aren't we?" Maureen asked impersonally.

"Yeah, mine's bad but yours is gonna be worse once my lawyer hears about all this."

"Then that should be soon," Maureen said sweetly. "If he's any good or even a little bit greedy, he'll be paying you an expensive visit in about an hour."

"Huh?"

"You see, he's about to get the kind of case most lawyers dream about. His worthy client, an innocent and very respectable citizen who was unlucky enough to have witnessed a crime the police are very interested in, is about to have her nasty, fat ass hauled before a judge who is going to lock her away as a material witness until this case is presented to a grand jury. Maybe longer, if her attitude continues."

"Huuhh?"

"Yes, I imagine your lawyer will be very happy defending your rights while he takes your case and your pocketbook as far as he can. Maybe even to the Supreme Court, if you can afford it. After that, you can think about getting even with us. We'll still be around."

It was a side of Maureen that McKenna had never seen. He watched Ms. Nasty as uncertainty showed on her face, followed by fear, but only for a moment. Then her personality reasserted itself and her face hardened into a look of contempt. She reached into her jacket and pulled out another cigarette and a book of matches. After she lit up she threw the match on the floor at Maureen's feet. "Bullshit," she said. "You can't do that. I know my rights and I haven't done anything wrong. I didn't see nothing and you can't do shit to me."

Maureen just smiled. "Ms. Nasty, I can see this is going to be fun," she said. Then she picked up the spent match, leaned over, and slipped it into the astonished witness's jacket pocket. "Now where were we?"

"Something about bullshit and you can't do that," McKenna said.

Maureen remembered. "Oh, that's right. Ms. Nasty, you are a liar."

"No I'm not," she said, still looking defiant as she dragged on her cigarette.

"Yes you are. Do you bathe?"

The question caught the witness off guard. "Of course I bathe," she answered after a moment's hesitation.

"And do you change your clothes?"

"Of course."

"Frequently?"

"Every day."

"Then I can prove you're lying. You're a witness and the judge will agree."

"How?"

"First of all, there's the call you made to 911. We'll do a voiceprint comparison and prove it was you. Then there's the fact that you have a tennis racket and a tennis ball was found next to the dead man. Finally, there's your shirt. There's sweat rings forming under your armpits. Since you bathe and change your clothes regularly, that sweat is from today. Now, it's five degrees outside and about seventy in here, so you were working up a sweat hitting your ball against the wall in the handball courts for at least a half an hour, I'd say. That man in the handball courts was poisoned. You were there when he died and you saw who killed him."

The witness reacted as if she had been punched, recoiling and rubbing her jaw as the air went out of her. McKenna thought she was ready to give in, but she still had some fight left in her. "Okay, I was there but I didn't see anything. He was on the ground when I got there, probably dead already."

Maureen just shook her head. "Ms. Nasty, you're still lying. You were in that park from 3:15, at least. The victim was alive and drinking there while you were there because he got a ticket from a cop at 3:20. Maybe he was alone then and maybe he wasn't, but we'll find out. The important thing is that you were there."

McKenna knew Ms. Nasty was on the edge when she took the last drag from her cigarette and looked around. Then she walked over to the administrator's desk, put the cigarette out in an ashtray, and sat back down, looking very dejected but still silent. Why's this so hard for her? he wondered. She's only a witness, so why won't she give it up?

Maureen must have been wondering the same thing, but she had the answer. "You weren't supposed to be there, were you?"

McKenna saw from Ms. Nasty's face that Maureen had hit it. As he watched, her hard, defiant expression changed into something soft and vulnerable as her lips quivered.

"You have a boyfriend, don't you?" Maureen asked softly.

"Yes." It came out in a whisper.

"And a husband?"

"Yes.

"And he suspects something?"

Ms. Nasty was holding back the tears. "Yes."

Now where did Maureen come up with that one? McKenna wondered, astounded. How could she know that there was not just one, but two men in this degenerate city who were so in need of abuse that they would voluntarily spend time with this woman?

Maureen wasn't dwelling on it. She took a packet of Kleenex from her purse and gave it to Ms. Nasty.

The witness needed it, her signal to break down. She took one Kleenex, and then another out of the packet and filled them with tears.

Maureen waited for Ms. Nasty to finish crying and compose herself before she said, "Tell me about it."

That was all it took. "We live in Queens, but my husband knows I used to have a boyfriend on Twenty-ninth Street, long ago. He thought that was over."

"But it's not."

"No, but I can't let him find out. I think he's looking for an excuse to leave me."

"That would be bad?"

"Yes. He's not an exciting man, but I love him. It would be very bad if he left. Bad for me and bad for the children."

"I see," Maureen said. "When did the press get to the park?"

"Right after the police and the ambulance. They set up their cameras and were talking to everybody. I couldn't let my husband see me on television on Twenty-ninth Street. All he does is watch TV, so he'd know for sure."

"So you decided to lie if you could get away with it."

McKenna's respect for Maureen grew as he recognized her strategy. Once a witness has been forced to admit that he or she is a liar, they stop trying and usually tell nothing but the truth from then on, however painful it is.

Ms. Nasty was having a hard time saying it as Maureen stared at her. "Yes, I lied," she admitted.

"And you're not going to lie to us anymore?"

"No."

"Good." Maureen took a pad and pen from her purse and passed it to Ms. Nasty. "I want you to write down your name, address, your home number, you work number, and any other number you might be at if we need you."

Ms. Nasty picked up the pen and started to write, then hesitated. "Will I have to go to court?" she asked.

"Maybe, maybe not. You will have to view a lineup when we catch this guy. That's why I need to know where you'll be all the time."

"Is my husband going to find out?"

"We're not telling him. We probably won't need you for a while, so you'll have time to come up with a story for him. Write."

She did. When she finished she handed the pad back to Maureen, who took another minute to read it over.

"All right, Helga, let's start over and see if we can be friends. I'm Maureen and the handsome one over there is Brian. It's his case, so he's the one who has some questions for you. Now, he's a nice enough man, but sometimes he has his moments and then he has a despicably low trust level, so keep it truthful," Maureen said, taking a moment to shoot McKenna a reproachful glance.

Of course Helga didn't get it, but McKenna couldn't miss Maureen's point.

"I have just one more question before we begin," Helga said to Maureen, looking embarrassed.

"Yes?"

"Is my ass really that fat?"

What's the matter, you got no mirrors in your house? was McKenna's first thought. But then he softened as he watched Helga stare at Maureen, waiting for an answer. Tough, hard, pain-in-the-ass Helga suddenly looked very fragile and vulnerable to him.

We have her where we want her, was his second thought, so he concentrated on sending a message: Maureen, just this one time, please lie.

If Maureen got the message, it just wasn't her style. "Helga, it could use some work. Keep up the tennis exercise and it'll improve in no time."

Contrary to McKenna's expectations, Helga took the criticism in stride. "Thanks, I will. Since you're the one who mentioned it, I just thought I'd ask. Men will never tell you, but a woman will let you know."

I guess I'm still learning, McKenna thought. Maureen was prepared to take the notes and Helga was staring at him expectantly, finally resigned and ready. "What time did you get to the park?" he asked.

"About three."

"You were alone?"

"Yes."

"Where were you coming from?"

"My boyfriend's apartment up the block."

"Where was he while you were in the park?"

"Taking a nap," she answered coyly. "I guess I tire him out."

And I guess I'll leave that one alone, McKenna thought. "Was the victim there when you got there?"

"Yes."

"Alive?"

"Yes. He was sitting by the fence at the handball courts, talking to another bum. I didn't pay much attention to them."

"Why not? Didn't they make you uncomfortable?"

"Them?" she snorted. "I could kick the shit outta both of them on my worst day. Besides, there's always bums in that park. Except for pissing all over the place, they never bother anybody there."

"What did the other guy look like?"

"Like the dead one. Maybe healthier, but dressed crazy. He had on brown leather gloves, probably cost more than everything else he was wearing. Had a scarf, too. Checkered yellow-and-red scarf with a blue coat. His colors were all wrong."

Which is why women make better witnesses, McKenna thought. As long as they're not scared, they generally remember things like colors and clothes better than men do. "Was he white or black?" he asked.

"White, probably Spanish. He was dark-skinned and had one of those scraggly beards the Puerto Ricans like."

"How tall was he?"

"A pip-squeak. Maybe five-two, kinda skinny."

"His hair?"

"Long and dirty. Mostly black, a little gray."

"How old?"

"Maybe forty."

"Was he wearing a hat?"

"No, no hat. He had that scarf around his head like a kerchief."

So our killer wasn't on the scene yet, McKenna thought. The one she just described definitely wasn't him. Too short, wears gloves, and no hat. I think our killer would wear a hat in July, just to make it harder to identify his face. "Any other people in the park?"

"When I got there?"

Strange response, McKenna thought. She must know who we're really interested in and knows he wasn't there yet. Might have to get tricky with her. "Yeah, when you got there," he said.

"Just a few other bums. No regular people. One bum that was there you got sleeping downstairs."

"Okay, you were playing tennis and the dead man and his pal are there. Did you talk to them at all?"

"Of course not. Like I said, I didn't bother them and they didn't bother me."

"Were they eating or drinking anything?"

"They had one of them big bottles of beer in a bag, passed it back and forth a few times."

"You were there when the cop first got there?"

"Cops. There were two of them and yeah, I was there. They came in and started busting the bums' balls."

"Was the killer there when the cops came in?"

"No, he . . ." She caught herself, but it was too late. "Wait a minute. I didn't say anything about a killer."

"But you were going to because you promised to tell us the truth, right?"

"Right," she said, smiling at him sheepishly. "I was just waiting to get to that part."

"And you didn't know it then, but you know it now since you watched the news on TV downstairs. You know that the other man you saw, that third man, is the one we want to talk to you about. You know he's the killer. Right?"

"I guess so."

"I just wanted to make sure we were clear on that. When did the killer get there?"

"I don't know, exactly. Before the cops came in."

"Well, when did you first notice him?"

"When he caught my ball."

"He caught your ball?"

"Yeah. I hit a fast shot off the wall and it got past me. I remember thinking that it was gonna go through the fence and I'd have to run out of the park and get it. But when I turned around, he had it."

"Did he say anything to you?"

"No. He just threw it back."

"What did he look like?"

"Like a bum, except his clothes were better."

"Then what made him a bum?"

"Because he was hanging out with bums and because they weren't his clothes. Except for the hat, his clothes looked like they were donated. They were too big on him."

"Too big?"

"Yeah, maybe two sizes too big. He looked like he was standing in a tent."

"Tell me about the hat."

"You know, it was one of them cheap hats that the sailors used to wear. The kind that roll up."

"A knit cap?"

"Yeah, a black knit cap."

"And the rest of his clothes? What color were they?"

"Black overcoat and black pants."

"Scarf?"

"I don't think so."

"Gloves?"

"No."

"You sure about that?"

"I'm sure. He wasn't wearing gloves when he threw my ball back."

"Shoes?"

"Black, I think. Maybe those black sneakers everybody's wearing."

"Now tell me about him. What did he look like?"

"White or Spanish like the other two, except lighter. Skinny and kinda tall."

"How tall?"

"Maybe five-eight, five-nine."

"Mustache? Beard?"

"No."

"How about his hair?"

"I couldn't see his hair. He had his hat on real low. He could be bald for all I know, or he could look like Elvis under that hat."

"How old was he?"

"Hard to say. Someplace between forty and fifty."

"What was he doing with the other two?"

"I wasn't watching, but I heard them talking."

"What language were they speaking?"

"English."

"And you didn't hear what they were saying?"

"I wasn't paying attention."

"What were they drinking?"

"Must've been the beer and the wine."

"Wait a minute. What wine?"

"The wine the cops took when they came in."

"Took from who?"

"From the dead guy. 'Course, he was alive then."

"What did they do with it?"

"Poured it out in the bushes by the fence after they gave the bums tickets. Poured out the beer, too."

McKenna's heart was racing as he saw the finish line in sight. To him it looked like another case solved by the man on post during the course of routine police work. "They gave them all summonses?" he asked hopefully.

"All?" Helga asked, confused. "Oh, I see what you mean. No, they gave them *both* summonses. The guy in the baggy clothes left as soon as the cops came into the park."

"The killer left?" McKenna asked, dejected. Then he grasped at a final straw. "Did the cops talk to him?"

"One of the cops stopped him on his way into the park and just touched his pockets with his stick. I guess he was looking for booze, but I don't think the cop talked to him. It only took a second."

"But you saw the killer leave?"

"Like I told you already a thousand times, I wasn't paying much attention to them. I guess he left, because I don't remember seeing him again."

So it's not a home run, McKenna thought, but at least I get a few more pitches. "What did the cops do with the bottles after they poured the booze out?" he asked.

"Threw them in the trash can."

"Bingo!" McKenna heard Maureen say under her breath. Not quite yet, he thought, but we're coming along with the increasingly marvelous Helga. Now for the million-dollar question.

"Helga, would you recognize this guy if you saw him again?"

It was the one question Helga had prepared herself for. "I don't know. Probably not."

So had Maureen. "Helga, c'mon. You don't really expect us to believe that you wouldn't recognize that killer if you saw him again, do you?" Maureen asked in an incredulous and derisive tone of voice.

"I really don't think I can," Helga said defensively.

Then Helga was administered a small dose of the reproachful Maureen. "Helga, wouldn't we be very foolish if we believed that?" she asked softly. "Especially after we heard you expertly describe him the way you just did?"

Apparently, Helga had been to kindergarten and had tried that very thing with her teacher once before. She realized that it hadn't worked then and it wasn't working now. "Well, maybe I would be able to recognize him if I saw him again," she acknowledged.

"Good girl," Maureen said, smiling benevolent approval. "Now tell Brian what happened after the cops left the park."

Helga smiled for the first time, astonishing McKenna that she was so happy to be appreciated by Maureen. He hadn't seen Maureen's technique practiced in over forty years, but remembered that it had always worked whenever Sister Mary Helen had used it on him. Involuntarily he touched his lips, remembering the times long ago when he had sported the same idiot smile.

"Not much to tell," Helga said. "I started working out again and I heard the two bums laughing for a while, but when I looked a little later there was only one. He was lying by the fence."

"You didn't see the other one leave? The one wearing the kerchief?"

"No."

"And then?"

"After a while I missed another shot and my ball landed by him. I went to get it and saw that he wasn't breathing and he wasn't moving."

"Did you try anything to revive him?"

Apparently the thought had never even occurred to the not-so-sensitive and very politically incorrect Helga. "Try and revive that bum? Good God, no! You saw what he looked like. I wouldn't even *think* of touching him. I did my civic duty when I called the cops."

"And right after that Detective Sanchez brought you here, right?"

"He the dopey prick who thinks he's Sherlock Holmes?"

McKenna smiled at the prospect of the small joy he was going to experience when he told Excellent Midtown Detective Cisco Sanchez that one. "Yes, I believe that's him."

"I've been here ever since," Helga complained. "Can I go now?"

"First I'd like you to come downtown with us and help one of our artists make a sketch of the killer."

That lovable Helga personality was back. "Are you kidding? You think I've got all night?" she screamed. "You might as well drive me right to divorce court after that. You don't understand a goddamn thing I told you about my husband, do you?"

"Helga, I've got an idea," Maureen said calmly.

"What?"

"You've been so nice to us that I want to do something nice for you. Why don't we leave Brian here? On the way to headquarters I'll buy you dinner and we'll talk about what to tell your husband. We're both smart girls and I'm sure that when we put our heads together we'll come up with something he'll believe."

As he watched Maureen talk to Helga, McKenna recalled watching Mighty Joe Young listening to "Beautiful Dreamer." Helga calmed right down and assumed the same blissful expression on her face that the big ape displayed in the movie whenever he listened to the song.

"You think we can?" Helga asked.

"I'm sure of it," Maureen said, then turned to McKenna. "That be okay with you?" she asked.

What could be better? McKenna thought. After all, he *did* have things to do and he *had* been dreading spending another hour or two with Helga. "Just fine, thank you."

Maureen and Helga were at the door when a thought hit him. "Helga! One more question, if you don't mind."

"Whaat??"

"If you had to, could you kick the shit outta the killer?"

She gave it hardly a thought. "Him? Easy."

"Are you sure? After all, he's skinny but he's still kind of tall."

"Makes no difference. You had to see him throw my ball back to me."

"What do you mean?"

"I mean he's weak and he's hurting. The ball bounced twice before it got to me and then he held his shoulder like he was going to cry. He's got something wrong with him."

"Which shoulder was he holding?"

Helga squinted her eyes as she tried to remember. "His left shoulder," she said. "He threw the ball with his left hand."

Now there's two fine pieces of information we almost didn't get, McKenna thought. We're looking for a lefty with something like arthritis. "Thank you, Helga. It's been a pleasure meeting you. Like Maureen says, you really are wonderful."

"I know. Everyone tells me that."

Instantly, McKenna knew that old Gestapo theory was right. Fear can make a person say anything.

12 Acting on the off chance that Lieutenant Ward was still in his office at 6:00 P.M., McKenna gave him a call as soon as Maureen and Helga had left. After all, McKenna reasoned, although it looked like he was suddenly working directly for Tavlin, it was a temporary thing; once his twirl through the spotlight was over, he would be back working for Ward again day in and day out. Ward had to be kept in the loop, happy and well informed.

As it turned out, Ward was in and he sounded happy enough already. Once McKenna had reported on his plans and activities, Ward was also well informed. "You're sounding very chipper," McKenna observed.

"Brian, why shouldn't I be? All afternoon I've been getting calls from chiefs wondering if I need anything and invitations from well-heeled reporters who like to eat in nice places. Then, all of a sudden, I'm told that overtime is no problem."

That was unusual, McKenna conceded. Because of the most recent New York City fiscal crisis, there had been cuts in the police budget so that every police commander had been tortured into compliance on holding down overtime. But the police department is a political animal, so when a newsworthy case erupts and public interest is titillated, all budgetary constraints are suspended as the department goes all out to capture the culprit and look good in the process. What usually follows is a round of promotions for the chiefs, a small pat on the back for the detectives who actually did the work, and a renewed round of edicts further limiting overtime. But while the case is on, detective commanders are free to dispense their largesse in the form of overtime to their best workers as well as to their pampered pets.

McKenna thought the system worked just fine. Despite their crying and whining on the subject, New York City detectives made pretty good money. When
working at time-and-a-half, the money was fabulous, and, consequently, they
usually worked twice as hard for it, whistling and smiling the whole time. At
those rates, the Bureau always got results.

"So you're happy?" McKenna asked Ward.

"I wasn't, until I asked myself the question, Since I suddenly have six detectives on overtime and the whole Homicide Squad at my disposal, shouldn't I also
be here?"

"It's your sacred duty to be there. Detectives on overtime can't operate effi-
ciently without the benevolent guidance of their lieutenant, who must also be on
overtime."

"Exactly what I thought."

McKenna was feeling good. "Then this case is a good thing, after all?" he
asked.

"A wonderful thing, as long as there really is a nut out there poisoning our
bums and, if there is, as long as you catch him in front of the cameras so I can
justify this enormous expense you're running up. Stay in touch, good luck, over
and out." Ward hung up.

McKenna started feeling bad. He ran the case over in his mind and concluded
that the whole thing was built on conjecture, without a single piece of hard
evidence.

Why would anyone poison Rodney Bailey and Juan Bosco, two people already
close to death? Mercy killing? Maybe, but then where did Benny Foster fit into
all this? Even when he was dead he certainly looked healthy enough, didn't he?

McKenna called the morgue and, after he waited while his call was shunted
to various offices around the building, Dr. Andino finally came on the line.

"Good to hear from you, Brian. I've been working long and hard, up to my
elbows in—"

McKenna knew what Andino was up to his elbows in and didn't want to hear
about it. "Have you found the poison yet, John?"

"A little testy, aren't we?"

"Sorry. I need some confirmation and support, and you're the only one who
can give it to me. Have you taken a look at the latest package I sent you?"

"Juan Bosco?"

"Yeah, Juan Bosco."

"Not yet. He's still in the waiting room while we check on his benefits and
coverage, but I did take a glance at him and he looks a lot like our Rodney Bailey
case."

"What have you done so far?"

"Found that both Benny Foster and Rodney Bailey both had slightly enlarged
spleens, which is something. That's the organ where poisons sometimes hang out
when the other organs are overworked, but we haven't found anything concrete
yet."

"That's it?"

"Like I told you, this is a time-consuming process. We have managed to
eliminate quite a few poisons."

"Maybe I can give you some help in that department. We have a woman who was there when Bosco died and she didn't even know it. Apparently there are no symptoms or sickness preceding death. No nausea, vomiting, or complaints of pain. He just lay down and died.''

"Can you give me an idea of the time frame?''

"From the time he was poisoned until the time our witness knew he was dead, about half an hour.''

"That indicates a toxic factor of five or six.''

"Does that help?'' McKenna asked.

"Does it? You've just eliminated about ninety-five percent of the poisons known to man.''

"Can you give me a list of the poisons you've already eliminated?''

"Give me a number where I can fax them to you, because you can't spell them and I don't want to look like a dope giving you my version of the way they sound.''

"Okay.'' McKenna took his department phone directory from his pocket and gave Andino the fax number of the police lab, then told him he might soon be in possession of the wine bottle that had contained the poison. If so, he would also forward that to the lab.

That was good news to Andino. He agreed with McKenna that knowing the possible reagents that his research had already eliminated would make the police chemists' task much easier and increase their chances for success. In any event, Andino was going to keep at it.

McKenna had one other thing on his mind, and needed some information from Andino to test a theory he was considering. "Do you know if Benny Foster had AIDS?''

"He didn't, but he was HIV positive. Had been for the last seven years, at least,'' Andino answered. "But he was either strong, lucky, or unusual. He hadn't developed any AIDS-related diseases.''

"Seven years? How do you know that?''

"I ordered his medical records from Bellevue Hospital. Seems Benny was a bit of a hypochondriac. He popped into the clinic there at least once a week for everything from ingrown toenails to headaches. He took pretty good care of himself, considering his lifestyle.''

"Did Rodney Bailey have a history at Bellevue?''

"Yep, a long one. He'd been a patient there off and on for the past six years.''

"How about the one today? Juan Bosco.''

"Him, too. He was an outpatient at the Bellevue AIDS Clinic. I see the direction you're heading in.''

Then an unpleasant thought hit McKenna. "I guess that means that Benny's girlfriend would have it, wouldn't she?''

"Good chance. Doesn't she know?''

"Probably not. There's a lot she doesn't know.''

After he hung up, McKenna felt a front of depression coming on. Since Foster had known that he was HIV positive, if he had infected that pitiful girl McKenna was prepared to be in total agreement with Maureen. Benny Foster should be roasting in Hell.

Next, McKenna called the 13th Precinct desk officer. There was no news on Chris Saffran. Finding the cop was becoming something of a problem; he was single and hadn't gone home after work. Sanchez was busy checking Saffran's usual haunts. McKenna asked the desk officer to check the summons box and see if Saffran had turned in the copies of the summonses he had issued that day.

Saffran had; the one McKenna needed was there. At 3:20 that afternoon, at the same time he had given Bosco a summons for drinking in the park, Saffran had also issued one to Julio Vargas of 421 East 30th Street for the same offense.

McKenna felt lucky, for he had just been handed the name of a man he needed to talk with, a man who had been with both the killer and the victim during the last hour of Bosco's life. It was no surprise to him that Vargas also had given his address as the Bellevue Shelter.

McKenna was set to go downstairs when he noticed a TV and VCR in a corner of the administrator's office. Knowing that the Public Information Unit videotaped all local news shows, he called the unit and told the duty officer that Chief Tavlin wanted a copy of the day's news tapes delivered to the Madison Boys Club as soon as possible.

Naturally, it would be done immediately, he was told. Anything for the chief, and please give him our warmest regards.

Then it was on to the interview of the homeless man Sanchez had brought in. He was white, bearded, about thirty years old, sleeping and snoring on the floor of the locker room downstairs. McKenna decided on a fix for him. Since he was hungry himself, he ordered in four bottles of soda and a large pizza pie with extra cheese, pepperoni, and lots of anchovies. As soon as the pies arrived and the aroma seeped down to floor level, the man started stirring. McKenna started on his first slice.

The man opened his eyes and watched McKenna finish his slice. "You hungry?" McKenna asked.

"Sure am," he answered, never taking his eyes off the pizza in the open box.

"What's your name?"

"Buzz."

"Dig in, Buzz."

The invitation didn't have to be repeated. Before McKenna had finished his second slice, Buzz was on his third. Five minutes later the pie was gone. McKenna only had the two slices, but still felt the thirst generated by the anchovies. He could imagine how Buzz felt, six slices in his belly, anchovies on his breath, and being hungover with the mud men running around in his mouth. Now that had to be a real thirst, McKenna figured.

That was when he took the first bottle of soda from the bag, opened it, and drank deeply, savoring every gulp while Buzz watched him.

"Man, you got any more soda?" Buzz asked.

"Only three more bottles," McKenna answered.

"You gonna drink them all by yourself?"

"Only if I have to," McKenna said before he took another long pull on his soda.

"What do you mean, *Only if you have to?*"

"What I mean is that I'd like to offer you some, but first I need some information."

"Information? No way. I ain't no squealer."

"I know that," McKenna said, then took another gulp. "What I need is information on a dead man. Whatever you tell me sure can't bother him."

"Who?"

"Juan Bosco."

"He's dead?" Buzz asked.

"Yeah. Don't you remember the ambulance and all the cops in the park a couple of hours ago?"

Buzz visibly strained his memory. After a minute, it came back to him. "I didn't know he was dead," he said. "I thought he was just sick again. He's got that AIDS thing, bad."

"He have any friends or family we can notify about his death? We have to do that, you know."

"I think he's got some family uptown, but he don't ever see them," Buzz said.

"And friends? How about his friends?"

"He ain't got no friends. Nobody wants to catch that shit from him."

"How about Julio Vargas?"

"Don't know the dude."

"Really. We know Bosco was with Julio Vargas in the park this afternoon the same time you were there. Didn't you see him?"

"No. I was in the park all day, but I didn't see no Julio Vargas."

"Who did you see with Bosco?"

"I saw him having a taste with Bongo, over by the handball courts," Buzz stated.

"I thought you told me Bosco had no friends?"

"Bongo don't count. He's crazy. He talks to anybody comes along."

"Does Bongo have AIDS?"

Buzz shrugged. "No telling who's got that shit, but he don't have none of them marks his skin."

"Is Bongo a short guy, wears a yellow scarf around his head?" McKenna asked.

"Yeah, that him. He's pint-sized, always wearing that yellow-and-red scarf like he was a woman or something."

"Does he live at the Bellevue Shelter?"

"Nobody lives at the shelter. He just stays there sometimes and keeps his shit there, just like everybody else," Buzz said. "Listen, can I get some soda yet?"

"Just a few more questions. Where does Bongo usually go at night, if he doesn't go to the shelter?"

"Some nights I see him up by Twenty-eight and Park, by the subway. Other times I see him at Grand Central."

"Where would he go when it's really cold?"

"Grand Central. When it gets real cold them railroad cops ain't allowed to throw you out. How about that soda? Man, I'm so thirsty I could drink piss."

McKenna passed him a bottle and watched him gulp it all down. It wasn't enough to quench the thirst the anchovies had caused. "Thanks," Buzz said. "You gonna drink the other two?"

"No, you are. Just got a few more questions and it's yours. You know how long Bosco's been on the street?"

"Longer than me, and I've been out here four years."

"One last question. You see anybody else talking to Bosco and Bongo by the handball courts?"

Buzz shook his head.

It was too much to ask, McKenna realized. The killer had been in and out of the park in about fifteen minutes, and by that time Buzz was in no shape to notice. He gave Buzz the last two quarts of soda and they were gratefully accepted. "You gonna be all right tonight?" McKenna asked.

"Could use some change, if you can spare it."

McKenna reached into his wallet and gave Buzz a ten-dollar bill.

It was received like it was a hundred. "Thanks," Buzz said. "You sure you got no more questions?"

The news videotapes arrived at the Madison Boys Club as McKenna was escorting Buzz out. The fact that Vargas was unusually short, rather distinctively dressed, and homeless caused McKenna to think that he shouldn't be that hard to locate. He called the radio dispatchers for the 13th and 17th Precincts and asked them to broadcast Vargas's description with the instructions that, when he was located, he was to be brought to the Madison Boys Club.

While he awaited the arrival of Vargas, McKenna decided to take the videotapes into the administrator's office. He started with the *Fox Five News* videotape of Heidi Lane's morning interview outside the station house.

After watching it the first time, McKenna's impression was that Heidi had arranged it so that the clip appeared to be one of those impromptu news conferences where the concerned reporter just happened to run across the harried detective leaving the station house. She had then asked a series of questions, all of which she already knew the answers to, but her reaction was one of stunned surprise to each of McKenna's revelations.

Aside from the fact that she had gotten him to reveal much more than he had wanted to at that point, another stunt Heidi pulled bothered him. Interspersed throughout the interview were many two-second reaction shots of Heidi looking either skeptical or incredulous as he answered her questions. The trouble was, he remembered that she had always been directly in front of him. There had been no camera behind him, so it would have been impossible for her cameraman to videotape her full-face reactions during the interview. He realized that Heidi had the reaction shots filmed by her cameraman after the interview and then had them spliced into the tape. It had been an ambush.

McKenna understood how she had done it, but he didn't understand why. He got along with most of the reporters in the city and couldn't remember having ever offended Heidi in the past. He had even promised her some preferential treatment and still she had chosen to abuse him on camera. The only conclusion he could draw was that, at the time of the interview, she had thought his suppositions and assumptions on the case were wrong, and she had used her power and bet her prestige that she was right. If she was, her stock would soar while his own would plummet.

We'll see about that, Heidi Lane, McKenna resolved. It didn't have to be this way, but you set the course, he thought as he started the *Fox Five News* videotape of Heidi's interview with Maureen at the 29th Street playground that afternoon.

Contrary to McKenna's expectations, this time it was Heidi who had been ambushed. Maureen had left very little of the TV journalist to be cleaned up by McKenna at a later time, if he was so inclined. After seeing Maureen's handiwork on the videotape, he wasn't. That would be sadistic overkill.

The taped segment began with Maureen, after McKenna had eluded Heidi. After a brief on-camera introduction as both women walked slowly toward the playground entrance, Heidi's first question to Maureen had been, "Detective Kaplowitz, do you agree with Detective McKenna's assessment that Benny Foster didn't freeze to death, that he had actually been poisoned?"

Maureen had stopped walking for a stunned reaction shot, like both she and Heidi had used the same director. Maureen's face said, *What's the matter? Are you a moron or something, asking such a stupid question?* What Maureen actually said for the camera had been, "Of course I do. He's a genius, you know, so anybody with any brains in the police department also agrees with him. That's why you see so many units and so much police activity here." Maureen had resumed walking, with Heidi in tow.

Heidi's next question had been, "So you think that the man who died here might also have been poisoned?"

In response, Heidi had been treated to another depreciating look as Maureen answered the question with a question. "Now we won't really know that until Detective McKenna gets a look at him, will we?"

They had reached the park entrance, but Heidi still insisted on another spanking. "So Detective McKenna thinks there is a serial killer poisoning homeless people in New York City?" she had asked in an incredulous tone of voice.

"Detective McKenna thinks there *might* be, but he's usually right," Maureen had answered as if it were one of the laws of the universe. "That's why every death of a homeless person is being thoroughly investigated. Murder is a sad and serious business, you know. It results in dead people. That's why responsible members of the press shouldn't bother Detective McKenna right now. He has work to do, catching a killer to save lives."

Heidi hadn't been ready to let it lie there, but she should have. She had brought her microphone to her face, ready to ask another question, but Maureen wasn't done with her yet. "Heidi, I think Detective McKenna needs me for something, so I have to go now. You're just getting in his way and risking people's lives with your silly questions."

Heidi had responded with the reporters' standard in such a situation, a very indignant, "Detective Kaplowitz, don't you and Detective McKenna believe the public has a right to be informed?"

According to Maureen's facial reaction, that had been another silly question. "Of course we do. That's why the police department has a Public Information Unit. That's where those fine reporters from the other networks go to get their questions answered. Good-bye." End of interview, and Maureen was under the crime-scene tape and into the playground.

There was a brief closing shot, with Heidi promising her viewers continuing coverage on this very important breaking story, but McKenna wasn't so sure. He surmised that Maureen's point had been well taken, since there had been no pressure from the press as they had left the playground that afternoon after Juan Bosco's body had been removed to the morgue. The press, including Heidi, had been grouped across the street and had filmed them leaving, but there had been no further interview attempts.

McKenna knew the reason was that Maureen had gotten away with a big, fat lie. Over the years he remembered being chased and interviewed by very responsible reporters while he had worked on newsworthy cases. Nothing wrong with that, he acknowledged. It goes with the territory. But Maureen had made Heidi appear irresponsible in her coverage of this particular story.

McKenna wondered why the Fox Five News executives had decided to run the interview that so abused their star reporter. He played news videotapes from the other networks and saw basically the same interview, except the bottom of the screen carried the legend COURTESY OF FOX FIVE NEWS. There was the reason the Fox Five executives had run it: They had no choice. All the other networks had crews present at the playground recording Heidi's interview. If Fox Five News hadn't aired it, all the other networks still would have, with or without Fox Five's permission.

Heidi had made a classic mistake and allowed Maureen to put her into an untenable position; instead of reporting the news, Heidi had become the news. The Fox Five News star reporter was fair game, and her bosses knew it.

McKenna watched the playground interview again, feeling uneasy and a little guilty about the prior assumptions he had made concerning Maureen and her conduct. In the end, he would rather have watched commercials for Rogaine or even the *Sally Jesse Raphael Show*; the news videotapes made him feel that guilty about his doubts about the woman with whom he was working.

Or maybe it should be the woman *for* whom he was working, McKenna realized, wondering.

13

Chris Saffran finally was located by Sanchez in an Astoria bar consorting with three ladies possessing astonishing good looks and dismally low morals. Sanchez was so impressed with Saffran's choice of surroundings that he immediately called the 13th Squad and took the rest of the evening off, merely mentioning to Saffran in passing that he was ordered back to work.

Saffran, being by nature a suspicious kind of guy and having dealt with Sanchez in the past, was very dubious about the detective's mission, motives, and story. He called the 13th Precinct desk officer and received the unfortunate news that, yes, this time Sanchez was telling the truth. Saffran was ordered to report back to work.

Fearing the worst—the scenario in which Sanchez happily pranced into the night with one or more of the young ladies in whom Saffran had just invested time and considerable money at the bar—the young officer reached into his bag of reliable, time-honored excuses, the ones that desk officers usually fall for.

"Gee, Sarge, I'd like to come in, but the pipes just burst in my basement. There's water everywhere and I don't know what I'm gonna do."

Not this time. "Too bad, Saffran. Call a plumber and get in here."

"Sarge, you won't believe this, but when my mother saw the water and the damage, she had a stroke. Right on the basement stairs, she had a stroke."

"That's terrible, Saffran. Call a plumber, call an ambulance, and get in here. You've got half an hour."

"And I tried to catch her before she fell, but she was so slippery because of the steam from the broken pipes. She slipped right out of my arms, fell down the basement steps, and she's still down there, under three or four feet of water. Sarge, I think my mom is drowning, if she's not dead already."

"Okay, Saffran. I'm gonna give you an extra five minutes to fish her out. Then call the plumber, call an ambulance, and get in here. In thirty-five minutes I expect you to be standing in front of this desk."

McKenna agreed with the 13th Precinct patrol sergeant who had told him about Saffran. He also thought there was something strange about the young officer standing in front of him in the administrator's office of the Madison Boys' Club, but he couldn't quite put his finger on it. It might have been the colorful tattoos that began at each of the officer's wrists and disappeared into the rolled-up sleeves of his sweatshirt, or it might have been the multiple earrings in the officer's right ear.

But McKenna decided that neither of those features was what bothered him, exactly. He had long since become accustomed to some of the transformations that took place in police locker rooms, those places where well-scrubbed, clean-cut, kind-of-military officers entered after a tour of duty and emerged ten minutes later looking very much like young Saffran.

The New Action Army, McKenna called it, and Saffran was definitely a member. He was dressed like a biker, in good shape, about twenty-five years old, and of indeterminate race. He could have been black, Spanish, or white with a dark tan. Maybe even Polynesian, he thought, entertaining the notion that the tattoos were the result of some tribal South Seas ritual.

McKenna concluded that what was so strange about Saffran was that the officer looked so very unhappy, even though he was on recall overtime. According to the current contract between the city and the PBA, Saffran had been called back to work after a tour of duty and was thus entitled to six hours' pay, even if he was needed for only five minutes. Therefore, Saffran should be almost ecstatic at the beating he was giving the city, but he wasn't.

"Where's Detective Sanchez?" McKenna asked, seeking to break the ice.

"Unfortunately, I think he's someplace nice by now," Saffran answered, obviously disturbed at the prospect and wishing Sanchez was someplace not so nice.

McKenna thought he understood and left it at that. He knew that Sanchez had a way of getting under a person's skin and thought his absence might be just fine. "I'm sorry I had to call you back in," he said.

"Okay, apology accepted. What's this all about?"

"Nobody told you?"

" 'Course not. I'm just one of the cops, remember? Bosses don't tell us nothing except where to go, when to get there, and what to do to keep *their* bosses happy. Sergeant just told me to get over here and see Big Shot McKenna. That's you, right?''

Big Shot McKenna? Okay. ''Yeah, that's me. You remember giving two summonses today for drinking in the park? One to Juan Bosco and one to Julio Vargas?''

''Uh-huh.''

''Do you remember stopping another man on your way into the park and checking him for bottles?''

''Uh-huh.''

''Well, I believe that man poisoned Juan Bosco.''

''Bosco's dead?''

''Yes. I believe the poison was in wine the killer gave him.''

''You mean the wine I threw away?''

''Yes.''

''You mean the wine I gave him a summons for drinking?''

''Yes, that very wine.''

''Awesome.''

For the moment, the philosophical implications of ''awesome'' were escaping McKenna. ''Think you'll be able to give me some help on this one?'' he asked.

''Yeah, it's a good thing you called me. I can help out a lot.''

''For instance?''

''For instance, you were right about the wine and about the guy we checked. He gave Bosco the bottle.''

''You saw that?''

''Sure. Me and my partner were in the firehouse across the street, warming up a little. Saw Bosco and Bongo having a taste over by the handball courts and—''

''Wait a minute! You know Julio Vargas as Bongo?''

''Sure. Off-the-wall, tiny dude. See him a lot.''

''Did you see anybody else by the handball courts?''

''Yeah. A blond babe, kinda heavy duty. Practicing her tennis stroke against the wall, really whacking the ball around.''

''Go on.''

''So we're watching them when into the park comes old Dracula. He saunters over to Bosco and Bongo and—''

''Wait a minute. Dracula?''

''Yeah, Dracula. The guy who gave the wine to Bosco,'' Saffran explained. ''He's one of the bums.''

''He is? Are you sure?''

''I guess so. Looks like them and he's always hanging out with them.''

''You've seen him before?''

''Yeah, lots of times. He's been hanging around the neighborhood a lot lately.''

''How long is lately?''

''The past month or so.''

''Do you know his real name?''

''No, sorry. Me and my partner just call him Dracula 'cause he dresses in black and looks like he's short a couple of pints of blood.''

''And you'd know him if you saw him again?''

"Sure."

"Can you remember if he was wearing gloves or not?"

"Sure. No gloves."

"Awesome. Go on."

"So anyway, from the firehouse we see Drac and the other two talking. Then Drac takes out a wine bottle and offers a taste to Bosco. Naturally, Bosco imbibes and then there's a little bit of a dispute. Seems to us that Bongo wants some wine, too, but Drac won't give him any. There's some mild pushing and minor grab-assing, so we decide to intervene before we head back to the station house."

"That was about 3:15?" McKenna asked.

"Yeah, right near the end of our tour. So, as soon as we leave the firehouse, they see us and start going through their routine. Drac gives the wine to Bosco and heads for the exit. Bosco and Bongo know what's coming, so they start swilling their stuff as fast as they can, before we get to them and pour it out."

"Who's swilling what?"

"Bongo's swilling his malt liquor. Quart of Colt Forty-five in the standard brown-paper-bag disguise. Bosco's swilling the deadly brew, but he's coughing a bit and doesn't get as much as he'd like. By the time we get to him he's only got half of it down."

"Aren't you forgetting about Drac?"

"Naw, I gave him the constitutional ████ over on the way in, but he didn't have anything."

"You mean he didn't have a ████"

"Yeah."

"So you let him go?"

"Sure. What else? We di████ ████o we really had no business with him."

"Did you talk to him? Yo████ ████ address?"

"What for? The names are us████ ████t until you get to know them and the address is always the same, always the Bellevue Shelter."

"I see. So you know Bosco and Bongo and you saw them drinking, so you didn't have to ask any information from them to give them the summonses, right?"

"Good thing, too, because Bongo was a little off this afternoon. Poor little dude couldn't remember his real name. Then he told me his ears were on fire, you know, really burning."

McKenna despaired on hearing this information about the personality quirks of his potential star witness in this case. "So he's crazy?" he ventured.

"No, not crazy, just a little confused. He remembered his name when I told it to him, and his ears weren't hot—they were cold. That's what was confusing him. The two feelings are pretty similar, if you think about it."

"Okay, I'll think about it later. How was Bosco doing at that time?"

"Like usual, all fucked up. Taking deep breaths and a little unsteady, but I've seen him worse."

"So you give them their summonses, then go over to the bushes and pour out their beverages, right?"

"Right."

"And then?"

"And then we bid them *adieu* and head back to the station house, end of tour."

"You didn't throw them out of the park and tell them to stay out?"

"Nope. My policy is never to tell anybody to do something if you can't enforce your rules. We were going off duty and wouldn't be there, so why bother?"

Good commonsense policy, McKenna conceded. "Did you see Drac again?"

"Yeah, he was hanging out across the street when we left, standing by the supermarket."

"Was he with anyone?"

"Nope, all by his lonesome, just watching us."

McKenna had been mulling over a tough decision while he had been questioning Saffran, but he needed to know just a little more. "Do you know most of the homeless people in the neighborhood?" he asked.

"The king knows most of the names and all the claims to fame of his less-than-royal subjects."

"The king? Is that you?"

"Speaking. King of the Neighborhood, Protector of the Peace, Enforcer of the Laws of God and Man, and Royal Overseer to all the miscreants great and small who dwelleth therein. Of course, I'm aided in my royal duties by my loyal assistant king, Police Officer Michael Hughes."

Saffran will do, McKenna concluded. I need someone operating close to ground level, and nobody in this job is closer to the ground than Saffran. Given, he could use a little polish, so I'm gonna have a tough time explaining to Chief Tavlin the hows and whys of this one. Maybe . . .

"Saffran, do you own a suit?"

"A suit? 'Course not. What for?"

"I was thinking of having you assigned to the detective bureau for the remainder of this case."

"Cool. So I need a suit for that?"

"It would make it much easier for me if you're wearing a nice suit, a white shirt, and a tasteful tie when I introduce you to Chief Tavlin. Something like I'm wearing would be fine."

Saffran took the time to give McKenna a good up-and-down inspection. "Your socks don't match your tie," he observed.

"They're not supposed to, once you leave Brooklyn. Your socks should match your suit, not your tie."

Saffran shrugged. "That's not what I heard, but if you say so."

"I say so. Let's not make a big thing out of this," McKenna suggested.

"Wait a minute. What happens when we catch the guy? Besides being used and abused and then thrown back in the bag on patrol, I'm also stuck with a suit I don't need?"

That really doesn't sound fair, does it? McKenna thought. "Maybe you won't get thrown back to patrol," he said. "I can't promise you anything, but you might need the suit some more. I think it all depends on how you do and what Chief Tavlin thinks of you."

"I'll give it a shot," Saffran said. "Just tell me what you want me to do."

"First thing is we're going downstairs. They have the trash cans from the park down there, so we're going to see if we can find the wine bottle Bosco drank from.''

"Shouldn't be too hard. Wild Irish Rose, pint size. Should be near the top of the trash can that was near the handball courts, right next to a bottle of Colt Forty-five.''

"Were you wearing gloves when you emptied the wine bottle?''

Saffran had to think it over before answering. ''No, I had just written the summons, so my gloves were off. Is that a problem?''

"Not much. If the bottle's downstairs, I'm gonna have you fingerprinted here and Bosco fingerprinted at the morgue. Any prints on that bottle not yours, his or some liquor store clerk's, must be the killer's.''

"Sounds good, but are you gonna be able to find him with just a couple of fingerprints?''

"Maybe, if he was arrested before or fingerprinted for something else. But that might take some time and I've got a better way.''

"What's that?''

"You. You're gonna give me a list of all the places you saw Drac in the neighborhood. Then you're going to go down to headquarters and have an artist's sketch made of him. I've got a witness down there right now doing the same thing, so you can see how close she is.''

"The tennis babe?'' Saffran asked.

"Yeah, the tennis babe,'' McKenna said, his opinion of Saffran still rising. ''She's pretty sharp, so between the both of you, we should wind up with a pretty close sketch of this guy.''

"And then?''

"Then you're gonna go home and get some sleep. First thing in the morning, you start working for me. You're gonna hang around the neighborhood and talk to every homeless person you know. Show them the sketch and see what they know about him.''

"What about the shelters? Want me to check them out?''

"No. I'll handle that. I want you to keep a low profile. Talk to people, but stay away from the places you've seen him. I'm gonna have every one of those places put under surveillance.''

"Why? Why don't you have me just look for him and lock him up when I find him?''

"Lock him up? For what?''

"Murder, right?''

"Wrong. We don't have a murder until the ME tells us we do. He still has to find the poison and tell us that's what killed our victims. Right now all we have is what we think are two suspicious deaths, nothing more.''

"Then I could lock him up for some other bullshit,'' Saffran suggested.

"Like what? Jaywalking? Littering?''

"Something like that. Then we'd get his fingerprints and find out if they match any prints you come up with on the wine bottle.''

"If you did that, all the fingerprint evidence we get would be suppressed in court. We'd lose it forever.''

"Why?''

"I'll tell you why by showing you how any Legal Aid lawyer would rip you up. He'd put you on the stand and ask you, 'Officer, how many jaywalking or littering arrests have you made in your police career?' What would you say?"

"None, I guess."

"Then our Legal Aid lawyer would say, 'Really, Officer? Is that because, in your entire police career, you've never seen anyone jaywalking or littering?' Answer that one."

McKenna got to see how Saffran looked when he felt foolish. "I guess I'd tell him, 'No, but jaywalking and littering just recently started pissing me off,' " Saffran answered after a long, embarrassed moment.

"Believe me, the court would look at your arrest as something they call a fishing expedition, made only to gain evidence of another crime. Even if you could get a DA to draw up a complaint for your bullshit arrest, any judge would throw it out and we'd lose all fingerprint evidence, forever. That's why we're gonna do it my way, not yours."

Saffran was a little chastened, the way McKenna wanted him. "Mind telling me what that entails?" the young cop asked.

"I'm still working it out, but right now my way is to first scientifically establish that we're dealing with murder. Then we find out who the killer is, figure out something on his motivation, and get enough evidence on him to have a DA draw up a complaint before we lock him up. Some of that might change along the way, but the important thing is to get enough to convict him for murder."

"And all you want me to do is ask around about him?"

"For now. I don't want him running into you so he gets scared and then gets lost. Understand?"

"Yeah, I understand, but my way might still be better. I think I should go out there looking for him and getting him scared, even if he does run. Otherwise, while you're busy building your case, this guy could kill again."

Although McKenna thought that prospect unlikely due to the publicity the case was receiving, the possibility still had to be carefully considered. According to procedure, the object of any investigation was to legally arrest and convict the person responsible for the crimes he had already committed. Stopping any future murders would be wonderful, as far as McKenna was concerned, but he was going to get his man and get him right. But it was a decision he wasn't one hundred percent certain about. "Heavy's the head that wears the crown," he said softly, more to himself than to Saffran.

"What's that?" Saffran asked.

"I said you may be right and I may be wrong."

14

Detective First Grade Joe Walsh of the Crime Scene Unit was a big, gregarious man, fifty pounds overweight, but he had a lion's mane of curly gray hair that still made him rather striking in appearance. He was famous throughout the department as the best crime-scene technician in the unit, which, according to Walsh, meant the best in the world. He also had a reputation as a showman who would spend hours displaying to anyone who showed the slightest interest his four thick scrapbooks, each filled with press clippings documenting all the famous trials in which Walsh had testified during his thirty years in the Crime Scene Unit.

Walsh hadn't been at the Madison Boys' Club when McKenna had arrived, but McKenna knew that Walsh would sniff major press coverage in this case and would be there. He was just as certain that, somehow, Walsh's picture would be somewhere in the first three pages of tomorrow's papers.

McKenna didn't mind at all. Having Walsh around certainly meant publicity for the case; having Walsh also meant that not a speck of physical evidence in the East 29th Street playground would remain unnoticed, undocumented, or unclassified. The best always comes at a price, and Walsh's ego had to be fed.

Walsh was bent over a table set up in the middle of the basketball courts, applying fingerprint powder to an empty Thunderbird wine bottle when McKenna and Saffran came down from the administrator's office.

"You're wasting your time on that one," McKenna said.

"Brian, I never waste my time," Walsh said without looking up from the bottle. "If anything, I'm wasting the city's time."

"That's not the one I need," McKenna informed him.

"That's too bad. Got four fingers on this one," Walsh said, shaking his head as he put the bottle down on the table. "If this were it, I'd have you halfway to getting your man. You'd be spending most of next week pasting pages in your scrapbook and all of next year admiring your front-page photos."

McKenna smiled as he shook Walsh's offered hand. "Joe, I've told you a thousand times. I'm not a publicity hound like you. I don't keep a scrapbook," McKenna said, forgetting to mention that his wife kept his scrapbook for him, but that the only time he ever looked at it was when Angelita was ignoring him while watching her *Oprah* reruns. He figured he hadn't even seen the sacred book in, what? A week, maybe. Could even be two, he thought.

It didn't matter, because Walsh obviously didn't believe him. "All the ink you get and you don't keep a scrapbook?" he asked skeptically. "What do you do with the paper when your picture's all over it? Just throw it out?"

"We just got a puppy for the baby," McKenna said, lying and thinking fast. "Need all the newspapers I can get my hands on. Most of the time I don't even get a chance to read them before I have to use them."

Wanting to change the subject McKenna introduced Saffran and explained who he was. Walsh gave the young officer a casual once-over, but made no comment about his appearance except, "You know, I was thinking about getting an earring myself."

McKenna couldn't imagine that. "Why would you?" he asked.

"Just to piss off the boss," Walsh answered, smiling. "Think that'll do it?"

McKenna understood at once. Inspector Scagnelli was the CO of the Scientific Research Division, the parent unit for the Crime Scene Unit, the Crime Lab, the Ballistics Unit, the Latent Fingerprint Unit, the Technical Assistance Response Unit, and the Photo Unit. Scagnelli had a lot of responsibilities and a lot to worry about, but still managed to spend most of his time actively hating Walsh.

It was all a matter of style. Scagnelli was an old-time detective boss and was a meticulously correct dresser; Walsh was in a dirty job and was a little loose about his appearance. There wasn't a press photo in existence that showed Walsh without his tie pulled down, his top shirt-button undone, or without fingerprint dust somewhere on his suit. Scagnelli hated those photos, but that wasn't all that bothered him. While he respected the job Walsh did, he was highly critical of his detective's flamboyant showboat style. Adding insult to injury, never once had Walsh given Scagnelli any credit during any of his many press interviews; for a detective not to mention his boss as his source of divine guidance was normally considered a capital offense in the Detective Bureau. However, since Walsh was a first-grader, a famous fixture in the Crime Scene Unit, and a past president of the Irish cops' Emerald Society, there wasn't much Scagnelli could do about it.

The worst part for Scagnelli was that Walsh knew it. He delighted in sending Scagnelli copies of every news photo and every newspaper article in which he was mentioned and, of course, Scagnelli was not. On those days Scagnelli talked to no one, had Maalox for lunch, and usually went home early. It was common knowledge throughout the Job that, in his own way, Walsh was trying to kill Scagnelli.

McKenna thought that Walsh wearing an earring on the front page of the *Post* just might do it. "Yeah, that'll work," he told Walsh. "Now you just have to do something wonderful for me to get your picture in the papers."

"No problem. Can you tell me exactly which bottle I should be looking at?"

"Empty bottle of Wild Irish Rose. It should have been in the trash can that was at the edge of the handball courts, probably right near the top of the can."

"Okay, come with me," Walsh said as he started across the basketball court. McKenna and Saffran followed him to a trash can standing in a corner of the large room with three rows of bottles, cans, and coffee cups arranged in front of it. There were two empty Wild Irish Rose pint bottles, one in the first row and the other in the last. The one in the first row stood next to an empty quart bottle of Colt .45 malt liquor.

McKenna had what he needed and smiled as he felt his heart race. Just to be sure, he asked, "The stuff in the first row come from the top of the can?"

"Exactly right," Walsh said as he pulled on a pair of latex gloves and picked up the Wild Irish Rose bottle by the screw-on-top threads at the bottle's mouth and held the bottle up to the light. There was something there, some moisture on the inside of the bottle at the bottom. "Looks like there's about ten drops of a red-colored residue present," Walsh said, making it official. "What now?"

"You think there's enough wine in there to do an analysis?" McKenna asked.

"Sure. We've got people who can do it, as long as they're careful and take their time. It'll be expensive and time-consuming, but I'll make sure it's done right."

"How?" McKenna asked.

"Simple. I'll just tell the inspector that I don't think his lab people can do it and that he should send the stuff to the FBI lab to get it done right. You know what that means, coming from me."

"That'll do it," McKenna agreed, glad he wasn't one of the department chemists. They were all in for a busy and aggravating day tomorrow, with a very nervous Scagnelli standing at their elbows at every turn. But there was more to be done. "You doing the paperwork?" he asked Walsh.

"If you want."

"Would you mark the Request for Laboratory Analysis: 'Test residue for presence of any known toxic level-five and -six poisons, excluding those on list faxed from Medical Examiner's Office this date.' You got that?"

Walsh scoffed. "Of course. That's it?"

McKenna decided to crank Walsh up a bit, mostly just for the fun of it, but also to get him working in earnest. "No, there's more, but first I need an honest answer. Are you really that good at lifting latent prints?"

Walsh was anything but modest. "Only the best there ever was," he answered, surprised that anyone would even have to ask.

"Think you could do it here?"

"I could lift prints in a sewer, if I had to."

"And photograph the lifts, if there are any?"

"There'll be prints, and I'll get them. Give you anything from wallet-sized photos up to a full-wall mural."

"Good. You'll have to take some elimination prints."

"Whose?"

"Saffran here, for one. He touched the bottle and I don't want to waste time getting his fingerprints from his personnel folder downtown."

"Okay, I'll do him," Walsh said. "Who else?"

"You'll have to go to the morgue and fingerprint Juan Bosco. Is that a problem?"

"Of course not. Are those the only ones you want?"

"I really only want the killer's prints, so who else would you do?" McKenna asked.

"That's up to you," Walsh said, holding the bottle up to the light again. "But if you get me really going on this bottle, I'll get the prints off it of the guy who made it and the guy who sold it. Hell, I'll even get the prints of any thirsty wino who just saw this bottle and wished he had it in his hand. That's a lot of elimination prints to be taken."

Maybe I overcranked him a little, McKenna thought.

After Saffran had been fingerprinted and went to see the artist at headquarters, McKenna found himself sitting in the administrator's office once again with nothing pressing to do for a while. He had been ordered by Tavlin to wait for him at the Boys Club, Maureen wasn't back yet, and until the patrol force came up with Bongo, there was no one to be interviewed by him. It was a lull he didn't relish because it meant one thing: time for paperwork.

That was another one of the mundane facts of life that never appear in the movies. Big-city detectives spend half their time documenting exactly what they were doing with the other half. Every step taken during the investigation must be recorded, including the substance of each interview of a witness or interrogation of a suspect, each on a separate report. A copy of each of these reports is then sequentially numbered and placed in the case folder in chronological order after review by a detective supervisor.

There are two reasons for this burden of paperwork. One, of course, has to do with supervision. Each detective supervisor has a minimum of eight men and women working for him, all usually carrying heavy caseloads. The only way he can stay on top is by reviewing the reports of his people and then issuing directives to keep the case on track.

The other reason has to do with courtroom presentation after an arrest has been made. In questioning a detective on the stand, both the DA and the defense attorney are now afforded the luxury implied by Lawyers' Maxim Number One: Never ask a question of a witness on the stand if you don't already know the answer. For defense attorneys that goes double when questioning detectives, a traditionally tricky bunch who delight in surprising them with unexpected answers to their questions, answers delivered in a believable, matter-of-fact manner, answers that the hapless defense attorney never wanted the jury to hear. The frequent result of this tactical mistake on the part of the defense attorney is that the future billing address for his client becomes a prison far upstate.

Lawyers hate that, since clients doing time generally are not worried about their credit ratings; they're worried about more important things, like scheming up their next pack of smokes or wondering whose derriere looks good in the showers while hoping it isn't their own. Sending these clients a bill for professional services rendered is generally acknowledged to be the waste of a stamp, a stamp that would be better used on a letter to Santa Claus. It doesn't help matters when the detective involved also writes the defense attorney's client a friendly, informative letter, asking the inmate to say hello to so-and-so, all other clients of his attorney, before reporting in an offhand fashion who the inmate's wife or girlfriend has been seeing in his absence.

This pen-pal activity on the part of detectives used to occur frequently and used to be a lot more fun before some spoilsport federal judges decided that, in the interest of fairness, the defense attorney should have access to everything the DA knows about a case.

The result in New York is called the Rosario Rule. It mandates that the DA is responsible to turn over to the defense the full and complete police file on the case, the implication of which is that there must really be a full and complete file. It wasn't long before appeals courts and prosecutors started insisting on it. Subsequent court decisions and common sense have held that this full and complete file must be compiled by the detective in a timely fashion, while the facts are still fresh in his mind.

The Rosario Rule took a lot of the fun out of testifying. Since the defense attorney knows in essence everything about the case and has the entire police investigation in front of him in black and white, no longer could a detective under pressure on the stand ad-lib as he went along. It used to be that the testifying detective was awarded points by his contemporaries based on the inventiveness, credibility, and originality of his responses under pressure, but no longer. Judges became cranky about ad-libbing under oath and even called it perjury, meaning that the offending detective got to send his messages to the subjects of many of his former cases by tapping them out on the bars of his cell.

Jail was one of those things that never happened to a first grade detective. According to legend, first-graders are models of investigative deportment, being stronger, braver, smarter, and faster than their lesser brethren, and certainly smarter than defense attorneys. Paperwork is a snap for these august beings, something they do quickly and perfectly without even thinking about it. It is expected of them, and they write tricks and complicated fall-back positions into their reports that those lowly defense attorneys only begin to comprehend as their clients are led away to begin their long stretch as guests of the state.

That was the legend, and McKenna was a detective first grade. As he typed away on the administrator's machine, his mind was working overtime as his fingers flew over the keys. He struggled against the legend as he tried to fulfill it. In truth, he hated paperwork and considered it an onerous but necessary burden. Still, practice makes perfect, and he had been a detective for a long time.

By the time Maureen returned with the sketches at ten o'clock, he had finished his reports on the interviews of Helga, Saffran, and Buzz and documented his visits to Citibank, Bellevue Morgue, the Photo Unit, and St. Francis of Assisi Church. His completed reports were totally unspeculative in nature; nothing Mc-Kenna wouldn't want to say in open court was there, but he wrote in such a way that inferences could be drawn from the total body of information, including the information not implicitly stated. It was a first-grade art form that would lead any supervisor or defense attorney reading the reports directly down whatever path McKenna chose to take.

He gave his completed reports to Maureen and she read them while he waited. ''Nice job,'' she commented as she handed them back. ''You managed to say it all without saying too much.''

McKenna considered that the supreme compliment from the acknowledged Grand Master of Documentary Double-Speak. He almost thanked her before he remembered that he should still be angry with her. Maybe I'm looking at this wrong, he considered as he watched Maureen watching him, that reproachful smile on her face again. She said I did good, but she's still looking at me like I'm a dummy. I think it's time to clear the air.

But now Maureen didn't think so. Before he could say a word, she handed him two sketches. ''We'll talk later,'' she said. ''Take a look at these first. I think you're going to like them.''

I'm beginning to really hate when she does that, McKenna thought as he studied the sketches. To him, they appeared to be identical sketches of the same man, but he knew they weren't. The artist's name was in the case information box at the bottom of each sketch, and the names were different. Consequently, McKenna felt like he was holding gold in his hands. He figured one sketch was based on the description of the killer that Helga gave to one artist, and the other sketch was based on the description that Saffran gave to a different artist.

Artists' sketches are frequently discounted by detectives as not being very reliable, but two virtually identical sketches drawn by separate artists based on the descriptions of two different witnesses meant to McKenna that he was looking at a very close likeness of the killer. He stared harder, trying to get a feel for his adversary.

The sketches were a front view of a white man in his forties wearing a black knit cap. There was no facial hair of any kind, and whatever hair he had on the top of his head was tucked under the cap. It was the face of a thin man, narrow, with an aquiline nose and sunken cheeks. Two large, baleful eyes stared back at McKenna, eyes that gave the face a pained expression. McKenna thought it didn't look like the face of a killer; his man looked sad, maybe kind, and not the slightest bit menacing.

"I was going to have them draw a composite based on both sketches, but I didn't see the point," Maureen said.

"You're right about that. Looks like we've got two very observant witnesses."

"I figured Helga would be good, but Chris was a real bonus. He's good and I like him," Maureen said.

Oh-oh, McKenna thought. Is Saffran gonna be another one of Maureen's boys? I hope not, because I don't wanna have to tiptoe around him. "He's a little rough around the edges, but he'll do," he said, hoping to end it.

It didn't. "He'll more than do. He's smart, he's witty, he's very observant, and he knows how to talk to people. I also think he'll be a good guy to have around."

Good God Almighty! "I agree one hundred percent, Maureen. I'm just flattered that he agreed to join our little effort. Anything else you think I should know about Supercop Saffran?"

"He sort of reminds me of you, in a way. You know, maybe when you were younger and better looking."

Then McKenna got it. She's just needling me with this Saffran thing, he concluded. But why? Why's she torturing me at every turn? I'm the aggrieved party, not her, right?

Before he could ask, Maureen did finally change the subject. "Anything on the guy that was with Bosco?" she asked.

Saffran didn't tell her that his name is Bongo while they were together at the Artists' Unit? Why not? McKenna wondered. "His nickname's Bongo and I haven't heard anything yet, but I'm optimistic. He shouldn't be hard to spot, but I guess none of the Thirteenth or Seventeenth Precinct units have seen him."

"That means he's either sleeping or hiding," Maureen said. "Or maybe he's staying warm by riding the subway, since Plan B is in effect again. He won't want to go to the shelter, so he'll run every time he sees a cop."

I should have figured that out myself, McKenna thought. With Maureen watching and wearing that amused smile on her face, he called the Bellevue Shelter. Julio Vargas wasn't there, he was told, so he made another three calls. He called the Long Island Railroad Police and the Amtrak Police, gave them Bongo's description, and asked them to search Penn Station and Grand Central Station for him. Then he called the Transit Police and asked them to broadcast Bongo's description to all their units with the instructions that, if he were located, he was to be held as a witness to a murder.

"You're putting a lot of effort into locating Bongo, aren't you?" Maureen observed as soon as McKenna hung up.

"Yeah, he's real important to me."

"Why? You've got a good enough description of the killer already, don't you?"

McKenna took just a moment to gloat. For once I've got her, he thought. I guess her pal Saffran didn't tell her much. "Didn't Saffran tell you that Bongo wanted some wine but the killer wouldn't give him any?"

"Of course not," Maureen answered at once, sounding hurt. "I don't interview your witnesses unless you want me to. It's your case, so naturally that's your job."

Oh yeah? McKenna thought. You didn't have much of a problem when it came to Father Hays. "So what did you two talk about that makes him such a wonderful guy?" he asked.

"We talked about cooking. He's taking a course in Korean cooking that I'm thinking of signing up for," she answered offhandedly. The implications of McKenna's revelation had just hit her and she was mulling them over in her mind.

Meanwhile, McKenna was mulling over the implications of Maureen's revelation. Korean cooking? he asked himself. That tough guy I'm counting on to help me out is taking a course in Korean cooking? And better yet, my trusty partner thinks that's just wonderful? Where am I and what am I doing here? And what happened to my police department while I was hanging out in headquarters for a year?

Maureen had reached her conclusion. "So we're not looking for a nut randomly poisoning homeless people," she said. "He knows who he wants. It's only them and nobody else."

"That's what it looks like, but I need Bongo to confirm it. I need to know what went down over one bottle of wine and three bums in the playground that leaves only one bum dead when there just as easily could have been two."

"I see," Maureen said. "Your killer's a maniac, but he's a discriminating maniac with motives of his own."

"That sums it up. We find his motives, we got the key to this guy. I'm hoping Bongo's gonna help us."

"You must have some ideas of your own by now," Maureen speculated.

"A few. For instance, I find it interesting that, counting Rodney Bailey, there's three dead we're looking at, and all of them are HIV positive."

"You mean Benny was HIV positive?" Maureen asked, stunned and surprised.

"Yeah, he was. Sorry I forgot to mention it, but I only found out myself a little while ago."

Maureen was sorry, too, and it showed. For a moment, McKenna was afraid she was going to cry, and he was sure the tears certainly wouldn't be over Benny. He knew Maureen was a very nice person, but the depth of her concern and feeling for Kerri surprised him. Watching Maureen fight back the tears made McKenna feel like crying himself. He wanted to take Maureen and hug her, but was saved from what could have been an embarrassing moment by his phone ringing.

It was Tavlin. The chief issued instructions and hung up.

McKenna took another look at Maureen and decided she wasn't going to cry after all. "We have to go," he said.

"Was that Steve?"

Steve again? Why do I find that so infuriating? McKenna wondered. "Yes, Maureen. That was *Chief* Tavlin and he wants us at the Seventeenth Squad office right away."

The Seventeenth Squad office was crowded when McKenna and Maureen arrived there at eleven o'clock. Every desk was occupied by a detective typing away, and there were other detectives going over their notes while waiting their turns to use the machines. The trash cans next to each desk were stuffed with empty pizza boxes, cans, coffee containers, sandwich wrappers, and dirty tin plates. Everyone appeared to be festively busy.

Mercurio, Birnstill, and Bender were there, along with some guys McKenna recognized from the Manhattan South Homicide Squad and many more he didn't. McKenna was warmly received by all as the benevolent originator of the scheme to get everyone overtime. It took McKenna five minutes of How-ya-doings, handshakings, and backslappings before he and Maureen made it through the throng to Ward's office.

In contrast to the scene in the squad office outside, peace and tranquillity reigned inside. Ward and Tavlin were sitting at Ward's desk playing cribbage while sipping their cappuccinos from Wexford cups. As befitting his station in life, the Midtown detective-lieutenant had dutifully rolled out his very best and shiniest cappuccino machine in order to entertain His Exaltedness, the visiting chief, properly. Since Tavlin was a Detective Bureau chief and not one of the rabble of common patrol chiefs, Ward had gone even further; properly complementing their beverages were two dozen exquisite-looking little fingers of Italian pastries resting on a silver tray on Ward's desk, right next to the pile of lace linen napkins. McKenna thought that the only thing missing was the butler.

He was wrong. "Good to see you two," Ward said to McKenna and Maureen. "Pour yourselves some cappuccino and freshen up our cups while you're at it, would ya?"

Of course they would; the amenities always had to be properly observed. Once everyone's cup was filled and properly freshened, and once McKenna and Maureen had tried some Italian pastries and complimented the lieutenant on his excellent taste when it came to selecting sweets and exotic coffees, and once McKenna and Maureen were on their second cup of cappuccino and even more pastries, Tavlin immediately got down to business. "Okay, you first. Tell me what you've been up to since I left you," he said.

McKenna did. He started by placing his reports on Ward's desk. The lieutenant followed McKenna's account on paper as he told Tavlin the results of his interviews of Helga, Saffran, and Buzz. Tavlin listened without saying a word while Ward turned the pages. "You're counting on this Bongo to give you an idea on motive?" Tavlin asked when McKenna had finished reporting.

"I'm hoping that talking to him will help me figure out why the killer didn't poison him when he just as easily could have. That might give me some insight into the killer's motives."

"Then I've got good news and bad news for you," Tavlin said. "We just got a call from the Ninth Precinct and Bongo's been located. The bad news is that he's in the psychiatric wing at Bellevue."

That was bad news, McKenna agreed. He would still interview Bongo, but anything he learned wouldn't be used in court by any DA trying to convict the killer. Under the circumstances, Bongo's testimony would be too susceptible to attack by the defense. "How did he wind up there?"

McKenna asked.

"At six P.M. an Officer Dante of the Ninth Precinct found him wandering around on East Fourteenth Street complaining his ears were on fire. Dante knew him and brought him into Bellevue. A Dr. Issacs working there also knew Bongo and admitted him at eight P.M."

That's one nut accounted for, McKenna thought. He fortified himself with another sip of cappuccino before he went on to the next nut. "This Officer Saffran I told you about is good and knows most of the homeless people in the area. I sort of told him he was assigned to the Bureau for this case."

"How much time does he have on the Job?" Tavlin asked.

"Can't be much. He's about twenty-five years old."

"Kinda young," Tavlin commented. "How's he look?"

"A little rough, but he'll act like a detective and he'll look like a detective by the time this is over."

Tavlin turned to Maureen. "What do you think of this Saffran?" he asked.

"I like him. He'll do just fine," she answered enthusiastically.

Tavlin then turned to Ward. "Could you take care of that for me?" he asked. "Tell them Police Officer Saffran is temporarily assigned to the Detective Bureau."

"Sure, Chief." Ward picked up the phone and dialed one of his secret numbers in headquarters. While he was busy changing Chris Saffran's job, status, personality, and lifestyle, Tavlin was busy munching on a miniature cannoli. "Have Saffran look me up sometime tomorrow," he said to McKenna in between bites. "I'd like to meet him."

"Sure thing, Chief." Now that wasn't so hard, was it? McKenna asked himself. All that remains for me to do is to transform the Saffran I know into the Saffran the chief expects to see. I hope that's some great suit he's buying.

"Where were we?" Tavlin asked.

"We're at the part where Joe Walsh gets involved," McKenna said.

Both Tavlin and Ward groaned at the mention of Walsh's name. "You sure you want that much publicity right now?" Tavlin asked.

"No, but we've got the wine bottle and Walsh says he'll get the killer's prints off it. Maybe someone else could get them, but why take a chance?"

"How's he doing with it?" Ward asked.

"Don't know yet. When we left he was still doing some of his secret Walsh-stuff to the bottle."

"That's all right," Tavlin said. "Rest assured that Joe Walsh will get your prints and he'll have them in time for the morning editions. What else?"

"Analysis of the little bit that's left in the wine bottle for the poison, but Walsh said he'd take care of that, too."

"He's gonna fire Scagnelli up again?" Tavlin guessed.

"That's his plan."

"Too bad for Scagnelli. I'd like to see him live through this, but Walsh will save me the trouble of firing him up myself," Tavlin said.

"Then there's this. Here's what our killer looks like," McKenna said, passing Tavlin the two artist sketches. "Different artists and different witnesses."

Tavlin and Ward were both impressed with the similarity of the sketches. "If you don't get him in the next two days, some publicity might not be a bad idea," Tavlin commented. "Just have to run either of these sketches in the paper and we'll be loaded with calls."

"Keep in mind we don't officially have a murder yet," McKenna said. "Until we do, I'd rather keep this as low profile as we can."

"Might not be possible. Between Walsh and your pal Heidi, the press is gonna be in a feeding frenzy. If I were you, I'd be prepared to say a few words tomorrow, just in case. Meanwhile, here's what we've been doing," Tavlin said, nodding to Ward. The lieutenant opened his desk drawer, took out a stack of reports, and handed them to McKenna. They were the interview reports of the Citibank customers. Each report had the bank surveillance camera photo of the interview subject stapled to the top of it.

"Don't bother going through them now," Tavlin said. "There's twelve of them there and the rest should be done soon. A total of nineteen customers who used the ATMs last night have been interviewed at home or work in either the city, Long Island, or New Jersey. A pretty expensive process to find out a lot of what you already know, but it would've had to be done anyway if this case goes to trial."

McKenna knew the chief was right about the interviews. Murder trials in which the press expressed an interest had become long, drawn-out, and very expensive affairs, with both the prosecution and the defense issuing subpoenas to everyone even remotely connected to the event. They all had to be interviewed.

But not necessarily now, by detectives on overtime, McKenna thought. Tavlin told me that Ray's taken an interest in this case, so the normal budgetary constraints must have been loosened considerably.

McKenna quickly found he was right. There was a knock at the door and Steve Birnstill entered. Birnstill gave another pile of interview reports to Tavlin. "That's the last of them, Chief," he said.

Tavlin went through them for a moment, then looked up and appeared a little surprised to see Birnstill still standing there. "Well?" he asked.

"The men want to know if they have to go home now," Birnstill reported.

"Yes, they have to go home now. But tell them to make sure they get their beauty sleep because I'm sure that McKenna will scheme up something else to put them all in a higher tax bracket tomorrow."

"Yes, sir. Thank you, sir," and Birnstill was gone, humming something from *Camelot* as he was out the door.

Only the police commissioner himself could inspire such largesse on the part of any chief, McKenna thought. I don't know what Ray's thinking, but the stops are out on this one. A small wink from Tavlin as he handed McKenna the new interview reports confirmed his thinking.

"Looks like we just spent about five thousand bucks to confirm what you already knew," Tavlin said. "The only one not interviewed yet is Cama. He's the main guy, so you can do him yourself."

"Does he know I want to talk to him?"

"Not yet, but he's available. After I talked to you at the Boys Club, I sent a team to his house to bring him here for you. He wasn't home, but the neighbors told them that he lives alone and works nights for Con Edison. So they called Con Ed. He's a supervisor at their steam plant, First Avenue and East Thirty-ninth. He's there now, a half mile from here and right in the precinct."

That was good news for McKenna, and he was happy to be interviewing Cama himself rather than reading about it on someone else's report; Cama was the only one of the bank customers who had seen Benny and the killer together, so whatever he had to say would be crucial. There only remained one thing left for Tavlin to tell him. "What did the customers after Cama have to say?" he asked.

"The next one shows up at one-fifty-five, a half hour after Cama. He sees Benny lying on the ground, just where you saw him this morning. Said he thought Benny was drunk and passed out, lying there on his back, breathing real heavy. Since Benny looked like he was dressed warm enough, he just went on his way."

"Dr. Andino will be interested in that," McKenna speculated. "Whatever the poison is, it takes at least a half hour to kill them."

"Barely. Next customer shows up at two-oh-two and Benny's dead," Tavlin stated.

"He said that?"

"*She* said that. She's a nurse at Bellevue, just got off work. Birnstill and Bender interviewed her and, at first, she denied seeing Benny. Then they showed her the picture of her looking at him on the way in and out of the bank. After some hemming and hawing, they broke her down and she admitted it. She went over and took a good look at him. She knew he was dead."

"Why didn't she report it?" McKenna asked.

"Basically, she knew Benny from the emergency room and just didn't like him. Him lying there dead was just fine, as far as she was concerned. You're gonna see the same kind of shit throughout those reports."

"Pretty callous," McKenna commented. "You'd think at least one of them would have called the police when they saw him lying on the ground in the cold."

"You'd think so, until you read all the interviews. Benny was a well-known but not-well-liked character in the neighborhood, so a few of them who saw him lying there wished he were dead, not knowing that their wish had been granted. In that neighborhood, with the Bellevue Shelter right down the block, they've become inured to the problem. For them, stepping over someone lying on the ground is like stepping over a crack in the sidewalk."

What happened to this great city? McKenna wondered.

16

The Con Edison Steam Plant on First Avenue and East 39th Street is one of two such facilities that provide something that is unique to New York among all the other major cities in the world. Many of Manhattan's skyscrapers are supplied with steam heat by the utility through pipes running under the city streets to these buildings, obviating the need for frequent oil deliveries that would further impede the already horrendous Manhattan traffic. Even those Manhattan residents and office workers whose buildings aren't heated with steam enjoy a small side bonus: The heat generated by the steam pipes running beneath the streets causes the snow to melt faster than in the outer boroughs, and sometimes not to stick at all.

McKenna and Maureen were witness to this phenomenon as they sat listening to the weather report in their car outside the Con Edison plant at midnight. The cold had abated considerably in the past few hours, and the warming temperatures had brought the snow. Although Queens was reporting a half-inch accumulation, in Manhattan outside the steam plant it was a dusting. A thin white layer stuck to the concrete sidewalks, but on the asphalt street there was only the slippery sheen of melted snowflakes reflecting the streetlights.

McKenna and Maureen were waiting outside because he had made a practice of not questioning a witness at his or her place of employment unless it was unavoidable. He knew that the police showing up unexpectedly to question a worker always set the rumor mill in motion, with the subject later trying to explain through the skeptical grins of his coworkers that his only crime was seeing something he wished he hadn't. Even if the person was believed, McKenna knew from past experience that the witness would be the weeklong butt of all the tasteless and corny jokes the pundits of the plant could contrive, so he had called Cama at the plant and asked for a meeting outside.

McKenna became optimistic at Cama's response. It wasn't, What's this all about? Cama just said that it would take him a few minutes to arrange for his relief, and then he would be out. McKenna figured that the visit was expected, which meant to him that Cama knew something.

A few minutes later Cama came out of the plant and McKenna recognized him immediately from the bank photo. He was in his twenties, stocky, and had a bull neck. To McKenna he looked like a tough guy, but he still looked too young to be a supervisor at the plant.

Cama took a quick look around and saw the four-door black Chevy the department called an *unmarked* car. McKenna reached around and unlocked the back door. "Pleased to meet you, Mr. Cama," McKenna said as soon as Cama was in. "I'm Detective McKenna and this—"

"I know who you are," Cama said.

"You saw the news tonight?"

"Uh-huh."

"And you knew we'd be coming to talk to you?"

"Yeah, if you were sharp enough."

"Sharp enough to get your picture from the bank cameras?" McKenna asked.

"Yeah. I stopped at the bank on the way to work tonight."

"To see if they had cameras?"

"Yeah, I never noticed them before," Cama said.

"But you weren't gonna give us a call?"

"Of course not," Cama said.

"Why not? Because you didn't want to get involved?"

"Yeah, that's part of it. This is gonna be a real hassle for me, right?"

"Shouldn't be too bad," McKenna said.

Cama didn't look like he believed that. "You telling me that if you get this guy, I'm not gonna wind up sitting in some filthy courtroom for weeks?" he asked.

"If we get him, you'll have to go to court, but it'll only be for two days, at the most," McKenna said. "What's the other part of it?"

"That's easy. The other part is, Why should I care if one bum kills another one? Not my problem."

McKenna didn't have an answer for that one. Either you cared or you didn't, he figured, and nothing he said was going to change how Cama felt about the homeless.

But to McKenna's dismay, Maureen had to try. "You could lose your job, and maybe you'd wind up on the street, just like them."

"Lady," Cama said, laughing derisively, "I might wind up on the street, but it wouldn't be for long."

"What makes you so certain?" she asked.

"Because I'm not like them. I'm not afraid to work, I'm not illiterate, and I'm not crazy. But the most important thing is that I've got some pride and a little self-respect. Before you'd see me out here panhandling change from strangers who don't owe me a thing, I'd do the right thing and kill myself."

"You'd commit suicide rather than be homeless?" Maureen asked, looking shocked at the thought.

"What's the matter? Suicide's not an option?" Cama asked, eying her coldly.

"It shouldn't come to that," Maureen answered.

"Oh yeah? Good people kill themselves every day over little things like their boss yelling at them, their wife screwing around on them, or their kids flunking math. Okay, that I can't see. But you tell those same people they have to be bums, and most of them would be standing in line on the platform to jump in front of the A train."

"And *that* you can see?" Maureen asked.

"Long as I'm not on the train and they don't make me late for work. It's their life and their decision to make, and I'd probably agree with them."

"You're a callous man, Mr. Cama," Maureen said sadly.

"You're wrong, lady. I'm as compassionate as the next guy. One of them asks me for some change, I always dig in and pass him a buck."

Now McKenna was mystified. "You do?" he asked.

"Sure. Don't get me wrong. I'm no cheapskate and it's not that I don't feel sorry for them. I just don't understand why they're still around. Lord knows we've got enough tall buildings, subways, rivers, and bridges in this town to give them their choice of exit."

Maureen threw her hands up. "Okay, say you're right and they should kill themselves," she said. "That still doesn't give anyone else the right to kill them, does it?"

Cama had to think a moment before answering. "I guess not," he conceded. "But like I said, I don't see why I should be inconvenienced because one bum poisons another."

McKenna saw his chance and jumped in. "So you think that both the men you saw outside the bank last night were homeless?" he asked.

"They both looked like bums to me," Cama answered.

"You know which one was Foster?"

"The black one."

"Right. Can you describe the other one to me?"

"White, maybe even a light-skinned Puerto Rican. About five-eight, dressed all in black, very skinny."

"Mustache or beard?

"No."

"How about a hair color. Could you see his hair?"

"No. He had on a black ski cap. Covered the whole top of his head."

"And the rest of his clothes?"

"All black. A long overcoat and black pants. Shoes were black, too, I think."

"Anything peculiar about his clothes?"

"Yeah, they looked too big on him."

"Nice clothes?"

"I guess, for a bum."

Now for the big question, McKenna thought. "Would you recognize him if you saw him again?"

"I guess so," Cama answered, noncommittally.

"Would you mind taking a look at this?" McKenna asked as he passed one of the sketches back to Cama.

Cama sat up, took the sketch, and studied it.

"Does that look like the man you saw standing with Benny Foster outside the Citibank last night?"

"No."

McKenna's heart sank as he watched Cama smiling back at him. "Are you sure?" he asked.

"Yeah, I'm sure. I'm sure it doesn't just *look* like him. It *is* him and nobody else."

"Mr. Cama, thank you so very much for breaking my balls. Might I add that it was done very professionally," McKenna said, trying to sound angry but not succeeding. Cama's identification had just vindicated him; the evidence was mounting that there was a serial killer poisoning homeless people for reasons of his own.

"Thanks. I've been told a few times I'm pretty good at it," Cama answered offhandedly. His attention was still on the sketch. "You know," he continued after a moment, "I'd forgotten about those eyes until I saw this sketch. There's no mistaking this guy."

"Remind you of anybody?"

"Dracula, of course. Don't you think so?"

"I'm beginning to. Just a few more questions before we take it from the top. Did you see him give anything to Benny Foster last night outside the bank?"

"You mean the wine?"

This guy just keeps getting better, McKenna thought. "Yes, Mr. Cama. The wine will do just fine," he answered. "Tell me about the wine."

"Not much to tell. They were standing outside the bank talking when I got there. They didn't look like they were bothering anybody, so I went inside."

"Did you hear what they were saying?"

"No, not then. While I was at the machine, I happened to glance outside through the window and saw Dracula take a wine bottle out of his pocket. Then Benny went to his cart and took out a cup. Dracula filled it up and Benny drank it down. When I was leaving, they were still talking. Benny had his cup out and Dracula was ready to pour him another."

"Did you hear what they were saying then?"

"I didn't pay any attention when I first left the bank, but when I was walking away, I heard them."

"What did they say?"

"I guess it was Foster who said, 'C'mon, give me just one more blast,' and I guess it was Dracula who asked, 'Are you sure you want another?' Heard that clear as a bell."

"Did Dracula have any kind of accent?"

"Not that I could tell."

"Was the wine red or white?"

"Red, in a pint bottle."

"Any brand you can remember?"

"No. I don't drink, so I didn't pay any attention."

"Okay, Mr. Cama. Like I said before, let's take it from the top. Tell me what you were doing last night and why you went to the Citibank."

It took McKenna only minutes to get the story. Cama had walked to the bank during his lunch break to deposit his paycheck and to withdraw $200.00 because he needed a new muffler for his car. He saw nobody else on the street until he encountered Benny and the killer outside the bank. Once he was inside, he spotted Kerri rolled up in her blanket under the counter, but he couldn't see her face and didn't know whether she was awake or not. He conducted his business at the ATM and left the bank. He described again his observations of Benny and the killer as he left, adding nothing new.

As Cama left the car and walked through the snow back to the steam plant, McKenna acknowledged to himself that he had been wrong about his witness. He realized that Cama wasn't too young to be a supervisor, but thought that he had chosen the wrong profession. Cama had the raw intelligence, the boundless ambition, the correct attitude, and the perfect personality to have been one of the youngest chiefs in the history of the New York City Police Department.

McKenna thought young Richard Cama was that good, or that bad.

17 One of New York's major hospital complexes begins on East 23rd Street and runs to East 34th Street, occupying eleven city blocks from First Avenue to the East River. Within this complex are the VA Hospital, the Hunter School of Nursing, most of the teaching hospitals associated with the New York University School of Medicine, and the enormous multibuilding city hospital occupying most of the acreage in the middle, the Bellevue Medical Center.

The formula used for determining which patients end up in which hospital is simple: Those with insurance and money are in the fine hospitals on the periphery of the complex; those without are squeezed to the center, to Bellevue. It is the largest of New York City's system of eleven municipal hospitals, all of them capable of providing fine medical care to the indigent and the police cases they were designed to serve, but all of them understaffed so that treatment is only administered after a long wait in a large room stuffed with the sick, poor, injured, and crazy people who prove by their presence there that they know absolutely nobody important.

Once treated, many of the walking wounded are sent back to wherever they came from, but the sick and injured who would benefit from a hospital stay are admitted. The exceptions are most of those who are brought to Bellevue suffering from mental illness. Years ago, in a move to save money, New York changed the method of treating the indigent mentally ill, closing most of the state mental institutions and instead providing outpatient care. The only people eligible for admission to the psychiatric wings of the city hospitals are those who are in imminent danger of seriously harming themselves or others. Most mentally ill do not fit into this category and leave Bellevue with nothing more than a prescription in their pockets for something that will slow them down a bit.

Since procedure mandated that the attending psychiatrist must give permission before a police officer can interview his patient in a psychiatric facility, McKenna asked to see Dr. Issacs as soon as he and Maureen arrived in the waiting room of the psychiatric wing. The clerk told them to have a seat while he located the doctor.

It wasn't long before Dr. Issacs came in. Tall and thin, in his fifties, he looked like he had the weight of the world on his shoulders but was managing to smile through it. McKenna and Maureen got up and introduced themselves to him.

"How can I help you?" Issacs asked, sounding like he meant it.

"We'd like to interview Julio Vargas," McKenna said.

"Bongo?"

"Yeah, Bongo. I heard you know him."

"Sure I know him. We're old friends. In the past couple of years I've seen him in all his personas and all his states. Does this interview have to be now?"

"Afraid so. We believe Bongo's got some information on a murderer who's sure to kill again."

"The poisoning cases?"

"Yeah, the poisoning cases. He doesn't know it, but he talked with the killer and was there drinking with the last victim right before he died."

"Well, for your sake, I hope the information you want from Bongo is in his pocket and not in his mind."

"We're hoping it's still hanging around in his mind."

"That was yesterday?"

"Right before he wound up here. Think he'd remember?"

"Yesterday he'll remember, although he might think it was last year. You see, he has a memory for events, but their placement in a time frame is a problem for him," Issacs explained. "Do you mind if I'm there during the interview? I might be able to help."

"I'd appreciate it, Doctor," McKenna answered.

"You realize that, if you're there, you might get subpoenaed someplace down the road?" Maureen asked.

"If I can help, I don't care. I can't do much for the homeless like Bongo under present policies, but I don't like the idea that there's someone out there murdering these poor slobs," Issacs said, smiling at Maureen.

"I agree," Maureen said, causing Issacs's smile to broaden. "Lord knows they've already got enough problems in the way of simple survival without worrying about someone out there trying to kill them."

"Detective Kaplowitz, aren't—"

"Maureen, if you don't mind," she interrupted.

Issacs didn't mind at all. "Okay, fine. Maureen, aren't you the Detective Kaplowitz who's a friend of Ben Rosen's?"

"Yes, I know him," Maureen admitted. "I guess you do, too, don't you? Rudy, isn't it?"

"Yes, Rudy," Issacs said, holding his hand out as he reintroduced himself to a kindred soul.

"My pleasure," Maureen said, taking Issacs's hand and holding it for what seemed to McKenna a couple of seconds longer than propriety demanded.

Now what the hell is going on here? McKenna wondered as he stood to the side, forgotten while Issacs and Maureen smiled at each other like teenagers. "Doctor, can you tell us some more about Bongo's condition?" McKenna asked, hoping to break the trance.

"Unusual case," Issacs said, turning back to McKenna and looking a little surprised that he was still there. "Thirty-six years old, reasonably good physical shape, born in Puerto Rico and brought here by his family when he was a child. He seemed to adjust to the move, learned English, and did pretty good in school. Sometime in his teens he developed schizophrenia and his life changed. He had periods of rationality, but became uncommunicative until some other complications set in. He has an unusual problem with his life force."

Issacs stopped and waited for a reaction, so McKenna gave him one. "His life force? Never heard of that one."

"It's an old concept. You see, man used to think of his life force as emanating from his heart. Later on, the thinking changed in most cultures and the brain became the place where it was thought the life force resided. But not Bongo. He has great respect for his life force, but thinks it's trying to leave him. He feels it move to various places around his body as it seeks an exit."

"He feels it? Like heat?" McKenna guessed.

"Yes, he actually feels it. To him it's warm, unless it gets into an extremity. Then it's hot. The hotter it gets, the more he worries that the heat of his life force is dissipating into the atmosphere. He's kind of scientific in that regard."

"So what does he do when that happens?"

"He rubs the location where his life force is hanging out, trying to move it to a new location in his body. He thinks that works because, for him, rubbing the life force seems to make the part of his body that's burning a little bit cooler."

"And this time it was in his ears?" McKenna guessed.

"Yes, he rubbed them raw. The abrasions have been treated and bandaged and should heal fine. I've sedated him a bit and have him believing his life force is moving back toward his heart. It seems to be working, for now."

"What happens when it finally gets to his heart?" Maureen asked.

Issacs smiled ruefully at the question. "After that I'll keep him here for another day or two, maybe longer if I can. At least he'll be out of the cold for a while."

"No chance of keeping him longer than that?" Maureen asked.

"I'd like to, but no, there's no chance," Issacs replied. "He's not violent, so he'll be discharged."

"Would you really be able to do anything for him if you could keep him?" McKenna asked.

"Keep him warm and keep his condition under control."

"But you wouldn't be able to cure him if you kept him, would you?" McKenna asked.

"There is no cure for schizophrenia, yet. Just control involving treatment with drugs," Issacs admitted. "But if I could keep him, he wouldn't be aggravating his condition by drinking."

"I see," McKenna said. "Could we talk to him now?"

"Follow me."

Issacs led them past a hospital guard sitting at a checkpoint to an elevator in the hall. They took it to the fourth floor, where there was another checkpoint at a locked metal gate. McKenna and Maureen signed in, the guard opened the gate with a key on his belt, and they followed Issacs down the corridor to Room 4296.

Through a small window in the door McKenna could see Bongo sitting cross-legged on his bed. He was wearing a hospital gown, his head was bandaged so that his ears were covered, and he was staring impassively back at McKenna. "He looks like he'll be okay to talk to," Issacs observed as he unlocked the door.

"Hello, Dr. Issacs," Bongo said as Issacs, McKenna, and Maureen entered the room.

"Hello, Bongo," Issacs replied cheerfully. "How you feeling now?"

"Much better, thanks. How you feeling?" Bongo replied softly. McKenna detected a slight Spanish accent and thought Bongo looked truly happy to see the doctor.

"I'm fine, thank you," Issacs answered. "Where is it now?"

"Right here," Bongo said, pointing to the base of his neck. "But it's going down. I think I'm gonna be okay this time."

"I'm glad to hear that. Feel like talking?"

Bongo shifted his gaze to McKenna and Maureen. "With you or with them?" he asked.

"With all of us. My friends here are hoping you can help them with some things they need to know."

"They cops?" Bongo asked Issacs.

"Yes. They're detectives investigating a murder."

"I didn't do anything wrong, did I?" Bongo asked frantically.

"Not a thing," Maureen said. "Mind if I sit down?"

Bongo didn't answer. He just looked at Maureen suspiciously, but she didn't appear to mind. She took his silence as a No and sat down at the end of the bed. Bongo reacted by making room for her, drawing his legs closer to his chest. She sat smiling at him while he fidgeted nervously, avoiding her gaze. After a few seconds Maureen said, "I'm sorry, Bongo. Do you want me to get up?"

Bongo had to look at her. He stopped fidgeting while he pondered Maureen's question as if it were a life-or-death issue.

McKenna watched Bongo watch Maureen, marveling at her technique; she had taken a potentially reluctant and very nervous witness and had given him some confidence with an insignificant action, making him feel he had some control of the situation he had unexpectedly found himself in. Bongo's face relaxed by degrees until the slightest hint of a smile tugged at the corners of his mouth. "No, that's all right," he said magnanimously. "You can stay there if you want."

"Thank you. I'm Maureen and this is Brian. We hate to disturb you, but somebody murdered your friend yesterday afternoon and you're the only one who can help us."

"My friend?"

"I'm sorry. Juan Bosco was murdered. He was your friend, wasn't he?" Maureen asked.

"Bosco's dead?"

"Yes, poisoned by the man you were both drinking with in the park yesterday."

"Yesterday in the park?" Bongo asked, confused.

"Yes, yesterday. About ten hours ago, right before the police brought you here," Maureen explained.

"Right before Dante brought you to see me," Issacs interjected.

"Dante? He didn't tell me anything about this, and he never lies to me," Bongo stated suspiciously.

"That's because he didn't know about the murder then. If he did, he would have told you and he would have told me. He never lies to me, either," Issacs said.

Apparently this Dante makes a practice of bringing people in to see Dr. Issacs, McKenna thought. Why does he do it and how did he get so popular with Bongo and Issacs?

The questions intrigued McKenna, but he put Dante out of his mind for the moment and remained focused on the confused and unhappy man sitting on the bed in front of him. "Bongo, doesn't it piss you off that somebody killed your friend?" he asked.

It caught Bongo by surprise. He looked up at McKenna, the spectrum of emotions passing across his face. Confusion was replaced by acceptance, followed by sorrow and then, briefly, anger. But the anger didn't last; sorrow returned.

That wasn't the emotion McKenna was looking for. He wanted an angry Bongo, a man who wanted vengeance. "So there you are, yesterday afternoon, you and Bosco in the park. Remember?"

"I remember."

"Then the murderer comes in, a filthy, cowardly, low-life sneak. This guy comes in to kill your friend for no good reason," McKenna said as he took the sketch from his pocket, unfolded it, and pretended to study it.

Sneaking a glance at Bongo over the sketch, McKenna was gratified to see that he had his total attention. "Sure is an evil-looking clown," McKenna commented. "I wish I'd seen him in person like you did."

Bongo looked ready to reach up and rip the sketch from McKenna's hands, so McKenna took a step backwards. The sketch was like a magnet, pulling on Bongo. He leaned toward it as McKenna stepped back.

"Oh, I'm sorry," McKenna said. "You know this guy, don't you?" he asked, holding the sketch up so Bongo could see it.

"Tony?" Bongo asked at once.

"Yeah, Tony. You know his last name?" McKenna asked, hope rising.

"No, nobody ever told me. You saying Tony killed Bosco?" Bongo asked incredulously.

"Yeah, I'm saying it because he did it. He put poison in the wine he gave Bosco. First he made believe he was a friend, and then he killed him in the sneakiest way one person can kill another."

"Are you sure it was Tony?"

"Absolutely certain. We've got lab reports that say the poison was in the wine and you know Tony gave the wine to Bosco. Now Bosco's dead and lying cold in the morgue. He's never coming back and Tony's walking around free, ready to do it again to somebody else. Think about that."

Bongo did, and McKenna was gratified to see his face contort into anger. "Bongo, you gonna help us stop him?" McKenna asked.

"Yeah," Bongo answered at once. "I'll help. What do you want me to do?"

"Just think hard and tell us what you know about Tony. You've got the key."

"I don't know him, really. I was only with him once before."

"When?"

The question stopped Bongo cold. His brows furrowed as he concentrated and McKenna could see that time was the problem. "Bongo, was it long ago?" he asked.

"I don't know. I want to help, but I just don't know."

"I understand," McKenna said. "Don't worry about it. Just think about the clothes he was wearing and the clothes you were wearing when you saw him. Was it winter?"

"Yeah, it was winter. It must've been. Tony was wearing his black coat and I had my scarf on. I remember now. It was in Grand Central, and I only go there when it's real cold outside."

"This winter?" McKenna asked.

"I don't know, but it was winter. I remember Tony told me he liked my scarf."

"Maybe I can help," Issacs said. He went to Bongo's closet and opened the door. Hanging on a hook inside were Bongo's clothes and folded on a shelf on top were a pair of brown leather gloves and the yellow-and-red scarf. Issacs took the scarf down, unfolded it, and held it out. "Was it this scarf Tony liked?" he asked Bongo.

"Yeah, that's the one. He really liked it," Bongo answered proudly.

"And do you remember who gave it to you?"

"Sure I do. Dante."

Issacs turned to McKenna. "It was this year," he said. "It was kind of cold out and Bongo was having a problem with his toes. His force was there heating them up, but the rest of his body was real cold. Dante bought him the scarf and gloves before he brought him in to see me. That was on January third, the last time Bongo was here."

"Thanks, Doctor," McKenna said, then turned back to Bongo. "You remember that now?" he asked.

"Yeah, I remember. So it was this year, right?"

"Right. How did you meet Tony?"

"Me and my friend Mickey were sitting in the waiting room when Tony came in. Mickey knew him."

"Where did Mickey know him from?"

"He didn't say. Just said he knew him."

"Was Tony wearing a hat?"

"Wool hat, same as in the picture."

"Did he ever take it off?"

"No."

"Were you drinking when Tony came in?"

"I wasn't, but Mickey was, a little. He likes his wine and Tony had some."

"Wild Irish Rose?"

"I think so. It was red wine."

"So Tony gave Mickey some wine, but you didn't have any. Right?"

"I had a little," Bongo said.

"You did?" McKenna asked, surprised. "Are you sure?"

"Yeah, I'm sure. Tony gave me a taste."

"Did you get sick?"

"No."

"Did Mickey get sick?"

"No. He liked it. Tony had another bottle and Mickey wanted more, so they went to the train yards to drink."

"The train yards? Where are they?" McKenna asked.

"You know, next to the station. The place they keep the trains they aren't using."

"There's an underground train yard that runs under Park Avenue, just north of Grand Central Station," Maureen explained. "It's huge. Most people in town don't even know it's there, but the homeless do. They go there to sleep and keep warm. Some of them even live there."

"Don't the police bother them?" McKenna asked her.

"Sometimes the AmTrak Police throw them out, but usually not when it's real cold out," she answered. "Ben Rosen sees to that."

McKenna didn't want to explore that subject, so he turned back to Bongo. "So you didn't go with Mickey and Tony?" he asked.

"No, I didn't feel like it. I stayed in the waiting room. I think I went to sleep."

"Have you seen Mickey since then?" McKenna asked, but thought he already knew the answer.

"I don't know," Bongo said.

"What does Mickey look like?"

"Ugly. He used to be fat, but now he's skinny. He's got them black marks on his hands."

"Like Bosco did?"

"Yeah, like Bosco. I think he's sick like Bosco."

"Is he white or black?"

"White."

"How old?"

"Maybe fifty."

"Do you remember what he was wearing?"

"Sure. The same thing he always wears, rain or shine. A long brown overcoat and a brown wool hat."

I'll worry about Mickey later, McKenna decided. "Now I'm going to switch times back on you, Bongo," he said. "I want you to think again about yesterday when you and Bosco were in the handball courts at the playground. It was real cold out and you were drinking some Colt Forty-five. Remember?"

"I remember."

"Tell me what happened when Tony came in."

"He just started talking to Bosco."

"Bosco knew him?"

"I guess so."

"Do you know where he knew him from?"

"No."

"What were they talking about?"

"Something about doctors and medicine, I think. I wasn't paying too much attention."

"What language were they talking in?"

"English."

"What language did you and Bosco usually talk in?"

"Spanish, but I don't think Tony knows Spanish."

"Why do you think that? No accent?"

"I think I heard a small accent, but Bosco knew him better than me and he talked to him in English. Why would he do that if Tony spoke Spanish? Bosco liked talking in Spanish."

Just because Bongo's confused doesn't mean he's stupid, McKenna remembered, content with Bongo's logic and reasoning. "Now tell us about the wine."

"Not much to tell. Tony took out a bottle of wine and asked Bosco if he wanted some. Bosco did, then he gave the bottle back to Tony and they kept on talking."

"But you didn't want any?"

"Not at first. I had some beer left and I like beer better."

"And then?"

"They was talking, but my ears started burning. I sat down and almost finished my beer, then Tony gave Bosco some more wine. I wanted to save some beer for later, so I asked Tony if I could have some wine. He told me *No*, said I'd get sick if I mixed the wine and beer. Got me pissed."

"Because he let Bosco have the wine and not you?"

"Yeah, and Bosco was no help. He said the same thing about me getting sick, so I told them both to fuck off and keep it all for themselves. Then Tony gave the bottle to Bosco and took off."

"That was just before the cops came in, right?" McKenna asked.

"Yeah, he left Bosco holding the bottle. I finished my beer real quick and Bosco tried to finish the wine, but he didn't have enough time."

"Then the cops gave you both summonses for drinking in the park?"

"I think so. I was having a lot of problems then, so I don't remember too much about it."

"Do you remember what happened after the cops left?"

"Bosco said he was tired and he was going to take a nap, so I just left. I felt like walking and then I met Dante."

"Do you know where Bosco kept all the rest of his things?" McKenna asked hopefully.

"He don't own nothing else, just what he had on him. Everything else got ripped off at the shelter."

The location of Bosco's possessions had been one loose end that had been bothering McKenna. He had hoped that there might have been something there to give him a clue about the relationship between the killer and his victims. Instead, all he got out of the interview with Bongo was something else to worry about. He felt certain that Mickey was another victim to be added to the list. As far as he could see, there was no good news except for the killer's first name, or at least the name he was using.

Bongo was staring at McKenna, waiting for the next question, but McKenna had none. He looked to Maureen, but she had nothing to add. She stood up and said, "Thanks, Bongo. You've been a big help."

"I have?" Bongo didn't look so sure.

"Yes, and we're happy you're still alive so that we were able to have this little chat. You're pretty lucky."

"How am I lucky?"

"You know that if Tony would have let you have that wine, then you'd be in the morgue right next to Bosco, don't you?"

"Yeah, I'm wondering about that."

"Wondering about why Tony wouldn't let you have the wine?" she asked.

"No, I was wondering if I wouldn't be better off if he had given me the wine. Do I look lucky to you right now?"

It was a question that Issacs, McKenna, and Maureen didn't want to think about.

After leaving Bongo, McKenna and Maureen followed Issacs through the checkpoints back to the waiting room. McKenna thanked the doctor for his help, but some questions had been gnawing at him. "Mind explaining a few things to me?" he asked.

"Officer Dante?" Issacs guessed.

"Yes, Dante. I take it he's in here frequently with people like Bongo?"

"Yes, especially in the winter when they have trouble coping with the elements."

"Why does he do it?"

"Aside from being a kind soul, Dante's got a brother who's a schizophrenic, so he learned everything he could about the affliction, even got himself a degree in psychology. He does whatever he can for those folks whenever he comes across one."

"I'm proud we've got people like him around," Maureen said.

I guess we've got these people everywhere, McKenna thought, surprised at the discovery but happy about it.

18 When they got back to the empty squad office at just after two in the morning, McKenna typed his report on the Bongo interview while Maureen went through the case folders in Ward's office, looking for the paper trail that would have been generated by the discovery of Mickey's body. McKenna had finished and had made a pot of coffee before Maureen emerged from Ward's office with a stack of case folders in her arms. She looked worried, which worried him.

While Maureen sat at her desk going through one of the folders, McKenna poured them both a cup of coffee, then sat down opposite her. He counted eight slim folders on her desk while he silently sipped his coffee, watching her and waiting. He finished his coffee before Maureen closed the folder and took a sip of hers. "It's not bad," she said.

"What's not bad? Those cases or the coffee?"

"The coffee's not bad. These cases are terrible. Not counting Foster and Bailey, in the Seventeenth Precinct alone we've got eight other cases of 'Investigate Aided–DOA' this month where the subject was homeless."

"That's a high number, I guess," McKenna ventured, making a mental note to go over the Rodney Bailey case folder. He didn't expect to find much because of the assumption that Bailey had frozen to death.

"Very high," Maureen said. "I just checked the files for January of last year. Found there were only three in this precinct last January."

"Is Mickey in there?"

"Right here," she said, pushing across the desk to him the case folder she had been reading.

It took McKenna a while to review it because a lot more work than he had expected had been done on the case. The initial complaint report stated that at 9:35 on the morning of January 9 the body of a male white had been found by an Amtrak cop in an emergency-exit stairwell of the Grand Central train yard. The 17th Squad had been notified and the case had been assigned to Detective

Mercurio. The body had been searched in his presence; found were thirty-two dollars and change, a Department of Social Services ID card, and an expired West Virginia driver's license. Both documents identified the deceased as Mickey Weyland, age forty-one. As Bongo had indicated, Mickey had been in poor health— five feet seven inches tall, about 110 pounds, Kaposi's sarcomas on his hands and arms. Mercurio had interviewed nine homeless people he had found in the train yard, but none could provide any information on the circumstances surrounding Mickey's death. Mercurio had recommended that the case remain active pending further investigation and autopsy.

Mercurio's second report on the case stated that he had done a computer check through NCIC, the National Crime Information Center, and had found that Mickey Weyland was not wanted for any crimes nor had he been reported as a missing person to any police department in the United States. Following procedure, Mercurio had notified the Missing Persons Squad since he had been unable to make a next-of-kin notification on Mickey's death.

A third report by Mercurio stated that he had located and recovered Mickey's personal effects at the Bellevue Shelter and he had determined the property to be of no investigative value in the case. The property had all been forwarded to the Property Clerk's Office.

Mercurio's fourth and final report on the case was dated January 12, three days after Mickey's body had been found. It stated that he had consulted with Assistant Supervising Medical Examiner Dr. James Wright. Wright had informed him that Mickey had died between ten and twenty hours before he had been found and that, after an autopsy and a review of Mickey's medical records from Bellevue Hospital, he had listed the case as "Death by Natural Causes." In Wright's opinion, Mickey had been in a weakened condition because of AIDS, and death had been caused by a combination of heart failure and pulmonary edema.

Mercurio had ended the report by recommending that the case be closed and filed. There was a notation by Ward at the bottom stating that he concurred with Mercurio's recommendation.

"It looks like we're opening a bag of worms," McKenna commented as he closed the case file.

"It doesn't get any better with these," she answered, tapping the pile of reports in front of her. "They all have to be looked at again, very closely."

"Are they all HIV-positive homeless men?"

"Six of them are."

"Anything else to go on in there?"

"Not that I can see. They're all closed cases."

"That's eight in just our precinct, but it's probably even worse than that. I think that every homeless death in Manhattan South in the last few months has to be reopened and given a very close look. There's a lot of trouble brewing here for the ME's office, and probably for a lot of squad commanders as well. I hate to say it, but Ward might be getting some big problems out of this."

"You're right about the ME's office, but Tommy's gonna be all right," Maureen said, smiling and confident.

Her reaction puzzled McKenna. "What makes you so sure about Ward?" he asked.

"Because last week I had a talk with him about all these homeless people dying all of a sudden and he called the ME's office."

McKenna was stunned by the information and Maureen's offhand delivery. "Last week?" he asked. "You suspected something was up last week?"

"Yes. But remember, it was just a suspicion."

"How?"

"Easy. I've been working in this squad for a long time and I usually catch no more than one homeless death a month," she said, then tapped the stack of case folders in front of her. "But two of these cases are mine and I didn't like the look of it. I asked the other guys in the squad about it and it seems that recently everybody's been getting more than usual. So naturally I went to Tommy about it. He also thought it was a little strange."

"So he called the ME's office?"

"What else could he do? They're the ones in charge of telling us what's a homicide and what's a death by natural causes. Unfortunately, he wound up talking to some pompous ass who was in charge there while Dr. Andino was away, a character named Dr. Wright. He just about told Tommy not to bother him with this homeless nonsense. Even gave him a little lecture, telling him how he has to expect to see a rise in AIDS-related deaths among the homeless."

McKenna had a hard time imagining anyone giving Ward a lecture. "And what did Ward say to that?" he asked.

"Just what you'd expect. He called Dr. Wright a few nasty names I can't repeat and hung up. Then he wrote the details of the call in the Telephone Message Log, so he's covered."

"And that's it?"

"As far as Tommy was concerned. He was happy, but I wasn't, so I went to see Father Hays to find out if some of his usual clients were missing," she said, giving him that kindergarten teacher smile.

"Oh boy," was all McKenna could say for a moment as he fidgeted with embarrassment like a schoolboy. I've had some very important things about Maureen all wrong, he had to admit to himself. She didn't discuss my case with anyone behind my back. She's so sharp that she was talking to Father Hays about it before I even knew I had a case, even before I got to this squad. The way she's looking at me, I know that she knows that she caught me acting like a dope. Maybe I can tough this one out. "And what did Father Hays tell you?" he asked nonchalantly.

The smile didn't change. "I just remembered," she said. "Didn't you want to talk to me about something?"

She's got me and I guess she's gonna make me suffer, McKenna thought. "Nothing I can think of right now," he said.

"Maybe it had something to do with a couple of snotty looks I thought I was getting this afternoon," Maureen suggested innocently.

Nothing to do now but take a well-deserved kick in the ass, McKenna acknowledged, but Maureen wasn't giving it. "Don't worry about it, Brian," she said as she reached across the desk and mussed his hair. "I was just having some fun with you."

"Well, then you got me good. But I'm sorry anyway. I should have known better."

"Apology accepted. Now where were we?"

Now that wasn't so bad, was it? McKenna asked himself, surprised at how good he felt. "You were gonna tell me what Father Hays said," he replied.

"That's right. He told me that he hadn't noticed anything and hadn't heard anything, but that he'd keep his ear to the ground for me. So then I went to the morgue to visit Dr. Andino's secretary."

"You know Sunshine?" McKenna asked, surprised for only a moment.

"Yes, she's a friend of mine."

"What did she have to say?"

"That she'd start going over the figures and tell Dr. Andino about it as soon as he got back from Italy."

"Do you think this thing would have been caught sooner if Dr. Andino had been here?" McKenna asked.

"Yes, or maybe even if you came here sooner."

"Me? How's that? It seems to me you've already done everything that should be done."

"Brian, you don't have to play modest with me," Maureen chided. "I know better. Why do you think Tommy gave the Foster case to you?"

"Because I was new and I was up. Since it had looked like Benny had froze to death, he probably figured I had some influence with the press and could tone it down. Looks like he was wrong on that one."

"The press angle might have had a little to do with it, but I don't think that was his main reason. He's smarter than that. By this morning he would have been suspicious of any homeless death, no matter what it looked like. He wanted to put his best detective on it, and it doesn't hurt that you've got some political muscle and can get things moving. He knows that if there has to be bad news for the chiefs, if you're the one giving it they'd be less likely to kill the messenger."

"Maybe. But Maureen, I've got a surprise for you," McKenna said. "You're his best detective."

For the second time that day, McKenna saw Maureen blush. "No I'm not," she said sincerely. "You think you're a little rusty, but you're the one and I'm not being modest. I think it's because you're smarter than me."

I am? McKenna thought, mystified by Maureen's conclusion after having watched her at work for a day.

At three in the morning, just ten minutes after leaving the station house, McKenna got out of the taxi at the Gramercy Park Hotel. He was home and feeling good, in spite of having just worked nineteen hours straight with another long day beginning in another couple of hours.

Part of his good mood McKenna attributed to the progress he had made that day on the case. While apprehensive about the number of bodies yet to be ascribed to the murderer, McKenna felt confident that he was going to catch him and stop the killing.

But that was just part of it. The main reason McKenna felt so good was the Gramercy Park Hotel. He loved the place and was happy every time he came home to it.

He conceded that living in the hotel was an extravagance, with the monthly rent for his suite eating up a major portion of his salary, but that bothered neither him nor Angelita. Money wasn't one of their problems since they had made a nice profit when they sold their Greenwich Village apartment a couple of years before, and they both had always figured that money was for spending. The convenience of living in the comfortable old hotel was worth the cost to them; although many of their friends considered them to be spendthrifts, for McKenna and Angelita the Gramercy Park Hotel meant Old World living at a price they considered reasonable. Set on Manhattan's only private park at East 21st Street and Lexington Avenue, all the places McKenna and Angelita liked to go were reasonably close to the Gramercy Park Hotel; it was a short taxi trip south to the Village for the restaurants and north for the theaters. Since McKenna hated driving and didn't even have a car in New York, the hotel's location offered another plus. At any time he could leave the hotel, hop in a cab, and be anyplace in Manhattan South in fifteen minutes, even with traffic.

Then there were the hotel's rooms. McKenna and Angelita both liked the furniture and the decor; it was warm and comfortable and made them feel at home, like it was their own place. For the moment, their suite was large enough for them and the baby, with one bedroom, a large sitting room, a small kitchen, two bathrooms, and plenty of closets.

Completing the at-home effect was the staff. Most of them had been there for many years, were proficient in the jobs they performed, and worked hard at anticipating McKenna and Angelita's every need. They were just nice people and McKenna treated them like family, with everything that entailed in New York in the way of gratuities. Since Christmas, the staff had been treating him like a kindly, rich uncle.

Still, as satisfied as they were with the hotel, both McKenna and Angelita were forced to admit they couldn't stay there forever. Janine was just three months old, but sooner or later she would need her own room. Where they finally wound up depended on whose point of view prevailed. They had a condo in Fort Myers Beach, Florida, and Angelita was all for McKenna retiring for good and returning there to live. On the other hand, while McKenna thought Florida was a great place to spend a vacation, he thrived on New York and had rediscovered during the long day that he loved being a detective. He knew he wasn't ready to leave yet, and knew that the consequences of that decision were going to be tough on him. Angelita would see to that.

Angelita was that most delightful of creatures, the greatest companion in every way that a man could have, as long as she was happy. The trouble with her was that there was no middle ground. She was either happy or unhappy, never just content. When she was happy, McKenna's life was wonderful. When she wasn't, he was miserable, and it wasn't because her treatment of him changed in any overt way. She was always loving, always solicitous, always keeping his welfare foremost in her thoughts. He was miserable when she wasn't perfectly happy mainly because he loved her deeply, but also because, when Angelita was unhappy, she disapproved of his choice of aftershave, never liked whatever tie he wore, hated the food at whatever restaurant he had chosen for dinner, and usually fell asleep at whatever show he had selected for them to see.

McKenna had learned through experience that it was the little things in life that can make a man miserable, and Angelita was great at working those little things. Lately, the danger signs had been there for him to read. On vacation in Florida, she had tried once again to talk him into staying there, and had almost succeeded. McKenna had been bored in his job in headquarters, but insisted that he wasn't ready to retire. Angelita had gone along with his wishes and they had returned to New York smiling, but McKenna knew something was up. She had made him try on four ties before he could pass her inspection and leave the hotel for his first day in the 17th Squad.

And tonight there was more trouble brewing for McKenna. Angelita was in her nightgown, sitting on the couch with headphones on while feeding the baby a bottle. Her eyes were closed and she hadn't heard him enter.

Unusual. Angelita's not that much of a music fan, McKenna thought as he stood there proudly admiring his wife and daughter. He thought they were the two most beautiful women alive. Working hard at it from almost the moment Janine was born, Angelita had dieted and exercised her way back into shape so that she once again looked like the woman he had married. The pregnancy had put a few lines on her face so that she finally looked her twenty-eight years, but he didn't mind and even preferred her new, mature look.

Janine was growing fast and had taken on most of the pounds Angelita had lost. Watching her suck her bottle, McKenna thought she was the prettiest, roundest, and most healthy-looking baby he had ever seen. Then he saw the case for his French tapes lying under the coffee table in front of the sofa, and was pleasantly surprised.

Languages were his hobby, not Angelita's. Rather than watch television, he usually preferred to sit and study from a taped Spanish, French, or Italian language course while Angelita read or watched her shows. He often had urged her to learn French, telling her it would be easy for her since she already spoke Spanish, and that French would be useful since they both enjoyed traveling in France.

Until that morning Angelita had resisted, always telling him that, although she loved the country, she wasn't particularly fond of the French and didn't care to speak to them in any language. As far as she was concerned, McKenna could handle making the reservations, ordering the meals, and doing whatever translating needed to be done while they were there.

McKenna's sense of pleasure at her change of heart didn't last for long. She opened her eyes, saw him standing there, and ended it with one simple question. "Does the name *Janine Courtois* sound familiar to you?" she asked as she shut off the tape player next to her on the sofa and took off the headphones.

At once McKenna knew he had a big problem, and he was at a loss for words. Before the baby had been born, they hadn't been able to agree on a name for her. Angelita had wanted names like Melanie, Erica, and Victoria, names that all sounded to him like characters in a soap opera. Instead, he had wanted to give her one of the Irish names that ran in his family, names like Margaret, Patricia, or Kathleen. Angelita had objected to all of them. They had discussed potential names for hours at a time without reaching agreement until one day in November, just days before her due date, McKenna had suggested *Janine*.

To McKenna's surprise, Angelita had liked the name, said it sounded classy. But first, of course, it had to be investigated. "Who do you know named Janine?" she had asked him.

"Nobody," he had told her, knowing Angelita. She got along with everyone he knew, as long as they weren't women under seventy with sexy voices. Never having given Angelita a reason to distrust him, McKenna couldn't understand her irrational little jealous streaks, but that was the way she was and he had learned to work around it.

"Then where did you get *Janine* from?" he remembered her asking. At the time, he had told her that he couldn't remember, but Angelita had him now. Janine Courtois was the name used during conversation drills by one of the instructors on his French language tapes. McKenna had always liked the way she sounded on the tapes as well as the way the French pronounced the name. So Janine it was, and both had been happy with the name until Angelita decided, out of the blue, to finally give herself a French lesson at three in the morning.

It was apparent to McKenna that Angelita considered the Janine Courtois question to be a serious matter that needed answering. "Okay, so our daughter's got the same name as some faceless girl in a language tape," he said, deciding to try the offensive. "What's the big deal?"

"The big deal?" Angelita repeated sarcastically. "Not much, I guess, except that you named our daughter after some French floozy."

French floozy? This one is getting out of hand fast, McKenna thought. Need some fast damage control. "Angelita, there is no Janine Courtois," he explained patiently. "It's just a made-up name. But if she did exist, I probably wouldn't like her anyway."

"Just tell me one thing. What did you like better? The name or the way your Janine on the tape sounds?"

"The name. Janine is a nice name, isn't it?"

"I used to think so, but now we're stuck with it."

McKenna decided to try backing out of the controversy. Sometimes the maneuver worked with her, and when it did, she would never bring it up again. Angelita believed in bringing things that bothered her into the open, but she hated fighting with him as much as he regretted it whenever he had done something to offend her. "Angelita, can we talk about this tomorrow?" he asked. "I've had a long day and I have to be back to work in a couple of hours."

It worked. "You're going back in the morning, after working all day and night?" she asked, concerned about him.

"Have to. My first case is turning out to be a big one."

"I know. I saw you on the news, but I don't think you're gonna be much good at playing cops and robbers tomorrow. You have to sleep, you know."

"I'll be fine," he assured her.

"Okay, if you say so. Got a minute or two to sit with me before you conk out?" she asked, moving herself and the baby to the end of the couch.

"Always time for that."

By seven o'clock McKenna was up, dressed in a fresh suit, and enjoying a cup of coffee in his living room as he browsed through the morning papers. He felt all right after his three hours of sleep, but not great. While he hoped for the java boost, his body was sending him a few signals that the days of getting by on catnaps were over for him. Whatever happened during the day, he resolved to give it eight hours' rest that night.

McKenna saw that his case was the featured story in both the *News* and the *Post*. The *News* headline was ASSASSIN STALKS THE HOMELESS with a front-page picture of Joe Walsh leaving the Madison Boys Club holding the Wild Irish Rose bottle in front of him cradled in a handkerchief. The *Post* banner read DON'T DRINK THE WINE and also showed a front-page photo of Walsh leaving the Boys Club with the wine bottle held in front of him, but McKenna thought there was something different about that one.

McKenna put the two photos side by side and compared them. It only took him a moment to discover that they had been taken at different times. In the *News* photo, Walsh's tie was at half-mast, with his shirt open and the tie knot someplace around his third button. In the *Post* photo his tie was a little snugger to his neck, with the knot around his second button. McKenna figured Walsh had posed as many exits from the Boys Club for the benefit of the press as MacArthur had made entrances, splashing ashore in the Philippines time after time as the cameras rolled.

Both papers detailed the discoveries of the bodies of Bosco and Foster and gave almost as much information about the murders as McKenna himself knew. What the papers didn't have was anything about the death of Mickey Weyland, but that was because only he and Maureen knew about it. As far as McKenna was concerned, he was just as pleased that they hadn't found out about it until after the papers went to press. He wanted to tell Andino about it himself so that the first information the ME received on another suspicious death wouldn't come from the newspapers.

Still, the press speculated that the police were worried that they were just seeing the tip of the iceberg. The reporters went to that usual high-ranking-police-official-who-asked-not-to-be-named and quoted him as stating that it was expected that the number of murders to be attributed to the poisoner would rise. The official refused to say more and suggested that the Medical Examiner's Office be contacted for further details.

Naturally, the Medical Examiner's Office was contacted, but Dr. Andino had told the press that he wouldn't have a statement until he knew more himself, since he still didn't know what poison had been used to cause the deaths. However, he did concede that if any past poisoning cases had been erroneously classified as "Death by Natural Causes," then his office bore the ultimate responsibility.

Both papers also ran the sketch of the suspect and asked for information from the public about him, printing a special Homicide Squad telephone number that had been set up and noting that all calls would be kept confidential. It was something that McKenna hadn't wanted yet. He recognized that, for some reason, Ray Brunette was working behind the scenes and promoting publicity for the case.

On page four the *News* carried a piece based on an interview with Joe Walsh. According to him, he had been called in because of the potential disastrous implications of the case. He assured the interviewer that he would help bring it to a successful conclusion and eventually succeed in ascertaining the identity of the murderer, stating that he had developed nine individual latent prints from the wine bottle that had contained the poison.

The *Post* gave McKenna the ink instead of Walsh. An article showed a file photo of him and gave a long and laudatory summary of his career, noting that he had chosen to return to police work as a detective, taking a sizable salary cut in the process, because he preferred fieldwork to his administrative duties in police headquarters. The article also mentioned McKenna's friendship and close professional association with the police commissioner, characterizing McKenna as a protégé of Brunette's.

While McKenna had never thought of himself as Ray's protégé, he was surprised at the accuracy of the information in the article until he noted that the byline read Mike Brennan. Brennan was a premier columnist, not a reporter, but he still did an occasional background news story and always managed to get his facts straight. McKenna had known him for fifteen years, saw him socially from time to time, and had always considered him a friend.

The last thing that caught McKenna's eye before he finished his coffee was a small piece on Page Six, the *Post*'s gossip page that reported on the after-hours activities around town of celebrities, politicians, socialites, and other people in the news. According to the columnist, she had been in Elaine's Restaurant, sitting near a table usually reserved for big-shot TV executives, when she overheard a rumor that a certain well-known, up-and-coming, glamorous newswoman working for Fox Five News had incurred the wrath of her bosses when she embarrassed the network by misinterpreting a recent news story.

For some reason he couldn't understand, McKenna felt sorry for Heidi Lane. He thought that she was a hard worker in a vicious and competitive business who had taken a gamble and lost. He didn't take it personally since he had developed a hard skin, having been abused in print a few times before by reporters who were otherwise very nice people. It was the nature of the business, he thought, considered himself a public servant and therefore fair game, to a point. As far as McKenna was concerned, Heidi had skirted the edges but hadn't yet crossed the line. He decided that, if the opportunity presented itself, he would give her a chance to get out of trouble.

Before leaving for work, he went into the bedroom to check on Angelita and the baby. Angelita had been up most of the night with Janine, and McKenna knew she was tired when she hadn't joined him for coffee. Both were sleeping, Angelita stretched out on the bed with the baby cradled in her arms.

McKenna decided not to wake Angelita, but she had heard him and opened her eyes. "Leaving?" she asked.

"Yeah, got to go."

"Could you try and get home on time tonight, no matter what happens?"

"Sure. I'll try," he promised.

"Thanks. Now kiss me good-bye."

McKenna did, but as he was leaving, Angelita called to him. "Be careful with that Heidi Lane," she warned.

"Don't worry about her. I have to deal with her, but I don't think she'll be giving me any more problems," McKenna answered from the bedroom door.

"Yes she will, if you give her a chance. She's got it in for you."

"What makes you think that?"

"Just a feeling, but I know a bitch when I see one. For some reason, she doesn't like you."

20 The cold spell had snapped and it had gotten so much warmer that McKenna doubted there would be a trace of the previous night's snowfall left on the streets by noon. During the ride to work he saw many doormen, supers, and shopkeepers clearing the snow from the sidewalks in front of their buildings with no more than a broom.

McKenna didn't see Heidi standing across the street from the station house until he got out of the cab, but by then it was too late. She had seen him first. She ran across the street to the station-house door, then stood waiting for him. For a moment McKenna thought about just walking away, but discarded the idea. Heidi knew he had to come to work sooner or later that day, and when he did, McKenna figured she would still be there waiting. She had him cornered and he could see no respectable way out except to talk to her. He looked up and down the block and saw no sign of her camera crew, so he put a smile on his face, squared his shoulders, and walked to meet her.

Heidi was affecting the 1930s waif look. She had her hair in a ponytail under a red wool kerchief and wore a long, baggy plaid overcoat that covered the tops of her high-button shoes. McKenna was sure that she had spent a small fortune on clothes to look fashionably homeless, but had to concede that, no matter what Heidi wore, she always managed to look good.

"What's the matter, Brian? You mad at me?" she asked, giving him a big smile.

"Let's just say that I don't feel like talking to you right now, Heidi."

Heidi's smile vanished, replaced by a little girl's look of embarrassment. "I guess you heard I'm in some trouble," she said.

"You mean you're in trouble for trying to make me look like a dope yesterday?"

"Yes, and I want to apologize," Heidi said, a picture of humility. "It looks like I was wrong and now everyone knows it. I should've been smarter and had more confidence in you."

I'm not buying this, McKenna thought. Have to keep in mind that this lady's a professional actress. "Let me ask you this," he said. "Suppose you were right and I was wrong. Suppose Benny Foster did freeze to death. Would you still be here apologizing to me after spanking me in public to boost your ratings?"

"Maybe, but it wouldn't have been today. If you were wrong, then we probably wouldn't have run into each other for a while."

"You're right about that, Heidi. They'd probably have me hidden away somewhere where I couldn't shoot my mouth off and you'd be filling in as an anchorwoman. When would we run into each other?"

"Maybe I like it better this way," Heidi said coyly. "Gives me a chance to straighten out with you. Like I said, I'm really sorry."

"Okay. Apology accepted. Anything else?"

"Yes. I'd like to apologize to you on the air."

The idea stunned McKenna. "Why would you do that?" he asked, eyeing Heidi suspiciously.

"Ratings, of course. I think the public would like it and they'd stay tuned."

She's right, McKenna conceded. In front of the cameras, she'd play it real sincere and remorseful and probably draw a lot of sympathy. "Heidi, I've got to hand it to you," he said. "You've got so many angles that, no matter what you do, you wind up a winner."

Heidi took it as a compliment and smiled graciously. "Thank you. Then we'll do it?"

"Let me think about it. When would this be?"

"What's wrong with right now? My crew's around the corner and I can get you interviewed in a couple of minutes."

So that's it, McKenna thought. She's using this apology bit to get another interview. Let's see if I can back her up a bit. "No good, Heidi. I'm not ready to do another interview yet. But you can tape your apology now, if you want."

Heidi's face told McKenna that his idea was entirely unacceptable. "That's not what I was planning," she said. "I have to apologize on camera right before an interview with you. That way the viewers can see you forgive me and they'll know that everything's all right."

"I've got nothing to say right now that's not already in the papers."

"When will you know more? Sometime this afternoon?"

"Maybe. I'll call you when I do."

"That a promise?"

"Yeah, it is."

"Good, but you can save the phone call. I've been assigned exclusively to this story, so I'll be out here in our van most of the time. That way you can't miss me."

"That's all you're gonna do? Just sit out here all day?"

"That's right. We've got another crew out working the human-interest angle talking to homeless people at the shelters, but unless something else big blows up in this town today, you're my story."

"Somehow that doesn't make me feel too comfortable."

"Don't worry about it. You'll do good and I'll make you look just wonderful. I promise, no more tricks."

Now why don't I believe that? McKenna wondered.

Maureen and Billy Mercurio were already in the squad office when McKenna got there. Maureen was preparing a pot of coffee and looked like she had gotten eight hours of sleep, but Mercurio seemed tired. Ward hadn't arrived.

Over coffee, McKenna asked Mercurio a few questions about the Mickey Weyland case, then told him the details of the interview with Bongo. Mercurio just took it in, giving no indication of his thoughts as McKenna told him of Mickey's meeting with the killer in Grand Central Station. At the conclusion of his account, McKenna waited for a reaction from Mercurio, but all he got was a wry smile.

"I take it you're not surprised at all this," McKenna commented.

"Yeah, I'm not surprised. How'd you know?"

"Because I read your case folder on this and I've never seen so much work done on a routine Investigate Aided case. Seems to me you thought something was up."

"At the time, it was just a hunch," Mercurio said, shrugging his shoulders, "Mickey was my second dead bum that week, so I was kind of suspicious. Unfortunately, I didn't get much to go on and the ME's office wasn't much help, either."

Ward came in with the newspapers under his arm and regally acknowledged his three detectives with a wave of his hand before he hurried into his office and closed the door behind him.

Maureen went to the coffeepot, made a cup of coffee, and carried it to Ward's office door. "Coming?" she asked McKenna.

"Sure." McKenna got up and followed Maureen in.

The lieutenant was seated at his desk, reading the report on Bongo's interview. He gave no acknowledgment of McKenna and Maureen's presence except to hold out his hand as he continued reading. Maureen placed the cup of coffee in his hand. Without looking up, Ward continued reading as he sipped his coffee. When he finished, he put the report and the cup on his desk and smiled. "Very nice," he said.

"Thank you," McKenna replied.

"Where do we go from here?" Ward asked.

Here goes the end of the good mood, McKenna thought. "There's been a complication, Lieutenant," he said. "It's not in the report, but it looks like we have one more murder than we did when you went home."

"Who? Mickey Weyland?"

"Yeah, Mickey," McKenna answered, impressed with Ward's powers of recall.

McKenna was wrong. What he thought was bad news for the lieutenant was good news somehow. "I'm not surprised," Ward said, his smile broadening. "If it wasn't for that knucklehead ME, we'd have been on to these killings a lot sooner. Can you imagine that snotnose Doctor Pompous Pea-brain Wright trying to give me a lecture?" he asked.

"Sure can't," McKenna and Maureen answered together.

"Sometime today, he's gonna learn that there's a new professor in town," Ward said. "Does Andino know about this one yet?"

"No, not yet," McKenna answered. "But I think he's given Wright a lecture or two himself by now."

"Not enough. Andino's just warming him up for me. How many other cases like Mickey's you think we got?" Ward asked McKenna.

McKenna turned to Maureen for the answer. "Possibly six in this precinct, maybe more," she said. "I think that all our Investigate Aided–DOA homeless cases for this month and maybe December are gonna have to be reworked."

"No problem," Ward said. "I've got the Homicide Squad working the phones taking calls on the sketch and I'll send those cases over to them to be reworked. I've also got them visiting the shelters and showing the sketch, so that should keep them busy." Then Ward opened his newspaper and pointed to the sketch. "Now which one of you is gonna tell me who this guy is?" he asked.

"He is," Maureen said, pointing to McKenna.

Thanks, Maureen, McKenna thought, then prepared to push himself away from the trunk and climb out on a limb. "I've got a theory, but I can't be certain of it until every homeless person who died this month is dug up and given another autopsy."

"Tough way to confirm a theory," Ward commented. "When do you propose all that be done?"

"As soon as either Dr. Andino or our lab identifies the poison the killer's using."

"Okay, suppose they find the poison and suppose all those bodies are autopsied. According to your theory, what do you think the results will tell us about the killer?"

"That he's been very busy and that he's only been doing people who are HIV positive. If that's the case, then my bet is that he's a doctor or a medical worker with some connection to Bellevue Hospital."

"You think all the victims are gonna be Bellevue patients?" Ward asked.

"Yes. Benny Foster, Rodney Bailey, Juan Bosco, and Mickey Weyland all were."

"And any others the ME reclassifies as homicides after they find the poison are all gonna have AIDS?"

"No, but they're all gonna be HIV positive. Benny Foster was, but he hadn't developed AIDS yet."

Ward leaned back in his chair, thinking over McKenna's theory for a minute while McKenna and Maureen watched him. "So you're saying that only someone with access to Foster's medical records would have known that he was HIV positive?" he asked.

"Right."

"And we know he only wants them because he let Bongo live?"

"That's what it looks like."

"That would be quite a scandal," Ward commented as he sat up straight. "Imagine the hue and cry we're gonna get when we snoop around Bellevue telling them we think one of their people, maybe even one of their doctors, has been poisoning their patients."

"It's not gonna make them happy," McKenna conceded. "Problem is, I've promised Heidi Lane a statement, so we're gonna be getting some more publicity on this."

"Unavoidable," Ward said. "It's even a good thing. We don't want any more cases than we've already got, so one of the things we've got to do is make sure that every homeless person in this city knows not to take any wine from anybody on the street. Publicity can only help us in that department."

"But it won't help us if I go snooping around Bellevue. The press is bound to find out about that and, even if we don't tell them what we're thinking, they'll jump to their own conclusions."

"So?"

"So, if it turns out I'm wrong, whoever's in charge at Bellevue is gonna go into a justifiable, target-seeking rage, and then we'll be huddled together in the bull's-eye."

Ward didn't give it a second thought. "That's where we'd belong, but it goes with the territory," he observed. "You've got your theory and it sounds like a good one to me. Go with it."

21 After leaving Ward's office, McKenna took a look at the Rodney Bailey case folder and decided there wasn't much to go on. On the morning of January 26 Bailey's body had been discovered in the service alley of a luxury high-rise at 128 East 37th Street. The building super had found Bailey's frozen body in two washing-machine packing cartons that the homeless man had pushed together to form a makeshift shelter against the cold. Detective Bender of the 17th Squad had conducted the preliminary investigation.

According to the super, at ten the night before he had taken the washing-machine cartons from the basement of the building and put them in the service alley for the morning sanitation pickup. He had stated that he didn't know Bailey, but had seen him at various times over the past few years panhandling around the neighborhood or hanging out with other homeless men at the St. Vartan's Playground at Second Avenue and East 35th Street.

Bender had noted in his report that Bailey was obviously in poor health, but that there were no injuries evident on his body. During the search of the body, $10.13 was found in Bailey's pockets, along with a wallet containing a Department of Social Services ID card and a medical appointment card that stated Bailey had an appointment with Dr. Suliman Rashid at the Bellevue AIDS Clinic on January 30.

The rest of Bailey's possessions were found in a shopping cart hidden behind another two washing-machine cartons in the alley. Bender had noted that both Bailey and his shopping cart were hidden in the alley and not visible from the street.

Bender's final report on the case stated that on January 29 he had conferred with Dr. O'Malley of the medical examiner's office. O'Malley told him that, after autopsy, he had determined that Bailey had frozen to death.

Bender ended his final report by requesting that the case be marked "Closed,

No Further Police Action Warranted.'' McKenna considered it interesting that Ward hadn't signed the report, but instead had drawn a question mark next to Bender's conclusion and initialed it.

McKenna closed the Bailey case folder and noticed that Bender had arrived and was sitting on Maureen's desk. Both watched McKenna as he got up and put on his coat. ''You going to the morgue now?'' Maureen asked him.

''Uh-huh.''

''What do you think of the Bailey case?'' Bender asked. ''Is it possible he's another victim?''

''You did a good job on it, but yeah, I think it's possible,'' McKenna said. ''I'm hoping Dr. Andino will be able to tell me for sure this morning.''

''Until then, we're gonna assume that Bailey was a victim,'' Maureen said. ''The Homicide Squad is going over the other cases, but Kenny and I will rework the Bailey case ourselves. Keep us posted.''

McKenna wasn't surprised that Maureen, like Ward, was suspicious about Bailey's death. But she had gone further and stated for the record that she thought Bailey had been murdered, which was good enough for the detective who had originally handled the case. Bender got up and took the case folders from McKenna's desk. He returned to his own desk and began to reread his work.

McKenna left without another word from Bender or Maureen, but getting to the morgue turned out to be something of a problem. Heidi's news van was parked directly across the street from the front door of the station house, and she bounded out as soon as he left the building. ''Sorry, Heidi. Not now,'' he told her.

McKenna's statement stopped her short. She looked disappointed but recovered quickly. ''Then when?''

''Like I told you, when I have something new to say.''

''Mind telling me where you're going?''

''I'd rather not, but I'll be back in a few hours,'' McKenna answered, trying not to sound brusque.

''And then we'll have our interview?'' she asked.

''Hopefully, if I learn anything new,'' McKenna said as he searched the street for his department car. He didn't see it, so he crossed the street with Heidi following. Then he saw it, parked in front of Heidi's van, blocked in by a double-parked marked radio car.

Not wanting to wait and give Heidi time to formulate any ideas about following him in her van, McKenna decided to take a taxi. He left her standing on the sidewalk, walked to the corner of Third Avenue, and hailed a cab. As he climbed into the backseat, he looked back. Heidi was standing by the side of her van talking into a radio.

''Where to?'' the taxi driver asked McKenna.

''Drive slow to the next corner. I'm looking for a friend,'' McKenna told him.

As the driver cruised slowly up Third Avenue to the corner of East 52nd Street, McKenna checked the parked cars on both sides of the block. Sitting in a rented Chevy three cars from the corner was Heidi's cameraman. He had gotten nervous when the taxi slowly passed his car and ducked down in his seat, but McKenna saw him.

''Wait here for a second. I'll be right back,'' McKenna told the cab driver, then got out and walked back to the Chevy. The cameraman was sitting behind the wheel with his engine running, trying to pretend that McKenna didn't exist. As McKenna knocked on the driver's window, he saw a portable radio on the seat next to the cameraman.

Heidi's man looked uncomfortable as he rolled down his window. For a moment, McKenna felt sorry for him. Having been burned himself more than once while working a surveillance, he understood the cameraman's predicament. McKenna remembered that it never felt good when the guy you're supposed to be tailing stops by to say, *"Hello, Officer. We're sure seeing a lot of each other today, aren't we?"*

"Sorry to bother you, but would you mind telling me your name?" McKenna asked as politely as he could.

"No bother," the cameraman answered, looking up at McKenna sheepishly. "It's Mike."

"Mike, could you give Heidi a message for me?"

"What's the message?"

"Tell her that I admire her persistence, but that if she keeps playing games with me Fox Five will be the only network not getting an interview. Got it?"

"I'll tell her."

"Thanks, Mike," McKenna said. "Hope to see you again sometime this afternoon, but not before. Understand?"

"Yeah, enough said. I'll see you this afternoon."

I guess I showed them, McKenna thought as he got back into his taxi.

22

This time McKenna breezed through the Sunshine obstacle and Andino met him at his office door. The ME looked exhausted past the point of caring; he had a two-day growth of beard, his eyes were bloodshot, his shoulders slouched, and his shirt was soiled with stains whose source McKenna didn't even want to think about. In spite of his physical state, Andino was all business. "C'mon in and let's work a few things out," he told McKenna as they shook hands.

McKenna followed Andino into his office and sat across from him at the ME's very untidy desk. It was covered with autopsy-report folders. McKenna could see that many of the pages inside the folders were dog-eared and that Andino had scrawled a long poison checklist on each of the report covers. From what he could see, it appeared to McKenna that Andino had scratched out each poison.

"I guess your lab's told you by now that your killer's been using some kind of cyanide compound," Andino stated.

"Not yet. They only got the wine bottle late last night and our chemists are all civilians, work strictly nine to five. I think they're getting their first look at it as we speak."

"Then we'll save them some time and conserve their sample. They're gonna need it later because your killer has come up with some innovations in cyanide poisoning. He's found a way to kill using less cyanide than has ever been used to poison anyone. That's how he's been getting away with it. The minute amount he's using doesn't register on our toxicological screening tests."

"How much cyanide is a *minute amount*?" McKenna asked.

"About as much as you'd get from sniffing some common household insecticides. For instance, I've got a pretty good nose and I can usually tell a cyanide case as soon as I open them up. Cyanide sort of smells like dirty socks, but I couldn't smell it when I opened up Juan Bosco. He had only one part cyanide to thirty thousand parts blood in him. I had to do some extensive testing to find it."

"You're sure he died from cyanide poisoning?" McKenna asked.

"Absolutely. Cyanide and something else, something we haven't come across yet. I suspect our killer has found an enzyme that dramatically enhances the effect of cyanide."

"So this new enzyme is also a poison?"

"No, legally the cyanide is the poison. The enzyme just combines with it to produce a synergistic effect in the human body when it enters the bloodstream. But the result is death by cyanide poisoning."

"Will you be able to find this enzyme?"

"No. There are so many enzymes running around in the human body, especially the diseased bodies that we've been dealing with in these cases, that I have no hope of isolating it," Andino conceded. "Your lab is going to have to come up with it because they're working with a better sample than I am."

"What makes their sample better?" McKenna asked. "They only have about ten drops of wine."

"With the advances in semimicro qualitative analysis, that makes no difference. What makes theirs better is merely a question of concentration. If the killer put three drops of cyanide in the pint of wine, they've got something close to a point-one-percent poison-to-wine solution. Once the victim drinks it and winds up with me, the solution is much less concentrated since it's been absorbed by the ten pints of blood in the body."

"Aren't there already a lot of enzymes in wine?"

"Yes. Not as many as there are in the human body, but there's lots of them," Andino conceded. "That shouldn't stop your lab people if you do your job."

"And what exactly is my job in this case?"

"You have to go out and get your lab something we call a control sample. Ideally, it will come from the same barrel of wine that the killer's wine came from so that his wine and the control sample will have all the enzymes in common, except one. That'll be the enzyme they should be looking at, the one the killer added."

He's right, but finding that control sample is gonna call for some real detective work, McKenna thought. I have to find out where the killer bought the wine and hope that store still has more left from the same batch. "Okay, I find the control sample, deliver it to the lab, and they isolate the enzyme. Then what? They duplicate it?"

"Probably not. Enzymes are pretty complex proteins, difficult to duplicate. Once your chemists identify the composition and form of the enzyme, they'd be better off finding out where it occurs in nature, which means finding which plant or animal in this world produces it."

"And if they can't?" McKenna asked.

"Then we lose. We'll know the victims were murdered, but you'll never be able to prove it in court because the amount of cyanide the killer's using is not enough to be considered a lethal dose under our present understanding of the poison and how it works. His lawyer would just say the victims weren't poisoned and we couldn't prove otherwise.''

"So catching the killer isn't good enough," McKenna said. "Without a confession, we also have to find this enzyme and then demonstrate to a jury that what has always been a less-than-lethal dose of cyanide combined with this mystery enzyme has been used by our killer to poison his victims.''

"Now you've got it," Andino said.

"How do you propose the DA present that to a jury?''

"Easy. He'll call me to the stand. I'll explain the signs of cyanide poisoning in a body and I'll testify that the bodies of the victims exhibited these signs, although I'll have to admit that they were misdiagnosed at the time. Then I'm going to tell them exactly how cyanide poisoning works. I'll then—''

"Sorry to interrupt," McKenna said. "First, why don't you tell *me* how cyanide poisoning works.''

"Certainly. The poison is usually a strong solution of either sodium cyanide or potassium cyanide. After it's ingested, it reacts chemically with the hydrochloric acid in the stomach to produce hydrogen cyanide, a deadly gas that prevents the blood from absorbing oxygen from the lungs. The red blood cells don't get the oxygen necessary for survival and the victim asphyxiates.''

"Like choking?" McKenna asked.

"Exactly. The victim feels dizzy and sits down or lies down. Then he faints and death soon follows. In some instances there are convulsions preceding death, but we have no evidence that happened in our cases and I don't think it did. The effect of the enzyme the killer's using with the cyanide was total, and death came too quickly after our victims went unconscious. Have I been clear enough?''

"Yes, I understood it," McKenna said. "Go on. What do you do for the jury next?''

"After that, it's simple. I'll take the enzyme, mix it with a minute amount of cyanide, put it in some Wild Irish Rose, set up a video camera, and then murder the largest chimpanzee we can find. When the jury sees the tape of our chimp sipping some wine and then croaking, it's my bet that your killer is convicted of every case you can legally connect him to.''

Not necessarily, John. First we'd need to have a jury smart enough to understand the basic science lesson you propose giving them, McKenna thought. Defense lawyers hate smart jurors in a case where there's going to be scientific evidence presented and they try to get a jury too dumb to understand the evidence. They succeed all the time.

The more McKenna heard from Andino, the more he despaired of convicting the killer, even if he did manage to catch him. Now for more bad news, he thought. "Got any idea how many cases we're talking about?" he asked.

"Some idea, considering I've got four positive victims so far among the bodies we still have here.''

"Is Rodney Bailey one of them?''

"Yes. We said he froze to death, but he's got the usual small amount of cyanide in him that Dr. O'Malley missed when we didn't know enough to look for it.''

That leaves three, McKenna thought. There's Benny Foster and Juan Bosco, but Mickey Weyland was killed more than three weeks ago, so he should be gone and buried by now. Andino can't be positive about Mickey yet, so that means that he's got a body here I don't know about.

Andino saw the perplexed look on McKenna's face and answered the question before it was asked. "Tyrone Lewis. Male, black, homeless, age forty. Got him in three days ago, thought he died of pneumonia. But since he was HIV positive, I decided to pull him from the freezers and give him a look myself this morning. He's got a touch of cyanide in him."

"Where did he die?"

"Men's Shelter, Bowery and East Third. Ninth Precinct, isn't it?"

"Yeah, which means our killer really gets around. So far, we've got murders in three different precincts," McKenna answered, then decided to turn the tables and tell Andino something he didn't know. "Now I've got one for you," he said.

"Which one of these unfortunates are you going to tell me about?" Andino asked, nonplussed, as he pointed to the autopsy reports scattered across his desk.

"Mickey Weyland, arrived here on January ninth. The last person he was seen with was the killer."

"Ah, Mickey Weyland," Andino said as he pulled a report from the bunch. "The train-yard case, wasn't he?"

"Yeah, but I'm afraid there's a problem with that one for you. My lieutenant had some suspicions and doubts on Mickey's death, so he called here and got your Dr. Wright. Turned out that all he got from Wright was a lecture explaining that an increase in AIDS-related deaths was to be expected by anybody who knew anything."

"I see. Wright's always been a charmer, loves talking down to people. But what's the problem for me?"

"My boss intends to come down here today to have a little chat with Wright."

"What's his name?"

"Tommy Ward. He's a heavyweight in the department."

"Nice guy?"

"I wouldn't go that far. I'd call him a tough guy, but I like him."

"Good. A tough guy is even better. You can even tell him that I'll hold Wright while he works him over."

"You really do hate him, don't you?" McKenna asked.

"Now more than ever. He's the kind who got where he is by going to all the right parties. He's wonderful to anyone who can help him, but he craps all over everyone else. When did Ward first talk to him?"

"January tenth, I believe."

"Then I intend to hold Dr. Wright responsible for every murder after January tenth. If he had addressed Ward's inquiry, it's possible that maybe ten deaths could have been prevented during the past three weeks."

The number staggered McKenna. "Wait a minute. Did you say ten?"

"Yeah, maybe ten deaths. Hope you forgive me, but I hate incompetence in high places. I checked the time sheets. While I was gone the latest Wright ever stayed here was six o'clock. Imagine that. The worst serial killer this city has ever known is running loose and our acting chief medical examiner is going home at six."

"Okay, Wright is a douche bag. Now can we back up here for a minute to the ten deaths? Could it be that many?"

"At least. Probably more if half the cases I'm looking at turn out to be positive for cyanide. We'll know by tomorrow night, after we dig them up."

McKenna was dreading the prospect, but knew it was inevitable. Any additional victims were going to wind up as his cases and, legally, bodies in a homicide were looked at as just another form of evidence. As with any other evidence, a proper chain of police custody had to be established and maintained by the investigating officer, so he had to be there when they were disinterred. "Are you sure you'll be able to tell if they're victims or not on the second autopsy?" he asked.

"What do you mean?"

"What I mean is that, during the autopsy, don't you drain all the blood before you turn them over for burial?"

"Sure, but now I know what I'm looking for and there will be enough dead red blood cells in their livers to tell me if there's cyanide there or not. Cyanide's got a pretty good shelf life."

McKenna saw no way around it. "When?" he asked.

"I'll be waiting here at nine tomorrow morning with one of our bigger trucks. How's that?"

"Just wonderful. How many orders am I applying for?"

"Twenty-one," Andino said as he gathered all the case folders on his desk and passed them to McKenna. "Besides the bodies we have in the building, that's every homeless death we've handled in January where I wasn't absolutely certain of the cause of death after reading the autopsy report. Now I have the big question for you."

"You want to know how I'm doing for a suspect?" McKenna guessed.

"Yes. I take it you have some ideas on where to look."

"Some. I think I'm gonna be looking pretty hard at the Bellevue staff."

"You think it's somebody with access to their medical records?" Andino asked.

"Yes, I do. He's killing Bellevue patients who are HIV positive, so it has to be someone with enough access to know that Benny Foster was HIV positive. I think our killer is a doctor or a pharmacist there."

"I agree," Andino stated. "He has to have quite a background in chemistry to come up with the mixture he's using and to have gotten away with it for so long."

"Can you suggest anyone at Bellevue who could help me out?"

"Jim Heaney. He's been their personnel director for a couple of years. Nice guy. When do you want to see him?"

"Sometime this afternoon would be great. I'd like to go to the lab and then get these court orders out of the way before I see him."

"Fine. Get to work and I'll set it up. Give me a call when you get to the DA's office and I'll fax you whatever statements you need to get the orders."

"Anything else I should know?" McKenna asked.

"Probably, but right now you know everything I know. We're both learning along the way, maybe you more than me."

"How's that?"

"You should have learned by now that maybe that cushy job you had in headquarters wasn't so bad after all."

John, are you out of your mind? What could be better than being a New York City detective working a big case? McKenna wanted to say, but didn't. "No, I guess it wasn't so bad," he said instead as he shifted the pile of autopsy reports and stood up. He stopped at the door to thank Andino, but the medical examiner was already asleep at his desk.

23

McKenna called Ward as soon as he left the morgue, told him about the Tyrone Lewis case in the 9th Precinct, and reported the details of the rest of his conversation with Andino. Except to say that he would have the Homicide Squad look into the new case, Ward took it in without comment. Then he had some news for McKenna. Inspector Scagnelli had called from the lab and wanted to talk to him, and Chris Saffran was in the squad office, waiting for him.

"How's he look?" McKenna asked, apprehensive about the impression that Saffran's appearance might be making on the orthodox squad commander.

"Fine. Why? He been sick or something?"

"No, I was just wondering if he had a nice suit on because I want to take him to the Silver Swan for lunch," McKenna ad-libbed.

"Of course he has a suit on. This is a detective squad office and he's going to be working here. Why wouldn't he have a suit on?"

"You're right, Lieutenant. You have him doing anything right now?"

"Everybody works. I got him typing up the case-assignment sheets for the Homicide Squad. He says he knows quite a few of the possible victims you and Maureen came up with last night."

"Can you spare him at eleven?"

"Yeah, he'll be done by then. The Silver Swan at eleven?"

"Yes, thanks. Have you heard anything yet from Maureen and Bender?" McKenna asked.

"Not yet, but when I do I'll let them know that Andino says Bailey was a victim."

McKenna next called Scagnelli at the lab. The police administrative aide who answered told him that the inspector was there, but wasn't available at the moment.

"Where is he? The bathroom?" McKenna guessed.

"Yes. He hasn't been feeling too well this morning."

McKenna wasn't surprised. "The newspapers?" he asked.

"You got it. Every time he sees one, he goes into a tirade about Detective Walsh. Carries on until he makes himself sick."

"And I bet everyone up there has at least one copy of the *News* and the *Post* prominently displayed on their desks, don't they?"

"I wouldn't want to say," the PAA replied. "However, it does seem that everyone up here is unusually well informed today."

McKenna imagined that they would be. Scagnelli was a nice man who had been in the Detective Bureau as long as anyone could remember and he was considered one of the department's scholars, having worked his way through pharmacy school at night. He was also considered one of the hardest working men around, which was okay for him but tough on everyone who worked for him since he expected the same dedication to duty from his subordinates that he exhibited himself. Even the hard workers hated it when he was around because he was always into every little task they were performing, standing over them with suggestions or polite constructive criticism. The result was that the entire Scientific Research Division was solidly in Walsh's corner. He was their hero and Scagnelli's Achilles' heel.

Before hanging up, McKenna asked the PAA to inform Scagnelli that he would be at the lab in ten minutes.

The police lab occupies the eighth floor of the Police Academy on East 20th Street, a few blocks from the Gramercy Park Hotel. Second only to the FBI Laboratory in Washington in the number of cases handled, there is a difference in the type of work performed. The main function of the police lab is to analyze and issue lab reports on the tons of illegal drugs seized by the department each year, so the majority of the personnel employed there are civilian chemists. However, like the FBI Laboratory, the police lab has a Documents Section, a Latent Prints Section, a Ballistics Section, and is equipped to do all the exotic tasks such as comparing paint samples in hit-and-run accidents and matching tool striations in burglary cases.

Police administrators across the country generally acknowledge that the quality of the work performed by the New York City Police Lab is superior, and the people who work there are proud of their reputation. They are even prouder of the fact that, because they are trained and equipped to handle such a myriad of tasks, rarely is it considered necessary by anyone to send any evidence to the FBI Laboratory for analysis or advice. Even to suggest sending anything to Washington was considered bad form in the police lab unless, of course, the person making the suggestion was Joe Walsh, a longtime first-grade detective and, naturally, above reproach. Any such suggestion made by Walsh was recognized by the lab staff for exactly what it was—another justifiable Walsh ploy to irritate the fine man who was driving the rest of them crazy.

As he stood at the open door of Scagnelli's small auxiliary office at the lab, McKenna's first thought was that Walsh might have overdone it this time. Scagnelli was normally one of those health nuts who jogged through their lunch breaks, never ate anything that tasted good, and whose top desk drawers were crammed with things like fiber wafers, vitamin supplements, and those "tasty little health snacks" that could make an ordinary man puke. Yet there he was, sitting behind his desk smoking a Lucky and using an empty bottle of Maalox as an ashtray as he read a chemical reference book. McKenna noticed that the trash can was filled with crumpled newspapers.

"I see you're having a tough day, Inspector," McKenna said, understating the obvious. "Want me to come back later?"

"That glory-hunting prick," was Scagnelli's only answer, but McKenna wasn't sure if the comment was meant to be heard by him.

McKenna waited for more, but there was nothing coming. Feeling awkward standing at the door, McKenna said loudly, "You wanted to see me, Inspector?"

Scagnelli looked up, only then noticing McKenna. "Come on in, Brian," he said, putting a polite smile on his face as he dropped his butt into the Maalox bottle. He stood and shook McKenna's hand, as courteous as ever. "Thanks for coming so quickly. I've got a problem for you, so pull up a chair."

"It's cyanide, but not enough to kill anyone?" McKenna guessed as he sat down, but regretted it at once because Scagnelli's smile faded into a frown as he slumped into his chair.

"Yes, it's cyanide. But how'd you know?"

"Dr. Andino told me, but it took him all night to find out what your people came up with in under two hours," McKenna stated, seeking to restore the smile.

Instead, Scagnelli got introspective on him. "I'm surprised he was able to come up with it all," he mumbled, more to himself than to McKenna.

"He's good, but like I said, it took him all night."

"Well, that's one bright spot," Scagnelli said. "It only took my two best men just under four hours. Of course, we were working with a more concentrated sample than Dr. Andino was."

Four hours? McKenna thought. He checked his watch and saw it was just after ten. "How did you get your chemists here so early?" he asked.

Scagnelli chuckled. "I heard some nonsense last night about Walsh recommending your wine be sent to Washington. According to that prick, our lab couldn't do it right. So I got up early this morning and kidnapped my two best men. Drove to their houses, pounded on their doors, and picked them up myself."

"I guess Walsh was wrong," McKenna offered.

"Sure was. Under four hours. It wouldn't even be in Washington yet if anyone listened to him. Unfortunately, we've still got work to do on it."

"You mean finding the enzyme?"

McKenna's question surprised Scagnelli, but only for a moment. "That Andino is sharp, isn't he? He put it together real quick," he said.

"Yeah, but he didn't have all the answers. He said something about needing a control sample to compare with the poisoned wine so you can identify the enzyme."

"Already working on it. Should know by tomorrow exactly what vat the wine in the bottle came from and exactly what store it was shipped to."

McKenna was relieved that what had sounded to him like a monumental task an hour earlier seemed to be child's play to Scagnelli. "How are you doing this so fast?" he asked.

"Nothing to it. Since all those product-tampering cases over the past few years, most manufacturers have come up with ways to identify dates of manufacture and lot numbers for each sample of their products. The Wild Irish Rose people encrypt the information in a code stenciled in two places on the bottle."

"You didn't have to send them the bottle, did you?"

"Never. When I called them up, I wound up talking to one of their senior vice presidents. Naturally, he was very concerned when I told him how his product was being abused, so he's sending someone here to read the codes."

"Very helpful of them," McKenna commented. "How are you doing with the fingerprints?"

It was like McKenna had lit a fuse. "What's the matter, you don't believe the papers? Walsh has just about found the guy. The rest of us are just part of his supporting cast, not worthy of mention," Scagnelli said, his voice getting higher and shriller with each word.

"Just asking, and no, I don't believe the papers," McKenna said as slowly, calmly, and softly as he could under the circumstances.

It worked. Scagnelli calmed down a bit, going from rage to plain anger. He took a few deep breaths, then reached into the trash can, pulled out the *News*, and opened the paper to the Walsh interview on page four. "Listen to what I have to deal with," he said calmly as he read the article. "Walsh says to this reporter, 'I was called in because of the potentially disastrous implications of this case.' " Scagnelli stopped to look at McKenna. "Now who called him in, I wonder. Was it you?"

"No."

"I didn't think so, and Lord knows it certainly wasn't me. Now, who would call that guy in? Chief Tavlin?" Scagnelli asked, then answered his own question. "No. Tommy Ward? No. So who could it have been?"

"Inspector, we both know that nobody called him in, but he did get nine latent prints off that bottle, didn't he?" McKenna asked, hoping to get back to the point.

"That's what Wonderful Walsh told the papers. Told them he lifted nine latents from that wine bottle and just about solved the case for you. Don't you feel relieved knowing that?" Scagnelli asked sarcastically.

"He didn't get nine prints?"

"Oh, he got nine, but now let's see just how wonderful a job Walsh really did. Five of the latents belong to the victim, Juan Bosco. We don't suspect suicide, so that's no help. Right?"

"It's some help, Inspector. It proves we have the right bottle."

"All right, but it doesn't help find the killer. Another two latents belong to a Police Officer Saffran from the Thirteenth Precinct. I understand that he's a little flaky, but he's not a suspect. Right?"

"No, I'm not seriously considering him as a suspect."

"So what are we left with?"

"Two latent prints."

"Right," Scagnelli said as he sat back in his chair, smiling. "Two, not nine. Big difference, and those two prints probably belong to some clerk in a liquor store."

"Probably. How good are these two latents of liquor-store clerks?"

It was the question Scagnelli didn't want to hear. Once again his smile was gone, replaced by a look of abject misery. "He got lucky. They look pretty good."

"Can I see them?"

Scagnelli lifted the chemical reference book on his desk. Under it were Walsh's report and a stack of five-by-seven photo enlargements of the latent fingerprints Walsh had taken from the wine bottle. Scagnelli rummaged through the photos, pulled out two, and handed them to McKenna.

"Yeah, he got real lucky," McKenna said, trying hard not to smile as he examined the two photos. They were almost perfect, and certainly the best lifts McKenna had ever seen. Although not a fingerprint expert, he would have no trouble classifying one of the prints himself if he knew whether it was from the right or left hand of the donor. The other latent lift photo showed only the top half of the donor's print, but not because of any shortcoming on Walsh's part; knowing Walsh, McKenna was sure it was because that was the only part of the donor's finger that had touched the bottle.

"I think you need eleven matching points from just one latent print to make a positive legal identification of a suspect, don't you?" McKenna asked innocently.

"Yeah, eleven identifying points," Scagnelli conceded.

"How many identifying points do you think this print contains?" McKenna asked, holding up the photo of the partial print.

"Maybe twenty-five," Scagnelli said glumly.

"And this one?" McKenna asked, holding up the full-print photo.

"Maybe a hundred."

"So when we find our liquor-store clerk, he won't be able to deny he sold someone that bottle of Wild Irish Rose, will he?"

"No," Scagnelli said.

"Let's say for a moment that at least one of those two latent prints belongs to the killer," McKenna suggested. "Is there any way of finding him with just the latent?"

Scagnelli chuckled at that. "See, that's where Walsh was cagey again. He said he'd 'ascertain the identity of the killer,' which is his way of saying, 'You tell me who you have in mind as a suspect, give me his prints, and I'll tell you if he's the guy.' That doesn't help you if you don't have a suspect in mind," he said.

McKenna knew Scagnelli was right, but he had hoped for more. "Don't we have a computer search system in place for identifying burglars on the basis of latent prints left at the scene?" he asked.

"Sure, but the only prints in the search file are persons arrested for burglary since 1976."

"Let's say for a moment that this is the killer's print," McKenna said, holding up the full-print photo. "One hundred points is about the best latent print anyone can come up with, isn't it?"

"Yes, but unless your killer has been arrested for burglary, his prints aren't in the search system," Scagnelli repeated. "I see where you're leading, but it can't be done. There's almost two hundred thousand sets of burglars' fingerprints in the system, so it takes the computer almost four hours to get a hit on one good print."

"Inspector, are you telling me it would be impossible to reconfigure the system to search our entire criminal history file if it turns out that this hundred-point print doesn't belong to a liquor-store clerk?"

"Presently, yes, it would be impossible. Our present computer doesn't have the capacity to store our complete criminal history file."

"Suppose we only did left hands?" McKenna asked. "Does our computer have the capacity to store all the left hands from our entire criminal history file?"

"Yes, but it would be very costly and time-consuming. I take it you're assuming the killer is left-handed and that, if one of those latents on that bottle is his, it comes from his left hand?"

"We know he throws lefty, so there's a good chance."

"I hate to sound callous, but, realistically speaking, the cost of what you're suggesting isn't worth solving, what? Three or four murders out of the fifteen hundred we have in this city every year?"

"Dr. Andino thinks we're talking about ten or more, and I think he's right." McKenna paused to let the number sink in. Scagnelli had no comment, but sat straight up in his chair. "If so, we're dealing with the worst serial killer in this city's history," McKenna added. "That's gonna generate a lot of media interest, and I'm talking about the national media. If we don't catch this guy soon, we're gonna be under a lot of pressure and answering a lot of questions, especially if he kills again."

"I see. You think they're going to be asking questions about those latent prints and what we're doing about them?"

"Exactly. If one of these prints belongs to the killer, then that's what reporters are gonna be asking me. Remember, we're in the nineties and everyone's programmed to think anything's possible with computers. I don't think they'll ask me anything about the department's budget."

"So it might have to be done, eventually, no matter what the cost or chances of success," Scagnelli commented. "But think about this. If your killer hasn't been arrested before and his prints aren't on file, we'd be wasting millions of dollars for nothing."

This guy certainly has a way with words, McKenna thought. But he's right. "I'm hoping it doesn't come to that. I hope we can get him without going through this whole computer-search business," he said.

"Then you better do it soon. You can bet that, with Walsh around, those reporters are gonna be asking questions," Scagnelli mused. "He'll be running at the mouth telling everyone how good his latents are, meaning, of course, how good he is."

"I'll try to keep that in mind."

McKenna was happy to leave Scagnelli and the Police Academy. He was sure that Walsh had Scagnelli just one or two headlines away from a complete nervous breakdown. McKenna couldn't understand why two such obviously competent people couldn't find a middle ground somewhere, but he didn't want to waste time clouding his mind with problems he couldn't affect. He was tired and already busy enough doing everything he could think of to identify his killer, but still he felt optimistic. As far as he could see, things seemed to be falling into place. In one day he had discovered that a serial killer was active and loose in New York, he was a few days away from learning the number of victims, he knew basically how the murders were being committed, and had developed a few ideas on how to find his man. The only thing he hadn't thought much about was the reason, real or imaginary, why his adversary was murdering homeless people who were going to die soon anyway.

As he walked to his lunch meeting with Saffran, motive was on McKenna's mind. He didn't notice the panhandler on the corner of Park Avenue South and East 20th Street until the man was directly in front of him. "Sir, can you spare some change?'' the man pleaded as he extended his arm, blocking McKenna's path.

McKenna was startled and stepped back to take in the panhandler, but a glance told him the man was no threat. He was emaciated, white, bearded, and somewhere between thirty and fifty years of age. Scrawled on a cardboard sign around his neck was:

I'M NOT GAY, BUT I'VE GOT AIDS
2 MONTHS TO LIVE

The man's extended arm held a coffee container with some change in it. The panhandler shook the cup, rattling the change, and repeated, ''Can you spare some change, buddy?''

This is a real sad case, McKenna thought. He reached into his pocket, pulled out two singles, and placed them in the cup. For a moment, the panhandler's face lit up, but then McKenna saw the man grimace in pain as he dropped his arm to remove the two dollars from the cup. ''You okay?'' McKenna asked.

''Yeah, I'm just living through the pain.''

''What hurts?''

''Everything, but especially under my arms. It hurts to raise and lower them.''

''Why's that?''

''B-cell lymphoma. It's a cancer in the glands under my arms. That's where the AIDS got me,'' the panhandler explained as he put the two dollars in his pocket. Then he looked closely at McKenna. ''You're that Detective McKenna that's been in the papers, aren't you?''

''Yeah, that's me,'' McKenna answered, a little surprised to be recognized by this man, so he took the time to give the panhandler another once-over. What struck him about the man's appearance was that all his clothes seemed to be too big for him, from his shabby brown overcoat to his pants. Even his shoes looked loose on him.

A number of thoughts hit McKenna that really piqued his interest. ''Those your clothes?'' he asked.

''Yep. Had 'em for years, but they used to fit me better. Why?''

''Just wondering.'' McKenna reached into his pocket, took out a twenty, and handed it to the surprised panhandler. ''I think we're gonna be pals,'' he said.

''Nice start for a friendship,'' the panhandler replied as he put the twenty in his pocket.

''Mind telling me your name?''

''Jake.''

''Just Jake?''

''Believe it or not, they used to call me Big Jake,'' he said, smiling ruefully. ''Now they call me Jake the Snake.''

''You got an appetite?''

''Some days I do, some days I don't.''

''How about today?''

''Today's a good day for me. I'm starving.''

''Good. You like German food?''

''Love it, but I haven't had it for years.''

"Then how would you like to be my guest in the best German restaurant around?"

"Sure, but why?" Jake asked suspiciously.

"Because I think you know some things I need to know. We'll talk while we eat, if you don't mind."

"No, I don't mind. Is it far? I'm not too good at walking anymore."

"Right down the block."

It took Jake less than a second to decide. "Deal," he said, then walked a few steps to the building line and picked up a trash bag that was resting there.

"Jake, if you don't mind, can you lose the sign?" McKenna asked apologetically.

"No problem." Jake took the sign from around his neck and placed it in his trash bag of belongings. Then he surprised McKenna when he took a brush out of his bag and ran it through his hair, possibly for the first time in days. It took him a minute to get the tangles out, but when he did, he reached again into his bag, took out a bottle of Vitalis, and applied a handful to his hair before slicking it back with the brush. "How do I look?" he asked when he was done, posing for inspection.

"Much better."

"Much better, but not great," Jake said with irony in his voice. He picked up the trash bag again and took a few steps toward McKenna, but the burden of the bag was obviously causing him pain.

"Want me to carry that for you?" McKenna asked.

"I dunno. Can I trust you with all my treasure?" Jake asked, smiling.

McKenna didn't answer, just held out his hand. Jake gave him the bag and the two men crossed Park Avenue South and slowly walked the half block to the Silver Swan.

McKenna liked the Silver Swan. Since it was only a few blocks from the Gramercy Park Hotel, he was a steady customer, going there as often as he could. Unfortunately, as often as he could was not as often as he would have liked. His appearances there were usually limited to the occasions when he could talk Angelita into taking a break from the hot and spicy Mexican, Indian, Afghan, and Turkish foods she favored. Whenever he succeeded, thereby providing himself with a gastrointestinal lifesaving session at the Silver Swan, she always pretended to be doing him a favor. But McKenna knew better.

For one, he knew that during her pregnancy Angelita had developed a thing for their potato pancakes smothered in sour cream. Naturally, she had wanted to keep that sinful proclivity a secret from McKenna, so she had enlisted the services of one of the hotel doormen to pick the goodies up for her, firmly instructing him that McKenna was not to be informed of these missions. That was in June, and as far as that experienced New York doorman was concerned, Christmas was right around the corner. He called McKenna at work that day, and every subsequent time Angelita went German on him, giving him the complete details of every one of her orders.

By July, it wasn't limited to the potato pancakes. Someplace along the line either Renatta or Mike, the owners of the Silver Swan, had wisely mixed some of their potato dumplings into one of Angelita's take-out orders, and another sinful habit immediately took shape. After that, sometimes it was the potato pancakes, sometimes it was the dumplings, but frequently Angelita had ordered both. Then she would spend the night doing penance in the form of exercise, amazing Mc-Kenna when she had gained only thirty pounds in the nine months despite her secret high-carbohydrate diet.

Still, time-honored matrimonial customs had to be maintained, so McKenna never let on and always had to beg in order to bring Angelita to the restaurant he knew she preferred to go to anyway. He was a traditionalist and expected nothing less from her.

When McKenna walked in with Jake, he got his usual ebullient greeting from Renatta, but Mike was behind the bar and somewhat more reserved as he eyed McKenna's new dinner companion and the trash bag McKenna was carrying.

Jake was certainly out of place and fidgeted nervously while McKenna answered Renatta's inquiries about Angelita and the baby. "And who's your friend?" she finally asked McKenna once the amenities were over.

"This is my new pal, Jake. He's helping me out on the case I'm working on."

"Really? Then you'll both be having lunch?" Renatta looked Jake up and down, but kept the polite smile on her face and whatever opinion she had of Jake's appearance to herself. "A table in the back?" she suggested tactfully.

"That would be fine," McKenna said. "I'm expecting another friend in a few minutes." Renatta didn't look pleased with that news until McKenna added, "He's a cop."

"Fine." Renatta showed them to the last table in the rear and gave them menus. "Anything to drink?"

"I'll have a Coke," McKenna said.

"Make mine a diet Coke," Jake said. "Trying to take off a few more pounds."

"No wine with dinner?" McKenna asked Jake.

"I'll have some if you do."

"Then I guess we're not having any."

"You got the problem, too?"

"Yep," McKenna acknowledged. "For me, one is too many and ten is never enough." He nodded to Renatta and she was gone. She returned in a moment with the two Cokes, a basket of German bread, and a plate of butter. "Are you going to wait for your friend before you order?" she asked.

"For the main course, yeah," McKenna answered, then ordered pea soup for himself and Jake. As soon as Renatta left, Jake started on the bread, smearing a piece of pumpernickel with butter. It was gone in three quick bites, but Jake was remembering his manners. He dabbed at the corners of his mouth with his napkin before he buttered another piece.

"I guess you're real hungry," McKenna commented.

"I feel hungry, but I haven't been able to eat much lately."

"You going for chemo?"

"Naw, why should I go through that shit? Be sick all the time, have all my hair fall out, and for what? If it worked and I was lucky enough to beat this brand of cancer I got, something else would just pop up to kill me."

Jake said it in such a matter-of-fact manner that McKenna didn't think he'd mind talking about it. "So you're just resigned to dying?" he asked.

Jake smiled, more to himself than to McKenna. "I used to think I was a fighter, but I'm just about ready to go," he said. "This AIDS has got me beat."

"What is it that gets you, mainly? The pain?"

"Pain's a part of it, along with the fatigue. But that's just the physical discomfort and I could live with it. The part that gets me is just knowing that, in a little while, I'm not gonna be around. Bringing your own mortality into sharp focus like that screws up your mind."

"Nobody lives forever," McKenna offered, but felt awkard as soon as it said it.

Jake didn't seem to notice. "But most of the people walking the earth right now expect to be around next year and are busy making plans for their lives. Mine's over and I know it. There's just nothing to think about and no plans to make. That's what's driving me crazy."

"Suppose you had something to do every day, something that you really wanted to accomplish before you died. Would that make it any better?"

"Like what?" Jake asked. "I'm not in shape to do much of anything."

Since meeting Jake, a theory had been forming in McKenna's mind, but he needed more information to test it. "How'd you get the disease, if you don't mind my asking?"

"Bad meat in the can," Jake said simply.

Jake's statement caught McKenna by surprise. "Wait a minute," he protested. "According to your sign, you're not gay. What is that, a lie to get more money from folks?"

"No, it's not a lie. Like the sign says, I've got AIDS, but I'm not gay," Jake said matter-of-factly.

McKenna wanted to pursue that immediately, but Renatta arrived with two large bowls of pea soup. He could see that Jake's mind, for the moment, was on the soup and nothing else. As soon as she put the bowl in front of him, Jake took a spoonful, then blew on it to cool it before sipping the spoon dry. "Delicious," was his only comment before he repeated the process, obviously enjoying himself while McKenna tried a spoonful of his own soup. It was too hot, so he just sat back and watched Jake.

He didn't have long to wait. Jake took only a few more spoonfuls before he pushed his bowl away, surprising McKenna.

"Hope you don't mind if I don't finish this, but I want to leave some room to try everything I can," Jake said as he again politely dabbed the corners of his mouth with his napkin.

"Suit yourself, Jake. Try anything you like."

"Thanks. You were saying?"

"I was asking how you got the disease."

"Jail sex."

McKenna understood at once. AIDS was running rampant through the jails. It had progressed to the point that New York City's jails were no longer overcrowded, but the funds and personnel necessary to treat the infected inmates was still causing the Department of Correction's budget to skyrocket. The city's main correctional facility, Riker's Island, had a large and well-equipped infirmary, but there were just too many AIDS cases among the inmates. Every day, busloads of inmates were brought for treatment to St. Claire's Hospital in Manhattan.

"Do you know who gave it to you?" McKenna asked.

"No."

"Were you a willing participant?"

"Of course not, but you know how jail is. I was a big guy, but it didn't help much," Jake explained. "In jail, in order to survive you have to go along to get along."

It wasn't the first time McKenna had heard that, but the man in front of him was living proof that the axiom didn't always work. "Let me ask you this. If you knew who gave it to you, would you kill him if there was a chance you could get away with it?"

"No."

The answer surprised McKenna. "Why not?"

"For one, he's probably dead already."

"But if he wasn't?"

"I'd let him live and suffer, just like I am."

That puts a big hole in my theory, McKenna thought, but maybe Jake's viewpoint is unique. How would I feel in his situation? he wondered.

Jake watched McKenna mull over the problem, obviously disturbed at the consternation the answer to his host's question had caused. "Mind if I clear a few things up for you?" he asked.

"If you could," McKenna answered.

"Okay. It's like this. I never expected to die rich at a ripe old age. I used to think that bad things always happened to me and I figured that wasn't going to change. So I'm really not too surprised at the shape I'm in."

"That's it? Just plain acceptance?" McKenna asked. "Seems like a rather magnanimous attitude to me."

"Not if you look at it the way I've come to see it. You see, I've done some thinking about my life and I've come up with a few conclusions that explain to me why things are the way they are. In my case, at least."

Jake had McKenna's total attention, but he appeared to have some reservations about revealing any more of his thoughts. While McKenna watched and waited, Jake picked up his spoon and shined it with his napkin, lost in thought.

"Please, go on," McKenna implored. "This could be important to me and we've got a deal. I need to know how someone in your situation thinks about it."

Jake put down his spoon, folded his hands in front of him on the table, and looked McKenna directly in the eye. "Why?" he asked.

"Because I think the killer I'm looking for is in much the same shape you're in."

"AIDS?"

"Uh-huh. I think he's got B-cell lymphoma, same as you. I have to know what's going through his mind."

Jake weighed McKenna's statement for a moment, then appeared to accept it at face value. "Okay, I'll tell you," he said as he leaned back in his chair and looked at the ceiling. "As close to the end as I am, it does no good lying to yourself. The way I see it, you get out of life what you put into it, and I haven't put too much positive effort into mine. I've wasted a lot of time and done some things I'm not proud of, so don't think I'll be missed.''

"Suppose things had been different for you. Suppose you'd worked hard all your life, did all the right things, and you had expected to die of old age, a rich man.''

"Okay, let's suppose that,'' Jake said, sitting up straight. "Then how'd I get it?''

"Let's suppose you'd worked so hard that you'd become a doctor. Then, through no fault of your own, you got AIDS from treating homeless patients, people you've come to think haven't put too much effort into their lives. Would that change your outlook?''

"I guess it would.''

"How?''

Jake thought the proposition over for a moment. "I'd be mad as hell,'' he answered.

"Mad enough to kill whoever you thought gave it to you, if he was still alive?''

"Absolutely. I'd make sure that worthless prick didn't outlive me.''

McKenna had finished his soup and Jake was savoring an appetizer of creamed herring when the new Chris Saffran arrived wearing a blue pin-striped suit, a yellow power tie, and a pair of well-shined black wing tips. Gone were the earring and the attitude. Saffran emanated confidence and looked like a rising young executive in a fancy brokerage firm.

McKenna was too astonished by the change in Saffran's appearance and manner to say anything as the new man took his seat as if it was his usual table at the Silver Swan.

Jake looked just as astonished as McKenna, but he recovered first and found his voice as he causally regarded the regal Saffran. "How you doing, Officer Saffran? For a moment I didn't recognize you.''

"I'm doing okay, Jake,'' Saffran replied as he snapped open his napkin and spread it on his lap. "Where you been keeping yourself lately? Haven't seen you around in a while.''

"Haven't been around. I checked myself into Bellevue for a couple of weeks to wait out the cold spell.''

"Good thinking. You feeling better?''

"Yeah, but not much. How about you? You still seeing that hot Chinese girl from the bodega on Third?''

"She's Korean, Jake, and that's been over for about a month.''

McKenna had hoped and halfway expected that Saffran would know Jake. After all, they both worked the same neighborhood and had for some time. However, he was pleasantly surprised at just how well the two men knew each other and smugly concluded that Saffran was the perfect choice for the mission he had in mind for him. "Before you two go catching up on old times, would you mind telling me how long you've known each other?'' he asked.

Both men had to stop to think. "I don't know, Jake," Saffran mused. "What's it been? Three years?"

"Closer to four, counting the time I was in jail," Jake replied.

"How'd you meet?" McKenna asked.

"Jake used to break into cars to boost the radio, but he wasn't very good at it," Saffran said. "I made a project outta him, locking him up a couple of times a month until some judge finally sent him away for a year."

"I wasn't that bad at it," Jake protested, his pride hurt. "I got plenty of radios you never caught me with."

"Oh yeah? How many? Twenty?"

"More than that."

"Twenty-five?"

"Maybe twenty-five."

"Okay, say twenty-five," Saffran conceded. "What'd you get for them on the street? Twenty dollars each?"

"Yeah, if I was lucky."

"So that means you made maybe five hundred dollars. Counting the five times I caught you where all you got was a trip to the slammer, you took a lot of chances, worked up a lot of sweats, and broke into thirty cars for five hundred dollars at the most, plus a year on Riker's Island. Right?"

"I guess so," Jake conceded, hoping to end the conversation.

But Saffran wasn't ready to let him off the hook. "Don't forget, Jake, I've seen your work. Real sloppy, no finesse. Whenever I found a parked car with the side window smashed, the radio missing, and two hundred dollars' worth of damage to the dashboard, I knew it had to be you."

Jake was finished. "All right, you're right," he conceded. "I wasn't very good at it. Satisfied?"

"Yes, perfectly," Saffran said, then turned to McKenna. "Next topic of conversation?"

"Okay, what I want you to do first is make a list of every place where you've seen the killer," McKenna said.

"It's not a long list. I've thought about it and I've only seen him four times."

"Where at?"

"The playground on Twenty-ninth and Second, Rutherford Park at Seventeenth and Second, Saint Vartan's Park at Thirty-fifth and Second, and hanging out on the corner at Thirtieth and Third."

McKenna was gratified that two of the locations were mentioned in reports on the murders. Benny Foster had been at Thirtieth and Third before he went to the Citibank branch and Rodney Bailey had been seen hanging out in St. Vartan's Park by the building super who had discovered his body. "Could you write it down, along with the approximate dates and times you saw him at those places?" McKenna asked.

"Sure." Saffran reached into his pocket, extracted a new Bureau-issued spiral notebook, and began writing on page one. While he was writing, Renatta appeared and took the lunch orders from the three men. After she left, Saffran tore out the page and handed it to McKenna. "Mind telling me what you're gonna do with that list?" he asked.

"Not at all. I'm gonna give it to the Street Crime Unit and have them set up surveillances at these places."

"Then if he shows up, they're gonna get the collar?"

"Like I told you, there is no collar yet. They're just gonna follow him, hopefully to where he lives so we can find out who he is."

"Just follow him? What's the matter, you still don't have enough on the poison to lock him up?"

This kid's a quick learner, McKenna thought. "That's right. Not yet."

"Well, it doesn't make much difference, anyway. Those guys from Street Crime are just gonna be wasting their time hanging out and getting hit for a ton of quarters by the bums. After all the publicity he's been getting, our man's gonna be laying low."

"He's right about that," Jake offered. "He'd have to be crazy to come out and try one of his stunts. Besides, what good would it do him?"

"Everybody knows the game?" McKenna asked.

"Sure. We're homeless, but we're not all stupid," Jake answered. "It's been in all the papers, and for those who don't stay up on current events, there were a couple of detectives at the shelter this morning showing that sketch, asking questions, and telling everyone not to take no food or wine from anybody."

Of course, they're probably right, McKenna thought. Unless he's stupid, the killer won't be parading around while his sketch is front-page in all the papers. And from what we've seen of the way this guy operates, we know he isn't stupid and he's in no hurry to get caught. The good news is that, just by letting on that we know about him, we've probably stopped the killings. So now what reason do I give Saffran for the surveillances? That they probably won't amount to much, but we're doing that old bureaucratic cop-out of covering all the bases? Okay. "We have to watch those places on the off chance he comes out, because if he got lucky and got away with it again after we know about him, the press would crucify us."

Saffran took the gibberish in stride. "Okay, and I guess we'd deserve it," was his only comment.

"But those surveillances aren't your concern. What I want you to do is talk to every person you know who's been on the street for a while. They may know him as Tony."

"Any idea where they might know him from?"

"I'd say Bellevue Hospital. I think our man is a doctor who's got AIDS, just like Jake here. I could be wrong, but it makes sense to me right now."

Saffran took a good look at Jake. "I see what you mean. Just like you, Jake, his clothes seem to be too big on him, like he recently lost a lot of weight."

"And we know he's in pain. Just like Jake, it hurts him to raise his arms," McKenna added. "According to Ms. Nasty, he looked like he was really hurting when he threw her ball back to her in the playground yesterday."

"Then why's he doing it?" Saffran asked. "Mercy killing?"

McKenna wasn't ready to expound on his theory yet, and didn't have to. Renatta arrived carrying their plates and the aroma of the food preempted all thoughts that didn't have something to do with eating.

Lunch went well. True to his plan, Jake didn't eat much, but he did manage to try everything and thoroughly enjoyed himself. He spent the meal chattering about how much fun he'd had and how much trouble he had gotten into during his drinking days. McKenna decided that, despite Jake's obvious suffering and a life of petty crime, his lunch companion was basically a pretty good guy with a fine sense of humor.

Saffran was another matter altogether. He ate his meal with studied determination, saying not a word during lunch. When he finished the last morsel on his plate, he bothered Renatta for her recipe for the sauerbraten gravy and wouldn't leave her alone until she finally took him into the kitchen to show him how to prepare it.

By the time they were having their coffee, McKenna was in a great mood, happy to have shared a lunch with two character types not likely to be found in any restaurant near police headquarters. He paid the bill, but Saffran insisted on leaving the tip. McKenna noticed that Saffran was a good tipper and far from being a cheapskate.

Once outside, there was an awkward moment while McKenna tried to decide what to do about Jake. He felt he should do something else for the man, but Jake read the situation and responded graciously. "Thanks for lunch and don't worry about me," Jake said as he took his trash bag from McKenna. "I had a great time, but I've got to get back to working my corner."

"See ya, Jake," McKenna said as Jake turned and walked back toward Park Avenue South.

"Not for long," Jake said over his shoulder with a wave of his hand, causing McKenna to grimace and count his blessings.

"Now what?" Saffran asked.

"You know a Ninth Precinct cop named Dante?"

"Sure. Nice guy, but a real bedbug. He's the one who brings all the nuts to Bellevue all the time. Most of them run whenever they see him."

"Sometime during your travels, I think you should talk to him," McKenna suggested. "Maybe he'll have some ideas since he's another guy who seems to know a lot of people in the neighborhood."

"Yeah, just like me," Saffran said, scoffing. "He knows all the people who don't count."

"Not quite. He doesn't know Chief Tavlin, but you will. Don't forget to drop in and see him."

"I won't. Do I look okay?" Saffran asked.

"Perfect. Where did you get a suit like that on such short notice?"

"Borrowed it from my brother."

"Really? What's he do?"

"Nothing worthwhile. He's a criminal attorney."

This is a pretty insightful guy, McKenna thought as Saffran turned and left.

McKenna acknowledged that one of the perks of being a somewhat famous former big shot was that he was spared waiting in line shuttling up the ladder of intermediaries and functionaries to see the people he wanted to see. On his way downtown he called J. Davenport Pinckney III, the man in charge of the DA's Homicide Bureau, and was told to come right on up. He was expected.

J. Davenport, as usual, was working his way through lunch, munching on a sandwich in his office while reviewing the activities his subordinate DAs had performed during the morning court session on their assigned cases. Except for those rare occasions when a big case came up, that was how he spent most of his time, supervising and directing his subordinates' cases rather than doing the thing he loved most—performing.

At heart, J. Davenport Pinckney III was an actor who just happened to be a lawyer, albeit a rather good lawyer. He was from the South, somewhere around Richmond, and had graduated at the top of his class from law school twenty years before. After knocking around southern courtrooms for a few years and learning well the tricks of the trade, he had established something of a good name for himself. The courtroom had been his stage and the jurors his audience. He had all the attributes associated with many successful stars of stage and screen: He was tall and thin, blond and good-looking in a boyish sort of way, possessed a distinctive baritone voice, and could even carry a tune if the part really called for it. But most of all he had a stage presence epitomized by two special tricks in his tool bag, his smile and his frown, and he knew how to play them. He looked like a nice guy, the kind of guy you wanted to know, so that when he smiled his special smile, everyone around him was happy. When he chose to wear his special frown, people were inclined to do something nice to relieve the pressure on the sincere, good-looking kid from next door. During his early career of performances, he had won some rave reviews from his audiences in the form of innocent verdicts for some of his guiltiest clients.

After some years, J. Davenport became bored with his small, rural audiences and decided he was ready to play the more critical jurors in the Big Time, so he had come to New York and joined the staff of the New York County District Attorney. His experience, his academic record, and his reputation eventually earned him a place in the Homicide Bureau.

J. Davenport had prospered there, winning many famous cases by careful preparation and his eloquent style, gratified that his performances were splashed across the front pages of New York's tabloids. Along the way he had met Brian McKenna, at the time a detective in the Homicide Squad, and the men had become friends on a professional level. They appreciated each other's talents, J. Davenport being grateful that McKenna never cluttered a prosecutor's mind and marred a performance by telling them technical things they didn't want to know about a case going to trial, things like the little tricks a good detective uses in questioning suspects and gathering evidence, and McKenna liked the way J. Davenport planned a prosecution and performed in court in such a way that the guilty man was always convicted by that jury of his peers, J. Davenport's appreciative audience.

"I was wondering when you were going to bring me something on this case," J. Davenport said as he rose to shake McKenna's hand.

"I only got it yesterday," McKenna answered as he took a chair in front of J. Davenport's desk. "I didn't want to waste your time until I had something for you."

"Or needed something from me?" J. Davenport guessed as he sat down.

"Now that you mention it, I do need something from you to get this case on track."

"What is it?"

"I need court orders to exhume twenty-one bodies from Potter's Field."

"Twenty-one?" J. Davenport asked, his face lighting up at the mention of the number. It was apparent to McKenna that headlines and visions of a courtroom packed with reporters were flashing across J. Davenport's mind. "You think there are twenty-one victims?"

"We won't know until Dr. Andino gets a look at them, but we have four positive victims at the morgue now."

"So there's a possible total of twenty-five victims?" J. Davenport asked enthusiastically.

"Probably not. Dr. Andino thinks that maybe half of them in Potter's Field are victims," he answered. "That would make fourteen."

J. Davenport's smiled faded a bit. "Have autopsies already been done on the bodies you want to dig up?"

"Yes, but we know what we're looking for now. If any of them are victims, Dr. Andino will know after he gets a look at them. You see, all these cases came up while he was on vacation."

"That's not going to look good at trial. How was the poison missed?"

"Because it's a new variation on an old theme. Minute amounts of cyanide, a usually much less-than-fatal amount, mixed with an enzyme that makes it more powerful," McKenna explained.

"Making it a type of poison that's never been used before?"

"As far as we know."

"Well, that will certainly be an interesting point at trial."

"If there is a trial," McKenna said. "Remember, I have to get this guy first and identify the enzyme."

J. Davenport dismissed McKenna's statement with a wave of his hand. "I'm not worried about that," he said, looking like he meant it. "You'll get him and your lab will identify the enzyme."

"I appreciate your confidence, but if we fail in either, there's no show. We might need a lot of help from you."

J. Davenport looked dismayed at the prospect of no show. "Whatever you need, just give me a call," he said. "But I see a bit of a problem in all of this."

"You mean proving that a minute amount of cyanide mixed with this enzyme is fatal."

"Yes. I'd like to hear how you propose to do that," J. Davenport said as he leaned back in his chair.

"Dr. Andino wants to administer the poison to a large chimpanzee while we videotape the whole procedure."

"You mean let the jury watch the chimp die?"

"Yes, I guess we have to."

"Good idea, but why go to the bother of videotaping it in a lab? We'll do it in court, right after the defense questions the toxicity of the poison. Can't you see it?"

McKenna could. He could see that chimp dying in court for the gratification of the jurors. Near the end, J. Davenport's eyes would fill with tears, and he'd be the first. Before that chimp finally died, J. Davenport would have the whole jury bawling, ready to fry the man who could do such an inhumane thing to another human being.

But J. Davenport was way ahead of him. "How's this poison work?" he asked.

"Well, the enzyme enhances the power of the cyanide to block oxygen from combining with the red blood cells in the body and—"

"I'm not interested in the chemistry," J. Davenport interrupted. "I mean, how do the victims look after they drink the poison."

McKenna knew exactly what J. Davenport meant, but he decided to have some fun. "You mean do they drop to the floor, suffer excruciating pain, uncontrollable spasms, moaning and foaming at the mouth before they are finally granted the release of death?"

"Yes, that's what I want to know," J. Davenport said, getting more excited at the prospect of the show in store.

"Sorry, nothing like that. From what we know, it seems the victims just lie down and die."

"Too bad," J. Davenport said, frowning. Then he had a thought that brought back his smile. "You know, the wonderful part is, I won't have to put this chimp on the witness list. The defense will never know what hit them, especially if we use a friendly-looking cuddly chimp."

"Maybe we could bring him in on roller skates dressed in kid's clothes."

"That would be nice," J. Davenport said as he closed his eyes and visualized the show, a very happy man. "A little too prejudicial for any judge I know, but it would sure be nice."

"I think we're getting a little ahead of ourselves," McKenna ventured.

"You're right," J. Davenport said, all business once again. "When do you want to dig up those bodies?"

"Tomorrow."

By two o'clock McKenna had twenty-one signed court orders in his pocket, but he felt a little guilty. He had used the prosecutor's enthusiasm for a prospective performance to get what he wanted in the shortest time possible, and he would probably use it again in this case. But while McKenna felt reasonably confident there would be an arrest, there would be no show. What he hadn't told J. Davenport was that he expected the killer to die in jail, possibly months before his trial could be scheduled.

26

After leaving the DA's office, McKenna called Andino from his cab and told him that he had the court orders.

"Where you going now?" Andino asked.

"Bellevue to talk to your pal, Jim Heaney. Did you call him?"

"Yep, he's expecting you. I told him that it's possible that one of his people is the killer."

"And what was his reaction?"

"As I recall, his only comment was, 'Oh, shit!' I think he's going to adopt a defensive posture, so try and remember: At heart, he's a nice guy."

"Don't worry. I'll go easy on him."

"Fine. See you in the morning. It's a dirty business, so don't bother dressing up."

Next, McKenna called Ward to report and make a big request. Although he didn't expect much in the way of results from the effort, McKenna still wanted the areas where his killer had been seen put under surveillance.

Ward agreed. "How many locations we talking about?" he asked.

"Six."

"Six? That's twenty-four men around the clock."

"More than that," McKenna said. "One of the places I need covered is Grand Central Station."

"Good God! Grand Central Station? It'll take ten men just to cover that place."

"I know. Sorry," McKenna offered.

"Don't apologize to me," Ward said. "I'm not paying for this, but there's gonna be a lot of happy Street Crime troops on overtime. Give me the list."

"Rutherford Park, Saint Vartan's Park, the playground at Twenty-ninth Street, the corner of East Thirtieth and Third, and Grand Central. I'm throwing in the Bellevue Shelter, too. He wasn't seen there, but he might be following his victims from there."

"You got it. They'll be covered starting tonight. I guess you don't want the press to know that Street Crime will be working here, do you?"

"Definitely not," McKenna said. "What good would it do for them to surveil locations if the press gets wind of it and prints where they're gonna be?"

"Then we can't have them report here. There's scads of reporters outside. I'll call the Street Crime Base and have the troops report direct to your locations."

"Can you have their bosses tell them that if the killer shows up, he's to be followed, not arrested?"

"Sure. I'll tell them to leave him alone unless he starts passing around the wine bottle. Meanwhile, it looks like Maureen's connecting your killer to Rodney Bailey. She and Bender found a bum who saw Bailey in Saint Vartan's Park with him last week. Same MO, seems they went off arm-in-arm to have a drink, but Maureen's guy wasn't invited."

"Lucky for him. You got him there?" McKenna asked.

"Yes, Mr. Lyle Lawton is here waiting for you."

Now if we can only pinpoint the day it was this guy saw them together, then I've got an eyewitness to help hang another case on our killer, McKenna thought. "He wouldn't happen to remember when he saw them together?" he asked.

"You mean was it the day before Bailey's body was found? Was it on the night of January twenty-fifth?" Ward asked, laughing and leaving McKenna little hope. "Now that would be just too easy, wouldn't it?"

"Yes, I guess that would be too easy," McKenna agreed.

"Well, don't despair. Mr. Lawton is a little sketchy on his date and time references and didn't even know what today was when Maureen first found him. It seems every day's Sunday for him, his day off. But she's working on him. Together, they're busy reconstructing his exciting week, taking a trip back in time. She'll get it for you, even if she has to have this guy hypnotized."

"I guess sometimes things are easy, as long as you've got good people doing your work," McKenna said. "Anything else?" he asked for the second time, hoping there wasn't.

"Just one more thing. I hope you'll have something to tell the press that'll clear them out of here soon. They're taking up every parking spot on the block."

"I'll think of something," McKenna promised. He hung up as the taxi pulled up to the Bellevue Hospital entrance. After some searching and shuffling around the vast complex of hospital buildings, he found the personnel office on the first floor of one of Bellevue's oldest hospital buildings. The receptionist announced his arrival to Heaney on her intercom, then told him to go right in.

The personnel director met McKenna at the door of his office, and he wasn't at all what McKenna had expected. Probably because of the atmosphere generated by the antiquated building, he had formed an image in his mind of what the personnel director would look like: a small, skinny, bespectacled man with a sallow complexion occupying a dingy office cramped with files. Instead he got Jim Heaney, an athletic type in his thirties sporting a sun-parlor tan and a friendly smile, standing in his large, newly renovated, well-lit, and nicely appointed office containing not one file cabinet.

McKenna noticed that he had been right about only one thing: Heaney was wearing glasses. But then Heaney took them off and put them in his pocket as he led McKenna back to his very clean desk. The only thing on it was a pen and pencil set and a computer terminal, and that was off.

This man's got a pretty good job, McKenna concluded. "You don't usually wear glasses?" he asked.

"Only when I play darts," Heaney answered, pointing to the dartboard on the wall behind McKenna.

I'm batting zero on this guy, McKenna thought as he turned around and took a look.

The dartboard was the standard circular variety with alternating pie-shaped zones pointing at the bull's-eye in the center. The alternating zones were all labeled either HIRE or FIRE, and the two-inch bull's-eye was labeled PROMOTE.

McKenna noticed that the three darts protruding from the board were stuck very close together in one of the FIRE zones.

"I've been having a bad day since Dr. Andino called," Heaney explained.

"Sorry," McKenna said as he sat in one of the chairs in front of Heaney's desk. "You know, I was expecting something different here," he commented.

"You mean lots of personnel folders cluttering up the place, file cabinets everywhere, and me in the middle living a life of drudgery?"

"Something like that."

"Well, that's the way it used to be until a couple of years ago. Then I got this baby," he said, tapping the computer monitor of his desk. "What I've managed to design here for myself is a modern paperless office. All the files I need are on the computer."

"Really? Even the old personnel files?"

"Not all of them. Anyone who left over two years ago isn't in the computer."

"Where are the old personnel files kept?"

"Someplace in the building, I guess. I don't know and I never asked. Never need them."

Well, you might, McKenna thought, but the heady personnel director wasn't finished. "See this?" Heaney asked, taking the pen from the holder on his desk and holding it up. "The only time I ever use it is to clean the wax outta my ears and sign my paychecks."

"Very impressive," McKenna commented dryly, realizing that he sounded impatient as soon as he said it. He needed Heaney as a pal, so he added, "It looks like you're happy with your system."

But Heaney had caught McKenna's tone. "I am, but let's get down to business," he said, replacing his pen in the holder. "Tell me, what makes you think your killer is one of my people?"

"The four victims we know about so far were all HIV positive and all were outpatients at Bellevue."

"Was it obvious they had the disease?"

"Three of them were in pretty bad shape, but one of them looked great. He was HIV positive but looked pretty healthy."

"I see," Heaney said. "So you concluded that the killer is someone who's killing only HIV-positive people, someone with access to their medical records."

"What would you conclude?"

Heaney again took a pen from the pen stand on his desk and toyed with it while he thought over McKenna's question. "Much the same thing," he admitted after a moment without looking at McKenna. "I'd be looking right here, but I've seen your sketch. It's nobody I recognize."

"And you know everybody working here?"

"By sight, at least. I'm in charge of hiring and firing and we have a pretty large turnover, but I know what all our people look like. Your guy is pretty distinctive looking, especially the eyes. He's not working here."

"How long you been here?"

"Seven years. Why?"

"Because I think it unlikely the killer still works here. I'm pretty sure he's got the disease himself."

"Is that why you think he's killing those folks? You think he got the disease here and he's taking revenge on anyone who might have given it to him?"

"Yes, that's what's going through my mind. Since the disease has an incubation period of approximately five years, it would have to be someone who was working here five years ago, give or take a couple of years."

"So say, what? Seven years? You must realize that you're talking thousands of people."

"Maybe I'll be able to make this easier for us. Could you give me a list of all your people who've claimed to have contacted AIDS from a patient?"

"Right now?" Heaney asked, suddenly smiling.

"If you can remember them all."

"I'll try." Heaney took a pad from his top desk drawer and placed it on his desk with a flourish. Then he wrote a big zero on the top page, tore it off, and handed it to McKenna. "I think that just about covers it," he said, still smiling.

"You've had none?" McKenna asked, stunned. "Not a single case of a patient infecting a medical worker?"

"Not one," Heaney answered smugly.

"But I thought it was a fairly common occurrence. One of the biggest medical centers in the country and you haven't had one case?"

"Nope. We've had a couple of scares, but that's it. We're careful with disposing of needles, but this whole thing about medical workers being infected by patients with AIDS is mostly just that—a big scare. There's only been seven documented cases of that happening in the entire country, and it hasn't happened here."

Well, that blows a big hole in at least a part of my theory, McKenna thought. But still, the killer must have something to do with this place. Four homicides, all HIV positive, and all outpatients here. "Is it possible there's a case you don't know about?"

"What do you mean? Of course I'd know about it."

"Then is it possible that one of your workers was infected here by a homeless patient and didn't report it?"

"Possible, but highly unlikely," Heaney answered, scoffing. "Any one of our people who caught it here would sue our balls off, and they'd win. We'd have to name buildings here after them, so why wouldn't they report it?"

So why wouldn't he report it? McKenna wondered, more discouraged by the minute. Am I wrong about this? No, I can't be, he decided. Everything points to the killer having something to do with this hospital. "I'd like to go over a few things with you and get your opinion. You ready to bear with me for a moment?" he asked Heaney.

"Sure. Shoot."

"How many HIV-positive workers have you had here over the past seven years?"

"I don't know, exactly. They're not required to report that they've got it."

"They're not?" McKenna asked, surprised. "Doctors and nurses don't have to tell you when they're HIV positive?"

"Nope. Some do report it, but they don't have to in this state. It's a matter of conscience. Everybody needs a job and there's not much risk of them infecting the patients, as long as they follow the procedures."

"The procedures?"

"Yeah, you know. AIDS is transmitted by blood transfer. If any of our people got it, they just have to be careful not to bleed into our patients' wounds. And I guess they have been. None of our patients have caught AIDS here from any of our staff.''

''But what about saliva?''

''Another big scare. Theoretically, it's possible to catch it from an infected person's saliva, but there's been no reported cases of that type of transmission in this country. Besides, we don't allow our people to run around spitting at our patients.''

''Okay, so you've got people working here now who have AIDS, and you probably did five years ago, right?''

''I'll concede that. There's a few cases I know about that are working here right now, but believe me, none of them come close to matching your sketch.''

''I believe you. Like I said, it has to be someone working here years ago, not someone who's still here.''

''Okay, say you're right,'' Heaney said. ''But if he didn't catch it here, what would be his motivation to kill poor bums with the disease?''

''I don't know,'' McKenna answered, shaking his head. ''But maybe the killer worked here, got AIDS somewhere else, and is taking it out on the homeless patients because they're easy. Or maybe it's mercy killing.''

''Or maybe the guy's a complete loony who needs no reason at all,'' Heaney suggested.

''No, that's not it. He's done a lot of planning and a lot of work on this. He's a man with a purpose who knows what he's doing.''

''Okay, suit yourself,'' Heaney said, shrugging his shoulders. ''What do you need?''

McKenna took the sketch from his pocket, unfolded it, and placed it in front of Heaney. ''Can you be sure this man wasn't working here five years ago?'' he asked.

''Like I said, we have a high turnover here,'' Heaney answered, staring at the sketch. ''Thousands of people have come and gone in the past five years.''

''So you can't be certain?''

''No, I don't remember that face, but I can't be certain. How good is that sketch?''

''I've been told it looks exactly like him.''

''Then I guess I'm gonna have to find out where those old personnel files are after all,'' Heaney conceded.

''Are their pictures in the files?''

''Uh-huh. A duplicate of their ID photos.''

''How about fingerprints?'' McKenna asked hopefully.

''Nope, unfortunately, no fingerprints. I'd like to fingerprint a few of these folks and find out where they've been and what they've done, but it's not required by law.''

''So you can't do it?''

''No. Our employees have quite a union, and if I tried it I'd be coming to work through a very nasty picket line. No thanks. If you go bothering too many people around here, you'll see what I mean.''

''It was just a thought. When will you be able to get a look at those files?''

''You think it's important, right?''

"Very."

"Then I'll start on it first thing in the morning. That soon enough for you?"

"Let me put it like this. On the off chance that I'm right, I think it would look very bad for this hospital if the killer goes to work tonight and gives us another victim after I talked to you today."

"That's if he is one of our people, right?"

"Yes, or one of your former people. I'll know for sure by the day after tomorrow if he is or not. Then we'll have to talk again, unless you find his picture in your files before that."

"What happens between now and then?"

"Dr. Andino is going to be doing quite a few autopsies on other possible victims. If he finds some more victims and they're all HIV positive as well as former outpatients of your place—"

"I get the picture, but I've got a question," Heaney said, holding up his hand. "Suppose you get one that's HIV positive, but not one of our patients?"

"Then I suppose we'll have to do some rethinking. But until then . . ."

"I'll start on those files tonight and work all night, if I have to. Good enough?"

"That would be very nice of you," McKenna answered condescendingly. "While you're going through them, could you pull the files of anyone even close to this guy?" McKenna asked, pointing to the sketch.

"You got it."

"And could you show it to the doctors, nurses, and pharmacists who've been here for a while?"

"Okay, but that's gonna take me more time. But why not show it to everybody who works here?"

"Because we know the killer's got quite a background in chemistry. I don't want to waste your time and maybe get their union mad at us."

"Okay, but now I've got a request," Heaney said.

"Whatever I can do."

"I don't want anything in the press connecting the killer to this hospital until there's some proof."

"Fair enough," McKenna said, offering his hand to Heaney. "There's some pretty sharp reporters out there and there's bound to be some questions, and maybe even some speculation, but they won't get anything from me until I've got some proof. That a deal?"

"Thanks," Heaney said, shaking McKenna's hand. "That'll keep this powerful hospital off both our backs."

"Now, do you mind if I ask you a personal question?"

"Not at all. I'm a pretty simple guy with not much to hide," Heaney said.

"What would happen to you if it turns out you hired the guy who killed many of this hospital's patients, giving it some very unfavorable publicity in the process?"

"That's an easy one," Heaney said while reaching into his top desk drawer. He took out a dart, and without seeming to aim, quickly threw it at the dartboard. It stuck square in the middle of the small group consisting of the other three darts, in the FIRE zone. "If that were the case, I guess I'd have more time to spend in Irish bars improving my game," he said as McKenna admired the accuracy of this not-so-simple guy.

27 The 17th Precinct station house had no back door, something McKenna had come to consider as a design flaw. East 51st Street was filled with news vans parked and double-parked, and there were reporters and film crews standing in front of the station house. From the corner, McKenna searched the block looking for Heidi, but didn't see her.

"Looking for me, Brian?" a sugary-sweet voice called from behind him.

McKenna turned to face Heidi, expecting to find himself in the glare of the cameras, but she was alone. "Where did you come from?"

"I figured you'd stand here when you got back, checking out the block. So I waited in there for you," she said, pointing to a deli on the corner behind her.

"Very sharp," McKenna said.

"What did you expect?" Heidi asked, brushing off the compliment. "So how was your day?"

"Not bad. Yours?"

"Pretty boring, standing out here all day waiting for you to accept my apology on the air, like you said you would. Remember?"

"I'll do it when we get a chance, but it's gonna be tough with that gang standing in front of the station house," McKenna said, pointing to the reporters down the block.

That got Heidi thinking. "You are going to make a statement today, aren't you?"

"I guess I have to."

"When?"

"After I talk to my boss. Probably in two hours."

"You going to give me any hints about how it's going?"

"No problem. There's more victims, but it's going reasonably well. That's all I can tell you right now."

"Good enough. Now, all you've got to do to get this apology thing out of the way is to acknowledge me after you give your statement. I'll handle it from there, okay?"

"Fine. I bet you'll be good, but are you sure you're doing the right thing?"

"Like I told you this morning, it'll be good for the ratings. Every kick's a boost, so there's no such thing as bad publicity in this business. The only thing that would help my ratings more is if I could manage to get arrested for kidnapping little boys, taking them to some fashionable hotel, and doing filthy things with them."

"I understand," McKenna said, not really understanding at all.

"I knew you would." Heidi treated him to her brightest smile and extended her hand. "Friends?"

"More like good professional acquaintances," McKenna said as he shook her hand and watched her smile fade. Then he turned, put his head down, and walked to the station house. He managed to get through the reporters by promising he would make a statement in two hours.

Upstairs, McKenna found Maureen sitting at her desk deep in conversation with a shabbily dressed white man in his fifties. As he was hanging up his overcoat, Maureen gave McKenna a sign that she was busy with her witness and would talk to him later.

Chris Saffran was also there. "I've got a present for you," he said, looking quite proud of himself.

"You've got somebody who knows the killer?"

"Yep, Donald Rosser. He's in there," Saffran said, pointing to one of the small interview rooms. "I didn't tell him, but he even knew his name was Tony."

At last, a breathing, sane person who knew the killer, McKenna thought, elated. "How long does he know him?"

"About a month."

"Where's he know him from?"

"Met him outside the Bellevue Shelter a few times."

"Are they friends?"

"They shared a few drinks together, that's all."

"They did?"

"Yep. Seems Tony's quite a friendly guy. Always got wine for his friends."

"Is Rosser HIV positive?"

"He says he's not and he looks pretty good to me, considering."

"Does he know any more of Tony's friends?"

"Yep. He gave me a list of people he knows that he's seen with Tony at one time or another in the past month."

"How many on the list?"

"Five. I know four of them, so I can guarantee you'll be talking to two of them as soon as I can round them up."

"Why not all four of them?"

"Because one of them is Mickey Weyland and another is Tyrone Lewis. It's now my understanding that both of those gentlemen have passed on."

They sure have, McKenna thought. The train-yard case and the Ninth Precinct case. "You knew both of them?"

"Sure. Mickey was all right, but Lewis was a low-life troublemaker, even before he got sick."

"When did you find out they died?"

"Just today, when I was typing some stuff for Lieutenant Ward. Their names were on a report he had me doing right before I met you for lunch."

"Were you surprised that you didn't know they died?"

"Not really. Besides getting locked up and checking into hospitals, a lot of these guys do quite a bit of moving around. Sometimes I don't see some of them for months. Besides, neither of them died in my precinct, so how would I know? Even Rosser didn't know they were dead until I told him. He had just assumed they were in a hospital, in jail, or staying at another shelter."

Saffran had just gone a long way toward answering a question McKenna had been asking himself: How could so many homeless have been killed without their friends noticing the trend and raising some kind of alarm? The answer was simple. These homeless victims were all sick and in a pretty fluid lifestyle. In most cases their friends didn't even know they were dead.

"You gonna talk to this guy?" Saffran asked.

"Yes, but first I have to talk to the lieutenant. Could you keep him on ice until I'm done?"

"You got it." Saffran went into the interview room and closed the door behind him.

McKenna took a deep breath, walked over to Ward's door, straightened his tie, and knocked.

"You get those reporters cleared out of here yet?" Ward asked as soon as McKenna entered.

"Not yet," McKenna said as he pulled up a chair.

"Well, what are you waiting for? They're a goddamn nuisance. I tried to get out of here to go see that Dr. Wright, but as soon as I left the building a bunch of them followed me, sticking microphones in my face. Had to run back here to hide."

McKenna could see Ward's problem at once. Ward was too sharp to take a chance and have some reporters follow him to the ME's office because that would focus attention on his role in the case, inviting lots more questions from reporters for Andino. He was much more comfortable letting his detective handle the press, for better or worse.

"That's one of the things I want to talk to you about before I talk to the press," McKenna said. "I'm thinking of saving you some trouble with Wright."

"What are you gonna do? Feed him to the lions?"

"With your permission. They're bound to ask me some questions about why the ME didn't catch these cases before now. I figure I'll take some pressure off Andino and let them kill Wright instead."

"I like it. I see you learned some lessons during your sojourn in the Puzzle Palace."

"I just paid attention and got to watch some chiefs at work who could have taught Machiavelli a thing or two."

"Yeah, they're good," Ward agreed. "What else are you gonna tell them?"

"That we've got four cases so far, but expect we'll have more. That we haven't identified the killer yet, but expect to do so. That this case is receiving the highest priority and that all the department's resources are being utilized in an effort to expeditiously end this menace to public safety. That we are receiving full cooperation from the DA's office and the ME's office. That—"

"So you're gonna give them the usual bullshit," Ward said impatiently.

"Yeah, I guess that's what I'm gonna do," McKenna admitted. "But this time it's true."

"They'll still think it's bullshit. What about Bellevue?"

"They're cooperating, but I promised not to mention anything connecting the killer to the hospital until we have absolute proof."

"I would have insisted on that. We don't need them coming down on us right now. And the fingerprints from the wine bottle? Walsh has got them primed to ask about them so that he stays somewhere near the center of the spotlight."

"I guess I'll have to dance around that until I hear from Inspector Scagnelli again."

"Didn't you talk to him this afternoon?" Ward asked seriously.

Uh-oh. I screwed up here somewhere, McKenna thought. "Not since I saw him this morning," he said.

"Well, he wants to talk to you, so maybe you'll be prepared and won't have to dance around those fingerprint questions. Check the Telephone Message Log.''

The Telephone Message Log! Good God! thought McKenna, angry with himself. Running a big case and I don't check the Telephone Message Log before coming in to talk to the boss? Worse, a message from an inspector that I don't know about? That's a real brand-new-detective boner I just pulled. ''Thanks, I will,'' he said meekly.

''Do that,'' Ward said curtly, then seemed to soften a bit. ''We're gonna be here for a while. You have dinner yet?''

What's this? McKenna wondered. Forgiveness in the form of a dinner invitation from the boss? ''No, sir.''

''Well, when you do, bring me back a sandwich. Ham and provolone on Italian bread, tomatoes, but no lettuce.''

Better than forgiveness, McKenna thought. Acceptance. Despite that stupid mistake, I'm in. ''Yes sir.''

As soon as he left Ward's office, McKenna went straight to the Telephone Message Log. There it was, in black and white, a message that came in at 4:10 P.M. instructing Detective McKenna to call Inspector Scagnelli at the lab as soon as he returned to the squad office.

McKenna checked his watch. It was 4:35. Not too bad, he thought as he dialed Scagnelli at the lab. He was just about to hang up on the tenth ring when Scagnelli picked up. He said, ''McKenna here, returning your call.''

''Got some news for you on your bottle. Had the Wild Irish Rose fellow in, a Mr. Sean Dougherty. He read the batch code off the bottle, called his company, and got the location they shipped it to. Grand Central Liquors in Grand Central Station. Shipped ten cases there on January twelfth. Dougherty and Walsh went over there and found they still had four cases left from the same batch. We've got our control sample.''

''Anybody there recognize the killer?''

''Walsh showed them all the sketch, but it didn't ring any bells. It's a busy store, so I'm not surprised.''

''How about the fingerprints?'' McKenna asked.

''Good news, so far. Walsh took elimination prints from the seven employees that were there from the day and night shifts. So far, no match to the prints on the bottle.''

''So far?''

''Walsh's got more work to do. There's two more to be printed—one of the owners and a guy they fired last week. I sent Walsh to do them, too. He should be back around ten.''

Scagnelli sounded happy about that, so McKenna knew it was bad news for Walsh. ''And where are they?'' he asked.

''The guy they fired lives in Harlem and the owner lives in Riverhead. They have another store out there.''

Harlem's close enough, but Riverhead? McKenna thought. Has to be a hundred and fifty miles round-trip. That'll keep Walsh away from his friends in the press and out of Scagnelli's hair for the rest of the night. ''He might not make it back by ten,'' McKenna said.

''He'd better. That's when he gets off and I told him he gets no overtime on this.''

"How you making out on the chemistry with the enzyme?" McKenna asked, thinking it time to change the subject.

"Just starting on that. I've assigned a lab crew to work twelve-hour shifts on it. Figure we'll have something in two or three days. Soon enough?"

"Great, Inspector. I appreciate it."

"One more thing. I ran your computer idea with the fingerprints past Commissioner Brunette. He says he'll authorize it, but only if we have to."

"I guess that means if I can't identify the killer any other way."

"I guess so. How's it look right now?"

"I'm thinking that, right now, it doesn't look like we'll have to."

"Good. I'll let you know when we come up with anything, good or bad," Scagnelli said before hanging up.

Next McKenna called Angelita to tell her he wouldn't be home till seven. The news wasn't well received. "I'm trying to be understanding, but you said you'd be home on time tonight," she said after a series of her impatient and annoyed sounds. She ended her little fit with, "You didn't get enough sleep last night and dinner's at eight tonight."

"Dinner at eight? What's the occasion?"

"It's the I-Can-Finally-Get-Back-into-My-Favorite-Red-Dress Day. Ray insisted we celebrate and he's buying."

"Wait a minute, Angelita. I didn't know anything about this."

"Really? He told me he left you a message."

Just great! McKenna thought. Another message missed, this one from the police commissioner, and I just looked at that goddamn book. He flipped back a page in the Telephone Message Log and there it was, the message that came in for Detective McKenna at two o'clock. It read simply: *Dinner at eight. Sotto Cinque.* There was no indication from whom the message came, but McKenna knew it could be only one person. Ray, Angelita, and he loved the place and frequently invented a reason to celebrate something there. "Cheer up," he told Angelita. "I'll be home at seven and we'll have a good time. I promise."

"Promise accepted. One more thing."

"I know. Keep the police talk to a minimum tonight."

"That's a good idea, but that's not it. Did you run into that bitch again today?"

"I talked to her, but only for a minute."

"You're not giving her another interview, are you?"

"Not directly. There's a bunch of reporters outside and I have to give them a statement before I go. She's one of them."

"Remember what I said. She's got it in for you."

"I can't imagine why, but I'll remember."

McKenna hung up the phone to find Maureen smiling at him from her desk. He was sure she hadn't intended to overhear his conversation, but she had caught the gist of it. "Having some trouble on the home front with Real Detective hours?" she asked.

"Yeah, I guess we're both a little spoiled after a year of that sissy nine-to-five routine. Are you and Mr. Lawton ready to impart some knowledge to me?"

"Yes. Mr. Lawton is now in a state of total recall and he's very anxious to tell you about some things he saw on the evening of . . ." Maureen turned to

Lawton, who was sitting across the desk from her, obviously awaiting his cue. "I'm sorry. I forget. When exactly was it, Mr. Lawton?"

"January twenty-fifth. I'm absolutely certain of it. I saw Tony and Rodney together in Saint Vartan's Park on the night of January twenty-fifth."

Besides what Saffran and Maureen had already told him, McKenna had learned a little more about his quarry from his own interviews of Lyle Lawton and Donald Rosser. It was nothing substantive, but still worthwhile. The killer's mannerisms and personality were beginning to take shape in McKenna's mind. He was getting a feel for him, an understanding of the way he thought and what he was like. Through further interviews with people who had seen and talked to the killer, he hoped eventually to know the man so well that he would be able to predict his next move.

As McKenna had already surmised, the killer had spent a lot of time over the past month hanging out in places where the homeless congregate, but his background was a mystery to his new friends. Like many of them, the killer had no past he wanted to talk about and he let on nothing about what his life was like before he first appeared among them. Both Rosser and Lawton had stated that they had first met him sometime that month and that "Tony" had never complained of any pain or illness. Rosser didn't think he was sick, just naturally skinny, but Lawton thought that Tony looked "unhealthy." Both men had only seen him dressed in black, apparently wearing the same coat and hat that he had worn when he had poisoned Benny Foster and Juan Bosco. Both also said that Tony was well spoken. Rosser thought Tony had a slight accent, maybe Spanish or Italian, but Lawton hadn't noticed it. Neither man had found him remarkable in any way.

Except for connecting the killer to the Rodney Bailey murder with Lyle Lawton's statement, nothing gained from the two interviews would have J. Davenport Pinckney III jumping for joy. However, McKenna was happy with the results.

Although neither Rosser nor Lawton had commented on it, that the killer was highly intelligent was a given. He had to be smart to do the things he had done and to have gotten away with it for so long, undetected. Both Lawton and Rosser had described Tony as friendly, a nice guy, but McKenna discounted their assessment. Since killing people isn't "nice," McKenna thought that the face the killer put on when interacting with the homeless was just another factor of his intelligence. He was what the textbooks call an "organized" serial killer, someone smart enough to know that being nice to your potential victims permits you to get close enough to kill them at your convenience. If you're going to be nice to your victims, to keep your projected persona straight you have to be nice to anyone who knows your victims. The killer had done that, even having gone to the point of "loaning" Rosser twenty dollars the last time they had met.

The picture that McKenna was forming of Tony was that of a patient, determined, and coldly calculating killer with a purpose. Standing out in the freezing cold for hours and hours, patiently awaiting his homeless prey while disguised as one of them, the killer was fulfilling his agenda one victim at a time. Whatever the reasons for his killing spree, they were intensely personal and not done to gain any criminal fame or notoriety. McKenna was sure that this killer would have been happy if his handiwork had remained undiscovered.

The killer was also clever and calculating enough to hide his pain and illness from his new friends, all potential witnesses against him.

After the interviews, McKenna asked Saffran how long it would take him to locate the other two homeless men Lawton had seen talking with the killer.

"Can't say, exactly. These guys don't exactly keep a regular schedule."

"Can I see your list?"

"Sure." Saffran took his notebook from his pocket, tore off the top page, and handed it to McKenna. The names *Slickman, Chingo, Mickey, Willie Boy*, and *Doo Man* were scribbled on the page in an almost illegible scrawl. A line had been drawn through Slickman's and Mickey's names.

"Rosser wrote this list?" McKenna asked.

"Yep."

"But he doesn't know any of their last names, right?"

"No, these guys go mostly by nicknames. But he was able to give me a description of each of them, so I know who four of them are. I've given those four summonses or locked them up for one small thing or another, so I know their real names."

"So Mickey is Mickey Weyland and Slickman is Tyrone Lewis, both deceased."

"Yep."

"Who are the other two you know?"

"I don't know for sure who Willie Boy is. There's about ten Willies out there that I know of and quite a few of them fit the description Rosser gave me. But I do know that Chingo is Felipe Santiago. He's a small Filipino, date of birth October 12th, 1958. He usually stays in the Men's Shelter on Third Street and hangs out in Rutherford Park. Doo Man is Reginald Baines, date of birth February 2nd, 1961. He's a black guy always wears a bandanna around his head, so they call him Doo Man, like he's got a good hairdo under the rag. He usually stays at the Bellevue Shelter, hangs out in the Twenty-ninth Street playground."

Now who else would know that? McKenna asked himself. Nobody, he concluded while congratulating himself for having selected the perfect man for the assignment he had given Saffran.

McKenna reached into his pocket, took out two ten-dollar bills, and offered them to Saffran. "Make sure those two get a good meal for their trouble."

But Saffran pulled only one of the bills from McKenna's fingers, saying, "You can pay for Lawton, but I brought Rosser in here. He's my responsibility, so I'll feed him myself."

The perfect man for the job, McKenna thought again as Saffran led Lawton and Rosser out. Then he sat down and started on his paperwork.

While typing out his reports on the interviews of Rosser and Lawton, another thought came to McKenna that brought his adversary into sharper focus. Bongo had posed a problem for the killer when he had poisoned Bosco, but he still hadn't poisoned Bongo when it would have been just as easy for him to do so. McKenna had thought that the killer might have a streak of humanity running through him.

After talking to Rosser, McKenna changed his mind. Maybe the reason Bongo was still alive was that the killer had been anxious to keep his mission a secret. "Tony" had known that the police, upon finding two dead homeless people in the same neighborhood around the same time, would be less likely to attribute their demises to natural causes. They would have looked deeper, and his existence and mission might have been discovered sooner.

As for motive, whatever private reasons the killer harbored for his homicidal spree, McKenna had drawn a different conclusion. That insight was something else he owed to Jake. Jake had said that, despite the pain and fatigue, life would still be bearable if he had plans to make and something to accomplish. Since he hadn't accomplished much in his life anyway, Jake didn't think that his last days would be a good time to change his ways.

McKenna thought the killer was different. The evidence was that he was an educated man of some accomplishments, so he looked at his own pending death differently. McKenna concluded that it was the killer's mission that made his life bearable, kept him alive and thinking through the pain and fatigue, ready and eager to go on.

28 McKenna took a good look at his audience. He knew some of the reporters from previous cases he had worked on, counted a friend or two among them, and recognized most of the rest by name. Standing in the front was Heidi Lane, smiling at him with her microphone held at her side. She gave him a wink and a smile when she caught his eye, just as he began his statement.

"As you all know, yesterday morning the body of a homeless man was found on the street at East Thirty-first Street and Second Avenue. At the time it had been assumed that he had frozen to death, but the medical examiner has now confirmed that death was actually due to a type of cyanide poisoning that, to our knowledge, hasn't been used to kill anyone in this country before. The ME investigated further and found another three recent cases where cyanide poisoning was the actual cause of death. Two of these cases had been diagnosed in error as death by natural causes. The third case had been incorrectly diagnosed as death due to hypothermia, which means only one person has frozen to death in this city this year, not three."

He stopped to let that point sink in, but saw that he was wasting his time. The expression he read on most of their faces said: Yeah, yeah, so what? Get on with it, would ya?

McKenna did. "All four victims were homeless men who were HIV positive. The suspect in these cases is the man we issued the sketch of yesterday. He hasn't been identified yet, but he's been positively linked to three of the four cases. He kills his victims by offering them wine that contains the poison. Death occurs in under half an hour after ingesting the poison."

The group remained silent and focused on McKenna, not realizing that he had completed his statement until he said, "Doesn't anybody have any questions for me?"

They did, so loud and so many at the same time that McKenna couldn't make out a single one. He just stood there, taking in the incomprehensible roar. Finally, Bob Tavis from the *Daily News* raised his hand and McKenna pointed to him. The reporters fell silent and many of the TV people shifted their microphones to Tavis.

"Are we to understand that the killer is targeting only gay men?" Tavis asked.

Wouldn't that be a political bombshell in this city? McKenna thought. We'd have the Marines called in here tomorrow. "No, Bob. That's definitely not what I'm saying," he answered. "All I said was that the four victims were HIV positive. We have no evidence to indicate that any of them were gay. Next question."

All hands were up, but McKenna pointed to Dick Yorkfield from the *Post* and the microphones shifted to him. He knew Yorkfield as an ornery, no-nonsense, intelligent guy and braced himself for a tough question, figuring it would be better to get the print guys out of the way first before going into the sound bites for the TV people.

"How is it that the ME missed those first three cases?" Yorkfield asked. "Didn't he do an autopsy on them?"

"Yes, all the victims were autopsied, but I have to explain something about the poison. The killer's adding an enzyme to the wine that amplifies the effects of the very small amount of cyanide he's using, an amount of cyanide so small that it wouldn't ordinarily produce death. The toxicological screening process that the ME's office was using couldn't register that small amount of cyanide, so the poison went undetected."

"What is this enzyme?" Yorkfield asked.

"We don't know yet. Nobody's come across it before, so both our police lab and the ME's office are working day and night to discover its chemical composition."

"When will you know?"

"I'm told it won't be for a couple of days."

McKenna wanted to move on to the next reporter and pointed to another, but Yorkfield wasn't done with him yet. The seasoned reporter yelled, "Let me get this straight. Four people were poisoned in this city in a week and, for whatever reason, the largest medical examiner's office in the country missed that fact and let this killer operate at will. Commissioner McKenna, don't you find something remiss there?"

There's no getting around this one, McKenna thought. If he's screaming about four cases, he'll be deafening when he finds out how many we suspect there really are. Only one way to go. "Yes, I do find something remiss there, and it's *Detective* McKenna now."

Seeing that some newsworthy dirt was about to be slung around town, more microphones shifted to Yorkfield. Nobody was about to interrupt him when he was on a roll like this.

"Whatever," Yorkfield said, waving his hand to indicate that he wasn't much impressed with this business of titles. "Detective McKenna, in your opinion, is it possible we need a new medical examiner in this town?"

The question was out, and sooner than McKenna had anticipated. He put the most serious look on his face he could contrive as microphones shifted from Yorkfield back to him. "No, it's not," he stated. "Dr. Andino is one of the most qualified medical examiners in the country, an internationally recognized expert in the field. I've worked with him many times in the past and know him as a diligent and dedicated professional. In my opinion, we're lucky to have him.''

The TV people didn't have time to shift their microphones back to Yorkfield before he shouted, "Wait a minute! Detective McKenna, would you care to explain the obvious inconsistency between your two statements?''

McKenna waited while two TV people who had been rushing back and forth between him and Yorkfield untangled their microphone cords so they could hold the microphones up to his face. "First, I'd like to explain that I've spoken to Dr. Andino about this matter and he told me that he takes full responsibility for the errors made by his office. However, I feel you should know that he was at a medical conference in Italy at the beginning of the month. After the conference he stayed there on vacation and only returned to work a couple of days ago. I might be overstepping my boundaries, but I hold him blameless for the errors made in his absence and appreciate the fine work he's done since he returned. You see, he was the one who came up with a new test that determined that yesterday's case was a cyanide poisoning, that Benny Foster didn't freeze to death.''

Out of the corner of his eye, McKenna saw Heidi's hand shoot up, but he ignored her for the moment. Instead, he remained focused on Yorkfield, anticipating the reporter's next question and trying to keep his face serious. It was hard because *Good-bye, Jimbo* was all he could think.

Yorkfield didn't disappointment him. "Who was in charge there while Andino was away?''

Remember, straight face, McKenna told himself. Look like you're searching for that name. "I believe his name is Dr. James Wright,'' he finally stated.

"Did Andino appoint Wright to his position?'' was Yorkfield's next businesslike question, asked just a second after McKenna got Wright's name out.

"No, it's my understanding that Dr. Wright was a political appointee.''

Finally, Yorkfield was through, but the way he was shaking his head and scowling gave McKenna the impression that it made no difference if Wright had been appointed for life by the College of Cardinals. By the time the *Post*'s morning edition hit the mayor at Gracie Mansion, Wright would be unemployed and whoever recommended him for the job would have some explaining to do. It would even happen sooner, if any of the TV stations were running a live feed on the press conference.

The prospect didn't make McKenna the slightest bit unhappy. Like Andino, he abhorred incompetence in high places, detested imperious attitudes, and held Wright responsible for an as-yet-undetermined number of deaths. So why take a chance? McKenna asked himself. Let's nail old Jimbo's casket closed tight and, incidentally, give Ward some good press and preempt these folks from pointing a nasty finger at the PD with their other hand. It's time to open that second big can of worms and get this press conference really boiling. "It's going to come out anyway, so I think you should know that it's a matter of record that, weeks ago, Lieutenant Ward expressed concern about a recent increase in the deaths of homeless people, all cases categorized by the ME's office as death by natural causes. He asked Dr. Wright to reexamine his findings in those cases, but Wright adamantly refused.''

"Who's Lieutenant Ward?'' came from a few voices at once.

He's sure not gonna like that one, McKenna thought. "Lieutenant Ward is the squad commander of the Seventeenth Detective Squad. He's my boss, the man I report to."

"You have a boss?" came a comment from the back, but McKenna couldn't see who said it and thought it best ignored. There were too many hands in the air and too many issues to be aired to give himself more trouble with that one. He pointed to Mike Sheehan, a retired detective and an old friend who was enjoying his retirement and making money by covering the police beat for New York 1.

"Brian, are you saying those cases are in addition to the four you've already mentioned?"

"Yes. They had been diagnosed in Dr. Andino's absence as having died from natural causes, but he suspects that some of them may be poisoning victims."

McKenna's statement had all hands waving in the air, with some reporters waving both hands, but he remained focused on Sheehan.

"How many cases is he looking at and when will he know?" Sheehan asked.

"It's going to take a couple of days to know for sure because all the bodies he thinks should be reexamined have been buried and must be exhumed. I've applied for and received twenty-one court orders authorizing us to do just that."

Sheehan was content to let it rest there, but he was the only one. Remembering the Public Information Unit's Axiom Number One—Always be nice to CNN because they're national and in a position to put a bad slant on a crime story that could hurt tourism, one of the city's lifeblood industries—McKenna pointed to John Brogan from CNN.

"Care to speculate how many of those buried cases are victims?" Brogan asked.

"I'm not qualified to venture a guess, but Dr. Andino fears that as many as half of them might be victims."

"I'm sorry, Detective McKenna, but let me make sure I heard you correctly," Brogan said. "Are you saying that's possibly eleven more, in addition to the four victims you already know about? Is that a possible total of fifteen victims in one month, all poisoned by the same man?"

"Yes, looking at it pessimistically, that's fifteen victims." McKenna held up his index finger to indicate to Brogan that he would accept only one more question from him.

"How many of those cases are HIV positive?"

"I don't know." Enough of this guy, McKenna figured, and pointed to Sue Richardson from Channel 9. But then Brogan breached protocol. "Do you have any idea on the killer's motives?" he shouted.

Don't want to answer that one today, McKenna thought. He ignored Brogan and gave Richardson his most gracious smile. She returned his smile, every bit as gracious, and asked, "Detective McKenna, do you have any idea on the killer's motives?"

Damn! If I say yes, next they'll ask me what they are and where I got my ideas from, McKenna thought. I can't drag Bellevue into this yet, so what's the answer? He settled for, "Yes, some ideas, but I'm not authorized to disclose that information. That would be up to the DA since he's the one who will have to establish motive for the jury at the killer's trial."

"Then you expect to make an arrest?" She asked.

"Eventually, but I can't say when."

To McKenna's surprise, Richardson just nodded and said, "Thank you." He pointed to Bill Patti of *Newsday* for the next question.

"How many people are now assigned to the case?"

"More than one hundred," McKenna answered. He thought he had given them enough for one night and figured the best way out would be to turn the show over to Heidi. He nodded to her and she lowered her hand. Sensing more developments in that newsworthy Lane-McKenna tiff, all cameras swung to Heidi.

Heidi was ready. She raised her mike and stared straight at McKenna with the perfect forthright expression on her face, the picture of the pretty little girl next door whom you just caught stealing a doll from your daughter's doll carriage. "Before I ask my question, I'd like to apologize to you for my conduct and attitude at our interview yesterday. At the time, I thought your assertion that Benny Foster had been poisoned was patently ridiculous and that was the way I handled the story. But we all know now just how wrong I was and how right you were. That's not to minimize my conduct yesterday. My treatment of you was wrong, I admit it, and I'm truly sorry."

As she lowered her microphone, a tear formed at the corner of Heidi's left eye. She maintained a stiff upper lip, her expression contrite and forthright, but her lower lip was trembling.

How did she do that thing with the tear? was all McKenna could wonder. His wonder turned to shock when first one, then another, then many more reporters began to clap.

God! If she's got some of these caustic, worldly, hard-ass skeptics bullshitted, imagine what she just did to those poor viewers at home, McKenna thought. As long as this story continues, *Fox Five News* featuring Heidi Lane is headed for a real ratings boost.

"No damage done, Heidi," he said. "What's your question?"

"Okay," Heidi said, looking professional in spite of the tear running down her cheek. "What made you first suspect that Benny Foster had been murdered, that he hadn't frozen to death like everyone else thought, including me?"

"It was when my partner told me there was something wrong. I wasn't the first one to suspect it—she was. She's good, so I suspect whatever she suspects."

"Your partner?" Heidi asked, taken aback.

"Detective Maureen Kaplowitz. If I hadn't been transferred to the Seventeenth yesterday, she would've had the Benny Foster case and you'd all be interviewing her today, not me."

McKenna could see that Heidi didn't savor that thought and, looking around the crowd, he judged that neither did anyone else. They had all seen the way Maureen had handled Heidi the day before and none of them relished the thought of being publicly tied in knots by Maureen. McKenna concluded that, as far as the press was concerned, he was the perfect man for the case.

Thinking it the right moment, McKenna ended the conference by promising to report on further developments the next afternoon. He then turned and walked back into the station house, but he didn't go back upstairs to the squad office. He had one more mission to accomplish before he went home, so he sat hiding in the ground-floor clerical office, looking out the window and watching the press pack up and leave for their offices to file their copy. Fifteen minutes later, figuring the coast was clear, he left the station house and headed for Third Avenue.

It was at that same corner that Heidi got him again. She was standing there, blocking his path, leaving him no way to avoid her politely. "I figured you'd be coming this way," she said, giving him her cat-and-mouse smile.

"Apparently you were right. So what's up this time?"

"My cameraman's filing my interview, so I'm off now. I just felt like talking to you."

"Can't right now, Heidi. I've got things to do tonight and I'm kind of in a hurry."

"Really? Business or pleasure?" she asked, raising one eyebrow and smiling that seductive smile.

She sure has total facial control, McKenna thought, but what is she really up to? "It's a social event."

"Is that where you're going now?"

"No. Now I'm on my way to get a sandwich."

"Just a sandwich. Good idea!" she said, looking as excited as if that sandwich was the best idea she had ever heard. "Do you mind if I join you? I'm starving."

Look at this, McKenna thought. She even has a starving face. "No, I wouldn't mind except it's not for me. I'm getting a sandwich for my boss."

That looked like devastating news to Heidi. "Too bad. We have a lot to talk about and I think it would be fun."

"Business or pleasure?" he asked, surprised at himself for even asking the question.

Heidi took a moment to look him up and down deliberately, leaving him with no doubt about what was on her mind. "Both. I live only a couple of blocks from here, but I guess now I'm just gonna go home by myself, wash my hair, and do some ironing," she said sadly, then gave him a rueful smile he had never seen before. "You know, I'd rather do anything instead of ironing. Maybe some other time? I still feel that I have a lot to make up to you."

"Heidi, you're a great-looking woman and I'm sure you know it. I'm really flattered, but there's something you should know about me."

"What? That you're married?" she asked teasingly.

"Yes, to a woman I love, the mother of my daughter."

"So you think that this you-and-I thing just isn't going to happen, right?"

McKenna had to stifle a chuckle at the thought of it. "I'm sure it would be fun, but I'm just as sure it's not gonna happen."

"Maybe not," she conceded. "You know, we were good together today. Better than—what did you call us? Good professional acquaintances?"

"Yeah, we're that and we're also great actors. Maybe even better than Tracy and Hepburn."

Heidi responded with her forthright stare, but this time McKenna felt she wasn't acting. "You know, I'm kind of embarrassed," she said seriously. "I really expected you'd go for it. See you tomorrow." Without another word, she turned and walked up Third Avenue. McKenna thought she was swinging her hips more than she had to for simple forward locomotion, but still appreciated her style.

Now what is that girl really up to and why? he wondered as he lost sight of Heidi in the crowd of pedestrians walking home. She's a problem, but nothing like the problem I'm gonna have after Angelita sees that show we put together tonight. That's sure not gonna play well at home.

McKenna got home at 7:30 and found Angelita in the bedroom. She looked ready, wearing her red dress with her hair up, her nails done, and her makeup on, but McKenna knew she wasn't even close. There were decisions to be made on choices not taken lightly by Angelita.

Draped across the bed was her black cashmere overcoat. McKenna was happy that important decision had already been made in his absence and required no input from him. But next to the overcoat were a black pair of high-heeled shoes and a black purse, a red pair of high heels and a red purse. He knew that issue had to be addressed but, to make matters worse, spread on the top of her dresser were her diamond necklace and her ruby necklace.

When he had entered the bedroom, she had been standing in front of the full-length dressing mirror, deep in thought, so he knew it was going to be some time before the final touches were completed to her satisfaction. There were just too many variables involved. Although Sotto Cinque was just five minutes away by taxi, he figured they were going to be late for dinner.

"Hi, honey. How was your day?" she said as she watched him come up behind her in the mirror.

"Fine. Making some progress," he answered, then kissed her on the neck as he held her around the waist from behind.

"And your press conference? How did that go?" She was still facing the mirror, pulling down her dress as he held her.

Is this a trap, or hadn't she seen it yet on TV? he wondered. No, she didn't watch it, or I would have heard about it first thing. "Okay. I managed to get through it without any damage."

"Did that bitch have anything to say?"

"As a matter of fact, she apologized to me on the air. After that, all she had was one easy question."

"Huumpph. She probably did that just to boost her ratings. Be careful of her. She's still trouble."

"Don't worry, I will," he said as he admired Angelita in the mirror. Every time he saw her, he felt lucky. What's this fine-looking little thing doing with me? he would always wind up asking himself. Great personality, great shape, smart as a whip, sexy as can be, and twenty years younger than me.

"You look great," he said, then took a look at himself standing behind her in the mirror and towering over her. Not bad, considering, he concluded. Tall enough, pretty good shape, and I still got my hair, whatever color it is. Starting to show some years, though.

In the mirror, she had caught him inspecting himself, and she smiled. "Not bad, considering," she said, then squirmed around so that she was in his arms facing him and looking into his eyes. "What really does it for me, though, is that you're the smartest man I know."

It was an old joke with them. "Not the smartest person you know?" he asked.

"No, but at least you're in the top ten. Once you grow out of this cops-and-robbers business, you'll probably make the top five," she said, having fun but meaning it.

It was an old song McKenna didn't want to hear again. He knew that she was so blasé about his job that she hadn't even bothered to watch his press conference on TV. For once it had worked in his favor and he was prepared to have a delightful time that evening.

Then she spoiled it, a little. "You look exhausted, Brian. We're going to get home early so you can get some sleep. Tomorrow's probably another long day, right?"

"Right," he answered dejectedly, knowing exactly what she meant. She was always overly concerned about his health, so they would get home early, he would go to bed, and go to sleep. What she meant was sleep, and that was it. He let her go and walked over to the bassinet.

Janine lay under her blanket in the fetal position, sleeping soundly with her thumb in her mouth. He wanted to pick her up and hold her, but knew that could provoke a catastrophe. Janine was a good sleeper, but when she was up, she was like Angelita—bright-eyed and busy. "Don't do it, or we'll never get out of here," Angelita warned.

"I won't. I'm gonna get ready. About ten minutes?"

"More or less. The baby-sitter's not getting here 'til seven forty-five."

Angelita was slipping into the black shoes when he left for the bathroom. Five minutes later he was back after running the electric razor around his face and brushing his teeth. She was again in front of the mirror, wearing the black shoes with the diamond necklace around her neck. "That looks just great," he told her.

"Really? I don't look too fat in this dress?"

"How can anyone look fat in a size four? You have no stomach and you look great from behind," he said. There was another tie on the bed, so he took the hint and changed ties before sitting in the corner chair, ready to begin. He knew that he'd be seeing every dress-shoe-necklace combination, so he sat back to enjoy the show.

Brunette was at the bar having a cup of coffee and talking to Mike Brennan when McKenna and Angelita arrived at Sotto Cinque at eight fifteen. The police commissioner and the *Post* columnist had their corner of the bar to themselves, sitting there like a couple of nobodys, seemingly unnoticed by the rest of the patrons. Of course everybody in the place knew who they were, but the haughty residents of the East Side of Manhattan customarily made a show of studied indifference when it came to their treatment of the many celebrities they encountered living and hanging out in their neighborhood. The hip East-Sider attitude was: Hey, I'm me and I'm real important, so who cares who you are?

McKenna got that treatment when he entered, but even this crowd couldn't help but notice Angelita. As the two new arrivals checked their coats at the door the eyes of the East Side were upon her, and she was even earning a few un-abashed stares, something that was never done here. Angelita pretended not to notice and did that little Angelita-thing he loved in those circumstances, holding his arm and looking admiringly up at him as they walked down to the end of the bar. Protocol demanded that they not show it, but they both felt great by the time they were next to their two friends. Brunette was standing and smiling, waiting to greet them, while Brennan was in his usual posture, elbows on the bar and staring into his martini.

In appearance the two men were a study in contrasts, looking as though they wouldn't even know each other. Brunette was in his late fifties, but seemed like he was in his forties. He was tall, dark, and handsome, a meticulous dresser, and exuded a personality based on his love of life and people in general. He was intense and impossible to ignore, the kind of person who, when he talked to you, somehow made you feel you were the object of his total attention and the only other person in the room with him.

Brennan was different—not just different from Brunette, but different. He was that type of person seen occupying corner stools in bars all over town, day and night. Although he was McKenna's age—forty-eight—he looked older than Brunette, and didn't mind at all. Everything about him suggested he could care less about his appearance and what people thought of him. He was out of shape and careless, even slovenly, in the way he wore his expensive suits; by his demeanor, he gave the impression that he had already met everyone he wanted to know.

But both McKenna and Angelita knew there were two things Brunette and Brennan had in common, two things that brought them together on a regular basis and made them friends. Both were observant, experienced in life, and possessed raw intelligence that gave them insight into what made people tick and what made them do the things they did. Together, they enjoyed talking about people and events in the news, picking apart what public figures said as opposed to what they were really planning to do, and speculating, both with benefit of some insider knowledge, about what was going on behind the scenes as a political story was developing and being brought to the public's attention.

The other thing they had in common was a love for the City of New York and the good people in it. They talked about what should be done and what, realistically, *could* be done to improve the lives of these good people. Where they differed was in how many ''good'' people they were talking about. Brunette optimistically put the number at 7 million out of the 7½ million people living in the city; Brennan, ever the pessimist, thought there were no more than 4 million worth any effort at all.

Each gave McKenna and Angelita a warm greeting in his own way. Brennan remained seated on his stool, but offered them a hint of a smile and a wave before returning to the contemplation of the contents of his glass. Brunette welcomed McKenna with a hearty handshake before turning his attention to Angelita. He kissed her on the cheek, saying, ''Creating quite a stir in that dress, aren't we?''

''Really? I hadn't noticed,'' she proudly lied.

McKenna knew that Brunette, always the perfect gentleman, was going to spend the next five minutes fussing over Angelita and her dress, so he bellied up to the bar next to Brennan.

Brennan gave him a pat on the back, but he was concentrating on something more important than polite conversation. His glass was almost empty and he was trying to get the barmaid's attention. She saw him and rushed to prepare another perfect martini for her famous steady customer. Then she gave the occasional customer his usual drink, putting a chilled glass and a bottle of O'Doul's non-alcoholic beer in front of McKenna.

Brennan took a moment to savor his first sip, then gave the waiting barmaid the okay sign, freeing her to attend to the needs of the other ten customers at the bar.

"You better catch that guy in a hurry," Brennan said as McKenna took his first long, good gulp of beer in weeks.

Oh-oh! This isn't just small talk. Bad news coming, McKenna thought. He put his glass on the bar and faced Brennan. "I'm gonna catch him, eventually. But I don't think he'll be able to kill again, so what's the rush?"

Brennan didn't look up from his own drink, which sat on the bar. "The rush is that two things are happening here that, I think, should put a lot of pressure on you, maybe even unbearable pressure. One of them is predictable, but the other one is just a feeling I have from some letters I've seen, something I'm trying to understand."

"What's the predictable one?"

"Ben Rosen. He's put together quite a letter to the editor that they're gonna run tomorrow. He calls for his usual things, but this time your killer has given him a soapbox to stand on because now people are going to be especially interested in what's happening with the homeless. Naturally, he blames what's happening out there on the government. He thinks the government isn't spending enough to alleviate the plight of those folks, so that's why they're out on the street being poisoned."

"And what does he think the government should do? Build more and better shelters?"

"At least shelters that they wouldn't mind going to? Sure," Brennan said, looking up from his drink for the first time. "Rosen states the obvious in paragraph one, and if that was all he was saying, I'd clap for him, give him my vote, then kick the soapbox from under him just to shut him up. But he goes on from there, laying blame on the government for everything wrong, like it's the government that threw them out on the streets."

Brennan thought he had stated his case sufficiently on that point and resumed his contemplative focus on the contents of his glass.

McKenna didn't get it. He recognized Brennan's ability to analyze a continuing news story and then tell his readers not what was happening, but what was *going* to happen. Being a cynic familiar with the dark side of human nature and also being something of a moralist, Brennan also told them what *should* happen if things were right and people were good, but things were never right and people were rarely good. If they were, it wouldn't be news.

So everyone wants this guy caught as soon as possible and there's gonna be some pressure, McKenna thought. But *unbearable* pressure?

Brennan glanced over and saw the confusion in McKenna's face, so he swung around on his stool to face him. "It's simple," he said. "Rosen is blaming the government for all the conditions that put the homeless in the shape they're in.

He blames it for the lack of affordable housing, for the loss of blue-collar jobs that those folks, in theory, should be doing, for the poor educational system that fails to train them to do those basic jobs that no longer exist anyway, for allowing drugs that destroy families and contribute to homelessness to come into this country, and even for failing to give some of them useful job training while they were in jail. Your problem is that a lot of what Rosen writes about has a grain of truth in it. He knows what's wrong, but he's got the wrong bogeyman. Unfortunately for you, he uses the common one, the government, that unseen entity that we've become conditioned to blame for everything that's wrong in this country.''

"So? Everybody blames the government for what's wrong in this country. Nothing new there," McKenna said.

"But as long as this killer is on the loose, Rosen's got his soapbox and people will be listening to him. The longer this goes on, the louder he'll get. Naturally, he'll be calling for new programs and massive shake-ups in a few of our bureaucracies, including yours. He'll make enough noise so our city politicians will feel the heat. Because they can't strangle Rosen to shut him up, they'll shift the heat to Ray and you and make every effort to make both your lives miserable until you catch your killer.''

"We've had heat before and we can take it," McKenna said. "Rosen's looking at this thing as a social problem, but basically it's just a murder investigation.''

"Fine, but I think that maybe you should hear about the other problem you might have developing around you.''

"You mean the one that's going to make the pressure on me really unbearable?''

"If it means what I think it could mean.''

McKenna was concentrating so hard on what Brennan was saying that he hadn't realized that Brunette and Angelita had completed their That-Is-Surely-The-Nicest-Dress-In-Existence-And-It-Looks-Like-It-Was-Designed-Especially-For-You ceremony and that they were standing behind him, waiting, so he was startled when Brunette put his hand on his shoulder.

"What's the matter? You're not hungry?" Brunette asked.

That's why Ray's in charge, McKenna thought. He knows that this is supposed to be Angelita's night and he also knows that she hates listening to police stuff when she's supposed to be having fun. But even though Mike's probably already told Ray what he's telling me, I still want to hear it right now, whatever he's got to say. "I'm starving, but can you guys wait just a minute?" he asked Brunette while watching Angelita's reaction. Then Brunette turned also to watch Angelita before answering.

She looked happy, content, and unconcerned. "Try and make it fast," she said. "We'll be waiting at the table.''

Brunette gave McKenna's shoulder a squeeze before he escorted Angelita to their usual table in the rear of the restaurant. McKenna turned back to Brennan. "You heard her, Mike. Can you make it fast?" he asked.

"Sure. I'll make it fast and let you draw your own conclusions. Today, just one day after you got on to what has been happening, my paper started getting what amounts to fan mail for the killer. Not just a stray letter from a nut or two, although we're getting those. But we're also getting lots of other letters and faxes, some of them quite sane and literate, with the writers using impeccable logic to make their points. Most of them are even signed."

"And tomorrow there's sure to be lots more?"

"The longer this case goes on with the killer still free, the more letters I expect we'll be getting each day."

"So that's the cause of the 'unbearable' pressure? You think we're going to wind up with copycat killings?"

"It's happened before in serial-killing cases, hasn't it?" Brennan asked.

McKenna got the point. "Yeah, it has, and in smaller and saner places than New York. In this city we have millions of people and more than our share of nuts. If it started here, it would be on a grand scale."

"Putting unbearable pressure on you?"

"Absolutely," McKenna conceded. "Join us for coffee after dinner?"

"I'll come over after you're all done eating."

Jack, one of the owners, was at the table talking to Brunette and Angelita by the time McKenna arrived and sat down. They were ready to order, so McKenna just had time to glance at his menu before ordering the hot antipasto appetizer followed by the eggplant parmigiana.

Over dinner, Angelita did have fun listening to Brunette expound on one of her favorite subjects—the antics of his four daughters. He had put three of them through big-name colleges and had then provided them with fancy weddings right after graduation. He speculated that the girls had been in a race to see who would be the one to bankrupt Dad, with the losers getting married in wedding chapels in Las Vegas.

According to Brunette, he and his wife, Ann, had outlasted them all except for his youngest, Ilene, but it hadn't been easy. They had forgone vacations for eight years and Ann had taken a job as a substitute teacher to keep his daughters in those pricey schools, followed by the expense of putting them in those made-to-order white wedding gowns. But Ilene was due to graduate in September and was very serious with a guy who was a nice enough fellow, even though he had shown a character defect when he had left the Faith, resigning from the NYPD to become a NYC fireman. Ilene was the one who would do Brunette in. Both his house in Queens and his vacation home Upstate were mortgaged to the hilt and he was living from payday to payday while struggling to pay off old college loans.

According to Brunette, his solution to the problem of the last impending wedding had been to take Ilene's young man to the garage, show him where the ladder was kept, and then fill his head with drivel by citing bogus statistics documenting the absolute truth that couples who had eloped had proven to be happier, wiser, and wealthier than those silly girls who had wasted their parents' life savings on a four-hour bash, because things always worked out better when the bride and groom's families never really got to know each other.

Brunette said the young man had bought it and had thus assured his position as Brunette's all-time favorite son-in-law. For Ilene's benefit, he and the young man were scheduled to have a massive falling-out the day after her graduation or the day before any appointment she might make to look at wedding dresses, whichever came first.

Of course, both Angelita and McKenna knew that Brunette's story was just so much wishful thinking and that Ilene would have her big wedding, but they let him talk without interruption. They thought it was good therapy for Brunette to talk about his girls, and it showed them that life was going on for their friend, that he was getting over the tragedy of losing his only son, a rookie cop killed in the line of duty the year before. The loss had devastated Brunette and, for some time, McKenna and Angelita had thought he would never recover. But slowly he was, and his two friends were delighted to see his love of life returning.

As McKenna had anticipated, throughout dinner not one word was mentioned about the case. However, as the waitress was clearing the plates away Brunette asked McKenna, "What's your schedule like tomorrow?"

"Potter's Field with Dr. Andino in the morning."

"Could you tell Ward I'll be by to see him at about two?"

"Sure." McKenna knew just what Brunette meant. Brunette wanted to discuss Brennan's theories with him, but he wouldn't violate the chain of command. Ward would have to be present while they discussed the case, so McKenna knew that Brunette was indirectly telling him to make sure that both he and Ward were at the office at two o'clock.

Brennan arrived carrying a fresh martini as coffee was served, and he immediately launched into a discourse on one of his favorite subjects, the deficiencies of the city's public school system. Out of the blue, Angelita stopped him by asking, "Do you know Heidi Lane?"

"Casually," Brennan answered. "She was a reporter at the *Post* for a few years before she got into television."

"Why do you think she treated Brian so badly yesterday?"

"Error in judgment, I guess. It surprised me because she usually treats the cops pretty good when she interviews them. I hear her father was a cop."

Brennan's simple statement sent a shiver up McKenna's spine. He looked at Brunette and found that his friend was staring at him, a worried look on his face. "I'll check it out," Brunette said.

"Check what out?" Angelita asked.

"He's going to find out if Heidi Lane is the little girl in the picture. If she is, it would sure explain a lot," McKenna answered.

He didn't have to say more. Angelita knew exactly what picture he was talking about. It was *the* picture, the one that had been lying at the bottom of McKenna's jewelry box since she had known him, the snapshot taken at a funeral that showed the little brown-haired girl standing on the front steps of a church bawling her eyes out as the casket passed her.

Angelita had only asked McKenna once what the picture meant and why he'd kept it, but he hadn't answered her. She had left the issue alone since then, figuring the picture was a remembrance of something in McKenna's life that had scarred him deeply. Some things are better left alone, she had concluded, and she hadn't seen or thought about the picture in years. But now the issue was back.

Brunette, McKenna, and Angelita didn't say another word as they silently sipped their coffees. Brennan noticed the change of mood at the table, but he didn't ask about it. He just politely excused himself and returned to the bar.

That's how it went at the table for the next ten minutes until Brunette asked for the check. None of them had said a word, each lost in thought.

As they passed Brennan on their way out, McKenna detached himself from Brunette and Angelita. "Sorry, just have to ask Mike one more thing. I'll meet you outside," he told them, then pulled up the stool next to Brennan at the bar.

"Seems I've been giving you bad news all night," Brennan said, once again staring into his glass.

"Yeah, you have," McKenna conceded. "But forewarned is forearmed, so I appreciate the news anyway. I have a request to make before I go."

"Whatever I can do," Brennan said, facing him. "What is it?"

"Can I see some of those letters? I'd like to get a feel for what some people are thinking."

"You know what you're asking me to do?" Brennan asked. "You must realize that showing the police letters that were sent to a newspaper, letters that were written by persons not suspected of having committed any specific crime, would be, I believe, a violation of what we in the Fourth Estate consider our First Amendment ethics."

"Yeah, but can I see them?"

"Sure. I'll make copies of them and send them all to you at the Seventeenth Precinct."

30

Is that you, Heidi? McKenna asked himself as he sat on the bed in his pajamas, staring at the old photo. If it is, it looks like you were about eight years old when this was taken, so that would make you about twenty-nine right now. That part seems right.

McKenna stared harder at the picture, looking for clues. If the brown-haired little girl was Heidi, then Heidi wasn't a natural blonde. He gave up and put the picture away.

Angelita came out of the bathroom looking ravishing in one of his favorite If-You-Can-Catch-Me-You-Can-Have-Me nighties, which was a pleasant surprise for McKenna. She figures I need some cheering up, he gleefully thought, and that'll do it. Looks like things are finally going my way.

It turned out that he could catch her, and while he got to bed at ten, early like Angelita had wanted, he didn't get to sleep until eleven.

The phone rang at 2:15 A.M., awakening both of them. It was Tavlin. "Looks like Street Crime's got him," he said.

"They're following him?"

"Nope, locked him up. Got him right after he killed another bum on Lex and Sixty-third, by Hunter College."

Hunter College? No surveillance locations near there, McKenna thought. What were they doing there?

Tavlin anticipated McKenna's question. "The team that got him had been relieved because both the cops have court in the morning. They were on their way back to their base when they saw the killer walking out of an alley. Except for his clothes, he fit the description, so they put him under surveillance and had another team check the alley."

"And they found a body?" McKenna guessed.

"Yep, but not poisoned. This time he slashed the bum's throat. So they radioed the surveillance team and they scooped him up at East Sixty-seventh and Lexington."

"East Sixty-seventh and Lex? Isn't that the block the Nineteenth Precinct station house is on?" McKenna asked.

"Sure is. He was just hanging on the corner there when they locked him up. Had a kitchen knife with a blood smear on the blade in his pocket, along with two sets of welfare ID and more than two hundred dollars in cash. One of the IDs was his, but the other one belongs to the dearly departed."

"The victim have AIDS?"

"They tell me it looks like he did. Sick and scrawny. Looks like he was sleeping when the killer cut his throat."

Makes sense, McKenna thought. Since all the publicity, the killer's not going to be able to pull off poisoning his victims since nobody out there's taking any wine from anybody. But he's still gonna get them, so he cuts their throats. No reason for him to keep it secret any longer and go with the poison thing. "Did the killer make any statements?"

"He's a little drunk and nobody asked him anything. The Street Crime cops figured you'd want to do the asking, so they just took him to the Seventeenth."

Smart cops, McKenna thought. Smart enough to follow the guy, smart enough to send another team to check the alley, smart enough not to question him, and smart enough to bring him to the Seventeenth instead of the Nineteenth. But why would anyone who'd just committed a murder go hang out on the station-house block? "Where are you, Chief?"

"On my way to the Seventeenth to take a look at the prisoner before I go to the crime scene. I just woke Ward up, so he'll be there, too. I'm gonna have a car pick you up in fifteen minutes. That enough time?"

"Should be."

"See you. I'm almost there," Tavlin said.

McKenna replaced the receiver and turned on the nightstand light. Angelita was sitting up in bed, staring at him and looking very unhappy. "You're going?"

"Yep. They got him, so it looks like today's starting out real early for me."

"Is Heidi Lane gonna be there?"

Is she? McKenna wondered. It's got to be all over the police radio and she said she only lives a couple of blocks from the station house. She'll be there, he concluded. "Maybe."

"I think it's time we talked about it."

"We will, but not now. Tavlin's got a car coming for me in fifteen minutes," McKenna said as he got out of bed. While Angelita glared at him, he went to the closet and selected a new suit, shirt, and tie, then went to his dresser and pulled out fresh underwear and socks. He was feeling uncomfortable under Angelita's gaze and thought he should say something else before he went to the bathroom to shower and get dressed. He was sure that Angelita wasn't going to be easily put off.

Then a wonderful thing happened. The baby woke up and started crying.

For some reason, the baby crying always made Angelita feel good, feel needed. She got up and stood over the bassinet, smiling for a moment before she picked up the baby. The crying stopped at once. With Janine in her arms, Angelita looked at McKenna with a reproachful smile on her face. "Did that mean old Daddy wake you up with his silly job?" she said into the wrapped bundle, but McKenna knew she was talking to him.

At least she's smiling, he thought. Thanks, Janine. You got me out of this one, so I owe you big.

By the time McKenna stepped out of the radio car at the corner of Lexington Avenue and East 63rd Street, quite a bit of work had been done and quite a few people were there. The street had been closed off and the block was crowded with marked cars from the 19th Precinct, the Crime Scene Unit, and Emergency Service, as well as many unmarked cars. The focus of attention was an alley 100 feet west of the corner. The area around the alley entrance was roped off with yellow crime-scene tape and an Emergency Service truck with searchlights on top was backed into it. Even from the corner, McKenna could see that the alley was illuminated like Times Square.

The death of this unfortunate certainly isn't going unnoticed, was McKenna's first thought as he scanned the large group of reporters huddled across the street from the alley. Heidi wasn't there, but Mike Sheehan from *New York 1* was broadcasting live from the scene. *Fox Five News* and *Eyewitness News* had their vans there with the large roof antennas raised, preparing to go live.

A 19th Precinct cop held up the crime-scene tape so McKenna could duck under. As soon as he turned the building corner, McKenna saw that it wasn't an alley at all, but rather a fifty-foot recessed delivery entrance in the Hunter College building. It ended in a loading dock and a large roll-down delivery door. Everybody was at the foot of a metal fire escape that ran up the side of the building. He spotted Tavlin standing among a group of cops and detectives. He didn't see the body, but guessed where it was. Hung from the second-floor landing of the fire escape were blankets and tarpaulins, creating a street-level tent-like shelter for the victim.

That's where he was, McKenna knew, inside his shelter, his presence there proved by the puddle of blood running onto the ground from under one of the hung blankets.

Tavlin detached himself from the group as soon as he saw McKenna. "Looks like it's all wrapped up for you, Brian," he said.

"Looks like it. Have you seen the prisoner yet?"

"Yeah. He's pretty close to the sketch. Had him weighed and measured. Five foot eight, hundred and thirty-one pounds."

Pretty close? Bad news, McKenna thought. My bank witness, Richie Cama, said the sketch looked just like the killer. That's much better than "pretty close." Worse, the guy we've got is skinny, but from what I know, he's at least ten pounds too heavy. Is it possible I've got two killers running around out here already? Could Brennan be so right so fast? "Mind if I take a look at our victim and get the preliminaries started?" he asked.

"No problem," Tavlin answered. "Crime Scene Unit already took all the photos they need." Then he turned to the cops and detectives assembled next to the victim's shelter and yelled, "Get those blankets and tarps down."

The response was instant. Two young cops ran up the fire-escape steps and pulled the blankets and tarps up onto the landing as McKenna watched. Except for the shopping cart jam-packed with the victim's worldly goods, the scene reminded him of the curtain going up to reveal the body of the hero in the last act of a macabre Greek tragedy.

Taking care not to step in the blood that formed a large tear-shaped puddle that began at a small cut on the side of the man's neck, McKenna and Tavlin stood over the body and took a good look.

He was lying on his back in an unzipped sleeping bag, tucked into another blanket covering all but his shoulders, neck, and face. They couldn't see much of him, but they saw enough to guess what his life and death had been like.

McKenna's first impression was that he was emaciated, sick, and frail, so thin that the polyester jacket he was wearing rested on his frame as it would on a wire hanger. He was a gray-haired white man, looking about fifty years old, clean-shaven, with ice-blue eyes, open and fixed on the moon in an empty stare. White, bloodless lips were pulled back in a grimace, pressed against a row of decaying brown teeth, the only discernible color on the man's face. The rest was white and waxen, totally devoid of color.

McKenna studied the puddle of blood and noticed that it was beginning to coagulate at the edges. Then he bent over and took a close look at the man's eyes. They were flat, sunken in their sockets, and glazed over, a fact that, along with the coagulated blood, caused some confusion for him. This man's been dead a couple of hours, he thought.

The more he looked at the body, the more convinced he became that he was right. His conclusion was buttressed when he touched the man's cheek. It was cold and dry. "The ME coming?" he asked Tavlin.

"Uh-huh. Notified at one-fifty-five."

"I'd like to get a body temperature while we're waiting," McKenna said.

"Worried about the time of death?"

"Very. I'd say he's been dead since midnight, at least."

"Spooky," Tavlin commented, shaking his head. "That would mean the killer sat in the tent with the body for a couple of hours before the Street Crime guys saw him."

"Maybe."

"Maybe? What else could it be?" Tavlin asked.

"What it could be is that he's not the killer."

"Then what about the knife? He had it on him."

"That remains to be explained, but unless the guy we've got has some serious medical training, he's not the killer. You see that cut?" McKenna asked, pointing down to the man's neck.

"Yeah, I see it," Tavlin said, bending over the body. "I see what you mean. Can't be an inch long, but he knew just where the artery was, sliced right through it. This guy's got no blood left in his head." Standing up, Tavlin yelled, "Get me an ambulance attendant over here."

The attendant was there in under a minute. Following McKenna's instructions, he stuck a thermometer under the victim's tongue, then held his mouth closed. Two minutes later he took it out, shook it, and held it up to the light. "I'm reading about ninety-one degrees," he said.

"How long would you say he's been dead?" Tavlin asked the attendant.

"Looking at him, I'd say about three hours."

"Thanks. That's all we need for now."

McKenna checked his watch when the attendant left: 3:10. "I'd say he's right on the money," he said to Tavlin. "It's about forty degrees out here and he's lost nine degrees of body temperature. Figure three degrees lost per hour and you've got this guy murdered before midnight."

"Okay, you've got me in your corner. Want to wait for the ME or do the search now?"

"Let's get it over with."

Tavlin went to the street and returned leading two 19th Precinct uniformed cops. They knew the drill and pulled on latex gloves as they approached McKenna and the body.

"Anybody know his name?" one of the cops asked.

Instantly, McKenna felt bad, and for the first time he pitied the man on the ground. What's the matter with me? he asked himself as he stared at the body. Have I been standing over so many murdered souls lately that their names aren't important to me? You've got a name and I didn't even bother to ask anyone what it is. Sorry.

Neither had Tavlin. He reached into his pocket and pulled out the Department of Social Services ID card that had been removed from the prisoner and read it. "His name's Daniel O'Sullivan," he said.

Following the standard procedure, one of the 19th Precinct cops was going to do the physical search while the other recorded the result. But first the victim had to be removed from the sleeping bag, so one of the cops lifted the body from the shoulders while the other pulled at the sleeping bag from the feet. As he pulled it off, an eight-by-eleven manila envelope fell from the folds and landed on the ground with a clunk. Written on the face of the envelope in large block letters was: *FOR DETECTIVE MCKENNA.*

"Don't touch that," McKenna said. "I need Crime Scene to dust it for prints."

Right on cue, Joe Walsh walked into the building recess. He looked as sloppy as ever, with his tie pulled down and a smear of dirt on the lapel of his overcoat. "Just happened to be in the neighborhood. Heard we've got this one wrapped up tight," Walsh said loudly.

Yeah, right, McKenna thought. Scagnelli's got him off duty right now, but where there's press, there's Joe Walsh. And we don't have anything wrapped up. But still, I'm glad he's here. "Good to see you, Joe. I heard Scagnelli had you really running tonight."

"Yeah, he had his fun running me around Harlem and then out to Riverhead, all for nothing as it turns out, but I'll get even. I always do."

"No matches to the prints on the bottle?"

"No, just like we all knew there wouldn't be. Those prints belong to your killer and no one else."

"Would you mind dusting that," McKenna said, pointing to the envelope on the ground.

"Not at all," Walsh answered while removing his off-duty pair of latex gloves from his pocket with a flourish. He put on his gloves, picked up the bulky envelope, stared at the message on the front, then turned it over and inspected the seal. "It's sealed tight," he said. "I guess you'll want blood type from the saliva if he licked it closed?"

"Please."

Then he took another moment to stare at the front of the envelope again. "Obviously a lefty writing with his right hand," he informed his audience.

Obviously? How could Walsh tell that just by looking at it in an alley? McKenna wondered. "That's what I figured," he said.

McKenna's statement slowed Walsh down, but only for a moment. He stared at McKenna shrewdly while he felt the envelope in his hands. "And I guess you'll want to know what's in it as soon as possible, right?" he asked.

"No, that's all right, Joe. Take your time and do it right. I already know what's in it."

"You do?" Tavlin and Walsh said in unison.

"Sure. Inside you'll find a white ceramic cup with embossed red lettering on the front, possibly the name Benny. In addition, you'll also find some sort of taunting cryptic message for me from the killer."

"If you say so," Walsh said, humbled. "You want anything else?"

"Yes, if you would. Street Crime's got a knife at the Seventeenth with some blood on it. I want to know if it matches this gentleman's blood."

"Sure." Walsh took his off-duty blood collection kit from his pocket and scooped some blood from the puddle on the ground into a vial. In contrast to his grand entrance, Walsh left quietly.

The rest of the search of the victim's body turned up little of interest to McKenna. There was no money or other identification, but the victim did have Kaposi's sarcomas on his skinny right ankle. However, the inventory of the items in the shopping cart turned up one thing that McKenna found curious. There was a plastic bag filled with vials of prescription medicine; they were all in the victim's name, but in the bag was also an appointment card. Like Rodney Bailey, Daniel O'Sullivan had an appointment to see Dr. Suliman Rashid at the Bellevue AIDS Clinic.

As the cops wheeled the shopping cart away, the medical examiner finally arrived. This time it was John Andino himself, a break in the usual procedure. Police cases, especially those occurring at night, were always handled by one of the junior pathologists in the medical examiner's office, and never by the ME himself. But here was Andino at 3:15 in the morning.

"I heard about this one on the radio, so I thought I'd handle it myself because I wanted to thank you for the way you handled that press conference," Andino explained to McKenna.

"I bet Wright didn't care for it too much."

"No, I don't imagine he did. He called in sick and I've been trying to get him all night. I think he's in that place where people go when they're 'unavailable for comment.' "

"And you won't be seeing him again?" McKenna guessed.

"Only when he comes in to pick up his last paycheck. What can I do to get rid of this body for you?"

"You can start by giving me your opinion on the wound and your best estimate of time of death."

"My pleasure." First Andino looked at the puddle of blood. "About two pints," he commented. Then he leaned over the victim and stretched the neck wound open with his fingers. "One-inch neck wound completely severing the carotid artery. Unconsciousness resulted in under five seconds due to loss of blood and oxygen to the brain. Death occurred within one minute as blood pressure dropped. In my opinion, this man was murdered by a doctor."

McKenna couldn't help himself. He had to take just a moment to preen for Tavlin's benefit, confident that things were going to get even better, prediction-wise.

They did. Andino looked into the victim's eyes, felt his face, then raised the dead man's arm and rolled down the jacket and shirtsleeve. He bent the arm back and forth at the elbow a couple of times, then examined the underside of the forearm. "Evidence of postmortem lividity and rigor mortis is beginning to set in," he said, then shocked both McKenna and Tavlin when he used his finger as a thermometer and stuck it in the victim's mouth. "Body temperature about ninety degrees," he said, then stood up, looked at his watch, and thought for a moment before announcing, "This man was murdered between eleven thirty and midnight. Anything else?"

"No, John. That's all I need," McKenna said before turning to Tavlin. "How about you, Chief?"

"I've heard quite enough, thank you. Let's go."

McKenna, Tavlin, and Andino walked to the street. Before Andino left, he reminded McKenna once again about their morning trip to Potter's Field, giving McKenna that little knot in his stomach.

Across the street, Heidi Lane had arrived and joined the group of reporters behind a row of police barriers. McKenna saw that, indeed, Heidi had gone home and washed her hair. But she had done more than that. She had a new hairdo, very blond and bouncy, with lots of curls. That, together with a shiny black vinyl coat, a very short black vinyl minidress, and black calf-length combat boots, made her look like a teenager. He also couldn't help noticing that she was talking to Joe Walsh, he on one side of the police barrier with the envelope under his arm and she on the other side.

Then one of the reporters noticed him and they all started waving, shouting his name, and calling to him. All except Heidi. She just barely raised her hand and gave him an almost imperceptible wave before resuming her conversation with Walsh.

What could they be talking about? McKenna wondered. Whatever it is, I don't think it means good news for me.

31

Only Ward and the two Street Crime cops were in the squad office when Tavlin and McKenna got there. Bad news travels fast, McKenna thought. If it were certain we had the right guy, there'd be plenty more chiefs here looking to link themselves up with a good headline. But now it's not, so none of them want to be pushed before the cameras to explain away a mistake. "Looks pretty bleak up here," he commented.

"What did you expect?" Ward asked. "You want the list of who was coming, but suddenly found another emergency requiring their presence?"

"No, but I'd like Chris Saffran here."

"I already called him. He just got off at midnight, but he's on his way back."

"Midnight? Why so late?"

"Street Crime wanted him. You'd be surprised how many skinny bums they found that matched the description from a distance, so I authorized the overtime for him."

Money well spent, McKenna thought. Although it happens to every cop sooner or later, there's nothing in police work so embarrassing as doing a full-blown surveillance on the wrong man. Nobody wanted to take a chance on that happening, and why should they? Saffran had seen the killer and could tell them whether someone they were watching was the right guy or not.

"We used him a couple of times," one of the Street Crime cops chimed in. "A lot of those bums out there should really eat more and drink less."

"And you are?" McKenna asked.

"Eddie Sorenson, a good friend of Johnny Pao's."

Young, sharp Sorenson figures he might be in trouble and knows Johnny Pao's one of my best friends, McKenna thought while stifling a chuckle. This kid's going far in this job.

But not as far as his partner, McKenna had to acknowledge when the older cop announced, "I'm Tommy Ryan and I introduced Eddie to Johnny Pao. Matter of fact, I'm the godfather of my good pal Johnny's first daughter."

"And I'm Brian McKenna, another pal of Johnny Pao. Looks like you two did some pretty good police work tonight."

Sorenson and Ryan cast sidelong, suspicious glances at each other before Ryan said, "We thought so at first, but now we hear you think we got the wrong guy."

"Maybe. But even if he is, it was still good police work."

"So there's no trouble over this?" Sorenson asked.

"Not for you. Where's the prisoner, in the lineup room?"

"Yeah, but he's taking a nap."

"Did he say anything?"

"Not a word. He's been drinking and you know how tiring that can be."

"What was his reaction when you jumped him?"

"Kinda funny. Almost like he was expecting us," Ryan said. "When we were coming up on him he took the knife out of his pocket and handed it to me."

"And it had blood on it, so you locked him up?"

"Yeah, without thinking twice."

I would have done the same thing, McKenna thought. "You had him under surveillance for ten minutes before you locked him up?" he asked.

"Yes sir."

"And what did he do during that time?"

"Not much," Ryan said. "He just walked up Lexington Avenue. Every once in a while he'd stop and look around for a few minutes, but then he'd start stumbling up the avenue again."

"Okay. Let's go take a look at him."

McKenna, Tavlin, and Ward followed Sorenson and Ryan into the dark viewing room. They left the lights off so that the prisoner wouldn't be able to see them through the one-way mirror that separated the viewing room from the lineup room, but they had nothing to worry about. Their man was slouched in a chair with his head resting on the wall behind him, sound asleep.

McKenna was immediately struck with how closely the man resembled the sketch. He was rail thin, dressed in a field jacket and a filthy pair of jeans, with a thin face that just about matched the sketch. "I want to see his eyes," McKenna said to Ryan. "Go in and wake him up, then have him write down his name and his date of birth."

Ryan left, closing the door behind him. A minute later he came into view in the lineup room, carrying a legal pad and a pen. It took Ryan ten seconds of shaking the seated man before the prisoner opened his eyes and squinted up at the cop, a confused look on his face. Gradually he focused and his eyes opened wider.

"The eyes are wrong," McKenna commented. "One thing my bank witness emphasized was the killer's eyes, and those aren't them."

After some protracted explaining, Ryan got the man to understand what he wanted. He placed the legal pad on the prisoner's lap and offered him the pen. The prisoner took it with his right hand and wrote on the pad, concentrating with his tongue sticking out of his lips.

McKenna had seen enough. He left the viewing room, followed by the other three.

"See what you think of this," Tavlin said as they waited outside the lineup room for Ryan. "He's drunk when he goes to visit his friend and finds him with his throat cut. He decides to tell the police and he brings the knife with the blood on it to show them, just in case they don't believe him. Then, for some reason, he gets to the corner near the station house and maybe changes his mind. That's when Street Crime grabbed him."

"Right, but I don't think he changed his mind. He was gonna go in, but he had to decide about the money," McKenna said, then turned to Sorenson. "He had more than two hundred dollars on him and the victim's ID, right?"

"Two hundred and thirty-seven dollars and eighty-one cents," Sorenson said.

"There was no money on the body, so I figure he went through his friend's pockets and took his money and ID. When he was grabbed he was in the process of deciding how much, if any, of that money he was going to tell the police belonged to Daniel O'Sullivan."

Ryan came out of the lineup room at that moment and handed McKenna the legal pad. Written on the top page in neat, childish handwriting was: *My name is Robert Esposito. I was born on May 12, 1951. This time I did not do nothing wrong. I swear to God. I do so declare.*

McKenna passed the pad to Tavlin. The chief took one brief look and said, "That man's no doctor. I can read every word. Now what?"

"Now we give him all the coffee he can hold while we wait for Chris Saffran to get here and tell us what we already know. After that, somebody has to go downstairs, explain things to the press, and tell them to go home. Finally, we'll have a little chat with Mr. Esposito before sending him on his way."

McKenna thought for a moment that he had pulled it off when the two bosses nodded in agreement with his analysis. He knew he was wrong when Ward stopped nodding, eyed him shrewdly, and asked, "What do you mean when you say *somebody's* got to go down and talk to the press?"

32 McKenna found that he had misjudged the reporters' reaction to his news. After answering their questions for ten minutes, he got the feeling they were absolutely elated about the developments of the evening, proving once again that bad news is always good news to lawyers, undertakers, and especially reporters. The story would go on and they anticipated titillating the public interest because now the killer was slitting throats, something they knew would sell more papers than his poisoning three or four people a week.

As they say in the business, the story "just got legs," so they were happy to accept without question McKenna's explanation that, after further investigation, it had been determined that the person arrested earlier in the evening was not in any way connected to the murder of another homeless person who appeared to be HIV positive. McKenna told them that Supervising ADA J. Davenport Pinckney III had been apprised of the results of the investigation and had ordered the prisoner released.

Through it all Heidi asked not one question. She was there with her microphone in his face, just like the other TV people, but all she had for him was a smug smile, a smile he found disturbing as he waited for her to ask the question about the envelope Walsh had been carrying under his arm, the one question he wasn't prepared to answer just then. If she was aware of the significance of the envelope, she hadn't shown her curiosity by the time he knew it was best to end the impromptu press conference.

That ending was prompted by the only question he didn't answer. When a reporter from one of the supermarket tabloids asked if it was possible that the killer had removed any of the victim's blood, McKenna threw up his hands, then simply turned and walked back into the station house. He knew that particular reporter's next question would have had something to do with teeth marks on the victim's neck, a question he would have felt ridiculous dignifying with an answer.

By the time McKenna got back upstairs, Saffran had talked Esposito into a state approaching coherence. The Street Crime cops had completed the voided arrest paperwork and were downstairs invoicing the victim's possessions. Mc-Kenna figured the only tasks left to accomplish before getting home for a couple more hours of sleep were to interview Esposito and await the arrival of Walsh with the package from the killer. But first he went into Ward's office to report the results of the press conference.

Ward and Tavlin were relaxing over coffee while comparing notes on which chiefs were up for promotion and which ones were on the downswing and headed for retirement. They suffered through McKenna's report without comment and resumed their gossip as soon as he finished.

That done, McKenna settled down to the Esposito interview. Esposito was lucid and ready to cooperate, and freely answered all McKenna's questions until the interview progressed to the point of personal finances. However, McKenna soon had it wrapped up to his satisfaction.

Things had happened pretty much the way McKenna expected. Esposito stated that the victim lived in his shelter in the building recess on East 63rd Street, so he had dropped in on his old pal O'Sullivan to sleep off the aftereffects of a bottle of wine. He had sobered up a bit when he had found O'Sullivan dead with the knife by his side. After that, he had taken the knife and gone through the victim's pockets, taking his ID and cash. Then he had started for the 19th Precinct station house to report the murder. Along the way he had realized that he couldn't quite remember exactly how much of the money in his pocket was O'Sullivan's and how much was his. He had still been trying to decide when the police arrested him on the station-house corner. Since the police hadn't asked him any questions, he had felt free to take a nap.

The interview slowed up when Esposito insisted that all but twenty dollars of the money the police took had been his, but McKenna couldn't see wasting any time on a small point. He agreed to return $217.00 to Esposito, then had just one more question for him. Esposito answered it, stating that he was sure he hadn't seen any sign of the killer.

McKenna thanked Esposito for his trouble, called down to the desk officer and arranged for the return of the cash, then sent Esposito off with Saffran.

McKenna was putting the finishing touches on his report on Esposito's interview when Walsh finally arrived at 4:00 A.M. He had two NYPD property envelopes with him, and he dropped them on McKenna's desk with a flourish. He appeared eager to show off his work, giving McKenna a Guess-What-I've-Got-For-You? look.

But first McKenna had some questions for him. "What were you and Heidi Lane talking about tonight?

Walsh's expression didn't change. "Nothing much. Why? I'm not allowed to exercise my First Amendment rights and talk to the press?"

"To a point. I was just wondering if the subject of the envelope with my name on it came up."

"Yeah, it came up."

"And?"

"And nothing. I told her that if she wanted to know about it, she should ask you. After all, it's got your name on it. She could see that."

"That's it? She didn't want to know where it came from?" McKenna asked.

"Sure she did. She's a reporter. Same answer. I told her to ask you."

"What made you go over and talk to her in the first place?"

"She called my name out and maybe I owe her a favor. Besides, who doesn't want to talk to a girl who looks like that? You catch that skirt tonight?"

"Yeah, I saw it. Very attractive."

"Did she ask you anything about the envelope at your press conference?" Walsh asked.

"No."

"Then you'll be hearing from her," Walsh concluded. "She's not gonna spill out something only she knows about in front of other reporters. She'll keep it to herself and ask you about it where no one else can hear the answer."

"You mean an exclusive?"

"Sure. She was the only one sharp enough to notice that I went into that alley with nothing in my hands and came out carrying an envelope with your name on it," Walsh explained. "She figures that has to mean something."

He's right, McKenna thought. Heidi's sharp, but I already knew that. "I'm sorry for giving you the third degree here, Joe," he said. "I was wrong about you."

"You mean you thought I gave her everything I knew?" Walsh asked with a face that said even he was astonished at such a thought.

"It had crossed my mind," McKenna admitted.

"Then I think it's time you knew something about me. I have a certain reputation for tooting my own horn when I do something good, but it's mostly just a show just to piss off Scagnelli. I know that, when something good happens, all the bosses scramble to stand in front of the cameras to get their awards. Meanwhile, the cops and detectives who really solved the case don't get a line. Agreed?"

"I've seen that happen a few times."

"But it doesn't happen to me. I see to that. But let me tell you something else. I've been on this job for thirty-five years and, no matter who gets the credit, my job is still putting bad guys in jail. Never once have I said anything to the press that screwed up anybody's case."

Is that possible? McKenna asked himself, searching his mind through as many of the cases Walsh was prominently involved in that he could remember. He could come up with nothing that countered Walsh's assertion. "I see. Sorry if I thought different."

"Apology accepted, but remember this: A well-informed citizenry is the cornerstone of democracy."

"What's that have to do with this?"

"I don't know, but it sounds good and it backs the chiefs off every time I say it. Now, let's get down to business. Did you take elimination prints from your prisoner and the Street Crime cop who handled the knife?"

"Yeah. Did you get any latent prints off the knife?"

"Three."

McKenna reached into his desk drawer and handed Walsh two fingerprint cards. From his pocket Walsh took a magnifying glass and three enlarged photos of the latent prints he had lifted off the knife. He spent a couple of minutes comparing the latents to Esposito's fingerprints. "I don't have to look at the cop's prints. All three are Esposito's," he announced. "Thumb, index finger, and ring finger of his right hand."

McKenna hadn't expected anything different, figuring that the killer would never leave a knife with his prints on it at the scene. "You have any good news for me?"

"I have lots of information," Walsh said, tapping the two evidence envelopes. "You ready for it?"

"Yes, but let's do this in Ward's office so the bosses can see it. That way you won't have to explain it twice."

"Who's in there?"

"Tavlin and Ward."

"Then let's go in."

"They meet with your approval?" McKenna asked.

"They'd have to," Walsh said. "Scagnelli cut off my overtime, so I'm working for nothing. That doesn't bother me, but when I'm working for nothing I make it a point never to talk to pricks and incompetents."

McKenna led the way into Ward's office and dropped his two envelopes on the desk. The bosses acknowledged Walsh's presence with the barest nods, which was good enough for him. He picked up the first evidence envelope, ripped it open, and took out a four-inch steak knife covered in fingerprint dusting powder. The knife was a cheap one, with a blue plastic handle and a stainless-steel blade. A red blood smear was still visible on the edge of the blade.

"What we have here is a cheap, very common knife, the kind that comes in a set of four that you usually pay three dollars for in places like Kmart, so that's no help," Walsh said. "There is a smear of the victim's blood on the blade, type O positive. There were three fingerprints lifted from the handle, all belonging to Robert Esposito."

Walsh dropped the knife on the table, picked up the second evidence envelope, and ripped it open. Then he paused for effect, making sure his audience was hanging on his every word. Satisfied that they were, he extracted the envelope that had been removed from the crime scene. It also was covered in white fingerprint dusting powder. "We're dealing with a sharp guy here," Walsh said. "There is not a single fingerprint on this envelope and it was sealed using water, not saliva, to moisten the glue on the flap. However, it does tell us something about the killer. The Document Section has confirmed my original analysis of the handwriting. 'For Detective McKenna' was written by a left-handed person writing with his right hand." Walsh paused again and proudly looked around the room.

McKenna expected at least one of the bosses to ask Walsh how he knew that with just a casual glance on East 63rd Street, but none of them wanted to give him the satisfaction. McKenna didn't either.

Looking slightly disappointed, Walsh removed a white ceramic cup from the envelope. It was covered in black dusting powder and had some sort of emblem on the front. On the top of the emblem was BENNY, written in large red letters. Below the emblem was 74–77, also in large red letters. "This is the cup Brian expected to find in the envelope, so you can see why he's a first-grade detective and not some lesser rank," Walsh explained, looking as innocent as an angel as he scanned the room.

McKenna didn't know if the bosses got Walsh's meaning, but it came through loud and clear to him. According to Walsh, a first-grade detective like himself and McKenna outranked the rest of them, or should.

Ward did get it. "Get on with this, will ya?" he said impatiently.

Walsh was obviously happy to get some reaction, whatever it was. "Certainly, Lieutenant. As you might have expected, there's not a single print on the cup. I'm going to pass it around and you'll notice that the emblem is the Attica Prison logo, indicating that Benny Foster was a proud man of some experience who we'll all miss dearly."

Walsh gave the cup to Tavlin, who indicated his impatience, and possibly his opinion of Walsh, by placing the cup on Ward's desk without even glancing at it.

"I can see that we're in a hurry, so I'll just go on," Walsh said, really enjoying himself. He took a folded piece of white paper out of the evidence envelope and opened it. The paper was covered with black dusting powder and there was a typed message on it. A corner of the page was torn off and there was a small burn mark on the page in the middle of the printed message.

"This piece of paper was found folded inside the cup. Not a print on this either," Walsh said. "There's a message on it, I assume for Brian, but I don't think he'll mind us reading his mail in this case."

Walsh looked at McKenna as if seeking approval, but McKenna wasn't getting in Walsh's boat with these two heavy guns looking to sink it. "Please go on," was the best thing he could think of to say.

"Fortunately for us, everybody's favorite slave driver, Inspector Scagnelli, had his best lab technicians working long hours through the night, so I was able to get them working on this right away. The message was printed using a bubble-jet printer. The ink was analyzed and found to be the type commonly used in a Canon BC-02 cartridge, but that's not much help because it's also the ink used to refill many other brands of bubble-jet printing cartridges. The paper is Xerox 4200 DP bond, also a very common brand."

Walsh held up the paper for all to see, and four sets of eyes strained to read the message, just as he expected they would. Not yet. He turned the paper around and read the message to himself before he began speaking again. "You'll notice that a piece of the paper was removed by the lab technicians to determine its type and brand," Walsh recited like a high school science teacher. "You'll also notice that they had to burn a small hole in the message during the spectrographic analysis of the ink, but of course the document was photographed before that was done. Before we go on, are we all clear on the procedure used?"

"What the hell's the message," Ward shouted.

"I see it's time to move on to the message, Walsh said without a hint of emotion. "It says, 'Congratulations. You should be looking at 13 cases right now, counting this one. I was beginning to think I would finish my work unnoticed. If you are going to catch me, you had better hurry up. I still have work to do and there is not much time.' He signs it, 'Hyde.' " Walsh turned to McKenna and said, "There's a rather lengthy P.S. for you after the signature, a couple of things of a personal nature."

"Read it," McKenna said.

"Okay. It says, 'I thought this cup was what you were looking for in the *garbage on 31st Street, so I decided to present it to you as a reward for work well done. Please do not let Heidi Lane intimidate you on the air. I find your reluctance to fight back demeaning in an adversary.'* '' Walsh put the piece of paper down on the desk. ''Is there anything else I can help you gentlemen out with tonight?''

Tavlin quickly scooped the paper off the desk, then looked directly at Walsh. ''No, Detective First Grade Joseph Walsh, not tonight there isn't. It's unfortunate that you're probably the best crime-scene technician in the country, just like you say you are, because you are the most insufferable man I've ever met. Please go home.''

It was the exact thing Walsh wanted to hear. ''Thank you, Chief,'' he said proudly. Wearing a big smile, he turned and left without another word.

''You know, I love that guy. He pisses me off so I can't see straight, but I love him,'' Tavlin said, surprising everyone. Then he took a minute to read the message before he handed it to McKenna. ''What I'd like you to do is read it and think it over. Then I want your impressions.''

McKenna did as he was told. He studied it for five minutes before he looked up. ''I take it at face value. I don't think he told us a single lie,'' he said. ''I think he's killed thirteen people and I'm certain that he's going to keep on killing until he gets all the people on his list, unless we get him first. I think when he says that there's not much time, it's because he's got AIDS and doesn't think he's gonna last long.''

''Why the message in the first place?'' Tavlin asked.

''The way I see it, he thought he was going to get all the people on his list and not even be noticed. Then we got on to him, but he doesn't mind. Turned his mission into a kind of contest, and he's starting to enjoy it. He's certain he's gonna win—so certain that he's making like he's giving us hints to keep us up to speed.''

''You don't think he planted legitimate hints in this message?'' Tavlin asked. ''It seems to me he did.''

''He told us things he figured we already knew or things we were bound to find out soon. He watches TV and knows we were going to find out through autopsies how many cases there are, so he told us. He knows that we have his description, so he told us there's not much time, figuring we already guessed from his appearance and his mission that he has AIDS. He also thought we'd figure out that he was a doctor, so he told us he was when he signed it 'Hyde.' ''

''Dr. Jekyll and Mr. Hyde?'' Ward asked.

''Yeah, he's telling us that he used to be the good doctor, but now he's the bogeyman. From this message, I'm taking it that we're right on track in this investigation.''

''He's certainly giving us a lot of credit,'' Ward said.

''He's only giving credit where credit's due, and he's right,'' Tavlin said. ''Brian had already figured out every one of the things hinted at in this message. We're right on track and this killer expects that we would be.''

McKenna felt his head swelling, but noticed that Ward didn't look very happy with Tavlin's observation. Ward thought about it for a moment, and then gave the only answer a squad commander can ever give a chief. ''I guess you're right,'' he said.

Tavlin turned his attention back to McKenna. "So what do you think? Is it possible he wants to be captured?"

"Absolutely not. I think he plans to finish his list and die in bed, a free man. But first he's gonna have some fun with us along the way and gain some fame."

"He can't get fame unless everybody knows who he is," Ward said. "That means getting caught."

"He doesn't want to be famous spending his last days in jail," McKenna countered. "He's looking for Jack the Ripper–type fame. Nobody knows who Jack the Ripper really was, but he was still one of the most famous mass murderers in history. That's how our killer wants to be remembered. To make it interesting and build up his image, he's toying with us with these hints."

"How do you account for his personal fixation on you?" Tavlin asked.

"I think it makes it more fun for him beating me than whupping a faceless bureaucracy. He likes it personal, sort of a Sherlock Holmes–Professor Moriarty thing. I'm something of a famous guy on this job, so he feels better beating me than simply evading capture by the department."

"I think you're right," Tavlin said. "He wasn't kidding when he wrote that he didn't like Heidi Lane pushing you around. If you don't look good, then he doesn't look that good beating you."

"Then why's he playing with your head, sending that cup to you?" Ward asked.

"Because, to him, these murders are now a gentlemen's contest, and opponents always play psychological games with each other. That's why his letter is so friendly and so condescending, and I have to admit he got me. I don't like knowing that he was watching me while I was searching for that cup, with him knowing all the time what I was doing."

"In line with that, there's another reason he sent the cup back," Tavlin said. "He wants to keep it a friendly game with you, but he also wants you on his side as much as possible. So he sends you that Attica cup as his way of saying that Benny was a prick who should have been done away with a long time ago."

"I agree," Ward said. "Whatever his motives, they make sense to him and I think he's trying to convince you that they should make sense to you."

"He's clever," McKenna noted. "But he's not as clever as he thinks he is, which is why we're gonna get him. He gave us more hints than he intended in his smart-ass message."

McKenna had their complete attention, but it took him a moment to arrange his thoughts. Too long, as far as Ward was concerned. "Are you gonna tell us about it?" he asked impatiently.

"Okay. First, there's his grammar," McKenna said, picking up the Hyde message. "Concise sentence structure with no misspellings, proving once again what we already know. He's smart and educated, but notice that there's not a single contraction in the entire message. He says, 'You had better hurry up,' not 'You'd better hurry up,' and 'There is not much time,' not 'There isn't much time.' Then in the P.S. he writes, 'Please do not let Heidi intimidate you,' not 'Please don't let Heidi intimidate you.' Rather stilted language for such a smart guy, especially for a guy who's trying to show us how smart he is. So why does he write it like that?"

"Because he wants to be totally correct for history," Ward ventured.

"Maybe, but I think there's more. We know that his English is so good that people who've talked to him aren't even sure if he's got an accent or not. But the message gives us a clue. I've noticed that people who speak English as a second language don't like using contractions when they write, even though they use them when they talk."

"Why? They afraid of making mistakes?" Tavlin asked.

"I think so. I've seen well-educated foreigners make mistakes placing the apostrophe in our contractions. Besides that, they believe that using contractions somehow makes their writing less correct."

"Okay, so he's foreign born, but speaks English as well as we do," Ward said. "How does that help us?"

"In a big way, if I'm right. We have two of his fingerprints from the wine bottle and we also think he had some connection to Bellevue. Unfortunately, Bellevue doesn't fingerprint their employees, so I thought we had no way to make a match."

"But Immigration fingerprints all aliens for their green cards so they can work in this country," Tavlin said, picking up the point. "If he was working at Bellevue, he had to be a legal immigrant. Immigration's got his prints."

"Right. Now, what I have to do is go back to Bellevue and get a list from them of all the foreign-born doctors who've worked there in the last seven years or so."

"I see a problem with that," Ward said. "Our multi-ethnic city administration has a policy of not cooperating with the Department of Immigration and Naturalization in any way. No city agency is allowed to give up the names of aliens, whether legal or not, to any law-enforcement agency. Lord knows I've tried a couple of times, but they don't. Bellevue's part of the Health and Hospitals Corporation, a city agency."

McKenna thought it was a valid point, but Tavlin glossed right over it. "In this case, the policy's gonna have to change," he said. "I'll see to it. Any more hints you see in that message?"

"It just confirms a few of our suspicions. Now we're sure he's left-handed. We suspected that his homeless routine was just an act to get close to his victims. Now we know it. Homeless people don't have computers and TVs, but this guy does. He watched my interview with Heidi Lane and his message is printed with a bubble-jet printer. I think the only time he goes near a shelter is when he's working, looking for his next victim."

"Very observant," Tavlin said. "But it brings to mind a very pressing question. I believe you're on the right track and that you are going to get him, eventually. What I need to know is, will it be before he kills again?"

"I don't think so."

It wasn't what Tavlin wanted to hear, McKenna knew. They were under pressure, and each death would make it worse. Much worse, McKenna thought, if Brennan was right about the psychology of the situation.

Tavlin recovered quickly. "I think it's time to wrap it up. It's late and we all need some sleep."

"What's the plan for tomorrow?" Ward asked.

"Let's see," Tavlin said, then turned to McKenna. "What are you doing tomorrow, Brian?"

"I'll be going to Potter's Field to dig up some bodies, then I have to be here at two because the PC is coming to speak to Lieutenant Ward and maybe I'll be needed. After that, I'll be heading to Bellevue."

"Wait a minute!" Ward yelled. "Back up! Brunette is coming here tomorrow?"

"Sorry, I forgot to mention it," McKenna said. "I'm sure a message on it will come up, so it would be in the Telephone Message Log by the time you got in."

Tavlin wasn't fazed by the news. After all, the PC wasn't coming to *his* office. He went to the door, but then remembered something. "Do me a favor and scratch out a report for the PC on what we discussed tonight and sign my name to it," he said to Ward.

"I'll take care of it," Ward assured him, apparently unconcerned with the prospect that "scratching out" that little report for the police commissioner meant slaving for hours over the typewriter, making sure all spellings were right, all commas were in place, and everything was in it without an extra word.

McKenna felt his first misgivings when he noticed that Ward was looking directly at him with a content smile on his face and knew it was time to go when the door closed on Tavlin. McKenna got up and made for the door himself.

Of course he didn't make it. Ward had been a squad commander for years and was much too sharp for a simple escape trick from McKenna. "Brian, would you mind hanging around for a couple of minutes longer?" he asked.

33 By the time Tavlin and Ward were safely tucked away under their sheets, McKenna was just waking up. The difference was that they were home, while he was still in the squad office and had used his typewriter for a pillow during his too-short half-hour nap.

McKenna prided himself on his paperwork abilities and had figured the report to Brunette would take him an hour, at the most. But then the fatigue had set in so fast and so severely that his fingers forgot where the keys were on the typewriter. It wasn't his brain that gave out, he knew, because his brain had no idea where the keys were in the first place. He had tried it before and knew that he couldn't draw a typewriter keyboard from memory for love or money. It hadn't made any difference in the past because his fingers knew. But not this time, and they had even resorted to chicanery to get a break; he had been typing mechanically when he noticed the unintelligible gibberish those tricky, tired fingers were putting on the page in front of him.

It was no use, he had realized, so he had rested his head on the keyboard and hung his arms at his sides to give his digits a break.

But now he was up, and for a moment he didn't know where he was or why. Then the phone rang again, and he knew that was what had done it, snapping him out of his nap. It kept on ringing while he went to the bathroom, washed his face, and brushed his teeth. He knew who it was and knew she would wait, although he hoped she wouldn't.

The phone was still ringing as he sat back at his desk. He picked it up. "Hello, Heidi. What is it?"

"Very good, Brian. But you mean *Good morning*, don't you?" Heidi said sweetly.

"Okay, Good morning. What is it?"

"I notice that Tavlin and Ward left. That makes you alone up there right now, doesn't it?"

"Where are you?"

"On the corner, freezing my buns and waiting for you. But I could be up there in a minute if you say the word."

"I already told you, Heidi. That isn't happening."

"Maybe, but I think we should talk anyway. We have a lot in common, you know."

"Meaning?"

"You know. We're both bright, ambitious people with good jobs and we're both working an interesting case from different angles. Not to mention we're both sexy, good-looking people with great bodies and an indescribable but temporarily repressed hunger for each other."

She was doing something soft and sexy with her voice that McKenna found disturbing in spite of himself. All he could think was: People don't really talk like that, do they? He wanted to change the subject, fast, but the only thing that came to mind was that other thing he didn't want to talk to Heidi about. He said it anyway. "You want to talk about the envelope, don't you?"

"Maybe, but only if you really want to. You owe me on that one, but that's just business and I'm not concerned about it right now."

What is this girl up to? McKenna wondered. "Yeah, Heidi. I'll bet you don't care about that envelope," was all he could offer in reply. It sounded weak to him.

"Okay, maybe I care just a little about it. That can come later, or maybe we'll just be too busy and forget all about it. Are you almost finished up there?"

"I've got a lot of paperwork to do and then I'm going home." He was satisfied with his statement, thought he sounded authoritative and in charge.

Heidi didn't think so. "We could go to my place, you know. It's closer than yours and tonight I think it makes more sense for you. Do you know what we could do there?"

"No, and I don't want to know," he answered, disturbed and worried by something she had said. How does she know her place is closer than mine? he wondered. Does she know where I live? Then he noticed that she was purring into the phone, describing her plans for the rest of the evening with him anyway. He listened with half an ear, at first, but then found himself paying close attention. He had gotten married late in life and figured he had gotten around as much as any single man before that, but Heidi was astounding him. Some of the things she was describing sounded physically impossible to him, unless one of them was a contortionist. He knew he wasn't, but she sounded like she really knew what she was talking about, so he guessed she must be.

McKenna thought about standing up and slamming the phone down with finality, but didn't think he could. "Heidi, stop it!" he yelled, glued to his chair. "I already told you, me and you together is a big never."

"I don't believe that, Brian. Sooner or later, it's going to happen," she said softly and reasonably.

"Maybe I don't believe it, either," he was astounded to hear himself say. What a minute! What's happening here? First the fingers and now this? he thought. Brain, you better assert some control over your appendages or we're all gonna be in big trouble. "I didn't mean that, Heidi. Forget it," he said.

"Yes you did, Brian," he heard her say as he hung up. He remained seated at his desk, staring at the phone and taking his time breathing and thinking.

There's more to this than her being a good reporter and this being a good story, he thought. Has to be, because if she wanted every story this bad, there'd be no state secrets left in the world. We'd be left with headlines blazing the real deal on every story Heidi covered and happy, smiling, physically exhausted cops, diplomats, politicians, and city officials stumbling around everywhere. So if it's more than the story, what is it? If she's Hank Lane's little girl, then she must hate me. Not love me to death, like the way she's acting like she does. So what would be her motive? Get me to give her secrets on this case, things that the press shouldn't know yet, and then disgrace me? Maybe.

He resumed work on the report, but it was slow going. Only half his mind was on the report. The other half was on Heidi and her motives. He was thinking furiously about it and was unable to concentrate. Then a chilling thought came to him: She's Hank Lane's daughter and she wants to get me in the sack. Then she's gonna expose me to Angelita, probably with pictures of me and her in those impossible positions she was talking about. She's probably even got her apartment wired for video and sound.

He pushed himself away from the desk and let his mind range over the potential consequences. She probably knows that Angelita's a Spanish woman, one of those insanely jealous, real-crazy-when-provoked Spanish women. All she'd have to do to kill me is prove to Angelita that we had an affair. Sooner or later I'd have to sleep, and then I'm dead, Angelita's in jail, and Janine grows up without a father. It's New York, so Angelita wouldn't go to jail for long under the extenuating circumstances, but just like Heidi, Janine grows up without a father. That's what's important to Heidi, he concluded. Sweet revenge that spans generations.

All of a sudden, a strange feeling came over McKenna. For reasons he couldn't quite understand at the moment, he wanted nothing more than to go home and hug his wife and daughter. His whole body acted on that feeling and his fingers flew over the keys, typing faster than he'd ever typed before, his mind clear and spewing out concise, detailed spurts of information to his fingers, so that thirty minutes later the completed report was on Ward's desk, proudly signed at the bottom, *Steven Tavlin, Chief of Manhattan Detectives.*

Now that wasn't so hard, was it? Why are these bosses always making such a big deal over these reports? he wondered as he put on his overcoat and went downstairs.

Before leaving the station house, he stood in the entrance foyer and checked both sides of East 51st Street. Satisfied that Heidi wasn't there, he sprinted to the corner of Lexington Avenue and hailed a cab. He made it.

34 McKenna heard the alarm go off at eight o'clock, but he ignored it, screwing his eyes closed tighter, huddling into his pajamas, and bringing the blankets over his head. Then came something he couldn't ignore. Angelita pushed herself up on her elbow, leaned over him, and turned off the alarm clock on the nightstand. Then she got under the blankets with him, put her head next to his, and whispered in his ear, "What got into you last night, you filthy animal?"

McKenna's eyes sprang open, but he moved not another muscle. He was frozen in fear. What's she talking about? he wondered. What did get into me last night and why am I such a filthy animal? For a moment he couldn't remember, but his ingrained Spanish-woman defense mechanism kept telling him: Make it good, make it good.

Then he did remember and he relaxed. What had happened last night with Angelita was fun, fun, fun. Then, to make matters better, Janine had awakened, just like he had hoped she would, and he got to hold her and walk her to sleep around the living room.

Now for the explanation, and it still has to be good, he thought. He pulled off the covers and looked at Angelita. She was smiling at him and looking very content.

"Can't us girls get any sleep around here at night? Really, Brian. Twice in one night, at two different times? We usually don't act like that anymore, do we?"

The way Angelita was smiling at him told McKenna that the explanation didn't have to be that good, after all. He looked around the room and spotted her red dress draped over the corner chair. "You see that red dress? My very favorite red dress?" he asked, pointing to it.

"Uh-huh."

"Well, when I came in here last night it was dark and I was bone-tired. Then I saw something. Do you know that red dress glows in the dark?"

"No."

"Well, it does. Believe me. Anyway, I saw that red dress glowing and I was so tired that I thought my little girl, the one with that sexy, great body, was sitting in the chair, wearing my favorite dress again for me, just waiting to do filthy things with me as soon as I got home. Then I held the dress and found out you weren't in it. You were here in bed, sleeping. Well, you know how I get sometimes when I get my expectations up, don't you?"

"Uh-huh."

"That's why you had to suffer again when I got home."

"Really?"

"Yep."

"Hmmm. You see that red dress over there?" she asked, pointing.

"Uh-huh," he answered turning again to look at it draped over the chair.

"Well, that's where it belongs from now on. Coffee?"

After showering and shaving, McKenna came out of the bathroom in the throes of a dilemma. Andino had told him that they were going to get down and dirty that morning but, looking through his closet, he was amazed to find that he had nothing but suits, and all new ones at that. No jeans, no Dockers, and not even an old flannel painting shirt. Just suits and dress shirts. It forced him to take a good look at his lifestyle.

He lived in Manhattan, loved it, and rarely left the island. In Manhattan, Angelita liked him in suits, and she liked dressing up and going to places where other people were dressed up. In theory, he was in charge of what clothes he bought and what he wore. Yet he couldn't remember being in a clothing store in a year and he was staring at a closet full of new suits. So suits it was: to work, out to eat, to the theater, and to all the PD affairs he always felt obligated to attend. But no matter how he rationalized it, he knew the situation he was facing was ridiculous and that Andino would have some fun with it.

As it turned out, Andino didn't have much to say about McKenna's attire when McKenna met him at the morgue at 9:00 A.M. Although the ME was dressed in coveralls and a field jacket, his only comment to McKenna on the subject was, "Nice suit for a dig. I guess I'm gonna be doing the dirty work."

"No, I'm gonna help out, John," McKenna protested.

"But I'm gonna be doing the dirty work?"

"You're the expert." They got in Andino's car and followed a large morgue wagon to City Island in the Bronx. After McKenna told Andino about the message and that the killer had claimed there was a total of thirteen victims, he dozed in the front seat while Andino drove. What finally woke him up was the loud horn blast. He looked around and saw that they were parked on a small ferryboat, still right behind the morgue wagon.

"Be there in about ten minutes," Andino said.

"Be where?"

"You've never been to Hart Island before?"

"No. Is that where Potter's Field is?"

"That's where it is. You've never been there?"

"No. I've never had a case before where the body had to be exhumed."

"I'm not surprised. We usually do only a hundred a year."

"So I guess you get up here quite a bit," McKenna guessed.

"Hardly ever. The place depresses me, so I usually send an assistant. As a matter of fact, the only reason you're sitting next to *me* right now is that this is the largest number of bodies we've ever exhumed at one time, so I figure it'll show up in our record books. Might as well have my name connected to the grand event for posterity."

If the place gets to Andino, it's sure to get me down, McKenna thought. "What's so depressing about the place for you?" he asked.

"Try seven hundred and fifty thousand people buried in a fifty-acre cemetery. Wouldn't that get to you?"

It did. The number shocked McKenna. "Three-quarters of a million unclaimed bodies buried in one small spot? Can there be that many?"

"That's what the records say. Since 1869 we've been burying them there, hundred and fifty to a grave. We do two to three thousand a year, but we keep it cheap. Use inmates from Riker's Island to bury them, pay them thirty-five cents an hour."

"And they go for that?"

"Sure. I understand there's inmates waiting in line for the detail, so they go on a seniority basis. They figure they get off Riker's for the day, get some fresh air, and get to make a couple of bucks in the process."

"Says a lot about Riker's, doesn't it?"

"Sure does. Tells me Riker's must be some shithole," Andino concluded.

"You're right about that," McKenna agreed. "Every time I go there, the smell lets me know what it must be like to live in a giant sneaker."

"If that smell gets you, you're sure not gonna like today's activities."

No, I'm not, McKenna thought as he watched Andino's face. Andino was smiling and enjoying himself at McKenna's expense, having a wonderful time, which led McKenna to conclude that he was in for a really rotten day. He didn't say another word for the remainder of the short ride.

When the ferry pulled into the dock on Hart Island, they were met by a smiling, happy-go-lucky correction officer who introduced himself as Carl Tufano. "You volunteered for this assignment?" was the first question McKenna asked him.

"Are you kidding? Of course I did. Thank God I've got the seniority. Gets me off Riker's Island, I get some sunshine and fresh air, and all the inmates wanna be here and give us no problems. Might be hard for you to believe, but it's the best job a CO can get."

Tufano got in the backseat and, as Andino drove to the cemetery, the CO acted as if the island had been in his family for centuries. He kept up a running commentary, pointing out the sights and expounding on the history of the small island, which was fine with McKenna—anything that delayed the task at hand was fine with him.

Tufano pointed out the old Nike missile base and the site of the old prison, and went on to explain that it had been used to confine prisoners ranging from Confederate soldiers during the Civil War to World War II POWs to city prisoners right up until 1982. According to Tufano, that was the year the old Potter's Field had been filled to capacity, so the living had been transferred to Riker's Island to make room for the dead.

McKenna would have been happy to stop at every point of interest and question Tufano for hours in order to expand his newly developed interest in small islands nobody knows about, but Andino drove straight to his objective and parked next to the morgue wagon. In front of the car was a row of pine coffins stacked three high at the edge of a long, deep ditch. At the far end of the ditch another CO and six inmates wearing thick work gloves, blue coveralls, and field jackets were gathered around a backhoe.

Andino took a list out of his pocket, left the car, and walked over to the coffins, ready to start work. McKenna was about to follow him when Tufano said, "Before I go, I need a copy of the court orders."

"You're not staying?" McKenna asked.

"Oh, I'll be around, but not close."

"Where?"

"About fifty yards upwind by the time you crack the first box."

"Really? Is it that bad?"

"Yep. Been through it a few times, but I don't do it no more. The bodies in those boxes aren't embalmed and some of them have been dead for weeks."

"What about the inmates?"

"I figure they'll hang around being helpful 'til they get their first good whiff. By the time you get to that second box, the smart ones will all be standing next to me."

What am I doing here? McKenna asked himself as he gave Tufano his copies of the twenty-one court orders. Tufano got out of the car, checked the wind direction by wetting his finger, then walked toward Andino and the coffins. He walked right past them without a word and kept going.

McKenna remained in the car, watching Tufano and not wanting to move. Tufano was just a speck on the horizon when he finally stopped, turned around, and waved.

You big sissy! Get out of the car and get to work, McKenna told himself, then did it. He walked over to Andino, trying to look as casual as he could. As he did, he noticed that the driver of the morgue wagon had elected to stay behind the wheel and wait.

If Andino noticed anything was amiss with McKenna, he didn't show it. The ME was busy checking serial numbers burned into the ends of the wooden coffins against numbers on his list. Then he took a black crayon out of his pocket and, while consulting his list, circled the serial numbers on two of the coffins.

"That's it? Only two?"

"Yeah. We got lucky. The rest are already buried, so we'll save these two for last."

"How does that make us lucky?"

"It's pretty basic. It's been warming up the last couple of days, so these two will be ripe. The other ones we want were shipped up here last week and buried when it was much colder. Since the ground heats up a lot slower than the air, they'll still be pretty cold."

"Where are they buried?"

"Probably right where that backhoe's sitting. It's really one long, continuous trench. Let's get them started."

McKenna followed Andino to the backhoe and the men gathered around it. "Where are the bodies from the beginning of the month to now?" Andino asked the corrections officer.

"Right underneath us."

"I need them up."

"All of them?"

"I guess so. I have to be able to see the serial numbers."

"I'll take care of it," one of the inmates said, then walked over to the backhoe, jumped in, and started it up.

McKenna sized up the inmate and decided that he was one of the toughest-looking men he had ever seen. Balding, about six-foot-six, maybe fifty years old, with tattoos covering his arms and a face covered with scars, the inmate looked like one of the bad guys in Wrestlemania.

"Thanks, Teddy," the corrections officer yelled up to him. Then to everyone else he yelled, "You folks better move back. Teddy's going to work."

The inmates didn't have to be told twice. They sprinted to the far end of the ditch and sat down to watch the show. McKenna, Andino, and the corrections officer thought it was prudent to follow their lead and joined them. Then Teddy got to work.

McKenna had never seen a piece of heavy equipment operated so expertly and so fast. It looked like Teddy was running on fast forward without a wasted motion. He started by digging a six-foot hole right in front of the backhoe and stopped when the heavy shovel barely touched the top of the first coffin. Then he swung the shovel over and dug down ten feet next to the top coffin.

Half an hour later he was done. Teddy had exposed one hundred coffins, stacked three high. To make things easier, he had dug a trench next to the row of coffins. He shut off his machine, got out, leaned against it, and lit up a cigar.

"Who is that guy?" McKenna had to ask the CO.

"Tough Teddy Two Fish. He was the vice president of the Brotherhood of Operating Engineers. Will be again when he gets out, I expect."

"What's he in for?"

"In his own way he kinda disputed some of the ballots in one of their elections, so he had to make a deal and take a year. He joins us every four years, right after their elections."

"I guess he always wins," McKenna said.

"Would you vote against him?"

"Probably not, but before I could say for sure I'd have to know what kind of dental plan they have," McKenna answered jokingly.

"The best. Teddy says that every time his members go to the dentist, they actually make money."

Why did I start talking to this knucklehead? McKenna asked himself. "Really?" he asked.

"That's right. Came straight from Teddy's own lips, God's honest truth."

McKenna had had enough and looked around for Andino. At first he didn't see him, then he looked down. Andino was already in the trench, circling serial numbers on coffins.

"Hey you guys!" the CO yelled to the inmates. "Get in the hole and help the doctor out or you'll all be in the general population tomorrow."

The threat propelled all the inmates into the trench so that Andino had more hands moving and backs straining than McKenna thought he could use. Might as well wait up here 'til I'm needed, he decided. At the other end of the trench he saw Teddy glance in, casually interested in the proceedings below. Like McKenna, Teddy had also decided the doctor already had all the manpower he needed and that his time would be better spent sitting under a tree and puffing on his cigar. Nobody disagreed.

Under Andino's supervision, it didn't take long for the inmates to get the other nineteen coffins out of the grave and onto the ground in front of McKenna.

Andino was the last one out of the trench. He went to the trunk of his car as McKenna watched him with some trepidation. When he returned, he was carrying a battery-powered drill with a screwdriver bit in the chuck. He stood over the first coffin in the row, read the serial number, checked his list, and announced to McKenna, "Our records indicate that coffin number 9600004 contains the remains of Avrim Randolph, male, black, age forty-six. Are you ready to document this exhumation?"

"John, I, for one, have total faith in your records. If you tell me Avrim Randolph is in there, then I believe you. I'll even swear to it. Go on to the next one."

"Can't do that. Believe me, mistakes are made all the time." Andino put on a pair of latex gloves, then took his power drill and unscrewed the first screw holding down the coffin lid. By the time he had removed the sixth screw, McKenna could smell something, but it wasn't the odor he had expected. It was familiar, but he couldn't quite determine what it was.

There were twelve screws holding the lid down. When Andino removed the last one and slid the lid off, the odor came to him, so strong that he had to close his eyes for a moment. It was some kind of insecticide. He opened them, looked into the coffin, and decided that Avrim didn't look bad, considering. He was wrapped in a blue paper blanket which Andino promptly ripped open to expose the dead man's right wrist. There was a plastic identification bracelet around it and Andino lifted the dead man's arm to read it while McKenna took out his notepad, ready to record the results of Andino's identification. "Avrim Randolph, died January first. ME Case Number 9600004," he read.

"He doesn't look like he had AIDS. He looks too healthy," McKenna observed, feeling foolish as soon as he said it.

"According to the autopsy report, he wasn't HIV positive. He's the first one who froze to death this year, January first, in the Bronx. It bears checking."

"Hey, I know the brother," one of the inmates announced as he looked into the coffin. "That be the homie that always be shufflin' the A and jivin' crazy on the Deuce for loose," which McKenna mentally translated as, "I am casually acquainted with the deceased. As a matter of fact, I have, on occasion, observed him on the subway, the A train to be precise. In addition, I have also seen him on West Forty-second Street acting crazy and putting on an exaggerated performance with the intention of panhandling change from persons passing by."

"Then perhaps you should be the one to say a few words over the deceased," McKenna suggested.

"No way. I ain't no jive-ass preacher."

"John, I suggest you get to the next case before our congregation is moved to tears."

Andino put the lid back on Avrim's coffin and replaced just four of the screws before moving on to the next coffin. "9600137. Should be Juliette Thompson, female white, age forty-six," he said, reading from his list. "She's the only female we'll be looking at. Found on January fourth in Corlear's Hook Park at East Tenth Street. Homeless, HIV positive, but the cause of death is listed as pneumonia." He unscrewed the lid and slid it off. Once again, the only odor was insecticide.

McKenna could see at once, just from her face, that the disease had ravaged her. It was thin and drawn, and even in death she looked like she still felt pain.

He tried to imagine what she looked like when she was younger, before the onset of the disease. Never beautiful, he decided, but maybe passably pretty. Andino tore the blue paper blanket, lifted her wrist, examined the bracelet, and made the identification.

For the next two hours and seventeen coffins, that was how it went. All the right bodies were in the right coffins and McKenna certified that fact in his notepad. Along the way he got to see for the first time the remains of one of his definite cases, Mickey Weyland. He looked terrible, but McKenna studied and memorized his face anyway. He had found long ago that it always helped him to keep the victim's face in the back of his mind when searching for his killer. Every time he had become tired or discouraged on one of those cases, he would re-member the victim's face once again, a face that always said to him, "I shouldn't be dead yet, but here I am. Keep going." And he would, renewing his efforts to catch the murderer, always reminding himself that it was his job to do the last thing government ever could do for the victim. He firmly believed that even the dead have the right to expect justice. So Mickey Weyland was there in his mind, along with Juan Bosco and Rodney Bailey. It wouldn't be long before he knew who they all were. He would commit all of their faces to memory.

Finally they were at the last two coffins. "I think you should have your men load the truck with the ones we've done before I open the last two," Andino suggested to the CO.

"Whatever you say, Doctor," the CO replied.

Five minutes later the morgue wagon was loaded. Andino then went through his procedure and unscrewed the lid on coffin number twenty. He wasn't halfway through before McKenna could smell the insecticide, but there was also something else. The pungent aroma of death was seeping through the lid. "How long has he been dead?" McKenna asked.

"Eight days."

Before Andino had removed the last screw, McKenna noticed that the audience wasn't that interested in this particular body. The inmates and the CO were slowly backing farther away from the coffin. When Andino finally pushed the lid off, McKenna could tell at once that they were acting correctly, under the circum-stances. The smell of decaying flesh was strong and nauseating and the body of the Caucasian man in the coffin had turned black.

McKenna had seen much worse, but it was something he would never get used to. To Andino, it was just another case. Once again, he ripped open the blanket, lifted the dead man's arm, and read the information for McKenna to record.

By the time Andino had screwed the lid back on the last coffin, McKenna's estimation of CO Carl Tufano had risen a notch. He was in the middle of the crowd in the distance, waving at McKenna.

"Just as I suspected, it looks like we'll be loading these last two bodies our-selves," Andino observed.

35 During the drive back to Manhattan McKenna couldn't get the smell of death out of his nostrils and felt certain that it was still clinging to his clothes, despite Andino's assertion that it was all in his head. Andino dropped him off at the 17th Precinct at 1:45, with fifteen minutes to spare before Brunette's arrival.

As soon as he walked into the office, McKenna could tell that something major had happened in his absence because there were only two people there at the busiest time of day. He was sure that those two were the reason everybody else was gone.

Sitting across from Maureen at her desk was Kerri Brannigan, dressed like a sixth-grader going out on her first date. She wore a frilly white print dress trimmed in light blue lace, white knee socks, and blue patent-leather half-heels. The clothes all looked new, but setting off Kerri's new look was her hair. Kerri had been to a beauty parlor. Her hair was professionally done in a Shirley Temple style complete with adorning light blue ribbons that matched her dress.

McKenna decided that Kerri had pretty good taste in clothes, in a twelve-year-old sort of way. But despite her new look, Kerri looked miserably unhappy, and so did Maureen. He then noticed that both Kerri and Maureen had been fingerprinted sometime that morning; they had cleaned their hands, but he could see the telltale gray smudges on their fingers. Between them on the desk was a manila NYPD evidence envelope. "What now?" he asked.

"Your killer has managed to get himself some good press. He's going to look like a hero in tomorrow's headlines," Maureen said. "As close as we can figure, he's given Kerri five thousand dollars."

"Five thousand dollars?" McKenna repeated, imagining the headlines as he slumped into the chair next to Kerri. "She saw him?"

"No, but it came from him. It was delivered to her room, probably by a messenger service."

"Her room? Where?"

"Ben Rosen and I figured that Kerri needed a break after Benny died, so Ben paid for a room for her at the Herald Square Hotel. He paid for the week, so this morning I went over there to give her the results of her blood test and explain what it meant to her."

"Explain it to me first."

"HIV positive," Maureen said quickly, glancing at Kerri to see if she understood. Kerri seemed unconcerned with her prognosis, so Maureen continued. "She wouldn't let me into the room, and she got me worried." Maureen stopped to give Kerri a reproachful look and Kerri lowered her eyes, looking like she wanted to cry. "I had to have the bellboy open the door, and then I saw what Kerri didn't want me to see. Toys, and lots of them."

"Toys?"

"Yeah, toys. All the things she should have had, but never did. Dolls, doll carriages, dollhouses, stuffed animals, play cribs. As you can see, Kerri also bought herself a lot of clothes. I asked her where she got all her new things, but she wouldn't tell me."

"Maureen," Kerri said, whining the name. "I already said I was sorry,"

"I know, Kerri," Maureen said, putting her hand over Kerri's. "I understand, but I have to tell Brian everything that happened. Okay?"

"Okay. I'll keep quiet."

"Just for now, honey. Brian will want to talk to you when I'm done telling him how smart you've been."

That satisfied Kerri. She smiled, made the motion of zipping her lips, and folded her hands on the table.

Maureen turned back to McKenna. "Kerri wouldn't tell me anything, so I searched her room. I found this under her mattress," she said as she reached into the evidence envelope and took out a stack of crisp, new hundred-dollar bills. The top bill was smeared with black dusting powder.

"How much is there?"

"Forty-one new, sequentially numbered one-hundred-dollar bills are what's left after Kerri's little spending spree. They were all dusted, but the only prints on them are Kerri's and mine."

McKenna picked up the stack and shuffled through the bills. Each one had dusting powder on it, so the bills felt like a stiff, new, powdered deck of cards. They were B bills from the Federal Reserve Bank in New York.

"I found this in Kerri's garbage," Maureen said, dumping the evidence envelope out on her desk. A folded 8½-by-11 piece of white bond paper fell out, covered in black dusting powder, along with a folded manila envelope.

McKenna unfolded the envelope. It had also been soiled with black dusting powder and was identical to the envelope Benny's cup had come in. Printed on the face in the familiar handwriting was:

KERRI BRANNIGAN
HERALD SQUARE HOTEL

"Left-handed man writing with his right hand?" he asked.

"Yes. There's lots of prints on that. Kerri's, the bellboy's, the desk clerk, and a few others we haven't identified yet. Probably the messenger's. But none of them match the prints off the wine bottle."

Next he picked up the folded piece of paper and noticed that a corner of the page had been torn off. "Xerox 4200 DP bond?"

"Yes, according to the lab."

"And the message inside is printed in Canon BC-02 bubble-jet ink."

"Yes."

McKenna unfolded the paper and read the killer's note to Kerri. It said simply: *Benny gave you AIDS, but it is not your fault. Enjoy the rest of your life.* Again, it was signed *Hyde.*

"When did she get this?" he asked.

"About noon, yesterday. It was delivered to the desk by a black messenger, dressed like he had a bike outside. The desk clerk had the bellboy bring it right up to her."

"Who else knew she was at the Herald Square?"

"Before this, I thought just myself and Ben Rosen. But even though Kerri's staying in the hotel, she's still been following her usual routine because that's all she knows. Yesterday she had breakfast at the Saint Francis soup kitchen like she always does. I figure the killer knew her routine, saw her there, and followed her to the hotel.''

Yeah, he would know her routine, probably from stalking Benny, McKenna thought. ''But she didn't see him?''

''She says she didn't. Insists on it, in fact.''

''Let me get this straight,'' McKenna said. ''This guy has his sketch on the cover of every newspaper in town yesterday, but he waits for Kerri outside a soup kitchen where there's hundreds of homeless people waiting to eat, and nobody sees him? Not a soul? Not even Kerri, who surely knows him because he killed her boyfriend the day before?''

''That's right,'' Maureen answered shortly, showing her exasperation with McKenna's line of questioning. ''It's the only way he could have found her, so that's what he did.''

''So he's got a very good disguise,'' McKenna reasoned.

''No, not a disguise,'' Maureen said patiently. ''The bum act is the disguise.''

The implications of Maureen's statement hit McKenna at once. ''You're right,'' he almost shouted. ''Unless he was sitting in a car following her, he wasn't in a disguise. He was there as himself, the doctor. The guy with so much cash that he can afford to drop five thousand off with Kerri. He was probably wearing a nice suit—''

''Padded,'' Maureen said, interrupting him.

McKenna hardly noticed. ''Right, a nice padded suit, good dress shirt and tie, well-shined shoes, a nice overcoat, maybe a scarf around his neck covering the bottom of his face. Probably a hat, too. A nice one, like a Homburg. And do you know what color his clothes were?''

''Something subdued, and anything but black.''

''That's right. He didn't have a stitch of black on anywhere. Nothing close to the description we gave the press. I'd say a brown suit, and he'd look the farthest thing from a homeless person you could possibly imagine. I'll bet he had the *Wall Street Journal* under his arm so he could walk into Bloomingdale's and the salesgirl would be right there for him with a big 'Can I help you, sir?' ''

''My, we are excited this afternoon, aren't we?''

''You bet I am. This explains a lot.''

''Like how he could get to Daniel O'Sullivan and kill him, but nobody sees him around? Or how come nobody recognizes him from the sketch?''

''That's right, but it gives me a warm feeling, now. Every time this guy tries to show me how smart he is, he trips himself up a little more.''

''You're getting pretty personal about this,'' Maureen commented.

''Yeah, he's coming into focus for me, and yeah, you're right. It is getting real personal because I've seen his work this morning. It's one thing to see him brag in writing about thirteen cases and it's quite another thing to see thirteen bodies stretched out in a row. That makes it real personal and now I know how he's doing it.''

''What? Killing people?''

''No. Getting away with it. He was in this town for years before he got sick, probably a doctor at Bellevue. But nobody recognizes the sketch because that's not the way he looked before he got sick. For all we know, he could have been a hundred pounds overweight. Then he gets sick and he leaves town. Could have happened years ago, but the important thing is that now he's back and nobody looks at our sketch and recognizes the doctor they used to know.''

"So then he's not living in the same place and seeing any of his old friends,'' Maureen speculated.

"Of course not. He came back here for only one thing—to kill the person who somehow gave him AIDS, but he's using the shotgun approach and killing anyone it might have been from his days at Bellevue.''

"There's one big problem with that theory. I read your reports, and what you're saying doesn't jive with what you're writing.''

"Wait a minute! You read my reports?'' McKenna asked.

"Of course I do. They're in Tommy's middle desk drawer, left side, underneath his bottle of Johnnie Walker Black,'' she answered, brushing aside his question. "According to what you write, Jim Heaney at Bellevue says there have been no reports there of any of their medical personnel getting AIDS from one of the patients there.''

"I know. It's perplexing, but Heaney's got to be wrong. From what we know, nothing else makes sense. All that I'm left to think is that our killer caught it there, and for some reason he didn't report it and sue the hospital like Heaney said he would have.''

"Maybe he's real rich, so rich that he doesn't care about the money. Since he knew he was going to die anyway, maybe he thought it wasn't worth the embarrassment to him, admitting he had the disease and then being the center of attention while he pursues his lawsuit,'' Maureen suggested.

"I thought of that already, and it makes sense except for one thing: Rich doctors don't choose to work in places like Bellevue. They prefer hospitals like Mount Sinai and Columbia Presbyterian, nice places where they can treat their patients from their fancy practices.''

"Then just keep thinking.''

"I am. What about the messenger services?''

"There's five pages of them in the Manhattan Yellow Pages. Tommy's got everyone out checking to see if any of them had a delivery to the Herald Square, but he thinks it's a waste of time.''

"He's probably right. This guy's too careful. He probably stopped a messenger on his bike, gave him twenty dollars, and told him to deliver the envelope to the Herald Square, right down the block. Naturally, that messenger's not reporting to his company that he made an extra twenty.''

"That's what Tommy says.''

"Any chance we can keep this quiet and keep it out of the papers?'' McKenna asked.

"None. I had to have the desk clerk and the bellboy fingerprinted, and they recognized Walsh right away.''

"Walsh fingerprinted them?''

"Probably a mistake on my part,'' Maureen admitted. "I wanted to get it done fast, so I called the Crime Scene Unit and he showed up.''

"So they see Walsh, recognize him from the papers, and put two and two together, which means they've probably called the press already. We have to come clean on this, which is very bad. Since they're gonna find out about this message to Kerri, I might have to tell them something about the one I got last night."

"I know," Maureen said. "Like I told you, your killer's going to get some good press out of this."

"You're right about that. They're gonna run with this and picture him as a benevolent, demented mastermind who delights in confounding and confusing his simple police department. He's gonna sell a lot of papers for them."

"Isn't that what he is?" Maureen asked.

"No, not the way I see it. He's smart, but he's not benevolent. He's taking time from people who had very little left. For whatever reasons he thinks he has, it's still evil, and evil things are done by evil people. And as far as being a mastermind, every time he shows off puts us closer to getting him."

"And what about giving Kerri five thousand dollars? That wasn't a nice thing to do?"

"He did it for the press, not for Kerri. He's too busy feeling sorry for himself to care about her."

"I'm not sure I agree," Maureen said. "Don't you think good people sometimes do evil things?"

"Yeah, sometimes. But not consistently, like this guy. No matter how you look at it, killing thirteen people is evil, and it's pure evil that's keeping him going through the pain. I just hope the press writes that in somewhere."

McKenna had had his say and got up.

"Where are you going?" Maureen asked.

"To go in and talk to the lieutenant and tell him how I made out this morning."

"You can't go yet," Maureen insisted. "I brought Kerri here so she could talk to you."

McKenna looked down at Kerri. It had appeared to him that she had been following their conversation with some interest, turning to one and then the other as they talked, but, as she had promised Maureen, she hadn't said another word. What could this poor, simple girl have to add? McKenna wondered.

"Okay." McKenna sat back down and faced Kerri. "What is it you want to tell me, Kerri?"

For some reason, Kerri looked scared. She looked at Maureen, who nodded encouragingly to her, but Kerri didn't say anything. Instead, her bottom lip began to quiver and her eyes filled with tears. "What is it, Kerri?" he asked. "You can tell me."

For a moment, he thought she was going to remain silent. Then the tears flowed from her eyes and she sobbed, "Maureen says you have to keep my money." Her shoulders shook and she covered her face with her hands.

McKenna hadn't given it any thought, but he did then. We might need it as evidence tending to connect the killer to Benny's death, he figured, but who cares? There's not gonna be a trial, anyway. Unless his victims' families serve him with a civil lawsuit that freezes his assets, a convicted killer can give all his money away, if he wants. Besides, if we voucher her money as evidence, the press will sob all over us. "Kerri, I don't want to keep your money. So don't worry about it," he said.

Kerri's hands flew from her face and she smiled so that McKenna thought she was going to hug him. But then she remembered something else and her eyes again filled with tears. "What about him?" she asked, sobbing and pointing to Ward's office door. "He wants to keep my money, too."

Him? Lieutenant Ward. Well, I'm sorry, Kerri, but that might be different, he thought, but didn't have the heart to tell her. Instead, he looked to Maureen for guidance.

"He doesn't want to keep it, really. I explained to her that he just wants to hold it as evidence and we'll get it back to her, sometime. Besides, he says it's better if we hold it because Kerri will waste it or lose it."

"Kerri, what do you want to do with the money?" he asked.

"Keep it and spend it."

"On what?"

"Toys and clothes and the hotel. I like the hotel."

"You want to stay there?"

"Yes, I want to stay there 'til I die," Kerri said adamantly.

Until she dies? McKenna thought. Stay in the Herald Square on $4,100 until she dies? Not likely. "Kerri, you have a lot of money now. But you're not gonna die for a long time," he explained.

"You're wrong, Brian. I'm gonna die soon."

McKenna looked to Maureen, wondering if she had told Kerri what HIV positive meant. Maureen shrugged her shoulders, looking as confused as he was. But Kerri had caught the exchange. "I've got AIDS, you know," she explained. "Benny gave it to me."

"Did he tell you that or did you read that letter?"

"I read the letter," she stated proudly.

"And what did it say?" he asked.

"I didn't read all the words, but I saw 'Benny' and I saw 'AIDS.' I'm not stupid, you know."

The press would just love this, he thought. Good killer gives dying girl money and bad police take it away. "Did you tell the lieutenant that might be a bad idea?" he asked Maureen.

"No, I didn't," Maureen stated. "Why should I? It's your case, remember? You tell him, give him whatever reasons you like, and he'll give it back."

"Just like that? You think it'll be that easy?"

"No."

36

"Do what you want with the money," Ward stated like it was a matter of no importance to him. "I was just making a few suggestions, that's all. She's just gonna piss it away or lose it, but if you say it's hers, I'm not gonna stop you from giving it back to her now."

"They were good suggestions," McKenna agreed. "Kerri needs someone to keep tabs on her finances or she *will* lose it. And I *am* going to invoice those bills as evidence. But in the meantime, I'm gonna try and get her cash replaced and have Maureen keep track of it for her."

"How you gonna get her money replaced?" Ward asked suspiciously.

"I said I was going to *try* and get it replaced. We'll know in a minute if I've got the juice." He took his department directory from his pocket, picked up the phone on Ward's desk, and dialed the number for the property clerk's office in headquarters. It was picked up on the ninth ring. "Property Clerk. How may I help you?" a brusque female voice answered, but her tone said, What are you bothering me for and how can I get rid of you?

"This is Detective McKenna from the Seventeenth Squad. Let me speak to whoever's in charge there," he said, sounding as pompous and important as he could.

"Yes sir."

Less than three seconds later, whoever was in charge came on the line. "Captain Ramos, Commissioner. Long time no see. I was just thinking about you."

Captain Ramos? Do I know this guy? McKenna wondered "Really? What made you think about me?"

"The tie. I caught you on the news this morning and you were wearing the same tie last night that I'm wearing today. Some coincidence, huh?"

Try as he might, McKenna couldn't remember the tie he was wearing the day before and he was sure he wouldn't know Captain Ramos if he fell over him. "It is a nice tie, isn't it? I bet it looks good on you."

"One of my favorites. But enough small talk. I know you're busy, so how can I help you?"

"We're vouchering forty-one hundred dollars and the invoice is marked 'Evidence,' but it's just a technicality. We're really just safeguarding it for the owner, but I want her to be able to spend it in the meantime."

"Let me see if I've got this straight, Commissioner. You're going to take her money and then the property clerk's office is going to loan it back to her, right?"

"Essentially correct, except we're gonna loan her different bills."

"That's a little irregular, isn't it?"

McKenna despaired at the mention of the word, knowing that "irregular" coming from a boss meant the same thing as, "Are you crazy? We're not going to do that."

"Yes, I admit it is. But if we don't do it, the department is going to get some bad press and then nobody's gonna be happy."

"And where do you want this money to come from?"

Where do I want this money to come from? McKenna asked himself. No idea, so it's easy to shoot me down.

But then Ramos shocked him. "I'd suggest the general disbursement fund. Easier to cover, as long as we get it back this fiscal year."

"Exactly what I was thinking."

"How do you want it? Fifties and twenties all right?"

"That would be fine."

"You want me to have someone deliver it today?"

Deliver it today? Really? "Can you spare somebody?" McKenna asked.

"For you? Sure. Catch you at the next dinner dance."

That Captain Ramos! McKenna thought, finally remembering the man. John Ramos, sat at my table at the last Hispanic Society dinner dance. Pretty wife who talked to Angelita so much all night about their supposedly wonderful winter vacation in Bolivia that Angelita almost had us going there. Bolivia! I *thought* I hated this guy. "Looking forward to it, John. See you there, and thanks."

"The money will be here," McKenna told Ward as soon as he hung up, trying not to sound like he was gloating.

"I'm impressed, Brian. Enjoy it while it lasts," Ward answered, looking totally unimpressed. "Now where's your pal? I've got my dress underwear on for his visit and the starch is sticking to my butt."

Where is Ray? McKenna wondered, checking his watch. Two-fifteen. It's not like him, the guy who always says, "I'd rather be an hour early than a minute late."

Brunette finally arrived at 2:30 and McKenna knew how it would go. In this setting, Brunette wouldn't be his old pal Ray; he would be the police commissioner, all business, and that's how it was. Brunette came in and waved a greeting as Ward jumped up and came as close to the military position of attention as he had since Korea. "Sorry I'm late. Sit down, gentlemen," Brunette said and took one of the chairs across the desk from Ward.

McKenna took the chair next to Brunette, ready to give any background information Ward might need.

"Where are we going with this, Tommy?" was all Brunette said to launch Ward into a twenty-minute synopsis and detailed analysis of the case.

McKenna sat listening, without saying a word, mystified by Ward's powers of recall after he realized that Ward had just about memorized his reports and was quoting them chapter and verse.

"Very good, so far. I agree with your conclusions," Brunette said, giving the barest nod to McKenna when Ward had finished reporting. "Now tell me what I can do to move things along for you."

"Immigration," Ward said. "We don't work much with the INS and I don't know anybody there. If and when McKenna gets his list from Bellevue, we're gonna want to get their fingerprints from Immigration quick. Scagnelli's gonna need time to compare them against the wine-bottle prints, and this killer isn't going to stop and wait around for us to identify him. If we're not fast, we're going to have another body on our hands."

"I'll take care of that," Brunette said, then turned to McKenna. "Tavlin will make sure you get that list from Bellevue. When you do, bring it down to Gene Shields. I'll have him ready to get you results fast."

McKenna knew that Brunette was just putting on a show for Ward's benefit. Gene Shields was the head of the New York office of the FBI and a good friend of theirs. Brunette knew that what he had just suggested would have been exactly what McKenna would have done anyway, but appearances had to be maintained for Ward's benefit.

Meanwhile, Ward was smiling, quite satisfied with himself, until Brunette said to him, "You've done a lot of work, but you're not doing enough."

Ward's smile vanished, replaced by a look of deep concern. "Commissioner, we're doing everything we can think of. Counting my men, Street Crime, the Homicide Squad, and the lab, there has to be a hundred people working on this, round the clock, and lots of them are on overtime. How much do you want to spend on this?"

"More."

"More?"

"Lots more, and I want it to show."

"Really, Commissioner, I don't think I could use more than another ten men on this, and that would be just to keep the overtime costs down."

"I know. You don't need them assigned to this case, but I do. It's getting national press, and we only get something like this every couple of years. Everybody knows about it, everybody's talking about it, and there's pressure building. The politicians and I are gonna want this guy caught at any cost, and that's the key phrase—at any cost. So for every man-hour you spend on it, I'm going to cry to the mayor and the city council like it's three. Get it?"

It took Ward only a second before he was smiling again. "I think so," he said. "It's February and the fiscal year ends June thirtieth. If I understand you right, because of the money spent on this unforeseen high-profile case, you'd like the money appropriated for the department to run out, say, maybe June fifteenth. Then you'll go to the mayor for an emergency appropriation, which you'll get."

"Only if you catch this guy and make it look like money well spent," Brunette corrected. "Otherwise, the politicians will let us starve. But go on."

"Then, since our budget will be bigger this year, through lies, deception, and calling in favors, you'll get it duplicated next year, maybe calling the extra money some kind of contingency fund."

"You've got it. So you know what I want?"

"Now I do. Every time somebody in the press turns on their camera, they're going to catch a detective assigned to this case interviewing a homeless person in a well-publicized, very expensive effort to catch the killer."

"Very good, but I have another reason for doing this. Right now it's not a good reason, but it might be later if things get out of hand."

From talking to Brennan, McKenna had a pretty good idea what Brunette was worried about, but Ward didn't have a clue. He sat on the edge of his chair, ready to follow and agree with Brunette's line of reasoning.

"I don't know if you've given it any thought, but I'm afraid of copycat killings," Brunette said. "To discourage that, I want a strong show of manpower working on this case. But if it happens anyway, I want you to have the manpower in place to end it quickly."

Ward was busy digesting this new potential problem when Brunette surprised him and said, "Give me your thoughts on that, would you?"

Apparently, Ward had no thoughts at all ready on that, but he wasn't going to say this to Brunette. Instead he said, "It's funny you mentioned that, Commissioner. Brian and I were just talking about that exact same thing right before you walked in. Brian?"

The spotlight shifted to the wings, but McKenna was ready. "The lieutenant mentioned to me that he was worried about copycat killings in this case, so he got me thinking. It's happened before when a series of killings goes on for too long, making the police appear impotent and unable to catch the killer. Then, for whatever reasons they might have, other nuts jump into the act, targeting the same type of victim as the original killer and killing them the same way. They think they'll get away with it, that everything will be blamed on the original killer, the one the police are concentrating on."

McKenna had given Ward all he needed—just a little time to think. "We were saying how that probably happened in Atlanta in the late seventies and early eighties," Ward said with a sincere, straight face. "They had twenty-seven murders of young boys, but when the police and the FBI caught Wayne Williams and looked at him closely, I hear they could only connect him to fourteen of the cases and wound up convicting him of just two or three. They had at least one copycat down there, but they were just as happy to close the case and end it to stop the killings."

"That's just the kind of information I need to take to the mayor while you're spending this money and getting ready, just in case. Any more copycat cases come to mind?"

"Not offhand," Ward admitted, then decided to sidestep the question. "But I think it's something we should be worried about. It was different when the killer was using his own specialized brand of poison. But now that he's just cutting bums' throats, hell, anyone can do that."

"Tommy, I've already figured that out," Brunette said dryly. "Do you know Vernon Geberth?"

"Sure, but I haven't spoken to him in years," Ward said. Then both men turned to McKenna.

When Geberth had been in the department, he had been the squad commander of the very busy Bronx Homicide Squad. Considered by many to have been the best homicide investigator in the department, he had taught the NYPD Homicide Seminar and even wrote *the* textbook on murder, *Practical Homicide Investigation*. But Geberth had been a little too well recognized by the press and a little too flamboyant for some chiefs used to hogging all the credit for themselves, so he had retired and developed a new angle. He went back to school, got his master's in psychology, and then started studying serial killings. He was right on the money so many times that he was kept busy touring the country, lecturing law-enforcement groups and giving them advice on their serial-killing cases.

Geberth was doing all right for himself in the murder business, so that, like many successful people, he was hard to get in touch with. However, it was common knowledge in the department that McKenna and Geberth were good friends.

"I'll give him a call," McKenna said.

"Good. Get all the copycat cases you can from him and get back to me," Brunette said, then turned again to Ward. "Last issue: How well do you know Ben Rosen?"

"Well enough to have formed a mutual hatred."

"Then I'm talking to you again, Brian," Brunette said. "How well do you know him?"

"Not at all."

"Perfect, because I want you to be his best friend. I'd do it myself, but I don't get along with him, either. I want him involved in this case, so ask his help."

McKenna wasn't looking forward to that and couldn't see the point, at first. But, like it or not, he started to see the sense in it. "Co-opting the enemy?" he asked.

"Exactly. Right now he's a gadfly, but if this goes on much longer, he's going to become a real pain in the ass. So I want him on the inside, knowing what's going on. Of course, he's probably gonna scream for more manpower, but that's perfect. Every time he screams, I'll assign more people. But if there's a copycat killing, I'm going to institute some drastic measures and I don't want him running to court blocking me with an injunction. You have to get him involved and make him see the sense of what we're doing."

"Suppose he doesn't want to get involved? He's got a reputation as an outsider, and I think he likes that."

"Just tell him we want to use him as our 'homeless expert.' He runs on ego and won't be able to resist."

McKenna wasn't enthused at the prospect, but he had no choice. "If you say so, I'll give it a shot."

"Sorry, Brian. I say so, and you have to make it good." Then he turned to Ward. "In case Rosen comes here, I want Brian to have his own office to give him some stature. I want pin maps and status boards, computers spitting out information—the whole deal. You can give him one of the interview rooms."

McKenna could see that Ward was appalled at the idea of one of his detectives having his own office but, of course, he didn't say so. What he said was, "Good idea, Commissioner. I'll see to it."

37

Brunette was no longer in the squad office by the time McKenna left Ward's office, but he hadn't gone far. Maureen opened the door and entered the office from the hallway, but McKenna could see the PC standing outside. Brunette also saw McKenna, so he waved as the door closed and then he was gone.

McKenna noticed that Maureen appeared worried, but as soon as she saw him looking at her she put a smile on her face. He wasn't fooled. While she would be the first to spot guile in others, he knew that she had never mastered the act of practicing it herself. Her conversation with Brunette meant bad news for him, he figured, and he suspected that it had something to do with Heidi Lane.

However, Maureen wasn't in the mood to tell him yet. She sat at her desk and resumed her game of war with Kerri. From the large stack of cards in front of Kerri, he could tell that the rich little poor girl was winning for once in her life. That would be Maureen's way, he knew, as he watched Kerri squeal with delight and add to her stack after her queen beat Maureen's ten.

There's no pushing Maureen, and bad news can always wait, McKenna figured.

He sat at his desk and called Vernon Geberth, but wound up speaking to his wife instead. Vernon wasn't home, she told him, but she expected to hear from him soon. He had been speaking at a conference in Idaho attended by investigators from the western states with ongoing serial-killer cases. However, he was on his way home and she said that he usually called her from O'Hare Airport in Chicago. McKenna gave her his cellular number and asked her to have Vernon call him.

Then McKenna pulled the sketch from his pocket and noted the artist's name on the bottom. Cartwright. He called the Artists Unit in headquarters and was put through to him. "Can you make me two more sketches of the subject's face, one making him fifty pounds heavier and the other a hundred?" McKenna asked.

"Sure, but no telling how accurate they'd be," Cartwright said. "I could put weight on his face, but your subject's really distinguishing feature is his eyes. Very sad looking, as I recall. If I put weight on him, I don't know if they should change or not."

"Let's assume his eyes look like that because he's been sick. Can you give that a try?"

"Tell you what," Cartwright said. "I'll give you four new sketches, add fifty and a hundred pounds to him, one with round eyes and one without for each weight. How's that?"

"Perfect, thanks. How long will it take you?"

"They'll be to you by tomorrow morning."

Next, a messenger arrived in the squad office with a box for McKenna. It was from Brennan at the *Post*, he saw from the mailing sticker. He was about to open it and see what kind of mail Brennan had been receiving when Kerri's money arrived from the property clerk's office.

As soon as the messenger left, McKenna gave the money to Maureen. "What are you going to do now?" she asked.

"Read some mail, then go to Bellevue."

"Forget the mail for now. I'll go with you to Bellevue and we can drop Kerri at her hotel on the way. I have to talk to you."

"That's fine, because I have to talk to you, too."

Maureen drove. During the trip she explained to Kerri that she was going to hold some of her money for her, but that Kerri could buy whatever she wanted. All she had to do was call, and maybe they would go shopping together.

Kerri didn't say much, but seemed happy with the arrangement. When they arrived at the hotel, Maureen gave Kerri three hundred dollars, all in twenties. "Will that be enough for now?" she asked.

"Sure," Kerri said. "It's a lot of money, right?"

"Yes, it is. If you want to, you can buy a lot of toys with that. When you need it, I have thirty-eight hundred dollars left that's all yours."

Maureen walked Kerri up to her room. McKenna waited in the car, wondering how Maureen was going to broach the secret she and Brunette shared. As soon as she came out of the hotel she got behind the wheel and started driving crosstown to Bellevue. "You ready to talk?" he asked.

"Sure. You first."

"I need you to introduce me to Ben Rosen. I have to be his pal," McKenna said, then explained the mission Brunette had given him.

"I'll do it and it might work with him, depending on what Ray means by the 'drastic action' he intends to take if there's any copycat killings," she said.

"He didn't explain it, but I figure he means to round up all the homeless and keep them somewhere safe if other people start killing them."

"Against their will?"

"Maybe."

"Then you'll have a tough time getting Ben to go along with that. He's a strong believer in constitutional rights, especially where the homeless are concerned. Unfortunately, sometimes he values their rights so much that he loses common sense. But if it doesn't come to that, he'll love being in on this case."

"What kind of guy is he?"

"Difficult."

"Do you like him?"

"Just between us, not much. But I overlook his shortcomings because he's smart, hardworking, and manages to get some good things done."

"How did you meet him?"

"At a soup kitchen," Maureen said.

"What were you doing at a soup kitchen?"

"Cooking, of course. Do it every Sunday for three hundred people. You oughta stop in sometime and try my stuff. It's not bad, you know."

"Where?"

"Saint Bart's, Park Avenue, right down the block from the station house. Good food, nice atmosphere, friendly, efficient service, but don't dress up."

"And Ben Rosen will be there?"

"Most Sundays. He's on the board of New York Cares, the charity that runs the soup kitchen. He's also one of their big contributors, but he's not afraid to pitch in and wash dishes."

"Then I'll be there next Sunday too."

"Don't make plans you're not gonna keep," she said. "That's the day after tomorrow, and you seem pretty busy to me right now."

"I'll make time. Now it's your turn. What do you want to talk to me about? Heidi Lane?"

"Yes, but it'll keep. We're almost there."

Maureen parked outside the hospital complex. They decided that McKenna would go see Heaney while she went and picked up a couple of sandwiches for them.

Heaney wasn't in his office, his secretary told McKenna; he was in the basement and had been for most of the day, but she could reach him. McKenna sat down to wait and picked up an old copy of *Time* from the magazine rack. By the time Heaney appeared, McKenna knew what the world had been worried about five years before.

Heaney looked beat. He was unshaven, his shirt was dirty and wrinkled, and he was wearing the same clothes McKenna had seen him in the day before. Knowing he was responsible for Heaney's condition, McKenna felt a little tinge of satisfaction. "How's it going?"

"Bad for you, good for me. Thanks to you, I've spent all night and most of today going through the old personnel files. I studied all their pictures and nobody close to your sketch, but I brought a few remotely possibles up for you to look at anyway.''

"You're right, that's bad for me. But how is it good for you?''

"Easy. If I didn't hire your killer, I've got me some good job security. C'mon, let's go in.''

McKenna followed Heaney into his office. Stacked on Heaney's desk was a pile of personnel folders. At Heaney's insistence, McKenna went through them, one by one. There was an ID photo inside each folder, and it took McKenna only minutes to conclude that Heaney was right: The killer wasn't in there.

"I went through more than thirteen thousand folders, so it looks like you were wrong,'' Heaney said with some satisfaction. "I also showed your sketch to all the old hands here. They'd all seen it in the papers anyway and thought I was nuts, but for the record, nobody knew him.''

"Did you show it to Dr. Suliman Rashid?'' McKenna asked.

"Rashid? What's your interest in him?''

"I just thought it interesting that two victims had appointments to see him.''

"Under the circumstances, I'm sure he'd like to be in a position to see them, but he's dead.''

He's dead? Coincidence? McKenna wondered. "When did he die?''

"Maybe three weeks ago. He was a nice guy, been here for ages. He was one of the few doctors we could get to work the AIDS clinic. Pretty depressing job, but he didn't seem to mind.''

"How'd he die?''

"Heart attack. Old Suli had a heart condition, had a couple of major attacks before. I guess the third one's the kicker. Matter of fact, I'm the one who sent the police to his house when he didn't show up for work and didn't answer the phone. Not like him—he was a very reliable guy.''

"So he died at home?''

"Yep.''

"Where did he live?''

"Flushing. Where else? Take Flushing off the map and this hospital goes under.''

McKenna had to agree. One stroll around the hospital would confirm that many of the professionals working there were originally from China, India, Pakistan, and the Philippines. It was common knowledge that many of them had chosen the Queens neighborhood as their community, so many that the subway line serving Flushing was nicknamed the Orient Express. "Did Dr. Rashid live alone?'' he asked.

"I think so. He's got kids here, all grown, but he's separated from his wife.''

"Do you know if there was an autopsy done on him?''

"Not for sure, but I doubt it. You know how Moslems feel about autopsies.''

"Yes, I know. Unfortunately, if one wasn't done already, I might need one now.''

"You thinking about digging him up?'' Heaney asked.

"If I can get the courts to go along.''

"Then you better have all your shots and your passport in order. His body was shipped home to Pakistan.''

Damn! Nobody's sending me to Pakistan, McKenna thought. It might be a coincidence, but the very untimely demise of Dr. Suliman Rashid bears some looking at.

McKenna's concerns must have shown in his face because Heaney said, "Cheer up, because it's probably gonna get worse. I've got your list here. Four thousand four hundred and two names." He reached into his bottom desk drawer, removed a bulky wrapped package, and handed it to McKenna.

"What list?" McKenna asked, staring at the package in his hands.

Heaney looked surprised at the question. "You know a Chief Steven Tavlin? Kinda pushy and obnoxious, but a real heavyweight, I guess?"

"I know him, but I never quite thought of him in those terms."

"I guess that's because you must always give him what he wants. Anyway, he came in to see me first thing this morning. Wanted me to give you the names, dates of birth, and green card numbers of all the foreign-born doctors, nurses, and pharmacists who've worked here over the past seven years. Naturally, I told him that wasn't possible, was against city policy."

"He was unhappy with your interpretation of the rules?" McKenna guessed.

"Sure was. He was very rude. After he left me, he stopped in to see the hospital administrator and made himself very unwelcome there. But my boss backed me up and I thought we were done with your chief."

"Until somebody else called, maybe from the mayor's office?" McKenna guessed.

"From the mayor's office?" Heaney said with a sarcastic chuckle. "Try 'Hiz-zoner' himself. Almost fell out of my chair when he told me that if you didn't have that list, then by this time next year we'd be treating nothing here but poor people's cats, stray dogs, and pet hamsters. He was also very rude, to say the least."

Isn't it wonderful being the chief? McKenna asked himself again. Of course I would have gotten this list eventually, but it would have cost me a dinner and a night of schmoozing and pleading with the newly compliant Jim Heaney. I think Tavlin's way is better.

Heaney obviously didn't agree and wanted no more experience with the Chiefly Art of Persuasion. "McKenna, do me a favor, would you?" he asked.

"Sure."

"The next time you need anything, and I mean anything, please just give me a call."

38

Maureen was waiting in the car with two fine sandwiches. "Dr. Rashid's dead," McKenna told her. "Heart attack."

"You don't believe in death by natural causes?" she asked as he took out his phone.

"Not anymore." He called the squad that covered Flushing, the 109th Detective Squad. Since all deaths occurring outside a medical facility required some kind of police investigation, he knew they would have records that would tell him more than Heaney could. He got the squad commander and asked him to check for an Investigate Aided, Suliman Rashid, about three weeks in the past.

"Here it is," the lieutenant said. "Dr. Suliman Rashid, 34-11 Parsons Boulevard. Detective Snyder handled it. DOA at home, January sixth. Case closed."

"Is Detective Snyder in?"

"No, comes in Sunday for a day tour."

"Then I need his home number," McKenna said, knowing that talking to Snyder would reveal more than the dull litany a routine closed-case report would contain.

McKenna caught Snyder in the middle of dinner with his family, but the detective was still eager to help. "I remember the case," he said. "Got the call from Bellevue. He'd been dead a couple of days and was starting to smell."

"He lived alone?"

"Yeah, but the neighbors called the family when we got there. They were there in no time. It was a bad scene."

"You notice anything suspicious about it?"

"Nothing. There was bottles of prescription medicine on his nightstand, mostly heart medication. His doctor's name was on the bottles, so we gave him a call and he came over. He examined the body, said Rashid had a chronic heart condition and that's what killed him. Heart attack. He signed the death certificate, so it was case closed."

"No autopsy?"

"Nope. No reason. Routine death at home, sixty-six years old, family and family doctor present and notified."

"What was Rashid doing when he died?" McKenna asked.

"Eating. He was sitting at his kitchen table and collapsed in his curry."

Snyder's answer caused the hair on the back of McKenna's neck to stand on end. "Think back. Was there any evidence he had any visitors before he died?" he asked.

Snyder took a moment before answering. "None. The place was immaculate and everything seemed to be in order."

"How about the kitchen? Any dishes in the sink?"

"No. It was take-out Pakistani food. You know, the kind that comes in those Styrofoam boxes. His wife told us that was what he usually ate since they separated."

"Where did it come from?"

There was a long silence before Snyder answered. "I don't know where it came from."

"There was no bag the food came in, no bill, no name of a restaurant anywhere?"

The silence greeting that question lasted so long that McKenna had to say, "Don't backpedal on me on this one, Snyder. Please, I've got to know."

"I'm thinking. Give me a minute," Snyder said.

McKenna gave him two before he asked, "There was nothing, right?"

"No, I don't recall a restaurant bill or a bag anywhere in the kitchen."

"Did you look in the garbage?"

"Now that you've got me thinking, I remember that the garbage can was empty. Not even a garbage bag in it."

McKenna remained silent, thinking. Then Snyder said hopefully, "Maybe he took his garbage out before he ate."

Does anybody do that when they've got hot food ready? McKenna asked himself. No, they eat first, then clean up.

"What happened to the food?" McKenna asked.

"The family cleaned it up." Snyder waited another minute before he asked, "Do I have a problem developing over this?"

"No, it's not your fault. Like you said, routine death at home. I'm the one with the problem, not you."

"What's the problem?"

"I'm chasing a guy who's been poisoning people without anyone suspecting anything. Then Rashid's name comes up, not once, but twice during this investigation. Then he dies three weeks before I want to talk to him. Dies while he's eating, no less, and I'm chasing a poisoner. Quite a coincidence, wouldn't you say?"

"What do you want me to do?" Snyder asked.

"Nothing you can do. Go back and finish your dinner and forget about it."

"You heard?" McKenna asked Maureen after he hung up.

"Yeah, I heard."

"You know what happened?"

"I know what happened if Dr. Rashid was the one who could have identified your man. Besides that, he would have been the first one to raise the hue and cry when his patients stopped showing up for their appointments."

"Then let's say that's the way it was," McKenna said.

"I see. The killer visits his friend Dr. Rashid with a big surprise, his favorite—an order of curry for two. Only one of the orders has something special in it that's not on the menu, so Rashid eats and croaks. Then the killer plants Rashid's face not in the poisoned curry, but in what's left of his own. He tidies up, wraps everything in the garbage bag, and takes it with him."

"So now we're stuck with two versions of the same event. The official, commonsense, routine version, option one, and the far-fetched, remotely possible, don't-make-me-laugh one. Which do you choose?"

"Put me down for option two," Maureen said. "It's bound to be a real crowd pleaser."

"Me too," McKenna said. "You know why?"

"Sure. Because option two will force you to look very closely at that AIDS clinic."

"That's one good reason, but there's an additional extra-points bonus involved with option two."

"What's that?" Maureen asked.

"Option two gives me another excellent opportunity to annoy my new pal Jim Heaney." McKenna dialed Heaney's number and his secretary quickly put him through.

"Didn't expect to hear from you again so soon," Heaney said. "What? Did you forget something?"

"No, but I need a favor."

"Anything. What?"

"Tomorrow morning, I need to talk to everybody who works in the AIDS clinic."

"Sorry, that one I can't do. Tomorrow's Saturday and the clinic is strictly a

Monday-to-Friday operation. With their union, even the mayor couldn't pull that one off."

"Okay, fine. Next best thing: I need the names and whatever addresses and phone numbers you have for anyone who's worked in that clinic over the last seven years."

"You got a fax number?"

"Uh-huh." McKenna gave him the number.

"Then stand by your machine. You'll be getting a transmission tonight. Anything else?"

"No, thank you. That'll do for now." McKenna hung up and turned to Maureen. "He hates me, you know."

"Of course he does. Let's do these sandwiches."

McKenna had figured that Maureen would bring up Heidi Lane while they ate, but she didn't. She enjoyed her sandwich in silence and tidied up the car before she turned to him. "Are you finally ready to tell me that Heidi is Hank Lane's daughter?" he asked.

"I guess I put it off as long as I could," Maureen said. "Ray checked Hank Lane's personnel folder. He had five kids. One of them was a daughter named Heidi."

"Did you know Hank?" McKenna asked.

"No, but I remember when he killed himself. I guess that makes me an old-timer, but it was quite a *Magilla.*"

Yes, it was, McKenna thought. It sure was.

Maureen watched McKenna closely, waiting for him to say something. After a long, uncomfortable silence, she said, "I guess you knew him."

"Ray didn't tell you the story?"

"No, he said you should. He thinks you feel responsible for his death."

"Then he's wrong both times. Hank was my partner for a while, but I don't feel responsible for his death. Some other people thought I was, and I did myself, for a while. But I've had a long time to think about it since then."

"And you're not going to tell me about it?"

"No."

"Fine," she said, but McKenna could tell by her face that she wasn't happy with his decision. She looked hurt, which hurt him. She started up the car, checked the traffic behind them, and threw the car into drive. "Since you don't want to talk to me, I guess you've figured out for yourself how to handle Heidi Lane. Right?" she asked.

The roadway was clear, but Maureen hadn't moved the car an inch. McKenna knew she expected a response to her question. Naturally he didn't want to give one because he didn't have a clue about how to handle Heidi. He decided on that old ploy that teachers used in similar predicaments. He answered her question with a question. "Why do you think Ray wanted me to tell you about it?"

"Because he thinks I know how to handle Heidi and knows that you don't."

Ray's right about that, McKenna thought. Maureen's already proven she can wrap Heidi around her finger and she knows I'm . . . What? McKenna searched his mind to complete his line of reasoning. His first thought was, *She knows I'm afraid of Heidi,* but he didn't like the way that sounded, even to himself. He decided on, *She knows I'm uncomfortable with Heidi.* Much better, he thought, but where do I go from here?

Maureen had her own ideas about where to go. She put the car back into Park with finality and said, "If I'm going to help, I have to know the story."

"I know, but I've never talked to anybody about this."

"Not Ray?"

"No."

"Not even Angelita?"

"No. She asked about it once, but no."

"Then it's time you did, so let's get you started. Once upon a time, long ago and far away, there was a good young detective who . . . Take it from there."

"It was a long time ago. 1977. But it wasn't that far away. I was a brand-new detective assigned to the Midtown South Squad. I don't know if Ray had anything to do with my assignment there, but he was the district captain."

"Third Detective District?"

"Yeah. He was in charge of the Midtown South Squad, the Midtown North Squad, and the Seventeenth Squad. His office was in the Seventeenth, so I didn't run into him on a day-to-day basis."

"But you were friends?"

"Yeah. Had been for a couple of years, but nobody knew that back then. Anyway, Hank Lane was my partner. He was older than me, a second-grader, had been in the Bureau for a while. At first, I really liked working with him. He was a hard-charger, fun to be around, and real bright. I learned a lot from him, and then I learned something I didn't want to know."

"That he was a crook?" Maureen guessed.

"Yeah, Hank Lane was a crook," McKenna sighed. "A real class act, but a crook."

"How'd you find out?"

"By accident. He caught a burglary case in the Garment District and I went with him. It was a Monday morning and it looked like the place got cleaned out by professionals over the weekend. The locks were sprung, the alarm was short-circuited, and all the clothes were gone. The owner was just about crying and had me feeling sorry for him."

"What was it, a put-up job?"

"Yeah, an insurance scam, but it looked good and we didn't suspect anything for a month. Then one night I picked up the girl I was going with at the time and she was wearing a new dress she had just bought."

"One of the stolen dresses?"

"I recognized it from the complainant's catalogue, but I didn't know if it was one of the stolen ones. Hank had taken off the next day, so I decided to help him out with his case. She'd bought it at Macy's, right around the corner from the precinct, so I went to talk to them. They had ordered that new line of dresses a month before from a wholesaler, a place that was also in the precinct."

"Let me guess," Maureen said. "You went to talk to the wholesaler and they said the dresses were delivered from the manufacturer right after the burglary, right?"

"Two days after. Our complainant had sold this wholesaler quite a bit of the stuff he'd reported stolen. Gave it to them at a nice price. Then gone up there over the weekend with some people to help him. Maybe his family, maybe some of his workers he trusted. Then they took the stuff to another location he'd rented and he offed the stuff as quick as he could.''

"So you told Hank about the work you did for him on his case?''

"Yeah, and he was real happy. Said I'd make a good detective someday.''

"But nothing happened?''

"Nothing I was aware of, at the time. Every time I asked about it, he'd tell me he was still building his case, that you have to be careful when you lock up rich businessmen. Meanwhile, he'd gone back to his complainant and held him up. Must have told him he could prove the burglary was staged and that he could be in major trouble.''

"How much did he get?''

"The amount claimed for the burglary was more than a hundred and fifty grand, so Hank had to walk away with at least fifty thousand of the insurance claim. Maybe more, but at least fifty.''

"What makes you so sure?''

"Because he pulled a fast one on me, and then I knew. But it was another month before I found out about it, a whole month of me asking him every once in a while about the case.''

"What did he do? Offer to split the cash?''

"Not subtle enough for Hank,'' McKenna said, smiling as he remembered it. "He put twenty-five thousand in my checking account. It was another month before I even found out he did it. Went into shock when I read my bank statement, until I figured it out.''

"How'd he do that?''

"On paydays he always went straight to the bank and cashed his check. I was single at the time and payday was always a surprise for me, so sometimes I'd give him my check to deposit for me since he was going to the bank anyway. After thinking about it for a while, I noticed that the deposit was made the same day he put my check in.''

"So he had your checking-account number, put in the cash, and made you look like an accomplice, just in case.''

"Yeah, but that's not the way it went down when I asked him about it. He denied it, but said, 'Maybe now you'll stop asking me questions when you don't want to know the answer, partner,' and he emphasized 'partner.' ''

"What was your reaction to that?''

"I said something like, 'I came on this job to lock up crooks, not to be a crook.' ''

"And?''

"He laughed at me. Told me to grow up, but he never admitted a thing.''

"You must have hated him after that,'' Maureen said.

"Funny thing was, I didn't. I never spoke another word to him, but I didn't hate him. I was single, no kids, cheap rent, and no bills, so I tried putting myself in his place. You know, mortgage, five kids, always wanting the best for your family. But I couldn't pull it off. I had no frame of reference for his situation.''

"So that's it? You just didn't talk to him?"

"At first, and it was obvious to everyone in the squad. They knew we'd had a falling-out, but neither one of us was going to tell anyone what it was about."

"You never thought about reporting him?"

"In 1977? Are you kidding? It never even entered my mind. Besides, I still liked Hank. Before that burglary, I'd even been out to his house for dinner."

"You met his kids?"

"His wife and his kids. Nice family."

"So you've known Heidi for a while?"

"As it turns out, I guess I have. But I didn't remember her, didn't even remember her name. They were just five kids running around, fighting with each other, and making a lot of noise at the picnic table outside while we were eating inside, as I recall."

"What about the money?"

"That got crazy. I took the twenty-five thousand out of the bank in cash, put it in an envelope, and put it in his desk drawer. Next day it would be in my drawer. I'd mail it to his house and he'd mail it back. I'd drive out to his house late at night, hide it in his garage, and think I finally got rid of it. The next month it would wind up back in my checking account. When I finally got transferred, it took me a few minutes to remember which one of us had it."

"How'd this transfer come about? Ray?"

"Yeah, the only time I ever went to him for anything."

"Really?"

"Yeah, really. I'm not saying he never helped me before with assignments, but that was the only time I ever asked him to."

"Did you tell him why you wanted to be transferred?"

"He asked, but I didn't tell him. But he did it and never asked me again."

"But he must have suspected. How long had it been that you weren't talking to Hank Lane?"

"Four months."

"It was one of his squads, so he must have heard about it and wondered what was up. Then you ask him for a transfer and won't tell him why. He's not stupid."

"I figure he put it together and took a good look at his squad. I think it's more than coincidence that I was replaced there a couple of weeks later by a spy from Internal Affairs."

"So Internal Affairs caught Lane?"

"No. I'm sure they tried, but Hank was much too sharp for them. I heard it took him less than two weeks to figure out exactly what the spy was up to, and then he let everybody know about the guy. Their spy wound up getting hassled so much that he retired."

"How'd Hank find out?"

"Easy. The spy was a second-grader, but Hank noticed right away that he was a lousy detective. He must have done something to get grade, Hank told himself, so he took a good look at their spy's career and thought it strange how many guys got in trouble as soon as he left a squad."

"So how did Hank finally get caught?"

"A year later the businessman he held up got grabbed on a swindle. He'd gone into a new business, sewing Gucci labels on some cheap imitations he was making. The Gucci people got crazy about it, wanted him in jail and were going to sue him for millions.''

"So he made a deal and gave up a cop?"

"Exactly. Told them about his dealings with Hank, and then that was all they wanted to hear about. Treated him like gold."

"Funny how it's always that way," Maureen observed. "Getting one crooked cop would always make better headlines than locking up some businessman for something dull like trademark infringement."

"We both know that. But once again Hank was too sharp for them. He had friends everywhere and somebody somewhere must have told him what was going down. You know the rest, don't you?"

"I think so. The way I heard it, when the two sergeants from IAD came to the squad to lock him up, Hank was waiting for them. He got the drop on them and took them into the men's room. Then he handcuffed them to urinals and made them do filthy things to each other while everybody else in the squad was outside, talking through the door trying to get Hank to surrender. I heard that Hank just kept laughing at them until he yelled 'Good-bye,' and then he killed himself.''

"How do these crazy rumors get started?" McKenna asked, but he had to smile at the version Maureen had heard. "He made them get undressed, but they never had to do anything to each other. He just made them watch while he blew his brains out. But Hank had two more jokes in store for them, the way I heard it.''

"Jokes? What could be funny about that?"

"Knowing Hank, I still get a chuckle out of it. First of all, he locked them up with two pair of those Spanish cuffs that nobody's got a key for. Emergency Service had to come up and cut them from the urinals. But the second one is better. Hank's gun was empty. No bullets in it.''

"Hank took them prisoner and locked them up with an empty gun?"

"Yeah, that would be his way. He knew what he was going to do and wouldn't want to take a chance on shooting a cop in case they put up a struggle, which they didn't.''

"But couldn't they see that the cylinders were empty? He had a revolver, right?"

"Yeah, but don't forget, the people in IAD weren't that sharp then. It wasn't like now where they take first-and second-graders and make them go there for a while. Back in those days, mostly all they could get was dummies they'd promised gold shields to.''

"So Hank killed himself with one of their guns?"

"Yep. That was his last joke on them so they could never cover it up and deny how it happened."

"The man was diabolical!" Maureen screamed.

"Like I told you, Hank Lane was a crook, but still a class act."

"What happened to you after that?"

"I was on vacation in Spain when it happened, so I didn't find out about it until I got back. By then, the funeral was over and Hank was buried, but I still had a few problems. Seems someone put together the fact that the spy arrived right after I left the squad and everybody knew that something had gone down between Hank and me."

"So they thought you turned him in?"

"Somebody did, but I don't know who. Somebody sent me a picture of Heidi at the funeral that made me feel miserable for a while, but I've straightened that out in my mind. Then for a couple of years I used to get dead fish in the mail on the anniversary of Hank's death, but that stopped years ago."

"Just one loose end," Maureen said. "What happened with the twenty-five thousand?"

"That was the one thing I beat Hank on. He didn't know it, but he had it when he died. I waited a few years for all the excitement to die down, then sent his wife a little treasure map of her backyard that showed her where to dig."

"And I guess she kept it?"

"I never heard of her returning it to the insurance company, if she even knew where it came from."

That was the end of Maureen's questions, for the moment. "I'm going to need some time to think about this," she said, then she put the car in Drive. "Where to?"

"The FBI office. Foley Square."

39 Gene Shields had been in charge of the New York office of the FBI through two city administrations and three FBI directors. Through the years he had been offered many positions that some would have considered a move up, but not Gene Shields. He could have been the U.S. attorney in Boston, a federal judge in Kansas City, or the deputy director of the FBI in Washington, but he had turned down all those opportunities without a second thought. Those positions entailed a move, something he would never consider. Although originally from Baltimore, Gene Shields was a New Yorker and couldn't live anywhere else.

Aside from the obvious professional concerns they shared, it was their common love of the town that made Brunette, McKenna, and Shields fast friends.

Maureen waited in the car and McKenna carried the package he had received from Heaney into the Federal Building, enduring the series of checkpoints before he was finally admitted to Shields's office.

Shields greeted him at the door, looking like a tanned and fit college professor. He and his wife had stayed a week with McKenna and Angelita at their condo in Florida two weeks before, so they didn't have much catching up to do. McKenna started to fill him in on the case, but Shields stopped him. "You just missed Ray," he said. "We spent an hour talking over your problems and ideas."

"So you know what I need?" McKenna asked.

"Yeah, some fingerprint cards from Immigration."

"Quite a few of them," McKenna said as he handed the package to Shields. "I got more than four thousand names from Bellevue, but I just scratched out all the women, all the blacks, and all the ones who are either too young or too old to be the killer. I didn't count what's left, but there's still at least a thousand names."

"No problem," Shields said. "I'll fax it to Immigration in Washington tonight and tell them I want the cards by morning. That good enough?"

"Just great. When you get them, could you have them delivered to our Latent Print Unit?"

"I'll get them there. I also asked Ray if you wanted any help from us on developing a profile of your killer, but he says you're gonna go with Vernon."

Touchy subject, McKenna knew. The FBI maintained a staff of agents, researchers, and psychologists whose mission was to study serial-killer cases and develop a profile of the killer for local police departments. Vernon was a one-man show and did the same thing by himself. It had become one of those rivalries that had taken on a life of its own. Not wanting to provoke any animosity, McKenna said, "Yeah, we're gonna give Vernon a try on this. Sort of keep it in-house."

Shields accepted McKenna's decision at face value. "You could do worse," was all he said on the subject, not committing himself to either side.

After leaving Shields's office, McKenna and Maureen hit heavy traffic during their return to the 17th Precinct. Once again Maureen was driving, but she wasn't talking. McKenna surmised that she was thinking about a solution to the Heidi problem. He knew he was right when she asked out of the blue, "Was Hank Lane a family man?"

"Yeah, he was. He didn't drink much, and if he wasn't working he was home."

They were about halfway back to the station house before Maureen spoke again. "I think I know what's happening in Heidi's head and I've got the solution for you. Ready to listen?"

"Sure. Go ahead."

"The way I see it, when Hank knew he was hot, he discussed it with his wife and told her everything but the truth. I think he put the whole thing on you."

"Why would he do that?"

"Because it was convenient. I'm not saying she believed him, but it was convenient."

"Why wouldn't she believe him?"

"Because she was just as guilty as he was. The way Hank handled that burglary leads me to believe he'd pulled some stunts before and made some extra bucks to bring home to his wife. At first she might not have liked it, but she took it. Probably told herself she wanted a better life for the kids. After a while, she came to expect that occasional tax-free bonus to keep things rolling smoothly. Everything was going along great until he started working with you."

"So he blamed me? He told her I was the cause of his problems?"

"That's what I think. You didn't do anything to trip him up but get yourself transferred from the squad, but that was the beginning of his problems. He was smart enough to spot the IAD spy and figured he had the problem licked until the businessman gave him up. But he also figured that the reason the spy showed up was that you had reported him."

"I don't think he believed that," McKenna said.

"Maybe not, but that's what he told his wife. He wanted her to keep thinking he was too sharp for them, so he blamed you."

"It wasn't me that got him, it was the victim turning him in. She couldn't blame me for that, could she?"

"Sure she did. Her husband was being chased and investigated, but you weren't. Don't forget, they both thought that you got some of the money, maybe half, but they didn't hear of anybody bothering you. Doesn't seem fair, does it? Then Hank committed suicide, and what do you think she told the kids after that? That their father was a crook?"

"I don't know what she told them."

"I do. She told them that the whole thing was your idea, that Hank never took any money until he started working with you. Now their father's dead, the kids sit back waiting for you to fall. So what happens?"

"Nothing."

"Wrong. While they blame you for their father's death, not only aren't you punished, but they watch you rise in the department. What kind of justice is that? they ask. Worse, they tell themselves that, if it weren't for you, their father would still be alive and getting the fame and credit you're getting."

"You think they all still believe that? His wife should know better, by now."

"Yes, she knows. She knew for sure when she dug up that money in the backyard. Like you said, she didn't give it back, but she knew. She'd thought you still had it and felt justified in putting the blame on you with the kids. But even though she knew, the lie was out and working and she saw no reason to change it. Let them go on believing that you're the bad guy and Hank was the good guy, she told herself. What's the harm? But now Heidi's playing dirty with you, so the truth has to come out."

Dirty? Maureen, you should know how dirty she's playing with me, McKenna thought. I could tell you things she told me, things you've never even imagined, but what good would it do? "So what do I do? Sit down with Heidi and tell her the truth about her father? I don't want to do that, and why would she believe me?"

"No, that's not what you do. You go to the source."

"Hank's wife?"

"If she's alive and still in New York. Is she?"

"I don't know."

"Find out. She knows the truth, so you have to make her see that she has to come clean with Heidi. She probably knows it already after seeing that interview with you and Heidi. Otherwise, either you or Heidi is going to wind up getting hurt for no reason."

"And if I can't get to her?"

"Then you have to talk to Heidi, but that's not the best option. That's bound to get too heated and emotional because you'll be giving her news she doesn't want to hear. It has to be done, but it's her mother's job to do it."

For the rest of the drive, McKenna ran Maureen's logic and conclusions through his mind. He could find no flaws in them and resolved to do as Maureen suggested. He took out his phone and called Brunette's office. As he expected, Brunette was still in. "Could you get me Hank's wife's present address?"

"Got it right here. Long Island, 30 Cooper Lane in Levittown. Same place—she hasn't moved."

McKenna knew where it was, but thought it strange that Brunette had the information at his fingertips until he figured that Brunette, like Maureen, had already examined the Heidi problem and had reached the same conclusion. Brunette confirmed it when he asked, "When you going to see her?"

"Sunday, if I can find the time."

"Make the time. This visit is long overdue," Brunette suggested before hanging up.

As Maureen was parking at the precinct, McKenna's cell phone rang. It was Geberth. "I was wondering when you were going to give me a call on this," he said, his tone of voice chiding McKenna.

"It's only now that we need you. Can we do dinner tonight and I'll run a couple of things by you?"

"Where?"

"Churchill's."

"That'll be fine. Will I be on the payroll for this?"

"I haven't cleared it yet, but I guess so."

"Good. Tell Brunette it's two-fifty an hour."

Well, Ray said he wanted to spend money on this case, McKenna thought. "What time you getting in?" he asked.

"Eight o'clock at La Guardia."

"Then it's Churchill's around nine. See you then."

McKenna hung up and they went into the station house through the crowd of reporters lounging outside. McKenna looked for Heidi but didn't see her. Many of the reporters yelled questions about the buildup, questions McKenna ignored, but they prepared him somewhat for the shock that greeted them upstairs. The squad office was very crowded with detectives from all over the city, all waiting for Ward to assign them something to do. Adding to the confusion were the workmen busy transforming one of the interview rooms into an office for McKenna. They were halfway through with painting it and his name was already on the door.

"Looks like the things Ray wants happen pretty quickly," McKenna commented to Maureen.

"What did you expect? I'm going home, but I'll see you Sunday at Saint Bart's. You should plan on getting there at eight."

"You're not coming in tomorrow?" he asked.

"Of course not. Tomorrow's Saturday and I'm off weekends."

That's right, McKenna thought. It's my case, not hers, so why would she be here on her day off? I'm on my own for the next two days.

The thought didn't make McKenna happy, but Maureen looked content enough as she signed out. As soon as she left, Ward called McKenna into his office and gave him the five-page fax from Heaney. "What do you think of that circus out there?" he asked.

"I know you don't need all those men now. Let's hope that you won't, but I guess they have to be assigned to something for the benefit of the press," McKenna said.

"What are your plans for the evening?"

"First I'm going to read Brennan's mail, and then I'm going to subject myself to a real session with the press. If the reporters don't know already, they have to be told about the money to Kerri. I'm also going to have to tell them about the two notes from the killer.''

''You going home after that?''

''No, I have to meet with Geberth and pick his brains. Then I'll go home and get some sleep, unless the killer hits us again.''

''You're tired?''

''Exhausted.''

''Then you've got nothing to worry about. Even though your killer's sick, he's been pretty much keeping the same schedule as you, busy every day. With all the people we've got out there looking for him, he'll be smart to stay home in bed tonight.''

''Let's hope so,'' McKenna said. ''I think we're getting close and it would be a shame to lose another victim to him now.''

40

Dr. Andino's call was switched to McKenna in the roll-call office, the quietest place he could find to read Brennan's mail. ''He wasn't lying to you,'' Andino said. ''Thirteen victims. They're all male and all HIV positive, and you'll be interested to know that they all have medical records at Bellevue. Interesting part is that they're all outpatients at the AIDS clinic.''

''That's great news, but I think he was lying. I think he's killed fourteen, not thirteen,'' McKenna said, then told Andino his suspicions on the death of Dr. Rashid.

''If you're right and he's not admitting to Dr. Rashid, then he must have a reason to hide it,'' Andino observed. ''I'd say that the AIDS clinic should be your new focal point.''

''It is. Could you fax me the list of victims?''

''You'll have it all in fifteen minutes.''

After hanging up, McKenna went back up to the squad office, made himself a cup of coffee, and stood waiting at the fax machine. True to his word, Andino sent the list of victims before McKenna had a chance to finish his coffee. He took the list to his desk and studied it intently. He saw that the first victim was Thomas Gately, male black, age forty-seven. His body had been discovered in the West Side train yards in the 10th Precinct on January 7, a date McKenna found significant since it was two days after Dr. Rashid died.

McKenna made a copy of the list and brought it in to Ward. The lieutenant was mulling over a roll-call sheet. ''Whatcha got now?'' he asked.

''The list of victims from Dr. Andino. There's thirteen of them in seven precincts, all in Manhattan. I need all the paperwork on them brought here.''

''Consider it done,'' Ward said, taking the list from McKenna. ''How many of them are ours?''

''We lead the list with four.''

Ward reacted badly to that piece of information. He sat staring silently at the list, but McKenna noticed that his eyes weren't moving and his face was getting red as it contorted in rage. Then he saw that a neck vein he had never noticed was pulsating and thought Ward's heart might be giving out. "Are you okay, Lieutenant?" he asked.

"No, I'm not okay," he said slowly and evenly, barely controlling his anger. "I'm not okay with four homicides, leading the list because of that asshole Wright. Firing's too good for him. He should be tortured and executed in public. You can bet I'd be there, right up front, sitting in a box seat eating popcorn with my wife and kids."

Ward warmed to the thought and McKenna watched as his anger slowly faded. Then he did read the list and asked, "This help you out any?"

"Quite a bit. He usually does one every two days, so I think I'm gonna get some sleep tonight after all. They were all patients at the Bellevue AIDS Clinic, so I think there's something you should know."

McKenna paused for a moment, searching for a way to put the best slant on what he was about to tell Ward. He had made up his mind not to mention the death of Dr. Rashid unless he was sure it was connected to the killer, but the evidence had mounted to the point that he was convinced that Rashid was the first victim.

There's no way to make this look good, he told himself, so he took a deep breath and told Ward about the death of Rashid, giving him the details of his conversation with Detective Snyder.

Ward listened without comment until McKenna had finished and then all he asked was, "This Snyder's just a third-grader, I hope?"

"I don't know," McKenna admitted.

"Let's see," Ward said, then opened his bottom desk drawer and removed a bulky computer printout. McKenna could see that it was a list of all the detectives in the NYPD. It took Ward only a minute to find Snyder's name. "Thank God," he said. "Detective Third Grade William Snyder. Been in the Bureau under two years."

The way Ward said it led McKenna to conclude that Snyder would have to be in the Bureau another fifty years before second grade came his way, if Ward had anything to say about it.

"I hope you're not thinking of squashing him, Lieutenant," McKenna said.

Ward looked surprised. "Are you condoning shoddy and unimaginative police work in an investigation?" he asked.

"No, but Snyder's new, and it was an honest mistake in a routine situation. Don't forget, we had no idea of the killer's existence when he poisoned Dr. Rashid. He was the first, so please let Snyder slide on this one."

Ward considered it before he said, "Okay, he'll live, as long as he doesn't show up in Manhattan working for me. I won't say a word about it unless I'm asked, but that's one you owe me, Brian."

"Thanks, and you'll get paid. That's a promise."

McKenna was happy to leave Ward's office and get back downstairs to roll call to finish reading the letters to Brennan and the "Letters to the Editor." Then he took a few minutes to sort out the information the letters contained.

He found that most of the writers took positions that generally conformed to those McKenna had expected they would. They deplored the conditions facing the homeless, called for more and better shelters, insisted on more research in the fight against AIDS, and railed against the killer in terms ranging from *inhuman* to *diabolical.*

However, twelve of the writers took positions McKenna found alarming. One writer stated that the killer had saved the city millions of dollars that would have been spent in welfare payments and providing medical treatment for the victims in their dying days. Others wrote that, while they didn't agree with the killer's methods, the city was better off without the extra bums urinating in the streets, tearing garbage bags apart looking for returnable bottles and cans, drinking in the parks, panhandling everywhere, and generally making a nuisance of themselves.

The three letters that McKenna found most alarming generally applauded the killer as a public hero who showed the courage to rid the city of vermin and make life a little easier on everyone else. They wished him success in his work, congratulated him on his progress, and said in so many words that he should be decorated, not prosecuted.

By the time he was finished reading, like Brennan and Brunette, McKenna saw a large potential problem looming on the horizon.

At 7:15 he decided that he could no longer put off the chore he had been dreading all night. He put on his overcoat and went out to meet the press. They were ready and waiting, with Heidi up front with the TV people. He tried to ignore her, but found it difficult. She was looking fresh, pretty, and was wearing her seductive smile.

McKenna began by making a statement, telling them that the number of investigators assigned to the case had been increased and that Andino had determined that there were thirteen victims to date, all males and all HIV positive. Then he told about the money given by the killer to a homeless woman and said that two messages had been received from him. He couldn't help but notice that Heidi's smile evaporated when he mentioned the messages. That didn't bother him. He was tired of games with her and glad to see that she was closer to putting her cards on the table. Then he opened up the floor for questions and instantly regretted it.

"Is it true that the killer gave the money to Kerri Brannigan, the girlfriend of one of the victims?" was the first question from one of the print people.

Glad I told them about that, McKenna thought. Maureen was right. That desk clerk and that bellhop have big mouths. "Yes, that's true."

"And where is she staying? Could you tell us?"

"I'd rather not say," McKenna answered, but it was in vain. "She's at the Herald Square Hotel," he heard another reporter say.

"Detective McKenna, could you please tell us why the focus of your investigation seems to have shifted to Bellevue Hospital?" It was Heidi, staring at him with innocent inquisitiveness, her microphone thrust in front of his face while she wore her on-camera smile.

It had to come out sooner or later, McKenna thought. Heaney has been asking too many questions on my behalf there, so the press was bound to have heard about it from one of the people he questioned. I told Heaney that I wouldn't mention Bellevue unless I was asked or unless I was sure the killer was connected to the hospital. Both those things have happened, so here goes. McKenna put on his own on-camera smile and said, "We've learned that all of the victims were Bellevue patients, so we're investigating the possibility that the killer is somehow connected to the hospital, possibly as a former employee who had access to their medical records.''

"Can you reveal to us the contents of either of the messages the killer sent?'' asked John Brogan from CNN.

"No. I anticipate that the DA will reveal those messages at the killer's trial.''

"Are you telling us that you're making progress in identifying the killer?'' Brogan asked.

Time for the first lie of the evening, McKenna thought. I can't tell them we're close because I can't take the chance that the killer will believe me and run. "No, unfortunately there's no specific progress I can point to. However, I assure you that all leads are being investigated and I'm confident that we'll eventually make an arrest and secure a conviction in this case.''

"Detective McKenna. Can you make a projection when 'eventually' might be? Do you think you'll get him before he kills another victim?'' It was Heidi again.

McKenna had had enough of being Heidi's pincushion for that night. "In answer to your questions, Heidi, no and I hope so,'' he said, smiling directly at her. Then he held up his arms and addressed the rest of the reporters. "Same time, same place tomorrow. Ladies and Gentlemen, thank you and good night.''

41 McKenna had chosen Churchill's as the site for his meeting with Geberth for two reasons. Decorated as an English pub–style bar-restaurant and serving good food in adequate portions, Churchill's generated a congenial atmosphere that favored conversation. The other reason was standing behind the bar when he walked in. McKenna's old pal Chipmunk, said by many to be the world's greatest bartender, was a source McKenna wanted to consult before he picked Geberth's brain because, by nature of his position, Chip always knew with clarity what people were thinking and talking about in the City of New York.

Before Chipmunk would consider opening office hours, the amenities had to be conducted and protocol had to be satisfied. McKenna had to be properly anointed by Chip with a handshake and a kiss on the forehead before going to step two of the proceedings. He poured McKenna a glass of O'Doul's and himself a beaker of something clear and potent from the rack, and then they raised their glasses to "airmen downed, soldiers killed in battle, and sailors lost at sea.'' Naturally, both glasses had to be drained before another word could be spoken.

"Okay, Brian, what do you need?'' Chip asked as soon as McKenna's empty glass hit the bar.

"It's that obvious?'' McKenna asked.

"Yep. You look worried and beat, so I figure it's something to do with your case.''

"It is. I need you to tell me how people see it. Not regular people, but the late-at-night nuts.''

"They like him, think he's smart, and think he's doing a pretty good job. They don't think you're gonna get him.''

"No sympathy for the homeless?''

"No, especially if they have AIDS. You know how some of these jerks are. They're mean, living marginal lives themselves. They love having somebody below them on the social ladder they can dump on."

"What I'm worried about is copycat killings. You know, guys get liquored up and start talking and then, later on, we have another victim with his throat cut. What do you think the chances are of that?"

"I think it's bound to happen if this thing drags on and is always on the news, but it won't be the crowd from here that does it," Chipmunk said after thinking about it a minute. "They might talk about it, but they're just pseudo–tough guys trying to sound crazy. Slobs, really."

"Where would they talk about it and then do it? The East Village?"

"The East Village and Uptown, not to mention all the hard-core loser joints in Brooklyn and Queens. You could go into one of those places, buy the bar a round, and drum up a slash-a-bum party in five minutes."

"Then I guess I've got problems coming," McKenna said.

"Maybe more than you know. Forget about the losers who'd do it on a whim. Think about the skinheads yet?"

"No, they haven't even crossed my mind. I didn't think we had a problem with them here."

"I hear they're getting big, just like in Europe," Chip said. "All low-class white trash who think Hitler was a pretty nice guy after all. They're slow thinkers and it takes a while for them to come up with an idea. But if this case goes on much longer, you might get a problem from them. They're real mean and have no pity."

"Thanks, Chip. Pour me another one, would you?"

"Really? There's almost no alcohol in those O'Doul's."

"I know. I'm just gonna drink and pretend and maybe wish there were."

McKenna was on his third beer when Geberth came in. His first thought was that Geberth looked different from his days running around the Bronx catching killers: older and a little grayer, of course, but he was putting on the years gracefully.

"You're looking good, Vernon," McKenna told him as soon as he got to the bar.

"Yeah, I know. Life's good on the outside."

He hasn't changed much, McKenna thought. "Aren't you going to tell me how I look?"

"Okay. You look terrible. I think you should get more sleep. Now, tell me what's happening in this case that I haven't read in the papers."

"Let's sit down and order first," McKenna suggested.

They did, and by the time they had finished their salads and the entrée had arrived, McKenna figured that Geberth knew as much about the case and the killer as he did. Both men were hungry, and McKenna was content to concentrate silently on his food, feeling it prudent to give Geberth time to digest the information he had given him before asking for his conclusions and advice.

As it turned out, McKenna didn't have to ask. Geberth was a faster eater than he was, and as soon as he finished his meal he said, "You've got an unusual one here. Most serial killers are sex driven—psychopathic sexual sadists who kill without pity."

"But not this one?"

"Nope. You've got yourself something rare—a classic mission-oriented serial killer. I can't tell you who he is. What I can tell you is how he thinks and some courses of action he'll probably choose, if that's what you want to know."

"I do, but that's not the most important thing I need from you. What most worries me is the possibility of copycat killings under the circumstances we have in this town now."

"Copycat killings? Even rarer, but they happen. Finish your food and give me some time to think about it."

McKenna did, but Geberth was still not ready. It wasn't until coffee arrived that he commented on the question. "Taking into account the hundreds of serial-killing cases we've had in this country, I can think of only three cases where there've been copycat killings during the same time frame and in the same locality the original killer was operating in. You already know about the Atlanta case, right?"

"Yes. Wayne Williams."

"Then there's the Green River murders, forty-nine of them to date. The killings generally occurred in the Tacoma-Seattle area in Washington, although some bodies found around Portland are thought to be linked to the same killer or killers. The murders have stopped and nobody's been caught yet, but some of the experts think there were two killers operating there."

"What do you think?"

"At least two."

"And the third case?"

"One pattern that fits your case in many ways. In LA between 1974 and 1984 they had a serial killer the press called the Skid Row Slasher. Turned out to be a guy named Vaughn Greenwood, cut the throats of eight homeless people in a ten-year period. When they finally got him, he said he was trying to rid the world of undesirables, but I think there was more to it than that, some sexual thrill-seeking on his part. But a couple of years after Greenwood started his spree, somebody else started killing homeless people in the same area, and in much the same way."

"He cut their throats?"

"No, but he also killed his victims with a knife. They called him the Skid Row Stabber and he wound up doing thirteen. When he was caught he was found to be another sadistic sexual thrill-seeker. Said he was inspired by the Slasher and that he decided to start when he saw the police weren't able to catch the Slasher."

"Do you think that will happen here?"

"Depends on a few things. I guess you know that the homeless aren't universally popular," Geberth said.

"I know that. I've been reading the mail the *Post* has been getting."

"Same thing happened in LA with the Skid Row cases. Now you have to consider that your killer has been working for only three weeks, but he's got quite a tally. Makes those deaths seem almost commonplace, like another one or two or five wouldn't be a big thing. If you don't catch him soon, I'd say the odds are fair that you're gonna have a problem."

"I'm convinced I will," McKenna said. "I've got to worry about rotten kids, drunks, skinheads, and now psychopaths. That's four groups, each one with an inclination to expand my case.''

"I think the only thing you really have to worry about is a copycat psychopath.''

"Really? Well that's a relief.''

"I'm not saying the others won't do it, but they'd be a one-time occurrence. They'd slash a bum on a dare, with very little planning involved. Jerks like them won't be your main problem.''

"Sounds like enough of a problem to me.''

"No, they'd be easy. You'd have them locked up in no time. Kids and skinheads would brag to their other demented friends and the drunks will be talking about it in bars, either before or after they do it. Given enough manpower, you'd have them in a day. Like I said, your real problem would be the psychopath.''

"And what do you think the odds are of one of them cutting loose?''

Geberth stopped, put milk and sugar in his coffee, stirred it slowly while he reflected on the problem, then took a few sips before he answered. "In a town this size, I'm sure there's more than one of them, seeing how famous your killer's getting. They're each admiring his methods and wondering why they didn't think of doing it first themselves.''

"But wouldn't they be in it for the fame?'' McKenna asked. "It involves getting caught to be famous.''

"Fame is just part of it, but they'd want the thrill of killing first. Once it starts, the copycat, or maybe copycats, will be trying to run the total way up.''

"So what do we do to prevent all of this from happening?''

"For the kids, the drunks, and the skinheads, just what you're doing. Massive display of manpower to prevent it, but if that doesn't work, catch them in a hurry with a lot of publicity and throw the book at them. That'll put an end to them.''

"And the psychopaths?''

"Just one way. They don't think much about the consequences of their actions, so you have to catch your killer before these other psychopaths get started and get that first taste of blood. It's that simple.''

Simple, huh? All I have to do is catch one killer to prevent the murders of some of the easiest victims imaginable, people sleeping outside all over town, maybe drunk, with their throats exposed to whatever crazy comes along, McKenna thought. Simple. "You got any good news for me, Vernon?'' he asked.

"As a matter of fact, I do, but it's only an opinion. I'm convinced your killer isn't a psychopath and I'm sure he doesn't want to get caught.''

"I agree, but how's that good news?'' McKenna asked.

"Because of his special brand of victim, your killer has to confine his operations to Midtown because that's where they are. Most of them are sick and they seem to stay close enough to the Bellevue Clinic. If you keep up the manpower show, he won't take a chance on killing again and getting caught. He'll wait you out, wait for the heat to die down before he tries again. That is, unless you get him identified first.''

"And what happens after we do that and put his picture on every front page?''

"That's easy, and he's prepared for that. He'll run.''

42

McKenna got to the crowded squad office just before 9 A.M. feeling well rested and better than he had since returning to police work. There had been no killings during the night, and he felt confident it was going to be his day. His own office was ready, which made him feel even better. As Brunette had wanted, Ward had it made quite impressive for a small place. All the furniture was new and a computer terminal sat on the desk. On one wall hung a large map of Manhattan's precincts with pins in it indicating the locations where the bodies of the thirteen victims had been found. Next to the map was a large status board with the thirteen names, dates of death, precincts of occurrence, and case numbers listed. McKenna noted with some consternation that there was room for many more victims on the board.

Feeling satisfied, he went back out to the squad office, made himself a cup of coffee, and watched the eight detectives in the office typing up their interview reports of all the homeless people they had talked to during the evening. It made him feel even better, thankful that he wasn't involved in the silly work in his case. Then he checked the Telephone Message Log and saw that Scagnelli had called for him at eight. The message directed McKenna to call him back at the lab as soon as he got in.

Inspectors at work at 8 A.M. on a Saturday morning and I don't show up till nine? Maybe I could have done with an hour less sleep, McKenna thought.

To McKenna's surprise, Scagnelli didn't sound the slightest bit annoyed. "Thanks for getting back to me so fast, Brian," he said pleasantly. "Just wanted to keep you up-to-date on how we're doing."

"With the enzyme?"

"Yeah, with the enzyme and with the prints. Good news first. We got your prints from Immigration, one thousand and nine of them. We're loading them into the computer and we should have them all scanned against the wine-bottle latents by one, maybe sooner if we get lucky."

Well, that is good news, McKenna thought. If I'm right about the AIDS clinic, by one o'clock I'll have a name for my killer. "That's great. And the enzyme?"

"We've isolated it. Unfortunately, it's a very complex protein and nobody here has seen anything like it. I don't think we'll be able to duplicate it anytime soon."

"Anytime soon? What does that mean, Inspector?"

"It means maybe not anytime this year without a major research budget," Scagnelli said, sounding depressed.

So what? McKenna wanted to tell him to cheer him up. This case isn't going to trial, we just have to make it look like we think it is. But he didn't think that was the way to go with the very correct and meticulous Scagnelli. "So what are your options?"

"We have to find where it occurs naturally in nature, just like your killer did. We're going to check it against the enzymes produced by every poisonous plant, insect, fish, and reptile known to man. I hope you don't mind, but we'd like to work it ourselves for a week before we send it to CDC."

"CDC?"

"Center for Disease Control in Atlanta. The feds."

"No, I don't mind. But why?"

"You kidding? We crack this one, it'll be in all the books and journals. I've got one or two people here who are documenting the work we're doing on it for their doctoral theses. I can't get them to go home for a break."

"How long you been there?"

"I don't know, really. In the excitement, I sort of lost track of time."

That's exciting? McKenna thought. Who would have believed it? "Take all the time you need, Inspector. And good luck."

"Thanks," Scagnelli said, then hung up.

Next, McKenna went into Ward's office with a copy of Heaney's list of AIDS clinic employees. He found the lieutenant sitting at his desk. There were stacks of hundreds of interview reports piled in front of him and a basket of case folders on the floor next to his desk. Since the lieutenant was on overtime, McKenna had expected him to be in a delightful mood.

He wasn't disappointed. "Morning, Brian. How do you like your new office?" Ward asked pleasantly, standing up so McKenna could see him over the reports.

"Fine, thank you. Did my new sketches arrive from the Artists Unit?"

"At eight-thirty this morning," Ward said, then sorted through the stacks of reports. He found the sketches and handed them to McKenna. They were numbered one through four in big, block letters at the top.

McKenna's first thought was that the new sketches didn't look like the same man everyone was searching for, but he had expected that. "I've got some busy-work for some detectives, if you can spare them," he told Ward.

"I sure can. I just hope whatever you've got in mind for them will get them to stop filling out these goddamn reports on every bum they see," Ward said. "Don't they realize I have to read and sign them all?"

What's he think? All those guys are out there working just to annoy him? McKenna wondered. "I guess they haven't come up with anything?"

"No, but Brunette's getting what he wanted. They all look really busy for the cameras," Ward said sarcastically as he sorted through the reports. "What do you want done?"

"Quite a bit," McKenna said, handing him Heaney's list and the sketches. "That's the names, addresses, and phone numbers of the two hundred and thirty-two people who've worked at the Bellevue AIDS Clinic during the past seven years. I need them all shown copies of those sketches and interviewed to see if they recognize the guy."

Ward went through the list. "I'll assign ten names to each team to get it done today," he said. "But why do you call it busywork? Seems worthwhile to me."

"Because the prints are in from Immigration and Scagnelli's running them against the wine-bottle latents. We should have the killer's name by one o'clock."

"That's all right. I'll send them out anyway and clear out this office. Now I've got something for you," Ward said, kicking the basket at the side of his desk.

"Those the case folders on the victims from the other precincts?" McKenna asked.

"Yeah. Now tell me something I don't know."

"Vernon says there's a strong possibility of copycat killings if we don't catch this guy soon."

"I don't need Vernon to tell me that. What else?"

"Nothing else. Now you know everything I do."

"Good. I hope you're right about the AIDS clinic," Ward said. "Get back to work, and thanks for sharing."

By 12:30 McKenna had gone through all the victims' case folders, learning nothing that he hadn't expected to find in them. They told of wasted, tormented lives and premature deaths, but he took the time to memorize all their faces, where they had died, and when.

Steve Birnstill had been assigned by Ward as the dispatcher and was seated at the desk in front of McKenna, sipping a cup of coffee with a copy of Heaney's list and Ward's Detective Assignment Sheet spread in front of him. His phone rang again and he listened to the reporting detective for a few minutes before scratching some more names off the list.

"Anything?" McKenna asked him for the tenth time in the last hour.

"Negative report. Nobody knows the guy in your sketches," Birnstill replied without turning around.

"How many so far?"

Birnstill ran his fingers down the pages. "That makes about forty people interviewed with nothing to report."

Forty? That's almost 20 percent of them, and still nothing, McKenna thought, growing more apprehensive by the minute. He decided his time would be best spent staring at the phone on his desk while awaiting Scagnelli's call.

It came at 12:50 and McKenna picked it up on the first ring. "Hi, Brian, got some news for you," Scagnelli said, sounding upbeat and raising McKenna's hopes.

"You got a name for me?" McKenna asked.

"From the prints? No, sorry. No hit."

No hit? I'm finished! McKenna thought. How is it possible that everything points to Bellevue and he's telling me *No hit?* "Are you sure?" he asked.

"Almost certain. Computers don't lie. Naturally I'll run your prints through again, but the match isn't there. Sorry, but it's not all bad."

"I'm listening, Inspector. I could sure use some good news right now."

"Then you'll love this. One of my people remembered reading something in an old *National Geographic* about a type of caterpillar and butterfly that manufactures cyanide in its body to discourage predators, so we've managed to get the article. It's called the passion vine butterfly, lives in Costa Rica and parts of Colombia. We got a hold of an entomologist from NYU, Dr. Kenneth Rowe. He's a top man in the bug field, world renowned, and he's agreed to help us look into it."

Yeah, I just love that, Scagnelli, you nitwit. What good does it do me to know how he's killing them if I don't know who he is? You think that's gonna save my bacon? McKenna felt like asking, but on reflection decided that would be a bad course of action. Instead, he took a couple of deep breaths and said, "Very nice of Dr. Rowe. You must be very excited."

"We sure are," Scagnelli said enthusiastically. "His name alone will add immediate recognition to our work here, but it gets better. According to him, certain types of passion vine butterflies manufacture an enzyme that enhances the effect of the cyanide. Birds eat one of those and they never want another. They remember the colors of the butterfly and go out of their way to avoid them. It's quite a successful species."

McKenna took three more deep breaths. "That's quite interesting. Does Dr. Rowe know of any cases where birds have died after eating those butterflies?"

"No, but he has observed them get quite sick. I think we're on the right track. We've got a real bug detective on our side now."

"Wonderful. Please keep me informed, Inspector."

"I certainly will. By the way, good luck in finding your man. Let me know if you need anything else."

After hanging up, McKenna spent five minutes staring at Ward's door, searching for the best way to give him the news. All the while his stomach was sending him messages. Then he remembered that he hadn't eaten all morning. He decided that, since bad news could always wait, lunch was the more pressing problem for the moment. He put on his coat and said to Birnstill, "I'm going for lunch. Be back in an hour. Want anything?"

"Sure, thanks. Could you get me a—" but Birnstill's phone rang again. McKenna watched in dismay as Birnstill listened, then crossed four more names off his list. "Sorry," he said as soon as he hung up. "Can you get me a hot pastrami on rye and a Sprite?"

"My pleasure."

On his way down the stairwell, McKenna met Saffran coming up. With Saffran was a small, shabbily dressed man who looked Hispanic to McKenna.

"We were just on our way up to see you," Saffran said.

"And is this gentleman Chingo?" McKenna asked.

"Yes, another friend of Tony's," Saffran said, turning to Chingo. "Detective McKenna, permit me to introduce you to Chingo, aka Felipe Santiago, currently of the Third Street Men's Shelter and Rutherford Park."

Chingo self-consciously extended his hand and McKenna shook it. "Could you gentlemen please wait for me upstairs?" McKenna asked. "I've got to get something in my stomach, but I'll be back as soon as I can."

"Take your time, Detective McKenna," Chingo said. "I got nowhere to go and nothing to do."

Me neither, McKenna thought.

43 McKenna went to Jameson's on Second Avenue, a couple of blocks from the station house, and ordered the leg of lamb. It was one of his favorite dishes and he was hungry, but when it came he found that eating did nothing to resolve that queasy feeling in his stomach. He knew he needed something more solid than food to calm his stomach; what he desperately needed was for something to go right, and soon.

But nothing was going right. He put down his knife and fork and reexamined the case in his mind.

How could it be *No hit?* he asked himself over and over. We know it's the killer's prints on the wine bottle and everything points to him working at Bellevue. All the victims are HIV positive and they're all outpatients at Bellevue Clinic. Some of them obviously had AIDS, but Benny Foster didn't. If he doesn't work at Bellevue, how else did the killer know Foster was HIV positive? But yet—No hit. No hit after we've run the prints of every doctor, nurse, and pharmacist at Bellevue even close to matching his description. How?

McKenna's ruminations were interrupted by his waitress. She was passing by and noticed that he had hardly touched his food. "Something wrong with the leg of lamb, Brian?" she asked solicitously.

"No, the food's fine. It's me. I've developed a little stomach problem."

"Sorry to hear that. Maybe you'd like to order something else instead."

"How about a pastrami on rye and a Sprite to go?"

"Sure. I'll have it to you in a couple of minutes," she assured him and was gone, leaving McKenna to his thoughts.

Could it be he's not a medical worker, but maybe a clerk or something like that at Bellevue? he wondered. No, can't be. With the potion he's cooked up, he's got to be a medical worker. Christ! Cyanide and an enzyme nobody's seen before? And even Andino said he must be a doctor to cut O'Sullivan's throat the way he did, so he must be. And if he's a doctor, he couldn't have also been a patient at the Bellevue Clinic. Doctors with AIDS don't go to the Bellevue Clinic with the poor and the homeless, McKenna concluded. They go someplace nice.

The waitress returned with Birnstill's sandwich and McKenna left Jameson's feeling worse than he had when he entered. He walked slowly to the station house, dreading his upcoming conversation with Ward. There were only a few reporters lounging around outside, and Heidi was not among them. McKenna considered her absence the only bright spot in an otherwise dismal day.

When he got up to the squad office, McKenna stopped briefly at his last remaining hope and gave him his sandwich. "Anything?" he asked Birnstill.

"Nothing but sixty-two negatives, so far."

"Thank you so much," McKenna said, then went to the interview room. Saffran and Chingo were there, playing poker for loose smokes. "Ready for us?" Saffran asked.

"Yeah, in a minute. I just have to stop into the lieutenant's office first for a dose of degradation and humiliation."

"Have fun," Saffran replied jovially.

McKenna put on his contrite face, knocked on Ward's door, and entered.

Ward was visible behind his desk, having come a long way toward completing his paperwork. "What can I do for you, Brian?" he looked up and asked.

"I'm afraid I've got some bad news."

"I already figured that out when you didn't come bounding in here at one o'clock," Ward said, sounding as disappointed as McKenna felt. "No hit on the prints?"

"Right. I still don't understand it, but no hit."

"Don't kill yourself over it," Ward said, surprising McKenna. "What do we do now?"

"I don't know."

Then Ward surprised McKenna even more when he smiled and said, "I hope this never gets repeated outside this room, but neither do I." For his final surprise, Ward cleared his desk by scooping the remaining reports into his trash basket. "Wanna pull up a chair and see what we can come up with by putting our heads together?"

McKenna had never seen anything like it. A squad commander, that class of person who lived and died by reports, defiling those sacred documents? He figured Ward was ready to snap and didn't want to be there when he did. "Could you give me a couple of minutes, Lieutenant? Saffran's got another guy outside who knows the killer and I'd like to interview him first," he said, hoping to be absent when the breakdown occurred.

"Sure, go ahead. Take your time, I'll be here."

McKenna went to the door, but stopped with his hand on the doorknob. "You feeling okay, Lieutenant?"

"Not great, but okay. Why? This reaction isn't what you expected?"

"Not at all."

"Then I guess the tough-lieutenant act fooled you?"

"Entirely."

"Good. Then let me tell you this before you go. If you haven't figured this case out yet, I'm not worried. You'll get that guy, sooner or later."

I love this man! McKenna thought. "Thanks very much, Lieutenant," he said, then opened the door.

McKenna had almost made it to the interview room when he heard Ward yell through the door: "But sooner would be better!"

Saffran and Chingo put down their cards as soon as McKenna entered the room. McKenna noticed that Chingo had a large pile of loose cigarettes in front of him, while Saffran was down to three. "You don't look too degraded and humiliated to me," Saffran commented.

"Ward could've killed me, but he didn't," McKenna answered, feeling like he had a new lease on life. "You ready to share some knowledge with me?" he asked Chingo as he pulled up a chair.

"What do you want to know?"

McKenna took his original sketch of the killer from his pocket and placed it in front of Chingo. "How long have you known this man?" he asked.

"Tony? No more than two months."

"Two months? You met him before New Year's."

"Yeah, before Christmas, too. I first met him in Rutherford Park maybe a week before Christmas."

"What was he doing when you met him?"

"Drinking in the park with Slickman."

"Slickman? You mean Tyrone Lewis?"

"I don't know if that's his real name. Everybody just calls him Slickman."

"That's his real name. Do you know that Slickman's dead?"

Chingo looked surprised at the news. "No. Haven't seen him around in a while, but dead is some serious shit. How'd he die?"

"Tony poisoned him."

"Damn!" was Chingo's original comment at the news, but then he decided to amend it. "Old Slickman was a wily dude, beat a lot of folks. Maybe he had it coming."

"Maybe, but he didn't do nothing to Tony," McKenna stated.

"Then why'd he do it?"

"We're still working that out. I'll let you know when we know for sure. How many times did you talk to Tony?"

"Lemme see," Chingo said, counting to himself on his fingers. "Seen him maybe four or five times."

"Where?"

"We was drinking together once down the block from the shelter, over on Bowery. Washing windows, panhandling, and drinking that old devil in between."

"Excuse me," McKenna said. "What were you drinking?"

"That old devil. Wild Irish Rose in the red."

"You were drinking and he was drinking?"

"You know I was drinking. And why wouldn't he be drinking? After all, it was his stuff. Maybe we'd sniff a little glue, too."

"Wait a minute! He sniffed glue?"

"I guess so. I never seen him do it, but it was his glue."

"His glue? Are you sure?"

" 'Course I'm sure. On the Bowery, when he was pulling out his wine bottle, the glue fell outta his pocket. So I picks it up and asks him, 'Do you mind?' and he says, 'No, go right ahead.' "

"So you sniffed his glue?"

"Yeah, but it wasn't that good."

"And he didn't sniff with you?"

"No, but he wanted it back. Said he was saving it for later."

Now what the hell does that mean, if anything? McKenna wondered. A glue-sniffing doctor? Can that be, or am I in left field with a hockey stick? He pondered the question until he noticed that both Chingo and Saffran were looking at him with bored expressions on their faces.

I'll figure it out later, if I can, McKenna decided. Now for the question I can't tiptoe around. "Sorry, Chingo, but now I've got to ask you a personal question."

"Go ahead. I ain't got nothing personal."

"Are you HIV positive?"

"What?" Chingo asked, loud and indignant.

"Sorry, but I've got to know."

"I ain't never been with no man and I don't shoot no dope."

"Have you ever been to the Bellevue AIDS Clinic?"

"No, of course not. I been to Bellevue, but never to no AIDS clinic. Why should I go there?"

"No reason. Just asking, that's all," McKenna said soothingly. "Where else did you see Tony?"

"Seen him outside the Men's Shelter on East Third and seen him once or twice in Grand Central."

"When was the last time you saw him?"

"Maybe a week ago. That was in Grand Central, when it was real cold out. Seen everybody there."

"When you saw him, what did you two talk about?"

"Mostly nothing."

"Nothing?" McKenna asked. "You must have talked about something."

"Not that I remember," Chingo said, his brow furrowed in concentration.

"It's important, so please keep thinking hard about it. Did you talk about any of the other homeless men?"

"That's it!" Chingo said, relieved. "Now I remember. He was always asking about the other fellas."

"Asking what about them?"

"You know. How they're doing and where they're hanging out."

"And where they sleep?"

"Yeah. He was asking where they crib."

"Who was he asking about?"

It was a tough one for Chingo. "I know he was asking about Mickey and about Chumpchange, but I don't remember who else."

McKenna turned to Saffran. "Chumpchange?"

"That's Beauregard T. Stafford, male black, about thirty-five years old," Saffran explained. "A regular jailbird, used to hang out in the East Twenty-ninth Street playground, but Dante tells me he'd seen him a lot on the Bowery. Until recently, that is."

McKenna recognized the name at once. Beauregard T. Stafford, the other Ninth Precinct case besides Tyrone Lewis. Discovered dead on January 17 in a small park at Bowery and Third Avenue.

"Do you think you'll be able to remember anyone else you talked about?" McKenna asked Chingo.

"Maybe later."

"Okay, let's go on. What was Tony wearing when you saw him?"

"Always the same thing. Always dressed in black, like Maverick."

Maverick? I sure like that one better than Dracula, McKenna thought. "And he looks like that sketch?" McKenna asked.

Chingo glanced down at the sketch. "He does now," he said.

"What do you mean, he does now?" McKenna asked calmly.

"What I mean is that this is the way he looks since he got rid of that rash," Chingo said, holding up the sketch.

"What rash?"

"When I first knowed him before Christmas, he used to have a rash on his face. But the last time I saw him, it was gone."

"Where was the rash?"

"All over the bottom half of his face and his neck. Real red and ugly. I asked him about it and he said he got it from shaving."

A rash from shaving, but now it's gone? What's that about? McKenna asked himself. Two things to ponder. A shaving rash and sniffing glue. Does it mean anything?

Suddenly McKenna stood straight up, knocking down his chair and surprising Chingo and Saffran so much that they ducked. "Do you remember what that glue smelled like?" he asked Chingo so loudly that the homeless man flinched.

"I guess so. I mean, maybe I do."

"Good. Wait here," McKenna told them, then almost ran out to Birnstill.

"Nothing yet," Birnstill said, startled by McKenna.

"Forget that. Get me one of the Street Crime sergeants on the line."

"Sure thing." Birnstill called the citywide dispatcher and asked her to have one of the Street Crime sergeants working the Midtown detail call the 17th Squad.

McKenna stood fidgeting and staring at the phone till Birnstill could stand it no longer. "You better calm down, Brian, or you'll be heading for the big one today," he advised.

"You're right. I will," McKenna replied. "I'll be waiting in the hall. Call me when you hear from Street Crime."

McKenna spent the next four minutes pacing and thinking in the hallway outside the squad office, but he would have sworn it was an hour. When Birnstill finally called him, he was at the phone in seconds. "Who is this?" he asked into the receiver, struggling to control his voice.

"Sergeant Winter, Street Crime Unit. Who's this?"

"Detective McKenna. I need one of the makeup kits you guys use when you do the decoys. You got one handy?"

"I don't know for sure. We might have one in the trunk of one of our cars. Want me to look?"

"I want you to do more than that. I want you to find one and bring it to me as quick as you can."

"Will do. See you soon."

McKenna hung up and saw that Birnstill was staring at him, wide-eyed. "Commissioner, weren't we a little strong with that nice sergeant?" he asked sarcastically.

"Maybe I was, but I didn't mean to be. I'll be sure to apologize to him and everybody else I get out of line with in the next hour. Now, please call the teams out there and tell them to stand by. They're not to show another person those sketches until they hear from me."

"Sure thing."

"I'll be in the hallway if you want me."

"Naturally."

It took Sergeant Winter twenty-two minutes to arrive with the makeup kit. McKenna knew it was twenty-two minutes because he had checked his watch six times while he paced in the hallway, waiting and thinking. Then he heard someone running up the stairs to the second floor, and a young sergeant wearing his shield on a chain around his neck came out of the stairwell carrying a briefcase.

"Is this what you're looking for, Commissioner?" Winter asked, holding up the briefcase when he saw McKenna waiting outside the squad office.

"I hope so, and it's *Detective* McKenna. Sorry if I sounded out of line, Sarge."

"No offense taken, Commissioner," Winter said as he handed McKenna the briefcase. "You need any help with the makeup?"

"No, I remember how to use it. I spent five years in Street Crime."

"Then you don't need me for anything else."

"No, but thanks a lot. I think you helped save my bacon with this."

The sergeant left and McKenna went into his office. He opened the briefcase, went directly to a pouch on the side, and pulled out a bushy black fake beard and two tubes of glue, one blue and one green. He put the beard back in the briefcase pouch and took the tubes of glue into the interview room. "You know what these are?" he asked Chingo, placing the tubes on the table in front of him.

"Sure. That's glue."

"Do either of them look like the tubes Tony had?"

"They both do."

"You don't remember what color the tube he had was?"

"Sorry, no."

"Don't worry, it doesn't matter," McKenna said. "Open them up and tell me which one it was."

"You want me to sniff glue here?" Chingo asked dubiously. "Sniff glue in the police station?"

"Yeah, I want you to really enjoy yourself."

"Okay, but I need a paper bag."

McKenna went back out to the squad office and rummaged through Birnstill's trash can. Birnstill had become immune to McKenna's antics and watched him go through the can with no more than passing curiosity. McKenna found what he was looking for—the bags the pastrami sandwich and the can of Sprite had come in. He took them back into the interview room and gave them to Chingo.

It took McKenna only a minute to discover that, when it came to glue, Chingo was a real connoisseur. The homeless man opened each tube and sniffed it delicately like the wine steward at the Plaza Hotel would sniff the cork of a bottle of Moulin rouge '78. Then he squeezed some glue from the blue tube into the Sprite bag and some glue from the green tube into the pastrami bag. He tried the green first, putting the bag over his nose and mouth and inhaling deeply three times. His eyes were slightly glazed when he lowered the bag. "This isn't the stuff," he told McKenna.

"How do you know?"

"This shit is too good, almost as good as airplane glue. Tony's was terrible, took me five minutes to get a good head."

"Okay. We'll wait a while before we try the other," McKenna said. Then he went outside and made Chingo a cup of coffee and gave it to him. Ten minutes later Chingo had finished his coffee and was ready. He covered his nose and mouth with the Sprite bag and inhaled deeply three times. When he removed the bag from his face he said, "This is the shit. Terrible."

"Are you sure?" McKenna asked.

"Sure I'm sure," Chingo said disdainfully. "You ask anybody, they tell you that Chingo knows his glue."

"Thank you, Chingo. You've been a big help. Could you wait here a couple of minutes more?"

"No problem," Chingo said, then he was hit by a thought. He held up the pastrami bag and asked, "Can I have this?"

"Of course not, Chingo. This is a police station, remember?" McKenna picked up the tubes of glue and went back out to Birnstill. "Could you get me one of the teams on the line? Any team will do."

Birnstill called the detective dispatcher and the phone rang a minute later. McKenna picked it up. "McKenna here. Who's this?"

"Detective Chaney, Two-six Squad. Sorry we got no hits on your sketches all day."

"Of course you didn't. You've got the wrong sketches."

"Huh?"

"Listen, Chaney. This is what I want you to do. Go buy a Magic Marker and draw beards on all four sketches."

"Beards?"

"Yeah, good ones. Put a little hair around the ears just below the cap, too. From now on, those are the sketches I want you to show. Got it?"

"If you say so."

"I say so." McKenna said, then hung up. "You heard?" he asked Birnstill.

"I heard."

"Good. Have all the teams call in and give them the same instructions."

Birnstill took it in stride. "If you say so."

McKenna replaced the glue tubes in the briefcase, then made himself a cup of coffee and sat at his desk, drinking and trying to relax. When he figured he had calmed down sufficiently, he picked up the briefcase and went in to see Ward. He found the lieutenant watching a soap opera on TV and looking very content. "I think we're making some progress," McKenna said.

"I've figured that out already," Ward said, then turned off the TV with the remote control.

"You have? How?"

"About a half hour ago somebody came in here and told me they thought you flipped, thought that maybe we should call an ambulance."

"Birnstill?"

"I'm not saying. Whoever it was, I told him that's the way great minds operate. You think they're crazy and then they come up with the big idea. What do you have there?" he asked, pointing to the briefcase.

"Thanks to Detective Saffran, the answer to some questions we didn't think to ask."

"*Detective* Saffran? Isn't it *Police Officer* Saffran, a uniformed cop temporarily assigned to the Bureau?"

"Maybe." McKenna put the briefcase down on Ward's desk and said, "How come we never tried to figure out what our guy was doing when he wasn't out killing people? We figured he was a doctor and that he spent a couple of years in this town, which meant he must have met a lot of people. Yet nobody knew him from our sketch. Why?"

"We already answered that one, didn't we? Didn't we figure it's because his appearance has changed so much because of the AIDS? You know, the drastic weight loss and everything."

"That should be why most of the people he knew back then didn't recognize him from the sketch, but not all of them. He must have had some friends who would know his face no matter how sick he got or how much weight he lost, right?"

"I guess so."

"But they didn't. Then think about what he's doing today when he's not out working. He has to buy groceries and leave his house sometime, yet nobody recognizes him. His sketch was on the front page of every newspaper in town, he's got a distinctive face with those eyes, and nobody recognizes him? Why?"

"Like you said, he dresses like money and projects a different persona," Ward said.

"That helps, but now I'm sure that's not enough. I'll show you how he does it." He opened the briefcase and took out the fake beard and the two tubes of glue. He looked at the tubes, thinking, then made his decision. He took the blue tube, spread it on the backing of the fake beard, then attached the beard to his face and pushed it into place. "I know it's not my style or color, but how do I look?" McKenna asked.

"Pretty professional job, but I'd know it was you under there," Ward said.

"Okay, but think about this. Say you've known me for five years, but you've never seen me without the beard. Then I get sick, lose fifty pounds, my eyes change, and I shave the beard off. Would you know me then?"

"Maybe not."

"Probably not, especially since I was a respectable doctor when you knew me. Now the police put their sketch of me in the paper. It's a sketch of some lunatic, a lunatic without a beard, who's out here poisoning and slashing homeless people. My bet is that you'd never connect the sketch to me, never even think of me."

"Probably not," Ward conceded.

"Now I'll tell you something else. He's living in some small town way outside the metropolitan area, the kind of place where they're worried about the prices farmers get paid for milk and corn, not what's happening here. He's got money, lives in a nice place, acts respectable, dresses nice, but doesn't go out much. However, every time he does go out, his beard is on, a real professional one custom-made for him. The only time it comes off is when he's working here in Midtown, so nobody in that small town recognizes him from our sketch, especially since they don't pay much attention to what's happening here anyway."

"Seems plausible."

"Plausible?" McKenna asked, trying not to sound sarcastic. "It's certain. It's the only reason we don't have him in jail yet."

"Okay, I agree. Now, where do we go from here to get him identified?"

"We already have gone from here," McKenna said, then explained how he had the detective teams add the beards to the sketches. "Hopefully, now one of the AIDS clinic people will recognize him and prove us right," McKenna said, making sure to put emphasis on "prove *us* right."

"I'm sure they will and I'm sure we are," Ward agreed. "But that beard still doesn't explain why we've got no hit on the Bellevue prints. A man's fingerprints don't change just because he gets sick and shaves his beard off.''

"I know, but he's a doctor and he was at Bellevue. I'm sure of that, so there's something in this we're not seeing yet.''

"It'll come to you. Now tell me how you got this beard idea.''

"I should have thought of it sooner, but Saffran's the one who should get the credit. He brought in a homeless guy he knew, a guy who had met with the killer a few times. Turns out he knew the killer before he went on his spree, knew him while he was still in the planning stage.''

"Saffran did this on his own?''

"No, but he knew who he was from only a nickname and brought him in to talk to me today. So then Saffran's guy tells me he saw the killer with glue and that back in December the killer had a rash on his face. Then I knew.''

"Just from that you knew about the beard? Pretty impressive,'' Ward commented.

"Actually, I hate to admit it, but it's not so impressive. You see, once I had the same rash. Got it from the glue on a fake beard.''

"You were wearing a fake beard?'' Ward asked, astonished. "When?''

"Years ago, when I was in Street Crime. You know Williamsburg, right?''

"Sure. Never worked there and never wanted to, but I know it's a tough Spanish neighborhood in Brooklyn.''

"Yeah, a tough Spanish neighborhood with a small Hasidic community right in the middle. You know how the Hasidic men dress on the Jewish High Holy days?''

"In all their finery,'' Ward answered. "Put on their best silk overcoats, their white stockings and their mink hats.''

"That's right. Their mink hats, each one costing about a grand. Anyway, back in the seventies those hats became quite a trophy item for the Puerto Rican bad boys in Williamsburg. They would swoop down on a Hasidic walking around in his finery and leave him bareheaded. You know what happened next, don't you?''

"I can imagine. The rabbis started screaming and, since the Hasidics vote as a block for whoever their rabbi tells them to, the politicians were listening.''

"Exactly. So for a couple of years when I was there Street Crime was in Williamsburg doing decoys for all the Jewish High Holy days. We'd dress a cop up like a Hasidic, paste a beard on him, and top him off with a fine mink hat. Then we'd put him out on the fringe of the Hasidic area and he'd stroll around muttering gibberish to himself. Before long, he'd get swooped by a group and five minutes later we'd be on our way to Central Booking with a load of trophy hunters.''

"And you played the decoy?''

"Yeah, but only a couple of times. It was fun, but I couldn't keep doing it because of the rash from one of the glues.''

"Only one of the glues gave you a rash?'' Ward asked.

"Yeah. It was a long time ago, but I think it was the green.''

There was a knock at the door and Birnstill entered. His face registered no expression when he saw McKenna standing there with the beard on, but he certainly wasn't going to let it slide. "Phone call for you, Rabbi. Detective Chaney thinks he found someone for you.''

"Switch it in here," Ward ordered, and Birnstill turned and left.

Seconds later, Ward's phone rang and McKenna picked it up. "What have you got, Chaney?"

"First one we went to after I talked to you is a guy named Mario Santos. He's an orderly at the AIDS clinic and he knows your man, the guy in sketch number four."

Sketch number four. The one with fifty pounds added and nothing distinctive about the eyes, McKenna remembered. "Does he know him from the AIDS clinic?" he asked.

"Sees him there, says he used to come in every once in a while to visit a Dr. Rashid, but he says nobody in the clinic understands it. It seems your man and the doctor were friends."

"Why doesn't he understand that?"

"Because the AIDS clinic isn't where he knows your man from. Years ago, before Mario got assigned to the AIDS clinic, he was an orderly in the emergency room. He says your man was, too. Doctors and orderlies aren't usually close friends like they were."

"He says the killer was an orderly?"

"That's what he says."

How can that be? McKenna wondered. An orderly with a degree in chemistry, maybe? No, can't be, but it explains the No Hit. We only asked Immigration for the prints of the foreign doctors, nurses, and pharmacists. Who would have thought an orderly could come up with a poison potion that nobody's heard of, that's very deadly, and very difficult to detect? It doesn't make sense, he concluded. There's more here. "Does Mario remember his name?" he asked Chaney.

"Hector De la Cruz."

"Where are you?"

"Queens. National Boulevard in Corona."

"I need to talk to Mario. Can you bring him in?"

"On the way. We'll be there in half an hour."

"Detective Chaney, thank you very much."

"Don't mention it, Commissioner," Chaney said, then hung up.

Commissioner again? I've got to tone down, McKenna thought as he replaced the receiver.

"Well?" Ward asked.

"We've got a name, finally," McKenna told Ward. "Hector De la Cruz."

"Then it looks like we're cooking," Ward said.

"That's what it looks like, but I don't want the pot to boil over. Can you have all the teams called back?"

"Sure, but why? Wouldn't finding more people who know your killer be better?"

"Yes, but we can do that later. For now, he's identified and that's enough. We find too many people who know him and then we tell them that the man they know is the killer that's always in the papers, and one of them is gonna wind up talking to the press."

"I see," Ward said. "And then he runs."

"Right. We have to keep him stupid about the fact that we now know who he is."

"So you're gonna talk to only one person, then swear him to secrecy?" Ward guessed.

"Exactly. So, if you don't mind, I've got a lot to do before he gets here," McKenna said, then turned for the door.

"Brian!" Ward yelled, stopping McKenna in his tracks.

"Yes?"

"Don't you think you should take that ridiculous beard off first? It's bad enough that Big-Mouth Birnstill's seen it, but if the press got a peek at you, then we'd both be standing in line at the Pension Section on Monday morning."

A little embarrassed, McKenna pulled it off with some pain since the glue had hardened and taken hold. "Better?" he asked as he rubbed his face.

"Much. Send *Detective* Saffran in here."

44 After giving Saffran the lieutenant's message, McKenna called Jim Heaney at home. The phone wasn't answered until the tenth ring. "Mr. Heaney, this is Detective McKenna. I need a favor."

"Goddamn it! I knew I shouldn't have answered the phone. You really caught me at a bad time."

Heaney sounded out of breath. "What were you doing when I called?" McKenna asked.

"Exercising. Really pumping up."

"Well, in that case, I'm sorry to disturb your workout, but I need you to go to your office."

"My office? Now?"

"Yes, now. Sorry, but it can't wait."

"What is it?" Heaney asked.

"You used to have an orderly named Hector De la Cruz working in your emergency room. I need everything you've got on him."

McKenna had expected some more moaning and groaning from Heaney, but he got none. Instead, Heaney said, "Why go into the office? I can access the hospital's personnel computer from my PC here."

"How long will it take?"

"Maybe five minutes. Is Hector De la Cruz the killer?"

"It sure looks that way. I'll know for sure when I get the information from you to get his fingerprints."

"Good work. Give me your number and I'll call you back in five minutes."

McKenna did, then spent time staring at the phone and waiting for it to ring. It took Heaney fifteen minutes to call back and, once again, he was out of breath. "You ought to slow down on that exercising," McKenna advised.

"Can't. I'm becoming addicted to a new workout routine. You ready for this?"

"Go ahead," McKenna said, pen in hand poised over his notepad.

"Hector De la Cruz. Worked for us for about a year, four years ago. January 6th, 1992, to February 2nd, 1993, all as an orderly in the emergency room. Date of birth March 21st, 1949. His social security number is 060-40-2939 and his alien registration number is D224543."

"Is his country of origin Costa Rica or Colombia?"

"Costa Rica. How'd you know?"

"Educated guess. You got his address?"

"Yeah, 712 Park Avenue, probably way uptown in Spanish Harlem. Apartment Twelve."

712 Park Avenue? McKenna thought. Sure, Park Avenue runs up to Spanish Harlem, but 712 is someplace in the low seventies on the old-money, very rich gold coast. "You got a phone number for him?"

"731-2911."

"You have anything listed about education?"

"Lemme see. Strange, it says college graduate here. Pretty unusual in one of our orderlies."

"Any mention of why he left Bellevue?"

"No, nothing."

"Next of kin?"

"None listed. I hope you don't need anything else because you've covered just about everything on my screen."

"Just his picture."

"I don't have that here," Heaney protested.

"I know that. I don't need it now, but somebody will be around to your office Monday morning to pick it up."

"I'll have it. Tell me, has this information helped you out any?"

"Enormously, thank you."

"And you're pretty certain he's the killer?"

"Almost positive. Now, I need just one more favor from you."

"Anything."

"I got some questions from the press about Bellevue last night, so there might be some reporters snooping around. If we let them know the killer's been identified, they're sure to publish it and he'll run. So you've got to stonewall any reporter that might show up and keep this whole thing just between us for now. Okay?"

Silence greeted McKenna's request, a period of silence so long that McKenna asked, "Mr. Heaney, are you there?"

"Yes, I'm here."

"Did you understand what I said? No talking to the press."

"Yes, I understood, but it might be a little late for that."

"What do you mean, *it might be a little late for that*?"

"There's someone here who wants to talk to you," Heaney said timidly.

Oh no! McKenna thought. Could it be?

"Hello, Brian."

Damn! Damn, damn, damn, damn! "Hello, Heidi. My, you are working very hard on this story, aren't you?" McKenna asked as sweetly as he could.

"Of course. It's Heidi Lane, not Lois Lane. At the moment, Superman's not my pal, so a girl's got to give it everything she's got to get ahead in this filthy reporting business."

"I see. Heidi, we have to talk."

"Haven't I been saying just that very thing?"

"Not just about this story. I mean we have to talk about everything."

"Everything? I've been saying that, too, but you haven't been listening," she said, giggling into the phone.

"Heidi, I can't let this story get out just now. If you identify the killer, he's gonna run. He's rich and I'm sure he's got places to hide."

" 'You can't let this story get out'? It seems to me you're not in charge of that anymore. I am."

"Yes, you are. What do you want from me?"

"We'll start with an exclusive, of course."

"Of course."

"And the rest we can talk about later. What time do you get off?"

"I don't know. Late, I guess."

"I'm at 413 East 54th Street, Apartment 6E. Come on over whenever you get off. I'll be waiting."

"It's not gonna be what you think, Heidi. We have a lot to talk about and that's what we're gonna do."

"Whatever you say for now, but we'll see."

"Fine. Can you put Heaney back on the phone?"

"Are you going to be mean to him?" Heidi asked.

"I think so."

"He's a nice man, so please don't be. As a matter of fact, consider that one of my demands as part of our deal. See you later, Brian."

It took Heaney another minute to come back on the line. "Detective McKenna?"

"Yes. Don't worry, Mr. Heaney. I understand. I know Heidi can be a persuasive girl and very hard to resist."

"That's a fact, but you never mentioned anything about me not talking to the press, did you?"

No. As I recall, it was you who asked me not to mention Bellevue to the press, McKenna thought. "No. I guess I should have, but I didn't."

"So do I have anything to worry about over this?"

"Except for a premature heart attack, I don't think so. As long as the identity of the killer doesn't come out before it's supposed to, I've forgotten all about this."

"Thanks, Detective McKenna. I owe you. Remember, anything I can do for you. Anything."

"Thanks. You better get some rest. Good night."

I don't have time to worry about this right now, McKenna thought. I have to forget about Heidi for the moment and keep thinking. What next?

As it turned out, Saffran was next. He came out of Ward's office, all smiles, and proceeded directly to McKenna. "I think that I'm in, thanks to you," he said.

"You've got it wrong," McKenna said. "Thanks to you, I'm in. What did the lieutenant tell you?"

"Said I might make a good detective someday."

"Funny. That's the same thing he tells me. What else did he say?"

"That he's going to keep me here to see if he's right."

"He's always right, so buy yourself some suits and welcome aboard."

"Thanks. What do you want me to do with Chingo?"

"Take him where he wants to go and go home yourself. I shouldn't need you again until Monday."

Once Saffran and Chingo left, McKenna called the lab and was happy to find that Scagnelli was still there. "You gonna be there long, Inspector?" he asked.

"All day."

"Good. I need another set of prints checked against the latents. They should come in by fax in an hour, if I can pull it off."

"Just one set?"

"Yes, but it's the right one."

"Then I'll do them myself."

"Just perfect. Thanks, Inspector."

Next McKenna called Gene Shields at home.

"You just caught me. We were going out for dinner," Shields said.

"Could you delay it?" McKenna asked.

"Sure, if you think it's important."

"You tell me. I think we've identified the killer, but I need his prints from Immigration to see if they match the latents on our wine bottle. If they do, then I can go the whole nine yards on this guy. Search warrants, phone records, bank records, et cetera."

"I'd say that's pretty important. I'll call the INS director at home. He's a pal of mine, so it's not a problem. Give me the info."

McKenna did, asking Shields to have De la Cruz's prints faxed to the lab.

Now just one more call to tie *Señor* Hector De la Cruz into a neat prison package, McKenna thought. What I need is information about De la Cruz that no police department in the free world can quickly provide, information that most of them aren't even equipped to obtain. So it's time to call my favorite private investigator, that master purveyor of privileged information, my old pal Bob Hurley.

He called the Holmes Detective Bureau and asked for the president. Of course Hurley wasn't in his office at five o'clock on a Saturday afternoon, but once McKenna gave his name, whoever answered the phone assured him that Mr. Hurley would call him right back.

McKenna believed it and didn't even take his hand off the receiver after hanging up. A minute later the phone rang. "Brian! I guess you need some real professional help solving your case."

McKenna had known Bob Hurley since his days in the police department. Like Vernon Geberth, Hurley was another not-so-humble guy who had recognized himself as the best at what he did and wasn't afraid to let it be known. McKenna had also learned through past experience that, when asking for favors or advice, abject humility was the best posture to adopt when dealing with the PI. "Yes, Bob. I need some help and you're the best guy—maybe the only guy in the city who can do it right for me."

"You're probably right," Hurley admitted agreeably. "If it's difficult and skirts the borders of legality, then I'm your guy. What do you need?"

"Everything you can find out about Hector De la Cruz, date of birth March 21st, 1949, and his social security number is 060-40-2939. He's an alien, originally from Costa Rica. Can you do that?"

"Can I do that? My boy, you give me your license plate number and, given enough time and money, I'll tell you who your grandfather was seeing before he met your grandmother. Now to more important matters."

"Money?"

"Yes, recompense. Is this a favor or am I getting paid for this?"

"You'll get paid, of course."

"By whom?"

"I can't have you and your methods showing up as a budget line in this case, so I guess I'll be paying you."

"I see. I take it Hector De la Cruz is the killer?"

"I'd say he is."

"Then I suggest an alternative method of payment, one that's much better than spreading filthy money around between friends."

McKenna knew what Hurley was suggesting because they had used his "alternative method of payment" in the past. "Publicity?" he asked.

"Yes. If you let it slip to the press that you've consulted with a private investigator in this case, and if they should happen to catch you coming in or out of my office, then you'd owe me nothing."

"That's a deal. Your office still in the same place?"

"No, I've moved to West 57th Street, right next to the Hard Rock Cafe. More fashionable, don't you think?"

"I guess so. How long will this take?"

"I'll call you in a couple of hours."

"Good deal. Thanks."

Next McKenna dialed Information and asked for a listing for Hector De la Cruz of 712 Park Avenue. No listing anywhere in Manhattan under that name, he was told. Then he tried Dr. Hector De la Cruz. Same answer.

"Where are the old phone directories kept?" he asked Birnstill.

"I'll get them," Birnstill said. "What years?"

"1991 to last year."

Birnstill got up and disappeared into a storage closet at the rear of the office. He came out carrying five dusty phone directories and placed them on McKenna's desk.

McKenna wiped the dust off the books with his handkerchief, then opened the 1991 book. There was no listing for a Dr. Hector De la Cruz. Then he tried the 1992 book. Still no listing. Nineteen ninety-three was next, and Dr. H. De la Cruz was there, with an office address listed as 712 Park Avenue. McKenna took a moment to congratulate himself as he stared at the page, then he tore it out and went to the 1994 and 1995 books. Dr. H. De la Cruz was still there, same address. Two more pages torn out and McKenna went to 1996. Dr. H. De la Cruz wasn't listed. McKenna closed the book and sat back in his chair.

Let's think this out, he told himself. He's a high-priced doctor in a very fancy neighborhood for three years. He's doing well and has so much cash that he can afford to get an office in the very fancy building he lives in. Life is good for him, but then he closes up shop last year, or maybe a little before. Why? Because he's got the virus, that's why. But none of this explains what our fancy Dr. H. De la Cruz was doing working as an orderly at the very unfashionable Bellevue Hospital in 1992 and the beginning of 1993. Let's try to get to the bottom of this.

He dialed Information in Albany and got the number for the New York State

Division of Licensing Services. He tried that number and, as he expected, got the recording that told him that the office was open Monday to Friday, nine to five. That didn't bother McKenna; he needed information that was in a locked office, but he knew how to get it. He called Brunette's office.

Brunette was in. "I hear things are coming together for you," he said.

McKenna wasn't surprised that Brunette knew about developments that had occurred in the last hour. He figured that Ward had called Tavlin with the update and Tavlin had called the PC. "I'm rolling along, but I need some help unlocking an office in Albany," McKenna said.

"What do you need?"

"Hector De la Cruz is listed as a Park Avenue doctor in the Manhattan phone directory for three years, from 1993 to 1995, but he worked as an orderly at Bellevue in 1992 and the beginning of '93. I need to know when he first applied for his medical license and when it was granted."

"You're thinking he had some licensing problems and was working as an orderly while he straightened them out?"

"It doesn't make sense to me because he was rich enough to have a place on Park Avenue, but it's the only conclusion I can draw. I want to know for sure."

"You will. I'm gonna call Albany and make somebody miserable. I'll call you as soon as I know."

"Thanks."

As McKenna hung up, a meticulously dressed detective in his sixties and a middle-aged short Hispanic man in his forties came into the squad office.

Detective Chaney and my new best friend Mario Santos, McKenna assumed. He got up and introduced himself, then brought the two men into the interview room. The three took seats around the table. "Is there anything you want to ask me before we begin?" McKenna asked Santos.

"Yeah. Is Hector the one who's killing all the bums?"

"That's what it looks like. Does that surprise you?"

"Sure does. He's a nice guy, maybe a little strange, but he likes them bums. Really likes them. Always used to go out of his way to talk to them and be nice to them."

"Where was that? In the emergency room?"

"Yeah, back when I first met him. I'd been there for a couple of years when he started working there, but right away he was always with the bums."

"There were a lot of homeless people in the emergency room?"

"Scads of them, and even more when it was cold out. They come in for everything, anything, and nothing. Drunk, headaches, backaches, stomachaches, drug withdrawal, you name it. 'Course, some of them were really sick, but lots of times they just came in to hang out with Hector."

"Hang out with Hector? Why?"

" 'Cause he had a place in his heart for them like no man I ever seen. He was always giving them money and hanging out with them when we weren't cleaning and mopping. Talk to them all night long about nothing, had them comin' in and making nuisances of themselves all the time."

"How much money are we talking about?" McKenna asked. ·

"That's one of the things I never understood about Hector. He was new, so he was making less money than me and I wasn't making shit. Still ain't. But he'd think nothing of reaching in his pocket and giving some bum with some bullshit story twenty bucks."

"Did you ever ask him about it?"

"That was another funny thing about him. He'd talk to bums all night long, but he didn't talk much to us."

"Us? You mean the other workers?"

"Yeah, us. It wasn't that nobody didn't like him,'cause he was pleasant enough and nice to everybody. But he was nicest to the bums."

"So what did he say when you asked him about giving so much money to them?"

"Always some stupid shit like, 'They need it more than I do.' "

"Did he strike you as being especially intelligent?"

"Hector intelligent? No, not especially. Stupid, maybe, giving all his dough to them bums."

"What language did you two talk in?"

"Spanish, mostly."

"How was his Spanish?"

"With me it was real good. Sometimes he used words I never heard of. But with the bums who knew Spanish he talked that gutter Spanish all the time. Sometimes I couldn't even understand him when he was talking to them."

"Did he have any friends among the staff?"

"Just Dr. Rashid, which is something else got everybody to wondering. A doctor friends with an orderly? Never seen that before, but they seemed to be real tight."

"Dr. Rashid used to work in the emergency room?"

"Yeah, for years when he first got to this country. That's where they start them all out."

"And what kind of guy was he?"

"Real nice. He was the one that got me swung over to the AIDS clinic when he started there. Much better job, but we wasn't what I'd call friends or nothing. Not like him and Hector."

"What did Hector and Rashid talk about?"

"I don't know. We all worked the midnight shift together, and sometimes when it wasn't too busy, which was almost never, Dr. Rashid would call Hector into the staff office there. They'd stay there together until something came up and one of them had to leave."

"I guess everyone wondered about that."

"Sure did."

"Anyone ask Hector about it?"

"I did, once. He gave me some bullshit about how Dr. Rashid was helping him out with his high school equivalency exam."

"And you knew that was bullshit?"

"Of course. You see, I was studying for mine then, too, and I always brought books to work so I could study when I got a chance. But not Hector. Never no books, but sometimes when I'd get stuck on something I'd ask him about it. He always had the answers right at his fingertips."

"Then that would make him smart, I guess."

"I guess so. Smart in books, stupid in life."

"Did Hector tell you why he was leaving?"

"No, didn't tell nobody. One day he just wasn't there anymore."

"When was the last time you saw him?"

"Last year, at the clinic. He was visiting Dr. Rashid."

"Did he visit him often?"

"Back then, every month or so."

"Was he different from when you knew him in the emergency room?"

"Yeah, real different, but still the same. He came in dressed in a suit whenever he showed up, looked like a million dollars. That was sure different, but he still goofed off with all the bums in the waiting room while he was waiting to see Dr. Rashid."

"Did you ever ask Hector about the suits?"

"Yeah, every time he showed up. He always gave me some stupid answer like, 'I passed my GED and got a better job,' or 'I got lucky and hit the Lotto.' But it was all bullshit and he was always laughing when he said it."

"Do you know if he and Rashid ever socialized together?"

"Yeah, I know sometimes they did."

"How do you know that?"

"One day when I was cleaning up in the doctor's office I happened to see his appointment book on his desk. I wasn't snooping or nothing, but it was right there. I saw that Dr. Rashid had a dinner with Hector marked down in his book at some Indian restaurant."

"So Dr. Rashid liked Indian food?"

"Indian or Pakistani. I don't know the difference, but I forgot to tell you this. Sometimes when Hector came to the AIDS clinic to visit Dr. Rashid, he brought bags of food from some Indian restaurant. Then they'd sit in Dr. Rashid's office and eat lunch."

"Okay, let's take it from the top. When did you start working at Bellevue?"

For the next fifteen minutes, McKenna went through Santos's history, taking notes this time, but he learned nothing new. When he had asked every question he could think of, he said, "Now I've got a request for you, Mr. Santos, and it's a big one."

"What is it?"

"When you get to work on Monday, a lot of people are going to be talking about how the police came to their houses and showed them some sketches. But we made a mistake because we showed them the wrong sketches. We didn't know that Hector had a beard."

"You didn't know that?" Santos asked.

"No, not until a couple of hours ago."

"He had a big, bushy beard. You couldn't miss it, he was real proud of it, always combing it out and shit."

"Still, we didn't know that, but we have a problem now. You're the only one in the clinic who knows Hector is the killer, but you can't tell anyone that you know about it."

"Why not?"

"Because then the press will find out and right after that Hector will find out we know. Then he'll run, I think, and we'll have a hard time catching him."

"So what do I say?"

"I want you to tell everyone at the clinic that the police were at your house and showed you some sketches, but that you didn't know who it was."

"So you want me to act stupid?"

"No. I want you to act smart, because right after we catch Hector, you're gonna get a day off because the mayor or some other big shot is gonna give you a medal and all the papers are gonna write stories about you, saying how you helped catch the killer. You're gonna be a hero."

"Really?"

"Absolutely, if you cooperate with me on this."

"You think I'd be able to get transferred?"

"To another hospital?"

"No, not another hospital. I like Bellevue and I got seniority. But this AIDS shit is starting to get me down."

"Where would you like to work?"

"I put in to work on the orthopedic floor. Those guys there don't do shit."

"When would you like to be transferred?"

"Now. Monday."

"How about when we catch Hector?"

"You are gonna get him?"

"Yes."

"You know, in a way that's too bad. Hector's a strange one, but he's still a nice guy. Looks like he finally came to his senses because those bums ain't nothing but trouble, always pissing everywhere and making lots of trouble."

"You don't want us to catch Hector?"

"I don't see why I should."

"Maybe you should think of yourself," McKenna suggested.

Santos did. "I hope you catch him soon because I'm sick of that AIDS clinic. You got a deal," he said, offering McKenna his hand. "Not a word outta me."

45 After Chaney and Santos left, McKenna went into his office and called Jim Heaney again. This time Heaney picked up right away. "Is Heidi still there?" McKenna asked. "No, she left right after you talked to her."

"Good. Are Dr. Rashid's things still in the hospital somewhere? I assume somebody cleaned out his office after he died."

"I guess so, but I don't know exactly where they are."

"I want you to find them and bring them to your office. Somebody will be there Monday with a search warrant for them."

"I'll do it as soon as I get in. Tell me, do you think De la Cruz killed Dr. Rashid?"

"Mr. Heaney, you of all people should understand that I'd rather not say, and I don't want any speculation in the hospital about it."

"Yeah, I understand. Sorry for asking. You need anything else?"

"Do you know Mario Santos?"

"Yeah, works in the AIDS clinic. Lazy, worthless good-for-nothing."

"You're wrong about Santos. He's a great worker and you love him," McKenna said.

"I do?"

"Yes, you do."

"Come to think of it, you're right," Heaney said. "I don't know what I was thinking of, but I love my old pal Mario Santos. I'd do whatever I could for him."

"I hear he put in for a transfer to the orthopedic floor."

"Come to think of it, he did. He'll be transferred there first thing Monday morning. I'll take him up there myself, introduce him around, and tell everybody what a wonderful guy he is."

"That would be nice, but wait 'til you hear from me before you do that."

"Whatever you say. Need anything else?"

"No, not at the moment, Mr. Heaney."

"Well, when you do, just give me a call. Anything."

"Thank you. See you on Monday."

McKenna figured he didn't have much to do until he heard back from Brunette, Scagnelli, and Hurley, so he made a cup of coffee and sat in his office, thinking.

Santos's revelations had shed a lot of light on Hector De la Cruz. McKenna figured that Rashid had known that Hector was a doctor, that it was one of the things that had made the two men friends and that, probably at Hector's insistence, he had kept that knowledge to himself. Since Rashid was the only person who could connect De la Cruz to the AIDS clinic, McKenna figured that Hector had murdered his friend before starting on his mission. If so, it strengthened his assessment that Hector had planned his crusade very well and that getting caught, or even having his work discovered, had not been part of his plan.

However, what he had learned from Santos had given McKenna more questions than answers. He tried to figure what had made Hector so compassionate to the homeless back then, especially when he took into consideration that they were the very people he was killing now.

McKenna decided he needed more information before he could come up with a theory, and until he got it, he figured his time would be best spent in catching up on his paperwork. He had a lot of catching up to do.

One hour later he was just starting his last report, the one on the interview of Mario Santos, when the meticulously dressed, almost-always-perfect Cisco Sanchez of the 13th Squad came into McKenna's office with a package under his arm. Sanchez put the package down on the desk with some pomp and flourish and said, "What's the matter, Brian? You don't talk to your old friend Cisco anymore?"

"Sure I do, but in case you haven't heard, I've been kinda busy," McKenna answered, noticing that Sanchez's package consisted of three large NYPD property envelopes taped together.

"I see. So do you ask your old pal Cisco to help you out with your problem? No."

McKenna had known Sanchez a long time and had been through it before with him. He conceded that Sanchez was a pretty good detective—an annoying one, but still a pretty good one. He also knew that the better Sanchez got, the more annoying he became, and that when he started referring to himself in the third person, Sanchez was at his absolute best and most annoying self.

McKenna braced himself for the coming ordeal. "What's in the package, Cisco?" he asked, hoping to get to the point a little quicker.

"Stuff."

"What kind of stuff?"

"Interesting stuff," Sanchez said, brushing the question aside. "You know, Brian, you should really be more polite and let Detective Sanchez finish what he was saying. Then maybe you'll learn something from him."

Cisco, this better be really good, McKenna thought. "I'm sorry for interrupting. Please continue."

"Now, where was I? Oh, yeah. So here you are on a big case with lots of press, the kind of case where everybody involved is getting lots of overtime. But do you get your old pal Cisco assigned to it? No, you don't."

"You're right, Cisco. I guess I should have thought of bringing you in right away. I was wrong and it'll never happen again. What's in the package?"

"Not yet. Do you remember who straightened out that crime scene for you at the Twenty-ninth Street playground?"

"Yes I do. It was you."

"And do you remember who it was who placed that nasty, fat bitch at your disposal so you could get the sketch that was on page one in all the papers the next day?"

"That was you, too."

"Yes, it was. And you know something? I took out my magnifying glass and put page one under it. I was looking for something nice at the bottom of the sketch, something like 'Sketch obtained courtesy of Detective Sanchez,' but I didn't see it. Was it so small that I missed it?"

"No, it wasn't there. An oversight."

"An oversight? I see. That explains it. It must be little oversights like that which kept Detective Sanchez from being assigned to this case."

"Cisco, this is a Seventeenth Squad case and you're assigned to the Thirteenth Squad," McKenna tried to explain.

"Artificial geographical boundaries which are never respected by great detectives," Sanchez countered. "For instance, this little thing here is a Ninth Squad case," he said, tapping the package. "But did that stop Detective Sanchez of the not-so-busy Thirteenth Squad from going over to the scene and lending his expertise to the very-busy-but-not-quite-as-good detectives from the Ninth Squad? No, it didn't. Of course not. Yet, Detective Sanchez is not assigned to this case when the Homicide Squad as well as everybody and his brother from squads all over the city are working it. Interesting, isn't it?"

"I had nothing to do with who came here, but what probably happened is that your squad commander felt he couldn't spare his best detective."

Sanchez appeared to consider that for a moment. "You're probably right," he said. "They're selfish pricks and they never give up their best men. I assume you're in a position to fix that?"

"Cisco, I'm just a detective now, just like you."

"Bullshit."

"Okay, I'll fix it."

"Then we have a deal?" Sanchez asked.

"Sure. Somebody has to fix all these oversights."

"Good," Sanchez said as he sat on the edge of McKenna's desk. "Does the name Juliette Thompson mean anything to you?"

Juliette Thompson? Where have I heard that name? McKenna wondered briefly before it came to him. How could I forget, when just yesterday I was looking at her in her coffin at Potter's Field? "I know the name and the face," he said. "Juliette Thompson, homeless female, white, age forty-six. Died of pneumonia on January fourth in Corlear's Hook Park, Ninth Precinct. Looked to me like she was once a pretty good-looking woman."

"I thought so, too. But she's not one of your killer's victims?"

"No. She was HIV positive, but not a victim."

"How about the name Hector? Does that mean anything to you?"

McKenna just about fell out of his chair. He tried a quick recovery, but of course Sanchez had seen it. "I see it does," Sanchez said. "How about the name Dante?"

"Yes, that name means something to me," McKenna answered, feeling fully recovered. "What's in the package, Cisco?" he asked again.

Once again, McKenna's question was ignored. "So anyway, nobody's telling him nothing or asking his advice, but Detective Sanchez's got his ear to the ground, like always, and what do you think he hears? He hears that your killer dropped off some money to a homeless girl named Kerri Brannigan. Interesting, Detective Sanchez thinks, but what does he do? What would a great detective do when he hears something interesting like that?"

"He investigates further," McKenna said.

"Exactly. So Detective Sanchez asks around and he finds that this money was all crisp, new one-hundred-dollar bills, sequentially numbered, all B bills from the Federal Reserve Bank in New York. Now he's really interested. Do you know why?"

"Because you found sequentially numbered, crisp, new one-hundred-dollar bills on the body of Juliette Thompson and those bills were B bills," McKenna guessed.

Sanchez looked hurt by McKenna's statement. "You're taking a lot of the fun out of this for me, Brian," he said. "Please don't do that again."

"I'm sorry. I won't," McKenna assured him. "Please continue."

"Since you already know, I might as well show you this," Sanchez said. He opened one of the property envelopes and removed a sealed clear plastic bag, the kind the NYPD uses to store vouchered money and jewelry. He gave the bag to McKenna.

McKenna didn't rip it open, but could see that the bag contained a stack of new one-hundred-dollar bills. The top bill was stamped NYPD—EVIDENCE and the serial number was B63402026H. He searched through his file folder and found the invoice for Kerri's money. The first serial number on the bills Hector had given Kerri was B63291035H.

It had to be more than coincidence, McKenna figured as he did some quick calculations in his head. These bills also came from Hector, he reasoned, and by subtracting the serial numbers he surmised that Hector had spent $21,000 from the time he gave the money to Juliette Thompson, which was sometime before she died on January 4, and February 1, when he gave the money to Kerri. "How much is here?" he asked.

"Twelve hundred dollars."

"Why is it stamped 'Evidence'? Did you suspect something in her death way back then?"

"Detective Sanchez suspects something in everything and thinks that finding twelve hundred dollars on a dead homeless person who died in a park is somewhat suspicious. Turns out that everyone's not as smart as him and he had to fight like hell to get it stamped."

"Fight with who? The Ninth Precinct desk officer?"

"Yeah. He reads the book and tells me that, since there's nothing suspicious about her death, the money should be deposited in the property clerk's account at the bank and that the property clerk will issue a check to her heirs. Asshole! Detective Sanchez had to really throw his weight around and wound up getting a two-day fine for insubordination, but the money was stamped and kept. That's the only reason you have it in front of you now."

McKenna could imagine the scene in the Ninth Precinct and knew that, according to the book, the lieutenant was right. The problem was that, unlike Detective Sanchez, the book wasn't always right. "I think those two days should be restored to you," McKenna said.

"So does Detective Sanchez. Now, where was he? Oh, yeah." He reached into another property envelope, removed a plain white envelope, and gave it to McKenna. "That's what the money was in."

The envelope had *For Dante* written across the face in a neat, feminine handwriting. "Does that mean anything to you?" Sanchez asked.

"Yes it does, but I'd be interested in knowing what it means to you."

"Simple. It means that, while Juliette Thompson might have been homeless, she still considered herself a patron of the arts. She obviously intended that the money be used to further promote the writings of the great Italian master who wrote Dante's *Inferno*."

It was better than any answer McKenna could have hoped for. "You're probably right," he said. "Now, what's this about Hector?"

"This," Sanchez said. He reached into one of the property envelopes, removed another plain white envelope, and handed it to McKenna. Across the face was written *For Hector* in the same neat, feminine handwriting. "What's inside?" he asked.

"A sort of good-bye love letter. Some of it doesn't make sense, but I suggest you read it."

McKenna didn't, at first. He sat staring at the two envelopes and the money, realizing that they were pieces of the puzzle. Unfortunately, it was one of those confusing thousand-piece puzzles that only senior citizens seem able to complete, but he figured he had a good start on it because the three pieces he was looking at had to be corner pieces. He couldn't see the picture yet, but he remembered his grandmother telling him when he was a boy: "You don't have to know what the puzzle's about, Brian. Once you find the corner pieces, all it takes is time and patience to complete it. Then you'll see."

McKenna opened the envelope and read the letter. Then he read it again. It didn't make much sense to him until the second reading, and then the pieces came together. It said:

My Dearest Hector,

I know I'm near the end, and God has been kind enough to grant me a small period of lucidity. I know you don't understand everything that has happened to us and between us, nor do I. I just want you to know that I accept my fate as God's will and urge you to do the same.

Hector, you are the kindest, gentlest, most generous man I have ever met. I know you have been looking for me, but as I told you, our last meeting was just what it should have been—our last meeting. Seeing me like this brings out qualities in you I never imagined you possessed, qualities I don't want to aggravate by my death. Forget the bitterness and be the man I love. It is my hope to pass unnoticed by all but you.

Here is something you might find funny. Try as I might, I can't remember your last name. I know you must have told it to me at one time or another, but you know how I am. The most basic things escape me most of the time.

Hector, I'm hoping you get this letter, but I don't see how you will. Therefore, I realize that I'm probably writing to no one but myself and God, to Whom I pray that you come to your senses. Don't blame our suffering on anyone else but me. I can't help what I am, but I know that everything is my fault—not their's. I urge you to forgive, forget, and make your peace with God. Once you do that, it all makes some kind of sense and doesn't hurt so much.

With All My Love,
Juliette

P.S. I am leaving the rest of the money you gave me to Dante. You know I've never had much use for money and I've always loved his poetry.

McKenna sat staring at the letter and was surprised when it went out of focus on him. Then he was embarrassed to realize that his eyes were filled with tears.

"Glad to see I'm not the only one it got to," Sanchez said, startling McKenna. "I cried like a baby."

"Quite a letter for a homeless woman," was all McKenna could think of to say for a moment as he reached into his pocket for his handkerchief. It was dusty from the phone books and didn't help, so he used his sleeve. It was a few moments more before he said, "Tell me about it."

"Damnedest thing I ever saw. I'll never forget it," Sanchez said. "Some kids found her in the park, wrapped in blankets and lying on top of one of the Con Edison steam grates. She must have known it was the end and had gotten ready for it. It was bitterly cold, but she had put her makeup on. Even the clothes she was wearing were new—a nice white dress, looked expensive."

"Where were the letter and the cash?"

"Tucked into her underwear."

"How was her face?" McKenna asked, feeling silly about the question. But he had to know after seeing her face in the coffin.

"She went out in some pain. I wish it weren't so, but that's the way it looked to me. I guess life's not fair."

"No, it isn't always," McKenna said.

"There's something else. Maybe I shouldn't have, but I was saving it for last." Sanchez reached into the last envelope, removed another clear, sealed plastic bag, and passed it to McKenna.

Inside the bag was a large, gold locket.

"That was in her hand when we found her," Sanchez said.

McKenna regarded the locket for a moment. According to the rules, only a boss or a DA could open one of the bags, but he caught Sanchez smiling at him and nodding encouragement. He ripped the bag open, took out the locket, and opened it up. There was a picture on each half.

On one side was a small picture of a younger, healthy Juliette Thompson and McKenna saw at once that he had been wrong about her. She had been more than passably pretty. She had been beautiful.

On the other side of the opened locket was the fourth corner piece of the puzzle. It was a small photo of a heavyset man with flowing black hair and a bushy black beard. He looked like the main character in a foreign subtitled black-and-white movie McKenna had seen as a boy. Hector De la Cruz looked like the Count of Monte Cristo.

McKenna put the locket down on his desk and stared at it. "Isn't it strange that all these things have been in police custody since January fourth, before the first murder even took place?" he asked.

"Sometimes that's the way it is. All the pieces of the puzzle are always there, but sometimes we don't know it and sometimes we don't recognize them when we see them."

"Funny you should say that," McKenna observed. "What tour are you doing today?"

"It's my day off, but I thought you should see these things. I come back to work on Monday morning."

"Then come here Monday morning. You're assigned."

"I thought so," Sanchez said. "Let's get this guy." He stood up, shook McKenna's hand, and was gone, leaving all of Juliette Thompson's treasures spread out on the desk. McKenna put it all in his bottom drawer and then dialed the Psychiatric Ward at Bellevue Hospital. He was told that Dr. Issacs was on vacation and wouldn't be back for a week.

Damn! McKenna thought. He dialed the 9th Precinct and asked for the desk officer. A Lieutenant Wickham answered. "This is Detective McKenna of the Seventeenth Squad. I need to speak to Police Officer Dante. Is he still there?"

"Sorry, buddy. He went home for the day," Wickham answered casually.

"Then I need someone to get in touch with him and have him report to the Seventeenth Squad. It's urgent."

"Didn't you hear me, buddy? I said he's gone for the day. That means he's off duty and he's not reporting anywhere for any detective," Wickham answered impatiently.

"And I said I want him here," McKenna said in measured tones.

There was a silence on the line for a moment until Wickham said, "I'm sorry. What did you say your name was?"

"Detective McKenna."

"Sorry, Commissioner. Got to have my hearing checked. Don't worry about a thing. Dante will be there if I have to go to his house and bring him there myself.''

"Thanks. That's very kind of you," McKenna said, then hung up.

I'm beginning to like this, McKenna told himself. I'm a detective again and I get to do all the interesting detective things without having to hang around head-quarters, pretending with the rest of the wannabes. Yet whenever I need some-thing, then I'm Commissioner McKenna for the moment. If that's always true, then this is a very wonderful life. Let's see.

McKenna went to Ward's door, knocked, and went in. Ward had wheeled out his very best cappuccino machine and it was on and steaming, leading McKenna to conclude that important company was expected soon. "How are we doing, Brian?" he asked.

"We're making progress, but I need something."

"Anything I can do."

"I need Sanchez from the Thirteenth Squad assigned here."

"Sanchez? That pompous pain in the ass?" Ward yelled. "I specifically asked that he not be assigned to this case."

"That might have been a mistake, Lieutenant," McKenna said, hardly believ-ing he was saying it. "Even though he's not assigned, he just contributed sub-stantially to this investigation."

"He did?" Ward asked incredulously.

"Yes, he did."

Ward took a couple of deep breaths, then smiled. "Maybe you're right, Brian. Never let it out of this room, but sometimes even I make mistakes."

"Then he's assigned?"

"Of course. You want him, you got him."

I love this man!

46 What is going on with this Hector De la Cruz? McKenna asked himself over and over. A man who turns out to be a Park Avenue doctor who was working as a hospital orderly, at Bellevue of all places, and now it turns out he had a homeless woman as a lover? Forgetting for the moment that he's the worst serial killer in New York City history, Hector still has to be quite a fellow with an interesting story to tell. I'm hoping to hear it directly from him, eventually, but I sure would like more background from Ray, Hurley, and Dante.

Not wanting to do another impatient spin in the hallway under Birnstill's scru-tiny, McKenna thought it best to put the subject out of his mind until his sources called. He phoned Angelita and told her he was going to be home very late, but he didn't know exactly when. He had been prepared to give her an update on the case and offer her all sorts of excuses like interviews that needed to be done and search warrants that had to be executed, but she showed little interest in his hobby that evening. All she said was, "You don't have to bother explaining, Brian. If I want to find out where you are and what you're doing, I'll just turn on the TV. This is really so convenient."

Was that sarcasm? McKenna wondered. "How's the baby been?" he asked.

"Just fine. She cut a tooth, said her first word, and learned to walk today. Tomorrow she wants to pick out a college. It all goes so fast, doesn't it?"

Yeah, it was sarcasm. "I'll be home as soon as I can."

"Fine."

McKenna figured the conversation was over until Angelita thought to ask, "Have you run into that Heidi today?"

"No, she hasn't been around. I guess she's off on Saturdays," he said. And that's the truth, he thought.

"Good. Wake me up when you get home."

"I will. Good night."

Angelita will have to be told about this Heidi deal sooner or later, McKenna thought as he hung up. She's gonna find out about it anyway when she sees on TV that Heidi has some exclusive coverage on this case.

It should be sooner, not later, but certainly not now, he concluded after a long minute of intensive thinking and worrying. Then the phone rang and he picked it up. "McKenna, Seventeenth Squad."

"Ready for some good news?"

McKenna recognized Scagnelli's voice. "Yes, Inspector, I certainly am."

"Two fingerprints on the wine bottle belong to Hector De la Cruz. More than a hundred identifying points of comparison on one print and twenty-three on the other."

"Thank you very much, Inspector."

Minutes later the phone rang again. It was Brunette. McKenna relayed Scagnelli's news and then he got some information from Brunette that buttressed a theory he had formed to explain Hector's stint as an orderly. "Hector applied for his medical license on November tenth, 1991, but it wasn't granted until November twenty-first, 1992," Brunette said.

"That's the day before he quit Bellevue," McKenna observed. "What was the delay?"

"Educational requirements. In 1978 he graduated at the top of his class from the medical school in Costa Rica and had been practicing down there for more than ten years. Unfortunately for him, our state medical board wouldn't recognize some of the courses he had taken in Costa Rica and insisted that he retake them here to be certified."

"And he did?"

"Yeah. While he was working at Bellevue at night he was going to the NYU School of Medicine during the day. It took him a year to meet the state board's requirements. They also put him through quite a rigmarole getting transcripts and course descriptions from Costa Rica before they deigned to grant him the license."

"Any marks or complaints on it?"

"Nope. It's clean. Are you gonna grab him soon?"

"As soon as I can."

"You have his address, right?"

"Yeah, but I'm sure he's not there. I think he's much too careful and has planned too far ahead to make it that easy for us. I have Hurley on it, so soon I'll know just about everything about him. He's rich, so I'm sure Hurley is gonna give me other addresses on him."

"Hurley? What's he want in return? Acknowledgment, publicity, and free advertising?"

"You know him. I figure it doesn't hurt, and he could do it quicker and probably better than we could."

"I hope you're not gonna admit that to the press," Brunette said.

"No, I'm just gonna picture him as a public-spirited citizen with some special expertise who volunteered to help us out with a few things. Meanwhile, this whole Hector thing is getting more complicated."

"More complicated than it already is?" Brunette asked.

"Much more." McKenna then told him about the Juliette Thompson affair. Brunette had lots of questions about it, but McKenna had no concrete answers, just speculative theories. Brunette offered no theories of his own, but said, "You realize that some of our tabloids are going to make him look like a misguided, lovesick hero after you get him, don't you?"

"Not much I can do about that. However, it certainly intensifies my desire to talk to him."

"Once this gets out, it's going to intensify the desires of every psychiatrist in the country to talk to him. If he was gonna live to see trial, they'd have scores of insanity defenses for him, all ready to be tried out."

"Let's hope it doesn't come to that," McKenna said.

"Yeah, let's hope, because there's a good chance that even J. Davenport Pinckney the Third with all the theatrics he could muster wouldn't be able to sway a jury against Hector if that letter ever gets read to them in open court."

"It's worse than that," McKenna said. "If he were to live to trial, I don't think he'd even need the insanity defense. He's rich, he can afford the best defense, and he'll be able to document that he's always been absolutely magnificent to the homeless before they somehow gave him and his poor lover AIDS. He'd get the sympathy vote and he'd walk, no matter how dead to rights we get him."

"Which means he might be killing with impunity right now," Brunette observed.

"Yes. I expect that if he lives to trial, he's probably doing just that."

"What are you thinking, Brian?" Brunette asked.

"No matter what story he has for his lawyer to make some jurors sob, I'm thinking that a killer's a killer. I guess you have to see the bodies lined up in a row to get a sense of how I feel about it."

"Don't let the flaws in our legal system get to you or it'll drive you crazy," Brunette advised. "The important thing for this department is that we stop the killings and bring him to justice. Exactly what justice consists of isn't for us to decide in this case."

"That's just what I'm gonna do, and don't worry. It's not gonna drive me crazy," McKenna said.

"Glad to see we're in sync on this one. Good luck."

After he hung up, McKenna got back to his paperwork. A short kid carrying a white paper bag knocked on his open door. McKenna figured it was a delivery boy, so he said, "I didn't order anything. Ask somebody else out there."

"I'm Officer Dante. I heard you wanted to see me."

What the hell? McKenna thought. He couldn't help himself as he looked Dante up and down. Looks about eighteen, five-foot-four, hundred and thirty pounds at the most, he thought. He didn't realize he was being rude until Dante said, ''I'm twenty-nine years old, five-foot-five, I weigh a hundred and twenty eight, and I've been on the Job almost five years.''

''I'm sorry,'' McKenna said. ''Come in. I've heard great things about you and I didn't mean to be insulting.''

''No offense taken, sir,'' Dante said, smiling as he entered and shook McKenna's hand. ''I know I look young and it happens to me all the time.''

Dante had a sincere manner and a genuine smile that McKenna liked. He looked to the bag and Dante said, ''I thought you might be hungry, so I picked us up some coffee and a couple of Danishes.''

''You know, I didn't realize it 'til you said it, but I am hungry. Thanks. Take a seat and let's eat before we get started.''

''Yes sir.''

''By the way,'' McKenna said as he bit into his pastry, ''my name's Brian and I'm not a *sir*. I'm a detective.''

''That isn't the way Lieutenant Wickham explained it,'' Dante said.

''He's misinformed. What should I call you?''

''Dante.''

Must have a horrible first name, McKenna figured. Then, without being asked, Dante said, ''Ignacio. Named after my father, but I don't really like the sound of it.''

Can't say I blame you, McKenna thought. How could there be two Ignacios in the same house? I guess life really isn't fair.

''I was wondering, where did you hear great things about me?'' Dante asked.

''From Dr. Issacs, for one.''

Dante reacted with a smile of pure satisfaction. ''Really?'' he said, but he obviously knew it was true.

''Really. From Juliette Thompson, for another.''

McKenna had Dante's total interest. He stopped chewing and asked excitedly, ''Juliette? You knew her?''

''No, I didn't. She mentioned you in a letter.''

''Juliette wrote you a letter?''

''No. Actually, she wrote it to Hector.''

''You know Hector?''

''Not yet. Do you?''

''No. She talked about him sometimes, but I wasn't sure he really existed outside of her mind. Sounded kind of too good to be true, if you know what I mean.''

''You thought she made him up?''

''No, not exactly made him up. She said he used to be an orderly at Bellevue and I'm sure she knew him. I just didn't believe that she was everything to him that she said she was.'' Dante took a bite from his Danish and grew pensive, staring into space. ''If he was like she said, I'm real glad for her. She had a terrible life and a bad end,'' he said, almost talking to himself.

McKenna could see that Dante really had cared for the homeless woman. He wasn't sure if he should tell Dante yet exactly who Hector was, but thought it best to put his cards on the table. ''I'm certain that Juliette's Hector is the man I'm looking for, the one who's been killing all the homeless people,'' he said.

"Jesus, what a shame!" Dante said incredulously. "Poor Juliette! What a tragic, wasted life, and then she winds up with a murderer. If it wasn't for her personality disorder, I think she could have been anything she wanted."

"In this business you don't see the happy people," McKenna commented, but noticed that Dante was getting pensive on him again. He decided that a break was in order. "Let's talk about it after we finish eating," McKenna suggested. To show he was serious, he took a big bite from his Danish.

McKenna ate slowly, but Dante finished his portion, drained his cup of coffee, and calmly asked, "Can I see that letter?"

"Sure." McKenna opened his desk drawer and took out Juliette's letter and the clear plastic bag containing the cash. He passed the letter to Dante and put the cash on the desk in front of him.

Dante didn't give the money more than a cursory glance. His mind was on the letter. As he read it, his eyes filled with tears. When he finished, he wiped his eyes with his sleeve and put the letter back on the desk. "Is there a bathroom up here?" he asked.

"Right outside, make a right," McKenna said.

Dante got up and left without another word. He didn't reappear until some minutes later. To McKenna's relief, he looked totally composed and ready to get down to business. "I'm sorry, but I get attached to some of those street people," Dante explained as he took his seat. "I know that it's considered unprofessional, but I do and I'm not ashamed of it."

"I don't consider it unprofessional and I would heartily disagree with anyone who does," McKenna said. "You should know that myself and one of the toughest detectives I know just about broke down when we read it."

"I can usually handle these things with a clinical attitude, but Juliette was a special case. She disappeared on me and the next thing I heard, she was dead."

"When was the last time you saw her?"

"A couple of months ago, before it started getting real cold."

"Did you know she had this money on her when she died?" McKenna asked, pointing to the cash.

"No. I didn't hear anything about that, but I was off when she died and some detective from the Thirteenth handled the case. I didn't even find out she was dead until a week after it happened."

"So you don't think she had any money the last time you saw her?" McKenna asked.

"I'm sure she didn't. She was broke, so I gave her a few bucks to get by. She never would have accepted it if she had any."

"Then I guess you haven't seen her since this meeting with Hector that she alludes to?"

"I guess not. As far as I knew, she hadn't seen him for years. She talked about him sometimes, but she hadn't seen him."

"Was Juliette schizophrenic?" McKenna asked.

"Yes, the worst kind. She was schizoaffective."

"What is that, exactly?"

"Basically, it means she was a schizophrenic and a manic depressive all wrapped in one very loose package. People who are schizoaffective have poor judgment, poor insight, and sometimes hear voices. They resent authority, usually have trouble with the law, change their names, dress flamboyantly, and are sometimes promiscuous.''

This kid's been making some good use of his psychology degree, McKenna thought. "Was she always schizoaffective?"

"No, not always. It's a personality disorder that usually first manifests itself at puberty, sometime in the teens. That's when it got her."

"I guess you really liked Juliette, didn't you?"

"Schizophrenics, and especially schizoaffectives, are hard to like until you understand how they think and what they feel that makes them act the way they do," Dante stated in a dispassionate tone. "I tried to understand her. It was difficult most of the time, but sometimes she came shining through. Then I liked her."

"From her letter, it appears to me she was fairly well educated. Was she?"

"To a point. She was smart, almost finished high school before it hit her. She was from what I guess you'd call a 'good family,' grew up someplace in Massachusetts."

"And her family gave up on her?"

"Not at first. They tried treating her at home, but her behavior got worse. Because, like I said, they were a 'good family,' they wound up having her institutionalized, then sterilized."

"Sterilized? Why would they do that?"

"Because Juliette became very promiscuous. Not her fault, really. It was just a facet of her personality disorder, a way of gaining affection and showing resentment for her family."

"Is that common?"

"No, nothing is exactly common with schizophrenics. They all find different ways to vent their rage and act out their inner insecurity and unhappiness. With Juliette it was sex, something her family couldn't accept."

"Isn't there some kind of cure or treatment?"

"Treatment, yes. There are some drugs like Clorozil and Escalith that help them control their behavior, but there's no cure."

"Was she under treatment or taking any medication?"

"Sometimes, when I could talk her into seeing Dr. Issacs. The problem with Juliette was that she hated institutions and would rather be on the street, especially the streets of New York."

"Because we don't institutionalize schizophrenics?"

"Not usually. Not unless they're dangerous, which she wasn't, or unless somebody else is paying for the treatment. Juliette's folks are dead, so even if she wanted treatment, which she didn't, there was no one around anymore to foot the bill."

"Do you think she had sex with Hector?"

"According to her she did. Called him her 'special lover,' only time I heard her call anyone a lover."

"But she had sex with others?"

"Many others. She was quite popular among the homeless crowd. She didn't particularly care for many of them, but she was always there for them."

"How long had she been HIV positive?"

"I guess since I've known her, but I never knew it until she started getting sick last year. She went fast."

"Did she receive any treatment for the AIDS?"

"No. Like I said, she hated institutions. To Juliette, a hospital was just another institution."

"I see. Would you say she infected many others?"

"Certain of it, but I'm just as certain that one of them infected her. You must know that AIDS is running rampant among the homeless."

"I know that. Can you give me any clues as to why Hector was attracted to her?" McKenna asked.

"I can only make some assumptions. When she bothered to take care of herself, which wasn't often, Juliette was a good-looking woman. Add in that she was very easy to get in the sack and you might have a pretty good basis for an attraction."

"How about her personality? Was it something you'd call attractive?"

"No, I'd call it terrible unless you agreed with her on two points. Juliette hated authority and she hated rich people. If you thought like she did, she could be quite agreeable."

"Then how did you pull off getting along so well with her? It had to be tough, being you're a cop and an authority figure."

"Not to her I wasn't. I'm not crazy about the rich, either, and I never told her what to do. I'd ask her to do things sometimes when she was getting out of hand, but I never told her," Dante explained. "I guess I'm not very forceful and not much in the way of an authority figure," he added.

"Most of the time, neither am I," McKenna admitted.

"Apparently you get away with it on this job. I don't. Once Juliette saw a sergeant chew me out good for talking to her for too long, and then she knew I wasn't real big on authority. She got quite a kick out of it."

"What about poetry?" McKenna asked, but immediately wished he hadn't come right out with the question because it caused Dante to blush right before his eyes.

"We both liked poetry," Dante said, placing both hands on the desk in front of him. "It's that simple, one of the few things we had in common. We like writing it and we like reading it."

"Did you write poems to her?"

"No. I wrote some poems *for* her, not *to* her, and she liked some of my weirder stuff. You know, the moaning kind of poetry when I'd try to write about all the things I think are wrong with the world and then make it rhyme."

Nothing should surprise me in this very strange case full of very strange people, McKenna thought.

"I don't know if it's important, but Juliette told me one of the reasons she loved Hector so much," Dante said, snapping McKenna's concentration.

"It's important to me. I want to know everything I can about the man."

"She said she loved him because he never tried to change her and he never disapproved of her or anything she did. No matter what, he was always nice to her."

"Then if he loved her, he must have been a very understanding man," McKenna speculated.

"Or maybe he just didn't waste time and energy trying to change things he knew he couldn't," Dante countered.

Maybe he's right, McKenna acknowledged to himself. As a doctor, Hector had to be familiar with schizophrenia and must have known that the prognosis for change and cure was nil. So what else do I need from Dante? Nothing more I can think of. "I'm going to make sure you get this money when this case is over," he said. "As far as I'm concerned, that letter pretty much constitutes a will."

"I don't want it," Dante said.

"I think you should get it."

"Why's that?"

"Didn't you give her money from time to time?"

"Yeah, but over the years I don't think it amounted to more than three hundred dollars. When it's over I'll take the three hundred. I think it would have made Juliette happy to know that she paid me back. The rest you can donate."

"Donate to who?"

"I think the Grand Central Coalition for the Homeless would be a good one. That'll rile the bosses and give me a little laugh on this job."

What's this? Another friend of Ben Rosen? McKenna wondered. "Do you know Ben Rosen?" he asked.

"Yeah, met him once or twice."

"What do you think of him?"

"He seems to work hard, but I'd say he's difficult, putting it mildly."

"So I've heard. Is that two more of those excellent Danishes you brought with you?" McKenna asked, pointing to Dante's bag.

"Sure is. Want another?"

"Serve 'em up and I'll make the coffee. Business is over."

"Have I been a help?"

"A big help, and thanks. I'm glad to see we've got people like you on this job."

Dante blushed, but he didn't seem to mind.

After they had finished their food, McKenna wished him well in his self-appointed mission and the young cop left for home. Then, while waiting for Hurley to call back, McKenna sat back and mulled over the implications of what he had just learned about Hector De la Cruz.

Maybe I've been looking at this wrong, he thought. Maybe he's not killing them because one of them gave him AIDS, indirectly through Juliette. Maybe he loved her so much that he's doing it just to kill the one who gave it to her. That would make him a better guy, I guess. Still a warped crazy and a killer, but somehow a better guy. But what did he see in her and why didn't he see her for years?

The questions tired McKenna and his impatience grew, so he called Hurley at his office. Hurley was in.

"Any news?" McKenna asked.

"Lots, but I'm gonna need another hour, at least. When I put the address in, all the bells went off and there's lots of information I think you'll need."

"Meaning?"

"Meaning that apartment is owned by the wife of Dr. Hector De la Cruz, the

Contessa Carmen Maria Suarez y Rodriguez. She's in the top one hundred women in the world when it comes to being filthy rich and there's lots to look into. I've got five people working on it, but I need more time.''

''Does he own any more real estate in town or close to it?''

''You mean does she, because all he owns is a house in Tamarindo Bay, Costa Rica. Besides the Park Avenue place, she maintains the usual digs in Beverly Hills, London, Paris, Barcelona, and Saint-Tropez. She also has a place in Jaca, Spain, and the one I think you'll be interested in, a house in Oldwick, New Jersey. Must be quite a place because the taxes on it are twenty-eight grand a year.''

''You wouldn't happen to know if anyone's staying at the Park Avenue or the Jersey place, would you?''

''You mean did I do something illegal and against my not-so-stringent professional ethics like call some well-paid friends in NYNEX and New Jersey Bell to check the phone usage?'' Hurley asked.

''That's what I mean,'' McKenna answered.

''Nothing but the service charge on the Park Avenue apartment. However, Jersey's different. They must have a caretaker there because there was usage all along, mostly local. Then last November it took a big jump, with lots of international calls to Costa Rica, Saint-Tropez, and Jaca, Spain. Last one was at two-twelve this afternoon to Jaca.''

''And you wouldn't happen to know where the contessa is?'' McKenna asked, knowing Hurley would.

''It just so happens she's quite a society item. According to a report last week on the society and gossip page of Barcelona's *Noticias de Hoy*, the wonderful contessa has been delighting blue-nosed invited guests at her Pyrenees retreat in—you guessed it—Jaca, Spain.''

''Any mention of her husband?''

''Apparently it's well known in European society circles that the doctor and the contessa are on the outs, so to speak. However, she's reputed to be very Catholic, so divorce is out of the question. Especially in Spain.''

''So they don't live together?''

''Haven't for a couple of years.''

''Any news on where he's been?''

''There's been lots of speculation, but nobody knows and she's not giving the reasons for the separation. Says it's a private matter. There's been no court actions in this country or Europe by either side, so it must be an amicable split.''

''Thanks for the news,'' McKenna said. ''Unfortunately, you've given me a big problem.''

''What? New Jersey?''

''Yeah. If I'm gonna take him there, I have to get an arrest warrant for him.''

''And you didn't want to do that?'' Hurley asked.

''No.''

''And why not? It should be just a formality.''

''Because an arrest warrant initiates a judicial proceeding against him, which means that then he has an absolute right to counsel. So before I can question him, his lawyer has to be present and Hector would have to waive his rights in front of him. No lawyer would ever let him say a word.''

''I guess you want to talk to him real bad.''

"Yeah, real bad. You say you'll have everything I need in an hour?"

"More or less, but there's a lot of paper coming out. Maybe you should stop by and pick it up. You might even get captured by a reporter or two on your way in or out," Hurley suggested.

"Then I'll be there in an hour, more or less."

47

Tavlin arrived at Ward's office just as McKenna started reporting the information he had learned from Hurley and Dante. The chief and the squad commander listened and then the three arrived at a decision and formed a plan. If everything worked out as they hoped it would, Hector De la Cruz would be in jail by midnight.

According to the plan, McKenna would go to Hurley's office and get whatever additional information the PI could provide. Then he would meet with J. Davenport and get the necessary warrants and subpoenas to wrap up the case. Tavlin would ensure that a New York judge and a New Jersey judge would be standing by to sign them.

Needed in New York were an arrest warrant for Hector, a search warrant for 712 Park Avenue, and a search warrant for Rashid's possessions at Bellevue. To make it appear later that whatever information Hurley might provide that night was legally obtained, McKenna would also request subpoenas from J. Davenport for Hector's Oldwick and Park Avenue phone records and all his bank records.

Needed in New Jersey was a search warrant for the Oldwick estate, signed by a New Jersey judge. Since, legally, that warrant would have to be executed by a New Jersey police officer, Tavlin would obtain cooperation from the New Jersey State Police.

The warrants would be executed that night to get Hector; the subpoenas would be served on Monday morning to solidify the case against him. The Park Avenue apartment and the Oldwick estate would be hit at the same time. To keep the press in the dark regarding the planned activities for the evening, Tavlin decided that the staging area for the raids would be the 13th Precinct station house. He would be there with the necessary manpower at ten o'clock.

McKenna had one thing to do that night that wasn't on the agenda, so he was happy that Tavlin was there. During his long career, the chief had commanded many operations of the sort they were contemplating that night, so the essence of the plan took shape in under fifteen minutes.

"Do you mind if I leave you two to iron out the details?" McKenna asked. "It's gonna be a long night and I want to grab a bite to eat before I go see Hurley."

"Fine," Tavlin said. "See you at the Thirteenth."

McKenna left the station house with a terse "No comment" to the reporters outside, but he wasn't going to eat. Instead, he had decided to use his downtime to get his meeting with Heidi out of the way and start her on her exclusive. Even though he felt he was close to arresting Hector, he couldn't risk having her reveal Hector's name and giving him enough warning to run. He feared that if he didn't show as promised, she'd arrange to go right on the air with her story. Besides, a deal's a deal, he told himself, and this meeting with her is long overdue.

Seven minutes and five blocks after leaving the station house, McKenna was standing in front of Heidi's building, marveling at what a wonderful industry television must be. Heidi's apartment was in a thirty-story luxury high-rise between First Avenue and Sutton Place, a very fashionable neighborhood. The building had all the amenities: a uniformed doorman, a concierge, and floor-to-ceiling windows in each apartment so that the occupants of the higher floors could look down and easily see what the little people were doing.

"Brian McKenna to see Miss Heidi Lane," he told the concierge standing behind his desk in the spacious lobby.

"Of course, sir. You're expected. Apartment 6E."

McKenna took the elevator to the sixth floor and stepped out into the carpeted hallway. He turned a corner and there she was, standing in her doorway, smiling politely and waiting to greet him.

He had expected Heidi, of course, but not this Heidi. She looked dignified and refined, dressed demurely in a sleek number that covered her knees and shoulders. Heidi offered her hand and said, "Thank you for coming, Brian. I have a little surprise for you. Actually, it was a surprise for me, too."

"What might that be?" he asked as he shook her hand.

"My mother's here. You remember her, don't you?"

That's a couple of surprises wrapped in one small statement, McKenna thought. I wanted to go out to Long Island tomorrow to see her mother and set things straight, but now she's here and something's happened. Heidi knows I've met her mother, which has to mean that she knows I know that she's Hank Lane's daughter, something she apparently didn't know before this evening. What's going on here? "Yes, I remember her," was all he said.

He followed Heidi in, down a short hallway to a small dining room that was off the kitchen. Janet Lane was seated at the dining room table with a half-finished cup of coffee and an ashtray containing four butts in front of her. She's been here a while, McKenna surmised, and I'd know her anywhere. Although it's been twenty years, Janet Lane looks pretty much the same if I subtract a few lines, wrinkles, and pounds from her and dye a few of those gray hairs, he observed. She looks none the worse for wear.

Janet Lane got up to greet him, surprising McKenna when she rushed over and gave him a hug. "Good to see you again, Brian. It's been too long, don't you think?"

"Yes, it has. Too long," he answered, not knowing what else to say as he hugged her back. There was a small embarrassing silence when she let him go, so he politely looked around the room. It was furnished exactly to his taste. The dining room table, the four chairs, and the credenza along the wall were painted a shiny, no-nonsense, utilitarian ebony black and there was silver everywhere, complementing it. The small chandelier above the table was silver, as were the serving set perched atop the credenza and the two ornate candlestick holders on the table. The only thing he didn't like was an abstract painting hanging on the wall picturing he wasn't sure what, but that had a silver frame, too.

Glancing through the archway into the living room, he saw that black and silver dominated there, too. The two sofas were black leather and the coffee tables and end tables were glass trimmed in chrome.

"I love the way you did this place," he said to Heidi.

"I hate it," she answered.

"What, the place or the furnishings?"

"Oh, I love the place, but everything else has to go if I stay here long enough," Heidi said. "I bought the apartment at an estate auction and all the furniture came with it. It's definitely not my taste, but I'm stuck with it for now."

"You're thinking of moving?"

"Might have to, unless I get a raise or an anchor job. I'm in way over my head right now in this place."

"I guess an exclusive on this story will move you along in that direction," he ventured.

"Yes, it wouldn't hurt," she answered, smiling wryly.

There was another embarrassing silence that Janet Lane ended. "Sit down, everybody," she said. "I think we have a lot to talk about."

McKenna and Heidi did as they were told, but then Janet seemed to have some second thoughts. "Heidi, why don't you go into the kitchen and make Brian a good cup of coffee. I'll have another, too, so take your time and do it right," she suggested.

"Of course," Heidi said, getting up. "Milk and sugar, Brian?"

"Yes, please."

Heidi looked pointedly at her mother, then turned back to McKenna. "Be back with the best cup of coffee you ever had," she said sweetly.

So they're gonna poison me, McKenna thought. Very good. Nice touch, considering the case.

Then Janet gave him another surprise as soon as Heidi had disappeared through the swinging door into the kitchen. "I'm sorry, Brian. I guess I let a lie live too long and people almost got hurt over it. It was convenient, but I realize now that it was too long," she said.

"Heidi knows?"

"Knows what? That her father was a crooked cop and not exactly the honest hero she believed he was?"

Pretty blunt, Janet. How do I answer that one? he wondered. "Does she know about that burglary scam?"

"Yes."

"And does she know that I had nothing to do with it that none of it was my idea or my doing?"

"Yes, she does now."

"And does she know that I didn't turn her father in, that I didn't make a dime off it and never would?"

"She does now."

"Now? Please define 'now,' Janet."

"I told her tonight. After talking to your partner, I saw that I had no choice."

"You talked to Maureen?" he asked, astonished.

"Yes. She stopped by my house today."

"In Levittown?"

"Yes, of course in Levittown. Said she happened to be in the neighborhood and thought we should talk."

Maureen just happened to be in the neighborhood? In Levittown, Long Island, no less? McKenna thought. Yeah, sure. That very Manhattan lady who probably couldn't get out of Queens without a map and a tour guide just happened to be way out of her element, in Levittown, Long Island, when, out of the blue at this critical time for me, she decided to drop in on someone she doesn't know, someone who just happens to be my old partner's widow. Right, Janet.

"Maureen's a bit of a good-natured, well-meaning busybody," he commented.

"Yes, she is," Janet agreed. "And it's a good thing for you. She's a nice lady, but you already know that."

"Yeah, she's the best."

"Anyway, she told me you were planning to visit me, but said you were so busy that she thought it better if she and I had a woman-to-woman talk. I think she was right."

Well, she certainly saved me an enormous and very unpleasant chore, McKenna admitted to himself. "So you decided you had to come in and talk to Heidi?"

"Of course. I'm a liar, but I'm not a monster."

"Care to tell me exactly what you told her?"

"I'll let her explain it, if you don't mind. I know she's got a lot she wants to talk about with you and she's been operating under some misconceptions her whole life, which is my fault."

"It's not all your fault."

"Well, mine and Hank's. We both always wanted the best for her and the rest of the kids, but maybe we wanted it too much. I was really worried about telling her."

"Is she handling it okay?' McKenna asked.

"Yes, she surprises even me. It was quite a shock to her, but she's strong. Much stronger than me, but I should have known that. Besides, she works so hard and she's such a good girl, don't you think?"

Heidi a good girl? Janet, thank God you don't know like I do just how hard and long your Heidi works to get what she wants, McKenna thought. It'd be enough to make your ears turn red, so what do I say to that one? "Yes, she's very smart and she's a nice girl. I have a feeling she's going to go far in the news business," he answered.

"Let's hope so."

At that moment Heidi came in carrying a silver tray with three cups of coffee on it. She placed one in front of each of them and sat down next to McKenna. "Let me know what you think, Brian," she said.

"About what?"

"About the coffee, of course. I'm just breaking in a new coffeepot."

McKenna took a sip from his steaming cup and savored it, a very difficult thing to do, considering what it tasted like. Yes, this could be the poison, he thought. "Very good. Excellent, in fact," he said. "Consider that pot broken in."

Heidi reacted as if he had just told her she was the most beautiful woman he had ever seen, smiling proudly with, McKenna thought, an unexpected touch of humility. She caught him glancing at her and she said, "So nice of you to say so, but my mom will probably tell you that I'm not much of a cook."

Mom wasn't quite ready to say exactly that, but then she hadn't yet tried Heidi's latest attempt at coffee.

"Nonsense. You're so busy and you're still learning. Someday when you calm down, you'll make some lucky man a wonderful wife," Janet said instead. Then she took a sip of her coffee, but her face couldn't disguise what she thought of it. "Maybe we should hope that lucky man is rich and likes to eat out a lot," she added.

Not very delicately put, McKenna thought. He, for one, was content to sit and sip his not-so-good coffee and was unhappy when Heidi put down her cup and asked, "Should I clear the air in here, or has that been done already in my absence?"

No, that's all right, Heidi. It's been done already, McKenna was ready to say. But not Janet Lane. "We weren't talking about the weather in here while you were gone, Heidi. I told him a few things. But since he's nice enough to drink this stuff with a smile on his face, I think Brian deserves some explanations from you," she said.

"Okay, let's do that." Heidi took a deep breath and faced McKenna. "My job is to report the news, but I do more than that," she said. "Occasionally, I get to scratch a public figure to see what's inside of them. I go sort of in-depth with them and I've found, with few exceptions, that they're all dirt and nothing like they're pretending to be for their publics. They're liars, cheats, and thieves who will do anything they can get away with to get what they want."

Heidi stopped to gauge the reaction to her statement. To McKenna, it was abundantly clear what Heidi was saying, but he could see that Janet was having problems with it. "What do you mean, you go 'in-depth' with them?" she asked.

"Exactly what you think I mean," Heidi said.

Janet didn't like that answer. "How can you do that?" she asked, obviously hoping it would get better.

It didn't. "Because, Mom, I'm dirt, too, just like they are. I'll do anything to get a good story from them or the promise of one in the future. How do you think I wound up in this nice apartment with this pretty-good-paying job in the first place?"

"Oh," was all Janet said in reply.

"Don't act so surprised, Mom. Since you wanted the air cleared, we'll get into your little act in a moment."

"So I'm dirt, too?" Janet asked.

"Yes, Mom, you are. Sorry, but if Dad was dirt, then you are, too. You had to be in it together, all the time pretending what a great cop he'd been and lying to us about that wonderful insurance policy he had. Proceeds of the crime and all that stuff, Mom. Makes you guilty, too."

"I see," Janet said.

"Mom, one thing I've learned is that not all dirt is bad. Daddy was a good husband and a good father and I still miss him. You did nothing but give to your kids, the best of everything. Great Christmases, big birthday parties, nice clothes, and we all went to good colleges, thanks to Daddy and you. Yet, I've never seen you take a vacation or go out to dinner on a lark. That still makes you a pretty good person in my book."

"So I'm a liar and a thief, but I'm still okay?"

"Yep, and if it makes you feel any better, I'm okay, too. I might be a devious liar and a spiteful slut while I'm working, but when I'm not, I'm a paragon of virtue. I'm nice to animals, children like me, and I'm a big tipper, so I guess that makes me okay in this town.''

McKenna sat stunned during this mother-daughter exchange. All he could think was: That's *really* clearing the air, Heidi. You cleared the oxygen right out of this room. Then they were through pummeling each other and they both looked to him for comment.

Time to change this subject, McKenna thought. ''You know, Heidi, I don't remember you ever doing any exposés on anyone.''

''That's because I don't. Just one exposé when you're starting out in this business, and nobody in this town talks to you anymore. I can't afford that. Besides, I'm not a hypocrite, so who am I to do an exposé on anyone?''

''So what do you do?'' Janet asked.

''Simple. I'm not exactly homely, so what I do is use my skill to get the story from whoever's got it or maybe to collect some future favors from those in the know. Consequently, I get a lot of calls when news starts breaking around town. Remember, the name of the game is: Get the story and get it first.''

Janet, please leave it at that, McKenna prayed, and for once his wish was granted. Janet had heard all she wanted to about her daughter's skill and methods of bringing home the story.

''Now on to you, Brian,'' Heidi said. ''You ready?''

''Fire away.''

''Fire away? This should be easy for you. How old are you, if you don't mind my asking?''

''Forty-eight.''

''Well then, and this is still hard for me to believe, but it seems to me that you're the oldest Eagle Scout I've ever come across,'' Heidi said.

A forty-eight-year-old Eagle Scout who's a cop? Can that be good? McKenna asked himself. ''What makes you say that?''

''Because at this moment in time, I think that the image you project and the person you are, down deep, are one and the same. Everyone who knows you tells me that you're a great detective as well as a good man, and now I think they're right. You might even call this realization a life-changing experience for me, a confirmed cynic when it comes to public figures.''

''I'm not much in the way of a public figure. I'm just a cop who happens to have a big case that drew a lot of media attention.''

''Don't kid yourself, Brian,'' Heidi advised. ''You've got recognition, that's what makes you a public figure. People know your face, know your name, and they trust you. You get Hector De la Cruz, and this case could open a lot of doors for you.''

''Maybe, but I like being a cop. That's all I want to do and it's all I'm going to do, as long as I can.''

''You know, if anyone else in your position told me that, I'd have a hard time not laughing in their face,'' Heidi said without a trace of a smile. ''But today, Detective Brian McKenna, you I believe.''

''And yesterday you wouldn't have?''

''No. Yesterday I was convinced that you were a lying, thieving, rotten dog who had everybody fooled,'' Heidi said while staring pointedly at her mother. ''I thought you were the man who hatched up a scheme that caused my poor, honest, misguided father to blow his brains out.''

"And you were gonna bring me down?''

"It's been my lifelong ambition. One way or another, I was going to get you and expose you as the man I thought you were. As a matter of fact, you were going to be my first exposé, and it was going to be a whopper.''

"How exactly were you planning to do that, if you don't mind my asking?''

"Brian, are you trying to give my poor mother a heart attack?'' Heidi asked, smiling and looking to Janet again.

So did McKenna, and he concluded that Janet Lane didn't look so good. She looked sick and very unhappy, but still interested. He assumed that she wanted to know the answer to his question, but he didn't think she should. "Forget I asked,'' he said to Heidi.

Heidi was prepared to show her mother a little mercy, but not much more than that. "Okay, but let's just say that sometimes men like to talk to me more than they should.''

All of a sudden, an image of Jim Heaney and Heidi popped into McKenna's mind. It was straight out of dull men's fantasy, and it wasn't pretty. There were whips, chains, and leather galore, with Heidi sweetly asking the questions, among other things, and Heaney panting the answers into her tape recorder. Heaney being Heaney, he really had no choice, McKenna realized. The personnel director was no match for Heidi and therefore deserved his understanding and forgiveness, maybe. "Okay, forget me for the moment. How did you get on to Jim Heaney?'' he asked.

"Brian, do you think you're the only one with a brain?'' Heidi asked. "When I heard you had all those homeless HIV-positive victims in Midtown, I went right to the AIDS clinic. People there told me Heaney had been around asking questions and showing your sketch. Then I called his office and asked for you.''

"And his secretary told you I had visited Heaney, but that I wasn't there just then,'' McKenna guessed.

"Exactly,'' Heidi said, smiling and obviously very proud of herself. "So I went to see our friend Jim, and you know the rest.''

"Yes, I know the rest. I have just one question for you, and then we have to get out of here,'' McKenna said.

"We?'' Heidi asked. "Where are we going?''

"We're going to pretend that you just got a call from a source who told you that I was going to see a famous private investigator in connection with this case. In about an hour, you're going to catch me coming out of his office and you'll ask me some questions, all of which I'll answer with 'No comment.' ''

"And then I'll talk to the PI?'' Heidi asked.

"Yes, but he won't tell you much right now. Later on, after we catch Hector, I'm sure he'll be willing to elaborate for only you.''

"Who's the PI?''

"Bob Hurley. You know him?''

"Office next to the Hard Rock Cafe?''

"That's the one,'' McKenna said, thinking, How come she knows that and I didn't?

"And when are you going to catch Hector, if you know?''

"Sometime tonight, I hope. You can't be there for that, but you'll still get a better story than anyone else."

"So our deal's still on, I take it?"

"Of course."

"Why? You don't have to, you know. As a matter of fact, you don't have to worry about me anymore."

"Glad to hear that, but a deal's a deal."

"And that's the only reason you're doing it?" Heidi asked.

"No. That's not the only reason. Let's just say that I wanna keep you in your apartment, for old times' sake."

"And that's it?"

Heidi was smiling innocently, but McKenna thought he heard her voice quiver. What's going on now? McKenna asked himself. Does the very cynical and quite experienced Heidi have something else going through her head? "That's it," he answered simply.

Heidi's smile vanished. "I never had a chance of getting you good, did I?"

"No, I don't think so. At least not with the plan I'm sure you had in mind."

"Heidi, for God's sake! Leave him alone," Janet yelled. "He's a married man."

Heidi ignored her mother, except to say, "That's right. You're married to what's-her-name, aren't you?"

"Yes, I'm married to Angelita."

"And, like you told me, you love her very much?"

"That was no lie."

"And she loves you?"

"So she says, and I believe her."

"And a deal's a deal. Right, Eagle Scout?"

"Yes, a deal's a deal."

Heidi's smile returned, but it looked a little forced to McKenna. "Okay, what's your question for me?"

"Long ago, right after Hank died, I used to get a package around the anniversary of his death."

Janet gasped and McKenna had his answer, but Heidi's face lit up. "And you want to know if it came from us?" she asked.

"Yes, I'd like to know, for the record."

"Was it usually a fish?"

"Always."

"Was it always a bluefish?"

"I believe so, as far as I could tell."

"And did it smell real bad?"

"It certainly did."

"And was it covered in maggots?"

"Yes."

"And did it get you furious?"

"Let's just say it got my mailman furious at me, and that cost me an extra twenty at Christmas."

Heidi and Janet could contain themselves no longer. Heidi put her hand over her mouth to suppress her laughter, then turned and pointed accusingly at her mother. Janet was doing no better keeping herself under control, but she was pointing to Heidi.

McKenna watched them for a moment, but then had to laugh himself as he imagined mother and daughter wrapping the old and smelly fish with great care. They all had a real backslapping session for a minute until Heidi was able to put on a straight face. When she did, she looked McKenna in the eye and said, "Sorry, but we know nothing about that." Then she burst out laughing again.

Whenever possible, leave 'em laughing, McKenna thought as he patted each one on the back and headed for the door.

48 Hurley looks good. The more money he makes, the better he looks, and he looks better now than he ever did, McKenna thought as he sat across the desk from the private investigator in his spacious, expensively furnished office.

Hurley was tall, thin, and compact. McKenna had worked with him when he was still with the NYPD and knew Hurley had to be sixty, but it was a good sixty for him. His blond hair was thinning and graying, but it made him look more distinguished rather than just older. As always, Hurley was dressed casually, wearing European-tailored trousers, a silk shirt, and loafers. His demeanor caused McKenna to surmise that, in business, a man doesn't have to wear a suit as long as he's the man in charge. Hurley clearly was, and he emphasized it by putting his feet up on his desk after passing McKenna a bulky folder.

"That should be everything you need to know about Hector and everything I could dig up on short notice on the contessa," Hurley said. "You want a synopsis?"

"If you don't mind."

"Okay. Hector was the easy one because there's a lot published about him. He's a local hero in Costa Rica and most folks down there know his story because it's a real rags-to-riches tale. He came from absolutely nothing. Mother was a prostitute who was thirty-nine when she had him, father's unknown. She came down with syphilis when he was six and they wound up homeless, living in the street together until she died when he was nine. Never even went to school until after his mother died."

"Sounds like they don't have much of a support system down there," McKenna commented.

"Not then, but they do now, and Hector's responsible for quite a bit of it. Costa Rica was strictly Third World then, but it's an up-and-coming place right now."

"Okay, so his mother dies. What then?"

"The nuns pick him up and he winds up in a Catholic orphanage. They start him out in school and it turns out the kid's a genius, excels in science, math, and languages. He becomes sort of the Catholic poster boy and everybody starts paying attention to whatever Hector's doing. Along the way he becomes the chess champion of Costa Rica when he's fourteen and then he really tickles everybody when he whups the champion of Nicaragua, a neighbor the Costa Ricans aren't very fond of. So he's everybody's favorite guy, and then he confuses them all and goes into the seminary."

"He wanted to be a priest?" McKenna asked.

"Yeah, surprised everybody except the nuns at the orphanage. One of them was interviewed by the local press down there and, according to her, Hector always had the calling. She said he was the closest thing to a saint she ever saw."

"Did he finish the seminary?"

"Yes, but then he didn't want to be ordained and he caused some controversy. Seems Hector didn't agree with the church's stand on birth control. Said that the Third World was overpopulated and getting poorer because of it."

"How about abortion?" McKenna asked.

"One of the questions he was asked. He's dead set against it, so he's not exactly a heretic and nobody's looking to burn him at the stake."

"So what's next for him? Medical school?"

"Yep. Gets a full government scholarship, something that's pretty hard to come by down there. Graduates at the top of his class at age twenty-nine, gets all sorts of offers to join the richest practices down there, such as they are, but money doesn't interest him. He opens up a free clinic in San José and works the barrios and slums."

"Treating the homeless?"

"Primarily, I guess. He gets even more ink down there because of his efforts, and soon everybody's donating to his clinic. Big multinational corporations like United Fruit as well as schoolchildren donating their lunch money. Then there's a drive to get him elected to what they call the Legislative Assembly, sort of like our House and Senate combined. He didn't run, but he was a shoo-in. Everybody in the slums wrote him in. So what do you think he does?"

Something bizarre, McKenna knew from the way Hurley was asking. A very deep man, a genius from the streets of the Third World who's almost a saint and who doesn't care about money, McKenna thought. "He declines the position?"

"That's right. Says that his work is more important. Their president himself had to go to the clinic to talk him into taking his seat. So Hector does, and then proposes some legislation that brings about socialized medicine in Costa Rica. Nobody could oppose a guy as popular as he was, so it passed. And that's what they've got now, cradle-to-grave medical care for everyone. They now have one of the highest life-expectancy rates in the world, and many Costa Ricans attribute that to him. Then he left politics and searched around for something else to do."

"Why did he leave if he was doing so good getting his programs passed?"

"Had to. Costa Rica is an old democracy with some strange ways. Nobody can be reelected. President serves for six years and the fifty-seven deputies serve for four."

"Didn't he go back to his clinic?"

"Sort of, but the challenge was gone for him. During his stint as a politico, Costa Rica became a tourist attraction, the money started pouring in, and everything got better for everyone, including their homeless. Supposedly, it's not much of a problem down there anymore."

"So what does he do, then? Collect butterflies?" McKenna speculated.

"I guess you know something about Hector that you didn't tell me," Hurley said, eyeing McKenna shrewdly.

"No, that was just an educated guess," McKenna stated as innocently as he could.

"It was a pretty good one because more than half of North America's species of butterflies are native to Costa Rica. They've got eighty thousand species and still counting. Hector became something of a lepidopterist, but that was just a hobby for him."

"A lepidopterist?"

"Someone who collects butterflies. That country's loaded with them, sort of a national sport down there."

"So that's his hobby. What was he doing that was serious and how does he get connected to the contessa?"

"He got into the environment and she always had been. At the time, a lot of Costa Rica's rain forest was being cut down to make way for cattle grazing. Hector was dead set against that, started up a protest movement, and before long he was getting headlines for his movement when he began chaining himself to the blades of bulldozers being used to clear the rain forest."

"And she heard about it?" McKenna guessed.

"Yes. She was in Spain at the time and was involved in a project to protect the Spanish wolves, among other things. That worked and she was looking around for another project. The rain forests in Costa Rica, Indonesia, and Brazil was it for her. So she started sending him money and he always wrote back to thank her and give her his ideas on the subject. His ideas started taking hold in Costa Rica so that now it's the only one of those countries where the rain forest is actually increasing in area."

"So she went there to see for herself and find out how he was doing it?" McKenna asked.

"Yes. She was impressed with the project, but even more impressed with Hector. You know what he looks like?"

"You mean what he looked liked then?" McKenna asked.

"Yeah, when she first met him."

"Yes, I've seen an old picture. Didn't impress me as particularly handsome."

"That's what they say, but Carmen Maria was supposed to be quite a beauty. So it wasn't his looks she fell for, and it sure wasn't money because he didn't have any. She was the one with all the gelt, so I guess everything was his mind and his personality as far as she was concerned."

"Could you give me the story on her?"

"Born in 1961 in Spain, second child and only daughter of Armando Suarez. Armando's fifty years old when she's born and she's the apple of his eye. There was Luís, a half-brother twenty years older than her, but Armando wasn't too crazy about him. The old man was strictly Catholic and Luís was a bit too spoiled, always knocking up one babe or another, got busted for possession of cocaine in Paris, killed a kid in a car crash, and got locked up for drunken driving, all stuff that drove Armando crazy."

"And cost him a fortune," McKenna observed.

"I guess, but money was never one of his problems. He was born to it and became one of Spain's industrialists, started their automotive industry going, making himself another fortune along the way. But back to Carmen Maria. She goes to school in Switzerland and France, does okay but not great. Her mother dies in

1980 when she's nineteen, she drops out of school for a while and lives with her father, I guess consoling each other. Then in '81 she goes back to Switzerland and finishes school. After that, in '82 she marries an Austrian count, Rudolph von Manstien. He's twenty years older than her, but it's his first marriage. In '84 Rudolph has the big one and drops dead while they're walking together along the street in Geneva. She buries him, then goes back to Spain to be close to her father. In '85 Armando kicks off. Same thing, heart attack. She's there for that one, too.''

"So everyone around her is dying. She couldn't have felt too good about that," McKenna observed.

"No, she didn't. Must've felt like the spider woman, so she went and got herself some counseling, something she could well afford. The count left her well off, but Armando really topped it off with a couple of hundred million.''

"And her half-brother, Luís?''

"One million, but this'll tell you something about her. Luís was in his sixties and still a bum. A rich bum, but a bum and a junkie. She tells him she'll split Armando's loot with him if he'll get himself cured and stay clean for a year. So Luís goes off to Tahiti and gets into a rich man's program there, supposedly trying hard. But he's a loser, overdoses on heroin in Tahiti in '86, nine months after Armando died.''

"So now everyone in her family is dead.''

"Yes, she's all alone and not feeling too good. That's when she starts getting into causes and starts giving millions away. Enter Hector, romance, and marriage in 1987. His work is basically done in Costa Rica, so he hangs out with her at all her houses all over the world for a couple of years. But he misses Costa Rica, so she buys him a house there in Tamarindo Bay and they set up housekeeping there. At first it's fine, I guess, but eventually she must have been bored out of her mind. So they move to New York. He tells one of the local papers that he'd love to stay in Costa Rica, but that the homeless problem in New York needs addressing and he's going to teach and open a clinic there. The Costa Ricans love it, sort of reverse foreign aid.''

"And that's when he runs into his licensing problems,'' McKenna guessed.

"I don't know about that," Hurley said, giving McKenna a small tinge of satisfaction. "The first time he shows up in the New York press is in 1993. By then he had opened his Park Avenue practice, but he started treating the homeless for free. They were hanging out all over the place and the co-op board had a fit and tried to have him evicted. Carmen Maria threw the best lawyers into the fray and they won, but she and Hector became persona non grata in society circles for a while. All during this time she's donating big-time to homeless causes all around the world, but especially here in New York. Then, two years ago, they pick up and leave. Go back to Costa Rica for a while, but last year she shows up in Saint-Tropez without him.''

"That had to be when the AIDS started hitting him,'' McKenna guessed.

"Maybe, but there's no mention of it anywhere in the press and neither of them was talking about it. He stayed in Tamarindo Bay for a while, then he began losing weight and people started questioning him about it. He told the local papers he had come down with cancer and was going to Europe for treatment. That was last June, and he hasn't been seen or heard from since.''

"I wish that were still true. You have his motor-vehicle information in here?" McKenna asked, holding up the file Hurley had given him.

"Yep. He's got a current New Jersey driver's license, clean. No cars registered in New York, but he's got two in Jersey, a Mercedes and a Jeep Cherokee."

"How about banking information?"

"Indications are that he doesn't have any money of his own, but she takes care of him. He's got a checking account at First Bank of the Americas. They have branches here and all over Latin America. On the first of every month a hundred thousand gets dropped into his account. Current balance is over half a million."

"Any withdrawals?"

"Lots of them, and all cash. Last June in Costa Rica he took out one hundred thousand in dollars. That had to be when he was leaving."

"And recently?"

"Seven separate nine-thousand-dollar withdrawals from their Park Avenue branch, all in cash. The first one was on November fifteenth and the last one was yesterday, so you should be able to get a recent picture of him."

Hurley's right, McKenna thought. He has to be on film somewhere in that bank. "Any credit cards?" he asked.

"All of them, no limit."

"When was the last time they were used?"

"Last June. He's been paying strictly cash, but if he changes his ways I've got a little bonus for you."

"You've got friends in the credit-card industry?" McKenna asked.

"Friends? No, not friends. Maybe they were friends when we were all on the Job together, but now I consider them high-paid employees of mine. You'll learn, if you ever wise up and get off that job, that banks and credit-card companies are top-heavy with retired NYPD, and I make it my business to keep in touch with most of them. That way, everybody's happy."

"So you'll know if he uses any of his cards?"

"The American ones. Five minutes after he gets clearance on a purchase if he uses his AmEx and any of his Visas or MasterCards, I'll know. But it's costing me."

"How much do you figure this whole thing cost you, so far?" McKenna asked.

"Counting manpower, gifts, and database searches, about eight or nine thousand."

"And how much does a full-page ad in the *Times* cost?"

"Thirty-five thousand at my rate during the week," Hurley said, then got the point. "Hey, I'm not complaining. A good story and getting credit where credit's due is better publicity than any lies I might put in an ad."

"In that case, I think you bought yourself a bargain on this case."

"Glad to hear it," Hurley said. "When, exactly, do I start collecting my just reward in publicity?"

"In about five minutes. When I leave here, Heidi Lane is going to ambush me outside. I'm not gonna tell her much on camera except that you, as a public service, have developed some information that might be of some use to us. Then she's gonna bring her crew up here and talk to you."

"And what do I tell her?"

"While the cameras are off and you're alone with her, whatever you want that won't send you to jail. But once you're speaking for the record, just tell her that you've developed some information that you can't talk about until you receive clearance from me. She knows who Hector is, but she won't reveal it yet."

"Sounds to me like you've developed an exclusive relationship with Heidi," Hurley observed, but wouldn't let it lie there. "She's been a little nasty to you, hasn't she? I mean, before all that public-apology nonsense."

"That was a misunderstanding," McKenna said.

"So what changed? Forgive my lewd and inquisitive mind, but are you tapping that fine little thing?"

"No, I'm not. I'll let you draw your own conclusions, but Heidi is Hank Lane's daughter. Did you know him?"

"Of course I did. Great cop and a fine man. Maybe a little too greedy for his own good, but he really went out in style. Gave the cheese-eaters a good, stiff scare and gave the rest of us a lot to giggle about. I like to think I would've gone out the same way if they were ever smart enough to get me good, which, fortunately, they weren't."

No, they weren't, but they sure tried, McKenna remembered. He had been at Hurley's retirement party ten years before and among the invited guests on the dais had been the Chief of the Internal Affairs Division. When he had been called upon to make a speech, he had good-naturedly said that he had hoped to throw a party if he could have gotten Hurley on any of the many scams he had been suspected of pulling off. Failing that, he had added, Hurley's retirement was still good news because it freed up ten of his investigators to concentrate on the affairs of the other persons sitting next to him on the dais.

McKenna remembered that, at the time, it had been considered quite a good joke on the chief's part. However, after Hurley left the Job, things and attitudes had started changing in the NYPD and, one by one, Hurley's pals were captured and fell. Some had gone to jail, some had been fired, and some had retired and were working for Hurley.

"You need anything else from me?" Hurley asked.

"Nothing I can think of at the moment," McKenna said as he stood up.

"You planning on locking up Hector tonight?"

"Hopefully. Then you can be the Hero of the Month by Monday's editions."

"That would be nice, but you want a word of advice from me?" Hurley asked.

"Anything you care to tell me would be appreciated."

"Then think about this. You know how many moves ahead a chess champion plans?"

"Eight, isn't it?"

"That's right. Eight, and Hector's a grand master and this is all a game to him. What I'm saying is that, if you miss him tonight, I don't think you're going to get him."

"Why? Because he's got contingency plans?"

"Count on it. If you miss him, he's gonna know you're on to him, and he's gonna run. I'm sure he's planned exactly how he's gonna get away."

"And where do you think he'll run to, if you've given it any thought?" McKenna asked.

"He's got the cash and he's been spending it. I'm sure one of the things he's been buying is IDs, but where he's going he doesn't need fake ID. He can show up as himself and be perfectly safe."

"I think we'd get him no matter where he went. This case has got national interest. Once we tell who Hector is and who he's married to, it's going international. So where could he hide? Cuba?"

"Nope. He'd go home."

"To Costa Rica?"

"Of course," Hurley said. "Home to Costa Rica. They have no extradition treaties with the United States, which is how Robert Vesco managed to live down there openly and in luxury for years while he was on our Ten Most Wanted list. It took our government ten years of pleading, and then the Costa Ricans just let him take off for Cuba."

"But Vesco was wanted for drug smuggling, stock swindles, and political campaign financing scams. Hector's case is different. He's a mass murderer."

"Not good enough," Hurley said. "When it comes to Costa Rica, he's got a country full of O. J. jurors on his side. He's a hero down there, and no matter how much evidence you show them, it'd all be bullshit as far as they're concerned. They'd never even consider giving him up to the *Yanquis*. He'd die in peace and contentment in his own country."

"Maybe you're right," McKenna said. "But for the moment, I've got nothing to worry about. Tonight's the night for Hector."

"Whatever you say," Hurley said as he swung his legs off his desk.

"I'll go one better than that," McKenna said. "This Job can't afford the black eye of letting this guy get away. If we don't get him tonight, I'll still get Hector De la Cruz. No matter where he goes, I'll get him."

"Whatever you say," Hurley said again, but McKenna didn't think the PI believed it.

49 Hector De la Cruz turned off the TV, deeply disturbed by the news. What had McKenna learned at that PI's office and why had Hurley appeared so confident during his interview with Heidi Lane? McKenna had looked surprised when she accosted him as he left the building on West 57th Street, and he had said nothing more than that Bob Hurley had provided him with some information that might prove useful in his investigation.

On the other hand, Hurley hadn't appeared surprised at all when the camera crew had knocked on his door, leading Hector to surmise that McKenna had tipped off Heidi that Hurley was going to be there. Hurley said that he had discovered, on his own, some information that he believed would help the police to catch the killer. But the PI's pompous demeanor originally caused Hector to discount Hurley's assertion as nothing more than a publicity stunt. However, it had been Hurley's closing comment to the reporter that maybe he'd talk to her again in a couple of days that worried him. Hurley's assertion had been accompanied by a wink, as if the two of them were sharing a secret.

Hector was also worried about the reporter's handling of Hurley. He had seen her interview McKenna before, and he had considered her to be something of a tigress. Yet he thought she had handled Hurley with kid gloves, not pressing him at all into revealing more. Why was that? Because it was possible something'd happening there, that there had been some developments that imperiled his security and his plan, he feared.

What could Hurley have told McKenna that would advance his case? Hector wondered. Nothing, as long as the police still hadn't learned his identity. But if they had, then that was different. He speculated that a good PI, operating without rules, could get banking, credit-card, and real-estate information much faster than the police could because of the cumbersome constitutional requirements they would have to overcome before the information would be made legally available to them.

Hector examined his past conduct, looking for mistakes he might have made, and came up with nothing. The police couldn't know who he was and shouldn't even know he was in the country. He had returned through Canada and had taken the trouble to cross the American border using a forged passport. Except for Suli Rashid and his housekeeper, Mrs. Sweeney, he had seen no one who knew him as Hector De la Cruz. Suli was dead and Hector was sure that Mrs. Sweeney, as instructed, had told no one he was back in Oldwick. She had accepted without question his explanation that he had come home to Oldwick to die with dignity and in solitude.

The truth was that while he expected the cancer to kill him, he didn't expect to die for months, and maybe longer. Against the odds, he was feeling better each day, and it seemed to him that his mission, along with the medical treatment, had combined to reinvigorate him.

Unfortunately, that treatment had been more costly than he had expected. On reexamining his movements over the past nine months, he admitted that money might be the only possible error he had made. He had expected that the hundred thousand he'd withdrawn when he left Costa Rica would last him a year. However, the chemo treatment in Switzerland, while it had gone a long way toward suppressing the cancer, had cost almost fifty thousand dollars and the black-market AZT he had been forced to purchase had set him back another ten thousand. So he had gone to visit the bank a few times, always taking out only nine thousand dollars on each visit, fully aware that the bank was required to notify the IRS of all cash transactions over ten thousand dollars. Had those bank visits in any way alerted the police to his identity? he asked himself. No.

Still, Hector decided that increased caution was in order, and that the night's planned operation would be the last for a while. He would leave and see what developed in New York in his absence before resuming his mission.

He had an hour to himself before he had to go, so Hector decided to devote himself to his latest obsession: Detective Brian McKenna. Three days before, he had visited the New York Public Library's main branch on Fifth Avenue, a building the size of a soccer field that was totally devoted to research. He had been amazed to find that, over the years, there had been 131 separate articles in the *New York Times* in which McKenna had been mentioned. He had made copies of all of them and brought them home to Oldwick for study.

What he had learned delighted him. This Brian McKenna would be a worthy adversary. After studying the articles, he had surmised that McKenna was hard-working, intuitive, honest, intelligent, courageous, popular, politically connected, and, most important, lucky.

Hector hadn't counted on a McKenna type when he had first undertaken his mission in New York, and had initially been disappointed when his opponent had discovered his work after only one day on the case. But since then Hector had developed a new way of looking at his mission, and his disappointment had been replaced by pure personal pleasure. He felt certain that he was going to hand the detective the first major setback in his long and successful career. It had become a game played for the highest stakes Hector could imagine—his life and freedom. As far as he was concerned, a game played against an inferior opponent was simply boring, no fun, and not worth playing, but this one was developing nicely and was bound to be loaded with new moves on the detective's part.

Hector relished the thought of placing McKenna in check for all the world to see, but realized that won games were sometimes lost by underestimating opponents and failing to perceive and anticipate surprise moves. That wasn't going to happen to him in this game, Hector resolved. Daring play was called for, but strategic retreat had to be kept ready as an option. However, the retreat must be dignified to keep the opponent off balance and unsure of himself, so Hector prepared a package and left it on the bed, just in case.

After finishing his studying for the evening, Hector dressed in a fresh shirt and tie and a clean suit, then he checked his appearance in the mirror. He decided that his beard needed combing and did that without removing it. Satisfied with his appearance, he went downstairs to inform Mrs. Sweeney of his plans for the evening.

As he had hoped, she had already turned in for the evening, but he wrote her a note anyway, telling her that he was going to Bethlehem to take in a movie. It was his usual story to her, and she believed that he must be quite an expert on the Spanish-language movies playing in Bethlehem. She didn't know that he hadn't seen one of them, but used the Spanish-movie routine so that she would never think to question him about the films.

He left the note on the kitchen table where she would be sure to see it if she came down during the night. Then he left the house, locked the door, and went to the garage.

Inside the garage were three cars. He ignored the Mercedes and the Cherokee and started up the Buick station wagon. The Buick belonged to Carmen, but was registered to Mrs. Sweeney at her Philadelphia address and had been provided for her use to do the shopping and visit her family when she was off, which was most of the time when he and Carmen weren't staying at the house.

After fifteen minutes of driving on the torturous winding back roads, he was at the east-west interstate highway, I-78. West led to Bethlehem and east led to New York. After another hour of driving at fifty-three miles an hour, he paid the toll at the Lincoln Tunnel. He saw by the large clock above the tollbooth that it was exactly 11 P.M. He was right on schedule.

By 11:05 he was in the city, heading crosstown on East 30th Street. At Lexington Avenue he made a right and drove south nine blocks. There the avenue ended at Gramercy Park. He drove around the park and found a parking spot on

Gramercy Park South. He made some final preparations, checked his beard in the rearview mirror, put on his gloves, wrapped his scarf around his face, and left the car, slowly walking east. He passed a few people on the street, but none gave the well-dressed, bearded man a second glance.

Hector stopped in front of an old brick synagogue, down the block from where his car was parked. It was Saturday night and the lights were on in the synagogue, but that didn't bother him. In fact, he had counted on it. The building stood alone, with an alley on each side leading to the rear. He stood and waited for ten minutes until there was no one on the street for a block in either direction. Then he entered the alley and walked to the rear of the synagogue, unseen by anyone.

There was a bamboo shed abutting the back wall. Hector had visited the location before and had done some research before he had learned the reason for the shed's existence. It was a Succoth hut, built to accommodate the synagogue's caretaker when he and his family observed the rituals associated with the Jewish holiday celebrating the harvest. The hut was used only a couple of days a year for the purpose for which it was intended, but Hector could see by the light spilling from the synagogue windows that someone else had decided to call the hut home, at least for that evening. A man was lying on the floor of the hut, wrapped in a sleeping bag. The squatter was sleeping, breathing loud and rhythmically. Next to him was a black plastic trash bag containing his possessions.

Hector smiled. Once again his information had proven correct; sleeping at his feet was the thin, weak man he wanted. He took a small penlight from his pocket, turned it on, and held it in his mouth, taking care that the beam didn't shine directly into his quarry's eyes. Then he removed a steak knife from his pocket, got on his knees, and bent over the sleeping man. He moved his head so that the penlight was shining directly on the side of the man's neck and he stared at the spot until he saw what he was looking for: the almost imperceptible pulse movement that indicated the presence of the carotid artery. He held his knife over the spot and was bearing down to make the small, fatal incision when a dog barked somewhere on Gramercy Park South and the man's eyes opened.

Hector still could have accomplished his purpose exactly as he had intended, but he waited a second too long, surprised by the terror in his victim's eyes as he struggled to remove his arms from the sleeping bag. Then Hector put his right hand on his victim's ear and pushed his head hard against the floor of the Succoth hut while he placed the blade of the knife on his victim's neck.

But the man knew what was coming, and although he was weak and dying, he was determined that his death not occur just then. As Hector began his incision, the man twisted his head against the pressure being exerted on his ear and overcame it. His neck turned, and although Hector could see that he had made a cut, it wasn't in the exact right place. There was blood, but it wasn't coming in squirts as it should have if he had succeeded in severing the artery.

Then the man did the one thing Hector hadn't planned on. He opened his mouth and screamed.

Hector sliced again, but the man was wildly thrashing inside his sleeping bag and pushing himself along the floor of the hut as Hector pressed his right hand into his ear, struggling to hold him still. The slice was ineffective, producing a long cut on the neck, but inches behind the artery. The scream continued and then the man managed to free one of his arms from the sleeping bag. It came out of the top of the sleeping bag and he waved it frantically in front of Hector's face, screaming all the while.

Hector knew it was time to leave. He dropped the knife, let the penlight fall from his mouth, and pushed himself to his feet. Then he walked toward the street with long, purposeful strides. The screaming continued. As soon as he reached Gramercy Park South, he looked around casually. There was no one on the street, but inside the fenced park was a woman holding a leashed golden retriever. She was staring at him and, after a moment's hesitation, she yelled to him, "Where's it coming from?"

Hector turned and made a show of listening, gratified to hear that the screams were echoing through the backyards of the buildings on Gramercy Park South. It was impossible to tell just which backyard the sound was coming from, but Hector turned and faced the woman again. "I think it's coming from the next block. I'm going to call the police," he yelled to her.

"Please hurry," she yelled back.

Hector did hurry, walking directly to his car. He took off his gloves and pulled his keys from his pocket, but his hands were shaking so much that it seemed to take forever to insert the key in the door lock of the Buick. When he finally got behind the wheel, he took some time to regain his strength and calm down before he started the car. The woman was still standing in the park when he drove by, and the screams were audible through the car's closed windows.

50 The business of obtaining the warrants and subpoenas with J. Davenport took McKenna longer than he had anticipated. The New York end of it went smoothly and McKenna quickly got everything signed there; the delay was encountered in obtaining the search warrant from the New Jersey judge for the Oldwick district. J. Davenport got him on the phone, but it took some time for the cranky judge to instruct him on the correct New Jersey format for the search-warrant application. It was only when everything was typed and worded exactly to the judge's satisfaction that he gave his approval and authorized the search of Carmen's Oldwick estate. The warrant was faxed to the judge and then faxed back to McKenna and J. Davenport, finally signed.

When McKenna arrived at the 13th Precinct station house at 11:05, he was stunned to see how much manpower the chief thought was necessary. There were forty detectives and uniformed cops crowded into the squad office. Tavlin planned to hit the Park Avenue apartment and the Oldwick estate simultaneously.

The Park Avenue end of it was a straightforward affair and would be handled by Ward. Tavlin had assigned to him five detectives and an Emergency Service team to execute that warrant. It read that the items they were to seize, if found, were Hector De la Cruz, poisons, wine, black men's clothing, makeup, fake beards, and B series one-hundred-dollar bills. McKenna considered that warrant to be an exercise in futility, but realized that the search had to be done.

The Oldwick estate was more complicated. Tavlin had arranged to meet the New Jersey State Police at the Oldwick exit on I-78, but they would be in for quite a shock. Since the chief had no idea of the size of the estate, didn't know if Hector had any surprises planned there, and didn't know what equipment the New Jersey State Police had at their disposal, he had pulled out all the stops. The search team would consist of a sergeant and ten detectives from the Homicide Squad, but going along for the ride were two Emergency Service trucks with heavy weapons, two searchlight trucks, two K-9 units, and, just in case, two teams from the Bomb Squad, complete with two of their bomb-sniffing dogs.

It was going to be quite a show, one that McKenna thought he'd almost rather miss. He was convinced that either Tavlin had slipped over the edge or, someplace along the line, the chief had garnered an enormous amount of respect for Dr. Hector De la Cruz. Deciding which became more difficult for McKenna when Tavlin informed him that there would be an NYPD helicopter over the estate.

At 11:30, just as the plans were completed and they were getting ready to move out, matters started going awry. The phone rang and one of the 13th Squad men grabbed it, then yelled to McKenna, "It's the desk officer downstairs. He wants to speak to you."

McKenna picked up and the desk officer asked, "Do you know a bum named Jake the Snake?"

"Sure do. Why?"

"Because he just wandered in. He's cut up pretty bad and he's screaming for you."

McKenna dropped the phone, bolted out of the office, and ran downstairs, followed by Tavlin and everybody else. He heard Jake screaming his name before he left the stairwell, so he wasn't hard to find. In front of the precinct desk Jake was lying in a pool of blood while a uniformed cop wearing latex gloves tried to stop the bleeding from his neck wounds by applying pressure with a towel.

"McKenna! I almost got that low-life cowardly prick for you," Jake screamed as soon as he saw McKenna standing over him. "I almost got him for you."

Jake was hard to ignore, but there was something McKenna had to know before he could talk to him. "Take the towel away and let me see it," he said to the cop.

The cop did as he was told, and McKenna leaned over Jake and took a look at the wounds, with Jake screaming over and over, "I almost got him for you, McKenna!"

McKenna saw that Jake had two cuts on the side of his neck and one of them was long, but not deep. Bright red venous blood seeped from both wounds, which heartened McKenna and led him to conclude that Jake was going to live if he received a transfusion and the bleeding was stopped. If the blood had been dark red arterial blood and had been squirting from Jake's wounds, McKenna knew it would have been a different story and good-bye Jake. Though Jake was badly injured, McKenna thought the homeless man was just as mad as he was hurt.

This looks too sloppy to be Hector's work, McKenna thought. Do we have our first copycat case lying here? he wondered.

"Did you see who cut you, Jake?" he asked.

"Sure I did. Almost got the prick for you, McKenna," Jake screamed.

"What was he wearing?"

"A suit. The prick was wearing a suit."

"Did you notice anything special about his face?"

"Couldn't see his face too good. The low-life cowardly prick was hiding behind a beard."

Damn! We're sitting up here planning to get him and he's outside getting us, McKenna thought. "Where, Jake? Where did it happen?" he screamed, almost as loud as Jake.

"Behind the synagogue. The cowardly prick tried to kill me behind the synagogue while I was sleeping."

"What synagogue, Jake?"

"The one by the park. By Gramercy Park."

The news stunned McKenna. He knew the location well. Hector had tried to kill Jake just two blocks from the 13th Precinct and across the park from the Gramercy Park Hotel, where he lived. "How long ago, Jake?"

"Minutes. Just minutes. I came right here to tell you, wouldn't let anyone stop me."

"Jake, did he have a car?"

"I don't know. Didn't see one."

"One more question, Jake, and then you're on the way to the hospital. Do you know someone named Chingo, kind of a short guy?"

"Of course I know him. Know him for years. Big-mouth little Filipino shit."

So that's how Hector knew where to find him, McKenna concluded. Chingo told him where Jake slept at night. There was lots of work to be done, and it had to be done fast if this situation was going to be salvaged.

McKenna started with the desk officer, a middle-aged lieutenant who was watching the proceedings with a detached look on his face. "I want this man taken to Bellevue by radio car. I want them notified and I want doctors standing by and waiting for him in the emergency room. I want him in his own room, he gets whatever he wants, and he gets guarded twenty-four hours a day," McKenna said.

The lieutenant didn't move. He just stood staring at McKenna with a confused, shocked look on his face.

"I want it done now, Lieutenant, before my friend bleeds to death on the floor in front of us!" McKenna yelled at the top of his lungs, surprising everyone in the room, including himself.

The desk officer snapped out of it at once. "Yes sir!" he yelled. "Didn't anyone hear the commissioner? Get this poor man to Bellevue!"

Two uniformed cops materialized from McKenna-knew-not-where and picked Jake up. As they rushed him out the door, Jake yelled, "Get that low-life cowardly prick for me, McKenna. Get him and hurt him good for me!"

"I will, Jake. Don't worry about it, I will," McKenna yelled back as the doors closed. He saw that the switchboard operator was talking frantically on the phone, to Bellevue, McKenna assumed. But he wasn't done with the desk officer yet. "Lieutenant, I want a crime scene established at that synagogue as soon as you can," he told the desk officer in a normal speaking voice.

"Yes sir. Consider it done."

The lieutenant picked up his phone and McKenna turned his attention to Tavlin. He found that the chief was staring at him with bemused interest. "He's gonna run now, Chief, and he's got a fifteen-minute head start on us," McKenna stated.

"I agree. What do you think should be done now?"

McKenna opened his mouth to speak, but Tavlin held up his hand, stopping him. The chief motioned the Homicide Squad sergeant over and said, "Take this down."

"Yes sir," the sergeant said, then took out his notepad and pen and readied himself to write.

"First of all, I want the descriptions and the plate numbers of that Mercedes and that Cherokee broadcast citywide," McKenna said. "I also want it to go to the Port Authority Police at all the bridges and tunnels, I want it to go to the New Jersey State Police, I want it to go to the Connecticut State Police, and I want it to go to every police department in those two states that are big enough to have a phone number. Got it?"

"Uh-huh," the sergeant answered, writing furiously.

"If either of those two cars are spotted, I want all the pursuit rules suspended. I want that car stopped and I don't care if they have to do a kamikaze and ram him to do it."

"Got it. Pursuit rules out the window," the sergeant said.

"I want the Jersey troopers waiting for us at Oldwick to get out of sight, but they're to be on the lookout for those cars, just in case he goes home for something before he skips."

"Got it. Alert Oldwick."

"I want men at every ticket counter and terminal at Newark, Kennedy, and La Guardia Airports. I want them all to have the sketch, with and without the beard."

"Got it. All airports."

"I want that Park Avenue apartment hit right now, and I want the area staked out in case he shows up there."

"Park Avenue done now. Got it."

"I miss anything?" McKenna asked Tavlin.

"I hope not, because you just doubled or tripled the number of men working on this case," Tavlin answered. Then he turned to the sergeant. "Get the PC at home. Use my name, get men called in on overtime, and pull whatever stunts you can think of, but get it all done," he ordered.

"Yes sir." The sergeant turned and disappeared at a trot into the stairwell.

"What now?" Tavlin asked.

"I don't think he's going there, but we are," McKenna said. "Oldwick, as fast as we can get there."

51 Tavlin led the caravan, with McKenna seated next to him mumbling his special ninety-mile-per-hour prayer. As they sped west on I-78, McKenna concluded between prayers that anyone traveling in a black Mercedes or a green Cherokee was going to be late to wherever they were going. All along the route, they passed cops from New Jersey police departments large and small, and most had a black Mercedes or a green Cherokee pulled over. They had passed so many by the time they reached the Oldwick exit that McKenna was sure that Hector wasn't in New Jersey or that he was using a different car, one they didn't know about.

Waiting for them in a gas station next to the interstate exit was a single New Jersey State Police car. One of the troopers got out of the car as the NYPD caravan filled the gas station parking lot. McKenna and Tavlin got out of their car and the trooper came over and introduced himself as Major Coswell. McKenna gave him copies of the arrest warrant for Hector and the search warrant for the Oldwick estate. Coswell gave them a cursory glance, took in the caravan once again, and asked McKenna, "Is there a war on or something?"

"No, we just like to overdo things. It's sort of our reputation."

"Well-deserved reputation, I see."

"Yes, it is," McKenna said, hoping Coswell would let it rest there.

Coswell was a gentleman, and he did. "I understand that this is your case and that we're just here to lend an official presence, but I hope there's not going to be lot of noise or things getting broken at the Suarez estate."

"Sounds like you like the place," McKenna observed.

"What's not to like?" Coswell asked. "Wait'll you see it. You'll agree."

"Ever been any trouble there?"

"Never. I've been living in this town most of my life and that house has been in the Suarez family as long as I can remember. They aren't the troublemaking type."

"Do you know any of the occupants?" McKenna asked.

"Never met the doctor, if that's what you're asking."

"How about Carmen?"

"Haven't seen her since she was a little girl. Years ago I used to see her father and her around town every once in a while, but they never spent a lot of time here and I don't exactly travel in their social circles. I take it the family only used the house when the old man had business in New York."

"Does anybody in town know the doctor?"

"I'm sure somebody must, but I don't know who. He didn't practice here and Carmen only used the house from time to time after her father died."

"Is there a staff at the house?"

"Used to be quite a few when Carmen was little and they had the horses, but now it's just the housekeeper."

"Do you know the housekeeper?"

"Don't know her name, but I know she's not from around here, originally."

"Does she have a car?" McKenna asked.

"I don't know," Coswell answered.

"Then let's find out," McKenna said. He and Tavlin got back in their car and the NYPD units followed Coswell's car through town and over winding country roads. Then Coswell made a left down a private road and the house came into view, set in the middle of acres of lawn.

McKenna's first impression was that the house didn't belong in New Jersey. Rather, he thought it belonged on a hill overlooking the Rhine, a point of interest for the folks on the château tour in the boats below. There was enough moonlight for him to make out a massive central three-story structure with a conical-roofed five-story tower on each corner. On one side of the house stood a separate three-car garage and on the other was a long stable. There was only one light on in the house, in a corner room on the second floor.

The road ended in a circular driveway in front of the house. By the time Tavlin stopped the car at the front door, the entire circular driveway was filled with police vehicles from end to end. "How many bedrooms, do you think?" Tavlin asked McKenna.

"I don't know. Twenty or thirty, I guess," McKenna answered. "If he's in there and he wanted to hide, it'd take us a long time to find him."

"Let's see," Tavlin said. He and McKenna got out of the car and met Coswell at the massive front door. Then Tavlin set about the business of securing the area around the house so that Hector wouldn't be able to leave unnoticed. Tavlin told the detectives to wait for him at the front door, then he walked around to the side of the house, followed by Coswell, McKenna, and an entourage of Emergency Service cops.

There was a side door that led to the garage. Tavlin posted two Emergency Service cops there, then asked McKenna if he wanted to search the garage before the house.

"No, we can do that later, but I want to just take a peek inside first," McKenna answered. He opened the side door of the garage and turned on the light.

There were two cars inside: a late-model black Mercedes and an older Jeep Cherokee. Both cars were covered with a fine coat of dust, but McKenna went over and felt the hoods anyway. Both were cold. He shut off the lights and rejoined Tavlin on his tour.

There was a rear door leading to the pool and cabana and another door on the other side of the house that led to the stable. Tavlin posted Emergency Service cops at all the doors, then had the searchlight trucks bathe the house in light from front and rear.

Seconds after the searchlights went on, McKenna could hear the helicopter approaching overhead. Coswell said nothing, but gave McKenna an inquisitive look.

"Please don't ask," McKenna said, and Coswell didn't.

It took a second stroll around the house before the chief was satisfied with the placement of his men. When they rejoined the detectives waiting at the front door, Tavlin turned to McKenna. "Ready?" he asked.

McKenna nodded and Coswell rang the front doorbell. There was no answer, so after a minute Coswell rang it again. Still no answer for another minute, then they saw lights coming on inside the house. A large, heavyset woman in her sixties, dressed in a nightgown and robe, opened the door. Her face went from anger to confusion when she saw all the detectives and uniformed cops at the door and the searchlights outside.

"Good evening, ma'am," Coswell said. "I'm Major Coswell from the state police. We have warrants to search these premises and arrest Dr. De la Cruz. Is he in?"

The housekeeper gave no answer, so Coswell offered her the warrants. She took them in her hand, then fainted dead away. Tavlin and Coswell managed to catch her on the way down and they carried her inside, but didn't know what to do with her for a moment. They were in an enormous hallway ending in a grand staircase. On each side of the hallway were closed double doors.

McKenna opened one of them and found that they were the doors to a large, formal sitting room. He stood back, giving Coswell and Tavlin room to carry the housekeeper in. They laid her on a couch and Coswell fanned her until she opened her eyes. Then a detective came in carrying a glass of water in one hand and an envelope in the other. He gave the glass of water to Coswell and the envelope to McKenna.

"Where did you get this?" McKenna asked.

"It was on the kitchen table," the detective answered.

The envelope was neatly addressed to *Mrs. Sweeney*. McKenna opened it and read the note inside while Coswell held up Mrs. Sweeney's head and gave her the water.

"Well?" Tavlin asked.

"Says he went to Bethlehem to see a movie and that he'd be home late," McKenna answered, passing the note to Tavlin.

In another moment, Mrs. Sweeney recovered sufficiently to swing her legs off the couch and sit up. She took in the group of men in the room with her, then directed herself to Coswell. "Could you tell me what this is about?" she asked.

"These men are detectives from New York City," he said. "They're here to search this house and arrest the doctor."

Mrs. Sweeney reacted as if she were hearing it for the first time. "Arrest the doctor? What for?"

"Have you heard about all the homeless people being poisoned in New York City this month?" McKenna asked.

"Yes, I've heard about it," she answered, becoming more alert by the moment.

"Dr. De la Cruz is the one who's been poisoning them," McKenna said.

"Impossible," Mrs. Sweeney said, standing up. "I want you people out of here right this minute."

"Mrs. Sweeney, we're not leaving until we search this entire house," McKenna said patiently. "Major Coswell has given you the warrants and everything is quite legal."

Mrs. Sweeney looked down at her hands and was surprised to see that she was holding the warrants.

"I know it's difficult for you to believe, Mrs. Sweeney, but the doctor has murdered at least thirteen people. We're sure of that. Then, tonight, he tried to cut the throat of another homeless man in New York City. That was about an hour and a half ago," McKenna explained.

"Impossible," Mrs. Sweeney repeated, but with less conviction. "He was up in his room when I went to bed."

"And what time was that?" McKenna asked.

"Nine-thirty, same as always."

McKenna nodded to Tavlin and the chief gave her the note. She read it and began to understand.

"How long has he been staying here?" McKenna asked.

"Do I have to tell you?"

"No, not at this moment. But if you don't, I will find a judge within an hour who will order your arrest as a material witness," McKenna said, taking a page out of Maureen's book. "Then you will be held in jail until a grand jury convenes in this case. I wouldn't like that and neither would you, so telling me what I need to know right now would be easier for both of us."

"You're that detective that's been on TV all week, aren't you?" Mrs. Sweeney asked.

Famous even in New Jersey, McKenna thought. How can that help me out with this difficult woman? "Yes, that was me. Unfortunately, the media is very interested in this case and I'm sure they'll want to talk to you, once they find out we're looking for the doctor."

"Am I going to be on TV?" she asked.

"Only if you want to be. They'd want to make you into the next Kato."

"That would be terrible," Mrs Sweeney said, but she didn't look like she thought it would be so terrible. "You know, this is very hard to believe. I've known the doctor for six or seven years and he seemed like such a fine man."

"From everything I know about him, he was a fine man," McKenna assured her. "Now he's sick and I believe that sickness has caused him to do some crazy things. Now he's a murderer and he has to be stopped."

"What do you want to know?" she asked.

"When did the doctor first come here to stay?"

"November fourteenth. Came by himself, looking terrible. He's got cancer."

"Has he been out of the house a lot?"

"Yes. He goes to his office in New York sometimes and he likes to go to those Spanish movies at night."

"Do you have a car?"

"Yes, but it's really not mine. It belongs to the house."

"But it's registered in your name?"

"Yes."

"What kind of car is it?"

"A Buick station wagon. Brown. It's a '94, I think."

"Does the doctor use that car?"

"Yes, whenever he goes out. I don't know why, but he likes it better than the Mercedes or the Jeep."

"I know why. Do you know the license plate number?"

"No. The registration is in the car."

"What's your first name and your date of birth, Mrs. Sweeney?" McKenna asked.

Mrs. Sweeney looked reluctant to give up that information, but she did. "Anabel. June 14th, 1930."

McKenna took out his cellular phone and called the detective dispatcher in New York. A minute later he knew that Mrs. Sweeney's car was a 1994 brown

Buick station wagon, New Jersey registration JSG 334. He instructed the dispatcher to put out a nationwide alarm on the car and to cancel the alarms for the Mercedes and the Jeep. When he finished, he returned his attention to Mrs. Sweeney. "How long have you been working here?" he asked.

"Since 1955."

"Do they treat you good?"

"Can't complain. When Carmen was little, the family spent a few summers here and it was a lot of work. You know, with the horses and the gardeners and all. But in the last ten years I don't think the house has been used for more than six months, total. The horses were shipped to Spain and a service takes care of the grounds now."

"So it's an easy job?"

"I manage to stay busy, but it's not a hard job."

"And I imagine you know every nook and cranny of this house?"

"Of course."

"Good. You and I will start with the doctor's room while the rest of these fine detectives look around."

Tavlin was directing the search teams as McKenna followed Mrs. Sweeney upstairs. She made a left at the top of the stairs and continued down a long hallway to a closed door at the end. She knocked, but there was no answer. She opened the door and touched a light switch on the wall.

The room was enormous and furnished in a heavy mahogany. It was more of a suite than a single bedroom, with a dressing room down a short corridor on one side and a bathroom on the other. Dominating the center of the room was a large bed. There was also a couch, a TV, and stereo entertainment center, a small stocked bar, and two dressers. It was a rich man's bedroom.

"Did his wife share this room with him?" McKenna asked.

"Oh, no," Mrs. Sweeney answered. "Carmen always had her own bedroom. It's at the other end of the hall."

Strange the way rich people live, McKenna thought. Then he spied a white envelope placed atop the pillow on the bed. With a sense of foreboding, he went over and picked up the envelope. *DETECTIVE McKENNA* was written on the outside in Hector's hand; he felt something stiff inside, and dropped it back on the bed. He turned to Mrs. Sweeney and said, "Please wait here, but don't touch anything."

McKenna left her there and returned minutes later with Tavlin and a Bomb Squad detective leading his leashed bomb-sniffing dog. "First have him check out that letter on the bed, then do the rest of the room," McKenna told the detective.

It didn't take long. The detective led the dog to the letter and got no reaction. Then he said, "Search," and let go of the leash. The dog pranced around the bedroom, the dressing room, and the bathroom, sniffing everywhere before he returned to his handler.

"There's not gonna be a lot of noise in here," the detective said as he leashed his dog.

"Thank you. That'll be all," Tavlin told him and the detective left with his dog.

With Tavlin and Mrs. Sweeney watching, McKenna picked up the envelope and opened it. There were a letter and a computer disk inside. Written on the disk label was *Mariposas*. He handed the disk to Tavlin and opened the letter.

"What does *mariposas* mean?" Tavlin asked.

"It's Spanish for butterflies. He's decided to help us out with the enzyme," McKenna answered before reading the letter. It said:

Dear Detective McKenna,

Since you are reading this, you deserve to be congratulated once again and I heartily do so. Although you have forced me to alter my plans to a certain degree, your involvement in this affair has provided me with unexpected pleasure. Ordinarily, I would look forward to our meeting someday, but I don't know if we ever will.

As a consolation prize and to save the fine taxpayers of New York the research expenses you were planning for them, I have enclosed the disk that documents my discovery of a new subspecies of passion vine butterfly and research I've done on the habits and characteristics of this remarkable creature. I hope you will forgive my vanity, but, as is my right, I have named it Heliconius hectorius.

In return for this favor, please have your men refrain from disturbing the house too much as my wife had no knowledge of my activities here and she needs no further problems. I'm certain that she will now be hearing from you and the media regarding my activities here and that alone will disturb her deeply and mar her reputation. Try to understand her position and be gentle with her. I predict you will find, as I have, that she is an exceptional lady.

As a favor to me, please thank Mrs. Sweeney for making my stay here as comfortable as she possibly could, under the circumstances. Beneath that rough exterior is a heart of gold. Under the pillow you will find $5,000. Please give it to her with my thanks and apologies and tell her that the Mercedes is hers until my wife can arrange a replacement car for the Buick, as I am sure she will.

With Warmest Regards,
Hector De la Cruz

McKenna was surprised to find that there was another page, and he read that one also. It said:

Dear Detective McKenna,

I expect that you will keep the preceding letter as some kind of evidence and that it will become a matter of public record. At the risk of being impolite and intrusive, I am enclosing this letter for your eyes only and will always deny its existence to save you any embarrassment.

Involving that private investigator was a master stroke on your part, so I hate to be critical. However, I think it would appear to the discerning viewer that both he and Heidi Lane were dying to divulge a secret they shared. Because of that, and considering myself that discerning viewer, you are reading this note in my absence.

I admit that the involvement of that very pretty lady in this affair makes me wonder exactly what is going on between you and her, but I leave that to you and your conscience with one word of advice. Fidelity in marriage isn't an option; it is a requirement.

The truth in that simple statement came hard to me and I hope you can profit from my misfortune. As you might have learned or guessed by now, I violated that dictum and am now a victim of my own infidelity. However, I don't fault God. As you know, I fault man.

Hector De la Cruz

As McKenna finished the letter, he was so deep in thought that he had forgotten he wasn't alone until Mrs. Sweeney asked, "What does he say?"

McKenna passed the letters to Tavlin and then he looked under the pillow. He found the wrapped packet of one-hundred-dollar bills and gave it to a very surprised Mrs. Sweeney. "Hector says to thank you for being so kind to him and he asked me to give you this," McKenna said.

"This is mine?"

"Yes. He also asked me to tell you that he's sorry he took your Buick, but you're to use the Mercedes until his wife can arrange another car for you."

"What a nice man!" she said.

"Yes, it would appear so," McKenna said dryly.

As Tavlin read the letters, McKenna sat down on the bed. The old supervisory axiom "Praise in public, criticize in private," entered his mind; that was exactly what Hector had done. For the world to see, he had praised McKenna's ingenuity and congratulated him. Privately, in the second letter, Hector had admonished McKenna for giving Heidi too much information, and, although the doctor hadn't spelled it out, he obviously suspected infidelity on McKenna's part. To make matters worse, Hector credited his escape as a side benefit of that infidelity.

What could I have done differently? McKenna asked himself. I didn't involve Heidi like he thinks. At first she was just sharp enough to involve herself and gain more information than I ever wanted to give her. But then I let her do that Hurley interview, and, because of that, Hector got wise and got away.

Or so he says, McKenna thought, reexamining the events of the evening. Hector left that note for Mrs. Sweeney, so it's probable he intended to come back this evening and we would have gotten him, Hurley interview or not. Maybe he was planning on leaving soon, but what caused him to flee tonight was his botched attempt on Jake. He's real careful and maybe he figured someone saw him at the synagogue. Maybe Jake was screaming, so he dumped the car and left according to some backup plan of his. But how and where?

By the time Tavlin had finished reading, McKenna .had finished his self-recriminations. "Nothing to say?" McKenna asked.

"I saw that interview on TV tonight. Maybe I might have had something to say, but I don't anymore."

"Why not?"

"Because Brunette saw it, too. He called me up and told me it was entirely appropriate. That's good enough for me."

Ray understands why I gave Heidi that break, but he saw a tip-off in it, too, McKenna thought. Now I wish I'd seen that interview myself. Then maybe I would have come right here, warrant or no warrant.

Tavlin wasn't going to waste any time on it. "Let's finish up this room," he said.

Tavlin searched the closet for the black clothing while McKenna went through Hector's dresser drawers. He stopped to examine a framed photo on the dresser. A woman he assumed to be Carmen and a healthy Hector were standing together somewhere in a jungle, and smiling with their arms around each other. McKenna concluded that, even in his best days, Hector wasn't much to look at, but Carmen Maria was another matter. She radiated class as well as beauty.

McKenna found nothing else of interest in the room and neither did Tavlin. "We're still a move behind while Hector's planning eight moves ahead," Mc-Kenna said.

"What do you mean, eight moves ahead?" Tavlin asked.

"Along with a lot of other things, he's a chess grand master and that's what they do. Plan eight moves ahead while we're wasting time here reacting to his last move."

"So what do we do now?"

"Let's finish up here and get to the Park Avenue apartment. I'm sure there's nothing here he wouldn't want us to see."

The search became a whirlwind affair after that, with detectives just looking for Hector under the beds and in the closets of the twenty-two bedrooms. Mrs. Sweeney reluctantly admitted Tavlin and McKenna to Carmen's bedroom at the opposite end of the hall from Hector's.

Architecturally, Carmen's bedroom was a mirror image of Hector's, but that was where the similarity ended. Where his bedroom was masculine, hers was unmistakably feminine. The colors were soft pastels and the bedspread on the huge double bed was trimmed in pink lace. On one dresser was a photo history of Carmen's life. There were pictures of her as a child, pictures of her riding horses, and pictures of people McKenna assumed to be her father, mother, brother, and her first husband, the Austrian count. There were also pictures of her and Hector in various places around the world, always in the same pose, smiling, standing side by side, with their arms around each other. McKenna gave each of them a cursory glance until one of the photos stopped him and riveted him in place.

It was a photo of Hector and Carmen in the familiar pose, with a twin-engine aircraft behind them and the skyline of Manhattan in the distance. McKenna recognized the place at once and a large piece of the puzzle suddenly fit. Hector and Carmen were standing in front of their plane in Teterboro Airport in New Jersey, the place where the rich kept their more expensive toys.

"Chief, get that helicopter down," McKenna said to Tavlin.

52 McKenna and Tavlin were in the air for ten minutes before they learned that they were an hour late. The NYPD copilot had contacted the Teterboro control tower and was told that Hector had filed a flight plan for Chicago and had left in his family's twin-engine Beech King Air at 1:05 A.M. The plane had been fully fueled, bringing it to its maximum range of 1,400 miles. The tower said that the plane had disappeared from the Teterboro radar screen at 1:15 A.M. still headed west on the flight plan for Chicago.

"Where do you think he's headed?" Tavlin asked McKenna upon receiving the news from the copilot.

"Not Chicago, that's for sure. South, I would guess, toward Costa Rica. He'll be flying low, but he's got enough fuel to take him to someplace in Florida or Texas."

Tavlin told the copilot to call back the Teterboro Airport and get the registration number for Hector's plane. When the copilot gave it to him, Tavlin called the detective dispatcher and instructed her to transmit an alarm on Hector's plane. Then he gave her the big order, and McKenna had no idea exactly what she would have to do to comply with it. Tavlin told her that he wanted local police standing by and on the lookout for Hector and his plane at every private airport within 1,500 miles of New York City. But he was a chief, so all she said was, "Yes sir. Anything else?"

"Yes. Please have a car standing by to pick us up at the East 34th Street Heliport," Tavlin said, and hung up. "The East 34th Street Heliport, and get a move on!" Tavlin yelled to the pilot.

It's wonderful being the chief, McKenna thought again as the acceleration pushed him back into his seat.

Half an hour later McKenna and Tavlin walked into Ward's office and found that Brunette was also there. McKenna gave him Hector's letters and Brunette read them.

"Pretty smug bastard, isn't he?" was Brunette's only comment as he folded up the letters.

Next, Tavlin reported on the evening's events and the steps he had implemented to apprehend Hector when he landed.

"That's throwing a pretty wide net," Brunette said, then turned to McKenna. "Can you think of anything else to do?" he asked.

"Knowing Hector De la Cruz like I'm beginning to know him, I'd say that he already has his own landing strip picked out and set up. He's either got more fuel there or a car gassed up and ready to go."

"To where? Costa Rica?"

"I think so. From what Hurley tells me, he probably thinks he'd be safe there."

"Good," Brunette said, surprising everybody but McKenna. He had given the matter a lot of thought and was gratified that Brunette had apparently reached the same conclusions.

McKenna thought it time to say something. "He might get to Costa Rica, but don't worry too much about that. I'll get him no matter where he goes."

Brunette gave McKenna a quizzical smile. "Even though we have no extradition treaty with Costa Rica?"

"Yes, of course."

"Thanks. That's what I wanted to hear," Brunette said, smiling broadly. "I knew I could count on you."

McKenna smiled back and the two of them enjoyed the joke until Tavlin asked, "Would one of you mind explaining this to me?"

"Should I?" Brunette asked McKenna.

"Please do."

"The important thing is that Hector De la Cruz is a mass murderer who will not live to trial, no matter where he's arrested. So if he makes it to Costa Rica, we're going to go public with our case against him and get folks in a real hanging mood. A formal request will be made to the Costa Rican government for Hector's arrest and extradition, which, I believe, they'll refuse," Brunette said, nodding in McKenna's direction.

"Yes, in the case of Hector De la Cruz, they'll refuse it, and they'll be within their rights under international law. So then I'll go down to Costa Rica, find Hector, and arrest him. Then I'll march him into their local police station, hopefully under the glare of the cameras from a member of our friendly local press."

"What good will that do?" Ward asked. "They'll set Hector free and lock you up, probably for kidnapping."

"Of course they will," Brunette agreed. "But as far as this department is concerned, we have an arrest in the case of the worst serial killer in the history of this city, and we'd be ready, willing, and able to demonstrate how likely a conviction would be. Case closed."

"So what happens? Hector's free until he dies?" Ward asked.

"Yes, unless McKenna can convince their government to change their minds about extradition. Hopefully, he won't succeed in that endeavor."

Now Brunette really had Ward going. "Hopefully he won't succeed? Why *hopefully*?" he asked.

"Because even though we can prove that he's as guilty as sin, he's cleverly built himself up quite a number of good defenses and a lot of sympathy. Even if he were to be extradited and live through trial, the chances are that he'd be acquitted by one of our juries and he'd walk out a free man. Then we lose and all our work means nothing."

Ward just shook his head for a few minutes as he pondered Brunette's interpretation of events. Then he said, "Okay, maybe I agree. But what about McKenna? What happens to him while all this is going on?"

"Why, he'll be in jail, of course," Brunette said.

"And you agree with all this?" Ward asked McKenna.

"Of course."

"Why, if you don't mind my asking?"

"Because we're planning eight moves ahead and we're gonna beat him. We're off the defensive and we're gonna give him a surprise he didn't foresee. He loses, and he won't die a hero. He'll die a cowardly villain who didn't face the music."

"But you'll be in jail," Ward said, unable to get accustomed to the idea.

"Yes, but it won't be so bad. At least I'll be beating the cold. I hear the weather's real nice down there," McKenna said, then laughed.

"Pardon me, but I don't see the humor in that," Ward said.

"Brian will be in some kind of jail, but it won't be that bad for him," Brunette said. "As a matter of fact, I think they'll make him quite comfortable. Don't forget, he's very popular here and he's just doing his duty as he sees it. Costa Rica's a free country and I'm sure they'll give him plenty of access to the press."

"Why would they do all that for someone who broke their laws and kidnapped one of their most popular citizens?"

"Because they're not stupid. Their economy is booming because of American tourist dollars and I foresee some kind of 'Boycott Costa Rica' campaign if they get too cranky with Brian. I've done some research on this, so consider the fact that they receive thirty-some-odd million dollars in foreign aid from us. I'll make sure that our government brings some pressure on them to keep him comfortable."

"But not to free him?" Ward asked.

"Of course not. All the time he's in jail we'll be crying to our press and he'll be talking to theirs."

"So what's the resolution, since we really don't want Hector back to stand trial?"

"They have to be permitted to save face and not knuckle under to the *Yanquis*," Brunette explained. "It ends when Hector dies or when they tell us that he's too sick to travel. Whenever they tell us that, we'd be ready to believe them as long as they keep him out of sight."

"And then they free Brian?"

"Yes, then we'll earnestly press for his release, they'll gladly free him, and he'll reluctantly come home to do the paperwork closing his case. Of course, I'll have to publicly give him some kind of medal," Brunette said.

"You mean something like a Distinguished Foreign Service Cross with Jailbird Cluster?" Tavlin asked.

"Something like that," Brunette answered. "What do you gentlemen think of this?"

"Before I answer that, am I to understand that you both independently came up with the assessment of this situation and the resulting scheme?" Tavlin asked.

"I don't know," Brunette said, then turned to McKenna. "Brian, have I said anything that wasn't already on your mind?" he asked.

"A few things. I didn't know about the foreign aid, so I hadn't thought of that angle. And to tell you the truth, I hadn't thought about bringing anybody from our media along when I lock Hector up, but I like it."

"I'm assuming you now have someone in mind?" Tavlin asked.

"Yes," McKenna answered simply, not wanting to expound on that subject. "Everything else the commissioner said has been on my mind since Hurley suggested to me that he thought Hector would make a break for Costa Rica."

"And it also came to you both independently that we would lose this case at trial if De la Cruz were arrested here and lived that long?" Tavlin asked dubiously.

McKenna looked to Brunette for help, but Brunette gave him the nod to continue. "No," McKenna admitted. "We had discussed that aspect of the case."

That was good enough for Tavlin. "Glad to hear that. For a moment there I thought I was looking at two bodies sharing the same brain."

"So tell me now. What do you think of the scheme, as you call it?" Brunette said.

"If I understand it correctly, as long as McKenna is willing to go to jail down there, then when and if Hector succeeds in escaping to Costa Rica, he's made a monumental error in planning by playing right into our hands. He'd be escaping to one of the few countries on earth where we could convict him without danger of losing at trial."

"You understand it as we understand it," Brunette said.

"He loses and we win. Of course I like it," Tavlin said. "I should have expected something very unusual was up when I saw you here at two-thirty in the morning."

"Really? I was in the neighborhood and decided to drop in on the search team at the Park Avenue apartment," Brunette explained innocently.

"And how did that go?" McKenna asked.

"Not too good, at first. No one was there and the place was locked up like Fort Knox. Fortunately, the concierge had the number of the alarm response company for the apartment and we got them there with the keys."

"Had Hector been there?" McKenna asked.

"No. According to the concierge, not in at least a year. It's quite a place, takes up two entire floors in the building, but what I loved was the decor. Hanging in frames covering every wall of the study was a butterfly collection that would make any museum proud. We took the whole thing and delivered it to the lab. I'm betting that *Heliconius hectorius* is represented there."

"With some luck, we'll have an airtight case built up against Hector," McKenna said. "It'll be fun telling the Costa Rican press their hero Hector has been using lethal butterflies from their country to kill our poor citizens."

Brunette looked like he was about to say something when there was a knock at the door. Kenny Bender came in and announced, "Good news and bad news, Commissioner. The Buick was found outside the Port Authority Bus Terminal."

"Makes sense," Brunette said. "After Hector screwed up with Jake, he knew we'd be watching the tunnels. So he dumped the car and took a taxi to Teterboro. What's the bad news?"

"Just got a report from the dispatcher that there's been a bum attacked in Brooklyn. The perps cut him while he was sleeping in Prospect Park, then they set him on fire. He's still alive, but he's in bad shape with burns. Got a fireman burned pretty bad, too."

"Any witnesses?" Brunette asked.

"The fireman's the witness. He was breaking the rules and doing some grocery shopping for the firehouse when he saw the fire and some skinheads running away. Pretty amazing, but he put the fire out by smothering it with his own body."

Brunette immediately turned to Tavlin and said, "It's started, but I want it stopped now. We're going to Battle Stations. I want one hundred detectives working on this case within the next hour and two hundred by morning."

"Yes sir. I'll take care of it," Tavlin said. Then he turned and left the office with Bender.

"What do you want me to do?" McKenna asked.

"Go home and get some sleep. You look exhausted."

"You don't need me?" McKenna asked.

"Not for this end of it. This is only peripheral to your case and I want you thinking only 'Hector.' For that I need you well rested and bright-eyed."

"Whatever you say. See you tomorrow," McKenna said. He quietly slipped out the door, happy with the knowledge that he might be the only detective in the Bureau who was going to be sleeping through the night.

53

Sunday, February 4   **Gramercy Park Hotel**

By seven-thirty the next morning, McKenna was dressed and enjoying his first cup of coffee while he watched the news on New York 1, the local news channel. He learned that four arrests had been made in the Prospect Park incident. The victim, identified as Moon Rivers, had died during the night at the Jacobi Hospital Burn Center. Joe Lavin, the fireman and new local hero who had tried to save his life, was also at the burn center, in satisfactory condition.

The cameras then cut away to the 78th Precinct in Brooklyn and the four prisoners were shown being led out of the station house for their trip to Central Booking and arraignment. They were an unusual-looking crew, four white men with shaved heads, earrings, nose rings, and tattoos on their hands and necks. They were dressed in prison coveralls, looking unafraid and defiant.

McKenna knew better and had seen it all before, many times. They had been through a life-changing experience, a scared night of crying, pleading, and lying. He was sure they had been tough when they had first been brought in, making snide remarks and proclaiming their innocence while smirking at each other. Then they had been separated and made to understand that what they had thought was a prank was murder. They had taken a human life, and because of that their own lives were over. Maybe.

They would have grabbed at straws. In the end, McKenna was sure that each of them had minimized his own role in the murder while pointing the finger at the other three. Each of them would have said it wasn't his idea and he didn't know what his friends were going to do. He was just there, an almost-innocent bystander.

Then came the Ray Brunette Show. He made his angry statement from inside the station house, describing the homeless victim as a forty-year-old black man who was bothering no one as he slept at his usual place near the southwest entrance of Prospect Park. At 2:00 A.M., four persons he described at various points during his statement as "cold, calculating miscreants" and the "scum of the neighborhood" crept up on him, woke him up, beat and taunted him, cut his throat, set him on fire with lighter fluid, and left him for dead. He praised Firefighter Lavin and said he had assisted in the investigation. When asked how the arrests had resulted so quickly, he credited a massive and rapid deployment of detectives and the complete cooperation of the community.

Then came the question McKenna had been waiting for. The interviewer asked Brunette if he thought this would be a death-penalty case and the PC had answered, "Of course. If the DA doesn't put these worthless, murderous, hate-filled miscreants on trial for their lives, then he's not the man I think he is."

No further questions or commentary were necessary to get Brunette's opinion on the crime and the people who committed it, so he simply smiled at the reporters and walked away from the lectern.

Then it was Jake's turn. New York 1 reported the details of the attack on him in Manhattan and interviewed him at Bellevue. He had bandages around his neck and was sitting up in his hospital bed, looking better than McKenna remembered him. He described the attack on him behind the synagogue and confided to the interviewer that he was sure his pal Detective McKenna was going to get the killer.

After Jake's interview, two sketches of Hector filled the screen, both with and without the beard. He was identified as a Park Avenue socialite doctor wanted in connection with the attack on Jake and the murders of thirteen homeless men during the month. The failed Oldwick raid wasn't mentioned.

McKenna surmised that either Ray or Tavlin had given the killer's identity to the press, but little else. There was nothing reported about his nationality or his marriage to Carmen, which didn't surprise him. McKenna figured the press would soon be given all the details as part of an orchestrated campaign to turn public opinion totally against Hector De la Cruz, discredit his motives, and dismiss his generosity as nothing more than an apparent ploy to curry public favor. That was step one of the plan to isolate him and set him up for the checkmate.

After he finished his coffee, McKenna called Brunette's cellular number. "Catch the news?" Brunette asked.

"Yeah. Was it a tough night?" McKenna asked.

"Naw, nothing to it once I got enough people there. They woke up the neighborhood looking for witnesses, but nobody saw anything. The main problem was that a lot of them knew the victim. Rivers isn't exactly the saint I made him out to be. He made a regular pain in the ass out of himself in the neighborhood, hanging out in front of the stores with an aggressive kind of panhandling attitude. Nobody we talked to who knew him had anything nice to say about him. Some folks even told us, 'Good riddance.' "

"Was the fireman any help?"

"Lavin? He was the key. He was able to give us some general descriptions, so we knew we were looking for skinheads. Turned out that was all we needed. The Seven-eight Squad has had some dealings with a bunch of them, so we went to visit one of the dirtbags at home. He still smelled like lighter fluid, so after that it was easy. Got a search warrant for the place and found the victim's wallet. Then he fessed up and gave up his pals."

"Were they as tough as they looked?"

"Babies. Went through a couple of boxes of Kleenex while they were ratting each other out."

"How about Hector? Any news on him?" McKenna asked.

"Nothing, no sign of the plane. I had to give his name to the press, but we have to talk before we give them any more."

"I understand. When?"

"Twelve o'clock at the Seventeenth good for you?"

"Good enough. I'm meeting Maureen at a soup kitchen at Saint Bart's today and I'm going to introduce myself to Ben Rosen, if he's there."

"Why Saint Bart's?"

"Because Maureen cooks there every Sunday."

"I'll be damned! I love that lady," Brunette said.

"Me too. Anyway, I'm gonna try to get Rosen on board for whatever you're planning to do with the homeless."

"I'm not sure what I want to do yet," Brunette admitted. "I'm hoping this copycat madness is over, but I don't want to take a chance. I'd like to get them all off the streets for the next couple of nights."

"And do what with them?" McKenna asked. "The shelters can't hold them all."

"I don't know, exactly. Maybe the armories, but I'll have to talk to the mayor about that first. Meanwhile, be nice to Rosen and explain our position to him so he doesn't leave you and head straight to court for an injunction. You can tell him I'm gonna assign cops to the shelters for the next couple of days since that's one of the things he always wanted."

"I'll try."

54 McKenna arrived in the basement of St. Bartholomew's Church a little late at 8:15. The place was already crowded with hundreds of homeless people there for the meal, and it looked like a good one to McKenna. He saw they had eggs cooked to order, sausage, bacon, hash, home-fried potatoes, toast, orange juice, and coffee. The service was complete with a host of volunteers acting as waiters and waitresses.

McKenna found Maureen in the kitchen with her apron on at a large griddle, filling orders and frying up eggs by the dozen. "Glad you could make it," she said, but he could see that she was too busy turning over eggs to chat. She was moving faster than any cook he had ever seen on KP, and so were the other volunteers working the large kitchen.

"What do you want me to do?" he asked, looking around and quickly realizing there was plenty to do. The kitchen was the one of the busiest places he had ever seen. At two other griddles volunteers were cooking the bacon, sausage, hash, and home fries. There was a large rotating toaster, and another volunteer was kept busy doing nothing more than loading in the slices of bread on one side and removing the toast from the other. One volunteer was rinsing off dirty dishes and another loaded the dishwashers. A constant stream of volunteers ran in and out, dropping off dirty dishes and shouting food orders.

"Put on an apron and start cracking eggs."

"Is Ben Rosen here?"

"Sure. Over there, but he's busy," she said, pointing toward the end of the kitchen.

McKenna saw that Rosen was indeed very busy. He was sitting on a stool peeling potatoes like Beetle Bailey, but much faster and with much more enthusiasm. Rosen was a very good man with a knife, working so fast that he kept two volunteers busy slicing his peeled potatoes into home fries.

So McKenna put on an apron and for the next two hours he was busier than he ever remembered being. Every time he got a chance, he looked over toward

Rosen. All the while, Ben Rosen peeled and peeled. The pace started slowing at 10:30 and McKenna got his first break of the morning, he thought. The griddle generated lots of heat and he backed away from it and wiped his face with his apron.

"Tired?" Maureen asked him, the first word she had said although they had just worked side by side for two hours. They had just been too busy for talk.

"No, Maureen. Not tired. Exhausted, but I'll keep it up as long as you do," he answered.

"It's almost over. Then a half hour to clean up and we'll be out of here." She went to the coffeepot, made two cups of coffee, and brought him one.

As they drank their coffee, McKenna glanced over at Rosen's corner and noticed he was gone. "He'll be outside getting things ready for the cleanup," Maureen said.

They finished their coffee, made a few more orders, and then the cooking part was over and the cleaning began. The volunteers were in and out with buckets of water while McKenna and Maureen scrubbed the griddle and mopped the kitchen. Just as everything was finally cleaned to Maureen's satisfaction, Rosen breezed in and gave the kitchen a quick inspection. He appeared satisfied, then offered his hand to McKenna.

Maureen stepped in to make the introductions, but Rosen waved her off. "Not necessary, Maureen," he said. "I've got a TV, so I know who Detective McKenna is, and I guess he knows who I am."

Yeah, this guy's going to be difficult, McKenna thought as he took his measure of Rosen. Looks and acts like Jimmy Cagney, right down to the pugnacious jaw. He shook Rosen's hand. "Of course I know who you are, Mr. Rosen," he said.

"Ben's my name. Not a bad job for a first-timer, Detective McKenna."

"Thank you, Ben, and it's Brian."

"Okay, Brian. What do you think?"

"I think that I'm glad we did this for free, because no one should have to work this hard for money."

Rosen liked the answer and smiled. "After a while you're going to see that working for money isn't as satisfying as working here," he said. "You'll find yourself looking forward to Sundays."

"Really?"

"Give it a try."

"I will," McKenna said. "Same time next Sunday?"

"Now you're talking," Rosen said. "I take it that it's more than coincidence that you decided to help out here today."

"To tell you the truth, I told Maureen I was gonna come and help out even before I found out you usually work here on Sundays."

McKenna could see that Rosen was disappointed at that answer. Play his ego, McKenna reminded himself. "But I have to admit that when I did find out you'd be here, I made coming here this morning a priority."

Rosen's smile was back. "Because you want something from me?" he asked.

"Yes. Everyone tells me you're the expert on the homeless in this city."

"You know, I was wondering when you were going to get in touch with me, especially since Hector De la Cruz was a friend of mine."

Not surprising, McKenna thought. Anyone who cares about the homeless as much as Hector used to would have had to run into Ben Rosen, sooner or later. "When you say he was a friend of yours, I take it you haven't seen him recently," McKenna said.

"No, I haven't seen him in at least a year, but that wasn't exactly what I meant," Rosen said. "What I meant was that if he's doing the things you say he's been doing, then he couldn't possibly be a friend of mine now."

"He is, Ben. Believe me. Hector De la Cruz is the one who murdered those thirteen homeless people."

"Not the Hector I knew. You're going to have to convince me."

"It shouldn't be hard to do," McKenna said.

"Don't be so sure," Maureen said. "Sorry, but I'm not going to hang around for this."

"Why not?" Rosen asked.

"Ben, like I've told you a thousand times, three hours a week is all I can stand of you," Maureen said good-naturedly.

"What did I do wrong today?"

"Nothing, yet. But if I were to see you being less than nice to my friend Brian, I'd have to bite your head off. I know the way you are, so I think it's better for both of us if I don't hang around."

Rosen considered Maureen's argument for a moment. "I guess you're right. I do get to be a pain in the ass at times," he admitted.

Maureen left McKenna to handle Rosen by himself. The two men sat in the dining area sipping coffee while McKenna outlined the case against Hector. As it turned out, convincing Rosen of Hector's guilt was very hard to do. Rosen interrupted frequently with questions only a lawyer would think to ask, questions on the veracity of the witnesses and questions on the admissibility of the evidence. McKenna tried explaining that Chingo and Jake could be presented as truthful witnesses, that the match of Hector's fingerprints with the prints found on the wine bottle was scientifically incontrovertible, and that Dr. Andino would be able to back up his findings as to cause of death by poisoning.

Rosen appeared skeptical after every explanation, leading McKenna to feel he was trying Hector's case before a very unsympathetic jury. "So that's your whole case against Hector?" he asked when McKenna had finished.

"That's it, so far."

"And what's his motive for these murders?"

"I think he's killing the people he thinks are responsible for Juliette's death and, indirectly, his own."

"I don't buy it because I know that man and it doesn't make sense," Rosen said. "He's been kind, compassionate, and generous all his life, especially to the homeless. The guy's a saint and a man like that doesn't throw his values out the window just because he's dying."

"Everything points to it," McKenna insisted. "That's just what he's done."

"And why would he change so? Tell me," Rosen said.

I sure don't want to say this to a lawyer like Rosen, McKenna thought, but I don't see a way out of it. "He's changed because he's gone insane."

"Ah-ha!" Rosen said. "Then he's not guilty. Out of your own mouth, he's not guilty."

"That's just my opinion. His sanity is a matter for a judge and jury to decide, after he's arrested."

"But you agree that, even if you do manage to arrest him, and even if some high-priced attorney doesn't rip your evidence to shreds and get him acquitted altogether, then he'll be found not guilty by reason of insanity if he lives that long."

"Yes, even though he did it, that's the way it'll probably work out," McKenna admitted.

"Okay. Just wanted to get that out of the way. What do you need?"

"You agree that he did it?"

"Of course. You've made a good case, but you've made me privy to evidence a jury might not get to hear."

"I didn't think I was convincing you."

"Sorry. I just wanted to examine your evidence from all sides before I told you anything that would harm an innocent man. Besides, I'm glad to know that whatever help I give you won't harm him too much. He's insane and can't possibly be punished."

"And you still like him?"

"I like the man he was."

"I do, too," McKenna admitted, then got down to business. "How did you meet him?"

"I looked him up at his office about three years ago. I never solicited money from him, but he had been sending my group some sizable checks for a couple of years. Curiosity got the better of me, so I went to meet him."

"And what did you think of him?"

"The same as everybody else. Brilliant man with a wonderful rich wife, and both of them more than willing to do whatever they could to help make the world a better place."

"I already know that. I mean, what did you think of him personally?"

"I like him, and I don't like a lot of people. He's a gentleman, an excellent conversationalist, and a great chess player."

"You play chess?"

"Yes, but not like he does. I won a few games, but I suspect he let me just to keep me interested."

"Do you know Carmen?"

"It's impossible to know Hector without knowing Carmen. They were always together and agreed on everything. It was like two halves of the same person."

"Did you know that he was an orderly at Bellevue?"

"No, not before you told me."

"Did Carmen know?"

"I don't know, but I'd say not. Why would she let him work as an orderly with all the money she's got?"

"You know him, so would you mind telling me why you think he did it?"

"I think it was a matter of pride. Don't forget, she married a big shot in Costa Rica, a famous guy. He might've been too proud to tell her that he had a hard time getting licensed here."

"So what do you think he did? Told her he was going to work every day as a doctor?"

"I don't know for sure. That was before I first met him, so you'd have to ask either her or him."

"I can't ask him right now, so it looks like it's going to be her."

"Are you going to go see her?" Rosen asked.

"If we can't locate Hector in the next day or two, I'm going to have to."

"When you do, please send her my regards and my condolences on this whole thing. She's a fine woman who's had a lot of tragedy in her life."

"I'll be sure to do that," McKenna promised. "Now I have a favor to ask of you."

"Let me guess. You're worried about more violence against the homeless like we had last night, so you want me to stand by and keep my mouth shut while you scoop them up and warehouse them somewhere until this whole thing blows over."

This Rosen's certainly no dope, McKenna thought. If he'd given me the chance, I certainly would have made it sound better. So how do I answer that? "Yes, that's what we propose to do. I'm sure you can see the potential for problems if last night's activities are any indication," he said.

"And where would you put them? In armories?"

"Yes."

"Even if they didn't want to go, in violation of their constitutional rights?"

"I guess so."

"Answer me this," Rosen said. "Why should I let you move the problem when you should be solving the problem?"

"Ben, we're the police. It isn't our job to solve the homeless problem."

"That's not the way I see it. You're the enforcement arm of government, and when you move somebody against his will because government can't solve the problem, then you're acting illegally and I'll stop you."

"Even knowing there's a chance that some of those people will be murdered because of your actions?"

"Yes. They're not children and they're not packages that can be moved around whenever their location poses a problem for the government. They're people with the same rights under the Constitution as you and me. They know the risks, so if they'd prefer to stay out there and take their chances rather than go to your shelters, what does that tell you about the conditions in those places?"

"I've heard what they're like. Crime, bullying guards, and less-than-courteous treatment. Suppose we put cops in the shelters and armories while this thing lasts?"

"Are you trying to make a deal with me?" Rosen asked.

"Yes."

"Okay, then let's deal. I don't want a token police presence. I want enough cops there to keep order, and I want supervisors there, too."

"Okay."

"I want everyone to get sensitivity training from my people before they're assigned there."

"What would this sensitivity training consist of?"

"We'll tell your cops how those people came to be homeless and in the wretched condition they're in. We have to develop empathy in our police, not just sympathy."

"What could you tell them that would do that?"

"We'll explain that the homeless are simply victims of an increasingly sophisticated society they just can't cope with. Maybe some of them aren't smart enough, maybe some of them lack the education, but there's no longer any room for them in the workplace like there used to be. Because of the technological revolution, the type of work that people with their skills used to do isn't done anymore in this country. It's done offshore, with less headaches for industry and at a cheaper rate. And it all happened in the last ten years, which is when the homeless problem first showed itself here."

"And how is it that the immigrants are hired and they're not?"

"Because the homeless who are capable of working come with too much baggage they picked up getting into the shape they're in. Some have prison records and problems with alcohol and drugs, qualities no employer wants. As for the immigrants doing the menial labor here, we get the cream of the crop from the Third World, people with families and strong support groups determined to make it here no matter what kind of work they have to do."

"Are you saying it's hopeless for our homeless?"

"No, not hopeless. I believe that everyone who wants to work in this country should be able to get a job commensurate with their skills. Our homeless are either unskilled or have skills that are no longer necessary in our society. So government has to step in. First they have to be housed and then they have to be trained to do the kind of work that's being done in this country right now. It will be expensive, but there's no quick fix for this problem."

"Okay. Let's make sure we both understand the deal," McKenna said. "If we provide the cops and you do the training, you'll let us bring them in?"

"No, but we'll help you talk them in if you set up the suitable accommodations for them."

"You'll have people available to do that?"

"Yes. Whenever you find someone who doesn't want to go, give us a call and we'll have somebody there in five minutes. But there has to be an understanding that, if any one of them is adamant about not going or he wants to leave the shelter once he gets there, then that's his right."

"Ben, you've got yourself a deal."

55 Brunette was waiting for McKenna in the 17th Squad office when he got there. McKenna could see that the long night had caught up with him. He looked beat and he downed a black coffee as McKenna explained the deal he had made with Rosen.

"It's gonna cost us, but we'll keep our end of the deal," Brunette said. "The mayor tells me he's talked to the governor and we can use the Sixty-ninth Street Armory on a temporary basis, but they have to be out of there by the weekend, when the National Guard needs it."

"That's all right. That gives us five days and this copycat thing should end by then, if it hasn't already."

"That's not what worries me. I think that once we get the homeless into the armory and off the streets, Rosen's gonna give us a hard time when we tell him it's over."

"Is that bad for you?"

"It's not good. If there's no crime in the shelters or the armories, Rosen will make a case for keeping the cops there. That'll cost the department millions, and it's not in the budget."

"More than five million?" McKenna asked.

"Probably not. Why?"

"Because isn't five million a figure you throw around a lot?" McKenna asked. "Don't you always say it costs five million in police salaries and overtime whenever the president comes to town?"

"Yeah, but we get some reimbursement from the feds for that. We wouldn't get anything from them to keep cops in the shelters and the armory, but it's more than money we're talking about. The people in the armory neighborhood are gonna scream when all those folks start showing up every night and hang around all day."

"But there'd be fewer people sleeping on the streets, at Grand Central, at Penn Station, and in the subways. Would sort of make the city seem like a better place, don't you think?" McKenna asked.

"Yes, I do, so I'm not gonna fight Rosen too hard. Just hard enough to force the mayor to put the extra money in our budget."

"I've got another budget problem to run by you," McKenna said. "Have you heard I've got Cisco working on this case starting tomorrow morning?"

"Yeah, Ward told me. He's not too thrilled and I don't blame him. Cisco's a good detective, but he's a real pain to have around."

"Then this'll be good. I want to send Cisco on a little vacation," McKenna said.

"Costa Rica?"

"Yep, Tamarindo Bay. Two hours after he gets there, he'll know everybody. In two weeks he'll be the mayor there, so if Hector shows up, he'll know it."

"Great. An all-expenses-paid undercover vacation for Cisco. That'll drive Ward crazy, but it'll keep Cisco out of his hair. What's next?"

"Have you heard anything on Hector's plane?"

"No, and all the private airports down South have been checked. No sign of him or his plane."

"Then here's how I think we should go. I'll give a sketchy press conference today and a major one tomorrow after we legally obtain Hurley's information."

"Today the evidence against Hector and tomorrow his background, after you serve the subpoenas?" Brunette asked.

"Basically."

"We're gonna have to put our heads together and write some copy so he doesn't look anything like a good guy. We want this case public, but we're going to have a hard time dealing with Hector's past and him giving away money whenever he got the chance."

"For starters, we can say that it's his wife's money he's been giving away, not his own," McKenna suggested.

"What do you propose to do about his wife?"

"She must've heard by now that we've identified Hector. Since she isn't involved, I'm gonna tip her off to what's coming so she can lock up and hide from the press."

"You got her number?"

"Yeah, got it from Hurley."

"It would be nice if you could get her on our side," Brunette commented.

"I'm going to try, but I don't know the relationship between them right now. She must know his physical condition and I'm assuming that's one of the reasons for the breakup. Maybe she hates him now."

"But she's still sending him money every month," Brunette observed. "Could be part of some settlement they worked out, but it would be nice if she cut him off and tells you if she hears from him."

McKenna checked his watch. "It's six-thirty in the evening in Spain right now. Want to give it a try?"

Brunette responded by handing McKenna his cellular phone. "I've got international service on that one."

McKenna flipped through the pages in his notepad until he found Carmen's number in Jaca, Spain. He dialed and the phone was answered immediately by a man. Speaking in Spanish, he identified himself and asked to speak to *Señora* Suarez y Rodriguez, adding that it was urgent.

"She is not available at the moment," the man said in French-accented English.

"Might I ask your name and your relationship to her?"

"I am *Monsieur* Picard and I serve as the *señora*'s personal secretary."

"Would you please tell her that it's urgent and that I must speak to her now on a matter concerning her husband."

"Urgent or no, she is unavailable at the moment," Picard said in a condescending way that irritated McKenna. "If you give me your number, I will give her your message when she becomes available."

"Thank you so much, *Monsieur* Picard. You have been so very kind," McKenna said, then gave him his cellular number and his number at the 17th Squad.

"She knows," McKenna said as he handed Brunette his phone back.

"Think she's heard from Hector?"

"I don't know, and there's no way to find out unless she tells us."

"Think she'll call back?"

"Yes. She loses nothing by talking to me, so I'll either hear from her or one of her high-priced attorneys. What's Hector's passport status?"

"U.S. passport, which Gene Shields has had suspended. Probably has a Costa Rican passport and Lord knows what else. I've got Shields looking into it."

"Do we have an extradition treaty with Spain?"

"Not exactly. We have a broad accord with them, with each request considered on a case-by-case basis. I'll have Hector's warrant lodged with the Spanish authorities. What's next?"

"We'll draft our statement, then I'll call Bob Hurley and orchestrate exactly what he's going to tell the press, for the moment. Then I'm going to talk to Heidi."

McKenna had expected some comment or questions from Brunette on Heidi, but he got none. Brunette just stared at him like he hadn't heard, but McKenna felt a need to explain himself. "I'm going to try not to piss the rest of the press off with this, but I promised Heidi some exclusive coverage on this case. In return, I expect she'll put our slant on the story when it comes to reporting on Hector and his motives.''

''I understand, and that's your business,'' was all Brunette had to say on that subject.

56

Monday, February 5   **17th Squad**

On the fifth morning since the discovery of Benny Foster's body, McKenna had walked to work without encountering a single homeless person along the way, which was something of a unique experience in the City of New York. They were in the shelters and the armory, having been brought to those places the night before in a well-publicized effort by the police department assisted by volunteers from Rosen's Grand Central Coalition for the Homeless.

The roundup had been a resounding success. With reporters watching and cameras running, the homeless had been talked in. Aiding the police in their efforts was the weather. It had gotten colder again; not cold enough for a Cold Weather Emergency to be announced, but cold enough to make sleeping outdoors uncomfortable. There had been no further attacks on the homeless.

Maureen was already in the office when McKenna got there at eight o'clock. She congratulated him on his success with Rosen, then told him that Cisco was in his office waiting for him. McKenna steeled himself for his meeting with the very tricky detective and went in.

Sanchez was sitting on McKenna's desk. ''Here as promised and waiting for assignment,'' he said.

''Good, and I've got a good one for you. You ever been to Costa Rica?'' McKenna asked him.

''No, never.''

''That's something you won't be able to say again tomorrow. Go home, pack for the sunshine, and pick up your passport.''

''When am I leaving?'' Cisco asked.

''This morning. American Airlines has an eleven o'clock flight to San José leaving from JFK and you're on it. There's a round-trip ticket waiting for you at the ticket counter there.''

''And when am I coming back?''

''I don't know, it's an open return. When you get there, go to the Holiday Inn in downtown San José. There's a room reserved for you for the next two days. Get used to the country, keep your ear close to the ground, and find out everything you can about Hector De la Cruz, which shouldn't be hard. He's a real big shot down there.''

''Is that where he's gone to?''

''I hope so. This is a very unofficial mission, so don't contact the police down there for anything.''

''No gun, no shield, no police ID?'' Cisco asked.

''Exactly. Keep a low profile, go as native as you can, and see if he's in town.

302

I hope to have a recent photo of him delivered to you at the hotel sometime tomorrow.''

"Fine. What if he's not in San José?''

"Then head for a place called Tamarindo Bay. It's a resort town on the Pacific coast. He's got a house there, so set yourself up in town, find his house, and watch it.''

"And what do I do if Hector shows up?''

"Do nothing but keep the house under surveillance and call me. Everything you should need is in here,'' McKenna said as he reached into his pocket. He took out an envelope and handed it to Cisco.

Cisco hefted the envelope in his hands. "Feels like money, and lots of it,'' he observed.

"Five thousand dollars of the taxpayers' green,'' McKenna said. "Only myself, Brunette, and Gene Shields will know you're down there. In case you get into trouble, you've got all Brunette's numbers in that envelope.''

"I won't need it, believe me,'' Cisco said. "Anything else?''

"Just stay in touch and give me a call whenever you think of it. Can you handle that?''

"Can I handle that? Detective Sanchez wants you to know that he is forever in your debt for assigning this mission to him. He will never forget you for this and will strive to spend all of the money you gave him as he enhances his tan and successfully completes his mission.''

"I figured as much,'' McKenna said, but he was talking to Cisco's back. Without another word, Cisco was gone.

What to do next? McKenna thought. Carmen. He used his credit card to call Carmen's house in Spain again. Once again, he wound up talking to *Monsieur* Picard and once again he was told that Carmen was not available.

"Did you give her my message yesterday?'' McKenna asked.

Picard hung up without answering.

Would I love to meet that guy! McKenna thought after calming down. Not having anything else to do for the moment, he caught up on his paperwork until Ward arrived at nine o'clock. Then he brought all the subpoenas he had obtained from J. Davenport in to the squad commander. There were twenty-four of them addressed to the main branch of every bank in town demanding all information possessed on the accounts and financial transactions of Hector De la Cruz. There was also a subpoena to NYNEX requesting telephone records for the Park Avenue apartment and one for New Jersey Bell requesting the telephone records for the Oldwick estate.

Ward shuffled through the subpoenas. "It's a shame to waste so much time and manpower to get information we already have, but I'll make it look good. Since the First Bank of the Americas subpoena is the only important one, I'll have Maureen serve it and get those photos for you. What are you going to be doing?''

"First I'm gonna have J. Davenport fax me one more subpoena for Hector's academic records at NYU. I'll pick them up, then go visit Jim Heaney with the search warrant to get Rashid's appointment books.''

"You expect to learn anything that can help you?''

"I don't know,'' McKenna said.

By two o'clock McKenna had eaten lunch and was back in his office with the appointment books and Hector's records from NYU. He had learned something from them. According to his appointment books, Rashid had been having lunch with Hector about once every two weeks for the past two years. The only books McKenna found in the doctor's belongings were from 1994 and 1995, so he wasn't able to learn how long those lunch dates had been going on. However, Hector's academic records made him believe that it had been much longer than that. As McKenna had expected, Hector had breezed through his makeup courses at NYU, earning an A in each one. What he hadn't expected to find was that listed as his graduate adviser was Dr. Suliman Rashid.

So Rashid knew Hector was a doctor the whole time he was working as an orderly at Bellevue, McKenna thought. It was a secret they shared, one that Rashid never divulged to anyone at Bellevue, as far as I know. Obviously, they were friends since Hector arrived in this country. So what kind of man has this Hector become that he could murder a loyal friend like Rashid? McKenna asked himself.

A monster, he concluded, and then he made a decision. He would talk to Brunette about it first, but he thought that the press would have a wonderful time feeding on the Rashid murder and it would tend to discourage any of the reporters from fixing a halo over Hector's head in their coverage of the story.

Then there was a knock at the door and Father Hays came in. "Am I interrupting?" Hays asked.

"Not at all," McKenna said. "Are you here to tell me that you know Hector De la Cruz?"

"Yes, I am. How did you know?"

"If Ben Rosen knows him, I figured you did, too. You travel in the same circles and it's just the way my luck's been running. Before I found out who he was, nobody knew him. Now it turns out everybody knows him and likes him. I bet you're going to tell me what a great guy he was."

"You're right again. He did some wonderful things for Saint Francis, so that makes him a great guy in my book. It's hard for me to believe the things he's doing now."

"Sit down and tell me about it," McKenna said. "Tell me how he's been giving you money for years."

Hays settled into a chair across the desk from McKenna. "I first met him four years ago. I heard his confession and then he asked me if I needed any help with our soup kitchen."

"You mean he wanted to help you cook and clean?"

"No, better than that. He wanted to donate to the kitchen and also provide some jobs. We're not in a residential neighborhood, so we were a little short on volunteers. He wanted to provide money so we could hire some homeless to work the kitchen."

"How much did he provide?"

"One hundred thousand dollars each year for the past four years. He and

Carmen were our best sponsors and really did more to keep the kitchen going than anyone else.''

"You know Carmen?''

"Yes, lovely woman. They used to stop in for mass in our humble neighborhood at least one Sunday a month. They're both very devout old-school Catholics.''

"Do you consider them to be friends of yours?''

"Yes, good friends.''

"Do you have any idea what's going on between Carmen and Hector right now?''

"Yes, but I can't discuss it with you. Let me just say that I know they've had some serious problems.''

"And you can't tell me about it because of something he told you in the confessional?''

"Yes. Actually, I heard both their confessions and tried to work things out between them, but it was no use.''

"Was the problem that Hector had contracted AIDS from a homeless woman he had an affair with?''

"I can't say.''

"Don't bother, Father. I'm saying it. I've got a few of Hector's letters I'd like to show you. I need some insight into him and I'm hoping you'll be able to tell me what you think's running around in his head.''

"I'd be glad to, but you have to understand that there are some confidences I can't violate.''

"I understand," McKenna said. He took the case folder from his desk drawer and removed the letters. There was the one found on the body of Daniel O'Sullivan, the letter to Kerri Brannigan, the letter found on the body of Juliette Thompson, and the two letters Hector had left for McKenna at Oldwick.

Hays took his time reading all of the letters. "I can't comment on Juliette's letter, but I'm able to make some observations about Hector's general mental state from his letters to you.''

So Hector did discuss Juliette in the confessional, McKenna thought. Maybe Carmen did, too. "Please go on," he said.

"It's only his actions that demonstrate he's insane, but the tone coming through those letters is the Hector I know. He's always been a kind person, especially tuned to other people's feelings and needs. For instance, I'm certain that he does feel sorry for Kerri Brannigan, which is why he gave her the money.''

"Are you sure it's not some kind of ploy on his part to seek favorable publicity?''

"Yes, but I'm sure he doesn't mind that side effect, if it comes. The other thing that comes through is that he has developed a genuine respect and affection for you, which isn't going to help you in your job.''

"I can deal with that," McKenna said. "I've gotten along well with some people I've locked up in my career.''

"You miss the point. Since your involvement, it's now become a game as well as a mission to him. Hector loves games and he's used to winning.''

"I take it you've played chess with him.''

"Yes. Before I played with him, I used to think I was pretty good at it. But I'm not in his league. I think that whenever I won it was because he let me just to keep me interested so I'd keep playing him."

"Ben Rosen told me the same thing," McKenna said.

"Just goes to show how nice a man Hector was. I've played Rosen and I'd never let him win. I know that sounds un-Christian, but Rosen's such a horrible winner."

"Unfortunately, I think I'm going to find that out for myself," McKenna said. "So you don't think any sign of his mental illness shows through his letters? Maybe a touch of megalomania?"

"I see that in there, but be careful. Knowing Hector, I'd assume that's just posturing on his part to throw you off and disguise his planning. Sometimes he does that when he's in a bind in a game, talks to you and builds you up, and before you know it, you're the one in the bind."

"I'll keep that in mind. Can you tell me when you received the donations from Hector?"

"The first of every year."

"And has it come through this year?"

"January first, same as always. But this time the check was only from Carmen, so I knew something was up."

At that moment Maureen came in, carrying a large manila envelope. She looked pleasantly surprised to see Father Hays there, and McKenna had to wait while they went through the Maureen kissy-huggy routine before she turned her attention to him. "You ready to see what the guy you're chasing looks like?" she asked.

"Let's have it."

Maureen opened the envelope, took out a stack of five-by-seven photos, and handed them to McKenna. "The best one's on top," she said.

McKenna could see that the best one was pretty good, for a bank surveillance photo. The surveillance camera was mounted high in the ceiling and the photo showed a well-dressed thin man in a suit and tie and wearing a beard accepting a stack of bills from a teller at the bank window. Hector was wearing his hair rather long and McKenna was sure that was to hide the place on the side of his face where the fake beard joined his sideburns. Although the photo was grainy, he was also sure that he would know Hector when he saw him. The date/time stamp at the bottom of the photo read: FRIDAY, 2-1-96 2:02 P.M.

Three days ago, McKenna thought. He passed the photo to Father Hays and asked, "This look like Hector to you?"

Hays looked shocked at Hector's appearance in the photo. "I never would have known that was him," he said. "He must be really suffering."

McKenna went through the rest of the photos, examined the account records. They showed a $100,000 deposit from the Banco de España on the first of every month since January of 1995.

"Come to any conclusions?" Maureen asked.

"Just that I want to talk to Carmen Suarez y Rodriguez very much."

"Are you going to?" Hays asked.

"Eventually. She's not answering my calls, so I'm probably gonna wind up ringing her doorbell."

"When you do, please try to understand her position. She's a fine woman and another one of the victims in this thing. She's going to be suffering long after Hector's dead."

"I will."

"And one more thing," Hays said.

"Send her your regards?"

"Please, and my condolences."

The news conference outside the station house had been a tumultuous affair, with every question imaginable about Hector and Carmen being thrown at McKenna in rapid-fire fashion. He had answered all questions as patiently and as completely as he could, trying to cast Hector in the worst light possible. To further his goal, he had divulged to the reporters the details of the suspected murder of Dr. Rashid, told them of the long relationship that had existed between the two men, and stated his theory that Hector had poisoned his friend to cover his tracks.

The news conference had lasted over an hour and, although Fox Five was represented, Heidi had not been there. McKenna knew she had better things to do than stand out in the cold, and there was no reason for her to attend. He had already given her a jump on the story and she had understood most of the details a day before her competitors.

McKenna also knew that, with the exception of the death of Dr. Rashid, most of what he had told the press was just for the record, since a tremendous amount of research had been done by the media in the preceding twenty-four hours. According to Hurley, there had been a mad rush by networks and newspapers to hire private investigators as soon as Hector's identity had been divulged. They had hired some good ones at exorbitant prices, but they couldn't get the best. Hurley had already humbly accepted a $25,000 retainer to work for Fox Five News.

As soon as he ended the news conference, McKenna headed home for another chore. Fox Five had scheduled an hour special on the case and Angelita had to be pampered and thoroughly placated before they sat down to watch it. A visit to the Silver Swan was in order, and he picked up all the potato pancakes and dumplings he could carry without feeling foolish.

McKenna had already laid the groundwork the night before, first telling her he helped Heidi and, after a period of shouting and hysterics by Angelita, finally managing to give her the reasons why. Convincing Angelita that his decision was the correct one had been tough for him, and he had gone all out, hiding nothing. After years of silence on the matter, he had told her about Hank Lane and then everything he knew about Heidi. Everything.

None of it had made Angelita happy, but in the end Angelita had finally admitted, with some reluctance, that she understood his reasons for advancing Heidi's career. She didn't agree with them, but under the circumstances he knew that understanding was all that he could hope for.

Angelita was already perched in front of the TV when McKenna got home at ten to eight. The baby was sleeping in the bedroom and Angelita was dressed in one of his favorite nightgowns. She was all smiles and looking her best, which, as far as McKenna was concerned, was as good as any woman could hope to look.

This isn't going to be so bad, he thought as he fussed over her, playing the waiter as he set up the folding TV trays and laid out her favorite goodies. Then he sat next to her on the sofa and she snuggled up to him while she picked at her food.

Everything was going just great until Fox Five's newest anchorwoman appeared on screen. Heidi was seated behind the news desk, demurely dressed in an off-pink business suit. She had darkened her hair two or three shades and wore it up, and she looked every inch the professional newswoman.

"Do you like that outfit?" Angelita asked.

"It's okay."

"How about what she did with her hair?"

"Not bad. She lost her floozy look."

"So you like it?"

Here we go, McKenna thought. "Like I said, it's not bad for her," he said as he put his arm around Angelita. "But you know I was never crazy about blondes."

"Not ever?"

"No, never," McKenna answered as he tried to hear what Heidi was saying without appearing to do so.

"I'd say she looks very nice and very professional. Wouldn't you?" Angelita asked.

"I guess so."

"Isn't it something how a slut can dress right, look so nice, and then fool everybody?"

"Yeah, that's really something."

And that's the way it went for the next hour. McKenna learned everything Angelita really thought about Heidi Lane while America learned everything there was to know about the murders in New York, the man suspected of committing them, and his fabulously wealthy wife. As long as Heidi wasn't on the screen, Angelita was fine and McKenna was able to hear what the rest of the country was listening to. Thanks to Hurley, the network had gathered a lot of information on such short notice.

After Heidi outlined the events of the past month, there followed a running commentary featuring Ben Rosen. He described the plight of the homeless while scenes of people sleeping on the streets during a cold New York winter night flashed across the screen. Then Heidi interviewed a retired medical examiner from Chicago, who explained how cyanide poisoning works. He ended by giving Andino a boost, stating that it was only because of Andino's skill and experience that the cyanide had been discovered in the victims' bodies.

After a commercial break, Heidi gave a detailed and flattering account of McKenna's career while news headlines of his more well known cases where shown to the viewers.

Angelita was very unhappy about that. "Where did she get all that information about you?"

"Not from me. She probably kept quite a file on me while she was plotting how to ruin my life."

"Well, isn't this some turn of events. Now she sounds like the president of your fan club," Angelita commented.

"Angelita, please!" he said. "I have no control over what she says."

"Sounds to me like a love-hate thing."

"It's not that at all. She's just a professional journalist doing her job and that's it."

McKenna could see that Angelita wasn't placated, but she let it rest for the moment. Then Heidi interviewed Vernon Geberth after describing him as the nation's leading expert on serial killers. He gave some background on serial killers and described the instances where there had been copycat killings. After some prompting by Heidi, he admitted that he had been contacted by McKenna for advice because Brunette had foreseen the possibility of copycat killings in New York. Geberth said that, as a result of his meeting with McKenna, Brunette had been prepared for the copycat attacks when they had occurred.

After Geberth's interview, Heidi's part of the show was over for a while and McKenna was able to concentrate on it in relative peace. Fox Five had obtained some file footage from Costa Rican television from a feature they had done on Hector in 1987. The presentation was in Spanish and Fox Five showed ten minutes of excerpts with English subtitles accompanied by commentary by one of their standard anchormen. In rapid succession the footage showed the streets in San José where Hector had been born and raised, an old picture of his mother, the orphanage where he had wound up and gone to school, his clinic for the homeless of San José, a scene of Hector playing chess in a tournament, his swearing in as a member of the Legislative Assembly, a demonstration where Hector had chained himself to a bulldozer, and, finally, a wedding photo showing Hector and Carmen arm in arm in their familiar pose.

McKenna learned one thing from the segment and he found it strange and disturbing, something psychiatrists would have a lot of fun dissecting. He thought that the old photo of Hector's mother bore a remarkable resemblance to the old photo of herself that Juliette Thompson had kept in one half of her locket, next to her photo of Hector.

It's possible I'm looking at this wrong, McKenna thought. If Hector was attracted to Juliette because of some fixation he had concerning his mother, then he's been running around with a few loose wires long before he got AIDS. He's probably always been a bedbug, but he hasn't shown it 'til now.

McKenna didn't get much more time to think about Hector because, after another commercial, the Carmen show was on. Fox Five had obtained photos of Carmen as a child with her father and mother, Carmen with her much-older brother, and wedding pictures of Carmen and the Austrian court. It was a segment cleverly designed to be a tearjerker, and each phase of Carmen's life was described, always ending with footage of her at a funeral or grave site. It was done in unhappy-little-rich-girl style and Fox Five managed to get its point across well.

The segment showed just how rich Carmen really was. *Lifestyles of the Rich and Famous* had run a show on her house in St.-Tropez, and portions of that show were repeated. *Architectural Digest* had done a feature on her Park Avenue apartment, and pictures from that article were shown. They had sent a helicopter to take aerial footage of the Oldwick house, and there were photos of her Paris apartment. They ended up the Carmen real-estate tour with a shocker for McKenna: Fox Five had a news crew live outside Carmen's house in Jaca, Spain. It was early morning there, but the viewer could see her house, a massive stone affair set into the side of a mountain.

A reporter standing in front of the house confirmed that Carmen was inside, but that through her personal secretary, she had declined to speak to reporters or comment on the reputed activities of her husband.

Reporters parked on her doorstep is just what that lady doesn't need at a time like this, McKenna thought.

Then Heidi was on again, this time interviewing a psychiatrist specializing in criminal behavior, and McKenna saw that Heidi had kept up her end of the bargain. He knew that she had interviewed a number of psychiatrists before she had found one who said the things McKenna wanted to hear. He told America that Hector De la Cruz's conduct indicated to him that the man was certainly disturbed, possibly deranged, but not insane under the legal definition of the term. According to Heidi's wonderful expert, Hector knew the difference between right and wrong and recognized that what he was doing was wrong. Therefore, in his considered opinion, Hector De la Cruz was a sane man consciously planning and performing evil deeds.

Heidi thanked her expert and then turned to the camera to bid her audience good night, but she didn't get a chance to reach the McKenna household. Angelita clicked off the TV with the remote control and silently resumed eating her cold potato pancakes and dumplings.

McKenna was searching for a way to snap her out of it when the phone rang. McKenna got up and answered it. "Detective McKenna?" a female voice asked.

"Speaking."

"This is Carmen Suarez. I'm sorry to call you at home. Am I disturbing you?"

"No, not at all. I was hoping to hear from you."

"I know. I hope you can forgive me for not returning your calls right away. I've been under quite a bit of pressure here and I've had a lot to think about."

"Yes, I know. I'm very sorry about that," McKenna said.

"You have nothing to be sorry about. It's not your fault. But I do have to speak to you."

"I'm listening."

"Did you just finish watching that news broadcast?"

"Yes. Did you?" McKenna asked, realizing it was three o'clock in the morning in Spain.

"Of course I did. I have a satellite dish and it came in perfectly. So you must know I have reporters camped outside, and tapping phones is not at all unusual here."

"So what are you saying?" McKenna asked.

"I'm saying that I would come see you, but I can't right now without bringing the world press with me. What I have to tell you can't be told over the phone."

McKenna glanced at Angelita. She was still sitting on the sofa, but her head was turned toward him as she listened to his conversation. She looked unhappy and McKenna knew that in another moment it was going to get worse. "I understand, Carmen," he said. "Sit tight. I'm on my way."

As frequently happened, McKenna had been wrong about Angelita's attitude regarding his trip. He could never tell whom she would like and whom she would despise, but for some reason she liked Carmen and felt sorry for her. After he hung up he expected some protest from her since she had always jealously guarded her time with him.

"Are you leaving tonight to go see her?" Angelita asked.

"Yes, she has to be interviewed and she can't come here," he explained. "Sorry, but I have to go."

"I understand," she said, surprising McKenna. "I know you have your job to do, but try to cheer her up while you're at it. Poor thing must be going out of her mind."

Isn't life full of surprises? McKenna thought. But "poor thing"? Carmen? It's just like Angelita to be wise enough not to equate money with happiness and it's just another reason why I love this woman.

58

Tuesday, February 6   **Pau, France**

Getting to Jaca had turned out to be a problem for McKenna. The last flight to Spain had already left New York by the time Carmen had called him the night before, so he had been forced to pack in a hurry and Brunette had managed to pull some strings to get him on the ten o'clock Air France flight to Paris. He had slept on the plane and was feeling fine by the time he had arrived in Paris that morning. From Paris he had taken a flight to Toulouse and then had caught another flight to the French city of Pau, which was as close to the Spanish frontier as he could get by air.

At the Hertz counter in the Pau airport McKenna found himself experiencing his recurrent language problem. The rental agent asked him questions in French and he answered in Spanish. He understood every word she said and thought he answered in French until he got that familiar blank look from her. Then he knew the problem was back.

At home he and Angelita frequently spoke in Spanish because they both wanted Janine to be bilingual, a definite asset in New York. For fun, he had also been studying French for years and they had taken many trips together to Quebec so he could practice. On his first day there, he would subconsciously translate the French into Spanish, the Romance language he was more accustomed to, and then find himself speaking Spanish to the French Quebecois.

With some difficulty, he corrected his thinking and answered the agent's questions in French. By the time the five-minute procedure was over, he had rented an Isuzu Trooper, he was thinking in French, and he was armed with a map and directions to Jaca, Spain.

By two o'clock, McKenna was having lunch on the veranda of a restaurant in the French border town of Urdos, high in the Pyrenees. He was overwhelmed by the magnificent mountain vistas, the cordiality of the manager, the cheerful attitude of his waitress, and the speed of service, all things not ordinarily found in Paris.

By three he was at the border and very glad he had rented the four-wheel-drive Trooper. It had snowed during the night and, although the roads had been cleared, the wind was blowing snow back on them and the going was slippery. Crossing into Spain was no more arduous than going through a tollbooth. He held his passport up for inspection by the Spanish customs agent and prepared for at least a question or two, but he was merely waved through without a word or a second glance.

Less than an hour later he saw Carmen's house. He had been worried about finding it, but recognized it from Heidi's broadcast. It was the kind of place that couldn't be missed. He was driving and looking at it for ten minutes before he reached the private access road.

The world press was well represented there, with many reporters and news vans from all over Europe parked on the grass at the entrance to the access road. Unfortunately for them, a sizable detachment of the Guardia Civil was also there. They had two of their cars pulled across the road, blocking it and preventing any of the reporters from reaching the house.

McKenna pulled right up to the roadblock with his shield out. His arrival immediately provoked some activity from the press. The reporters saw him, left their vans, and ran toward his car. But they weren't as fast as the Guardia Civil. The Spanish cops formed a cordon around his car, keeping the reporters back while a sergeant came up to McKenna's window.

"I'm Detective McKenna of the New York City Police Department. The se-ñora is expecting me," he said in Spanish as he offered his identification.

The sergeant briefly examined McKenna's shield and ID card before giving it back. "This is a tragic business, isn't it?" he asked.

"Yes, it sure is."

"Please be as gentle as you can with the contessa. She's one of our national treasures," he said, then signaled to the cops in the cars blocking the road. They moved their cars so McKenna could pass through, and after a half-mile drive straight uphill he was at the front door of the house.

The door was open and two more uniformed cops were there talking to a formally dressed, distinguished-looking man in his fifties. The man wore a mon-ocle, something McKenna had never seen except in movies. He left the cops and walked to meet McKenna. "I am Henri Picard and I owe you an apology, De-tective McKenna," he said, offering his hand. "I hope you will forgive my brusque treatment of you on the phone, but things here were very unsettled at the time."

"I understand, Monsieur Picard," McKenna said. "I'm sure this has been a tough time for you folks here. Think nothing of it."

"Thank you. The señora is waiting for you. Would you come with me, please?"

They went to the front door, but had to stop for a moment when the two cops surprised McKenna with a salute. He returned it and said in Spanish, "I know. I'll be as gentle as possible with the señora," which was apparently just what they wanted to hear.

"Gracias, Señor," one of them said as McKenna followed Picard inside and down a long, wide entrance hall. At the end of the hall there was a grand staircase on the right and a set of large double oak doors on the left. They stopped in front of the doors and Picard asked, "May I take your coat?"

"Certainly."

Picard helped McKenna out of his overcoat and draped it over his arm. Then he knocked on one of the doors, swung them open, and announced, "Detective McKenna."

It was a large library with the bookshelves filled from the floor to the twenty-foot ceiling. On one wall directly opposite the doors a fire blazed in a large stone fireplace. In the center of the room two large sofas faced each other separated by a coffee table. Carmen was seated on one, wearing jeans and a sweatshirt. Her dark hair was in a ponytail, she wore no makeup, and her eyes were puffy. McKenna could see that she had been crying, not recently, but sometime during the day.

The other sofa was occupied by a man McKenna recognized. For a moment he was surprised to see Charles Schenley sitting with Carmen, but it quickly made sense to him; Schenley was regarded by many, including himself, as one of America's best criminal defense attorneys.

McKenna didn't like him, but it wasn't because he was a defense attorney. What bothered McKenna was the old-boy, big-school, condescending attitude that Schenley showed toward everyone but wealthy clients and jurors.

Carmen stood up as McKenna entered the room and Schenley followed her lead. Picard left, closing the doors behind him.

"Thank you for coming so quickly, Detective McKenna," Carmen said, offering her hand. "Strange as it may seem, I've found myself looking forward to meeting you all day."

McKenna noticed at once that Carmen had that something, that self-assured presence. He politely shook her hand and said, "It's a pleasure to meet you. I'm sorry it has to be under these circumstances."

"Thank you. I believe you know Mr. Schenley."

"Yes, I do," McKenna answered and left it at that.

"Señora Suarez has hired me to represent her husband in the action you've commenced against him," Schenley announced. "I understand that you've obtained an arrest warrant and that a copy of that warrant has been lodged with the Spanish authorities."

"You understand correctly."

"May I see a copy of that warrant?"

McKenna reached into his pocket and handed it to him. Schenley snapped the folded warrant open and read it with a look of concentration on his face.

McKenna thought Schenley was showboating for Carmen's benefit and he wasn't going to let him get away with it. "I think you'll find it's the standard form listing little more than your client's name, charge, and docket number. There are really no secrets to ponder in it."

"It's my job to make sure that everything is in order," Schenley answered pointedly, then offered the warrant to Carmen. "Everything appears to be in order."

She looked down at the warrant with an amused look on her face, but didn't take it. "Unlike yourself, Mr. Schenley, I don't think Detective McKenna lied to all those reporters when he said he had a warrant and I don't think he's traveled all this way to show us a bogus document. He's been described to me as rather competent.''

That's telling him, Carmen! McKenna thought. But described by whom? he wondered. TV or Hector?

"I'm sorry, Detective McKenna," she said. "Mr. Schenley has advised me that he should be here while I talk to you. While I really don't see the point, I'm new to matters of this sort and I followed his advice. He feels that you're here to trample my rights and to trick some information from me that I shouldn't be giving you.''

"With or without Mr. Schenley, would I be able to do that, even if I wanted to?'' McKenna asked.

"Probably not,'' she admitted.

"I think it's time to inquire whether or not the señora is one of the targets of your investigation," Schenley said.

"No, of course she's not," McKenna answered. "She's been described to me by people who know her as a fine lady and totally aboveboard.''

"Who might those people be?'' Carmen asked.

"Father Hays and Ben Rosen, two people I think I can believe. Both of them asked me to give you their regards.''

Carmen smiled, but said nothing.

"I'd like to point out that she's been separated from her husband for a year and had no knowledge of his alleged activities until quite recently," Schenley continued. "I'd also like to add that Señor De la Cruz has committed no crime in Spain and that the señora has had no contact with him since your warrant was lodged here.''

"All that's a given, as far as I'm concerned," McKenna said to Schenley, then turned to Carmen. "When was the last time you had contact with him?''

"Sunday night,'' she answered at once.

"By telephone, I assume,'' McKenna said.

"No, he was here.''

McKenna was stunned by her answer, and many questions quickly formed in his mind, but then Schenley cut in.

"Madame, you shouldn't answer his questions yourself," the attorney said to her in French. "I think it best that I answer them, and only those I think appropriate. Keep in mind that he is a policeman here only to get information from you, some of which might prove embarrassing to you later on. He looks and acts pleasant enough, but he's not your friend.''

What a cagey bastard! McKenna thought as he stared at Schenley with the blankest look he could contrive. He knows I speak Spanish, but have I got a surprise for him!

So did Carmen. "Monsieur Schenley, you are being rude to a guest I've invited into my home," she admonished, also in French. "I'm forced to accept the fact that my husband is a murderer many times over and that he may kill again. I'd say we're past the point of worrying about what's embarrassing and what's not.''

"Not necessarily, Madame," Schenley answered, still in French. "This man needs information that only you possess, so we are in a position to demand certain concessions.''

"I disagree," she said emphatically. "I still love my husband, but it is time for us to accept the consequences of his actions, and he must as well. In any event, I think we both owe this man an apology. Think of how he must feel as we both go on with him standing here."

Schenley looked appalled at the thought of apologizing to McKenna and very unhappy at the way Carmen proposed to handle the situation.

"That's all right, Monsieur Schenley. You don't have to apologize. I understand that you're just doing your job as you see it," McKenna said politely in French.

In just one second, the surprised look on Schenley's face paid McKenna back for all his hours of study. Even if he never spoke another word of French for the rest of his life, the time and effort had been worth it for that one moment of pure pleasure.

Carmen giggled like a schoolgirl, but it took Schenley a moment to recover sufficiently to say in English, "I see I've underestimated you, Detective McKenna."

"A little, but you were right about a few things. I am a policeman here investigating murder. However, I didn't appreciate it when you made me sound like an inquiring whore without morals or a shred of decency. I would never use anything Carmen told me to harm her or her fine reputation."

Schenley opened his mouth to say something, but then glanced at Carmen. She was smiling and obviously enjoying his discomfort. "I see," he said.

"And so do I," Carmen said to McKenna. "I'm sorry about that French business. It was rude of me to let it continue as long as it did." Then she turned back to Schenley, offered him her hand, and said, "Thank you so much for coming, Mr. Schenley, but I feel comfortable enough to speak with Detective McKenna alone."

Schenley looked down at her hand in shock. He was a man unaccustomed to dismissal, but learned quickly and proved nimble enough. He lightly took her hand and bent over, kissing it in the European fashion with his lips never touching her hand. "Thank you so much for having me, Contessa," he said when he straightened up. "Your company has given me great pleasure." Then he turned to McKenna and said, "In the event you apprehend Hector De la Cruz, you are not to question him in my absence."

Schenley turned and left with as much dignity as he could muster. When he got to the door, there was no need for him to open it. Picard opened it from the hallway and was waiting there with Schenley's overcoat over his arm.

How did Picard know Schenley was leaving? McKenna wondered as the doors closed on them both.

"Lawyers," Carmen commented.

"Yeah, lawyers," McKenna agreed.

"We have a lot to talk about. Would you care for a drink while we talk?"

"Just coffee for me, please."

"Fine. I think I'm going to need something stronger for myself, if you don't mind."

"Not at all."

McKenna expected her to do something about ordering drinks, but she didn't.

Instead, she sat on the sofa and curled her legs beneath her. McKenna took her cue and sat opposite her on the other sofa.

"Where do we begin?" she asked.

"For the moment, not at the beginning. Were you expecting your husband on Sunday night?"

"Not exactly. He had called me on Friday and told me he would be coming to see me, but he didn't say when."

"What time did he get here?"

"About six Sunday night."

McKenna quickly did some time-zone calculations and concluded that Hector was here when he had first called Carmen from his office, after the press had been given Hector's name. Had Carmen heard about it before Hector arrived? It was a question he decided not to pursue, for the moment. Instead he asked, "Did any of the servants see him?"

"Just Monsieur Picard, but that is the same as nobody if you're worried on my behalf. He has worked for my family for thirty years and is fiercely protective of me."

Just goes to show how wrong first impressions can be, McKenna thought. The more I know about Picard, the more I like him. "How long was your husband here?" he asked.

"No more than a couple of hours."

"Did he have a car?"

"Yes, but I don't know what kind. He parked it at the end of the driveway and it was dark already."

"Would Monsieur Picard know?"

"He might, but he'd never tell you, no matter what I said. You see, Monsieur Picard doesn't see the world in terms of right and wrong. For him, it's just us and them and we're always right, as far as he's concerned. Besides, he likes Hector."

"I see. What did Hector tell you?"

"He said that he had killed some people who deserved to die, but that the police had discovered his actions and were searching for him. He said he never intended that they find out what he had done, but that he didn't mind for himself that they did."

"I guess he really shocked you."

"Of course. The Hector I knew would never even think of killing anyone, no matter what they'd done."

"So how do you explain the inconsistency?"

"Obviously, he's gone insane."

There it is, on the table, McKenna thought. Although it's not our official position to admit it, I won't lie to this fine lady. "I'm very glad you realize that," he said.

"Why?"

"Because I wanted to be sure you recognized that the man we're dealing with now isn't the same man you used to know and love. The disease has changed him, and not just his appearance. It's changed the way he thinks and it's certainly changed the way he acts."

"I know that now, but aside from his appearance, he still seemed the same to me when I saw him on Sunday."

"In what way is he the same?" McKenna asked.

"In many ways. For instance, he was inconsolable over the homeless man who was attacked. He said that, because of him, an innocent man had been horribly murdered. He shook and cried so much that I had to hug and comfort him the way a mother hugs her baby."

"And that worked?"

"Yes, it always does. But that's another story."

Not if I can pry it out of you, McKenna thought, but decided that later would be better. "In what other ways do you think he was the same?"

"In the way he thought about me. Remember, at grave risk to himself, he traveled here to prepare me for the publicity and to try to console me."

"He was worried about what people might think about you after they knew what he had done?"

"Yes, but that wasn't his main concern."

"It wasn't? He had to realize all the trouble his actions would cause you and how people would be talking and thinking when they found out about it."

"Yes, he realized that. However, after he talked to me, I wasn't worried about what people thought. I realized it was just a short-term problem."

"That must have been quite a talk. Can you tell me what he told you?"

"I'd rather not," Carmen said, lowering her eyes. "It's a little embarrassing."

"Even so, I wish you'd tell me. I have to know exactly how Hector thinks right now and you're the only one who can tell me. I have a lot of embarrassing questions for you, all things I need to know, so let's get the first one out of the way."

"You won't repeat it to anyone or put it in any of your reports?"

"Not if you don't want me to. Do you mind if we establish some ground rules?"

"No."

"Okay. First of all, I guarantee that you will never be called as a witness in this case. Second, I will tell only one man the details of our conversation, but that would be the same as you telling a secret to Monsieur Picard. Once I've explained our arrangement to him, I'm certain he'll never repeat it to anyone."

"Who is this man? Your confessor?" Carmen asked.

"Just about. He's my best friend, but he's also the police commissioner. I wouldn't do anything behind his back, but don't worry about him. We sort of think alike and he'll see things my way."

"The police commissioner would conspire with you and withhold information to avoid embarrassing me?"

"Absolutely. Aside from him, anything you tell me in confidence will never be mentioned again by me in writing, in conversation, or in testimony. I also won't tell you a single lie as long as you tell me you'll do the same."

"Aren't those some rather unusual promises for a policeman to make, especially since you're speaking on behalf of the police commissioner?" she asked.

"Yes, highly unusual."

"Then why are you making them?"

"Because everyone I've met who knows you has asked me to be nice to you. That has to count for something, don't you agree?"

"I'm flattered, but I have to admit that it makes me feel good to hear it."

"Then you'll love this. My wife doesn't know you and doesn't like many people, but she likes you and she also told me to be nice to you. I don't like living in my house when Angelita's unhappy, so you've got my best deal. What do you say?"

"You want to hear something funny?"

"Yeah, I could use a laugh."

"Hector told me you'd be coming, sooner or later. He told me that I could trust you."

That's not exactly hysterical, McKenna thought. Why would he tell her that unless he wants to get caught? And if he wants to get caught, then why am I having such a hard time catching him?

"I take it you don't think that's funny?" Carmen asked, while watching him closely.

"No, it just confirms my belief that there's a lot I need to know about Hector. Anyway, what about our deal?"

"You know, I do trust you. You've got one," she said, extending her hand across the coffee table. They shook hands like the captains of two opposing teams.

Carmen immediately began fulfilling her end of the deal. "Hector told me that I shouldn't worry what people thought of this because throwing dirt at me was obviously unfair. He said that once people realized what they were doing, they would stop. Like I said, it wasn't Hector's main concern and he didn't think it should be mine."

"Then what was his main concern? Why did he feel he had to come here and console you?"

"He thought that I would blame myself for all this. He was afraid I'd think that, if I hadn't left him, then none of this would have happened."

"And how did he go about doing that?"

"By pointing out that, before I left him, we had talked it over and we had both agreed that it was the correct thing for me to do. He said that what he had done since hadn't changed the logic of that decision, that it still had been the correct thing to do."

"When did you leave him? When you discovered he was HIV positive?" McKenna asked.

"No. He told me as soon as he knew himself, but it was never the same after that. I stayed with him for another few months, but I couldn't forgive him while I was with him every day. It took time and separation to do that."

"Did he succeed in convincing you?" McKenna asked.

"He tried," she said, then covered her face with her hands and began sobbing softly.

I'm handling this wrong, McKenna thought. What can I tell her that will snap her out of this? "Surely you can't blame yourself for Hector killing people in New York while you're here in Spain," he tried.

It was the exact wrong thing to say. Carmen took her hands from her face and stared him straight in the eyes through her tears. "Of course I do. Don't you see it?'' she asked. ''If I hadn't been so stubborn and so proud, then none of this would have happened. I left him at the time he needed me most.''

It was too much for her to bear. Carmen began sobbing uncontrollably. ''I left him to die alone, to go insane and die alone!'' she said through her sobs over and over, the first few times in English, but then in Spanish.

McKenna didn't know what to do or say to comfort her, but Picard did. The doors swung open and he came in carrying a tray. On it were a silver coffee service, two cups of coffee, and a drink that McKenna guessed was a Campari and soda. He put the tray down on the coffee table and looked at Carmen with the most tender look McKenna had ever seen on a man. He pulled her to her feet as easily as he might pick up a large rag doll and held her. Carmen's face was pressed into his shoulder and her arms hung limply at her sides as she shook and sobbed. He began talking softly in her ear, speaking consoling words in the strangest-sounding language McKenna had ever heard.

After a while, Carmen responded. She kept her face pressed into his shoulder, but her shaking and sobbing abated and she placed her arms around his waist for support. Then she began speaking into Picard's chest in the same strange language while she cried softly.

Picard looked at McKenna as he held Carmen. ''Perhaps you should leave us for a while,'' he suggested. ''The house is yours, so make yourself comfortable wherever you like.''

''Certainly,'' McKenna said. He stood up, looked at the coffee on the tray, and picked up a cup. Then he picked up the other one as well, carried them into the hallway, and placed them on the steps of the grand staircase. He went back and closed the double doors to the library, then sat on the steps staring at the closed doors.

59 It was a long wait. The language business had bothered McKenna until he realized that, although Carmen was Spanish and Picard was French, they were both Basques, that ancient people living on both sides of the Pyrenees and sharing a common heritage and language. He also understood that, while Carmen had previously been under psychiatric care to help her deal with the tragedies in her life, she would be going back for more treatment. Combining personal tragedy, the Hector affair, and all of the world's problems in one kind and sensitive mind was a sure-fire formula to produce guilt beyond human endurance and could lead nowhere else, he thought, but to long sessions on the psychiatrist's couch.

By the time Picard opened the doors again, McKenna had finished his second cup of coffee. ''I know it's difficult under these circumstances, but please don't make her cry again,'' Picard said as he picked up the empty coffee cups.

''I'll sure try not to,'' McKenna assured him. ''Is she going to be all right?''

''Yes, she is. Fortunately for us, she's one of God's gifts to the world, a living saint walking among us. Unfortunately for her, the path to sainthood is paved with sorrow, but she's strong and she'll endure.''

Picard said it so sincerely and with such conviction, as if it should be obvious to everyone, that McKenna was surprised to find himself almost believing it. He went into the library again, closing the doors behind him.

Carmen was once again seated on the sofa, looking puffy-eyed but composed, sitting straight up with her hands on her lap. Her drink was on the coffee table in front of her, half-finished.

"Please sit down," she said. "I can't tell you how sorry I am and how silly I feel."

"I'm the one who should be sorry," McKenna said as he resumed his seat. "I made you cry and I feel almost as bad as you do about it."

"Don't worry about it," she said, then surprised him when she reached across the table and squeezed his hand. "Sometimes I'm such a baby, but I promise not to do that again. What do you want to know?"

"Did you know Suliman Rashid?"

"No, but I know who he was and I know what you think. There was extensive coverage in the Spanish press today on the news conference you gave last night. I think you're wrong about that."

"Why? Because you don't believe that Hector could kill a friend?"

"I don't believe that he could do that just to cover his tracks. Although I recognize that he's an insane murderer, I know he's not a cold-blooded monster."

"Okay, we'll leave that one alone. Did you know that Hector worked as an orderly at Bellevue?"

"Not until I read about it this morning. It was quite a shock for me."

"You thought he had spent a year working nights at Bellevue as a doctor?"

"Yes, and this should make you laugh. I also believed he was teaching at NYU during the day for that first year in New York."

"Why do you think he didn't tell you what he was really doing? Was it because he was too proud to admit to you that he wasn't a doctor as far as the State of New York was concerned?"

"No, that certainly wasn't it. There's nothing proud and pompous about Hector. He's very self-confident and has a fine sense of humor, so I'm sure he must have been quite amused at New York's attitude on his qualifications."

"That's it? Amused, not mad?" McKenna asked. "The most famous doctor in Costa Rica can't get a license to practice in New York, and that only would have amused him?"

"Yes. That's the way Hector was."

"Then why didn't he tell you?"

"Because he didn't want to make me feel bad. You see, he loves Costa Rica and wanted to stay there. But we left, and it was because of me that we did."

"You didn't like it there?"

"I loved living there, at first. It's such a simple, refreshing life and it's a beautiful place. But it's not for me, all of the time. I was used to a different life."

"You don't have to explain that to me," McKenna said. "I've already tried the idyllic lifestyle and I almost went out of my mind."

"Yes, there was that aspect of it. But, believe it or not, I have many responsibilities. I'm on the boards of most of my father's companies and I believe our investors should get something for the confidence they showed in him. I had a hard time doing that from Costa Rica."

"Do you know how he got AIDS?"

"Yes. He had an affair with a homeless woman and she gave it to him," Carmen stated simply.

"Did he tell you he loved her?"

"No, he said he cared for her deeply, but it wasn't love. I know he loves me. He has me on a pedestal and almost worships me."

With Carmen's simple statement, many suspicions solidified in McKenna's mind. If I'm right, there are secrets here that have to be aired briefly, he thought. Then I have to put them back under the blanket and keep them hidden again for Carmen's sake. "Do you know the woman he had this affair with?" he asked.

"I never met her, but I know her name. Juliette, and he was her Romeo in another forbidden love story."

"Do you know what she looked like?"

"No, but Hector told me she had been pretty before she got sick."

McKenna took Juliette's locket from his pocket, opened it, and gave it to Carmen. At first she glanced at it as if she wasn't interested, but then something in the photo caught her eye and she stared at it intently.

"Remind you of anyone?" McKenna asked.

"Yes. I see the resemblance to Hector's mother, if that's what you're asking."

"And what does that tell you?"

"Something I should have known. It's certainly not his fault, but Hector has always been insane."

"Why should you have known it?"

Carmen looked at him and he knew she didn't want to answer. She took a sip from her drink, then put the glass back on the table and stared at it for a moment before she answered. "I should have known because Hector couldn't have sex with me under normal circumstances."

"But you found a way?" McKenna asked.

"Yes, we found a way," she said with her eyes lowered.

McKenna knew that was all she wanted to say on the subject and he felt uncomfortable going on, but he needed to know. "Will you tell me about it?" he asked. "Remember our deal. Talking to me is like talking to yourself."

"That doesn't make it any less embarrassing."

"I know, and I'm sorry about that."

"Okay, I'll tell you," she said, but took a sip from her drink before she did. "At first, I tried the sexy lingerie, but that didn't work. Then I read some books that made me blush and tried everything in them, but it just made Hector uncomfortable. He said he preferred just to hold me and that was enough for him."

McKenna thought back to all the photos he had seen of Hector and Carmen together, always in the same pose with their arms around each other's waists. Those photos had told him that the two were certainly friends, but there hadn't been one photo he had seen that shouted that they were lovers. "Was that enough for you?" he asked.

"No, I wanted to have children. We both did."

"So you figured he was impotent?"

"At first I did. Then one night we got stuck in Puntarenas. It's not too nice a city, very poor and run-down."

"Is that in Costa Rica?"

"Yes, on the Pacific coast. We were driving home from San José and we were going to take the ferry from Puntarenas to Nicoya, but the ferry had broken down. I wanted to drive back to San José, but then Hector found this hotel he wanted us to stay in. I had never been to a place like that."

"A dump?"

"The worst kind of place you could imagine. The roof leaked, it hadn't been painted in years, the plumbing was barely functional, and we could hear activity in the other rooms all night long, if you know what I mean."

"And that's where Hector found himself?"

"Yes, that's where he found out who he was. He performed in a place that cost us two hundred colones for the night, and I think we paid tourist rates."

"How much is two hundred colones in dollars?"

"Maybe a dollar fifty."

"What was your attitude?"

"I was miserable, but I pretended to be happy. It was an unexpected solution to what I'd thought was an insoluble problem. We wanted to have children, so we worked at it. We went to a few more places like that. But as much as they affected me, they affected him even more. He became so different in those run-down hotels, and he wanted me to be different, too."

"What was different about him?"

"His mannerisms changed and he spoke a kind of Spanish that I had only heard before in movies, like he was from the gutter."

"He was from the gutter. Remember?"

"I always knew that, but he had worked his way up. Anyone will tell you that Hector is a refined gentleman."

"Except when it comes to sex?" McKenna suggested.

"Yes. Hector had to set the mood for himself. He would sit outside the hotel on the curb and talk to people for hours before we went up to the room."

"You mean he wanted to hang out and talk about nothing, but he wanted to do it in gutter Spanish?"

"Yes."

"And did he talk to homeless people there?"

"Homelessness isn't a problem in Costa Rica anymore, but I imagine many of them had been homeless at one time."

"Did he want you there while he did this?"

"Oh, no. I usually waited in the car. I only came when he called me, when it was dark and he was ready to go up to the room."

"And then I bet he wanted the lights to be out?" McKenna guessed.

"Yes."

"And he didn't want you dressed in lingerie from Paris."

"No, he didn't. He liked me to wear trashy rags."

"And he wanted you to talk in gutter Spanish."

"Yes."

"And it was all over very quickly."

"Yes. I loved him, so let's just say I thought it was a quirk I was willing to put up with. Maybe I suspected what was going through his mind, but I wasn't sure until you showed me that picture of Juliette."

"Did you ever suggest treatment for him?"

"I suggested it, but knew he wouldn't do it. Hector's a doctor who doesn't believe in psychiatry. He says it's not a science, just sets of opposing theories. He called it the 'practice of continuing treatment with no cure.'"

"Did he ever talk about his mother?"

"Yes, but not much. He said she did whatever she had to do to keep them both alive. He said she was very brave, but when she got syphilis she went insane and then it was really hard on him."

"Did he love her?"

"Very much. That picture we saw on TV was the only one he had of her, but thousands of copies were made of it in Costa Rica. He cherished that picture and I'm sure he's got the original with him now."

"What did he think of people with venereal diseases?"

"Very little. He saw no reason for venereal diseases to still exist. He agreed with the church's position that prohibits sex outside of marriage and he called all those diseases the price of promiscuity."

"Yet his mother died of a venereal disease and he is himself. Did you two ever discuss that?"

"Only once, when he told me he was HIV positive. He said his mother was a prostitute who had sex to keep them both alive. He didn't blame her disease on her; he blamed it on whoever gave it to her, the person who infected her in return for a little pleasure."

"But she must have given it to many others."

"To survive. The way he sees it, she had no choice."

"And how does he see his own disease? Who does he blame for that?"

"Himself. Only himself. He thinks it's his penance for betraying me and all the things he believed in."

"How do you see it, if you don't mind my asking?"

"As another disease, like TB, smallpox, and measles. I don't think of disease as the price for sin. Everything I've been taught tells me that we're all on trial in this life for our souls. God's reward and punishment comes in the next life, not this one."

"Does Hector believe in capital punishment?"

"Yes. He has the Old Testament view on that, that 'eye for an eye' type of thinking."

"That jibes with the theory I'm forming about what's been running through Hector's mind, why he's been killing the people he has, and how he justifies it to himself."

"Are you going to tell me this theory?" Carmen asked.

"Yes, I am. I'm hoping you'll correct me whenever you think I'm wrong."

"Go on. I'm ready."

"Hector was born poor and homeless and highly intelligent in the Third World with no father and a prostitute for a mother. That's a pretty bad start in life, but it got worse for him before it got better. I'm assuming that, when he was very young in those years when the psyche is forming, he saw his mother doing all sorts of things with many, many men, and those guys weren't what any woman would consider a high-quality lover. He wasn't going to school, so he had to be there watching at least some of the time."

"It makes sense, but why wouldn't he have told me about it if he had?" Carmen asked.

"Because it would be one of the things he'd want to forget. Maybe he almost had by the time he met you, but there had to still be subconscious images bumping around in his head, causing some damage. Tell me, were there ever any women in Hector's life before he met you?"

"No, I'm sure there weren't. He would have told me if there had been."

"Given, Hector's no Adonis, but he's not ugly and, considering his stature and popularity in Costa Rica, I'm sure he was what most women would consider a very good catch. But he gets to be thirty-nine and there's nothing at all happening before you come along. Why?"

"Because he knew about his sexual problems?" Carmen ventured.

"Of course he did. Like all men, he had sexual fantasies. He might have repressed them, but you can't do that while you're sleeping. He knew what it took to get him going, so he knew just what he was doing when he dragged you into that hotel in Puntarenas. He was under pressure and knew what he had to do."

"You mean that I had him under pressure?"

"Yes. You wanted children, and you had mentioned something about a psychiatrist to him. He knew what was going on in his own mind and didn't want it brought into the open air. He couldn't perform with you because he idolized you and for him sex was a filthy affair. So you wound up in a dump in Puntarenas and he made love to his mother with the lights out and under the same conditions he associated with sex."

"That must have been horrible for him when he had to think of it like that, if he knew what he was doing," Carmen said.

"He knew, but I'm thinking it had to be horrible for you."

Carmen grew visibly introspective at McKenna's comment. She picked up her drink and finished it, then stared through McKenna into space. McKenna thought she wasn't going to comment until she said, "In the back of my mind, I guess I always suspected what was going on with Hector. But I love him, so every time after the first time, it was always my idea. Another three times, but it always took me days to talk him into it."

"Because you really wanted children?"

"Yes, but mostly because I wanted him happy. But our kind of sex didn't make him happy. After we left those places, he was always so guilty and pampered me so much that it even got on my nerves, and I like to be pampered."

"Tell me what you know about Juliette Thompson."

"Not much. Two years ago last November Hector told me about her. He told me he was HIV positive as a result of one sexual encounter with her. That was quite a scene."

"Did he tell you where and how it happened?"

"It was in an abandoned building somewhere. He said it just happened, like it was something he had no control over. I believe that now. I can see now that he loved her like he loved his mother."

"Did he tell you he wasn't going to see her anymore?"

"Yes, and he didn't for a long time. But I know he saw her after I left him."

"How do you know that?"

"Hector told me. We're friends and we talked on the phone all the time. Saw each other every couple of months, too, mostly in Costa Rica where our visits wouldn't get reported in the gossip columns."

"What did he propose to do about Juliette when she first got sick?"

"Nothing. I wanted to provide for her and get her treatment, but he told me she hated rich people and wouldn't even talk to him again if she knew he was rich. He said she liked living on the street."

"When did Hector first get sick?"

"Last May, in Costa Rica. He hadn't been feeling well and had been losing weight, so he had been spending a lot of time there. We both knew it was going to come, but he was surprised that it came so fast and hit him so hard."

"B-cell lymphoma?" McKenna asked.

"Yes. I wanted to go see him, but he told me not to. He was worried about my reputation, I think, but he was emphatic about it. He said we'd see each other again, but last Sunday was the first time I saw him in over a year."

"Do you know where he went after he left here?"

"I asked him where he was going, but he wouldn't tell me. All he said was that I'd never see him again, but that it was for the best."

"Then let me put it another way. Do you have any idea where he was going when he left?"

"Yes, I have an idea."

"Are you going to tell me?" McKenna asked.

"Probably, after you tell me a few things. What do you expect will become of my husband if you catch him?"

"Depends on where I catch him. How long do you think he has to live?"

"I'm not an expert on these things, but he looked pretty bad. However, he told me he's been feeling better."

"Months?"

"Maybe months."

"Then if I catch him in Europe, he'll die in jail here fighting extradition to New York. It'll be a very messy, very public affair, but I assume you'll keep him supplied with the best lawyers."

"He'd have the best lawyers, but I don't think that's going to happen," Carmen stated. "He doesn't particularly care for Europe, so I don't think he'll be here long and he might have left already."

"My assumption is that he plans to die at home, in Costa Rica," McKenna said. "That would be best for all of us. Hector, you, and me."

"Are you telling me that you don't want to catch him in Europe?" Carmen asked.

"It's complicated, but yes, that's what I'm telling you."

"And you don't want to catch him in New York?"

"I did before, when he was still killing. But we interrupted his mission and now I hope he's not stupid enough or feeling well enough to go back there and continue it. If he does, I'll get him there."

"If he returned to New York, do you think he'd kill again?" Carmen asked.

"Why else would he risk returning except to continue his mission?"

"Which is?"

"To kill every homeless man who might have infected Juliette. This time, before he dies, he wants to make sure he kills the man who killed his mother. Hector wants him already roasting in Hell when he gets there himself.''

McKenna instantly regretted saying what he thought Carmen already knew. Her eyes filled with tears and he thought she was going to break down again, but she didn't. Instead, she got up and went to the fireplace. She stood there for a moment, staring at the flames. "Hector doesn't think he's going to Hell," she said softly, but McKenna thought she was talking to herself, not him.

He didn't know what to say. He wanted to comfort Carmen and tell her that Hector wasn't responsible for his actions and wouldn't be punished in this life or the next.

As it turned out, it wasn't necessary to say anything to comfort Carmen. She put a log on the fire and returned to the sofa, calm and composed. "Go on," she insisted. "Tell me why would it be best if he went to Costa Rica."

"Because then we're all still losers, but we all come out with something. Hector gets to die at home in bed, I get to successfully close out our case against him, and you're spared the ordeal of watching him die in prison."

"You'll have to explain to me how that works."

McKenna did, giving her his and Brunette's plan. "Let me get this straight," she said when he finished. "You're going to arrest him in Costa Rica, but you're the one who's going to wind up in jail?" she asked.

"Yes, but I won't be there long."

"Only until Hector dies?"

"No, only until he's too sick to travel."

"But for your plan to succeed, you're going to have to vilify him in the press?"

"Carmen, you have to admit that he is the villain in this, don't you?"

"Yes, but he's done so much good during his life."

"Then that's the way I'll handle it. I'll say that Hector was a very good man who went very bad."

"You're not going to say he's insane?" Carmen asked.

"No, I can't. My official position has to be that he's the bad guy, and that's that. But I wouldn't worry about that. You've got Schenley."

"What will his role be?"

"To prepare the American public for the trial that's never going to be. Every time he opens his mouth, reporters will be turning their mikes and cameras on and he'll present his insanity defense at every opportunity, countering all the bad things the NYPD and the Manhattan DA's office will be saying about your husband."

"I think Mr. Schenley will like that role," Carmen guessed.

"He'll love it. Now, tell me. Where do you think your husband went when he left here?"

"To the only place in Europe he truly loves, the place he goes to whenever he gets a chance. I think he went to Lourdes, to pray and to confess his sins before he dies."

60

All the reporters were out of their vans and waiting for McKenna at the base of Carmen's access road. He stopped at the Guardia Civil's roadblock and the sergeant approached his car again. "I need a favor," McKenna told him. "I'm heading back to France, but I don't want to talk to any reporters and I don't want them following me."

"Is twenty minutes enough of a head start?" the sergeant asked.

"That would be fine."

"I was just thinking that it's time we checked their press credentials. Then I'll call ahead to the frontier and make sure they're checked again there. Just give me a minute." He talked into his radio for a moment and McKenna saw two of the Guardia Civil cars block the road leading north to France. Then the sergeant signaled to the police cars blocking the access road and they backed up to permit McKenna to drive through. He drove slowly through the crowd of reporters, ignoring their shouted questions, then turned right on the highway as the reporters rushed to their vans. The cops manning the new roadblock let him through, then sealed off the road again. In his rearview mirror, McKenna saw the Guardia Civil questioning the reporters in the first van of a long line.

Half an hour later McKenna breezed through the French border, then stopped at a phone booth in Urdos and called Brunette's office. In was noon in New York and Brunette was there. McKenna briefly summarized what he had learned from Carmen, then asked Brunette to lodge Hector's warrant with the French authorities and also call the police in Lourdes, fax them Hector's picture and description, and have them start checking the hotels there for Hector.

"You think he's still there?" Brunette asked.

"I hope not. He's got a day head start on me and I can't see him staying there two days, if that's where he went. He knew I'd be talking to Carmen and, for some reason, he told her she could trust me. I'm sure he figured she might tell me about his love of the place."

"So he should be on his way to someplace else by now," Brunette said.

"If he's smart, and we know he is. I'm gonna make a good show of it in Lourdes, though. I think he wants us to focus our attention in Europe while he breaks for Central America, and I'm not gonna disappoint him."

"Good thinking," Brunette said. "Spend some time there and make some noise."

Lourdes was bigger than McKenna had expected. Located in the foothills of the French Pyrenees at the intersection of two small rivers, it is a town of bridges, winding streets, and old buildings, dominated by a cathedral at one end and an ancient fortress set on top of a steep hill rising from the center of town.

After fifteen minutes of driving through the deserted winding streets, many of them crossing the rivers more than once, McKenna found himself at the gates of the cathedral and concluded that all streets in Lourdes ultimately led there, to one of the major Catholic pilgrimage destinations in Europe.

McKenna had learned the story in school and knew it well. Catholic school-children are taught that a miracle occurred in Lourdes in 1858: Mary, the mother of Jesus, appeared a number of times to a poor young girl named Bernadette. According to the legend, the woodcutter's daughter had been gathering firewood outside town near a small cave when she saw Mary in the cave and received messages from her that became part of Catholic doctrine. When Mary appeared for the last time, water sprang from the cave where she had appeared. That site became known simply as "the grotto," and miraculous healing qualities are attributed to the waters still flowing from it. The cathedral had been built on top of the grotto.

McKenna passed the cathedral a few more times before he finally located the town's police station at ten o'clock. The lieutenant in charge of the station had already heard from Brunette and had received the faxed photo of Hector. He told McKenna that he had also received instructions from Paris instructing him to cooperate fully, and he did just that; he was polite, deferential, eager to help, and he had called in extra men and assigned them to search the hotels in town.

"I am sorry to inconvenience you like this," McKenna told him.

"No problem at all, Monsieur," the lieutenant assured him. "Except for an occasional avalanche in the mountains, reuniting lost children with their parents or classmates, and directing traffic around the cathedral, we don't have much to do in the way of police work here. People come to Lourdes to be good, not bad."

McKenna hadn't been there ten minutes before a unit reported by radio to the lieutenant. They had located the hotel Hector had stayed at the night before, but he had checked out at one that afternoon. "I assume you would like to speak to the manager?" the lieutenant asked McKenna.

"Yes, I would."

McKenna drove behind the lieutenant through town to the Hôtel d'Annecy. It was a small, old, family-owned hotel, located near the railroad station and at the opposite end of town from the cathedral. There was a police car parked in front, among the four cars McKenna assumed belonged to the guests of the hotel.

The manager and two gendarmes were having coffee in the dining room when McKenna and the lieutenant walked in. The manager was a congenial fellow in his thirties who introduced himself as Monsieur Durand, but he would entertain no further questions until the lieutenant and McKenna were seated with cups of steaming café au lait in front of them. Then followed ten minutes of informal pleasantries between Durand and the lieutenant, during which they inquired on the health of each other's families and the progress of their children in school. After that, there were observations and predictions on the weather, a short discussion on the winter tourist season, and some general rejoicing by the lieutenant, the manager, and the two gendarmes because the Lourdes high school soccer team had finally beaten those filthy heathen children from the Tarbes high school.

McKenna sat drinking his coffee and listening, not at all disturbed by the wait. He thought it was the best cup of coffee he had ever had. Finally, Durand turned to him and asked, "What can I tell you about Monsieur Robles?"

"You've seen his picture?" McKenna asked.

"Yes," Durand said, nodding to the gendarmes. "I'm certain it was him."

"His name isn't Robles, it's De la Cruz and he's murdered fourteen people," McKenna said solemnly.

McKenna had been expecting a horrified reaction to his statement, but got nothing but a polite, inquiring look from Durand. Finally, McKenna had to ask, "You're not concerned that a mass murderer was here at your hotel among your family and guests?"

"Not at all."

"Why not, if you don't mind my asking. Don't you believe me?"

"Of course I believe you, but permit me to tell you something. Nobody leaves Lourdes the same as when they arrived here. You tell me he *is* a murderer, but I tell you that he *was* a murderer. Like many others he came here to rejoin the Christian community, and I'm sure he has done so."

"Did he tell you that?"

"No, he didn't have to. I've seen it happen many times."

"You talked to him?"

"Yes, of course. I registered him and showed him to his room when he arrived last night, my wife and I served him breakfast this morning, and I checked him out this afternoon."

"How did he seem to you?"

"Very pleasant."

"Did he seem to be sick?"

"Oh, yes, but that is not unusual. Many sick people come to Lourdes in pain and complaining about everything. But they always feel better when they leave."

"And Hector. How did he look to you when he checked out?"

"Much better. He had been to the cathedral and I could see he had prayed at the grotto."

"Did he have much luggage with him?"

"I don't know. He only brought one suitcase from the car."

"What kind of car was it?" McKenna asked.

"A green Renault with French plates."

"You didn't get the license number, did you?"

"No. Sorry."

"May I see his registration card?"

"Certainly." Durand went outside to the desk and returned with the standard French hotel reservation card. He gave it to McKenna with a shrug in the lieutenant's direction.

The only information on Hector's card was M. Robles for name and Madrid as the address. The boxes for passport number, nationality, make of auto, and registration number were blank.

"Not a lot of information here," McKenna commented.

"Why should there be?" Durand asked in reply.

"Isn't it a French law that certain information is required of foreign guests in hotels?"

"Oh, I see," Durand said. "Yes, it's a law, and a good one for other places. I believe its purpose is to protect hotels from theft by unscrupulous guests, but we don't need it here."

"You've never had an unscrupulous guest?"

"In Lourdes? No, never," Durand said, amused by the question. "My family has run this hotel for eighty years and we've never had a problem from a guest nor lost so much as a towel. On the contrary, our guests go to the grotto and leave in their rooms the towels they've appropriated from other hotels when they check out. It's always been quite a problem for us returning those towels to hotels all over Europe.''

''I see,'' McKenna said as he noticed the lieutenant and his men nodding in agreement with Durand's violation of that silly law.

The lieutenant was right, McKenna decided. Being a cop in this town must be a really boring job. ''How did Hector pay his bill?'' he asked.

''In francs.''

''Did he give any indications about where he was going?''

''Yes, he did. He asked directions for Paris.''

''Is the room he stayed in still available?''

''Yes, it is. Would you like me to show it to you?''

''No, that won't be necessary. I'll take it,'' McKenna said, then turned to the lieutenant. ''Thank you very much, Lieutenant,'' he said. ''You can have your men discontinue the search.''

''Are you sure he didn't leave here and check into another hotel in town? Most people spend two days here.''

''No, he's gone. He's seen the town many times before and knows it well,'' McKenna explained.

''Should I notify the Paris police?'' the lieutenant asked.

''You'd do better to notify the Nairobi police,'' McKenna said, but saw that his answer had perplexed the lieutenant. ''I don't know exactly where he's going next, but one thing is certain. It isn't Paris,'' he explained.

''Oh, I get it. This man is very clever, no?''

''Yes, he's very clever. Thank you.''

After handshakes all around with Durand, the French police left and McKenna went out to his car, returned with his suitcases, and Durand handed him a hotel registration card. McKenna wrote simply *B. McKenna, New York*, and handed it back to Durand. Completely satisfied, the manager showed McKenna to his room.

It was in the front on the second floor, overlooking the hotel entrance and the parking lot. The clean, small room was spartan, containing just a double bed, an armoire, a dresser, and a nightstand. There was an ancient TV on top of the dresser and a telephone on the nightstand. The decorations consisted of a crucifix over the bed and two religious prints on the walls. In contrast, the bathroom was large, well lit, and modern.

''Breakfast is served beginning at six and the cathedral opens at seven,'' Durand said. ''Will there be anything else?''

''No, thank you.''

Durand left and McKenna showered before he began his search of the room. He found it in the first place he looked, under the mattress in the center of the bed. The envelope was hotel stationery and addressed to him. He opened it, took out the letter, and read:

Dear Detective McKenna,

Once again, congratulations are in order. You may be unhappy to know that I'm feeling much better, for the moment. You should spend some time tomorrow walking around this wonderful town and make sure to visit the cathedral. Although I did not get to do much sightseeing myself today, you might also find the fortress interesting and there is a funicular running to the top of the mountain just south of town. The view from the top is breathtaking and I recommend you take the time to see it.

Whatever else you do, don't miss the breakfast. Madame Durand is an excellent cook, the croissants are fresh, and the butter is sweet and homemade. The coffee is so good that I'm inclined to believe they are using a Costa Rican blend.

I have been reading the papers and have noticed with some interest that your department has undertaken a major publicity campaign against me. I'm astounded at how much you have learned in such a short time, but must admit that I am offended by one major error. I look forward to discussing this with you and hope to set the record straight. Au revoir.

Hector De la Cruz

P.S.: Of course I am not going to Paris.

What could be the error? McKenna wondered. Echoing Carmen's sentiments, his conclusion concerning the death of Dr. Rashid was the only possibility that came to mind.

He was tired, so he set his alarm clock for 6 A.M., climbed into bed, and turned out the light. Hector, I look forward to discussing it with you, too, was his final thought before sleep overtook him.

6 **Tuesday, March 12** **New York City**

Hector's whereabouts were still unknown, and little progress had been made in the case since McKenna had returned from Europe five weeks before, but the hue and cry from the press continued and public interest remained high as sightings of the now notorious criminal were reported all over the world. Most of them had been investigated by local police departments and ultimately had been found to be either unsubstantiated or a case of mistaken identity. However, almost a quarter of the sightings had been in Costa Rica and formal application had been made to the government there in each instance, requesting investigation and verification, but the requests had never been acted upon and, after the first ten, not even acknowledged.

Constant pressure on the NYPD for Hector's arrest came from all quarters of the media, save one. Fox Five seemed always to be first to report on any new development in the case, however minor, and Heidi had a built-in five-minute spot on every *Fox Five News* broadcast, five days a week. She had become known among viewers as the Hector Girl, and Fox Five had garnered a reputation as the Hector Channel. It didn't hurt the station's ratings, so Fox Five's increasing popularity intensified the desire among executives of the other networks for a successful end to the case. Through their commentators, they were vocal in this desire and put as much pressure as they could muster on the NYPD, citing, of course, the grave danger Hector posed to public safety as their main concern.

The viewers became bored with the rhetoric and the national networks' efforts to present them with real news stories and, in ever-increasing numbers, they tuned to Heidi and Fox Five—especially on Wednesdays and Thursdays, the days she broadcast her piece from on location in Costa Rica. She did man-in-the-street interviews there, in which every Costa Rican interviewed invariably extolled Hector's virtues and proclaimed him innocent of the trumped-up *Yanqui* charges. She also documented Hector's life in Costa Rica, taking her American viewers through the slums of San José where he had spent his childhood, to the orphanage where he had grown up, to his clinic, through the rain forests he had saved, to his old seat in the Legislative Assembly, and to his home in Tamarindo Bay.

The male viewers were the first to notice that the tropical heat was getting to Heidi because every week she wore less and less as she broadcast from Costa Rica. They watched on, secure in the knowledge that what little they couldn't see of Heidi wouldn't be long left to the imagination. It had been rumored she was to be featured in an upcoming issue of *Playboy*, and advance orders for May issues had nearly broken all previous records.

The Wednesday and Thursday broadcasts had been Heidi's idea, an effort on her part to balance the news and keep it lively. She called those the Good-Hector Days, since the rest of the week consisted entirely of Bad-Hector Days, thanks to Bob Hurley. He had done his homework and earned his pay as he managed to locate every living relative, schoolteacher, army buddy, minister, priest, social worker, lover, or cellmate of each of Hector's victims. Those willing to say the right thing and shed a tear on demand had gained their five minutes of fame as they were interviewed on camera by Heidi.

For the viewers' gratification, those interviewed had extolled the virtues not immediately apparent in the poor victims as they struggled through their sad, misguided lives before being so ruthlessly murdered. Between tears the aggrieved sobbed for justice, but somehow always ended up wishing that wonderful Detective McKenna luck in his endeavor to catch the heartless killer.

There was more to Heidi's spots, and some of it was real news of the few developments there had been in the case. She was the first to report that the police lab, assisted by Dr. Rowe from NYU, had cracked the secret of the enzyme Hector had combined with the cyanide to poison his victims. During his interview with Heidi, Inspector Scagnelli had modestly admitted that most of their success should be attributed to the computer disk Hector had left McKenna at Oldwick.

The disk chronicled Hector's discovery of a new species of passion vine butterfly in 1988 near the Costa Rican town of Arenal. He had been in the forest observing butterflies when he saw a bird known as a jacamar swoop from a tree and take a passion vine butterfly in flight. He observed the small bird land on a branch and begin eating the butterfly, but the jacamar soon let it drop from its beak. A minute later the bird also dropped from the branch, falling to the forest floor a meter away from its discarded prey.

Hector watched the jacamar die, gasping for breath as it exhibited the classic signs of cyanide poisoning in its death throes. He noted that less than three minutes elapsed before the bird died.

Only a wing, the head, and half of the thorax had remained of the butterfly. Hector wrote that the large black, red, and yellow passion vine butterfly appeared to belong to the species *Heliconius cydno*, but he noticed some small coloring differences in the red pattern on the wing between the highly toxic butterfly he had found and all the other less-toxic *Heliconius cydnos* butterflies he had studied in the past.

Hector recorded taking the jacamar and the butterfly remnants to his lab in San José. There he dissected the bird, and his findings perplexed him. Although he had watched the bird die from what he had assumed to be cyanide poisoning, he was able to find only minute traces of cyanide in the bird's bright red deoxygenated blood. He had theorized that the butterfly manufactured an enzyme in its body that had enhanced the toxic effects of the cyanide that all species of passion vine butterflies possessed in their bodies. He called his new species *Heliconius hectorius*.

Hector documented many other expeditions to the forest around Arenal in 1988, '89, and '90, but he failed to find another *Heliconius hectorius* until 1991, when he located a group of twenty-three of them. He reported that the rare, toxic butterfly slept with other members of its species at the same place in the forest every night. He took ten of them to his lab and dissected them, but was unable to isolate the enzyme from the butterflies' bodies, although he was certain of its existence.

He had conducted further experiments. He made a paste from a piece of the abdomen of one of the butterflies, dissolved it in alcohol, and fed one drop of the solution to a rhesus monkey, mixed in with its food. The monkey had become sick within minutes, but recovered.

Experimenting further, Hector added half a milligram of potassium cyanide to one drop of the butterfly/alcohol solution, and had then fed it to another monkey with its food. The animal sickened and died within five minutes of ingesting the poison. Concluding that experiment, Hector reported that death had occurred in the test animal after it had been administered less than ten percent of the amount of cyanide ordinarily necessary to kill an animal of the monkey's size and weight.

Hector conducted more experiments and had documented the deaths of more monkeys. His last experiment recorded on the disk had been conducted in July of 1993. Citing a lack of proper research equipment, Hector lamented that he had never been able to isolate the enzyme.

Scagnelli told Heidi that it hadn't been necessary for Hector to isolate the enzyme to produce his cyanide concoction and poison his victims. Hector had simply repeated his experiment, making a paste from the insects' abdomens, dissolving it in alcohol, mixing in a minute amount of cyanide, and then dissolving a few drops of his solution in a pint of Wild Irish Rose.

Dr. Rowe of NYU had also been interviewed by Heidi in another spot. From Hector's collection taken from the Park Avenue apartment, he had identified two *Heliconius hectorius* butterflies. Knowing what the species looked like and armed with Hector's description of the place near Arenal where he had discovered the butterflies, he had traveled to Costa Rica and returned after two weeks with nine live butterflies. Within another two weeks he had isolated the enzyme, reproduced it in the laboratory, and killed another two monkeys.

There had been other developments indirectly linked to the case, but those hadn't been covered by Heidi in her spots. The weather in New York had become considerably warmer and an early spring was forecast, but, since there had been no further attacks on the homeless in over six weeks, it was becoming more difficult for the police to talk them into the shelters at night as the temperatures rose. Most of the cops on the beat had given up trying, and Ben Rosen screamed his criticism of the NYPD's efforts at least once a week on one news show or another, but never on Fox Five. Headquarters ignored him, and the cops working the streets had quickly gotten the message, wasting no more time trying to talk the homeless into the shelters.

No disciplinary action had been taken at this noncompliance, and Rosen had screamed louder, whenever he got the chance. However, most of his time was spent organizing counterdemonstrations in response to the well-attended protest demonstrations organized by the Upper East Side and other residents' associations who wanted the armories returned to their original purpose and the homeless out of their neighborhoods. As the number of homeless in the shelters and armories declined each night, everyone except Rosen concluded that he was fighting a losing battle, and a boring one at that.

Over the weeks, McKenna had found himself with very little to do, so he had more than enough time for lunches with Heidi. They became good friends. Her antics and methods in her rise to stardom amused McKenna and she loved hearing unabridged stories of her father's escapades in the police department. They caught up on the years and, on occasion, she teasingly called him Uncle Brian. He protested whenever she said it, but in reality he didn't mind at all because he had come to regard her as his naughty-but-nice niece. Heidi's attitudes and plans regarding McKenna during the first week of the case were never mentioned again by either of them.

McKenna had told Angelita of his lunch meetings with Heidi and she had accepted it after some initial protests. He had offered to include her, but Angelita had declined, saying she already had enough friends. McKenna suspected that Angelita preferred to hate and distrust Heidi and that she was afraid she might find something to like or respect in the rising young reporter.

Cisco was still on station in Tamarindo Bay and reporting daily on his surveillance of Hector's house, but there had been no sign of the doctor. Cisco found that Hector had a man looking after the house, but the caretaker lived outside of town and only spent a couple of hours each morning there, tending to the grounds and tidying up. His name was Victorio and, naturally, he had come to view Cisco as one of his dearest friends. He had told Cisco that he hadn't heard from Hector in two months.

As far as McKenna was concerned, the lack of positive information from Cisco, though distressing, was something to be expected, even after another $10,000 in expenses. Since returning from Europe, McKenna and Carmen had corresponded by mail since she still distrusted speaking over the telephone. They both still agreed that Hector would ultimately go home to die.

McKenna wasn't feeling too good when he arrived at the squad room at 9 A.M. He and Angelita had been at Bellevue all night, staying with Jake when he died. It had been a sad affair; Jake had never left the hospital after the attack six weeks earlier, but that wasn't what had killed him. It was the cancer and, near the end, Jake had wanted to die. What saddened McKenna was not so much Jake's death, but rather the unfulfilled promise. He had promised Jake that he would get Hector for him, but hadn't been able to fulfill that commitment in time.

McKenna wanted to do something, but all he could do was wait. It wasn't his move yet. Maybe today will be the day, he hoped once. He checked his assignment sheet and was disappointed again. For the second day in a row there had been no Hector sightings reported in the city, so he had a cup of coffee with Maureen and discussed her cases. It had become a standard routine, since there was very little to discuss about his own case that everyone in America hadn't heard already. Most days during the past month he had done nothing more than have breakfast, read the paper, have lunch, attempt the *Times* crossword puzzle, talk briefly to the press, and go home.

McKenna had spoken to Ward and asked to be put into the case rotation until Hector was located, but Ward wouldn't hear of it. "How would it look if the detective in charge of the most important case this department is handling showed up at someone's house because they had reported that their neighbor's kid had pinched their daughter on the ass, inflicting lifetime scars on the poor little darling?" he had asked.

McKenna hadn't been able to come up with an answer, but Ward had made a few more points. "Keep in mind that the press thinks you're working on this case twenty-four hours a day," he had said.

"But there's nothing to do on it right now."

"We know that, but they can't be let in on the secret."

"So what do you want me to do all day?" McKenna had asked.

"Just what you're doing now, most of the time. Nothing, but make sure you do it here every day."

So McKenna did nothing most days, and did it as best he could. This day started no differently. By ten o'clock he had finished reading the *Times* and was ready to go to breakfast when a DHL messenger arrived with an overnight letter from Carmen.

McKenna was surprised and excited as he signed for it. Letters from Carmen usually arrived on Fridays, and he had received one the Friday before. In it she had commented that she was still a prisoner to the press and hadn't been out in six weeks. She worried that she might be losing her mind, but said that her stockholders couldn't afford the speculation in the press a psychiatrist visiting her home would be bound to cause. She didn't say it, but McKenna knew that she fervently wished the whole affair was over.

The messenger left and McKenna opened the letter. It was the shortest one he had ever received from Carmen. She said that she had awakened Saturday to find that Monsieur Picard was gone, but he had left a note. She apologized for not informing him earlier, but she hoped that he would understand and forgive her. Included with her letter was a copy of Picard's parting note to her.

Picard's short note was in French. In it he told Carmen that it was almost over, and that he would be back when it was. He asked that, if she must inform Detective McKenna of his absence, would she please wait two days before doing so? If she couldn't, Picard wrote that he would understand. He closed by asking her to be strong and to pray for Hector and him.

McKenna noted that Carmen had given Picard the two days before writing, but that was fine with him. He was prepared and ready to go. He had a suitcase sitting in his office, packed for the tropics, and another one at home packed the same. In addition, he had a round-trip open ticket to San José, his passport, international service on his cellular phone, and $2,000 in colones. He wanted to wait and hear what Cisco had to say when he reported in at noon, but the last flight for San José left at eleven.

He pondered his dilemma for a moment, and then remembered something that brightened his day. It was Tuesday, so he could wait to hear from Cisco and still make it to Costa Rica that day after all. Heidi had become a big shot, so she and her film crew would be going down that afternoon on the Fox corporate jet for her Wednesday and Thursday broadcasts. His passage on her plane would be considered highly unusual by the other networks if they ever found out about it, but it fit his plan perfectly for a number of reasons.

He went into Ward's office and gave the squad commander the news. It was well received at first, but then Ward looked worried. "So it's finally come," he said.

"If I'm right, it has," McKenna agreed.

"And if you're right, you're headed to jail."

"Yeah, but it shouldn't be so bad, if I'm right."

"Let me know what Cisco has to say," Ward said.

As soon as he left Ward's office, McKenna called Angelita and told her his trip was finally on. In the interests of domestic tranquillity, he neglected to mention his manner of transport. Still, Angelita was unhappy, but she had known this was coming sooner or later. She would meet him for lunch before he left. Then he called Brunette and got a slightly better reaction. It would be three for lunch at 12:30.

McKenna was in his office and staring at the phone when it rang at exactly noon.

"Looks like we've got some developments," Cisco said.

"Hector's there?"

"I didn't see him, but there's a Nissan Pathfinder with Nicaraguan plates parked in the driveway."

"Did you see anybody?"

"Yeah, a tall guy in his fifties, distinguished looking in a snotty sort of way. He's sitting on the front veranda, looking around and reading the paper."

"Tell me he's wearing a monocle," McKenna said.

"How'd you know?"

62 Considering all the publicity he had received, McKenna had expected that the Costa Rican Immigration officials would question him closely about his purpose in their country as soon as they read his name off his passport, but that didn't happen. McKenna attributed the pleasant surprise to his manner of arrival and the company he was in.

The weekly arrival of Heidi Lane and her staff had come to be regarded by the officials as a routine visit by dignitaries, and they were given special treatment. Instead of having to wait in line for processing in the international arrivals terminal, Immigration came to them as soon as the Fox plane was parked in its regular spot on the tarmac. While everybody was still seated, Heidi's director collected all the passports and gave them to the official waiting at the door of the plane. Minutes later, McKenna had his stamped passport back in his pocket.

The sun was setting as they left the plane. Two vans with drivers waited for them on the tarmac. McKenna, Heidi, and her cameraman carried their luggage into one van while the rest of the film crew took the other. The film crew would be staying at the Gran Hotel downtown and they would register Heidi and her cameraman there as well, but Heidi told her driver to take them to the municipal airport at La Sabana. A small chartered plane was ready for them, and an hour later they landed at the Tamarindo Bay airport.

Cisco met them, deeply tanned and tropically resplendent in a multicolored flowered shirt, khaki shorts, and Dock-Sides loafers. He had let his hair grow and had it pulled back into a short ponytail.

McKenna started to make the introductions, but Heidi stopped him. "Don't I know you?" she asked Cisco.

"Sure you do. We had drinks together a couple of weeks ago when you were here filming your spot at Hector's house," Cisco said. "La Mesa del Capitan, remember?"

"Yes, I remember. And didn't you tell me at the time that you were a rich real-estate developer looking at properties here?"

"I could be, but I probably forgot to mention to you that I'm stuck with this crazy police-work hobby."

"That's what you call your act here? Police work?"

"No, I call it high-quality police work."

"You sure fooled me," Heidi said, then turned to McKenna. "I swear, I thought he owned the town."

Probably does, by now, McKenna thought. "Cisco's very resourceful," he answered.

It turned out that Cisco also knew Heidi's cameraman, Mike. Cisco had shown him around town one night while they had been filming a few weeks before, and McKenna assumed it must have been quite a time; Mike was deferential to Cisco, apparently holding him in high regard.

Cisco led them to his car, a rented Range Rover. They loaded the luggage into the back, then piled in, and Cisco drove them to town on the badly rutted dirt road. Minutes later they were in town, and McKenna could see that there wasn't much there, but it was obviously undergoing major changes. The road ran close to the beach with old hotels and restaurants lining it on both sides, but new homes, stores, and small hotels were under construction on every available lot. McKenna strained to see the ocean, catching only glimpses of it through the trees. "What's so special about this place?" he asked Cisco, but it was Heidi who answered.

"Wait till you see the beach, and then you'll know," she said. "As you can see, this town has been discovered. Life is simple here, the food's great, the views are magnificent, and everything's cheap by our standards."

"Speaking of food, you folks want to eat first or go straight to the villas?" Cisco asked.

"Eat," Heidi said.

A minute later Cisco pulled in front of an old restaurant on the beach, La Habana Cafe. A thatched roof supported by log posts covered the dining room, but the walls were only three feet high to permit an expansive view of the bay. They got out of the car and went in. Their party was immediately greeted like visiting royalty. The manager, the waitresses, and the waiters all had come to the door to greet Cisco. Once they were seated at a table right next to the beach, even the cook and the dishwashers came from the kitchen to say hello to him.

The restaurant was only half full, but many nationalities were represented among the diners. Besides English and Spanish, McKenna also heard Italian, German, and French. Heidi was right, he saw. Tamarindo Bay had been discovered, and he could see why. It was beautiful, a wide horseshoe-shaped expanse of water lined with forested hills buffered by white beaches. The waves began far out in the bay, just before a small island in the middle, and even by moonlight McKenna could see that a few surfers were out taking advantage of the high tide. A cool ocean breeze just barely disturbed the clothing, causing McKenna to think that the temperature was just perfect. He could see the lights of houses on the beach and in the hills all around the bay.

"Where's Hector's house?" McKenna asked.

"On the beach, about a mile north of here," Cisco said, pointing.

"And where are you staying?"

"Captain Suiza's Villas, the same place you'll be staying. Real nice, on the beach, and right down the road from Hector's place. You can stay with me and I rented another villa for Heidi and Mike right next to ours."

"Can you see Hector's place from yours?"

"No, but there's some dense woods across the road from his house. I've made an observation blind there and spend a lot of time doing nothing but watching."

"Has Picard left the house at all?"

"Only once, as far as I know. Drove into town this afternoon and I found him there at one of the grocery stores. Spent the equivalent of two hundred dollars, then he went to a liquor store across the street and bought a couple of bottles of cognac. He drove straight home, put the car in the garage, and has been there ever since."

"As far as you know," McKenna observed.

"Yeah, as far as I know," Cisco said defensively. "I'm only one man, but I give it an honest twelve hours a day of sitting in the woods and watching that house. It was empty when I left last night, but when I got there this morning the

Pathfinder was in the driveway and Picard was sitting on the veranda. Now you know as much as I do.''

"Sorry, Cisco," McKenna said. "I didn't mean to sound critical. I'm sure you've been working long and hard.''

"Let's not get carried away. I've been working long, but not hard," Cisco said, smiling. "Sitting sunrise to sunset here isn't like sitting in a filthy tenement watching a joint in Harlem. Besides, I've managed to find myself some nighttime diversions, so I'm not complaining.''

"But still no Hector?" McKenna asked.

"Maybe he's there, but I haven't seen him."

"What about the caretaker? You talk to him?"

"I was watching the house when he showed up for work this morning. Picard was sitting on the veranda, they had a talk, and then Picard gave him an envelope. Victorio left without doing a thing, but I found him in town after I talked to you. He was doing a little celebrating, so I had a couple of beers with him. He said Picard gave him a month's pay and told him to take a vacation.''

"He knows Picard?"

"Sure, from when Hector and Carmen lived here."

"Picard didn't say anything about Hector to him?" McKenna asked.

"No, but I don't think it would come up. According to Victorio, Picard's the man in charge of the help and he always does whatever Picard tells him to do. This time he was happy to do it.''

"He's got to be in there," Heidi said. "Why else would Picard be here and why else would he give Victorio a month off?"

"I don't know, but this just seems too easy," McKenna said.

"This has been easy?" Heidi asked. "You've chased this man across two continents. Let's get this over with so I can get it on film.''

"I have to be certain he's here before we can do anything," McKenna said.

"So what do we do until then?" she asked.

"We have no choice but to wait."

"How long?"

"Until we see him."

"Suppose he doesn't show himself in the next couple of days?" she asked.

"Then you and your crew will go back to New York. I'll stay here with Cisco, watching and waiting. If we see him, we'll do it when you come back next week.''

"Let me get this straight," Heidi said. "If you don't see him tomorrow or Thursday, then I'm going back to New York without you?"

"Yes. Like Cisco says, he's only one man. Between the two of us, we'll watch the place twenty-four hours. If Hector's there, we're bound to see him.''

"Your absence is going to cause a lot of speculation in New York," Heidi observed.

"I know, but we'll have to work around that. The important thing is that, thanks to you, I've managed to slip legally into this country without the authorities noticing that I'm here. I don't know if we could pull that off again next week, so I'll stay.''

"And what if you don't see him tomorrow, Thursday, or during the week I'm gone? What then? Wait another week?"

"I don't know," McKenna admitted. "I'll think of something." He saw that his answer had made Heidi unhappy, but he couldn't think of anything else to tell her.

"Anyone mind telling me what you're going to do after you see him?" Cisco asked, but the waitress had arrived to take their orders and McKenna didn't answer just then. "Well, what?" Cisco asked as soon as she left.

"It's complicated, so let's not worry about it until we're sure he's here," McKenna said.

McKenna's refusal to say more made Cisco as unhappy as Heidi, but they both snapped out of it when the food arrived. Everyone had ordered one or another of the local seafood specialties, and their plates came heaped with food. It looked and smelled delicious, so they all dug right in. Nobody was disappointed and the conversation turned from Hector to Costa Rica. During dinner, Cisco, Mike, and Heidi talked about the weather there, the people, and the cheap cost of living. McKenna didn't say much and only listened with half an ear. Hector was still on his mind as he ate. Agreeing with Heidi, he acknowledged that everything pointed to Hector being in the house, but he wouldn't have been surprised if there was just another letter waiting for him. He was getting tired of that and wanted finally to meet the man face-to-face and end it.

After dinner Cisco drove them to the Captain Suiza Villas. There were seven of them, new, spacious thatched-roof cottages surrounding a large kidney-shaped pool. The complex was separated from the beach by a narrow band of landscaped forest, but the sound of the surf pounding on the beach was clearly audible.

Cisco had already registered them, had the key, and was eager to show Heidi and Mike their accommodations. He pointed out their exterior light switches, wiped his feet on the doormat, and unlocked the door.

It was nice. Besides a large living room and dining area that faced the pool, there were two bedrooms with a bathroom in each, a small kitchen, a laundry room, and another bathroom. The furniture was new and comfortable, the lighting was soft and indirect, there was a CD player and cable TV, and the place was immaculate.

Heidi and Mike had become used to the good life and made no comment, but McKenna was impressed. "Our place is like this?" he asked Cisco.

"The same. You've got to take the good with the bad, I always say. You want to take a look at Hector's place?"

McKenna did. Heidi and Mike had already seen it, so they decided to wait in their villa.

It was a few minutes' walk down the dark, unlighted road. The forest canopy completely blocked the moonlight so that McKenna could hardly see Cisco until they were in front of the house. It was a spacious home with a separate two-car garage, located on a landscaped one-acre lot surrounded by a four-foot masonry wall. Like Captain Suiza's Villas, Hector's place was separated from the beach by a narrow band of forest. Except for one exterior light near the front door, the house and grounds were in total darkness and the windows were all shuttered, so McKenna couldn't tell if there were lights on inside. He stood staring at the house, trying to imagine Hector and Carmen living there together in happier times.

It was difficult. To McKenna, it looked like a country retreat, large enough to be considered opulent by Costa Rican standards, but certainly nothing like the homes Carmen was used to. After having seen her estates in Spain and New Jersey, he had a hard time imagining her living here.

"Seen enough?" Cisco asked.

"For now. Let's go back and get our last good night's sleep. Starting at dawn tomorrow, one of us is going to be watching that house until we see Hector."

63

McKenna and Cisco had spent a long and frustrating week watching Hector's house, seeing plenty of Picard but nothing of Hector. The Frenchman hadn't left the grounds and had spent most daylight hours sitting on the veranda, reading, but it looked to McKenna like that was about to change. At 11:50, ten minutes before McKenna's noon relief, Picard had backed the Pathfinder out of the garage and parked it by the front door. Before going back into the house, he checked the oil, inspected the tires, and raised McKenna's hopes. Just as Cisco showed up to relieve him, Picard emerged from the house carrying two suitcases. He loaded them in the back of the Pathfinder, then drove off toward town and the world.

"What now?" Cisco asked.

"If he doesn't come back, I'm going in tonight."

"To arrest Hector?"

"No, just a quiet look around to see if he's there."

"And if he is?"

"Heidi's getting back tonight, so I'll do it tomorrow."

"I think it's time you explained to me exactly what we're doing here," Cisco said adamantly.

McKenna thought so, too. "Once I know he's in there, J. Davenport is going to formally request his extradition, even though we have no extradition treaty with Costa Rica. Once he does that, the Costa Rican authorities will realize that we know Hector's here."

"They might not even know themselves he's here," Cisco said.

"Maybe not, but they'll know once J. Davenport makes his request. Then timing becomes crucial. They'll never give up their favorite doctor, so I have to go in and arrest Hector before they have a chance to put this house under police guard to prevent exactly what I intend to do."

"And then bring him to the police station in Tamarindo Bay while Heidi films it, right? They're sure not gonna like that," Cisco observed.

"I know, but then the ball will be in their court."

"Chances are that they'll cut Hector loose and lock you up," Cisco observed.

"Maybe, but our case will be cleared by arrest."

"Is it that important?"

"Yes. I spoke to Brunette this morning and he tells me that he's been under a lot of pressure since I left town. There's been a lot of speculation in the press about where I am and what I'm doing. They're almost screaming for results, so, one way or another, this thing has to end soon."

"And Heidi? What's she been doing?"

"Screaming along with everyone else, but not quite as loud. She knows that if it leaked that I was down here, the Costa Ricans would put it together and the show would be over. I'd say that Heidi and the Fox people have been magnificent."

"Magnificent? I'd say that little Heidi kept her mouth closed and set herself up for a great story."

"Then I guess it just depends on how you look at it," McKenna said.

McKenna picked up Heidi and Mike at the airport at 10 P.M. and gave her the news.

"So tonight's the night and tomorrow's the day?" she asked as they loaded the luggage into the Range Rover.

"Hopefully."

"So Uncle Brian's feeling good about going to jail in the Third World," she asked playfully.

"Uncle Brian's feeling great about it. You hungry?"

"I'm always hungry."

McKenna drove them to La Habana and he surprised them with how much he ate. He felt like a man on death row, eating his last good meal for a long time. Cisco was on duty in the woods, so they took an order to go for him when they left. After dinner, McKenna took them to their villa, then delivered Cisco his meal. Picard hadn't returned, the house was in darkness, and nothing was stirring. McKenna told him that he'd be back at 2:00 A.M.

"Before you go, tell me just one thing about this," Cisco said.

"Okay. One thing. What?"

"You've got no gun, no shield, and probably no handcuffs, right?"

"That's right."

"Suppose Hector doesn't like your plan for him and decides he doesn't want to go to the police station. What then?"

"Then I'll have to drag him. Shouldn't be too tough in his condition."

"Suppose it gets tough?" Cisco asked.

"Then maybe I'll need some help," McKenna conceded.

"You mean maybe you'll need someone to keep you company in jail, don't you?"

"Yeah, I guess that's what I mean."

"Well, if it comes to that, you tell your pal Brunette that I expect to be earning overtime rates for every hour I'm in there with you."

"Thanks, Cisco. I'll tell him."

64 The alarm went off at 1:30. McKenna got up, took a shower, then dressed in the darkest clothes he had with him. Then, for the third time, he inspected the tools Cisco had bought for him in town. The gym bag contained most of the items McKenna had seen in burglars' kits over the years: a flashlight, a screwdriver, a hammer, tape, pliers, a crowbar, and a venetian blind slat. He put them all back in the gym bag and left to meet Cisco.

Although they weren't supposed to participate in any part of the night's activities, he wasn't surprised to see Mike and Heidi sitting on their veranda waiting for him. Mike had his camera and lights slung over his shoulder. Heidi knew what McKenna was planning, and if she had enough confidence in Mike to tell him about it, then that was fine with McKenna. They joined him as he passed their villa.

"I hope you two realize that tonight's visit is strictly off the record," McKenna said as he walked.

"We know. Don't worry about us," Heidi said.

"Then why the camera?"

"It always goes where I go, but it doesn't go on unless you say so," Mike said. Then he reached into his camera pouch, took out a portable radio, and gave it to McKenna. "Just give me a call if you need me for anything. It's charged and ready to go," he said.

"Thanks, Mike. I was wishing I had one of these," McKenna said. He put the radio in his gym bag and the three walked on in silence. By the time they met Cisco in the woods, McKenna was on pins and needles.

"You sure you're ready for this?" Cisco asked.

"Yeah, I'm sure," McKenna answered. He searched his mind for some smart comment to make, but couldn't think of one that fit the way he felt. So all he said was, "See you later," then he left them and walked through the woods to Hector's veranda while thinking of all the things that could go wrong.

Maybe Picard was supposed to meet Hector here, but Hector never showed, was one thought. That one was followed by *Maybe he's dead already.* There were more, but he put them out of his mind as he stood in front of Hector's door in the glare of the single exterior light. He tried the doorknob; it was locked, so he walked around the house trying windows. Each one was covered with a steel shutter, but he tried them all anyway and found them all locked tight. The side door was locked and the double doors in the back leading to the pool were shuttered.

He decided that the the side door was his best bet. He put his gym bag on the ground, took out the crowbar, and inserted it in the doorjamb just above the doorknob. As he applied pressure, the doorjamb creaked before the door sprang open with a loud crack. The interior of the house was dark and he waited a moment, listening. He heard nothing but the surf and wind, so he put the crowbar back in the bag and took out the flashlight and radio. He put the radio in his belt, gave a wave to the woods, and went in, leaving the gym bag outside.

He was in the kitchen. As he shined his light around it, he saw that it was large, clean, and modern. He left it, passed through a formal dining room, and found himself in the entrance hallway by the front door. There was a stairway leading up on the right, but he ignored it for the moment and searched the ground floor. He quickly realized that the house was bigger than it looked from the outside. There was a living room, a library, an office, a pool room, a den, and two bathrooms, but no sign of Hector.

He went back to the entrance hallway and climbed the stairs as quietly as he could, but not as quietly as he would have liked. The stairs creaked and it sounded like thunder to McKenna. When he got to the top he waited and listened, but heard nothing but his own breathing.

There was a wide hallway on the second floor with six rooms spaced along it. Four of the doors were open, but the doors at either end of the hallway were closed. McKenna decided to search the open rooms first and it didn't take long. Each was a bedroom with a separate bathroom and a walk-in closet. It took only moments to go through the closets and look under the beds, but still no sign of Hector.

McKenna stood in the hallway, his nerves on end as he thought about which room to try next. He decided to try the one at the left end of the hall first, thinking that, if this house was laid out the same as the Oldwick estate, then the bedroom on the left should be Hector's and the one on the right should be Carmen's. He stood in front of the door for a moment, took a deep breath, then opened it.

The smell of death immediately assailed his nostrils. From the doorway, he shined his light inside and saw that there was a body lying on the bed, under the covers. There was an IV stand next to the bed and an intravenous line was running to the arm. He shined his light around the room, saw nothing suspicious, then slowly approached the body, noticing that, the closer he got, the worse the smell was. Dead about three days, he thought as he shined his light on the face.

"What the hell?" McKenna heard himself say as he stared down at the mannequin. As the lights came on, he wheeled around and saw Hector sitting in a chair in the doorway of the walk-in closet, dressed in a suit and tie, with a cocked pistol pointed at McKenna's chest in one hand and the remote switch for the lights in the other. He was clean-shaven, his hair was cut short and dyed gray, and he looked thin and sick, but nowhere near death. "So we meet at last, Detective McKenna," he said, smiling politely. "I have been looking forward to this."

"Me too, but I wasn't expecting it to be under these circumstances. Nice little joke you pulled on me," McKenna said, struggling to bring his nerves under control as he tried not to stare at the gun. Although Hector was smiling as if a neighbor had just dropped in, McKenna was sure the doctor would shoot him if he tried anything.

"Sorry. I felt a little melodrama was necessary to put us in a position to talk," Hector said. "I assume you are unarmed?"

"Yes," McKenna answered, raising his arms and still holding his flashlight. Hector looked offended by his action.

"Please put your arms down, Detective McKenna," Hector said. "I believe you and I do not think we will be telling each other lies at this point. Would you please turn that flashlight off and take a seat on the bed?"

McKenna did as he was told. "Where's that smell coming from?" he asked.

"Sorry to make you uncomfortable. There is a dead goat under the bed."

"Three days?"

"Four. Monsieur Picard tells me it smells awful, but my sense of smell is just about gone. I see you have a radio, so I assume you have some people outside."

"I do."

"Is one of them Heidi Lane?"

"Yes, she's here."

"Does she have a news crew with her?"

"Just a cameraman."

"Excellent. We will ask them to come in a little later, but first I have a few questions for you and I am sure you have some for me."

That's an understatement, McKenna thought as he regarded Hector. The doctor was smiling back at him, but McKenna could see he was in pain. "How are you feeling?" he asked.

"Terrible. Yourself?"

"Not too good, either. I guess I wasn't cut out to be a burglar."

"A burglar? Nonsense. You are an invited guest in my home."

I guess I am, McKenna realized. He wanted me here for whatever reason and he played me perfectly. But why? Not just to chat, I'm sure, but that part should be interesting enough. "Okay, questions," he said. "Who's first?"

"Me, if you do not mind. My first question is rather personal, and you don't have to answer it if you don't want to, but it is something I have been wondering about."

"Me and Heidi?" McKenna guessed.

"Yes, Heidi and you. The change in your public relationship over the past two months has intrigued me."

"It was complicated at first, but now it's simple. I like her and we've become close, but not in the biblical sense. I'm a married man and I love my wife. That answer your question?"

"Not entirely, but it will do. Next, what made you suspect that Benny Foster had been poisoned?"

"Initially, I didn't suspect a thing. The credit goes to my partner. She's very intuitive and you were leaving too many bodies around in one month. She noticed and became suspicious."

"That would be Detective Kaplowitz?"

"Yeah, Maureen Kaplowitz. She's smart and I wound up looking good. Until tonight, that is."

"I see, but she did nothing about her suspicions until you came on the case. Am I correct in that?"

"Partially. She did what she could, but I'm sort of a heavyweight in the department and I got a few breaks."

"From me?"

"Yes, from you. You made a few mistakes."

"I agree, but I think they would have gone unnoticed if it were not for you. I consider it bad luck that you were assigned to the Seventeenth Precinct when you were."

"Thank you," McKenna said. "I'll take that as a compliment."

"It was meant to be, but let us get on to more important matters. How was Carmen when you left her?"

"She loves you dearly and I'm sure she's praying for you. This is very hard on her, but she'll pull through."

"After I am dead?" Hector asked casually.

"Yes, after you're dead. You really shocked her with your routine, but she loves you in spite of it."

"Does she think I am insane?"

"Fortunately, yes."

"Do you share her opinion?"

"Yes. Just between us, I do," McKenna said, expecting some reaction, but Hector's face didn't change. "Don't you see it?" McKenna asked. "You must be to have done the things you did."

"Yes, I see it, and I agree. I must have been insane, but let me assure you that I am not insane now and I see things clearer than I ever have."

"But that really makes no difference now, does it?" McKenna asked.

"I guess not, if we are talking about a legal defense for me. We both know my crimes will never be described before judge and jury. Correct?"

"Correct."

"I am glad we both realize that. Now I would like to point out your one glaring mistake. I hope you will believe me and I hope you will correct it later."

"Dr. Rashid?"

"Yes, Dr. Rashid. I did not kill him and the thought never even crossed my mind. He was a good friend who simply died of a heart attack. I tried everything I could to resuscitate him, but it was no use."

"I see," McKenna said. "You didn't call the police because they would have had questions and you didn't want anyone to know you were in town. I'm assuming you hadn't killed anybody yet, but you had made preparations."

"Yes. Talking to the police would have been inconvenient at that point and I saw no reason to help them clarify their paperwork. So I cleaned up and left."

"Was Rashid of any assistance to you in selecting your victims?" McKenna asked.

"No. I would not think of involving my friend in this and he provided no assistance. Somehow, you have taken the wrong road and still managed to arrive at the right place."

"Then how did you know who to kill?"

"How did I know who to kill?" Hector said, smiling as he repeated the question. "Detective McKenna, exactly how much do you think you know about me and my motivation?"

Time to be very careful, McKenna thought. He's the one with the gun. "Doctor, I know things about you that you'd never tell anyone else. I know what makes you tick, but I'm not in a position to get you mad at me."

Hector looked from McKenna down to the gun in his hands, then chuckled to himself before he looked up. "I am not going to shoot you for answering my questions," he said. "I realize Carmen must have told you about Juliette and I expected you to draw some conclusions from that."

"I already knew about Juliette before I went to see Carmen and I knew why you were killing," McKenna stated. "I think I told Carmen more than she told me."

"You knew about Juliette?" Hector asked, stunned for a moment. "Again I have underestimated you, Detective McKenna, and I am forced to acknowledge that you are right. You probably do know more about me than I would care to tell anyone, but we are way past that. What was your question?"

"If Rashid didn't help you, how did you know who to kill?"

"Simple. Juliette told me. Two years ago, when we first found out she was HIV positive, we would sit outside the AIDS clinic for hours. She pointed out the men she had been with. Most of them were showing symptoms and she was not, yet, so it had to be one of them."

"And you figure that, whichever of them gave it to her, they knew they had it when they did?" McKenna asked.

"What would you think?"

"The same, I guess. So you were seeking revenge for Juliette, not yourself."

"For myself, I have nothing to seek vengeance for. My punishment is the price of sin and betrayal. We did not know that Juliette had AIDS during our one time together, but I do not think it would have made much difference to me if I had known. I will not try to explain it to you, but I do not regret the happiness Juliette and I shared."

"Do you regret killing those people?"

"I try to, but it does not come easy for me. I know them too well. Before I got sick, I made it my business to investigate their habits and find out who they were."

"Was it a tough investigation?" McKenna asked.

"Rather easy for me. I walk their walk and talk their talk, as they say. I knew them all. Ate, drank, and panhandled with them. And talked with them, a lot."

"Philosophy?" McKenna asked.

"Yes, the philosophy of living. Found that they are all takers and don't worry about anybody but themselves. Talked about Juliette with them, too. Invariably, they described her as a good piece of ass when she was in the mood. They knew what they were doing when they infected her, but they did not care."

"Is that when you decided to kill them?"

"No. I had thought about it and even made some plans, but I did not make a final decision until I returned to New York. When I saw what had become of Juliette, saw her suffering, I knew they had to die."

"And you started killing them in January?"

"Yes, after I heard that she had died. All in all, I think I did a pretty good job of it."

"That doesn't sound like regret to me," McKenna observed.

"It's not. It is called gloating, but I pray for the ability to regret my actions."

"Why?"

"Because it is part of the formula. In order to be forgiven for your sins, you have to regret them. I am happy to say that, at times, I do experience some remorse, so I'm within the guidelines and I have a shot at salvation."

"You went to confession at Lourdes, didn't you?" McKenna asked.

"Yes. I went there, I prayed, I felt remorse, and then I went to confession."

"And you were forgiven?"

"Yes, I confessed and received absolution, with the usual contingency clause."

"Penance?"

"Yes. The penance the priest gave me was what you would expect. Prayer, good works, and the reason you're here."

"Your confessor told you that you must surrender to the authorities for your absolution to be effective?"

"Unfortunately, yes. So I intend to surrender to you for punishment, in a manner of speaking."

"Didn't you say your case would never be heard by judge and jury?"

"I leave the details to your imagination. For the moment, I am in charge, but I am tired and in more pain than you can imagine. I am ready to be interviewed by your reporter friend and conclude this affair."

McKenna did use his imagination and suspected that he knew Hector's intentions. They didn't sit well with him. "Is there a chance that you're going to kill me?" he asked.

The question amused Hector. "It is a possibility, Detective McKenna," he said. "It all depends on you."

"And how about Heidi and her cameraman? Is there a chance you'll kill them, too?"

"Same answer. You can tell her that I might kill her, but that I will grant her an interview before I do. I am betting she will be disposed to take that chance."

McKenna found that Hector was right. He called Heidi on the radio and described his situation to her. She fussed a little and expressed concern for his safety before he gave her Hector's interview offer and all it entailed. "Don't let that wonderful man go anywhere. We'll be right up," were Heidi's last words before she went off the air.

"Mind answering a few more questions while we wait?" McKenna asked Hector.

"You want to know where I have been and how long I have to live?"

"Yes."

"Before I tell you, am I correct in assuming that you do not intend to charge Monsieur Picard with any crime?"

"I wouldn't think of it. I respect loyalty. As far as I'm concerned, he was never here."

"Thank you. It is a pleasure to be dealing with you, Detective McKenna. Monsieur Picard has many friends, some of them quite wealthy, and all of them value his friendship highly. Thanks to him, I have spent the last six weeks in some comfort in Mexico, Nicaragua, and here."

"How did you travel?"

"I came here from Nicaragua by boat, by yacht, really. It was not much of a problem since my country does not have anything that you would call a coast guard. Between the other countries I traveled in disguise on private planes."

"Are Monsieur Picard's friends all Basques?"

"A very interesting, resourceful, close-knit group, wouldn't you say?" Hector answered, avoiding the question in his own way.

"I'm learning that," McKenna answered. "Now for the last part of the question. How long do you have to live?"

Hector didn't answer. He just smiled at McKenna. Then they heard movement downstairs, signaling the arrival of Heidi and Mike.

"We're up here!" McKenna yelled, then heard them coming up the stairs. "Well? How long?" he asked Hector.

"I think we both know the answer to that one."

The door was open, but Heidi knocked on it anyway.

"Come in, please, and join Detective McKenna on the bed," Hector ordered.

Heidi and Mike sat down next to McKenna, but neither of them looked happy about it. McKenna thought it was because Hector had his pistol trained on them, but that wasn't it at all. "What is that god-awful smell?" Heidi asked, crinkling her nose.

"I assure you it is nothing that will show up on film," Hector said. "I hope you will forgive me if I sound brusque, but I am getting tired and want to get this over with, here and now. Cameraman, what is your name, please?"

"Mike."

"Mike, please get your equipment ready."

"Yes sir," Mike said. He pulled his camera and lights from his bag, hooked them up, and turned them on. He looked through his lens at Hector and made an adjustment before he said, "Testing, one, two, three," as he looked at a gauge on his belt. "Ready when you are, Doctor. We've got picture and sound."

"Good. Heidi and Mike, would you please go stand by the far wall?" Hector asked, pointing.

They did as they were told and stood watching Hector, awaiting further instructions. "Mike, I want you to focus on whoever is speaking, but I also want you to be prepared to capture Detective McKenna and myself in one frame in our present positions," Hector commanded.

"Yes, sir." Mike focused on McKenna, then widened his lens angle and focused on them both. "Detective McKenna, could you scoot down the bed a little?" he asked. "I'm not getting all of you."

"I don't want to do this," McKenna stated.

"I really must insist, Detective McKenna," Hector said. "Please indulge me."

"And if I don't?"

"I am not usually a braggart, but I really am quite a good shot. If you refuse, I will shoot you in the leg. I believe you know what that feels like, don't you?"

McKenna did know, and wasn't surprised Hector knew he had been shot in the leg once before. He didn't answer, but shifted his position on the bed.

"That's fine. Thanks, Detective McKenna," Mike said, then turned back to Hector.

"Heidi, you may make an opening statement. Inform your audience that you are all invited guests in my home and make the introductions," Hector ordered. "Then you may ask me five questions. After that, you may ask Detective McKenna whatever you like and he may answer as he chooses. At the conclusion of the interview I will make one final statement. Is that clear?"

"Should I mention anything about the pistol?" Heidi asked.

"I would prefer that you let your viewers draw their own conclusions."

"What happens after the interview?" Heidi asked.

"If you follow my instructions implicitly, you will all leave. If not, you will die, but I see no reason to tell your viewers that."

"Will you be coming with us?" Heidi asked.

Hector found the question amusing. He turned to McKenna, seeking to share the joke, but McKenna just stared back at him. "You can take me with you, if you like," Hector said. "I am ready to begin."

So was Heidi, ready for the moment she had been waiting for her whole life. She patted down her hair as Mike focused on her and began as soon as he gave her the okay sign.

"This is Heidi Lane of *Fox Five News* broadcasting to you from the home of suspect Dr. Hector De la Cruz in Tamarindo Bay, Costa Rica. It is two forty-five on the morning of March twentieth and Dr. De la Cruz has graciously invited us here for this exclusive interview. Good morning, Dr. De la Cruz, and thank you for having us."

McKenna had to stifle a laugh as Mike swung his camera to Hector. The doctor kept his pistol trained on McKenna's chest, but waved at Mike with his free hand. "Good morning, Heidi, and thank you for coming," he said with a gracious smile on his face.

Mike swung back to Heidi. "Also invited by Dr. De la Cruz and here with us now is Detective Brian McKenna of the New York City Police Department. He is the officer in charge of the investigation of Dr. De la Cruz's alleged crimes in New York last January and he believes that Dr. De la Cruz is responsible for the murders of thirteen homeless people and also the murder of Dr. Suliman Rashid, a man Detective McKenna believes was a close friend of Dr. De la Cruz's. Good morning, Detective McKenna."

The camera swung to McKenna, but he sat motionless without saying a word. Mike stayed on him while Heidi went down on her knees and pleaded with her hands. Finally, he could take it no more. "Good morning, Heidi," he said. "It's a pleasure to be interviewed by you once again."

Mike stayed on McKenna long enough to give Heidi a chance to get up and compose herself before he swung back to her.

"Dr. De la Cruz has consented to answer five questions regarding this case," she said. "Dr. De la Cruz, are you ready to begin?"

"Yes," Hector said before Mike could swing his camera around, so he remained on Heidi.

"Dr. De la Cruz, did you, as Detective McKenna believes, murder fourteen people in New York last January?"

Mike swung to Hector.

"No, I did not. Detective McKenna is wrong, but I understand how his error is possible," he said, then paused for a moment and smiled while Heidi gaped. "I killed thirteen homeless people who were infected with AIDS and were spreading the disease every time they got the chance. I poisoned twelve of them, killed another by slashing his throat, and tried to kill a man I know as Jake the Snake, but I was unsuccessful. However, I want to emphasize to you that I did not kill my friend Dr. Suliman Rashid."

McKenna could see that Heidi was thinking fast as the camera swung back to her. He was sure that Hector had surprised her, answering in one statement at least three of the questions she had intended to ask him. But she was composed and ready by the time Mike was on her.

"Did you kill those people because you believe that one of them is responsible for infecting you with AIDS?" she asked.

"No, I killed them because I am certain that one of them gave the disease to a dear friend of mine, killing her," Hector said into the camera. "Her name was Juliette Thompson and I am sure that Detective McKenna can give you the details later. I would just like to say, before her name and memory are sullied, that although she was homeless and promiscuous, she was a fine person. She was also mentally ill, and her promiscuity was a side effect of her illness. Juliette had relations with all the men I killed, and all of them knew they were taking a chance of infecting that poor, helpless soul with their disease."

"Scientifically speaking, only one of them could have given her AIDS," Heidi said when the camera swung back to her. "It makes no difference to you that you killed twelve innocent men to kill one man you consider guilty?"

As the camera swung back, Hector smiled at Heidi as if her question was silly. "I will answer your question with an analogy," he said. "Suppose I create a firing squad composed of thirteen homicidal maniacs, people who do not mind killing and care for no one but themselves. I place an innocent victim at the stake in front of them and tell them that they can shoot her if they like, if it gives them pleasure. I also tell them that they cannot be prosecuted in any court of law if they do decide to shoot her. Then, I load their guns. I load twelve with blanks, but they don't know that. I load only one gun with a real bullet. Then I tell them, 'At the count of three, fire if you like.' They all fire and the innocent victim is killed, murdered by one shot. Now, I ask you this. Are the twelve people who fired blanks innocent and is the man who fired the fatal bullet the only one who is guilty of murder?"

McKenna didn't know whether Heidi was faking or not, but she looked confused by Hector's question as Mike swung back to her. The look remained on her face for a while before she put on her professional smile and asked her next question. "Considering your present troubles, Dr. De la Cruz, do you feel any remorse for having killed those men?"

"Remorse?" Hector asked, then appeared to ponder the question for a moment before he answered. "I was seeking justice where none would be forthcoming from any police agency or court in the United States. So I took the law into my own hands. I killed them the way they killed Juliette. Most of them were seeking a little pleasure in a taste of wine. Like her, they got their pleasure and they got death without knowing it was coming. Unlike hers, it was a quick, painless death. It was justice, of a sort. However, in seeking justice, I have broken the laws of God and Man, and for that I am sorry. I realize now that I was wrong to do it, so you can call that remorse, if you like."

"I don't know what to call that," Heidi said, for the benefit of her viewers. "When you first contemplated killing those people, did you think you were going to get away with it, to go unpunished without your crimes being detected?"

"To tell you the truth, yes, I did expect my actions to go undetected and, considering my circumstances, I did not expect to be punished for them. Not in this world, at least," Hector said, then smiled at McKenna. "However, I had not counted on people like Detective McKenna and Detective Kaplowitz taking an interest in my actions, so what I had intended to be a private matter is now a public affair. As a result, I sit before you in disgrace, a confessed murderer soon to be punished for my crimes.''

"Are you going to surrender to Detective McKenna, waive extradition, and return to New York for trial?'' Heidi asked quickly before Mike could swing back to her.

"Heidi, I'm sorry,'' Hector said. "I believe I have already answered your five questions. I am not feeling well and growing tired of this. However, I will answer your question after my statement.'' Then he turned once again to Mc-Kenna. "Besides, I am interested in hearing what Detective McKenna has to say.''

Mike followed Hector's gaze with the camera and stayed on McKenna. Heidi was again on her knees, urging him to speak.

"I'd like to take this opportunity to admit that I was probably wrong concerning the death of Dr. Rashid. I now believe that Hector De la Cruz had nothing to do with his death.''

"Do you find fault with any of Dr. De la Cruz's statements?'' Heidi asked, off camera.

"No, I don't think he told a single lie. After listening to his viewpoint, I can understand why he did what he did, but I can't condone it. Dr. Hector De la Cruz, by his own admission, is a murderer many times over,'' McKenna said, hoping Heidi would leave it at that.

She didn't. He watched in dismay as she got up and brushed herself off, then gave Mike a signal. He focused on her and she asked, "Can you tell us how you happened to be here in Costa Rica for this interview?''

McKenna didn't like being put on the spot, but he didn't fault Heidi. He knew it was a question that had to be asked, one her viewers everywhere would be wondering themselves. It was time to come clean, he knew. Not squeaky clean with the whole story, he hoped, just passably unsoiled. "I came here hoping to locate Hector De la Cruz so that the New York district attorney could present the Costa Rican authorities with a request for his extradition. Now that I've done that, I expect that request will be made and I hope that the Costa Rican authorities will honor it.''

"Just one more question, if you don't mind,'' Heidi said.

Heidi! I do mind, McKenna thought, but then Hector saved him.

"Heidi, I believe Detective McKenna has answered all the questions he should be asked and I'm ready to make my statement,'' Hector said, off camera.

Mike quickly shifted back, close in on Hector.

"I would like your viewers to be able to gauge Detective McKenna's reaction to my statement,'' Hector said, and Mike shifted position to cover them both with the camera.

"First of all, I want to thank my countrymen for the unwavering support they have shown me,'' Hector said. "Unfortunately, I am not worthy of that support. I am guilty of the crimes Detective McKenna has charged me with, and he is doing his duty as he must. I apologize to the nation and only hope that, years from now, Costa Ricans will remember me for the good things I have tried to do here my whole life and hope that they will forgive me for the evil I did when I left my wonderful country. We are a good people who rarely find reason to leave our beautiful, beloved homeland. I know now and am living proof that no reason is good enough. I went insane when I left Costa Rica, and now I must pay for that insanity. That is as it must be.'' Hector turned from the camera to McKenna and held up his pistol. ''Detective McKenna, do you know what kind of gun this is?'' he asked.

''It's a Heckler and Koch nine-millimeter automatic.''

''In your opinion, is one shot from a pistol like this in the hands of an experienced marksman capable of causing death?''

''Yes,'' McKenna said, suspecting where the conversation was leading and not liking it at all.

''And how many rounds does this gun hold, fully loaded?''

''With one in the chamber, fourteen.''

''I assure you that this pistol is fully loaded with fourteen rounds and that I am an experienced marksman. I know that you are as well, so you have some work to do. Under the pillow behind you is another Heckler and Koch nine-millimeter automatic. Please get it,'' Hector said, keeping his pistol trained on McKenna's chest.

McKenna reached under the pillow and found the gun. The hammer was cocked. He put it down on the bed next to him.

''I have confessed that I am guilty of the crimes with which I'm charged. Do you believe that I am guilty?''

''Yes.''

''Do you believe that I should be punished for my crimes?''

''Yes, but only if you are found guilty in a court of law.''

''Detective McKenna, I already said it. I am guilty. Do you believe, if I waived extradition, that I would survive to receive my just punishment in the State of New York?''

''No, we both know that you'd die before sentence could be pronounced, even if there was a trial.''

''Am I correct in stating that New York now punishes the crime of murder with a sentence of death?''

''That's the law, but nobody's been executed by the State of New York in thirty years.''

''Then I will be the first in a long time and you will be my executioner. I believe in justice and demand it be applied in my case. There is one round in that pistol next to you. Please stand up and hold the pistol by your side.''

''And if I don't?''

''That decision you will have to make, but first I think you should have the facts. In a moment, I am going to begin counting. If I am not dead by the time I get to three, I am going to start shooting. I will shoot thirteen rounds and you will be the first to die. Then I will shoot Heidi and her cameraman, out of sheer spite and anger. I will keep shooting, even after I'm certain you all are dead, but I will save the last bullet for myself. In the end, I will still be dead, although seconds later than I should be. Now, can you can see how illogical it would be of you not to comply with my request?''

''Hector, please don't do this,'' McKenna said.

''You know that I must. I must warn you to shoot to kill. If I have any life left in my body at the count of three, I will start shooting. I do not anticipate an open casket, so aim where you think best.''

"Hector, what you're asking me to do is called suicide. It's a sin and you'll burn in Hell."

"I call it justice," Hector countered. "I expect to be able to plead my case before the Pearly Gates, and maybe I will win. I believe you know Mr. Schenley?"

"Yes."

"So do I, unfortunately, but he said something once to me that stuck. He said, 'Give me one shred of an argument and, given enough time and the right jury, I'll get you an acquittal, no matter how guilty you are.' Now, please pick up the gun and stand up."

"I think you're bluffing," McKenna said, not making a move.

"Only one way to find out, but I advise against it. One . . ."

"Hector, for the love of God, please don't do this," McKenna pleaded.

"Detective McKenna, do your duty. Two . . ."

McKenna fired while seated and Heidi screamed and screamed.

65 Thanks to Heidi, McKenna had to spend at least one extra day in jail, the first one, and it wasn't pleasant. After he had killed Hector, Heidi remained in the house with him waiting for the police to arrive, but Mike vanished. Not trusting the Costa Rican authorities with her only copy of the videotape, Heidi had sent Mike to get a copy made. That proved to be quite a problem in Costa Rica at three o'clock in the morning.

McKenna realized that he was in for a bad time when the two Costa Rican policemen finally arrived at four o'clock. One of them wept openly when he saw Hector's body. He then searched McKenna and placed him in handcuffs, not too gently, while his partner knelt beside the body and prayed for an hour. During that time they asked McKenna not a single question, and he thought it better not to disturb them by volunteering information when he heard the threats they shouted to Heidi in Spanish every time she opened her mouth.

Eventually, Heidi got the point and she sat on the bed, sobbing about what a wonderful man Hector was, stopping occasionally to complain politely about the smell.

McKenna suspected that what Heidi really had meant to say was, "What a great, newsworthy murderer that Hector was to give me that wonderful, Pulitzer Prize–winning interview. But God, it smells awful in here. Can't you two jerks smell it?"

Heidi was a model of decorum by the time the sergeant arrived at five o'clock. Then the questioning began, in Spanish. Heidi didn't understand a word, but she responded to each question by smiling and pointing at McKenna.

Under questioning, McKenna explained exactly what had happened, but they weren't inclined to believe a single word he said and obviously regarded him as they might regard Nero while he was feeding Christians to the lions.

The coroner arrived at six. Naturally, he had been a friend of Hector's and he declared the death a murder without asking any explanation whatsoever from McKenna.

The cops then dragged McKenna down to the broken side door. They had many questions about that and the tools in the gym bag, but by then McKenna had decided that silence was golden.

By six-thirty, Heidi had been placed under guard in her villa. Cisco had wisely managed to make himself scarce, apparently seeing no point in keeping McKenna company in the one-cell Tamarindo jail while a lynch mob numbering in the thousands shouted outside. Every policeman in Guanacaste Province had to be mobilized outside the jail to protect McKenna's life. For a while, he thought they were doing a wonderful job. Then he watched one platoon of his protectors go off duty, take off their shirts, and immediately join the mob shouting for his painful-as-possible death.

At noon Brian Newman of the American embassy arrived in Tamarindo Bay and he tried to help as best he could, but his best turned out to be not so good for both McKenna and for him. After repeated attempts, he was finally admitted to McKenna's cell. "I've never seen anything like this," he told McKenna. "These are normally very kind, peace-loving people. You've managed to really strike a chord with them." Then they watched from the cell window as Newman's car outside experienced the worst case of spontaneous combustion either of them had ever seen. While they were watching, they dodged fruit and everything else small enough and light enough to be thrown through the cell window. "At least you won't starve to death," was Newman's parting comment as he left, on foot, to advise all American tourists to clear out of town.

Things began changing for the better at 5:30 that afternoon. McKenna noticed that the mob outside his cell had dissipated considerably, and a few people remaining waved to him and even shouted his name. Then, at 5:45, the comandante visited McKenna and deferentially escorted him to his office to watch some TV.

Mike had gotten through, and copies of the tape had been distributed to TV stations all across America and Costa Rica. Unfortunately for McKenna, no one had thought it necessary to give one to the police in Tamarindo Bay and they had to see it on TV, the first time at five o'clock. McKenna watched the rerun at six, and then he was informed that his new cell was the *comandante*'s office until some small details could be straightened out. Meanwhile, he was given the menus of every restaurant in town and told to pick whatever he wanted, whenever he wanted.

On Thursday morning it was decided that the facilities at the Tamarindo jail were not up to the standards of a dignitary such as McKenna and he was driven to the large, stately home of a very rich government official on the beach in Flamingo, fifteen miles away. The house came complete with pool, sauna, exercise room, motorboat, and servants galore. The owner, a Mr. Estoriz, greeted McKenna at the door and said in perfect English, "I was a good friend of Hector's and apparently he held you in high regard. My house is your house until some small details get straightened out. My family and I will be moving out to ensure your complete privacy."

Things were beginning to make sense to McKenna. "Mr. Estoriz, by any chance, are you Basque?" he asked.

"Why, yes I am, originally. Now, of course, I'm Costa Rican through and through."

"You wouldn't happen to know a Monsieur Picard, would you?" McKenna wanted to know.

Estoriz smiled and repeated, "My house is your house." Then he left without answering.

By Friday afternoon, after a morning of fishing, McKenna realized that he really had it good when Cisco showed up at the door to his prison with Heidi. Cisco came to formally offer his surrender, insisting that he had committed the same crimes as McKenna, whatever they were, and that he therefore deserved the same treatment. The Costa Rican cops listened politely before throwing him out, but he kept coming back. Finally, after consultation with their superiors in San José, they gave up and accepted his surrender. They then issued him his prison gear, consisting of six towels, a new bathing suit, a fishing pole, and a set of water skis.

McKenna had been relaxing at the pool watching TV with Heidi during Cisco's surrender negotiations. Hector's wake was still on, as it had been for the past two days, and they watched the thousands of mourners file by his open casket. Cisco passed them there with nothing more than a wave as he was on his way to the kitchen to order up a meal.

Heidi gave McKenna plenty of news during her visit. She told him that apparently the Costa Ricans, nationally and en masse, had come to regard the Hector affair as a wonderful Greek-style tragedy, with a story line much like those in the *novelas* they loved to watch on daytime TV. In them, there are no villains, only heroes in conflict with each other as they struggle to work out their tragic destinies in order to make the loyal Costa Rican fans cry all the way to the store to buy whatever the sponsors of the show are advertising. Consequently, McKenna was a hero while Heidi and her Fox Five crew had been given national carte blanche, going wherever they wanted.

Heidi had also broadcast a show from Hector's home, soon to be a national monument, and had discovered some of his little tricks. McKenna had wondered how Hector, a sick man, could stay awake while waiting for him. The answer was that he didn't. Heidi had discovered all sorts of hidden little infrared electric eye devices Hector had installed all around his house. Whenever McKenna had crossed a beam, a signal was sent to the band Hector wore around his arm, causing it to vibrate. He had woken up for the show.

"Do you know how they're doing with straightening out those 'small difficulties'?" McKenna asked her.

"Slowly, I imagine. You have to keep in mind that these folks argued for twenty years and even formed political parties over what would be their national bird."

"Fine. Now, tell me honestly this time. What was the last question that you wanted to ask me, the one that Hector wouldn't let you ask?"

"Like I've been telling you, I was going to ask you if you were the greatest detective there ever was," Heidi said with her lying smile, the one he had come to know.

Angelita arrived on Thursday night in a government-provided chauffeured limousine, which was really nothing more than a black Nissan taxicab in disguise. She took one quick look around the house and immediately decided that prison life was for her, but McKenna feared that things were about to turn a little too lively for his tastes since Heidi was still there.

As it turned out, his fears were groundless. The two women talked quite a bit, by themselves and without incident. It seemed to McKenna that they treated each other cordially, though icily correct, but he suspected that they really liked and respected each other. He even thought that they might eventually become friends, long after he was dead.

EPILOGUE

Saturday, March 23 **Flamingo, C.R.**

After a tough morning of waterskiing around their splendid prison course, McKenna, Cisco, and Angelita were lying poolside, watching Hector's state funeral in San José on TV. Thousands of dignified mourners were there, dressed in their best, all come to comfort Carmen. McKenna thought that she looked like she was holding up well, but Angelita didn't agree. "She's going to collapse," she predicted. "It's not an act. She's trying to smile, but that poor girl is definitely suffering."

Sure enough, five minutes later Carmen did collapse as she stood outside the church while Hector's coffin was brought out. Picard and Mr. Estoriz were there to catch her. Picard whispered into her ear and held her close while she sobbed into his chest.

Everything stopped for five minutes as people around Carmen sobbed along with her. Even the TV commentator and a few members of the honor guard were crying.

To McKenna's complete surprise, Angelita rolled over to him, hugged him, and started crying herself. He let her continue for a while, then dried her eyes with a towel before he dried his own.

Cisco thought it was time to take a swim and he stayed underwater a long time before he came up, rubbing his eyes. He saw McKenna looking at him and he shrugged. "Too much chlorine in this pool, don't you think?" he asked, then went under again.

McKenna and Angelita went back to watching the TV. Carmen had stopped shaking. Picard let her go and dried her eyes with one of the hundreds of offered handkerchiefs. She pulled herself erect, nodded to the crowd in thanks, and followed the casket to the waiting hearse.

The ceremonies went on for another two hours, exhausting both McKenna and Angelita. They went to their room and took a nap, but were awakened by Newman knocking on their door. Angelita got up and McKenna answered the door.

"You're free to go," Newman said, handing McKenna his passport. "The government has a plane waiting to take you to San José."

"But we just got here," Angelita protested.

"Do we have to leave right now?" McKenna asked.

"No. I was told to inform you that you can stay as long as you like. For you, they'll keep that plane waiting on the runway until it rusts and falls apart."

They stayed, but McKenna had a hard time sleeping that night. He couldn't stop thinking about Hector. He wished things could have worked out differently, but knew that was never possible once they had embarked on their collision course. McKenna realized that it had ended the only way it could. Hector's sad life had ended tragically, but it certainly hadn't been a wasted, empty life. He realized that Hector loved games, and everything had been a type of a game to him, a challenge to be met and won. If he couldn't win, he would settle for a draw.

That's what it had been to Hector, McKenna thought. The new game of murder and revenge, patent pending. McKenna knew that he could never beat Hector in chess, and after watching him in action, he also decided that he would never want to sit at a poker table with Hector, in this life or the next. Hector was just too good at bluffing to be beaten.

It had all been a bluff that night. Hector had known he couldn't win, so he had settled for his draw. He had died as part of his plan, winding up being considered a tragic hero in Costa Rica and as a cunning, mad criminal in the United States, forever famous in both places.

Hector De la Cruz had gone out in style. After his last performance, McKenna realized that the doctor had never intended to kill him, Heidi, or Mike, no matter what decision McKenna made in his house that night.

As every schoolchild in Costa Rica knew by then, Hector's pistol hadn't been loaded.